The Field Researchers Files

by A.E. Hellstorm

In the Hands of the Unknown; *Claire, 2008*
Lost; *Octavius, 2010*
Of Darkness Born; *Caesar, 1973*

Upcoming books
The Living Wall; *Caradoc, 1969*
In the Shadows; *Odette, 2011*
A Crack in the Door; *Team O, 2012*
Crossing the Line; *Claire, 2002*
In Deep Waters; *Odette, 2014*
The Game is on; *Omega, 2006*
In Enemy Territory; *Cicero, 1941*
Not for Your Eyes; *André, 2016*
The Golden Fleece; *Artemis, 1918*

Short Stories
The Thin Man; *Newton, 1989, (upcoming)*
The House in New Orleans; *Minerva, 1986, (upcoming)*
Down the Rabbit Hole; *Lisa, 2002, (upcoming)*
FR-Files, Short Story Collection, *(upcoming)*

LOST

a novel about

the Field Researchers of the Golden Fleece Society

Octavius, 2010

inspired by the world of H.P. Lovecraft

by A.E. Hellstorm

Copyright

This book is a work of fiction. Names, characters, places, and events are the products of the author's imagination or are used in a fictitious way. Any resemblance to actual events, locales, or persons, living or dead, is entirely coincidental. This book is loosely inspired by the world created by H. P. Lovecraft.

ISBN: 978-1-9992530-3-5 (e-book)
ISBN: 978-0995283213 (printed book)
Published by: Hellhag Productions via CreateSpace.
Website: www.hellhagproductions.com
Facebook: www.facebook.com/A.E.Hellstorm
Soundtrack list on Spotify: Lost
Cover layout and design by Flying Elk Photography
Beta readers: Mikael Hellström, Emma Fryksmark, Melody Bell, Owen R. O'Neill (Thank you. What would I do without you?)
Line editor, context editor, content editor: Emma Fryksmark
Edition: March 2020

Acknowledgment

To Allie; a huge thank you for making this book into something I hadn't planned originally. You're awesome, as always.

Thanks to Siobhan Buck and Jeff Elder, who graciously let me use their RPG characters Strawberry and Miles in the story. Allie's Geek Squad wouldn't be the same without them.

Emma Fryksmark has been a tremendously helpful resource and provided great advice and lots of laughter during this journey. I would especially like to give you a heartfelt 'thank you' for loving the characters.

Dr. Cecilia Gordan gave me good advice in all the medical aspects, just like last time. Thank you again. You're great.

Owen R. O'Neill has, through his honesty, given me so much great feedback and even inspired me to make some changes in the end chapters to something fuller and better.

Melody Bell forced me to open the lid to my box and check out the surroundings, helping me getting new perspectives on the events and the characters.

Jeannette Moore has been fabulous support in all aspects.

Thank you, Gabriel, Martin, Simon, Cilla, Micke, Emma, and Niklas, for all wonderful, fantastical, and imaginative evenings and nights. Love you always. PS. If you didn't know it, you changed my life completely, and I can't thank you enough for it.

To the Goodreads' group *Support for Indie Authors* in general, and to Owen, Jenycka, Dwayne, Charles, and Hayden in particular.

As always, to my wonderful and supporting husband, who also helped me tremendously with creating the hierarchy system as well as the teaching methods of the Western Shore

University, and who also gave me plot ideas for upcoming books.

Above all, to all the muses who graciously were with me during the creation of this book. You took me all by surprise. Thank you. Your presence has been so much appreciated and loved. (And please, stay.)

Glossary

WSU – Western Shore University in Detroit

GFS – Golden Fleece Society

FRT – Field Researcher Team

FR – Field Researcher (Field agent of the Golden Fleece Society)

R – Researcher (Academic of the Golden Fleece Society)

Star Student – Student at WSU who studies to become a Researcher or a Field Researcher

The Wing – The Star Student lodgement at the WSU

R.A. – Researcher Assistant (Star Student Trainee)

P.I. – Principal Investigator (Team leader)

SiC – Second-in-Command

SAC – Special Agent in Command

I.C. – Intermediate Course

R.P/Project/P. – Research Project (cases that the FRs are involved in)

Field Researcher name – Codename for Field Researchers

Researcher name – Codename for Researchers

Team A/The Faculty – The board of the Golden Fleece Society

Originals – First generation of Researchers and Field Researchers of the Golden Fleece Society

CSI – Crime Scene Investigator

DSI – Death Scene Investigator

Sub-Dep – Substance Department

Hom-Dep – Homicide Department

Cast

Team A
Anna (real name unknown)
Armand (Henry Wittinger)

Team B
Dr. Bernard (real name unknown)
Sister Banafshe (real name unknown)
Sister Blaise (real name unknown)

Team O
Principal Investigator: **Olwen** (Sally Oakley)
Second-in-Command: **Octavius** (Carl Hansen)
Ophelia (Miriam Goldblum)
Omega (Pieretta Williams) *Intermediate Course*

Part One

so lost

Chapter 1

The early morning sun stretched its rosy rays over the horizon. As Carl drove through the quiet and lush suburb, he took his time to enjoy the view. For the first time in weeks, the sky promised to be blue instead of gray, and there wasn't a single cloud to cover the radiant sun. Even though the air that found its way in through the open car window was chilly with a scent of late snow, it couldn't diminish the hope of coming spring.

A smooth left turn onto Juniper Hill Drive placed him outside the small white brick house where Amanda lived with their daughter. The car clock told him that he was just in time for the hearty breakfast he, his ex-wife, and their daughter always tried to share on Saturdays. Pleased that the previous late night hadn't made him oversleep too much after all, he turned off the engine.

He had just gotten out of the car when the front door swung open, and Sarah came rushing out, barefoot on the cold pathway. With a laugh, he held out his arms and caught her. He twirled her around, hugged her hard, and breathed in her special scent. She laughed too but squirmed out of his embrace. Instead, she took his hand and eagerly dragged him with her.

"Come, Dad! Come! I have a surprise for you!"

Inside, the warm and welcoming scent of newly baked bread met him. Without even letting him properly greet Amanda, who stood in the doorway, smiling at them, Sarah dragged him along to the kitchen table, packed with bread, coffee, cheese, and strawberries. A plate with scones stood on a cake stand in the middle of it. With a tug at his heart, Carl realized that Sarah had used the recipe he had shared with Amanda all those years ago when they were younger and more naïve than they were today. He hadn't expected her to keep it after the divorce. She was definitely not a baker.

Proudly, Sarah displayed the breakfast table. "I made them myself, Dad."

"Did you now? Wow, they look super tasty, Peanut," he said enthusiastically and kissed her on her head. She beamed at him.

"Come, try them. Mom told me how to do, and I've set the table too."

He admired the artistic flair she had given it with colorful hand-drawn name cards on the plates and cut-out paper flowers. Then, she tugged at his hand, and, laughing, he sat down. Amanda left the doorway and joined them. She winked at him as he took a big bite out of one of the scones. Surprised, he thought it was pretty tasty, especially for a first attempt. Sarah watched him intensely as he chewed and swallowed. Then, he gave her a big smile.

"Did you really bake this?" When she nodded vigorously, he continued. "You're really talented! What a treat. Thank you."

Sarah lit up, and her cheeks flushed by the praise. She took her chair and placed it close to him before sitting down. Then, she eyed Amanda.

"Aren't you going to have any, mom?" she asked.

"Course I will," Manda smiled and reached for the scones.

Over breakfast, they decided to spend the whole day at Riverside Park since the day promised sun and not rain, instead of going to the indoor playground as they first had planned. While they packed the picnic basket, Sarah chatted about all the things that had happened since Carl had seen her last. Listening to her cheerful and excited voice that only stopped long enough for her to catch her breath, lured out a smile on his lips. It was as if they'd been separated for months and not only for a week. Manda kept in the background as always, but her face was soft whenever her gaze fell upon their happy daughter, and as always, he was forever grateful that she was a sensible and loving woman that let him take part in Sarah's life, instead of shutting him out after their divorce. He glanced at her with an amused smile as she came over to put the sandwiches in the basket. *'Letting me take part in Sarah's life', eh? She would kill me if I didn't.* Brimming with the amicable love that he would always hold for her, he gave Manda a half-hug. Her green eyes behind the thick-framed glasses were surprised and questioning, but he just shrugged with a smile.

"And do you know what she said, Daddy?" Sarah asked, referring to her drama teacher.

"No, what?"

"That I'm a good actor. Do you think I am?"

"I do."

"And that I should go to the audition on Friday in two weeks. Do you think I should?"

"Why not? As long as your mom thinks it's a good idea."

"She does. Don't you, mom?"

"I said," Manda said with a smile, "if it doesn't affect your homework, I can't see why not."

"It won't," Sarah replied with conviction. "And it's on Fridays so you can pick me up afterward if you want to, Daddy."

Manda laughed. "She's got it all sorted out already. Wait with all the plans until you know if you've got a part."

"I think I will," she said confidently. "So, do you, Daddy? Want to pick me up?"

A spark of insecurity flashed over her face for a split-second before she managed to hide it. At the sight of it, the pain in Carl's heart made him short of breath, but he was better than she at hiding things, so he just smiled lovingly at her and ruffled her hair.

"Of course I do, Peanut."

She beamed at him. "Good. It's settled then."

Carl and Manda shared an amused glance over her head, and then Manda took the picnic basket and said over her shoulder, "Last out to the car is a squirrel!"

12

Laughingly, Sarah set off and was out of the door before any of them had the time to blink.

The drive to the park was a short one, and as soon as they got out, Sarah took his hand and held on tight. Together, they skipped all the way over the parking lot to the steep wooden stairs that led down to the wild-like nature trails. Amanda laughed behind them as she tried to keep up.

Carl loved these kinds of excursions when he got to spend a whole day of quality time with his daughter. During days like this, he was completely satisfied with everything. It wasn't until he returned to his empty and quiet apartment that the longing for being something more than the fun "weekend-daddy" became overwhelming. Sarah's warm hand in his and her happy, radiant face as she smiled up at him, made that longing of being a full-time daddy nearly unbearable.

As he bent down and kissed her sun-warm hair, regret welled up inside him, as it usually did when he thought about the decision he had made all those years ago. It wasn't Manda's fault. When they decided that it was best for everyone that they sold the old apartment and found separate places, she had wanted him to take two weeks every month with Sarah. God, she had been so angry with him when he told her that he couldn't do that, and she accused him of being paranoid and stupid and letting his work take over his life. In a way, she'd been right. He had indeed been paranoid back then, but he couldn't blame himself. At that point, he and his teammates in N had been involved in that damn, terrifying Newton-project. It was the first and only time he had received death threats, and it had scared the hell out of him, especially since the killers had gone through with one of their threats and murdered Nigel's cousin. Just the thought of exposing his daughter to those lunatics had brought him to the brink of panic. Manda had always believed that he had exaggerated, but even now, six years later, he wasn't as sure about that as she was. At least he had managed to overcome part of the paranoia during the past two years. Now, he

13

would love the two weeks a month with Sarah, but the opportunity to talk with Manda about a change hadn't come up yet. If he was entirely honest with himself, part of the reason he hadn't brought it up was that he was afraid Manda would say no. *I'm just silly. Why would she say no? There's no reason for that.* He glanced at Manda. Her face bore the calm, intelligent demeanor behind which she sometimes tried to hide her real feelings when she was together with him. He knew it to be a defense mechanism from the days that led up to the divorce. Every time he saw it, he regretted the things he had said and done back then, all of which led to her to distance herself from him.

Eventually, I'll talk to her, he promised himself. *But not today. Can't talk about Sarah when she's around to listen. I also need to prepare first, so I know how to phrase it properly.*

Satisfied with that thought, he smiled down at Sarah as she suddenly stopped and got down on her knees.

"Look, Daddy!" she breathed. "A squirrel! And it's so close. Do you think it will take a nut from my hand?"

Careful to not scare the curious animal, Carl kneeled too and handed her a nut from the small plastic bag in his pocket.

"You can try."

She took it between her thumb and her index finger and stretched out toward the squirrel. The whiskers shivered slightly when the animal saw the treat, as did Sarah's hand, and then, the squirrel took a couple of cautious steps forward. Sarah sat completely still, and Carl barely breathed beside her, as eager as she was that the squirrel would take the nut. It took a few more steps forward, but just then, there was a loud commotion behind the bend of the wooden path, and the squirrel disappeared into the undergrowth. A small boy and his large golden retriever came rushing through the bushes, laughing breathlessly at everything and nothing.

Disappointed, Sarah stood up but didn't say anything as the pair continued their running, and a couple of adults showed up at the bend, laughing too as they jogged after the boy and the dog.

"I'm going to leave some of the seeds and nuts here, Daddy," she said when it was all quiet. "I don't think he'll come back now, but when he does, I want him to be able to find what I promised him."

"Yeah, go ahead," Carl agreed.

"That was sad," Manda said behind them. "I was so sure he would come all the way to you. Next time, sweetheart."

With a concentrated expression, Sarah dug out a little hollow in the soil where she placed seeds and the nuts from Carl's bag.

"There," she said, eventually, looking pleased. "I hope he'll be happy when he finds it."

"I'm sure he will," Manda said, but Sarah glanced at Carl, wanting his reassurance.

"You know what?" he said, and she shook her head. "He's sitting in that tree right now, just waiting for us to leave so he can get all the goodies."

"How do you know?" she asked, wide-eyed.

"Do you hear that sound?" She listened and nodded as she heard the shrill, angry sound coming from the tree Carl had pointed at. "It's him, warning all the other squirrels and birds from coming here, telling them the food is all his."

A bright smile lit up her face, and she took both Manda and Carl's hands and pulled them along. "Let's go then."

Smiling at each other over Sarah's head, they followed her along the bend in the path, which led down to the river.

After a couple of hours, they had hiked the shortest trail all the way around, watching birds, feeding more squirrels, and even seen a beaver dam, which had excited Sarah to no end, and now they returned to the open meadow behind the parking lot. As they slowly walked toward the cars, Carl glanced down at his still energetic nine-year-old girl, and with an ulterior motive, he led the conversation toward

Sarah's favorite subject, her future dream of becoming a police officer. For a while, they chatted about the different kinds of professions within the police corps and the FBI, respectively, before Carl, with a very innocent appearance, said, "You know what I and everyone else did to become FBI, Peanut?" Intrigued, she shook her head. "Exercised. Every single day. That's what you need to do. You won't get into the Academy otherwise."

His serious, book-loving, never-want-to-exercise-ever-even-if-her-life-depended-on-it daughter, gave him a suspicious look, and he managed, with some difficulty, to keep a straight face, while Manda smiled broadly at him behind their daughter's back.

"Okay, Dad," she said eventually, and with a surprised grin of his own, he jogged over to the car to get the soccer ball out from the trunk. "Did you plan this?" she shouted after him when she saw, and he couldn't help laughing. "You did! I know you did!"

"Yeah, I did," he admitted when he came back. "But it's true, you need to exercise when you're a policewoman. How do you think you'll be able to catch the bad guys if you can't run as fast as they can?"

She squinted her eyes as she always did when she thought something through, and then she nodded at him. "Alright, we can try."

At her words, a light-hearted astonishment washed over him. *Wow, I should have tried that tactic years ago!*

"Great!" he said happily. "Let's go over to the goal over there. Take the ball. You'll be the goalkeeper for now."

As she ran over the field with the ball under her arm and the long copper-red braids bouncing on her back, Manda came up beside him.

"Good job," she said, still smiling, and started to put her own thick sandy-blond hair into a ponytail to get it out of the way.

"Thanks." He didn't even try to hide how pleased he was.

16

She laughed at him and poked him on his shoulder. "You look like a kitten who's fallen headfirst into a bowl of whipped cream."

"Well, I have, haven't I?"

"I admit, it was good," she said and corrected her green glasses that had gotten stuck in her hair. "I would never have thought about it. If we can get her interested in some kind of sport this way, I'm not complaining."

"I hope we can. Soccer's a great beginner sport, and I'd love it if she could get some friends in the process too."

"Agreed," Manda said with emphasis. "Especially if this theater thing doesn't work out."

"Are you coming?" Sarah shouted at them. "I could have brought my book otherwise."

Both of them laughed and began jogging toward her.

They played for almost an hour, and Carl was amazed by how quickly Sarah picked up on the rules and by how much fun she had. When they sat down at the picnic table to have some hot chocolate and sandwiches, her cheeks were rosy, and her gray eyes glittered.

"That was fun!" she exclaimed. "I like the rules. They make sense. It's like math. You have to calculate how to kick the ball to avoid the opponents."

Carl shared a quick, astounded look with Manda, before smiling and tugging at one of Sarah's braids. "Haven't really thought about it that way," he said, and it was her turn to give him an astounded look.

"I thought you'd played this game before."

"Uh, yeah, I have."

"Well, there you go."

"Yeah, there you go, Carl," Manda grinned at him, and he chuckled.

When they had finished their picnic, they packed Carl's car and went back home to his ex-wife's and daughter's small house. Sarah was unusually quiet, and Carl could tell she was tired, so he didn't object when she put on a movie and cuddled up on the sofa with her soft blankie and her old stuffed kitten. Manda went into the kitchen to start their dinner, and Carl followed to help her, but she ushered him out.

"I got this. Go sit with Sarah."

He nodded and went back to the living room and sank down beside his little girl. Immediately, she curled up in his arms and pulled the blanket around both of them. As with everything she was interested in, she was intensely concentrated and indulged herself completely. Rather than watching the boring and irritating film himself, he used the time to study this little copy of himself, and as usual, he was filled with wonder and overflowing love for this little being he had been part of creating. Her eyes gleamed as they followed what was happening on the screen, and her sensitive face was like a sky of emotions as she reacted to the events. Carl glanced at the screen when Sarah covered her mouth with her hands. The Dread Pirate Roberts and the vapid princess had just fallen down into the Fire Swamp. Why Westley continued to love this idiotic girl was beyond him, and he had to admit that he wasn't entirely pleased with Manda for letting Sarah watch the movie in the first place. First of all, she was too young for it, and secondly, Buttercup was definitely not a good role model for a girl. He could have come up with several films much more suited for their daughter, but the damage was already done, and he was not going to instigate a fight with Manda over it. As he looked back at Sarah, his cell phone suddenly rang. With a slight scowl, he noticed the unknown number. *Damn telemarketing chasing me the whole week. Can't they let me be on a Saturday evening, at least?*

"Yeah?"

"Carl Hansen?" The dark female voice sounded vaguely familiar. It had to be the telemarketing woman he had spoken with earlier in the week. He suppressed a sigh but didn't make any efforts to sound polite when he answered, "Yeah?"

"This is Bethany Miller, Miriam's sister, you know? We've met once. How are you?"

Surprised, he frowned. *Beth? What the hell?* A sudden tingling sensation of something wrong made his skin prickle. *Didn't know she had my phone number.* Without thinking, he put on his trusting voice. "I'm just fine. And you?"

"Fine. Um, Miriam isn't with you, is she?"

The tingling became stronger, but as he casually put his foot up on the coffee table and rested his hand on his leg, no one would have been able to tell that he was on edge.

"Sorry, no. Why?"

"Just— We were supposed to meet tonight after work. You know, have dinner, go out dancing, but she hasn't shown up. I— I thought she might've forgotten about it."

Slightly concerned, he drummed his fingers on his legs. *Yeah, right, Beth, and you don't believe that either.*

"That's not like her," he said calmly.

"I know, but I kind of hoped she'd be with you. I mean, you do meet sometimes." Carl frowned at Beth's uncertain voice but didn't say anything. *What the hell's going on? There's something she's not telling me.* She inhaled like someone who was about to dive from a high cliff. "She doesn't answer her phone, and she's not at home. I know I'm silly, but I can't— I can't help thinking, you know, that she might've been in the store when it— When it blew up…." Her voice trailed away, embarrassed.

"What?" Carl put his foot down on the floor and straightened up. Sarah changed her focus from the film to him and gave him a worried glance. With a reassuring smile, he caressed her hair, and she relaxed.

Beth sounded nervous as she gave up a fake laugh. "I told you, it's silly—"

"No, wait. What store?"

There was a slightly astounded pause in which Carl's heart rate raised, and his hands got all sweaty.

"You haven't heard? It's all over the news. It's Kroger's on one o' ninth, you know, the one Mimi usually shops at."

Carl's mouth was suddenly completely dry, and he had to swallow hard before he could talk. "No, I hadn't heard. When did this happen?"

"About an hour ago."

"Alright, I'll check it out. Can I reach you on this number?"

"Yes, yes, you can. And thank you." She hung up, and with a concerned frown, Carl put the cell phone back into his pocket.

"What was that about?" Manda asked behind him. When he looked up at her, she stood leaning against the doorway to the kitchen. The light behind her illuminated her hair, and for a moment, the thought flashed through his mind of how beautiful she was. Then, he pushed the thought away and casually rose from the sofa to not alarm their daughter. So Sarah wouldn't hear, he took the few steps to Manda and said in a low voice, "It was Miri's sister calling, asking if I knew where she was. She hasn't shown up for their girls-night-out."

"Miri? That must be Miriam, right? Your girl?" Carl glared at her, irritated by the slip of the pet name he only used between him and his teammate, but Manda just smiled. "Well, she should be. She's good for you. Anyway, not my business, is it?"

"Correct."

"Well, why are you still here? Go find her. She probably needs you."

Carl just rolled his eyes. "She's not some kind of damsel in distress, you know. She's quite capable of handling herself. If she weren't, she'd not be FBI."

Manda poked him. "Just look at my big hero here." When he didn't respond to her teasing, a slight frown appeared on her forehead. "Has something happened?"

Carl glanced over his shoulder at Sarah, who seemed to be enthralled with the movie, but just in case she was trying to fool them, he lowered his voice even more when he turned back to Manda.

"A Kroger's on one-hundred and ninth blew up an hour ago."

Manda stared at him in sudden shock. "Why haven't you been notified?" she asked quietly when she found her voice. "Shouldn't you be at work?"

"It's not my table. It's Homeland Security." Carl exhaled nervously and let his hand comb through his copper-red hair several times. Then he cleared his throat. "Problem is, it's Miri's store, and she hasn't shown up to a date with her beloved sister when she's a reliable woman. It's probably nothing, but I have a feeling I should check it out."

"So just don't stand here. Go." Manda followed his gaze as he watched their daughter watch TV. She placed a gentle hand on his arm. "If there's nothing to worry about, you can come back tomorrow. We'll go to the zoo as planned and eat out. You know you're always welcome here."

He gave her a grateful look and squeezed her hand. "Thanks, Manda." She waved away his remark, and he walked back to the sofa. "Sarah—"

She immediately paused the film and watched him sincerely with those big, gray eyes of hers. "Dad, you have to go. If Miri's hurt in that explosion, she'll need you, and if she's not, other people need you."

Carl chuckled and tousled her braids. "Nothing escapes you, right, Peanut?"

"Of course not, Daddy. How could I become a police officer if I don't pay attention to what's happening around me?"

When she continued to watch him with that precocious face, he sighed, but slid down on the sofa and hugged her hard, feeling the earth trembling love for her that always welled up inside him, as he mumbled in her hair, "You're going to become an awesome police officer, Peanut."

21

"I know. Now go, Daddy."

When he rose, Manda had already brought his bag to the door and held his jacket in her hands. He put on his shoes before freeing her from the jacket and the bag.

"You be careful now, as usual. Let me know tomorrow if you can make it to the zoo. We're going to be there at ten."

He nodded, and she gave him a friendly kiss on the cheek before he left.

As he stepped out of the house, the sun had already set, and its remaining rays colored the sky rosy. The cold wind that ruffled his hair held more than just the promise of late snow, he noticed, when a single snowflake landed on his cheek. With a shiver, Carl zipped up his jacket and wished he had the old tuque his grandma had knitted for him when he was ten. It had finally fallen apart last winter after almost twenty years of faithful service.

With a glance up at the flaming sky, he reflected that the winter this year was very stubborn. It was already mid-April, but it felt like late February. Usually, the spring flowers bloomed abundantly by this time, but this year only the most hardened flowers had dared to poke their heads up. He missed their colors and gentle form. *Who wouldn't?* he thought as he hurried down the pavement to get to his car. *Anyone from Alberta would,* he continued his chain of thought, thinking about how long and bitterly cold the winters were where he grew up, and when spring finally arrived, flowers were few and in short supply. *I'd be emotionally blind to not appreciate them,* he concluded and stopped at his bottle-green Toyota Prius.

For a moment, he hesitated before he pressed the unlock button on the keychain. It had been a great day, and the thought of having to end it with a disaster felt... *Sad? Depressing? Terrible? No.* He shook his head, couldn't find the right word. Instead, he stole another precious moment, indulging in the splendor of the dusk, while contemplating how his love and need for beauty and colors was something people didn't know about him. *Most aren't curious enough to figure it out either.* The thought backstabbed him, and he scoffed. *Yeah, it's true. So what? It's their loss. I don't give a damn.*

Miri was one of the few who had taken the time to get to know him. After the Project in Alaska two years ago, she had filled his room with flowers, and their colors and scents had eventually reached him through the grayish darkness in which his mind had hidden, and comforted him. That, together with Sarah's loving presence and Miri's visits when she calmly read to him, drew him back. He owed her, and he was well aware of that. He also liked her a tiny bit more than was comfortable. Since he hadn't liked her at all at the start, she had somehow managed to unnoticed slide under his skin and arouse feelings he never had expected to have for her. And now she might be in danger. Carl tried to laugh at himself and his searching for a phone booth to change into his Superman costume.

"She's FBI," he muttered to himself while anxiously jingling his keys. "She'll manage." He refused to think about how exactly she'd be able to avoid getting blown to pieces by a bomb.

Still lingering, he brought out his cell phone and pressed the three to fast dial her, but a mechanical voice answered him, telling him, "The customer you have dialed is currently not available. Please, try your call again later".

Nervously, he fiddled with the phone a few seconds before putting it down into his jeans pocket. While trying to decide what to do, he opened the door and got into the car. Beautiful sky or not, the wind was damn cold. Drumming his fingers on the steering wheel, he pondered his options. There was no point in heading to her apartment since Beth had already checked it. If DSI-officer Andy Gorlois had called Miri and the other angels into work, she would've let Beth know, so he could rule out that scenario. Nothing else popped up in his mind. Instead, he decided to drive directly to Kroger's. Not that he actually suspected her to have been there when it exploded, but just to be on the safe side, to be able to tick it off the list. The thought struck him that he would probably find her there working while she'd forgotten everything about Beth and their girls-night-out. Carl began to breathe easier. That scenario sounded much more likely than her being in the store at the wrong time, especially since she lived just a block from it and would have heard the explosion.

Just as he was about to insert the ignition key in his car, the cell phone rang. This time, he recognized the phone number, and he grimaced.

"Boss."

Alan Bai's voice was more stressed than usual and almost drowned out by background noise. "Carl, we need you at one-hundred and ninth and thirty-fourth. A bomb's detonated at Kroger's. Massive mess. Everything's blown to smithereens. We need everyone we can get. Even SWAT's been alerted."

SWAT? Goddamn! It's that bad? The image he had in his head of one or maybe two broken walls began to give away for something bigger. *It can't be the whole store, can it?* "I'm on my way. How many survivors?"

"Hard to say. A handful, I think, from outside. It's chaos, Carl. Our own little nine-eleven."

Carl clenched his teeth, couldn't believe what he was hearing. "I'm out of town. I'll be there within the hour. Is agent Goldblum there?"

"Haven't seen her, but it's possible. I guess the president himself could be around here without us noticing."

Alan didn't joke, he never did, and Carl wasn't in the mood for laughing. "What about Sharon and David?"

"I've called them in too."

"Alright, I'll be there ASAP." He hung up and started the car. Immediately, the radio turned on.

"—massive cordon guarded by police as far as a block away on each side. No one of authority will answer my questions, but what we know so far is that no organization has taken on any responsibility for the bombing. From where I stand, I can see ambulance crews taking care of a few people, firefighters clearing debris, and even FBI working alongside. There's a canine unit as well, and a bomb squad, probably searching for other detonations as well as survivors. We haven't gotten any reports of how many victims are expected, but seeing as the bomb detonated at six-fifteen p.m., Kroger's was most likely filled with people shopping for dinner. This is Nicola Brett for CBS Radio. Stay with me as we continue to follow up on the biggest terrorist attack in the United States since nine-eleven."

Carl switched off the radio and logged in to FBI NAC on 167 while concentrating on driving as fast and safely as he could. Every ten minutes, he made a new attempt to reach Miriam without any result. He didn't want to admit that it began to worry him immensely. Sternly, he focused on the radio instead.

The encrypted FBI channel didn't reveal any direct news. There had been no threats before the detonation. The bomb squad suspected there had to have been more than one bomb to create this kind of damage. The FBI worked frantically to find a connection between the store's owner and the bombing. So far, the only survivors were found in the parking lot outside the store. It would take days to locate all the victims. *And months to identify them,* Carl thought with a cold feeling in his stomach.

When he closed in on the area, it became harder to get through. People were milling around everywhere, both on the street and the sidewalks. Cars were carelessly parked halfway out in the street, and people had stopped their cars in the middle of it just to gawk. Irritated, he honked at them and got some ugly fingers as an answer. Eventually, he just gave up and parked his car in a nearby parking lot. Yes, he knew it was for residents only, and no, he didn't care that he was going to get a ticket and maybe towed. He grabbed his CSI bag and struggled to get through the mob as quickly as possible. As he jogged toward the blocked off area, he hauled out his cell and called Beth.

"Have you found her?" Beth sounded breathless and near tears.

"Not yet. I've been called in. My guess is that she's already here working. With all the chaos, I'm not surprised if she forgot to notify you. I'll tell her to call if I see her."

A relieved gush of breath was heard from her. "I'm so stupid. Of course, she's working. Thanks, Carl. I'm going home now, but I'll keep my cell on." She hung up, and Carl put down his phone again, cruising around people, trying to get through the growing crowd of spectators. The air was filled with a dark-gray smoke that smelled of chemicals and dust, and a sweet, burnt odor he hadn't smelled in nearly four years, except for in his nightmares. He closed his eyes for a moment and swallowed, gathering strength to push away the past and concentrate on the present. Determined, he opened his eyes, pushed himself through the crowd, and finally reached the cordoning. Before the police officer in charge could tell him off, he shoved his ID badge under her nose.

"Where's HQ?" he asked when she opened the barricade slightly to let him slip through.

"At the end of the parking lot. You'll see it. The big van." She pointed down the smoky street, and he nodded, leaving her behind as he half-jogged toward the scene. When he turned around the last house, he stopped mid-step. The smell and the smoke were overwhelming here, but it was the absence of the well-known store that stopped him. He'd been here numerous times during the past two years, shopping with Miri for their Friday dinners, and now there was only rubble and a few walls left standing. It looked like a war zone.

Silently, he tried to take it all in. The image he had had of just a couple of damaged walls would have been laughable had the sight not been so shocking. He had no knowledge of explosives at all, and it bothered him that he felt so clueless about the situation. How much was needed to create such damage in the first place? How many people were involved in this? How many casualties were there? Several ambulances stood around with the crews tending to more people than he expected to be alive after seeing this disaster.

"Carl!" Alan Bai, Special Agent in Charge of Carl's unit, hurried toward him. His usual proper demeanor looked dirty, and his face was soiled with sweat and ashes. "You're here!" he said unnecessarily. "Great! You can join Sharon and David. They're interviewing the victims at South Side Hospital."

Carl nodded, relieved that his two elder colleagues were somewhere safe, and looked around, feeling dazed. The magnitude of it all eluded him, it was impossible to grasp it; the dark-gray smoke that clawed in his throat and lungs, the cries of injured people, the blood on the rubble, the frantic voices of the rescuers.

"This looks really bad, boss," Carl remarked, shaken. Even though he tried, it was impossible to hide the shocked and unnerved tone in his voice.

"It's actually better than we thought initially," Alan said pleased.

Carl gave him a skeptical side-glance. "Really? In what way?"

"There are quite a few survivors, more than were expected initially. Some of the witnesses have quite the story to tell. I've spent the last hour interviewing the conscious ones here, and most of them say the same thing."

"Which is?" asked Carl, swallowing his irritation when Alan stopped to catch his breath. It was no use to try to hurry him. Alan spoke in more complex ways than needed. Not that it mattered since he was one of the best profilers in the field. Carl just dug up more patience than he usually needed every time he had to work closely with the man.

"Quite remarkable. Nine people, two teenage girls – one black and one Chicano—"

"Hispanic," Carl mumbled and got a glare back.

"One male postal officer in his fifties – white," Alan continued, "four cashiers – all women of different ages – two

27

of them white and two black, one young dad in his twenties and his five-year-old son – both white, all tell the same story."

"Which is?" Carl asked again, drumming his fingers on his leg.

"Carl, we have a hero here!" Alan's eyes gleamed, and his grimed face brightened with a smile.

"Well, that's good. Not very unusual that someone steps up in a crisis—"

"No, no, WE have a hero. FBI has a hero."

"Alright?"

"All these people survived because of one woman, Carl. They all heard her shout over and over from different parts of the store as if she was running around."

The tingling sensation came back to Carl with full force to the point where it was almost overbearing, and his heart hammered heavily in his chest.

"Alright, what did she shout, Alan?" Somehow, he managed to hide the strain in his voice and sound casual.

"'FBI! There's a bomb in the store! Get out!' And people began to run toward the entrance. Not even five minutes later, everything exploded."

Carl swallowed hard. "What happened to the woman? Do you know?"

Alan shook his head. "She's not out here, so she's probably in there somewhere. Dead, I suppose, but you know, as soon as we know who she is, she'll be celebrated as the hero of April seventeenth. And she's FBI. That's great! We need some positive light for once."

"So, you're suddenly in the marketing department, are you?" Carl sneered and left. It felt like someone had kicked him repeatedly in the stomach. He refused to cry. He promised himself he wouldn't cry until he knew for certain, but he needed to find her – and he needed to call Beth. The thought made him cringe.

Behind him, Alan was shouting, "Where are you going? I need you over at the South Side!"

Carl spun around and walked back to his superior, towered up over him, and looked him straight into the eyes, utterly emotionless. Alan took an insecure step back.

"Agent Miriam Goldblum lives one block from here. This is her store. She's not at home. She doesn't answer her phone. She missed a date with her sister this evening. You're telling me a female FBI-agent warned people here. How many other female FBI-agents use this store? I don't care about South Side. I'm going to look for her."

Alan's face had the most ridiculous expression of shock he had ever seen in a superior before, but he didn't like to laugh at people. Instead, he stomped away to the clearing site where someone gave him a white mask to cover his mouth and nose.

He didn't know how many hours he worked, but night fell, and numerous spotlights lit up the whole area. A helicopter hovered overhead, filming their work. When dawn broke, Carl's whole body ached. He had never worked this hard for this long in his entire life, and he had never seen so many wounded people at the same time. Seeing all their pain and agony made him want to cry, and to be able to continue working, he had to try to shut off that overflowing well of sympathy and sorrow that he felt. Somewhere, he found the strength to push himself harder. They all did, he realized. No one wanted to stop because they all knew that every single pause might mean that someone under this rubble lost their battle with death while the person who could have saved them had a cup of coffee.

It was eight in the morning when they found Miriam's badge. Alan had stopped hours ago trying to reassure him they would find her alive. At this point, Carl could tell that they all had a feeling that most of the people still buried under the rubble hadn't made it, even though no one said it out loud. When he stood with the badge in his hand, swaying with exhaustion after clearing debris for twelve hours, Alan awkwardly patted his shoulder and said, "There's always a chance, you know. She could be lucky, you know. Quite a few people in these kinds of situations are, you know, um, lucky…" Then, he fell silent, sighed, and walked away.

Carl stood alone a couple of minutes and looked at the dirty ID photo with Miri smiling at him. During the night, the same story had been told over and over from surviving witnesses as they got dug out from under the rubble, how she had run through the store, trying to get people out, and when the customers all fled, she went to the back, to warn the employees. A young butcher told him that she had rushed in, waving her FBI badge and screaming at them all to get out.

"She was right behind me, sir, and then, just black."

The butcher had been hit in the head by a partly crumbled wall and suffered a concussion and two broken legs, according to the paramedics, but he – like most of the surviving victims they found – was going to make it. They had found sixteen dead so far, and nearly seventy alive. The talk of the bomb squad was that the numbers would have been the reverse if Miri hadn't been there. She had managed to get people away from the epicenter, and she was indeed talked about like a hero. When they heard from the butcher that she'd been behind him just as the bomb detonated, they started to clear the debris in that area, but they only found her badge. At least they knew it was her now, Carl thought, and he really had to call Beth. He had put it off for so long now, wanted to be sure before he called.

A hand was placed on his shoulder, and he jolted. Alan's exhausted face scrutinized him. "I'm going home now. You should go too. You need to sleep. The SWAT team just arrived to relieve us, all of us, who took the night shift."

Carl nodded. "I'm just going to put this in the van," he said, the words coming out with some difficulty.

"Do that. We'll reassemble at eight hundred tomorrow morning in our briefing room if we're not needed here. I've already notified Sharon and David too."

Carl nodded and walked away to the HQ van. In the organized mess, he found unused evidence bags. He took one of them and put Miri's badge in it and wrote the serial number on it with a permanent marker and in the evidence journal as well. In the corner of his eye, he saw the side door to the van open and a SWAT officer coming in. She closed the door carefully behind her and came up beside him.

"Hi, Octavius. I thought it was you," the low, melodic voice said.

For once, he was taken entirely by surprise, and he looked down at the officer with wide-opened eyes. She took off her helmet, and the long, brown hair fell down, framing her heart-shaped face and beautiful almond eyes.

"Olwen?" he said, unbelieving, even though he shouldn't be surprised. He knew his other superior worked as a SWAT officer nowadays.

"Not so loud." She looked him over. "Have you been here all night?"

"Yeah."

"Is it true what they say about Ophelia?"

Without answering, he handed her the badge. She took it and scrutinized the photo. Then she gave it back to him. "I'm sorry."

"Yeah, me too."

"She's not been found yet?"

"No. We searched in the back area where a witness says he saw her just as the bomb detonated, but nothing yet. Just this."

Olwen handed him a floor plan over the store. "Can you show me?" With the marker he tightly held in his hand, he circled the place where they thought Miri was. "Thanks. You're on your way home now, right?" He nodded, his throat aching when he thought of doing something as ordinary as taking a shower and sleeping when Miri— Olwen gave him a penetrating glance and seemed to think something over, but then she shrugged and reached into her pocket. "Here," she said. "It'll help you sleep."

He took the pill from her without looking at it. "Thanks."

31

She turned and opened the door. "I'll see you around," she said and headed out. Carl just nodded, tired to his bones.

Chapter 2

He didn't call Beth until he sat in his car. The smell of burnt flesh and dusty concrete oozed from his clothes and skin. The only thing he wanted to do was to go home, take a long, hot shower, swallow that sleeping pill, and black-out until tomorrow morning, but he had this one duty left to do.

"Hi, Carl." Her voice was quiet, and he knew that she already knew.

"Hi, Beth." His own voice was nearly unrecognizable. The silence stretched out. "I'm sorry," he managed to say eventually. She didn't answer but drew a deep, shaky breath. "We found her badge an hour ago."

"Okay."

"I don't want to—" No, he wasn't going to say something stupidly comforting they both knew wasn't true. Instead, he said, "We've only found her badge, nothing else."

"I understand."

"We're... we're still searching."

"It's alright, Carl. Thank you." The silence stretched out once more. Carl rubbed his neck and let his hand continue up and run through his hair. Beth sighed again. "If you don't mind, I'm going back to... to..." He could almost see her waving her hand as she struggled to find words.

"Yeah. Take care, Beth."

"You too."

They hung up, and Carl covered his face with his hands, but he couldn't cry. After a while, he managed to compose himself enough to start the car and drive the twenty minutes home.

Coming into his small apartment was like entering a bubble of quiet harmony. The sienna colored walls in the living room complemented the Persian carpet on the warm golden hardwood floor. Together with the soothing incense that seemed to infuse every room, he felt his shattered nerves relax. Getting rid of his clothes was the first thing he wanted to do. He couldn't undress fast enough. Naked, he went into the microscopic kitchen and threw his clothes, his jacket, and shoes into the cupboard beside the trash can. He never wanted to see them again. As he stood in the apartment, looking around, everything seemed to remind him of Miri. In his mind's eye, he could see her sitting on the sofa, smiling at him, as she had yesterday evening. It felt impossible to understand that she might never come here again, that they might never again sit together on the sofa, drinking tea and chatting about books and movies, history and philosophy, that she might never again share a home-cooked meal together with him, and that he might never again have the chance to let her know that he really liked her.

With a stuttering breath, he sternly cut off the thoughts. Instead, he hurried into the shower and let the hot water flow over him. The vanilla-scented soap washed away the last fourteen hours of grime, sweat, sorrow, and anxiety, and together with the sleeping pill Olwen had given him, he managed to calm down and drift off to sleep, not even an hour after he came home.

When he woke up from a restless dream that he didn't remember, the room was dark. He glanced at the alarm clock. Four a.m. He turned around on his stomach and sprawled in bed, wishing he had someone special to embrace. As he loosely hugged his pillow, he somehow managed to drift off to sleep again.

One and a half hours later, the CD alarm went off. This morning he had the pleasure to be lulled awake by the ambient dark-jazz of *Bohren & der Club of Gore*. As he lay there, listening to the music, he felt drained. His face and pillow were damp. He must have been crying in his sleep. Slowly, he rose from the bed, and couldn't help groaning. Every single muscle hurt, and under the lingering scent of vanilla, he thought he could still smell burnt flesh. He turned up the music, grabbed the lighter on the bedside table, and without bothering to put on a robe, went around the apartment lighting candles and incense. Standing naked in the living room, he stretched his body, warming the muscles. Eyes shut, he let his mind disappear in the movement, the music, and the calming scents as he performed the program. Afterward, he took another steaming hot shower until he felt totally relaxed, and the vanilla won the battle over the burnt flesh.

He was struggling with finishing his breakfast when the phone rang. He glanced at the display window.

"Alan. Damn it." Filled with foreboding, he answered. "Yeah?"

"Yes, um, Alan here." His boss's voice still sounded stressed out. "You know, let's just skip the whole briefing room meeting. We'll do a short phone conference instead."

Relief flowed through him that Alan didn't call to tell him they'd found Miriam dead.

"Alright."

"Okay, wait a minute, I'll just connect Sharon and David. Um, just a second."

"Hiya, Sharon here." The older woman's voice was high-pitched and cheerful as usual.

"David here." David's mature voice was deep, warm, and trusting, and as always, it reminded Carl of Caesar. Both of his colleagues were excellent interviewers and had about eighty years' experience between them. None of them was a personal friend to him, but they were a pleasure to work with, and he always enjoyed taking part in their vast knowledge.

"Yeah, I'm here too."

"Good, good." Alan's nervous voice broke in. "Alright, let's start. No one really believed we were going to finish the cleanup quickly, right?" Carl kept quiet, but the other two hummed in agreement. "Of course we didn't. So, I've worked out a schedule with the other departments and the SWATs. We need to get to the victims ASAP, right?"

"Right," Sharon agreed. "Those poor people."

"Sharon and David, you're both too old to work with the debris clearing. You continue with the interviews at the

South Side, and contact those who have been released already. Don't forget to keep clean records and journals."

Carl rolled his eyes. It was so typically Alan to try and teach the seniors their job even though they'd started working as FBI when he wasn't even born yet.

"Don't worry, Alan." David's reassuring voice didn't sound offended. They all had more patience with Alan than he deserved. "Sharon and I worked out a good system yesterday. We'll hand it over to you this afternoon."

"Good, good. Carl, you and I will continue at the site, clearing debris. We're not night-timers, so I've worked out a schedule of our usual eight to five shifts."

"Oh, that's great!" Sharon chirped, saying what Alan wanted to hear.

"Yes. The contractors who are involved now say it will take about a week to clean up the place. I don't think we'll be working onsite that long; we've got more important work to do, but for now, they need all they can get, firefighters, contractors, us, to get all the dead bodies up from there." He paused. Carl clenched his teeth at the disrespectful tone. It was no use saying anything. Alan wouldn't get it. In all his life, Carl thought, he had probably never encountered anyone who was so good at profiling people, but who had no clue at all about social graces. Alan cleared his voice nervously when no one said anything. "Anyway, I'll keep in contact with you, David, during the days, and I'll come over to South Side every now and then, just to check in."

When Alan paused again, Carl's eyes narrowed. *And as usual, you don't even acknowledge Sharon and her competence! Asshole.*

"Sounds good, Alan," David said. "We'll have the reports ready for you, as long as we know when you're coming."

"Of course, of course. I'll be over at three. Carl, I'll see you at eight onsite. Any questions?" He waited slightly, but no one said anything. "Good, good. I'm on the phone if you need me."

The conference call ended. Carl sighed relieved and let his hand comb through his hair. Then, he glared at the cupboard with the trash can and went over to gather his clothes from the night before. He wasn't going to throw away new clothes every day, but he refused to wear these until necessary. Instead, he hurled them into a black garbage bag and placed it at the door. Time showed seven-fifteen. He could still grab a coffee from his regular shop if he wanted to, but his stomach felt sore and uncomfortably full from the one sandwich he had managed to eat. Unwillingly, he took the garbage bag with his used clothes, carried it down to his car, and drove directly to the site.

Coming back only twenty-four hours after he had left it, didn't reveal much of a difference. It still looked like a war zone with people milling around hauling debris. Honestly, it didn't look like anyone had worked at the site at all, and he'd be damned if that sickening smell didn't linger all over the place still. Clearing the site in just a week, as Alan had said, seemed more than a bit optimistic.

In the HQ van, he grabbed the event log to see what had happened during the past twenty-four hours. The victim's report was the first he checked with slightly shaking hands and an anxious lump in his throat. There were now eighty-seven survivors, but he couldn't see Miri's name anywhere, and twenty-one deceased. The description of those who hadn't been identified didn't match Miri. Carl felt torn. He was relieved to see that she wasn't among the dead, but the fact that she hadn't been found yet was alarming. He tried to put it out of his mind. If he was going to be able to work at all today, he couldn't search for Miriam under each and every pile. He would go crazy in the end, breaking down, wondering if he had searched at the wrong place, wondering how injured she was, if she was slowly bleeding to death or suffocating— *No! Stop it right there! I am going to go out and MOVE DEBRIS, nothing else, and I'm going to do it slowly and carefully and meticulously, so I don't miss anything or mess anything up.*

He took some deep, shaky breaths and pulled his hand through his hair several times. When he felt relatively prepared – *I'm never going to be fully prepared* – he went out, looking for the coordinator to get a location to start at, not caring to wait for Alan, who was late anyway.

"You're under Alan Bai, you say? Not sure I know where you're supposed to be, but if you don't mind, you can help out at the epicenter. Report to Special Agent in Charge Qiu over there." The FBI-agent pointed with his whole hand, and Carl nodded.

Carefully, he trudged over the uneven surface until he reached the sweaty and tired agent. Several dogs were sniffing around the perimeter.

"Reinforcement? Great," she said before he had even had the chance to introduce himself. "So what we're looking for in particular are pieces of a stroller. Here. Take a look."

Carl put on his unreadable mask when she gave him five evidence bags containing different deformed metal parts and pieces of dirty green fabric.

"A stroller?"

The agent nodded grimly. "Yes, we've found what we think is the bomb carriage, and that's a stroller.

"Was, um, was there a baby in it?" *Why wouldn't there be a damn baby in it? People just love destroying others' lives. Damn it!*

"It's possible, yes, but we haven't identified any yet, although we have found the person of interest, at least what's left of her."

"Her?" Carl repeated, somewhat surprised, but the SAC rattled off the information at a rapid pace as if she had done it too many times already.

"We've found a severed head that corresponds to the damage a suicide bomber suffers when wearing a bomb-belt and it's a female head. The stroller parts found corresponds to damage that would occur if it'd been filled with detonations." Qui paused and picked up a bunch of see-through bags from her FBI-carrier. "Here, take some e-bags. And speaking of detonations, if you find something, anything, that looks like parts of copper wires, plastic tubes, and suchlike, place them in bags too." She took a quick breath and looked down at his hands. "Good, you're already wearing gloves. You can start over here. If you find any body parts, let me know."

With a hard knot in his stomach, Carl began to search for whatever could be of interest while trying not to think of what the SAC had told him. He felt a little lost in this more or less unknown territory. *Miri should've been here,* he thought without being able to stop himself. *She's the one who's good at finding things, seeing things. Me, I'm just second class.* Despite that, he found a whole bunch of evidence. What surprised him was the large number of bomb pieces lying around. He had not expected that many parts to survive the blast. A couple of hours of thorough searching made him fill up several e-bags, and it was almost lunchtime when he came close to the bomb unit.

"How can you cram so many explosives into one single stroller?" he overheard a younger man say, bewildered. "I mean, a stroller?"

"That's no problem," an older officer answered. "What worries me is where the hell she got them from."

When they noticed him listening, they silenced and walked away. Carl shuddered at the thought of how many casualties there would have been if Miri hadn't somehow been alerted and managed to warn people.

He hadn't caught one single glance of Alan the whole morning, and he suspected his SAC had found something 'more important' to do. Not that he was surprised. As long as Carl had known him, Alan had never been enthusiastic about working with his hands or getting dirty.

Suddenly he stopped his slow, methodical search. Something was half-buried under some debris. *No, no, no, please let it be something else.* Reluctantly, with sweaty hands and hard-beating heart, he crouched and carefully removed the debris. That horrible smell wafted up toward him, and he choked violently. A terribly burnt face without eyes looked up at him. He stumbled backward, sliding over the debris, and somewhere far away, he heard someone shouting at him, but he couldn't make out what. Everything spun around him, and he wasn't aware of what was happening. A hard slap on his face woke him up, and he turned on the side and vomited.

"First time, boy?" a rough voice said beside him.

Carl avoided shaking his head. "No, not the first time, and that's the problem," he gasped.

"Well, first time or not, you can't lie here. Can you walk over to the van? You're too big for us to carry."

"Yeah..."

With the help of the SWAT officer, he managed to get up on his feet and stagger to the van.

"Here, have some water," the older man said kindly, after leading him to the only chair, and gave him a bottle. Gratefully, Carl drank deeply. "You wanna talk about it?"

"No." *Can you please just get out of here?*

The other man suddenly scrutinized him with squinting eyes. "Wait a minute, you're not that agent who was almost burnt alive, right? In that huge scandal four years back? Star Student?" Shocked, Carl jerked his head up and stared at the African-American man with eyes wide open, before racing his hand through his hair several times, without answering. The officer patted him on his shoulder. "Thought I recognized you. Name's Jones, but I don't believe you remember me. Don't worry. I'm not telling anyone. You just take your time, and maybe you'd better ask your superior to give you the rest of the day off and to be placed somewhere else. No one who's been through what you've been through should have to work with this."

"Thanks," he managed to croak.

The older man patted him again, rose, and went out. Finally, he was alone.

The images in his head came unwanted, no matter how hard he fought to keep them out. Accompanying the shaky film in his mind were the sounds, the horrible screams, and the smell. Oh, God, that smell...

It was a sunny day. Carl knew that because when he tilted his head, he could see the beautiful blue sky above the bundle of gray houses that served as a fortification. Eight long, sturdy stakes made out of wood decorated the round grass-clad yard. Carl couldn't see them properly, but he thought they had once served as telephone poles. If nothing else, they were uncomfortable enough. He tried once more to ease off the pain from where his hands and feet were chained to the stake, but to no avail. Though what frightened him was the terrifying foreboding that he was going to hurt more, so very, very much more before the day was over.

They were all here; he, Ned, Nigel, and Nadir from Team N, and Uranus, Uriel, and Ursula from Team U, and they were all chained to stakes. There was one empty stake, and the reason for that was why Carl was the only prisoner honored with a gag. It had already made his mouth completely dry, and his tongue felt like it had doubled in size. He hadn't believed he'd be able to talk the guard into letting the young Star Student research assistant go, but he'd had to try. She was only seventeen and had her whole life ahead of her, and whatever these mobsters had planned for them, he was sure none of them would get out alive.

Yes, he was afraid; he was crap-my-pants-afraid. He didn't want to die. He was only twenty-five and had a five-year-old daughter who needed him. He wasn't finished with life yet. None of them were. He looked at the others. Ned, who had remarried only a few months back and was going to retire next year, Nigel— Well, yeah, Nigel might be finished with life. Carl had never understood why the Faculty still let him be active. The guy was so damn nervous that he exploded if an ant looked at him the wrong way. But even if he was crazy, he didn't deserve to die in the hands of mad religious zealots who didn't have an ounce of empathy for others. Then there was Nadir, who always loved to laugh. The two of them were real friends in a way Carl had never experienced before, not even with Simon and Sonia. He

41

watched the members of FRT U where they were strapped up just opposite him. He didn't know them well enough, but they sure as rail tracks get wet in the rain had better things to do with their lives than end it here, today. And everything because of a stupid, damn mistake. No, he didn't blame Nigel. The guy was obviously irrational, but the Faculty should have known better than to send him with them.

On the other hand, one could have thought Nigel should've known better than to light that damn cigarette, but he was a chain-smoker and crazy on top of that, and after a whole day without his kick, he was about to do something tremendously stupid. Ned saw the signs as well as Carl, so eventually, he told Nigel to take two puffs of his cigarette, nothing more. Apparently, Nigel only heard the "smoke your cigarette" part because he sneaked away, and when Ned finally went to get him, four cigarettes lay at his feet, and he was smoking away on the fifth as if it was going to be the last one he ever had. Well, as it looked now, he might've been right about that part.

As if things weren't bad enough, Nigel also decided that this was the perfect time to knock Ned unconscious for having the guts to reprimand him. Carl didn't know if it was the lit cigarettes or Nigel's shouting, or both, that gave them away, and it didn't matter. The Faculty's mistake to send Nigel on this Research Project when he was clearly unstable would end with the deaths of seven Field Researchers.

Something stirred at the main entrance. A group of men and women entered the yard. In the middle, Carl recognized his guard, hands bound together with a rope. The group steered the former guard toward the last empty stake and started to haul him up, all the while he was shouting and screaming and kicking and squirming to get away. Carl felt sick to his stomach. So, because of his actions, someone else was going to die here today anyway. Not that he regretted anything. He would do it again if it meant Danielle managing to get away.

It took them about fifteen minutes to get the screaming, squirming man up on the stake, and his feet, hands, and stomach chained. Around his neck, a bag of some sort was hung. Meanwhile, about fifty people gathered around, watching silently. Some of them had drums hanging around their necks. A woman Carl hadn't seen before walked to the middle of the yard. She was clad in a red cape, and her shaved and oiled head gleamed in the sunlight.

"We have gathered here today to take part in the execution of these heretics," she began in a deep voice that seemed to reach throughout the fortification. Carl suspected that she had some kind of amplifier to be heard without shouting. "These seven police officers," she continued with conviction, "came here to try to destroy our community. They failed, just as every other association will fail. The-All-in-One stands behind us and will protect us."

"Yog-Sothoth," the crowd breathed.

"These people are dangerous. They have powers unknown to us, and they were sent here to try our faith. Our brother was weak, and he will be punished. That man!" The woman pointed toward Carl, and the crowd murmured. "That man deceived our brother. He will not only suffer the cleansing fire, but he will also watch all the others burn before him. He will have plenty of time to contemplate his sins and rethink his path in life."

"Y'ai'ng'ngah."

"Helgeb, light the cleansing fire for our brother."

The former guard on the stake began screaming again. "NO! I will repent! Please, I will repent!"

"Yes, brother, you will."

Carl's heart hammered like crazy as several of the audience members gathered wood from a woodpile he hadn't noticed before and placed it underneath the guard's stake. He watched the others, and he could see the same shock and disbelief on their faces as he felt on his own.

"Wait!" Ursula shouted, and the cape-clad woman turned to her.

"Yes, heretic, what have you to say?"

"I'm... I'm pregnant. You can't burn an unborn baby."

There was a slight pause, but Carl couldn't see the woman's face, so he didn't know what she was thinking.

"Well," she said eventually. "We could. It has happened before, in another enclave." *Oh, God,* Carl thought, bewildered, *there are more of these lunatics?* "We, however, are not barbaric. An unborn child does not share its mother's sins." She looked at the men who had taken them out to the yard. "Did any of you notice if this woman is pregnant?"

"I thought she was just fat," one of them mumbled.

"Rip off her clothes. I want to see if she speaks the truth."

Obligingly, the man went over and shred Ursula's clothes. Pain flashed across her face as the chains bit into the flesh, and her arms were stretched out. With her upper body naked, Carl could clearly see her baby bump. Around the fifth month, he would say, from his own experience.

"Take her down," the woman said. "We'll keep her here until her baby is born. If she has come around to our way of thinking by that time, she'll live. If not, she'll burn, and we'll raise her baby as one of The-All-in-One's own."

Carl stared at the woman's back. If she didn't understand that there would be people searching for them, she was more delusional than he had been led to believe. Eventually, they would find this place, if not this week, then the next one at the latest. It wasn't as if the Faculty didn't have the Teams' coordinates and knew exactly what kind of RP they were assigned to, and since Ned had failed to contact them during the last couple of days when they'd been prisoners, a search party might already be on its way. He didn't have any high hopes of being alive when the rescue team came, but at least Ursula would live.

Ursula was taken down from the stake and staggered along when another woman with long blond hair brought her inside the fortification. While she walked away, she kept her

44

gaze on the ground as if she was ashamed for being rescued from the execution. *Don't be ashamed,* he thought. *Live and take care of your baby.*

"I'm pregnant too!" Nigel suddenly shouted, and everyone on the stakes, except the guard, laughed.

The red-clad woman glared coldly at him. "Trying to be comical will not help you, heretic. You will soon try your ridicule on the burning flames." She nodded toward the blond, heavyset man who Carl thought was her executor. "Helged. It is time. Bring the cleansing fire to our brother. May he find atonement in pain."

The guard started to scream again when the blond man lit a torch and to the sounds of slow-beating drums solemnly marched up to the stake and set the wood on fire. The crowd began to chant something Carl didn't understand as the flames reached higher and higher. Unable to look away, he saw how the flames closed in on the guard's body and licked his feet. Soon the guard's screams were not screams of fear, but of pain, unbearable pain and agony, as his bare feet turned black and cracked in the fire. A violent churn in his stomach made Carl retch behind his gag. He couldn't look anymore! He couldn't see this! The guard screamed and screamed, and the fire roared. Tears of shock and compassion fell from his eyes and wet the gag.

"Faitho, make that man look. He will not be allowed to escape his punishment."

Carl glanced around toward the assembled people to see who Faitho was. Worriedly, he saw a heavyset man with a huge butcher knife making his way toward the stake. As soon as the man stood at the foot of it, he fixed his emotionless eyes on Carl and held up the knife. Even now, with the threat of being burnt alive, Carl tried his best to wiggle away from it. Then, Faitho moved his hand so quickly that he barely saw it. A sharp flash of agony pierced his shin, and he inhaled painfully. Blood dripped from a wide, but shallow wound in his leg. Faitho pointed toward the burning stake with the knife, but Carl, filled with defiance, continued to look down

45

at the butcher. Once more, the man pointed with the knife toward the scorching flames, but Carl refused to look. If it was so important that he watched people burn, then they had to try harder and by other means than some flesh wounds. The thought hit him that this might be a way for him to stall for some time.

The butcher cut him deeper in his shin, and Carl groaned behind the gag. It hurt like hell, and blood flowed freely down his leg. With a gaping mouth, Faitho attempted to talk, but only grunts were heard. Nauseously, Carl saw that his tongue had been cut off at some time. The man began to wave with the knife as if to force him by will to look at the burning man, and Carl saw incipient fear in the butcher's eyes, not fear for him, but for what he'd suffer if he didn't manage to make Carl watch. Even now, when he was this scared and nauseous, a small wave of empathy hit him.

Faitho started to slap Carl's thigh with the broad side of the knife, and through the pain and fear and compassion, Carl forced himself to grin around the gag at him and at his desperate attempts to make him look. Driven to desperation, the man raised the knife and swiftly thrust it deep into his thigh and rotated it. If he could, he would've screamed, but the pain was too extreme. Only raw groans slipped out of the gag, and red waves of pain flashed in front of his eyes. Then, everything went black.

When he regained consciousness, some weird metal construction held his head up at an uncomfortable angle, but the tired pain in his neck felt like nothing compared to the intense pain in his leg. Gradually, he became more and more aware of the pain, until it crept up through his whole body and made his eyes water and his entire body cringe in futile attempts to get away. Weak groans slipped out of the gag. As soon as he opened his eyes, he saw what was left of the guard. The whole body was blackened and scorched. The feet and half the legs were gone, just burnt away, and the head— What the hell had happened to his head? It looked like it had exploded, partially. Waves of nausea rushed through him, everything started to spin, and he fainted again.

Next time he regained consciousness, the pain had subdued to a dull aching. Exhausted, he noticed that the shadows in the yard were deeper and darker. *Early evening. We've been here all day.* His head was still pinned to whatever contraption they used to make him look straight ahead, and his whole body ached, but it seemed as if someone had a bandage on his hurt leg. Apparently, they didn't want him to bleed to death. He glanced at the others, but thanks to the contraption, he couldn't see all of them. Nigel had lost consciousness for some reason, and his body hung slumped on the stake, but Ned and Uriel seemed to still be aware of what was happening around them.

"He's awake!" someone shouted, and the red-clad woman turned toward him. Had she been there all day too?

"Good. For being so weak, you have caused us quite the ruckus." She looked him steadily in the eyes with a solemn expression, before continuing, "Therefore, you will have the privilege to name which three shall be burned next."

He stared at her, still dizzy, didn't really think she was serious. *Are you kidding, lady? What makes you think I'd do something like that?* As if she knew what he was thinking, she made a gesture with her hand, and two young teenage boys came forward carrying armfuls of fresh birch branches.

"If you name them, they will be strangled before the fire is lit. If you don't, these green branches will be placed in the woodpiles, so the fire will burn slowly, which will be much more painful and take them longer to die. Take off his gag. I want to hear what he has to say."

Carl felt the first tendrils of panic. She was serious. She didn't lie. How could he choose which ones who were to die? If he chose three, how would the rest of them die? If he refused to choose, how could he sentence people to a slower and more painful death? Wildly, he stared at the others.

"I volunteer," Ned shouted suddenly.

"I volunteer too!" Nadir's voice was heard from his left side.

"I too," Uriel said.

For the first time, the woman smiled. "You have loyal friends, heretic. I hope you deserve them." She turned toward the man who had lit the fire under the guard. "Helged, bring the garrote."

Helged immediately went over to a sandbox and picked up the garrote. *A sandbox? They keep these things in a sandbox? How often do they execute people here?* Two other men brought a larger stepladder and put it down under Ned. Ned looked straight at Carl and smiled kindly.

"I'll see you on the other side, Nero. Thanks for all the good times."

Deep sobs heaved Carl's chest, and tears fell from his eyes. They blurred his sight so much that he didn't see the details of Ned's face when the garrote was placed around his throat and tightened, but he heard the sickening choking sounds for an eternity. When they finally stopped, Ned's head hung lifeless, his tongue sticking out between his lips.

"Look!" the woman shouted. "The heretic has feelings! He cares for his friends." The crowd laughed loudly, and the drums beat a sensational tune. "Let's burn the body before the soul escapes. Helged."

Still crying, Carl saw Helged douse the woodpile and Ned's body with a liquid that smelled like benzene. When the man lit it with his torch, the whole stake went up in flames with a deafening roar. Helged worked quickly. Ned's body hadn't even perished in the flames before he proceeded to Uriel. Uriel didn't say anything. He only looked straight ahead when the garrote was placed around his throat.

Beside Carl, Nadir prayed in Arabic. It was a du'aa he hadn't heard before, even though he knew about it. It was a du'aa invoked when tragedy struck.

"We are from Allah, and unto Him we return. O Allah, take me out of my plight and bring to me after it something better."

48

As Uriel let out the last gurgling chokes, something broke inside Carl. With a burning hatred he had never felt before, he promised that if there were a life after this, his ghost would not rest until these people suffered as much as he and the others had suffered here today.

"Catch the heretic's soul, Helged. Don't let it slip away."

"*To Him, we belong, and to Him, we shall return.*" Nadir's voice was calm and soothing. Carl wished he could move his head and look at him, that he could talk to him.

The benzene stung Carl's nose, and the heat from the flames burned his right side as they engulfed Uriel's body. This new pain awoke the pain from the deep knife wound. Lightheaded from agony and fear, grief and hatred, he tried to convince himself that this was a better death, had to be a better death, than what the guard had suffered, but every kind of consolation felt empty.

"*O Allah, surely Carl is under Your protection, and in the rope of Your security, so save him from the trial of the grave and from the punishment of the Fire. You fulfill promises and grant rights, so forgive him and have mercy on him. Surely You are Most Forgiving, Most Merciful.*" Nadir's voice quieted a couple of seconds. "Carl," he whispered urgently in Arabic, "don't forget that revenge and hatred will eat your soul. Bear love and forgiveness in your heart. Allah will see the deeds of the wrongdoers for what they are and do with them what He sees fit. My love for you is like the love for a good brother." Carl cried again. He heard the step ladder be put down on his left side, and heavy feet climb it. "Laa 'ilaaha 'illallaahu," Nadir cried out.

Carl wished that he could scream, that he could move, that he somehow could save them. The fact that he couldn't, pained him more than anything he had ever experienced before. Nadir's death du'aa broke off and choked. This time, Carl closed his eyes.

When the heat from Nadir's death pyre reached him, it felt like the breath of a giant dragon that burned his left side. The smoke from the fires lay thick and heavy over the small yard. *There's no wind here,* Carl thought dazed. *Nothing that can blow away the smoke.* The suffocating smell of burnt flesh made him retch under the gag.

"Now, heretic, only one more of your friends is left to suffer for your crimes, but you have yet another choice to make. Either you or he suffers the green branches' slow fire. The other one gets doused and burned quickly."

One more? Does she mean Uranus? What about Nigel? Is he dead? Carl realized that Nigel hadn't moved on his stake during the whole strangling and burning. He was still hanging slumped. *Something must've happened when I was out. Why didn't they burn his body too if they're so eager to catch our souls? Was he too crazy for them?* The thought of Nigel being too mad for these madmen made him giggle hysterically underneath the gag, but only wheezing sounds broke through. The giggle died away soon enough. At this point, he felt so drained that all he wanted was to end all of it. It hurt everywhere, except in his leg, which he couldn't feel any longer. That was an extremely bad sign, but he was too far gone to care anymore. What did a lost leg matter when he was going to burn anyway?

"Remove his gag. I want to hear his verdict."

At that moment, a gunshot echoed around the yard, and the red-clad woman slumped. There was a sudden shocked silence before the crowd screamed and ran toward the main entrance, stopping short when they were met by several SWAT officers aiming at them with their shotguns. Carl saw Helged frozen in place, still with the torch in hand, but he abruptly composed himself and rushed toward the stake where Uranus hung. Carl stared at his fellow FR. The relief on his face from the sight of the SWATs got replaced by unbelieving terror as Helged doused Uranus and the pyre underneath him.

"No! No! Stop him! Oh, God in Heaven, stop him!" Uranus pulled the chains violently and screamed louder. "God, shoot him! Shoot him! I don't want to die! I don't want to die!"

The sticking smell of benzene penetrated the sickening smell of burnt flesh. The roar and heat of the fiercely burning fire reached him, and Uranus screamed, high-pitched shrieks of agony that ripped Carl's soul apart. Helged stood in front of the stake, watching the man burn. His arms were up in the air, and his lips pronounced words Carl could not hear. Through the roaring fire, another gunshot blasted, and Helged went down. The shot fuelled the crowd who uncertainly had lingered around the entrance and let themselves be surrounded by the SWATs. Everyone cried out with rage and attacked the officers unarmed. Several more shots were heard, and people fell. The yard echoed of screams of fear and pain and frenzied fury, but Carl was only aware of Uranus' horrible wails until they abruptly ended. He barely noticed how the people at the door were overcome, and the ones still living taken away. Too many lay unmoving on the ground. The next moment, everything was quiet except for the dying fire and the never-ending wails in Carl's head. He wanted to claw his scalp to get them out of there, but his hands couldn't move. Two SWAT officers left the others and approached Nigel.

"Oh, my God, look at his head. He can't be alive."

"No. He's not."

"Shit, man, these people suffered. Burnt alive? Can you believe it? And the one still burning— I've never seen anything like it."

"The damn bastard managed to douse him with something. He just went up. God, I'm shaking."

"At least we got him. Oh, my God, Jones, that guy over there, he's still alive! He's looking at us!"

"Shit! Get him down! Get him down!"

The two SWATs rushed across the yard toward him, and not being able to stop himself, Carl cried.

Chapter 3

The memories slowly faded away, leaving Carl trembling uncontrollably. When he buried his face in his hands, he realized that his cheeks were wet with tears.

Alright, breathe now, breathe. You can't get a panic attack here. Breathe, goddammit, breathe!

He took some deep shattering breaths, trying to calm down, trying to steer his thoughts away to something else, touching on Miri, but shied away immediately. *No, can't go there now, just can't. If I do, I'm done for.* In his mind's eye, he saw himself on the floor in a fetal position, helplessly crying with sweat covering his clammy face. Desperately, he searched for something else, anything else, detached from him that could help him calm down, but his mind was blank from everything that wasn't work-related. *Okay, fine, work. Um, work what? Uh...* He took another deep breath and felt something stir. *Um, alright, what happened after the RP? It changed everything. That's good, I can concentrate on that.*

Jones was right, he thought. The whole RP had become a huge scandal. The Golden Fleece Society had nearly been kicked out of the FBI, something that had never happened before. The only thing that had saved them was a massive reorganization. The entire Faculty got sacked, and a new one was chosen. Amongst other decisions, the new Faculty decided that before any FR-Team was allowed on a Project, they had to undergo a psychological evaluation to establish if they were fit to operate. No Research Assistants were allowed to take part in any Projects that could involve violence. The Faculty also had to report coordinates and updates from the different Field Research Teams that operated within the FBI to a specially appointed SAC at the FBI HQ.

All in all, Carl thought it was good news. The FRs were FBI-agents too, after all, and they had a responsibility toward the FBI as well, not only toward the Faculty. He only wished they could have gotten rid of the silly Field Researcher names too, but the Faculty decided to keep them.

A week after the new Faculty had taken on its responsibility, one of its members, Anna, visited Carl at home since he was a convalescent. He appreciated that she did. It showed him that the new Faculty cared about injured Field Researchers, and it created another kind of relationship than what had existed before. The new members weren't the faceless Faculty anymore; they were people he could finally connect with.

"The names have lots of symbolic and ceremonial worth and value," Anna had explained to him. "They're part of who we are. They define us as a unit and give us a sense of belonging." He had to concede the point, but now, when he was wearing his third FR name, it also stood for all he had lost. Not only that, sometimes FRs like him, who had gone through several names, also had a hard time remembering what name to answer to in the heat of a moment. It was easier for someone like Caesar, who never had changed his name until he became Faculty.

Now, two years later, he had come to accept that he never would be able to get over that Project, no matter how long he spent in therapy. Sometimes, when the thought of it struck him from out of the blue, or when he woke up from nightmares, or smelled the horrible odor of a barbecue, he still felt guilty about being the sole survivor. Honestly, he didn't count Ursula and Danielle. They hadn't been there. They hadn't seen everything. They were the lucky ones. At those times, the thoughts wouldn't leave him alone, and he waddled through oceans of what-ifs. If only he had been unconscious half an hour longer. If only he had had the opportunity to talk before Ned volunteered. They used to call him *Golden Tongue Nero*. Surely, he'd been able to say something to, if not stop the executions, at least stall for more time.

At least, he had stopped screaming, "It's not fair!" in his lonely apartment, but that didn't mean that he still didn't feel that way.

Sometimes when it was truly bad, he lay in his bed crying inconsolably, seeing Ned's lifeless head with his tongue hanging out, or Nadir's badly burnt and unrecognizable body of which he had caught a glimpse when the SWAT officers removed the cage-like device his head had been fastened to. At these times, it wasn't any of the psychiatrist's words that managed to calm him down, but the imagined presence of Nadir and his comforting du'aas. *Yeah, and the Xanax. Don't forget your beloved pills, Carl,* he thought bitterly.

To be fair, he didn't take them at times other than when an anxiety attack struck, and together with the therapy sessions he actually managed to attend, he was now able to accept that he couldn't have done anything to stop the events from happening.

The therapy went on for half a year before he had been appointed a new FRT, the C, where he became Cyrus, and then another half a year of therapy before C accepted the damn Research Project where he got those claw marks on his back. In retrospect, he'd probably needed more than a year in therapy before going on a new RP. *Yeah, I screwed that one up pretty badly. Can't believe Caesar kept me considering what I did. Well, when all's said and done, I'm glad he decided to give me a second chance.*

When he entered C, he had promised himself that he wouldn't make any new friends and that he would be cold, professional, and distant. He knew that something would happen sooner or later that would make him lose them anyway, and he couldn't go through that again. For a year and a half, he had managed to keep that promise before Miri somehow found the key to his feelings without even trying, and now the day he feared had come, the day he might find her dead.

Carl drew another shaky breath and drank the rest of the water Jones had given him. The panic attack had stalled and disappeared, thank goodness. He wouldn't give in. He was needed here, and now he knew what the worst parts would look like. The next burnt body wouldn't catch him off guard.

Still a little unsteady on his feet, he stood up, grabbed a couple of wet wipes from the table, and wiped the sweat and grime from his face before heading out. The sun was peeking out from behind the clouds, and he squinted against the harsh light.

While walking back to the epicenter, he saw Jones coming toward him with a concerned frown.

"You're white as a sheet, boy. Sure this is the right place for you?"

Carl clenched his teeth. "I'm not giving in," he said defiantly.

Jones looked at him with respect. "You're one tough cookie. What's your name again?"

"Carl Hansen."

"Yeah, that rings a bell. I'm Jones, as I said. Mike for my friends." The big African-American man looked him over. "So, you've got Scandinavian ancestors or what?"

Carl didn't show that the question surprised him, even though he saw through the attempt of redirecting his thoughts. With a trembling hand, he tugged at his hair, grabbing some strands and let them glide through his fingers, feeling too confused and dazed to grasp everything going on around him.

"Dad's grandpa was Danish," he managed to say eventually.

"Thought so. I know you can't tell from the looks, but family legends tell of some Scandinavian blueblood in my veins too." He gave up a thundering laugh as he held up his dark hand and looked at it. Carl tried a smile for the first time that day, tried to normalize things, and got a friendly nudge on the shoulder. "You look better already." Then the older man let his gaze wander around the scene. "What a mess. Never thought anything would happen in nice quarters like this. D'you know if they've found the girl yet? The one everyone's talking about?"

Carl swallowed hard and shook his head. "No, she's still missing." His voice cracked, and he cleared his throat quickly, but not quickly enough.

Mike stopped mid-step and scrutinized him. "No, no. Don't tell me you know her."

"Miriam Goldblum. My co-worker and my… my girl." A slow blush he couldn't control crept up on his face, making it burn. *Why the hell did I say that for? 'My girl'? Am I for real?* Anxiously, he tugged at his hair again. *God, I'm such a mess. I hope she never hears about it. It would be so damn embarrassing.*

Mike gave him a long look, and Carl met his gaze, tired to his bones. A huge hand landed on his shoulder.

"You're one unlucky man, Carl. I'm sorry, my friend."

The thought that he should be offended touched him, but he didn't take offense. Instead, the genuine sympathy this man radiated worked as a healing spell.

"Thanks."

"Okay, let's try to find her," Mike surprised him. When Carl looked at him with inquiring eyes, the officer took up a thumbed and folded sheet of paper and a pencil from his breast pocket. "You know," he said while carefully unfolding it, "I'm one lazy bastard and don't like to work more than I have to, so I've been studying the reports coming in. Here, take a look." Carl looked obligingly at the map in Mike's hands. "This place here and this one here," he showed with his pencil, "—have been thoroughly searched. They're positively empty of victims. Here's the epicenter. This area here—" He drew a circle around the epicenter. "—we're ninety percent certain being empty of victims, thanks to your brave girl. That leaves this area here. As you can see, this wall here separates the store from the employee area." Carl followed Mike's explanation with keen interest and, for some reason, growing hope. "Here's the customers' washroom, just before the big double doors that lead to a common storage area. Behind this door here, lies the meat department. Over here, at the other end's the bakery and over here's the produce. This place here's the dairy. Right?" Carl nodded. "So your girl ran this way, from what I've figured out. She started here, right, 'cause she must've seen the bomb carriage. She ran over here, according to witnesses, and continued here, according to other witnesses. That way, she covered most of the store, probably relying on people over here getting the drift and following the herd. Right?" With another nod, Carl saw everything in his mind's eye. "So, she runs back again, past the epicenter and the washrooms, which had to take more than some guts, through the doors here and here, to the meat department where a young butcher tells us she was right behind him when it blew."

"I thought you said you're lazy," Carl remarked, and Mike laughed.

"Believe me, I am. That's why I'm doing thorough research before jumping into the crockpot, to minimize the workload."

"Yeah, makes sense."

Mike grinned. "I knew you'd get it. Anyway, she's not been found here—" He drew an X on the map. "—where the butcher boy said she was. Thing is…" Mike pulled another map from his chest pocket. "This here's the basement. As you can see, the bearing wall goes right under the X here. That means—"

Carl suddenly filled with hope. "She's there," he said with certainty. "She must be. There's still hope."

Mike smiled at his suddenly beaming face. "Let's go and dig up your girl, Carl."

Together with three others, they cleared debris for five hours at the spot Mike had chosen before they found anything. It was Agent Hawkins and his border collie Cutie who directed them. Cutie had sniffed around for a while when she suddenly marked, and Carl's heart skipped a beat. They immediately started to clear away the debris, and not even ten minutes later, they found the damaged floor. Cutie whimpered eagerly, and Carl had to restrain himself from

57

jumping down into the hole. *Safety first,* he had to remind himself. *She'll not be helped by a couple of broken legs.* Another agent, Mbeko, carefully checked the floor's durability before he lay down on his stomach and flashed his light down into the hole.

"It's the basement, alright, and it's pretty intact. There's only one pile of rubble down there. A wall that collapsed, most likely. Oh, my God, I see something! She's half-buried under it. Help me down."

Carl's legs collapsed under him, and he had to sit down.

"Easy now, my friend," Mike said. "Easy now. Breathe."

Carl became aware that he was holding his breath, and he forced himself to take deep, calming breaths. His heart hammered like crazy, and his throat felt as dry as a thousand-year-old column in the desert. Mike gave him a new water bottle, and he drank deeply.

From down the hole, they heard Mbeko shout, "It's only a coat, nothing else. I need some assistance to remove the pieces of the wall."

Carl immediately stood up, and Mike helped him down before providing a ladder and extra light. The cold room was empty and smelled faintly of vomit. Carl looked around, but couldn't discern any source to the smell. Instead, he walked over to Mbeko, who stood at a large heap of rubble that covered the stairwell. It seemed to come from a collapsed wall and an upper floor. Behind him, the rest of the men climbed down before helping Cutie down the ladder. The border collie sniffed around and marked at several places, including at Miri's one-of-a-kind bright-red coat which lay half-buried high up under the rubble.

Carl cleared his throat. "Yeah, it's hers."

"Okay, she can't be far away." Mbeko flashed the light over the rubble again. "Agent Goldblum? Can you hear me? Help is on the way. Can you make some kind of noise, so we know where you are?"

The five men held their breaths, but no sound was heard. Tears burned in Carl's eyes, and to hinder them from spilling, he flashed the light at the coat. Several light-brown strands of hair were stuck under a big piece of concrete, and blood stained the broken concrete pieces underneath. Carl inhaled shakily and brought out an e-bag.

"It's her hair and some blood," he said, trying to sound calm and professional. "She's been here if nothing else."

Mbeko came up beside him and studied the area. Then, he frowned. "It's a weird position. She seems to have been sliding down on the rubble and then got stuck under it. If you look here at how her coat is placed, I'd say she was conscious and managed to break free." Carl followed Mbeko's gestures and nodded with growing hope, but the agent spread out his arms and frowned, clearly concerned. "But if she was, where is she now? It doesn't make sense."

"She must be under here somewhere. Maybe she got trapped a second time," Mike interposed. "Let's clear it."

It didn't take long. An hour later, the area was cleared, but no Miriam was found, and there were no other traces that she'd been here; not under the broken wall, not in the collapsed elevator, not under it, and not in the also collapsed stairwell. Even the spots Cutie had marked were without traces. They all looked quietly at each other.

Eventually, Mike broke the silence. "She's been here. We have the evidence; her hair, her coat, blood. There's no way she's been able to get out of this place on her own, and we were the first ones clearing this site."

"She can't just vanish into thin air," Mbeko said with the same troubled expression Carl had seen numerous times when ordinary people encountered something that shouldn't be. He looked around the enclosed area one more time, even more thoroughly than last time, trying to figure it out, trying to find somewhere, anywhere, she could have gone, somewhere she could have become trapped, but there was nothing.

Mike just shook his head. "Honestly? I don't get it."

The older man glanced at Carl, who tried to wipe away his tears without them noticing. *Failing with that too,* he thought with bitterness completely unlike him, but he was so damn tired of getting his soul ripped apart again and again.

Mike's voice was very gentle, "Go home, Carl. You've been here all day, and it's been very emotional for you. You need to sleep."

Carl nodded. "Yeah. Thanks." He took Miriam's coat and climbed up the ladder into the early evening.

The whole drive home, he tried to create an empty space in his head, but the thoughts clamored and wanted to get in. *Go away,* he growled at them. *Just fuck off!* They didn't listen, and images of Miri's broken body haunted his mind.

As soon as he got home, he threw himself and the coat on the sofa and buried his face in the red fabric. It didn't even smell like her anymore; it just smelled of concrete and dust. Finally, the tears ran freely, and he curled up on the sofa, sobbing.

It wasn't until he woke up that he realized that he'd fallen asleep. He felt completely drained. In a way, he welcomed the emotional hibernation. Right now, it felt better than the raw pain and sorrow.

As Carl sat up on the sofa, his whole body protested. He grimaced, but it was also a relief having something else to wrap his mind around instead of Miriam. With her coat in his arms, he wandered over to the big window. The night was dense, but everywhere he looked, light penetrated the darkness. High above, the stars competed with the city lights, but their faint glow nearly disappeared in the competition. For a while, he just stood there, looking out at the dark sky and the city's nightlife, without thinking, while cradling the coat, but eventually, he composed himself and went to the minuscule hallway where he hung the coat in the closet.

"You'll have to come here and get it yourself, Miri," he mumbled as he brushed off the worst of the dirt with a clothes brush. "Until I find your body, I'm not accepting you're dead. So there."

When he felt relatively satisfied, he put the brush away and stripped off his own dirty, sweaty clothes at the door. On his way to the bathroom, he saw the answering machine blinking and pressed the button.

"Carl?" It was Manda's worried voice. "I saw the news. Do you want me to come over? Or do you want to come here? I know you probably want to be alone, but I don't think you should. Please, call me, okay? Sarah sends her love."

The machine whirred.

"Carl." He grimaced when he heard Alan's voice. "I've got a message from Dean Henderson at homicide. Your presence is required at HQ tomorrow. A murder case with a child witness. You're supposed to check in with Mr. Henderson at ten a.m. Sleep in and be representative. You know how important our job is."

Carl sighed and went into the bathroom, where he lit some of the tea lights instead of turning on the bright bathroom lamps. A quick glance in the mirror showed him that he'd already lost some weight. His face looked sunken and hollow-eyed. *I need to eat, I guess,* he thought listlessly, but shrugged the thought away and turned on the hot water. He wasn't hungry. After the shower, he went to his bedroom to try to get some more sleep. Instead, he lay awake for three hours, fiddling with his cell phone and repeatedly clicking and refreshing the FBI's missing person's list from the bomb site until his alarm went off.

Mechanically, he brushed his teeth, combed his hair, washed, and put on deodorant and eau de cologne, before dressing properly for a day at the office. His eyes felt like they were filled with sand, and his stomach was as hard as a date pit. At least he'd be doing something, not just sitting at home, wallowing in the loss.

"I'd go stir crazy," he mumbled and rubbed his sandy eyes.

Before leaving, he reluctantly called his ex-wife. To his relief, he only reached her answering machine. In an unnaturally happy tone, he recorded his message.

"Yeah, thanks for checking in, Mand. Um, I've been called into the office today, so I won't be at the site. If it's Miri you're wondering about, she's, um, not been found yet. I don't know when I'm off, but probably too late to drive to your place anyway. Don't worry about me. I'm good. Tell Sarah I love her too."

Liar, he thought as he hung up. *Well, maybe it's not a lie if the person you tell it to knows you well enough to recognize it as one,* he continued his chain of thought, but then, he shrugged. *Honestly, it doesn't matter how I feel. She can't do anything about it anyway.*

As he was about to walk out the door, he took up the folded newspaper that lay on the floor at the front door. A big photo of Miri was on the front page with the words *FBI-HERO!* all over it. He looked at it, indulged in the smile and the happy look in her eyes. With a finger, he stroked her cheek. Then, he took the whole paper to his closet, where he had an empty shoebox and put it inside.

Leaving his apartment, he drove to the big gray building where he spent most of his days trying to get people to remember things correctly and to tell the truth, or if that wasn't possible, to at least try to discern what were lies. Not always the easiest of tasks, but at least it was never boring. He took the elevator up to the third floor. Usually, he took the stairs, but his body protested at the mere thought of more exercise. When he knocked on the door to Dean Henderson's office and peeked in, the SAC of the homicide department talked on the phone and just gestured at him to take a seat, and threw a thin file to Carl as he obligingly came in and sat down. While flipping through the few pages, he half-listened to Dean's distinct New York City accent.

"No, sir, we've just started the investigation. There's no reason for the media to link her to Joanne Siegler's death at this point. We've nothing specific right now that connects them. Yes, of course. I'll keep in touch." Dean hung up and adjusted his glasses. "Thanks for coming in, Carl. I know you've been busy at Kroger's. This case here turned up on our table yesterday, and there's only one witness, a young girl, four years old, so we wanted you for this."

Carl nodded. "What are the circumstances?"

"An elderly woman, Karen Smith, found the girl walking on I-95 in the middle of the night and took her to a local police station."

"I-95? Isn't that the discontinued one in New Jersey?"

"That's right."

"What was an old lady doing there in the middle of the night?"

Dean shrugged. "You tell me. We haven't had the chance to interview her yet. I'm putting Sharon on that one."

"Yeah, she's good with that. Sorry, I interrupted you. Why was it handed to us?"

"Long story short, NJPD found a car with Michigan State plates and a murdered woman in the front. On check-up, she's a university student at MSU, single, no kids, so the NJPD got suspicious about all the kid stuff in her car; you know what I'm saying? Turns out the kid's missing from Cincinnati. Case gets turned over to us."

"Does she have a criminal record? The student, I mean." Carl flipped through the few pages one more time and pulled out a school photo of a smiling young woman.

"None whatsoever. Her grades are tops. Comes from a clean middle-class family. No connection between her and the kid."

"So, we're actually looking for a third person, eh?"

Dean grinned. "That's what I'm talking about, Carl. We've put Allie Harris on the case today."

Carl raised his eyebrows as he recognized the name. "Allie Harris? I thought I heard you say there's no connection between this case and that of Joanne Siegler?"

Dean gave him a broad grin. "Let's just say I'm following a hunch. Allie might be young, but she's the best specialist we have on serial killers."

"Alright. Am I assigned to this case too, or just here for the interview of the child?"

"Right now, just for the kid. We'll see later on if that changes, know what I mean?"

"Sure thing. So, what are the details of the child? She's from Cincinnati. What else?"

"Name's Ariel Wing." Carl's lips actually made an attempt to form into a smile, and Dean caught it. "I know, right? Parents these days. What's wrong with Teresa or Sophie? No way, now it's Belle and Aurora and Jasmine. Damn Disney." He paused and corrected his glasses. "Anyway, Ariel Wing turned four on January thirteen. Parents are Alexis and Jason Wing, both born and bred in Cincinnati. Nothing special. High school sweethearts. He's working as a computer engineer; she's a kindergarten teacher. No economic problems, no criminal recs, no history of violence, no known enemies. Kid's at a day home during work hours and gets snatched from the high-fenced backyard when the provider makes lunch. This was April eleventh, so little more than a week ago now. Provider Lucia Hernandez never saw the perpetrator. When she came out to get the girl, she was just gone."

"Huh." Carl drummed thoughtfully with his fingers on the chair's arm. "She's been with the kidnapper a few days, eh?" Dean nodded. "Well, hopefully, she'll be able to give me some kind of description, even though she's very young. When can I meet her?"

"A social worker will be here with her at eleven-thirty."

"Alright, that'll give me enough time to go through the file and set up the room. Anything else? Anything I need to know about the student? Name, for example?"

"Right. Stephanie James. Twenty-one years of age. Studied to become a lawyer. Missing from the university since April eighth. Well, that's it.

"Alright." Carl stood up. "See you later, then."

"You just go ahead. I'll be here if nothing calls me away."

Carl nodded, took the folder, and left for the child interviewing room. It was bright and sunny with airy yellow curtains and a fairytale landscape painted on the walls depicting an enchanted forest, a mountain with a castle on top of it, a lake, and a meadow with lots of flowers. The moss-green rug on the floor went tone in tone with the painted grass on the wall. It was big and soft and fluffy, and he'd seen numerous kids hide their toes and hands in it and some who even lay down to snuggle on it, pretending they were in the fantasy realm they saw on the walls.

When he first started as a child interviewer, the room had looked like any other interview room; gray, boring, and intimidating. He had fought for years to change it to this, and last summer, he had finally gotten the approval. The results with the children had become so much better, just as he had predicted. What he hadn't expected, however, was that it quickly became the favorite place for FBI people who wanted to steal a couple of minutes of quiet and calm whenever it was unoccupied.

From the cupboard, which was painted with flowers and butterflies, he brought out cookies and juice boxes and placed them on the kids' table. He was glad he'd managed to drive by the store and pick up some fresh blueberries and a fruit tray. Cookies were fine, but he liked to make the kids feel a little bit extra special.

He cut and filled small bowls with pieces of strawberries, grapes, and chunks of pineapple and honey melon, before bringing out his special things from his child victim interview bag; the old-fashioned-looking tea party set with roses and violets, and the four stuffed animals. He set the table with the porcelain and placed the stuffed kitten,

65

puppy, teddy, and bunny on small chairs around it. On the tiny plates in front of each animal, he put a blueberry each, before placing the rest of the berries in a bowl of their own. At last, he scrutinized the result and felt satisfied. It looked perfect. Different kids acted and reacted on different cues, but the tea party almost always worked, even with boys, at least up to a certain age.

On the old CD player, he put on a cd with carefully chosen tunes by *Bohren & der Club of Gore* on low volume. He had often found the ambient dark-jazz soothed both the kids and the adults.

Time showed eleven o' five. While he waited for his clients to arrive, he sat down crisscross on the carpet and read the file again. There wasn't much to go on, more than what Dean had already told him, but he memorized all the details and tried to figure out what was left out since it was obvious that quite a few case details were missing. Irritated, he realized it was too vague to work out, and restlessly, he flipped through the pages without being able to concentrate. With a grimace, he closed the file, hid it under the rug, and brought out his cell phone instead. Quickly navigating to the FBI page on the missing, dead, and surviving people from the bombing, he anxiously read the lists over and over, hoping for some miracle, but Miri's name was still under the missing persons. A few times, he clicked and refreshed, clicked and refreshed the page, but nothing changed.

When there was a knock on the door, he turned off his cell phone, tossed it into his work bag, took a deep breath to regain his professional persona, and called out, "It's open."

To his satisfaction, it was Elliette Burns who came with the little girl. Not that the other two social workers he occasionally interacted with were bad, but he and Ellie had worked together for six years, and she knew exactly how he wanted the scene.

The girl held Ellie's hand and looked curiously at the surroundings. She didn't seem traumatized, Carl reflected with relief, even though she had a nasty looking bruise on her cheek. Her short brown hair had been neatly combed, and he guessed it was the always meticulous Elliette who'd provided the brush. Her own blond hair was neatly formed into an elegant bun at her neck, and her makeup was discreet and sophisticated, making her brown eyes and high cheekbones stand out.

"Hi, Carl," Ellie said and kneeled down to the girl's level. "This is Carl, Ariel. He's very nice, and he'd like to invite you and me over for tea. What do you say? Do you want to have some cookies and juice?"

The girl nodded eagerly but didn't let go of Ellie's hand. While the social worker stood up and closed the door behind them, Carl waved cheerfully to Ariel.

"Hi there. I have some friends here who'd like to meet you." He took the bunny from its chair and waved its paw at the girl. In a high-pitched voice, he said while jumping the bunny up and down, "There she is, there she is! Can I say 'hi' now?" In his regular voice, he looked at the bunny and said, "Sure you can, but you'll have to wait 'til she sits at the table with you."

Ariel giggled, and Ellie smiled and tugged her along to the table.

"Nice to meet you, Mister Bunny," Ellie said and shook the paw. Ariel took the paw too.

"Nice to meet you, Mister Bunny," she repeated.

"Nice to meet you too, Ariel. These are my friends, Puppy Pie, Kitty Kat, and Teddie Freddie. We love tea parties. Do you?"

"Yes, I do, Mister Bunny."

Carl took up the stuffed cat and changed his voice to a slightly more feminine version, "I love strawberries. They are my favorites. What's your favorite?" Ariel pointed toward the grapes. "Those are my favorites too," Teddie Freddie said with another version of Carl's high-pitched voices. "Do you want to share with me?"

Ariel looked at Ellie, who nodded encouragingly. "It's okay, Ariel, I've known Teddie Freddie for a long time, and he's the best sharer." She put some fruit on a plate and handed it to Ariel. For a while, they ate and played and managed to get some great giggles out of the girl. When Carl felt that she trusted him enough, he took up Teddie Freddie, who seemed to have caught Ariel's heart the most and put on the voice recorder.

"I heard a bad person took you from your ma and dad, Ariel," he said in Teddie Freddie's voice. The girl nodded with big eyes and hugged herself. "And I know you have bad dreams." She nodded again. "Do you know what I do when I have bad dreams?" Ariel shook her head. "I hug someone I trust and tell them about my bad dream. Do you want to tell me?" Ariel nodded and held out her arms. Carl put Teddie Freddie in her hands, and she hugged the bear hard. "Do you want to tell me about that person who took you?" he asked in his own calm and reassuring voice.

"He was very bad," she whispered and hugged the teddy even harder.

"How was he bad?"

"He was bad to the lady."

"What did he do to the lady, Ariel?" As he led her through her memories, he was careful to keep his tone soothing and gentle. Ariel looked him trustfully in the eyes as she hugged Teddie Freddie tightly to her chest.

"He made her cry and bleed. She needed a Band-Aid. But she was sleeping, and the bad man went away. He didn't come back. The lady didn't wake up."

"What did you do, Ariel?"

"She was sleeping, and I was hungry."

"Did you have anything to eat?"

"No. I wanted to go home to Mummy and Daddy."

"What did you do then, Ariel?"

She looked down, and two red spots covered her cheeks. "I was bad," she whispered, distraught.

"Why?"

"I went out. I wanted to go home. Don't tell mummy."

68

"I won't tell her."

Ariel looked up at him with a pleading look in her eyes. "A lady gave me fries. Mummy says it's bad to eat things from strangers, but I was so hungry."

"That's okay, sweetie. Mummy won't be angry."

"Okay." She sighed, and Carl saw the first signs of tiredness in her appearance. Despite that, he decided to ask a few more questions before trying to get a description out of her.

"When he took you, was the lady in the car?"

Ariel nodded. "Yes, but she didn't say 'hi.' She just cried. I got scared."

"I understand, sweetie. Was there anything else that made you scared?"

"I didn't have my car seat. And I didn't have my mummy. And he hurt me because I didn't want to be on the floor, but I didn't want him to hit me anymore, so I was on the floor anyway." Carl felt his chest clasp in sympathy with the frightened girl, and as a tear trickled down on her cheek, Ellie hugged her gently. It was time to change the subject so he could get a description out of the girl before she became too upset to work with him.

"Ariel," Carl said, "can you tell me what the bad man looked like?" From his bag, he took out a large piece of hard plastic from which several pieces of human hair in different colors hung. He could see interest flashing back into her eyes, and the tears were forgotten.

"Is this hair?" she asked and fingered a dark-brown strand.

"Mhm."

"Look!" she giggled and put her own light-brown hair beside a matching color on the plastic piece. "And you have this one." She pointed to a copper-red shade. "And you have this one, Ellie." She pointed to a honey-blond shade. Carl did a mental happy dance. She was spot on.

"What color did the bad man have?"

69

Without hesitating, she pointed toward an ash-blond nuance. "And the lady has this one." She fingered on a walnut-brown strand that matched Stephanie James' on the school photo he'd seen of her. Carl brought out several pieces of hard plastic, each of them with a different skin tone. He pointed toward his own arm and took up a sheet with a very pale color and placed it beside his arm. She giggled again as she compared her own skin to the different pieces.

"Which one did the bad man have?" he asked her, and she pointed to a skin color slightly darker than Carl's own, which fit into the type one category of the Fitzpatrick skin typing test.

"Very good," he praised her while bringing out a new piece of hard plastic. This one was translucent and had pairs of eyes printed in a row on it.

"Which color did the bad man have in his eyes?"

Ariel frowned uncertainly. "He had glasses, just like grandma."

"Alright." Carl put the eyes away for now. Instead, he took out a sheet with different shapes of glasses. "Can you show me what they looked like?" Ariel didn't hesitate. She pointed toward the big, round ones. "Good job!" he praised her again and brought out another sheet, this one of different lip sizes. With a concentrated frown, she studied them before decidedly pointing at the thinnest lips.

Several other hard plastic sheets found their way out of Carl's bag, these ones with different styles of beards in various colors, including a beardless half-face. Ariel immediately pointed toward a goatee on the sheet with blond beards. The next pile of sheets had different hairstyles in the same colors as the beards. He chose the one with ash-blond hair and showed her. She studied them thoroughly and pointed toward a neatly cut style.

The last plastic sheet he brought out was shapes of faces. Ariel looked at them and frowned uncertainly. Carl placed the skin tone on the floor and chose the blue pair of eyes, which seemed to be the most likely choice if he continued with the Fitzpatrick scale, and placed it over the first face that was oval-shaped. Then he put the sheet with the lips and the beards on top of it and placed the goatee over the face, the hair, and lastly, the big, round glasses. As soon as he put all of the sheets together on top of the skin color on the floor, Ariel shook her head.

"No, he was fat," she said decidedly, and Carl nodded. He replaced the oval face with the round, burly face, and Ariel turned sickly pale. She swallowed hard and hugged Teddie Freddie. Carl removed the sheets immediately and looked sincerely into her eyes.

"Thank you so much for helping Teddie Freddie and me out. I couldn't have done this without you." With wide-open eyes, she nodded seriously at his words, and he continued, "You're a very brave girl, and you know what? I have a baby Teddie Freddie, who wants to follow you home, and every time you have a bad dream, you just hug him, and he'll help you." He got out a small replica of the big teddy bear from his bag and gave it to her.

Ariel's face brightened with excitement, and she hugged the teddy hard. "Teddie Freddie," she whispered and closed her eyes.

Ellie smiled at him over the child's head and made a thumbs-up. "Anything else?" she mouthed, and he shook his head. She nodded and stroked the girl over her hair. "Shall we say bye to Carl and his friends?"

To his surprise, Ariel shook her head and stared at the different sheets of facial features.

"Can I do the lady, too?" she asked.

"Absolutely," he said, positively surprised and gave her the female sheets.

While she worked, Carl and Ellie watched her anticipatorily, and little by little, Stephanie James' face took form.

Carl shook his head admiringly. "It's spot-on," he said to Ellie. "Just spot-on. Amazing."

71

They smiled triumphantly toward each other over Ariel's head.

"Well," Ellie said, "now you know how accurate your sketch is."

"I do. I really do." He leaned forward and ruffled Ariel's hair. "You did an awesome job, Ariel. Give me a high-five."

She grinned proudly and gave him a high-five. Then, she suddenly yawned.

"Tired," she said and put her thumb in her mouth while hugging baby Teddie Freddie.

"Let's go back, Ariel. Your mummy and daddy will probably arrive soon."

"Mummy and Daddy? YAY!" Apparently forgetting how tired she was, Ariel flew up onto her feet and tugged at Ellie's hand.

As Ellie got pulled toward the door, she turned toward him and said, "I don't think I've ever told you how clever your system is."

Then, she and Ariel were out of the room, and Carl sat alone on the floor with the different sheets spread out around him. Stephanie James' face looked solemnly at him, besides that of her killer. He studied the face of the murderer and wondered why he had walked away from the car, leaving the girl alive so she could describe him. *Maybe he wants to get caught? Or maybe he doesn't think a young child can be a trustworthy witness?*

Sighing tiredly, he shrugged and stood up. With the pile of sheets in a firm grip to keep them in place, he went out to the copying machine and printed five copies of each. As soon as he had the two faces in his hand, he went back into the room and placed the facial parts back into his bag. Before cleaning up, he decided to go back to Dean with the copies.

"Ah, Carl. Did you get anything?" Dean asked as soon as he entered the office. Carl handed him the sketch of the killer. The other man studied it thoroughly. "So, this is our murderer," he mused. "Great job, as always. Anything else?" Carl handed him the sketch of Stephanie James. Dean glanced at it before looking up at him, amazed. "It's spot-on, Carl. Wow, this is hole-in-one!" he exclaimed enthusiastically. "We need to get this murderer-sketch out to the public ASAP. Maybe we'll catch him before the week's over. Did she tell you anything else?"

"Yeah, she witnessed the murder, but she doesn't seem to understand what happened."

"Thank goodness," Dean commented in earnest, and Carl nodded.

"I have the interview here," he said and showed the small voice recorder. "Do you want it?"

"Absolutely. Better yet, send it to my email when you've transferred it to your laptop. I'll hand it over to Allie later on, together with the sketch. Thanks, Carl, I don't know what we'd do without you."

The rest of the day, he spent cleaning the interview room, writing a psychological evaluation over Ariel Wing, and transcribing the interview from recorder to document, all of which he e-mailed to Dean at the end of the workday. When finished, he sat in his tiny office, restlessly drumming his fingers on the desk. Now, what? He didn't want to go home, and he didn't want to drive all the way to Amanda and Sarah, and he didn't want to return to Kroger's, even though they'd probably welcome him there as a couple of extra hands that could move more debris. If he was going to be completely honest with himself, he had to admit he was too exhausted and didn't trust himself with doing a good job. *No, Carl, that's not what you're afraid of,* he corrected himself. *You're afraid you're going to be the one finding Miri, burned, crushed, and dead.*

Abruptly, he rose from his desk, trying to rid his mind of the vivid image of the burnt body he found yesterday. Unable to decide what to do, he collected his material and took a detour past David's and Sharon's offices. David's was empty, but he found Sharon writing away on her computer.

She had colored her hair purple with white streaks in it this time, he noticed, and it looked great.

"Hi, Carl. What a pleasant surprise. You look tired."

"Mhm, thanks," he said drily, before admiring her hair again. "You, on the other hand, look audaciously fresh. Your hair just rocks. May I invite you out on a date?"

She laughed out loud and blew him a kiss. "Just you wait until I write that on Facebook," she grinned at him. "A thirty-year younger man wants to take me on a date." Intensely fanning herself with her hand, she continued humorously, "Look at me blushing. My friends will be green with envy." Then, she grimaced and patted the computer screen. "However, I'm already occupied by this demanding lover. I have so many reports to write that I'll probably sit here 'til midnight."

"Any news about Miriam Goldblum?"

She shook her head, suddenly serious, and the glance she threw him sideways didn't escape him. Did everyone know about his feelings for her nowadays? If so, how the hell had that happen? When had he become this transparent? He felt unpleasantly naked as he tugged at his hair.

"Sorry, Carl," she said in a genuinely caring tone. "I haven't heard anything but what we already know. And she's still missing. Look." She gestured at her computer screen and fiddled with the mouse. The next moment, the now painfully familiar FBI page dedicated to the bombing showed up. He glanced at it and nodded, hadn't expected anything else.

Clearing his throat, he changed the subject. "What about this lady you interviewed, Karen Smith? Why was she walking on I-95 in the middle of the night?"

Sharon readily followed his cue, no doubt out of her usual kindness. "Ah, yes, you interviewed the girl today, right? Well, it wasn't as suspicious as it sounded initially. She's a night owl and takes her dog on long, nightly walks. Her coat was full of white dog hair, and she showed me a photo of it, a big scary beast. Gave me the chills all over, just to see it in the photo, but then again, I don't like dogs. One of those sons of Bill bit me as a child. Can't stand them since."

"Right, I remember now. The leg, eh?"

"Right you are." Her eyes glittered. "I know it's a huge disappointment for you, but I'm not going to show you. Sorry, love. Oh, my friends would all faint if I told them you wanted to see my leg. They're so conservative." She laughed and winked at him as he shook his head at her, amused. "Anyway, you need to move on, sweetheart, so I can finish before dawn." She blew him another kiss, and he took his leave in a much better mood, which probably was her intention. *The ups and downs of working with a whole bunch of profilers. You can never hide anything. On the other hand, you can never hide anything.*

Instead of going home, he drove to the store and bought some bread, shredded vegetables, and more grapes, as well as a small bag of birdseed, before heading down to Lincoln Spring Park. It was his favorite place to relax. Every time he came here, the vision of the urban planner amazed him. There was something magical about it, like stepping into another dimension. How the wilderness and the tamed nature blended together was incredible. The streetlights were formed like blooming trees and almost hidden amongst the greenery. When dusk set, they spread a soft light that transformed the whole park into a fairy realm. In the middle of the park surrounded by weeping willows, a lake had been hidden away.

Carl walked the winding path that led him there. The soft ripple of water and the wind's gentle dance with the willows' leaves soothed him. He chose a wooden bench near the lakeshore that looked like it had grown from the ground and been altered by forest elves. At this time in the early evening, very few people visited the park. Carl could only see a couple sitting on a bench at the opposite side of the lake, but he doubted that they had even noticed him. They were too engulfed in each other.

As he pulled out big hands of shredded carrots and grapes in halves for the ducks, and bread for the swans, all the birds came waddling up toward him and grabbed at the pieces he threw out to them. He found their cooing relaxing. One swan was especially bold and came all the way up to him, craving some extra attention. Carl smiled and gave it a big piece, which it swallowed in a second and loudly gaped for more. As he continued to feed the birds, he occasionally glanced toward the kissing couple and felt a huge emptiness. Not once during these past two years had he taken Miri here. It was too romantic a place, and he'd been afraid coming here with her would have given her the right signals for once. He shook his head in regret. What a stupid way of handling their feelings, and what a lack of respect for her.

Suddenly, he realized that he'd fallen into the same trap he'd silently berated other men for falling into, by taking away her choice. He felt his cheeks burn with shame. *How could I do that? I'm no better than Caesar.*

How bad would it have been if he'd let her know that he wished for something more than friendship? The worst thing that could've happened was her telling him no, and he was a grown-up man, he could take a no. It would hurt like hell, but at least it would be her choice, not his patronizing idea of what she might or might not want.

He sighed and gave the big bird the last piece of bread. For some moments, it tugged at his pants, but eventually, when it realized that the goodies were gone, it gave up and waddled back to the lake.

In his mind's eye, he saw Miri's delight over the birds and the serene beauty. He promised himself that if he were ever granted a new chance, he would take her here and feed the birds with her, and walk the winding gravel paths with her as the sun set and the magical lights lit. Then it wouldn't matter if she read him right. *I wouldn't mind,* he thought. *Not at all.*

She was as sensitive to beauty as he was, and she would love this park. There were so many nooks and crannies and cubbyholes everywhere, and so many deliberately hidden gems; fountains and brooks and small decorated bridges, sculptures, and flower arrangements, not to mention all the squirrels. He had a distinct feeling that she'd love the squirrels. They were practically tame, and many picked food from his hand if he was patient enough. It wouldn't matter that they weren't a couple; just sharing this place with her would be enchanting enough.

The thought that this was a daydream that most likely would never come true made his throat ache. Before he started to cry again, he took the empty bread bag and left the lake and the entwined couple. He entered upon another magical path flanked by blooming cherry trees. The highest branches had been braided together to turn the path into one long archway. The gravel crunched quietly under his feet, and the wind's soft rustling made some of the pale pink petals glide through the air down on the path. At times like these, he wished he were a poet or an artist or a photographer who could capture the aching beauty he saw. As it was now, he could only honor it by immersing himself in the serene feeling he believed he would have felt entering a church, had he been religious. The path took him to a fork in the road, and he chose the right one, which would lead him to another favorite spot of his.

The little glade he stepped into was abandoned by people, which he was thankful for. In the middle, a small artificial mountain had been created, and, on top of it stood a birdseed house in the shape of a small fairy-tale castle. He went over to it and swung open the roof. The hinges had recently been oiled, he noticed. They didn't squeak this time. He opened the bag with birdseed and filled the castle to the brim. When spring arrived, there weren't as many people buying birdseed, and Carl found it more or less empty. He regretted that the sun had already set and that he wasn't going to see any birds by now. He took the empty bag and threw it into the tulip formed garbage bin before following another path out of the glade. Time showed eight p.m. The park gates would close in one hour. He wasn't in any hurry.

At the loud, unexpected sound of his cell phone, he jumped, heart in throat, and birds shrilled, frightened, from the trees around him. As quickly as possible, he muted the phone and answered.

"Yeah?" The static made him grimace, and he held the phone some distance from his ear. "Hello?" The static continued, and he was just about to hang up when he thought he heard a voice trying to get through. "Hello?" he said again, heart throbbing like crazy. "Miri?" The static just went on, and he shook his head. *I must've imagined it.* He listened a little while longer, but no voice came through. Slowly, he took the phone from the ear and hung up, feeling apprehensive. *Could it have been her?* Inhaling deeply, he fast-dialed her number with trembling hands but hung up when the usual automatic voice let him know that the customer couldn't be reached. The damn tears began to fall, and he wiped them away, grateful no one else was around. The serene atmosphere was gone, and he walked faster to get to his car.

The phone rang again, and his heart jolted.

"Miri?"

"Carl? It's Alan."

He suppressed a sigh at his boss' nervous voice and put on his own happy one, knowing that Alan needed to observe his body language to see through him.

"Boss. How's it going? Did you just call me?"

"What? No, no. Um, I have good news for you. The reports you wrote today were very successful. The young woman, um, what's her name now again? Hardy, Harolds, Harvey, something. Uh, that chubby woman, you know? The so-called serial killer expert?" Alan paused, but Carl kept quiet, clenching his teeth at the disrespectful tone. "Uh, she wants you to work with her. You're supposed to meet her at eight a.m. tomorrow."

Relaxing, and with a pang of satisfaction in his chest, he said, "Oh. Wow. Yeah, that is good news." This time he was genuinely sincere. It was fabulous that he could perform professionally enough for the renowned expert to be impressed, even now, when he was struggling to cope with this new tragedy.

Alan cleared his throat in his usual annoying way, and continued, "Don't forget you're representing us, so look nice, be clean, and shave."

Carl rubbed his face and shook his head while trying not to laugh or sigh. *He's just, I don't know, incredible, or something.*

"Sure, Alan, don't you worry," he responded and put on his trusting tone,

"Good, good, I know I can trust you."

"Uh, boss?"

"Yes?"

He didn't want to ask. It would make him vulnerable in front of a person he deeply despised, but he needed to know, and Alan was good at sniffing out secrets. "Any news about agent Goldblum?"

The silence on the other side was hard to interpret. Then, Alan said, slightly surprised, "No. Why do you ask?"

Carl closed his eyes momentarily and suppressed a shaky sigh. "Just curious," he answered, couldn't sound as casual as he wanted to, but Alan didn't question it.

"So eight tomorrow, don't forget."

He finally hung up, and Carl tried to laugh at the whole situation, but, instead, he was near tears. With great effort, he composed himself. Shaking his head, he went over the absurd conversation in his mind. *People definitely come in all shapes and forms,* he thought and stroked his chin and cheeks, *but Alan's in a class of his own.* As he already knew, he wouldn't need to shave for another couple of weeks or so. Trying to clear his mind, he quickened his steps as he walked the long way to his car and reached it just in time for the park gates to close.

Chapter 4

A young woman, around twenty-five years of age, stood at the end of the table, looking through some documents when Carl entered the assigned office at eight a.m. sharp. Her long honey-blond hair had probably been neatly braided an hour ago, but now several thick strands of hair had escaped and framed her face. She was dressed bohemian-like in a long flowing, dark-blue shirt, and wide jeans. Amused, Carl thought of Alan and his angst over Carl not being formally and properly dressed.

When he closed the door behind him, she looked up and came toward him with her hand raised in greeting. As he took it, he couldn't tear his gaze from her face.

"God, you're beautiful," he heard himself blurt out. Not even a second later, he realized that he had said it out loud. Suddenly frozen in place, a mortified hot blush burned his face, and he wished for nothing else than a huge hole to open up beneath him. *Oh, God, please, don't let her think I'm hitting on her or trying to make her feel uncomfortable.*

As he stared at her without knowing what to say, she looked amused.

"Why thank you," she said with a grin and a slight accent, which he couldn't place, while shaking his hand vigorously before letting it go. "You're not bad-looking either." It was as clear as crystal that she was teasing him, and he ran his hand through his hair several times.

"I'm, um, I'm sorry… I usually don't say things like that. I didn't mean— well, I did mean, but you're very intelligent-looking too— I mean—" *Good God, shut up, Carl, for everything holy in this world!*

A burst of heartily and contagious laughter found its way out of her. "You're sweet. I think I'll like working with you. It's Carl, right?" He nodded, still with hot burning cheeks, but relief filled him that she didn't seem insulted or upset. He couldn't even remember the last time he had made such a fool of himself. Probably not since high school. "I'm Allie. And don't worry, you didn't offend me. On the contrary." She winked at him, but the next second, the smile disappeared as she thoroughly studied his face. "Oh wow, you've been through some rough times lately. I'm sorry. I won't tease you anymore." Her voice was suddenly full of empathy.

Bewildered, Carl felt as if he had lost his footing. "How did you know?"

She smiled kindly. "I'm a profiler, remember? And I'm good, so trying to hide your feelings won't work with me. Sorry, but we'd better be clear about that part from the beginning."

He couldn't stop pulling his hand through his hair, and she gave him a direct look that managed to be honest, amused, and understanding at the same time.

"You're a hurricane," he said, almost fatigued, and she laughed.

"I'll take that as a compliment too." With that, her voice took a more professional tone. "Anyway, let's go over here." To his surprise, she took him by his hand and pulled him over to the short side of the table where all her documents were messily laid out. "How much have you been briefed?"

"Just the big picture, I'd say. Not very detailed. I got this." He handed her his thin file. She took it and quickly browsed through the few pages.

"Yeah, some important details have been left out in your report. You need much more info if you're going to be able to help me out." She handed back his file. "You probably wonder why this is now under-the-table considered a serial killer case, am I right?"

"Yeah."

"Okay. Take a seat." She sat down as well and nodded at his documents. "So, just to make a few things clear. First, your background is in forensic psychology and profiling, specialty child witness interviewer, right?" Carl

81

nodded. "Since I got your report yesterday, I've talked with people about you, and you have an excellent reputation." She took up a notebook and found a page. "Intelligent, highly perceptive, very empathic, great with both children and adults, usually manages to create trust with both victims and perpetrators, could become anything within the field." She glanced at his awkward appearance and gave him a gentle smile. "Sorry, didn't mean to embarrass you. I just want to make sure I get the best one for this case. Are you the best?"

He felt even more awkward but managed to not scoot around on the chair. "I'm good. Might even be among the top ten, but I usually let others decide that."

She studied his face for some seconds, before looking down at her notes once more. "Okay," she said eventually, clearly thinking him through.

He sat motionless on the chair beside her and didn't know how to feel about the situation. She seemed to be more straightforward and honest than most people he had ever worked with, and that disturbed him slightly, even though he couldn't put his finger on why. As the seconds ticked by and she still looked down at her notes, he suddenly felt that he truly wanted to work with whatever it was she hid from him.

He took a deep breath and looked her over. "You're used to working alone," he said, and she gave him a surprised glance. "And this is a case you find difficult. Otherwise, you wouldn't have asked for assistance, but you don't want to spill anything to the wrong person. You're not comfortable with the situation right now since you thought I'd be more upfront about my competence. If you have to work with someone, you'd prefer that they're more outspoken than you think I am. You've heard a lot of good things about me that speak well of my ability as a profiler, but you've also heard some negative things, which makes it hard for you to come to a decision. You thought that when we met, you'd be able to make this decision immediately, but now you're not so sure anymore, and that frustrates you immensely."

She stared at him with slightly parted lips and an astonished face. Then, she closed her mouth for a second before giving up a friendly laugh.

"Okay, I'm impressed," she said smilingly. "And you're on." She gave him another penetrating glance. "Just as you said between the lines, I like honesty, and I'm straightforward, and I'd like to have open communication between us. If you think I'm condescending in any way, let me know. I won't take offense. Too many people think I'm looking down on them as it is. You don't need to get in line."

He raised an eyebrow but smiled as he thought of the difference between this young woman and Alan Bai. He admitted to himself that so far, he preferred Allie Harris.

"Deal."

"Good." Without any more hassle, she returned to the report. "Okay, so you have files of Stephanie James and Ariel Wing. Thing is— Here, take a look." She rummaged around amongst her papers on the table and handed him a crime scene photo, which he hadn't seen before. It showed him Stephanie James sitting slumped in the drivers' seat with the head wound clearly showing. She had obviously been shot point-blank. It was gross, of course, but he'd seen worse. What immediately caught his attention, though, was the big sign that hung around her neck on a string. Written on it in big, capital block letters was the word *HELP!* He stared at it.

"Huh."

"Yeah, this is confidential, of course."

"I can see why."

"Thing is—" She handed him another crime scene photo. "This is Joanne Siegler. She was found on April third in Boston, but according to the coroner, she'd been dead for about three, four weeks."

This photo showed another young woman in a greater state of decomposition, sitting in the same position as Stephanie James, with a headshot just like her, and a sign around her neck with the word *HELP!* clearly printed.

"Okay. Is it the same handwriting?"

"We think so, yes. Here's another one." Allie put yet another photo in front of him. "This is Philippa Tyrnon, found December twelfth in Pittsburgh. As you can see, they're all about the same age, they have brown hair, similar complexion, and weight, and they share the same sign and head wound. The same bullets have been used in all three cases. They're from a Raven MP-25."

"A cheap enough pistol," Carl mused. "Yeah, I can definitely see why you think it's a serial killer. The pattern's as clear as glass."

Allie gave him a crooked smile. "It looks like it, right? But, here's the thing; only Stephanie James had a child in her car, a child without any kind of connection to her."

"He's developing his style? Stephanie's the last one, right?"

She gave him an appreciative look. "Not bad at all, and I'd probably agree with you, hadn't this victim been found." Another photo landed in front of him. Carl studied it thoroughly. "Peter Lee, forty-two years of age, found on December fourteenth not far from Philippa Tyrnon. The coroner says he died two days after Philippa's murder. There's no connection between the two victims except for this sign."

"*No one could help,*" Carl read.

"She's from Philadelphia, he's from New York, both found in Pittsburgh. He seems to have jumped from a bridge, or at least, that's what someone wanted us to believe."

"And he can't be the killer, obviously."

"Nope." She gave him another photo. "Here, you see his wrists had been bound long and hard enough to nearly cut off the blood circulation to his hands."

He studied the photos, and several different ideas swirled through his head, but since this was an entirely different subject than he was used to, he wasn't certain about any of them.

"Alright, enlighten me. I know almost nothing about serial killers and their psychology. You're acting as if this is weird. Why is it weird?"

She gave him another appreciative look. "Most people don't ask me that question, even if they have no clue whatsoever. I'm happy you did. That means I can give you an explanation that can help you help me later on."

Carl smiled in return. He liked this straightforward young woman.

"My pleasure."

"So." She took a pen and a blank sheet of paper and began to scribble. "Let's skip the whole lecture on how someone becomes a serial killer. That's not relevant right now. When it comes to serial killers, they're placed into one of the following categories: organized, disorganized, or mixed." She wrote down the three words and circled them. "The one we're dealing with is most likely in the organized category. They usually plan their murders and have specific ways of carrying them out. They might use the same *modus operandi* on all their victims, or choose only dark-haired women, or only prostitutes, or one-legged retired pirates." She looked amused as she quickly drew a one-legged pirate lying on the ground with crossed-out eyes. "They're also usually quite knowledgeable of forensic science, which means they own the scene, so to say."

"It's harder to find their traces?"

"Yeah. So, in this case, it's definitely the same person who killed the three women, no question about it. What troubles me, though, is the rest. They don't belong to the pattern. The handwriting specialist says it's the same person who wrote all the signs, including the one on Peter Lee, but why the difference? Why start with one victim and one M.O, to continue with another victim, different M.O, to go back to the first type of victim and M.O in two different cases? And why suddenly kidnap a child and let her go? If it had been a development, then there should've been a man around in Woodbridge and in Boston, as well, and the child wouldn't

85

have lived." Allie paused and sighed. Then, she pointed to the different categories. "Some people would probably feel attracted to put this person in the mixed category since he doesn't move his victims from the crime scene, but that doesn't ring true, if you get my drift. The kidnapping of Ariel Wing and the homicide of Peter Lee are both thoroughly planned, and not the impulsive act that disorganized serial killers tend to commit. The choice to leave the victims at the crime scene is also very deliberate."

"Alright, I admit, I'm baffled. There's no history of serial killers who change M.O or murder victim preferences?"

"Well, now you're stepping into another kind of category; the motive. This whole subject is more complex than what I'm giving you now, but, well, you know, time." Allie scribbled on the sheet of paper again. "So, motive gets divided into four different categories. The first is power and/or control – Ted Bundy is a good example in this category since he used rape to control women. The second is mission-oriented – like Joseph Paul Franklin, who killed his victims out of racist beliefs. The third is visionary – psychotics who think they communicate with some kind of being – that's like Son of Sam, who believed he got messages to kill from his neighbor's dog. The last one is the hedonistic category – people who enjoy killing for its own sake. The hedonistic one is also divided into three different categories." She scribbled again. "Lust, like Jeffrey Dahmer, who murdered boys and performed necrophilia and cannibalism on them; comfort, that's for your own profit – many female serial killers are placed in this category; and thrill. Coral Watts is a good example. He used to become very excited when he was about to murder someone, according to witness reports." Allie looked critically at the messy sheet of paper but shrugged. "To make it even more confusing, all these motives can overlap each other."

"Yeah, makes sense it's not simple. It's humans we're talking about, after all."

The self-critical expression disappeared, and Allie beamed toward him. "I like how you're wrapping your mind around this, Carl. You have potential."

He laughed and waved away her remark. "No way, serial killers are too scary for me."

She grinned. "Give me half a year, and I'll turn you into a great serial killer expert."

"Yeah?"

"You bet." They smiled at each other before Allie focused on the sheet of paper. "But to return to your question, depending on what your motive is, you can change M.O. or preferences, but it's not common. What's usually the case with serial killers who change, is that they suffer from some kind of mental illness, like psychosis, which in turn puts them into the disorganized category. Of course, it's not that static, but it's usually that way."

Carl frowned. "And mental illness doesn't coincide with the profile of this killer, eh?"

"Right. Told you you have potential." He just smiled and shook his head. As she studied her scribbling, the self-critical expression returned. "Well, this explanation isn't entirely correct. I mean, many serial killers, not only the disorganized ones, suffer from some kind of mental illness or psychopathy, but the most common trait is that they were abused or neglected as children and never managed to develop empathy." She paused and sighed, and the sheet of paper she just used got shoved to the side. Instead, she grabbed a new where she wrote *Edward Edwards* at the top. "Here, let's take an example of one killer that shows likeness with the one we're dealing with. In nineteen seventy-seven and nineteen eighty, Edward Edwards committed two double murders. In the first one, William Lavaco and Judy Straub were shot to death point-blank in the neck while sitting in their car. This happened in Ohio. In the next one, Timothy Hack and Kelly Drew disappeared in Wisconsin. They were found two months later. Timothy had been stabbed several times, and Kelly had been raped and strangled. In nineteen ninety-six, Edwards shot his foster son Danny Boy Edwards to get hold of the insurance money." She wrote down the names, the two different states, and the words *shotgun, stabbing, rape/strangulation,* and *pistol,* beside them.

Carl watched with keen interest. "And you'd like to put him in the organized category even though he's using so many different M.O's and jumps between motives?"

"Yes, mainly because of four reasons. The victims were moved from the crime scene and hidden. The murder of Danny Boy was planned way ahead and included Edwards persuading him to desert the army so he could kill him under the pretense to hide him. Edwards was never confirmed mentally ill. He was also labeled very charming, a trait he shares with several organized killers, like Ted Bundy, for example."

"Did he ever explain why he used so many M.O's?"

Allie shook her head. "No, unfortunately not. He's still in prison, though, awaiting trial. Maybe he'll give us an explanation one day. Anyway, enough with lessons before it gets too confusing. Let's get back to our killer." She shoved the sheet his way and took back the first one and pointed with the pen at the names of Peter Lee and Ariel Wing. "What does disturb me is that if it's not a development like we talked about, and if he didn't make a mistake, well, what is it then?"

"Um, part of the pattern?"

"Exactly." She looked at the paper with a grim expression.

"But if it's a pattern, then there should be more victims."

"Yep."

Carl inhaled as the thought struck him hard in his gut. "Oh…"

"I'm thinking about requesting a new search in all the areas where they found victims, but I haven't decided yet."

"Why not?"

She glanced at him sideways. "Well, you know how it is with the politics between the FBI and the local PDs. According to the PDs in Woodbridge, Boston, and Pittsburgh, they've searched the areas thoroughly. I need to have more than a hunch to request a new search."

"Yeah, I get it." He looked at the messy table and tried to prevent a sigh. How she ever would be able to read something out of this mess was beyond him. "So, what do you want me to help you with?"

She smiled mischievously at him. "Don't think I don't see that resigned look of yours. I know I'm a mess. Here. Take these things and copy them and organize your pile as you want them. When you're done, get us both some Frappuccino's or something with lots of yummy muffins and get back here. You need to read through the files and the reports and study the photos and familiarize yourself with the case. That's done best with mountains of caffeine and sugar. I'll help you with any questions you have."

He gave her a playful salute. "Yes, ma'am, will do."

She laughed at him and waved him away.

Copying everything took just about an hour, so he went to Starbucks before getting started on organizing the work, and came back with two large Frappuccinos and a whole box of sweet baked goods.

Allie's eyes lit up when he placed them before her. "Oh, yeah, I'm definitely going to enjoy working with you. Awesome!"

She dug in on the sweets while continuing to write on her laptop, and he began to go through the documents. The only sounds during the next couple of hours were the rhythmic clicking of keys from the laptop and the quiet rustling from the documents when he handled them. The more he read, the more intriguing he found the case, and soon, he began to take notes.

When Allie stood up and put the lid down on the laptop, he was surprised to see that it was already lunchtime.

"Hungry?" she asked, and he shook his head.

"Not really, but I probably need to eat anyway. What kind of food do you like?"

"Anything, honestly, but I'm a sucker for Asian."

"Asian it is then."

She hooked her arm with his in a friendly grip and walked with him to a newly opened, nearby located Mongolian restaurant that he hadn't visited before, and soon enough, they were enjoying plates of tsuivan.

"So," she said between mouthfuls, "tell me a little about yourself."

"About me?" he asked, surprised, not used to people querying.

She nodded. "Mhm."

"Um, wow. What do you want to know?"

"Well, did you always want to become law enforcement, for example?"

He laughed a little. "Well, I guess. I have an uncle who was in the RCMP—"

"RCMP? Royal Canadian Mounted Police?" she interrupted with a slightly surprised tone.

"Yeah."

"You're Canadian?"

"I thought that was as clear as water from my accent."

She unexpectedly stuck her tongue out at him, and the gesture reminded him about Miri. For a moment, it was hard to breathe. Then, he forced the thoughts away and made an attempt to laugh at her instead. It was clear that he didn't fool her.

After a quick, sharp look at him, she said, "I'm not good at hearing the origin of accents, to tell the truth," she admitted, and he was happy that she didn't ask about his reaction.

He cleared his throat. "I'm usually pretty good at it, but I honestly can't place yours."

She looked amused. "I've gotten lots of suggestions over the years. The most interesting and unexpected one was

South African. It's actually Swedish, but I've lived here since I was ten, so I guess it's not that obvious anymore."

"Swedish? With a name like yours?"

She laughed again. "Is Anna-Lena Gustafsson better sounding? My mom married Leonard Harris thirteen years ago, and I changed my last name to his. Allie is short for Anna-Lena, obviously."

"Leonard Harris? Why does that name sound familiar?"

A slightly awkward expression quickly flew over her face but disappeared immediately.

"He's the director of the opera house," she said blandly and took a sip from her Coke.

"Right! I knew I'd heard it before." Curiously, he looked at her, wondering what she tried to hide from him, but she just waved it away with a smile.

"You're really good at steering the questions away from yourself, Carl. We were talking about you and your Canadian ancestry. How did you end up in the US?"

"Hm, well, I went to university here, and then I kind of stayed. Got my green card and swore the oath and everything."

"Aha, what university did you attend? The one here?"

"Uh-uh, the Western Shore University in Detroit."

"Western—? Wait a minute!" Unexpectedly, she looked at his fingers, and amazed that she knew what it was, he held up his left hand with the tiny Star Student ring on his little finger. She beamed. "You're a Star Student! How cool is that! Wow!" Fanning herself with her hand, she smiled broadly and a bit teasingly at him. "I think I need your autograph." With an amused smile of his own and a flamboyant gesture, he scribbled his name on an unused napkin and handed it to her. Allie laughed at him. "I definitely need to frame this and put it up in my bedroom. But," she said after looking at the napkin, "I thought you used different names, like code names or some such?"

Surprised, he gave her a penetrating look. "Well, yeah, we do. How did you know? It's not common knowledge."

For a second, she looked guilty, and he couldn't understand why. "Sadly enough, I didn't get to know about the Star Student program until I was almost finished with my Ph.D., but it caught my interest – a lot – and I did lots of research about it."

He squinted with a feeling that she hid something from him. "Shouldn't be in any search engine," he commented suspiciously. When she shied away, he knew that he was right.

With a mischievous glance in her eyes, she looked back at him. "Well, I have a good friend who's great at finding stuff on the internet. She helped me out. Your code names were one of the things she found, and that sparked my imagination a lot." There was a slight pause in which they studied each other. Then Allie grinned at him. "So, tell me, what's yours?"

Even with the suspicion that what Allie's friend had done wasn't entirely legal, and that Allie was more than aware of that, he decided not to ask about it, and let her drag him away from the subject. He leaned back on the sofa and saw Allie relax too.

"Mm, right now it's Octavius, but I started out as Nero, and went on to Cyrus."

"Why do you change? Or wait a minute," she said hastily when she apparently saw him shut down his feelings, "that was a bad question. Sorry, I take it back, and we'll pretend I didn't ask."

He shook his head at her in amazement. "You are good. Really good. I'm not used to people reading my emotions as easily as you do. Most people actually think I don't have any feelings at all."

"Sorry. Can't help it."

"Hey, it's okay." He paused with a slight frown. "I think. At least, it will be okay when I get used to it. Anyway, let's talk a bit about you now."

"Not feeling comfortable anymore?" Her voice had a slight tone of teasing, but it was friendly, and he didn't take offense. "So, now it's my turn to ask what you want to know."

"Well, what do you do in your spare time, for example?"

"Aha, getting away from work-related things, are we?" She continued to tease him, and he couldn't help smiling at the tongue-in-cheek-look that spread over her face. "Well, I'm busted. No use in denying it, I'm a huge geek. I have a place I share with my best friends, and we're all geeks, playing roleplaying games almost every weekend, and such."

"Alright, now it's my turn to say 'oh' and 'ah,'" he joked, falling into the lighthearted tone she used. "I've never played, but I've always been intrigued by the concept. What kind of RPG do you play now?"

"Hah, you even know the short for it. Wow, you're cool." Her tone was downright excited and genuinely pleased, and he couldn't help but smile at her enthusiasm. "We've just started a superhero game; last week," she continued. "It might sound silly, but it's actually really fun."

"And what superhero do you play?"

"Invisible Girl. She's fun. I like her."

He glanced at her. "Yeah, I bet it gets on your nerves being stared at all the time."

Allie looked surprised at his hint of her being beautiful. Then, she laughed. "Wow, you're good too."

He grinned. "Profiler, you know." Then, he winked. "With a good reputation."

She laughed. "Got that. Guess I'll hear it a lot in the upcoming weeks." He just grinned. She cocked her head and gave him a curious look. "Well, if you're really that interested, you're more than welcome to visit on Friday. We're playing our next session then." With a deep, hurting tug at his heart, he thought about his lonely apartment and how he would have spent the Friday with Miri, if— "Hey, what's wrong?"

Allie's voice was suddenly gentle, and she took his hand in hers.

At this point, he'd figured out that this touching thing she had going on was a part of who she was, and that physical contact was immensely important to her. She probably didn't even reflect on the fact she did it.

He cleared his throat and hesitated. He didn't want to talk about Miri. He and Allie had just met, and they weren't friends, even though they liked each other. Talking about Miri would make him cry again, and he already spent too much time crying at home. Besides, he definitely did not want to cry in front of his new boss.

"I just— I just might come over. Could be fun."

She raised her eyebrows and gave him a crooked smile. "Alright, I'm not going to probe right now, since we need to get back to work, but I'm not letting you off the hook this easily, just so you know."

He raised his own eyebrows, and she nudged him, amused.

Back at the office, she went professional again. It fascinated him that she could be so good at keeping her private space and her workspace so separated. Very few people he knew managed to do that.

"Any questions so far?" she asked.

"Well." He brought out the three different reports on the murdered women. "I don't know if I'm on the wrong track or not, but when I look at the coroners' reports, there's one thing that struck me."

"Aha, what's that?" she asked with an anticipatory gleam in her eyes.

"Look here." He took his pencil and circled the dates of death. "Stephanie James, dead on April thirteenth. Joanne Siegler, dead around March tenth, Philippa Tyrnon, dead on December eighth." He took up his calendar and flipped up the year overview and pointed to the different dates. "Both Stephanie and Philippa were murdered on a Tuesday in the first half of the month. Joanne has an approximate date of death in the first half of the month too. If it's a pattern, she'd probably been murdered on Tuesday the ninth."

Allie gave up a little cheer and nudged him appreciatively. Carl felt a bit baffled at her sudden outburst.

"You don't know how happy I am that I followed my hunch and asked for you to join me on this case – and that I didn't tell you to leave. It was close, just to let you know." She cocked her head and gave him a probing glance.

He just smiled at her. "Yeah, I know."

A broad smile broke out on her lips. "Course you do. You're good. And that's what I'm talking about," she continued. "That you saw this pattern means I was right; you do have a knack for this kind of work. Yes, you're absolutely right about the dates. You've actually got an A on the test." The smile she gave him had a teasing hint, but then her voice got serious again. "But there's another thing, which is quite disturbing. Since our murderer seems so keen on following a pattern of dates and numbers, then I'm afraid we've only found three out of five girls."

A chill went down his spine as he looked at her. "January and February."

She nodded. "Yep. And there's no way for us right now to figure out where to find them. I mean, look at this." She grabbed him by the arm and brought him to the large map that hung beside the crime map on the farther wall. "We have an area, but it's a damn big area. Philippa: abducted and murdered in the state of Pennsylvania. Joanne: abducted in the state of Vermont, murdered in the state of Massachusetts. Stephanie: abducted in the state of Michigan, murdered in the state of New Jersey."

"They're all north-eastern states. And if we put Peter Lee into the pattern as well, he was abducted from New York. And Ariel was abducted from Ohio."

"Yeah, so if he moves around this much, the rest of the victims can be anywhere in this range, including West Virginia, Virginia, Washington DC, Maryland, Delaware, Connecticut, New Hampshire, and Maine."

Carl puffed frustrated. "Don't forget Quebec, Ontario, and New Brunswick." When she turned her head toward him, looking shocked, he continued, "Well, we have to be prepared that he might've crossed the border at some point."

"Goddammit! We need to get the M.O. and your sketch to the RCMP ASAP. Fuck!"

"I'll do it. I have contacts."

She gave him an appreciative look. "Thanks, Carl. Great thinking. I never even reflected on the Canadian states. I feel like an idiot."

"Provinces," Carl corrected calmly.

"Sorry, what?"

"The Canadian provinces."

A slow blush covered her face until she was blossoming red. Carl felt sorry for her, but before he could say something, she shook her head in self-disgust but shrugged it away a moment later.

"Typical American, right? I'm sorry. Anyway, I was going to say that the sketch is very well done. I'm impressed you got so many details out of a four-year-old."

"Well, it's a system I find works great with younger kids. I've gotten different transparent sheets printed for me with all facial features, except noses since they're too hard to discern in a straightforward-looking face, and I treat it like a game, or a puzzle, where they point out the different eye and hair colors, lip sizes, and so on. Ariel had been with this guy for some days, and she also has an excellent eye for shapes and colors, which was a great bonus. Obviously, not all kids have it. She pointed out the correct color of her own hair, my hair, and the social worker's hair, for example, without me even asking. When I put all the pieces together at the end, her reaction told me it was pretty spot on. She also puzzled together Stephanie's face without any problem at all. I think I have a copy somewhere in my other file." He went over to his bag and handed her the sketch.

Allie studied it thoroughly before giving him a respectful look. "Wow, this is very impressive. What a great way of doing it. Can I keep it?"

"Sure, why not? Anyway, I'd better contact Cody. What do you want me to include?"

"Just the M.O and the sketch. We don't want the media to get their hands on this yet."

"Sure thing."

"I need more caffeine after this shock. Do you want some too?"

"Absolutely. Otherwise, I'm going to steal yours when you come back."

Laughing, she headed out while he brought out his laptop. After the e-mail had been sent, he spent the rest of the afternoon continuing to familiarize himself with the case and take notes. He didn't find any more obvious patterns, but he had a feeling that there was something else, something he could see if he only looked at it from the right angle. It frustrated him as well as incited him.

Eventually, Allie stretched her arms up in the air and yawned. "I'm done for today. I suggest we break here. It's four thirty-five anyway, and I'm quite cooked." As she stood up and began to put her disorganized mess into a disorganized pile, she said thoughtfully, "You know, I have a feeling we're both closing in on him as well as fumbling around in the dark. Like Clarice Starling in *The Silence of the Lambs* when she's in that room with the killer in the end, and she can't see him, only sense his presence. You know what I mean."

"Ah, so that's what I'm feeling. The thought just struck me that I need to look at it from another angle, you know, and then I'd discover something important, but I just can't seem to find the right angle."

She nodded. "I think it'll come. We just need to be patient." Then she walked over to him and, to his astonishment, gave him a hug and a light kiss on the cheek. "See you tomorrow." She grabbed her trench coat from the hook and went out the door. Carl put his hand on his cheek, where the kiss burnt. *What a weird thing to do. We don't even know each other.* Then he shrugged and placed his documents and files in a neat pile, but instead of leaving them at the office, he put them into his bag. The nagging feeling of being close to finding something important didn't leave him alone, and he wanted to have the chance to study the documents at home.

For once, the air wasn't chilling his bones when he stepped out of the building, and he took deep breaths of the invigorating spring breeze. It wasn't warm enough today to drive with his window open, but at least it was a promise of those days not being too far away.

When he came home, the stagnant air in his apartment made him grimace, and he hurried to open the windows. The curtains shimmied as the wind gently drifted through the rooms. He glanced at the time. Five thirty. He should probably eat, but the tsuivan still felt like a piece of concrete in his stomach. Instead, he opened his tea cupboard and chose a refreshing raspberry-lemon variety that worked well with the spring scent. He put some pieces of sweet German rock sugar in the mug as well. When the water boiled, he poured it onto the tea infuser. The two fresh fragrances blended together, and he took deep breaths of the lovely scent. Then, he cuddled up on the sofa with all the documents and switched his iPod on low. Finally, it felt like he could relax and concentrate again.

He placed all the reports on the young women at the side since it was a pretty clear and straightforward pattern. Instead, he brought out the report on Peter Lee.

In his mind´s eye, Carl created a huge painting with the two actors placed where they had been found: Philippa in her car, Peter under the bridge. Then, he zoomed in on the man. Why was he there? What was so important that he needed to be placed in the painting? Allie had said that this killer seemed to focus on numbers, like dates. If that were the case, there should be other numbers that were important too.

He checked the report again. Peter Lee had disappeared on his way to work Tuesday, December first, and here was a Tuesday again. Carl made a note about it in his notebook. Philippa Tyrnon had disappeared two days later, on Thursday the third. Then Philippa had been murdered five days later on Tuesday the eighth, and Peter had been murdered on Thursday the tenth. According to the DSI reports, there were no traces of Peter in Philippa's car, so the killer had probably kept him somewhere during the days between the disappearance and the murder. That meant that the killer had money of some sort since he traveled so much. He probably paid for a motel room, the kind where you could reach the rooms without going through the reception. Otherwise, he would have been noticed, Carl was quite sure. A man and a woman going to a room didn't raise any eyebrows, but two men still did. Carl frowned at the all-present, everyday hypocrisy when it came to the view of whom people chose to have sex with. *Anyway, parenthesis.* He concentrated on his files again.

Peter Lee must've been gagged and bound since no one had noticed anything strange. According to the report, there had been urine and feces in his trousers when he was found, which also meant that the killer either liked to humiliate others or that he simply didn't care that his victims had physical needs. There had been no food in the stomach at all, so he had a feeling that the last option had more relevance than the first. So, two days after Philippa was shot while sitting in the front seat of her car, Peter was tossed from a high bridge and immediately died of his injuries. There was still the 'why', but since the killer most likely spent money on him, he must be important for the final picture, which in turn meant that the killing of Peter Lee wasn't a mistake. Allie must be right, there had to be other victims yet to be found.

In his mind's eye, he panned back to Philippa's car and added more details to the painting. It was December and most likely night if it followed the same pattern as Ariel had described. That meant that it must have been relatively cold.

99

Out of curiosity, he grabbed his laptop and searched for the weather conditions of the night in Pittsburgh. Not too bad. Only minus two C, and not a lot of snow, only point seventy-nine centimeters. *What's that in inches, now again?* A quick search gave him an answer. *Point three. Not much at all.*

Once again, he saw the painting in his mind; Philippa's navy-blue Ford, parked in an abandoned area with quite a few old factories around. The ground was lightly covered by snow, and it was chilly enough for the breath to be seen. Philippa was in the car, slumped over, and then the back door opened, and a child jumped out, starting to walk away.

Yes, this felt true. The reports told of the back left door being open. Carl began to scribble down a table.

December	Philippa Tyrnon, Peter Lee	Pittsburgh, PA	Missing: 1 child
January	None found	?	Missing: 1 woman, 1 man, 1 child
February	None found	?	Missing: 1 woman, 1 man, 1 child
March	Joanne Siegler	Boston, MA	Missing: 1 man, 1 child
April	Stephanie James, Ariel Wing	Woodbridge, NJ	Missing: 1 man
			10 victims missing!!!

As he grimly stared at the table he'd created, the phone suddenly rang. He frowned when there wasn't any phone number on the display.

"Yeah?" The static was so loud he had to pull the phone away from his ear. "What the hell's going on? Miri? Is

100

it you? I can't hear anything. Just damn static. Miri?" He listened some minutes more, but nothing changed. "Damn it. I'm going to hang up now. Miri, if it's you, please call again right now, alright?"

He put down the phone and waited. The minutes went by, slow as batter, as he kept staring at the phone with a rapidly beating heart, but nothing happened. "Damn it, Miri," he said quietly when twenty minutes had passed. "I wanted it to be you."

He hurriedly checked the FBI list on his cell again, but it didn't reveal anything new. *She's dead. You know she is. Stop trying to pretend she's not.* The thought hit him hard out of nowhere. It created a deep, hurting pain in his heart, and squeezed his chest so he couldn't breathe. He crouched, and his whole body strained and locked itself in its position. The breaths wheezed in his throat, clawing themselves out, hurting him on their way. Finally, the tears broke free, and amongst them, the anger.

He hit his fist into the soft pillows and yelled, "Damn it, Miri! Why did you have to die? Why did you— Why the hell did you die? I want you in my life, damn it! I just— I just want you in my life!"

The anger left him as suddenly as it had arrived, but the tears continued to flow, and he couldn't control his rapid, hurting breaths. Recognizing the signs, he rose from the sofa and quickly went into the bathroom. As he drenched his face with ice-cold water, he hoped that the physical shock would calm him down. It didn't. Instead, he felt the old symptoms from the execution aftermath coming over him; the hyperventilation, the tremble, the chest pain that made it hard to breathe, and the splitting headache. With quivering hands, he located his Xanax. He nearly dropped the pill on the floor, and the water in the glass coiled violently as he brought it to his mouth. When he was about to put it down beside the sink, it slipped through his fingers and shattered with an explosive crash that made him flinch. He looked at the mess, paralyzed for a moment, and just left the bathroom. Instead, he went into his small bedroom and sat down on the queen-sized bed, buried his face in his hands, and hoped for the medication to start working soon. He didn't know how long he'd been sitting there without being able to stop crying when the trembling in his body finally began to subside, and his breaths came in longer intervals. The expected and welcomed drowsiness rolled over him, and he could undress and curl up under the duvet, hugging the pillow as a comfort. Sleep was instant.

Chapter 5

The morning after, Carl felt lethargic and unattached to his body, not as welcome a feeling as the drowsiness had been yesterday night. At least, he could function, even if he wouldn't be on top today. As a secondary thought, he hoped that Allie didn't have any more 'tests' for him. He would be failing them miserably if she did. Without bothering to clean up the glass shatter in the bathroom, he just grabbed his toothbrush, the paste, and a new towel, and fixed himself in the kitchen. Some part of him felt disgusted, but the other part just shrugged. *Can't do this now. Maybe tonight. Or tomorrow.* The headache was not as bad as yesterday, just a quiet throbbing along his hairline. He glanced tiredly at the fridge. If he ate now, he'd throw up. *If I don't start to eat properly soon, I'm going to look like a damn ring wraith.* Then he shrugged. *I don't care.* Instead, he brewed himself a soothing cup of chamomile and lemon balm with lots of honey and poured it into an insulated travel mug. He wasn't particularly keen on the thought of eight hours of work, but on the other hand, he wasn't keen on anything today.

Of course, the wind was arctic and harsh, despite the radiant sunshine, when he came out of the building complex. He tightened his jacket, but it didn't seem to help. *Great. It's going to be one of these 'Murphy-loves-you'-days,* he thought grumpily as he quickened his steps, and indeed, it didn't look better when he got caught in a traffic jam halfway to work. He tried to force himself to relax and stop clenching his teeth. *Zen. Just think Zen, Carl.* As far as he could predict, this was going to be a long-lasting one. He took up his cell phone and dialed the number Allie had given him yesterday, but only reached her answering machine.

"Yeah, it's Carl. I'm stuck in jelly on ninety-fourth. Don't know how long it will take. Wish I had a flying car instead. Anyway, I did a little bit of extra research yesterday, so it might compensate for this. See you ASAP."

As he waited in the unmoving line of cars, he turned on his iPod and closed his eyes, letting himself appreciate the extra time to relax instead of fretting over something he had no control over.

Eventually, the cars started moving forward again, and at long last, he finally turned onto sixty-ninth and nineteenth. As a conciliatory gesture, he stopped at Superfresh and bought smoothies and a fruit tray as well as bagels, soft cheese, and cherry tomatoes. When he came into their room, Allie lit up where she sat behind her laptop.

"Morning. Nice seeing you."

She studied his face, and he was happy she didn't mention his rough looks. *She probably thinks I was out partying yesterday,* he thought worriedly. *Really bad for her impression of me and my work performance if she does.*

"May I offer a peace treaty for my late appearance?" he tried.

She laughed and came over to him, giving him first a hug and a light kiss on the cheek before digging into his bags.

"Mm, do you want to be late tomorrow too?"

Relieved, he chuckled, and the day seemed brighter. He didn't even mind the kiss much. *It's just who she is. She's not even reflecting on it. I guess I'll get used to it eventually.*

"Mango or strawberry smoothie?"

"I'd go for mango. I love mango, especially the ataulfo ones. Believe it or not, but I can eat ten in a row and still long for more." Smilingly, he handed her the mango and took a sip of the strawberry. "So, you said you'd done some research," she said and tilted her head while watching him. "What did you come up with?" He dug out his notes and the short table and handed them to her. She glanced over them and grimaced. "Yeah, I think you're right. Damn it. I've been too occupied with his personality to reflect over the practical dimensions. I hope it won't backfire on us. Anyway, my mistake, but yes, this seems very likely. We should get the sketch to the different motels around Pittsburgh, Boston, and Woodbridge ASAP. Maybe someone will remember him. I'll e-mail Rick Summers. He'll get that train going." Carl nodded. Rick at the hom-dep was an excellent choice for that task. She glanced at his notes again. "I like your table. Very clear. Sadly enough, probably very accurate as well. Maybe you could work on the missing persons' files around the north-eastern states we talked about yesterday."

"Sure thing. I'll start immediately."

He sat down with the laptop and logged in on the FBI's missing persons' files. While working, he managed to drink his whole smoothie and eat some fruit without throwing up.

The day went by slowly but steadily. In the afternoon, the sky darkened, and a rattling rain whipped the windows. Allie bought tea from the FBI cafeteria, and it felt rather cozy sitting in the lit room listening to the angry rain and the clacking of keyboard keys.

Eventually, he looked up from his screen and waved his notebook at Allie. She immediately took the chair beside him and looked at him expectantly.

"Alright," he started. "There's a guy from New York who seems to fit in with the pattern. He's forty-five years of age, brown-haired and slim, and he disappeared on his way to work on April fourth. That's a Sunday, though, but he's self-employed in the security area. It's also two days before Stephanie was abducted and seven days before Ariel was abducted. Name's Ian Field."

"And it's New York," Allie mused. "That could be significant since Peter Lee was from there too. On the other hand, it might not mean a thing, seeing as none of the girls come from the same area. Anything else?"

"Yeah. I believe New York does have significance. Three other guys seem to fit into this pattern, too, and they're all from Queens; they're all in their forties with brown hair, and they all disappeared at the beginning of each month on their way to work. Theo Sullivan disappeared Sunday, January second. It's a taken name. Birth name is Tadeusz Szlaga. He's a play writer, quite successful, apparently. Basil Stokes disappeared Tuesday, February first. He's a computer engineer. Nothing special about him. James O'Connor disappeared Tuesday, March second. He's also a computer engineer, but works as a professional blogger at the side and offers to ghostwrite to other companies. Here's his website."

Allie glanced at his notes before grimly scrutinizing him. "There's a feeling, here," she said eventually, and pointed to her stomach, "that you've found them." They looked at each other in silence for a couple of moments, before Allie focused on his records again. "You know what I don't grasp?" Carl shook his head. "Why pick his male victims from New York and his female victims from all over? And why being so meticulous about New York, and not just New York, but Queens in particular, for the men, and the university student thing going on amongst the girls? I mean, yeah, it's clear it's a pattern, but only in some ways. In other ways, he suddenly doesn't seem to care. I don't know yet if it makes sense or if I'm missing something." She frowned. "Question is; where are they now? Where were they murdered? And it's the twenty-second today. We don't have many days to break the chain. He's not going to stop now. He's never going to stop."

The certainty in her voice made a cold shiver run down Carl's spine. With an uncomfortable shrug, he tried to shake it off.

"Well, Ian Field has to be around the Woodbridge area, eh?"

"Yeah, you're right. By the way, did you find anyone else? Before December, I mean?"

"None that followed the pattern."

She gave up a relieved sigh. "At least that's reassuring." She stared at his notes again and pointed toward the photos he'd printed out of the victims. "And what's with all the brown-haired people? Is that his issue?" She puffed frustrated and raised her hands. "Honestly? I don't know."

"But, Allie," Carl put on his encouraging voice, and she glared at him, clearly seeing through his attempt to calm her down. He felt a bit shaken but let go of the encouragement. "How long have you been working on the case? Since Tuesday, eh? That's only for two days. Give yourself a break."

She suddenly grinned. "Sorry, this is how I am. Better get used to it. I'll fret about it until the day we hopefully break it."

"Fair enough. I don't mind."

She laughed and nudged him. "Yet."

"Yet," he agreed calmly.

"Anyway, you've done a great job, Carl. You're such an asset. Thank you."

A pleased smile appeared on his lips, and he chuckled at himself, but after working with Alan Bai for eighteen months, working with Allie was refreshingly simple and enjoyable. There were no fire pits to navigate around or suddenly slip and fall down into, and no ego to carefully boost. It was just one incredibly happy, generous, and satisfied person doing a job she knew she was exceptionally good at, without any need to brag.

She went back to her own chair and began wrapping up the workday when suddenly her cell phone rang.

"Yeah? Yep, it's me. Aha. Yeah?" She listened for a while, and then her face suddenly beamed. "No way? You're kidding me! Woot! Thanks, Dean. Awesome, awesome news!" As she hung up, she made a happy, improvised dance on the floor. "You know what, Carl?" she said and stopped twirling around, still grinning at him like crazy. "I think we'll catch him. He shouldn't have left Ariel alive. That was his mistake."

"We've got a lead? No way! Not this early?"

She laughed happily, danced toward him, and gave him a smacker and twirled a couple of extra rounds before stopping again.

"Told you that sketch was awesome! Someone at a remote motel on the outskirts of Woodbridge recognized him on the sketch. He paid cash under the name Johnny Brown in advance for six days. He kept to himself, denied room service, like cleaning, never spoke to anyone, and didn't come by the reception once. The room was neat when they finally entered it after he left. DSI's on their way now to check it out, and who knows, there might actually be something left to find. Woot!"

Carl felt his heart hammer, and a broad smile lit up his face.

"They're sending Andy and his Angels?" he asked her, sternly refusing to think about the missing Angel of the team.

"I certainly hope so. Gorlois's the best, by far, and his girl team's just amazing. If anyone can find anything, it's them."

"Johnny Brown?" Carl mused, trying to steer away from the painful thoughts. Miri hadn't been an Angel for more than nine months, but she'd been elated when she got promoted. "The name must be fake. He'd pay with card otherwise. You don't pay that much money cash if you're clean."

"Uh-uh, no clean flour in that bag, that's for sure. What a great end to this workday. I'm so damn happy!" She threw her arms around him and gave him another smacking kiss on his cheek. Then she danced back to her laptop and shut the screen. "If I weren't already occupied for tonight, I'd ask you out for a drink, but I think we'll save it until we have him safely where he's supposed to be, and then I'm up for a black-out night. Anyway, I need to go. I suggest you do the same, and we'll meet at eight as usual. And, um, I know I sound like a mom, but try to get some sleep. You need it, and it'll be late tomorrow night. Game nights always are."

He grinned. "Yes, ma'am, will do."

She let her mess on the table lie as it did, and on her way out, she stopped and kissed his cheek lightly. He smiled at her back when she let go of him and left. She must be the most genuinely happy and carefree person he'd ever met. He wasn't used to all the kissing and touching, but he had to admit that it was an agreeable way of expressing oneself that he almost envied her, at least when it was as disarming as what she did. He couldn't help a sudden shiver running down his spine, and the hair from standing up on his arms, when the image of Alan Bai suddenly starting to touch and kiss, popped up in his mind. *Go away, hideous thoughts,* he thought with horror, but the image seemed etched in his mind by now. *Damn it, anyone else, fine, but not him! He's revolting. Well, maybe not physically, but his personality—* No. No, stop it now, Carl. *Think about something else, anything else.*

As Carl gathered his things together, he sternly steered away from the thoughts of a kissing Alan Bai to the unexpected turn of events. *It can't be this simple, can it? Seems unlikely. There's something we're missing, I'm quite sure. We can't be breathing down his neck already. It would be fabulous if we did, but—* Suddenly, the tiredness came over him again, and he shrugged away everything that was even remotely work-related. He was too exhausted to even think about anything except a hot shower and his comfortable bed.

The drive home was uneventful, and as soon as he entered his apartment, he dropped his bag on the floor, grudgingly abandoning the thought of a hot shower and brought out the broom and the vacuum cleaner instead. He couldn't shower before he'd fixed the mess in the bathroom. While he was at it, he decided to continue with the rest of the apartment. The kitchen sink got a tough makeover since he didn't enjoy the thought of skin flakes all over his dinnerware. After that, he reluctantly opened the fridge for the first time in days and grimaced disgustedly at the sour smell that wafted out at him. *Oh, God, it's the Swamp of the Eternal Stench right here, in my fridge!* Resigned, he chuckled and began to clean it out. It hurt to throw out all the vegetables and the berries, as well as the leftover dinner from last Thursday. As he lifted the lid, the white mold made him grimace, and his nostrils twitched at the foul smell. *Should've put it in the freezer. These microbes are definitely advanced enough to create a religion and a political system of their own at this stage. Probably voting too.* The milk had gone sour, as well, and the bread had turned green. When he finally was done, there were mostly empty shelves staring back at him. *Now, what?* He didn't want to go to the store at this time, and he didn't feel like waiting forever for food delivery. *I'm not that hungry anyway. I'll buy things tomorrow. Or on Saturday.*

He closed the fridge and went to the bathroom, where he brought out his prescription medication. There were still some pills left from his long breakdown after the execution. He weighed an unopened container with Zopiclone 7.5 in his hand and tried to decide. Eventually, he opened it and swallowed one of the pills. He needed his sleep. He needed to function. Above all, he needed to shut off all the thoughts he knew would torture him if he didn't fall asleep.

"I'm sorry, Miri, but I... I just can't think of you tonight," he murmured. "I just— I just can't. I just want some peace tonight. You understand, don't you?"

He let his hand comb through his hair and glanced at his gaunt appearance in the mirror. The shadows under his eyes were dark and harrowing, and there wasn't any light in his eyes. Sighing, he turned his back on the ghost that looked at him. The claws of anxiety stroked him lightly over his spine. Desperately, he struggled to keep them at bay and hold on to an every-day-routine, so before he got caught up in either the nervousness or the artificial drowsiness, he took a quick shower and changed his bed linen. He wanted to feel fresh all over tonight. It had been too long since he felt completely clean. When the yawns overwhelmed him, he felt grateful for the quickly built-up soothing wall in his mind that kept all the painful thoughts at bay. Finally at ease, he cuddled up in bed and embraced the pillow. He didn't have to wait long before sleep took him away.

The next day, he felt much better. Thanks to the pill, he'd managed to sleep ten dreamless hours straight without even tossing and turning, and he almost felt hungry, to his own surprise. Since he didn't have anything at home, he waited for breakfast until he arrived at work and ate the last bagel leftover from yesterday.

When Allie came in at eight, he was already sitting at his laptop, going through state after state of missing women and children. It was going to be a long and tedious day of research, and a day filled with other people's pain over missing loved ones. He could take the tediousness, but each face he saw filled him with something that resembled grief. He knew all too well that these people, in most cases, would never come back, and the families would never get closure, and he knew all too well what that felt like. There were families, of course, who didn't care, but he liked to think that they were in the minority. He couldn't imagine anything worse than a missing person no one missed.

In his mind, he could hear Manda teasingly say, *'You're such a big softy, Carl. If people only knew you're just a big fluffy heart under that tough shell of yours, you'd be in trouble.'* Irritated, he frowned. When did she say that? Years ago, and it still irked him. It also irritated him immensely that *Runaway Train* played over and over in his mind, especially since he knew just a few lines of the song. Eventually, the irritation he felt boiled over, and he pushed the laptop away and took a tour to the washroom.

"Okay, what?" Allie asked when he came back again.

He frowned at her, but she seemed unaffected. Frustrated, he pulled a hand through his hair. "I just feel like we're wasting so much time, searching for people all over the states on the Internet."

"Okay, you might be right. What would you like to do instead?"

He gave her a suspicious look, but she was absolutely genuine, and he decided to give it a shot.

"We could go and look for ourselves, Allie. It would take us, what, five, six hours max to get to Pittsburgh? If we leave at six a.m., we'd be there around elevenish, or noonish at the latest, and then we could spend six hours looking around before going home again. We know the pattern, we know what we're looking for, and we know what area we need to search. As soon as we find the child, we're in the

111

clear, and we can request new searches. And fuck the damn politics! We're trying to catch a damn serial killer, for crying out loud. You said it yourself; he won't stop, and we only have about a week left to stop the next kidnapping. We can't waste our time searching the damn Internet!" He stared angrily at her and realized that she, in turn, was beaming at him.

"Carl, you're the best! God, I think I'm falling in love with you right here and now. When do we leave?" She laughed at his shocked expression. "I think you're right, is all. If you want to, I'll call Kevin and tell him we're skipping tonight's session. Catching a serial killer is damn more important than playing Invisible Girl." She glanced at the time. "It's ten now. If we leave right away, we'll be in Pittsburgh around four-ish, and we can rent motel rooms somewhere, so we don't feel stressed about the time, and then we can concentrate on searching the area until we find the kid."

"Okay." Carl chuckled a little and felt a bit wild and crazy, suddenly going on a road trip. "Let's go."

The drive with Allie through the northern state's landscapes was pleasant. She played lots of classic rock and sang frisky to her favorites without being ashamed of her lack of singing voice. In between, they talked. She inquired more about the Star Student program, and he was surprised and happy about her genuine interest, even though he didn't tell her anything about the secret aspects of the program.

Then, he got to know about her childhood in Sweden and about the unlikely situation that led to her mom and Leonard Harris meeting and falling in love, and the move here. Then, she asked about his childhood in Canada, and he told her about his big extended family, and how happy and caring, and warm and funny they'd been together when he was a kid, and how everything changed when his parents disappeared when he was twenty.

"Everyone suspected murder, but they were never found, and there were no leads, nothing. The trail couldn't even go cold, 'cause it was never warm. Truthfully, I've never been back. I eventually let my Uncle Pete and Aunt Shukriyya sell the farm and put the money into an account so they'd have something if they'd ever come back. They won't, I know that, but when my daughter Sarah's old enough, that money will go to her university education. I know Ma and Dad would like that." He sighed and looked out of the window. "There are way too many disappeared people in my life," he muttered and thought about his parents, about Sonia and Simon, about Miri. He could feel Allie's probing look, but he didn't want to talk about it.

They sat silent for a while, but eventually, Allie cleared her throat. "The worst thing is the helplessness," she said, and Carl gave her a surprised glance at the unexpected line. "I have a sister, Aggie, or Agneta rather. She hates my guts. I don't know why, but she's always competed with me about everything; grades, looks, boys, you name it, and always felt herself falling short, for no good reason at all. I mean, it's not like she's not smart or good looking or lacking attention, but for some reason, she thought she'd never manage to raise herself to my level, that she'd never beat me, as if it was a race. I won't go in on every sad turn of event, but eight years back, she ran away. She was fifteen. We were worried sick. At that point, we didn't even know if she was dead or not. She was one of all those missing people on the FBI's list. Last year, she was finally found. She'd married a guy, a drug addict, who'd made her into one as well. He'd hit her so badly she had to be hospitalized, and that's when it was discovered that she was reported missing, but the worst thing was…" Allie fell silent and dried a tear from her eye. Carl didn't rush her, and eventually, she continued, "He had killed their youngest child, a boy, just beaten him to death. His name was Sunshine, and he was only two years old. We didn't even know she had children." She sniveled, and more tears fell. Carl felt shocked and devastated and put a comforting hand on her shoulder. She drew a deep breath. "Goddamn, I wasn't going to cry. Anyway, she and Twilight and Golden-

Ray live with Mom and Dad now, and, hopefully, they're going to heal. Dad, Leo, I mean, understands how important it is for them to go to therapy, so he pushes that part. I'm staying away, 'cause Aggie can't stand the sight of me. For some damn reason, she blames me for all this shit."

Squeezing her shoulder gently, he hoped the compassion he felt seeped through to her.

"You can't take responsibility for her life, Allie."

She wiped away more tears. "I know, but it's not easy when she fills the kids' heads with her hatred for me. Anyway, that's my sad story."

They drove in silence for about twenty minutes, but the quiet felt calm and caring. It fascinated him that they didn't need words to comfort each other. Thinking about it, it felt as if they'd known each other for years, not just for a few days. The only person he'd felt like that with before was Nadir.

Eventually, they started to talk about the case again, and she gave him the profiler report she'd finished in the morning. As he read through it, he nodded in agreement.

"Yeah, I think it's hitting the bone here," he said when he finished. "But there are a couple of things I wonder about. You say his killing didn't begin until last year, that something triggered him, but it's something that's been growing inside him for some time. Why do you think that?"

"Good question, Carl. I like how you nail the difficult parts first." She fell silent a couple of moments while passing by some slower driving cars. "It's a very distinct pattern. I've never seen anything like it before. These things don't just pop up out of the blue. They're created somewhere or sometime, like a trauma, as I wrote, that hasn't been treated. He probably wasn't even aware of it being a trauma, or if he was, he probably didn't want to go to a psychologist. I'm quite sure he grew up in surroundings that viewed people with mental disorders and psychological issues as 'nuts' and 'idiots,' and that he'd been ostracized had he gone to therapy.

He might even have suppressed his own trauma to such a degree he didn't even remember it.

"And then something happened that pushed him over the edge. Maybe you should mention that in your report."

She glanced at the sheets of paper in his hands. "I thought I had."

He skimmed through the report again. "Sorry, no."

"Huh. Okay. Guess I missed that part then. No problem. It's not supposed to be in until Monday anyway. Can you make a note of it somewhere?"

"Sure." After finding a pen in his pocket, he wrote, *Ostracized if seeing a psychologist, not aware of trauma? Not remembering trauma?* on the side.

"Great. Thanks." After a short pause, Allie said, "I'm starting to get hungry. Do you want to wait with lunch 'til we've found ourselves a motel, or shall we stop at the next place we see?

"Let's eat now. When we're there, I just want to get out to the scene."

"Okay. I hear you."

Within fifteen minutes, a roadside restaurant turned up, and they had themselves a bland lunch. It was hard getting the food down. They were both sitting in their own thoughts, and Carl felt his stomach whirl with butterflies. They were so close to the city now, and he just knew that they were going to be lucky today. It felt as if the child was hovering around them, waiting to lead them to the right place.

"You done?" he asked when he saw her moving her food around on her plate rather than eating it, even though she'd just told him how hungry she was. She exhaled and nodded. Without another glance at her food, she stood up and headed for the exit.

"You know," he said as they approached the car, "let's skip the whole motel thing and go directly to the scene."

115

Allie gave him an understanding glance and nodded. "Okay."

As soon as they got into the car, she brought out the map and studied it. "We're not too far away, actually," she mused. "This is the place, and we're here. It's just a couple of kilomet— miles, I mean. Are you good at reading maps?"

"Yeah. You concentrate on driving. I'll do the rest."

"Okay, good." She fastened her seatbelt and started the car.

The afternoon sun was bleak and jagged as it unsuccessfully tried to hide behind the gray clouds. Carl and Allie sat quietly in the car, driving for another thirty-five minutes before they parked at the abandoned factory complex. During the ride, the atmosphere in the car had been so thick that it felt like he needed a sword to slice it. He wasn't superstitious, but he refused to look in the rear-view mirror in case the child was there, looking back at him. He could see that Allie was affected too. Her face was rigidly tense, and as soon as she'd parked, she opened the door and got out. As he was about to follow her, he thought he saw a movement in the corner of his eye. His breath got caught in his throat, and rapid fingers ran over his back, made his hair stand up, but then he forced himself to breathe normally and relax. If there was a child around, he or she only wanted them to find him or her. Carl closed his eyes for a moment, and certainty grew inside him. *It's a he, I know it's a he. It doesn't work with the pattern, but it's a boy.*

Uncomfortably tense, he got out of the car and walked over to Allie, who studied the local map. The wind was chilly and felt like it breathed on his exposed neck. He buttoned the jacket and huddled, but it didn't help.

Allie pointed at a spot on the map. "Okay, we're here. Let's go here, where they found Philippa's car. We'll use that as a starting point."

Carl nodded, and they started walking. Neither of them talked. It was probably his imagination, but he thought he heard faint footsteps behind him. He refused to look.

As they walked to an open space formed like a courtyard in between three-story buildings with broken window-glass in the panes, they saw the spot immediately. The yellow police tape lay abandoned on the ground.

Allie looked around. "Where do you want to start?"

Carl followed her gaze and tried to think like a little child, trapped inside a car together with a dead woman in the middle of the night.

"If I'd be him," he started, and Allie gave him a curious look at his specific use of gender, but didn't say anything. "If I'd be him," he said again, "I'd want to go home. These buildings would scare me. I wouldn't go in. I wouldn't know where home was, but I'd go toward any kind of streetlight."

They looked around.

"Hard to see streetlights from here," she said, and he nodded.

"If I didn't see any, I'd follow the wheel tracks."

Allie brought out the report and browsed through the pages.

"That way," she said and pointed, and they walked toward the right entranceway. While they walked, his thoughts swirled around in his mind. *How far did he get? Was he caught by the killer, or did he suffer from some injury? Did he freeze to death? Did he get hit by a car and left for dead?* The wind blew around him, and he put his hands in his pockets.

"Damn chilly here, don't you think?"

"Mm, yeah, maybe," Allie answered absentmindedly as she searched the surroundings. They had left the factory complex behind and stood at the edge of an open field. The road they followed turned right again and would eventually connect with the highway. Straight ahead was a field that continued for a while until it was interrupted by a low hill. To the left stood a grove of trees. Allie looked expectantly at him, and he took a deep breath of the brisk air to clear his mind.

"Yeah, If I'd be him, I'd probably follow the road," he said doubtfully.

"But?"

"Call me crazy or something, but I'd like to check out the grove."

"Okay."

They walked in silence, but Carl felt an anticipatory presence tugging at his hand. *Yeah, my little friend, we're getting there.* The washed-out grass from last year frazzled under their feet. *It's weird, almost no fresh grass around. What kind of spring is this anyway?*

They stopped at the edge of the forest and looked around. The undergrowth was thick and could easily hide a small body.

"Do you want us to separate?"

Carl shook his head. Then he closed his eyes. Even if the presence he felt only originated from his mind, it was strong enough for him to give it a chance. *Which way, little one?* He felt a mental tug forward and followed it. Allie trotted after him. For a while, they stumbled around, trying not to break their ankles, but soon the ground began to slope, and the undergrowth thinned out. They slid down and stood at a little brook. Carl felt an urge to go to the left and followed the brook upstream. The peat that covered the ground was soft and wet. Soon enough, his shoes were soaked, and a squishy sound was heard from his feet. Absentmindedly, he grimaced and carried on.

After a while, they found the origin of the water, but this wasn't the place. Instead, he wanted to walk more to the right. Allie followed him quietly. The ground soon lost all the undergrowth and became sandy instead of moist.

Just as Allie said, "Are you sure he'd be able to make it this far?", Carl saw him.

He stopped dead at the edge of a deep sandpit, and Allie managed to walk right into him. Instead of saying something foul, as anyone else would, she came up beside him and looked the same way he did. They glanced at each other, and without a word, they began to slide down into the sandpit.

The pitiful little body lay sprawled out on the ground. It showed clear signs of being eaten by animals, but it was also clear that it had been left alone for quite some time, since the body had darkened and dried. He was dressed in a bright red winter jacket, blackened jeans, and winter boots, and he lay on his stomach with his face down.

Suddenly, Carl heard Allie sob quietly beside him. He turned and saw tears running down her cheeks as she watched the little body on the ground. Without saying anything, he embraced her, and she cried into his jacket. He lifted his gaze up toward the brink. The poor boy must've stumbled into the pit in the dark without being able to get up afterward. Compassion and sorrow filled him as he thought of the lonely child, slowly starving to death without anyone there to save him. Tears blurred his own sight, and he hugged Allie closer.

Just then, there was a movement up at the rim. He looked up, and through the tears, he thought he saw a child looking down at them before turning around and disappear among the trees.

Part Two

time in between

Chapter 6

It was late at night when they finally left the grove. Allie looked devastated in a way Carl had never seen her before.

"You'll have to live with me clinging on to you for a while," she said, holding on tightly to his hand. "I don't want to be alone. I… I keep seeing his little body in my mind over and over again." The tears fell again. At this point, her eyes were sore and red from all the crying. "I'm an academic," she continued in a low voice as he put an arm around her shoulders to console her. "I'm not a field agent."

It wasn't until then that Carl realized that this was the first time she had ever seen a dead body. He didn't say anything, just gave her the physical contact she needed and let her talk.

"He was so little," she said quietly. "You probably think I'm stupid, not realizing how little he was, but you work with kids all the time. You see kids all the time. Me, I just see them in photos and read about them in damn, fucking REPORTS!" Her voice suddenly shrieked in anger before breaking, and she started to sob; deep, harrowing sobs.

Carl stopped and pulled her into his arms, embraced her hard. Her whole body shook and trembled as all the shock and horror struggled to find an outlet. A long while later, she finally stopped crying and managed to breathe again. She rummaged through her bag, locating a package of tissues and blew her nose a couple of times before putting on hand sanitizer.

"Let's go," she mumbled. "I want to get out of here."

The place was empty now. Both the police and the ambulance crew had left long ago. Only Allie's car was left, looking lonely and abandoned, just as Stephanie's had in the photos.

Allie had been able to keep herself together throughout the many hours of reports and DSI searches and the forensic investigation of the body. They had found a name in the boy's jacket; Ernie, but no surname and no phone number. If they were unlucky, it was an inherited jacket or one that had been bought at a thrift shop, but for now, they called him Ernie. Allie had contacted Dean and requested a new search of the other areas in Boston and Woodbridge. Now, all her nervous energy had disappeared, and she looked like a washed-out dishcloth.

He had to drive to the other end of town before he found a motel that seemed both suitable and affordable, while Allie sat without talking in the passenger seat, looking out at the passing street lights.

At the check-in counter, she quietly asked for a two single-bed bedroom instead of a room each. Carl didn't say anything about it. It was as clear as crystal that she needed his presence right now. She didn't speak again until they were safely locked in together in their room. With frustrated moves, she threw the content of her bag on the bed at the window, grabbed new clothes, and with a mumble about a shower, she left and went into the bathroom. Carl rubbed his neck and continued up; let his hand comb through his hair in slow, soothing motions.

He understood her. Had they been at the office, getting a notice about Ernie having been found, they'd probably celebrate, but now… It had become more intimate than she had anticipated, more personal. He believed that she never would forget Ernie. Nor would he. His mind shied away from the thought of the child's presence, if that was what it was, but he couldn't deny the fact that he had found the body with that presence' help. Without it, he admitted, he wouldn't even have searched the grove in the first place.

Allie came out from the bathroom, her damp hair glimmering in the light, dressed in a nighty that looked like something she might've worn as a teenager, a soft white cotton thing that reached to her knees and had a worn-out image of two teddy bears hugging in front of a big heart. Not what he'd expected her to wear, had he thought about it, but it suited her personality perfectly.

As she threw all her things on the bed down on the floor and crawled up in her bed, he went into the bathroom for a shower too. The floor was all wet with the used towel lying in a heap on the toilet lid, and the small shampoo flask standing without its lid on the floor of the shower. Her used clothes lay in a crumpled bundle on the floor beside the flask. It irked him, like him being a cat, and she brushing him the wrong way. *God, she's messy. I wouldn't be able to live with her longer than a weekend,* he thought and cringed. Since he couldn't leave it be, he picked up her clothes and folded them neatly, used the already wet towel to clean up the water from the floor, and put the shampoo bottle at its place on the shower shelf. Then, he exhaled and felt like he could relax. His own shower was short since the temperature was too uneven to enjoy. At least, he felt clean.

When he got out, she had fallen asleep, still half-sitting up in the bed on top of the duvet. She looked cold, and her cheeks glistened with more tears. After hesitating a moment, Carl went over to her and tried to pull the duvet away and place it on top of her, but she woke up and looked at him, confused.

"Sorry," he said. "It just looked so uncomfortable. Here, lie down. You're going to get cold without something on."

She nodded and lay down, and he spread the duvet over her. In a minute, she fell asleep again. Without being able to restrain himself, Carl picked up her things from the floor and placed them in tidy rows on top of the drawer before getting into his own bed. As soon as he turned off the light, sleep overwhelmed him too.

The few hours went by way too fast, and when he slowly and unwillingly woke up, he felt almost gluey in the head. Allie sat on the bed, nudging him repeatedly.

"Mm?"

"Morning."

"Mm… morning… What time is it?" His voice was thick, and his breath didn't smell that great. He flopped an arm over his face.

"Seven."

"Seven? On a Saturday? Why aren't you still sleeping?"

"Kevin called. He was worried about me. I forgot to let them know I wouldn't come home last night. I just told him I was going after a serial killer."

"Kevin?"

"Yeah."

Carl forced his left eye to half-open and tried to focus on her dim face. "Why do I feel like we're cheating on someone?"

She laughed. "Well, we're not, so I don't know."

He shook his head and grimaced. "God, I feel hungover. Not fair." He stretched out and yawned and pulled himself up to half-sitting. Allie was already dressed and looked less haunted than she had the evening before. "So, seven?"

"Mhm. I thought we could have breakfast and then leave, so we're home relatively early. What do you say?"

"Are you always this early-birdie?"

She shrugged and grinned. "Today, I am, apparently."

"Not fair," he muttered, but rose from the bed and put his feet on the floor, feeling slightly dizzy and with a low throbbing headache. *Too many nights lately, with too little sleep,* he thought grumpily as he went into the bathroom to get himself ready. When he got out, he noticed that Allie had already packed her things and was ready to leave.

"Thanks for folding my stuff," she said. "I know I'm a terrible mess."

He waved away the remark. "It was nothing."

"Well, for me, it was something, so thanks."

He smiled lightly, feeling some of the grumpiness disappear. "You're welcome, Allie."

124

He didn't have much to put back in his bag, so only a few minutes later, he gestured indistinctively at the door. "Shall we?"

She nodded, and they went down to the little canteen. Carl managed to eat a sandwich and drink a bland cup of bag tea before his stomach protested.

"You want me to drive today?" he asked when they walked out into the gray morning. The air smelled of rain, and the ground was wet.

"Yeah…" She hesitated. "Well, no, not really. Sure, I'm tired and such, but I've got a thing going on with my car. That you got to drive it at all is very rare."

"Alright."

"Thanks, though."

They got into the car and started the long drive home. This time, they didn't talk much. Both were mulling over their own thoughts, thoughts that resembled the cloudy day outside. Since Allie had claimed the wheel, Carl soon took advantage of the six-hour gap of doing nothing and napped. She woke him up as she turned onto sixty-ninth and nineteenth.

He yawned but felt more alert than in the morning. "Oh, wow, thanks for letting me sleep. I think I needed that." He looked around as she turned into the FBI's huge parking lot. "And thanks for taking me back to my own car."

"No problem. It was mostly out of self-interest anyway, since I didn't want to come and pick you up on Monday."

He chuckled. The smile she gave him was faint, and she had dark smudges underneath her eyes. When she parked, he took her hand in his, and she looked slightly surprised.

"You know what, Allie?" She shook her head. "I never got to say it yesterday, but you were great. First time is hard, really hard. You tell me I have the potential of becoming a forensic serial killer psychologist. Well, you've got the potential of becoming a field agent. So there."

With another, more genuine smile, she placed her hand on his cheek and leaned in and gave the other a light kiss.

"Thanks, Carl. I think I needed to hear that. I'm going home now to sleep some more, and then I'll see you on Monday."

He nodded and got out of the car. Before heading to his Toyota Prius, he watched her drive away.

Instead of going directly home, he stopped by at Superfresh and bought himself some food. It was time to try to start to eat again.

He had just gotten home and through the door with all the groceries when his cell phone rang. This time, there was a number on the display window.

"Yeah?"

"Hi, it's me again."

Carl smiled amusedly. "Hi, Allie."

"Didn't want you to miss me too much, so I was going to invite you over. We're playing tonight instead. Want to come?"

He didn't even reflect on the craziness of the suggestion. "Sure, I can do that."

"Great! You can come around six."

When she'd hung up on him, he checked the time. Almost three p.m. He'd be able to take a well-deserved hot shower, and even cook and eat something before he needed to leave. He could live with that.

At five forty-five, Carl stood outside Allie's penthouse complex. To his surprise, it was situated in the posh quarters around Lincoln Spring Park and had a view over the section with the lake. Now, when he thought about it, he knew that Leonard Harris was considered one of the richest, if not the richest, persons in the state. No wonder his stepdaughter could live like this.

The doorman greeted him gracefully, which made him feel awkward, and the awkwardness followed him as he took the luxuriously decorated elevator to the top floor and

126

rang the bell. At least the elevator didn't take him directly into her apartment. He got some time to compose himself. While he waited to be let in, he looked up at the glass ceiling and around at the big potted plants that stood everywhere, and at the expensive art on the walls. He couldn't think of anyone else he knew who lived like this. Suddenly, he felt underdressed and uncomfortable and completely out of his league. Then, the door opened, and Allie stood there smiling at him, robed in a sleeveless flowing dress that looked like a dress version of Van Gogh's *Starry Night*. Her hair was loose for once and spread over her shoulders like a golden waterfall. *God, she's so beautiful,* he thought but managed to keep the thought in his head this time.

She draped her arms around him and kissed him lightly on the cheek. Immediately, his awkwardness disappeared, and he smiled back at her. She looked rested and more relaxed and happy than she had been since yesterday afternoon.

"Hey there, glad you could come. Come on in and meet the rest."

As soon as he'd taken off his shoes, she took him by the hand and pulled him into the big, airy living room. Three comfy sofas stood in a half-circle around a big table, hand-painted in the style of Alphonse Mucha. A golden retriever puppy came sliding over the hardwood floor and greeted Carl enthusiastically. He kneeled, and suddenly, he had his arms full of a happily wiggling soft body and got his face eagerly licked.

"Clackety, down!" Allie ordered sharply, and the puppy plopped down on its butt. "Good boy, good Clackety," she praised him and patted him vigorously. "He's Strawberry's," she said as if that explained everything, "but I'm trying to teach him some manners."

Eight other persons milled around or sat on the sofa. Allie waved her hand and raised her voice to get their attention. "Hey, all! This is Carl." Then she continued to introduce the other ones. A tall, handsome-looking African-

American guy who radiated with tons of charisma shook his hand. "This is Kevin, our game master."

Kevin was also dressed in seventies-inspired clothing with an airy tunic in a warm orange nuance and wide harem like trousers.

"Nice to meet you, Carl. Hope you'll like tonight's session. It's just the beginning of the adventure, so don't expect too much action. We're mostly concentrating on character development at this point."

"That sounds great. It's not the action part I'm interested in anyway, more the whole concept."

Kevin grinned and patted his shoulder. "I like your attitude."

"This is Ted." A heavy brown-haired guy with glasses, goatee, worn jeans and a Grateful Dead T-shirt waved amused at him. "And this is Strawberry." Allie pointed to a wisplike woman who sat crisscross beside Ted on the sofa, crouching over her laptop, lost to the world. Her long flaxen hair hung like drapes around her face. Ted nudged her repeatedly, and eventually, she looked up.

"What? Oh, um, hi," she mumbled, looking at him, but her thoughts were clearly somewhere else. Then, her gaze wandered back to the screen again. Ted shrugged and smiled.

"This is Ardy and Andrea. They're pretending not to be a couple." Everyone laughed, and the tomboy-looking blond young woman grinned while the dark-haired guy with glasses and sensitive face blushed heavily. Carl grinned too at the obvious, failed attempt to look like they weren't attracted to each other. "This is Steve. His twin brother Scott usually joins us, but this term, he's in Greece digging up ruins."

Carl's interest immediately peaked. *Must introduce Miri to him someday*— The thought snuck up on him and backstabbed him before he could prevent it, and his chest tightened. Without noticing, the fit Asian guy smiled openly at him and waved, and Carl could find a few seconds to compose himself before Allie turned toward him again. "And last, but not least, Laurie and Miles. They have some kind of relationship going on." The tall, thin guy frowned at Allie, but she just smiled back, unaffected.

"Yeah, just like you and Kevin have 'some kind of relationship' going on," the likewise tall, African-American woman interposed with a teasing smile. Allie grinned and nudged her, before turning back to Carl.

"We're KKs," she explained, but Carl felt himself looking confused.

"FFs," Kevin corrected her, calmly.

"What's that?"

"'Fuck friends.'"

Carl felt the anticipation rise in the room as everyone seemed to wait for his reaction. This was clearly some kind of test of new people's personality and moral compass.

"O... kay..." he said and tried to control an awkward blush. "Fair enough."

When everyone laughed, Allie turned to him again. "Rules in this house are: there are no rules as long as we respect each other. You can drink and eat what you want from the kitchen, go anywhere in the common areas, and have sex with whoever you want if they're willing." She shrugged at his shocked expression. "Most of us have hit the sack together at one point or the other. No big deal."

"Wow..." Embarrassed, he tugged at his hair. "Um, alright. The last part might take a while to adjust to, but fair enough."

Kevin's heavy hand patted him again, and he gave him a kind smile. "You're cool. I think you'll fit in here quite nicely if you don't let Allie scare you too much. She's very prone to the dramatic and exaggerates a lot and likes to shock people."

Allie stuck her tongue out at him, before turning back toward Carl. "Sadly enough, he's right."

Then, she got caught as Kevin put his arms around her and gave her a big, deep kiss. As far as Carl could tell, she seemed to be at least half in love with Kevin, and him with her.

Laurie came over with a beer in one hand and a Coke in the other. She had just kissed Miles passionately goodbye at the door. "Which one would you like? Beer?"

"I'll stick to Coke, please. Isn't Miles going to play?"

Laurie smiled and handed him the glass bottle. "Nah, he's not really comfortable being around here, not really part of the gang. A little too reserved to enjoy the tone, you know. You're FBI, right?" Carl nodded. "Yeah, so is he, just like me and Allie and Strawberry, but you know, he's more into the outdoor interests, like hunting and such. Right now, he's meeting his more 'manly' friends at one baseball game or another."

"Sounds kind of clashing," he commented, and Laurie laughed.

"I know, right? But somehow it works. We have common grounds too, which is good. We usually spend lots of time together at his cabin in Massachusetts, hiking, and fishing."

"Nice. So, FBI, eh? Haven't seen you around. What do you do?"

Before Laurie could answer, Kevin turned toward him with Allie still comfortably cuddled up in his arms. *They look absolutely stunning together,* Carl reflected. It was rare to see a couple who seemed to belong together as much as they did, without being a couple.

"So, you can sit around and watch tonight, and if you like it, we'll meet some evening this upcoming week and create a character for you. If you have a concept you like, great, but if not, we'll find something that suits you."

He nodded and liked that Kevin had said *that suits you,* not *that suits the game.*

Everyone assembled around the table with character sheets, dice, things to drink, fruit and chips, bread and dips, and antipasto. It was a minor feast, in Carl's opinion, and as everyone dug in, he helped himself to a plate as well, while Clackety, to his immense delight, jumped up on the sofa and shamelessly placed himself in his lap. Kevin put on some ambient music on his laptop, lit the candles, and dimmed the lights. Everyone went silent, watching him expectantly.

"It's December twenty-fifth, nineteen-hundred-and-ninety-three," Kevin began in a schooled voice. "It hasn't been snowing at all this year. On the contrary, it has been so unusually warm that flowers and strawberries can be found in the gardens, and the meteorologists are growing more and more concerned about the weather, especially since they can't seem to find any logical reason to why this is happening." He paused dramatically and looked them over. "There are, of course, some people who know exactly why." The players around the table grinned, and Kevin continued as he addressed Ardy, or rather his character, "Victor, you've summoned friends and foes to your castle. The excuse you've used is your annual Christmas party, but the real reason is, of course, something entirely different."

As the hours went by, Carl found the evening both entertaining and satisfying. Both the game and the story were intriguing and well thought through, and contained much more psychological depth to the characters than he had expected from a roleplaying game. It was also great watching all these people interact with each other, and to his surprise, he felt that they included him in their warm, slightly mischievous, and frivolous friendship without even reflecting on it. It charmed him more than he was prepared for. The thought struck him that he'd never been part of a group of friends like this before. It fascinated him that most of them shared the same need for physical contact that he saw in Allie. They touched each other, leaned on each other's shoulders, held hands, hugged, nudged, and even kissed, and they radiated warmth, love, and respect. The fact that they so naturally included him in their comradeship touched him deeply. Laurie, Ted, Andrea, and Kevin all put their hands on his shoulder or arm or leg when they talked with him, and nudged him when he, to his own surprise, cracked a joke, like it was no big deal. It was like coming home to his own warm and noisy family. For the first time in years, he relaxed in a big group of people, and just allowed himself to go with the flow. The only one who seemed more reluctant and secluded was Strawberry, who didn't play, and mostly sat with her laptop during the evening, but the others respected that as well and let her be with them on her own terms.

It was two in the morning when they decided to break off the game this time. Kevin dealt with what he called 'experience points.'

"So, one for being here, as usual. Everyone gets one for roleplaying. Did anyone learn anything?"

"That there are ordinary people in this world," Ardy said while cuddling together with Andrea. "And they don't like superheroes who can read their thoughts."

"Especially if the superhero in question is rude enough to comment on them," Andrea grinned, and everyone laughed.

"Okay, seeing that Victor comes from that kind of background, yeah, sure, go ahead. Anyone else?" They all shook their heads. "No danger in this session today, no heroics, and no success so far, obviously. Steve and Laurie, you, on the other hand, get one extra XP each for your wonderful scene."

"Woot!" Steve exclaimed with hands in the air, and everyone laughed again, as Steve and Laurie did a high-five.

"That's it, folks."

As people began to wrap their character sheets and dice together, Carl pushed himself up from the sofa where Allie and Clackety had cuddled up beside him during the game. It hurt to wake up the deeply snoring puppy, but it was time to leave.

"Thanks for inviting me. This was awesome and quite intriguing, and yeah, Kevin, I might actually take you up on your offer."

Kevin patted him on the arm and smiled broadly. "Cool! Wednesday, here, at seven? We'll treat you to dinner."

Carl felt a broad smile of his own breaking through. "You've got a deal. And I think I have some ideas for a character."

"Awesome! Looking forward to it."

As he went to the door, Allie trotted after him. "Thanks for coming," she said as he put his shoes on. "I'm so happy you had a good time. Sometimes it's boring to just sit and listen."

"No, no, it was great. Thank you for inviting me. As I said before, this is something I've always been curious about."

As he stood up again, she leaned in and gave him the usual friendly kiss on the cheek, and now, when he'd seen these people interact so physically with each other, he felt that he could accept it and even welcome the contact.

"You're sure you're leaving? There's always room for one more overnight guest here."

"Yeah, in your bed, Allie!" Ted shouted, and everyone else laughed. Carl, on the other hand, felt a violent blush cover his face and an awkward and surprising tug in his lower abdomen at the unexpected thought. *No, no, that's not a path I want to go,* he thought bewildered.

Allie grinned when she looked over her shoulder at the others. "Fuck off," she suggested friendly, and Ted snickered.

Then, she took Carl completely by surprise by easily putting her arms around his neck and kissing him softly. At first, he stood as passive as a statue, shocked and wildly blushing, as the others laughed at them in the way genuinely good friends do when they know each other inside out, but she snuggled into his arms like a playful kitten, and he forgot the rest of them. With a slightly spinning head and pounding heart, he ignored the voice in his head telling him what an extremely bad idea this was, and drew her closer into his arms and returned her sweet, teasing kiss. She tasted light of beer and a distinct Allie-taste that aroused him way too much. *Oh, God, what the hell am I doing?* Her body was gorgeously full and

133

curvaceous and pressed toward his in a way he couldn't misinterpret. Without even wanting to stop himself anymore, he gave into her softness. When was the last time he had kissed someone? Six years ago, maybe, before he and Manda felt too uncomfortable being physical together. Allie's lips were so sweet, so eager and willing, and her fingers caressed his hair, sending shivers of pleasure down his body. He closed his eyes and just enjoyed the moment. Too soon, after an eternity, she let go of his lips, but her fingers continued to play with his hair. Her eyes were a bit cloudy and aroused, and a tender smile played on her lips.

"Are you sure you don't want to stay?" she whispered, her lips almost touching his. "No one would mind."

For a moment, he was tempted to say yes, and his body tried to convince him to not be a fool. As if it had a life of its own, his hand caressed her cheek, and she leaned toward it. He let his other hand comb through her amazing hair and twirl it. It was soft as silk and smelled richly of vanilla and coconut.

"Honestly?" he said with a low, hoarse voice, feeling his body ache with arousal. "I wouldn't mind, but it's not really the right time for me now. Ask me again in a couple of months if you're still interested."

The smile on her lips was slow and sexy and made him short of breath. "You have yourself a deal." She closed the short distance between their lips, eased in her tongue, and yearningly touched his before she slowly let go of him, leaving him aching for more. She looked him straight in his eyes. "I look forward to that day, Carl."

He felt himself blush again. "Damn it. Me too."

With a low, sexy laugh, she opened the door and let him out.

As he was standing alone in the small private foyer, waiting for the elevator, his inner was in complete turmoil of conflicting feelings. He didn't want his body to react to Allie's attempts, but her warm, lovable personality and genuine interest – despite her being half in love with Kevin – made him feel more appreciated and giddier than he had in a long time. She didn't know anything about Miri, so he couldn't blame anyone else but himself for the situation that had occurred. The raw pain that hit him when he thought about Miri and how he never was going to see her again made him want to scream and cry and bang his fists on the wall.

"No," he muttered, his voice cracking on the word, "I can't lose hope. She's out there, somewhere. I just wish—" Backing away from the unrealistic notion that she might be found alive after all this time, he dried his wet eyes and cheeks. With a ragged breath, he checked the time. It was way too late to call Alan, but while waiting for the elevator, he sent a quick text, asking if he'd heard any news about Miri.

Then, he forced himself to think about something else. Getting another anxiety attack was not part of his agenda, especially not here. Instead, he thought about Allie and how embarrassing it would be on Monday. Then, he shrugged tiredly, finding that he didn't really care. He liked Allie. She was fun and sexy and totally unpredictable, and it felt like they were becoming friends.

"And I don't want to lose that friend," he muttered, "so Monday's gonna be embarrassing, but then we'll both forget about this incident."

As if it was a cue, the elevator arrived, and he got in. The night porter at the entrance nodded at him and told him to have a safe drive home.

When he exited the beautiful, warmly lit-up vestibule and entered the darkness outside, he huddled from the chilly wind, hurried to his car, and drove home in the cold, lonely night. Finally, at home, after swallowing a Zopiclone, he fell into his bed and dreamless sleep.

Chapter 7

Since Carl had thought they both would be feeling awkward seeing each other again on Monday, it surprised him that Allie was as happy and natural as usual when he hesitantly walked into the office, trying hard not to blush. Eventually, her 'what's the big deal' attitude made him relax, and he could talk naturally with her again, even though he, most of the time, made serious efforts to look like he was deeply buried in work. It would be easy to pretend the incident had never happened – if he only could force himself not to think about it, but his traitorous mind trotted back there, again and again, not caring about the fences he fought to build up, and replayed the kiss over and over. He could swear that Allie was amused on his behalf, but it didn't bug him as much as he thought it would.

He sighed and squirmed, glancing covertly at her. At the moment, she sat at the far end of the table, reading through the files while taking notes.

It was silly to not admit that he appreciated her, and it was not because she had kissed him and wanted him to go to bed with her. *What the hell, Carl, are you thinking about this again? Stop it! It's not the place. It's not the time, and it's not something I want to do toward Miri. Doesn't matter that we never had anything going on. I have more respect for her than that. She's worth more than this from me. And I don't need more trouble in my life right now. Adding sex to the relationship with my boss—* It's NOT the right way to go. He felt better for a moment until a low voice whispered in the back of his head, *Even when she's gorgeous and sexy and willing, and really turned you on?* He scowled, took a deep breath, and forced his thoughts away from how it felt when she kissed him. *No,* he thought, *it has nothing to do with that. The reason is that there are very few in this world that don't give a damn about pretense and fewer yet who act it out with that kind of easygoing charm. So there.* His mind just laughed at him.

At lunch, he had managed to compose himself enough to ask her about it, and the fact that he felt that he could, convinced him even more of how special she was.

"I've been thinking about you," he began but cut off the sentence at her immediate amused expression. "Okay, that came out wrong." She rested her chin in the palm of her hand and looked expectantly at him with raised eyebrows, and that amused little smile still playing on her lips. "What I meant was, well, you're very special— No, this doesn't... work."

"Keep digging," she suggested teasingly, and embarrassed, he chuckled.

Inhaling, and feeling as if he was falling, he tried to compose himself again. "Alright, I have my big shovel in hand, ready for duty."

She laughed and blew him a kiss. "Okay, I admit, I'm bad, but it's quite fun."

Finally, he saw an opening. "This is what I mean, Allie. How many people do you know who would say something like that in a situation like this?"

"Quite a few."

"Alright, you're lucky in that case. For me, meeting this kind of disarming honesty is very rare."

Her face got an intrigued expression. "'Disarming honesty'? What do you mean by that?"

"Well..." He thought it over for a moment. "For the most part, people aren't honest. They say, 'wow, you look good in that color' while actually thinking you look like a dead-drunk lobster." Allie laughed but gestured at him to go on. "And inside, they gloat because they actually look better than what you do. Or they say you did a good job, even though you didn't because they want to be nice and not hurt your feelings. Or they smile at your face and talk dirt about you behind your back. These are the kind of people I usually meet. Then, we have the people who are immensely proud of their own honesty, and say things like, 'good lord, did you drink the whole night through? You look awful!', or 'sweet

Jesus, please try to calm down, you just embarrass everyone.' This is honesty that hurts. You, on the other hand, manage to be honest and nice at the same time, and you don't hide your feelings, and you don't seem to be ashamed of your feelings either or care about what people think of you. That, for me at least, is very liberating, very special, and very attractive. I don't need to be on my guard with you, which, of course, means that I sometimes manage to say things that come out completely wrong. Had I been with anyone else, I'd fret for weeks over the part I did wrong, and I'd go over it in my mind again and again until it's become a huge mountain, but you— You're just completely acceptant of everything around you."

To his surprise, Allie's eyes were moist. She took his hands and kissed them sweetly. "Aw, Carl, this is probably the most beautiful compliment I've ever received. Thank you." She dried away a tear that had managed to find its way down her cheek, and then she smiled. "Look at what you managed to do. I didn't expect that." She sniveled while still smiling. Eventually, she inhaled. "You know, you're right, there are way too many people like that, and I try my best to avoid them. They only make your life miserable, and I'm not interested in that. Honestly, I don't try to hide my feelings because I realized years ago that, in the end, it will only backfire, you know, and I'm the one who's going to suffer from it. Life's too short for that kind of stuff. I mean, yeah, I'm quite aware that there are many people whose nerves I really irk, and who don't get my style or my sense of humor or my views on life, or think I'm a slut for admitting I like sex and that I – heaven forbid – enjoy sex with different people, both guys and girls, whose personality I find attractive, without any strings attached. And you know, I don't care. How they feel about me is not my problem. I can't change because they see me as an irritating stone in their shoe, or because I challenge their views on life. Even if I would change to please them, I'd irk someone else, so I'm better off being myself. At least one person will be happy about it, and that's me."

Carl smiled admiringly at her. "You're incredible, Allie." This time, it didn't surprise him when she went up from her chair, came around the table, and gave him a warm, hard hug.

When she sat down again just in time for the food to arrive, she said, "Okay, my turn."

"Your turn what?" he asked, suddenly suspicious.

"Well, we seem to play *Truth or Consequence* without the consequence part. You had your question, so now it's my turn."

He squinted cautiously. "Why do I suddenly have a bad feeling about this?"

She grinned. "Probably because you're a great profiler."

"Yeah? I knew you'd have a good answer."

Allie laughed heartily, then turned serious again. "Okay, so tell me about it."

"About what?" he asked to stall for time he knew was already wasted.

She just shook her head at him. "You know. About what happened. You obviously haven't talked about it with anyone, and as far as I can tell, it's just growing inside you like a tumor."

He kept his silence and picked at his food. He had completely lost his appetite. The look she gave him managed to be stern and compassionate at the same time. *How does she do that?*

"You know I'm here," she said. "You know I'm a good listener, and you know I care about you." He gave her another suspicious look, and she laughed amused. "Come on, Carl, we just talked about it!" When he didn't answer, she came around to the sofa where he was sitting. "Scoot in. I want to sit here too." Obligingly, he did what she asked. She half-turned toward him and placed his hands on her lap, holding them comfortingly. "I'll tell you again," she said

139

when he glanced up at her. "I like you a lot, Carl. You know that. I mean, it's not like I don't prove it several times a day. You're a great person, compassionate, fun, and sincere. That I want to take you home and have sex with you is just a bonus, and it's not that you're unaware of it. I mean, after Saturday it's pretty obvious. You don't need to be a profiler to notice that." The grin she gave him was both teasing and kind.

Carl didn't know which way to look, feeling embarrassed but amused and cared for at the same time. "You're just amazing, Allie. You know, I feel really lucky to have met you."

Her face softened, and she looked touched, but with a glint of mischief in her eyes. "Even though I drive you crazy with my huge mess?"

He laughed, feeling caught. "Yep, even then."

They smiled at each other, and Carl felt happier than he had in a long time. For years, he'd distanced himself from people in an attempt to not get hurt again. To experience this kind of loving friendship without feeling the need to fight it… It suddenly dawned on him what a rare gift it was.

"Anyway," she said eventually, "stop trying to change the subject now. I'm sorry I'm destroying your appetite, but you need to get this off your chest. You're thinking about it all the time, and it's devouring you. Just tell me what happened as if I'm not here. You'll feel better afterward. Promise."

"I've never been on this end before," he said, feeling a bit grumpy. "I've told you, I'm not used to people reading my emotions. Honestly, it's not very pleasant."

"Yeah, it's scary if you try to hide them. Maybe you need to learn how it feels. Or what about not hiding them at all?"

He gave her an irritated look, but she just met his gaze with that honest look of hers. He sighed and knew he was defeated.

"You might be right." He fell silent, and Allie waited patiently. "Well, I don't know where to begin…" He played around with her fingers while struggling to find the words. "Um, I have a co-worker. She… she was at Kroger's…"

Allie looked stunned, and then she caressed his hands gently. "I'm very sorry to hear that, Carl. Do you want to tell me about her?"

He exhaled but felt comforted by the warmth of her hands and her obvious compassion. "Um, well, her name's Miriam. I call her Miri. When we met, what was it, three and a half years ago now, she was in a relationship with another co-worker. Honestly, I like him a lot, respect him tons, and trust him completely, but, um, for various reasons, he and Miri didn't function together as a loving couple should, but they weren't even aware of it. None of my business, so I never engaged in it. Their relationship, their problem, if they didn't ask for my opinion, which they didn't, of course."

"So, what didn't work between them?"

"Well, I guess she looked up to him as a father figure while he wanted to protect her. I mean, it's not necessarily a bad thing trying to protect someone you love, and he did love her, but the way he treated her was— Well, it was actually bad. He held her back, gave her the strong impression that she was weak and fragile, and useless in all other areas than her specialty."

"Hmm, yeah, those relationships are difficult."

"And she let him turn her into this shy and insecure person that isn't really her." He puffed frustrated and frowned.

"And that irritated you."

"Immensely. Goddamn, she's a smart, intelligent, highly talented woman, and extremely good at her work. I mean, the way she steps into a room and just sees everything at first glance. It's like magic. There was no reason at all for her to think of herself as second best or third best, or inferior to Caesar. I mean, yeah, she can be damn annoying too, but

141

that doesn't exclude her other traits. We're all annoying at some time or the other."

Allie smiled briefly. "So, what happened between them?"

"Well." He sighed and looked down at their entwined hands. "It might've been my fault, actually. Not that I feel very bad about it. Don't get me wrong, I wouldn't purposely try to break a relationship, but I might give them a nudge to think outside the box sometimes. And when it came to Miri and C, I wasn't even interested in getting involved from the beginning, and honestly, I was never on talking terms with either of them. I mean, Miri and I didn't even like each other for the first year and a half. Then this Project happened, this case, and we were forced to start to communicate without having C mediating for us, mostly because of some weird – and I mean really weird – shit happening around us that, you know, cut us off from everyone else and we had to put our differences aside. We didn't have any other choice." He could see a gleaming professional interest light in her eyes, and he smiled. "No, no, the Project is classified. Sorry."

"Bummer. I was afraid you'd say that. Well, go on, what happened then?"

"Yeah, lots of things obviously, as usual in a Project like that, and it ended with us getting reinforcements and me taking over the team. I blended our two teams together and separated Miri and C, pushed her to stand on her own two feet, to trust her own instincts. Not only because of personal reasons but also 'cause I wanted to make our two teams work together, to get to know each other and feel like one." He paused, thinking back at the difficulties they'd experienced. "There was some friction in the beginning," he continued, "and it was extremely important in the situation that we all knew each other and completely trusted each other. Ah, well, it became a damn mess anyway…" Carl fell silent a couple of seconds, reluctantly thinking about Oona. He still went to the cemetery occasionally to put flowers on her grave. Then, he thought of the long aftermath during which he'd fought so hard to pull himself back to reality, leaving the nightmares behind. He shook his head and sighed. "Whatever. When we got back home, she eventually left him. As I said, it wasn't my intention, but the result of her realizing she could manage on her own without anyone protecting her that led her to that decision. I can't say I wasn't pleased when I got to know about it. At that point, we'd become really good, close friends, and eventually, I realized I— Well, I liked her a little bit more than a friend. It surprised me a lot, actually. She's not... not the kind of person I'd, well, fall for, I guess. At least not as she was back then. After she left Caesar, she finally began to develop into the person she actually is, strong-willed and funny and independent. I was so happy for her, and then she... then she..." To his horror, he heard his voice crack on the edge of tears.

Allie squeezed his hands comfortingly. "She died?" she asked gently.

Carl shook his head. "I... I don't know. I don't want to think about that possibility. She hasn't been found yet."

"Okay." Allie paused. He could tell that she thought Miri was dead but appreciated that she didn't say it. Instead, she said, "You love her." His head jerked up, and he stared bewildered at her. She gave him a surprised look. "You didn't know?"

"Um..."

She continued to caress his hands, calmingly. "Okay. That can happen. Does she know?"

He shook his head again, feeling dazed. "Um... Well... Probably not. She's, um, not good at reading people."

"And you haven't told her you have feelings for her?"

"No."

"Would you if you got the chance?"

"I— Maybe."

"Why just maybe?"

"Um, well, I honestly try not to think about what I'd do, if— Life's what it is and if— If she's... if she's dead, I'd just torture myself going through scenarios that will never

143

happen." Carl swallowed to try to get rid of the aching lump in his throat. Allie nodded. He inhaled and decided to get everything out while he was at it. "But there's one thing that keeps coming back to me."

"What's that?"

He avoided her gaze and felt a need to tug at his hair, but she was still holding his hands.

"It's so weird," he stalled. "I honestly don't get it."

She tugged his hand. "Go on, tell me."

"Yeah… We found her things, you know, her coat, her badge, some strands of hair that had been torn off, and some blood. It was as clear as crystal that she'd fallen through a crack in the ground floor to the basement and got caught under a collapsed wall. There was absolutely no way out of there. The elevator and the stairs had gone to pieces; the hole she went down through had been blocked. Everything was sealed – but she wasn't there!" He puffed again, feeling frustrated. "I don't understand it, Allie. I don't understand it. Where the hell did she go? How could she not be there?"

She frowned. "That does sound weird. I'm not good at CSI, but— Are you sure there wasn't any other crack she could've fallen through or into? Maybe one that was blocked by debris or something you didn't see?"

He shook his head. "No. We were five people down there, including a canine handler with his dog, looking for her, scrutinizing every inch, moving every single piece of concrete. Cutie marked several spots, so yeah, she'd obviously been there, and yet— Nothing. Nothing at all. It's like she disappeared into thin air. I check the lists several times a day. She's the only one who's still missing."

Allie frowned intrigued. "Very strange, very weird. No wonder you won't give up on her being alive."

He puffed. "I'm just afraid I'm fooling myself, Allie, that I'm keeping hopes up where there aren't any, and… and everyone else acts as if she's gone. I can't even talk about it with anyone, 'cause I don't want them to… to, well, I guess, pity me."

"No, you're right, Carl. It is strange that she disappeared from a sealed area where she obviously was stuck and hurt, maybe not badly hurt, but still. It doesn't ring true. She has to be somewhere."

An enormous wave of relief flowed over him, and he squeezed both her hands with his. "Thank you, Allie. Just— Thanks."

She was clearly engrossed, and as she looked at him intently, his heart hammered a bit faster with hope. "You know, this is very intriguing. Maybe we could—" Just then, Allie's cell phone rang. She grimaced. "Sorry," she said to him as she put the phone to her ear. "Yeah?" While listening, her facial expression turned shocked. "What?" She urgently started to look for something in her jacket and finally got a hold of a pen. She grabbed an unused napkin. "Do you have a name? Aha... Okay... And he's from New York, you said, right?" She scribbled down the name *Theo Sullivan* on the napkin and continued with writing *New York* after. "Okay. They didn't find anything else around, did they? No? Okay. When can I get the photos? Yeah, sure, the report can wait, if I get the photos. Mhm, yeah, that's my e-mail. I'll check it as soon as I get back to the office. Yeah, thanks." She hung up and watched Carl, devastated. "They've found another one, in Niagara Falls. Everything matches, hands bound, fell from a bridge, the damn sign around his neck. He's been there for a long time. Damn it! Damn it, damn it, damn it!"

Carl immediately stood up and waved to the waitress before turning toward her again, grabbing his jacket. "Come on, we need to get back." Then, he glanced grimly at the napkin. "Theo Sullivan. He's on my list."

They got their uneaten food in takeaway boxes and rushed back to the office. As they walked in, Carl stopped surprised. Alan Bai was standing at the table, looking through the material. Allie frowned, and then, she briskly walked toward him and took the documents from his hands.

"I'm sorry, sir, but this is classified material," she said coolly. "The door was locked. How did you get in?"

Alan put on the high-and-mighty air Carl knew all too well, and instead of answering her, he turned toward Carl. Behind Alan's back, Allie frowned even more and crossed her arms over her chest.

"Carl, I've got complaints about you," Alan said, and it felt like a stone hit Carl in the head out of the blue.

Confused, he blinked. "Um, alright. Sorry to hear that. What kind of complaints?"

"You acted unprofessionally at the Kroger's site last Monday in a way that made people ask for you to be removed from there."

Carl frowned, feeling at a loss. "Um, I'm not sure I follow you."

Alan glared at him. "Don't try to act condescending, Carl. You know what I'm talking about. You acted out when you searched the site together with the bomb squad."

He held a futile hope that the others didn't notice the pained expression that flashed across his face before he managed to get it under control.

"You mean when I found the burnt victim?" he asked calmly.

"I don't know all the details of what you found, but yes. This is not acceptable, and I'm extremely displeased with your behavior."

Carl let his hand comb through his hair and puffed. "Um, if you want my apology, you have it. Finding that burnt victim took me by surprise. None of the other victims I saw were burnt. I didn't expect to see that."

"It doesn't matter. What matters is that people reacted to your display."

"My display?" Anger rose in him, but he managed to control it.

"The way you acted was unacceptable, and I can't trust you to commit to your work properly anymore."

The anger tried to break free. "What the hell, Alan! I'm a profiler. The people I'm interviewing are rarely burnt to death. This incident won't happen again. I don't understand why this is a problem or why you're treating it as one."

"I'm your SAC, Carl. If you have psychological issues you can't handle at work, and you get complaints, and people ask me to get you out of there, then it's my goddamn problem!"

As Carl watched his SAC's arrogant demeanor, the anger fumed. "You've read my file, I assume, so you know exactly what kind of 'psychological issues' I have and why. What the hell, Alan, I've been in your team for over a damn year, and I've always done my job well. You've never had a reason to complain before. Anyone could've 'acted out' in that situation."

"You vomited and made a scene in a professional environment. That's not acceptable. And you're asking everyone involved about Miriam Goldblum as if she's the only one who matters. You're giving all of us a bad name, making us look like a joke and like we can't handle rough situations. And you're making a scene now. I can't keep you. I want your resignation before this workday has ended." Alan's tone was final.

The whole world stood still for a moment. Carl stared at him in disbelief. "My— My resignation? What the fuck, Alan?"

"There's nothing more to discuss, and there's no reason to use vulgar language. You can leave the resignation in my inbox. I'll see to it that you get the rest of this month's wages."

"Agent Bai," Allie interposed, still with her arms crossed and an even deeper frown on her forehead, "you might want to reconsider—"

Alan immediately turned his righteous gaze toward Allie. "You, young lady, have no voice here." Obviously satisfied, he turned his back on them and walked out of the room. The door closed silently behind him.

Dumbstruck, Carl flopped down at the table and tugged helplessly at his hair.

147

Allie sat down beside him and puffed angrily. "What a damn asshole. What an idiot! What a damn *jävla skitstövel!* He has no right to treat you like this. I'm going to talk to someone about it. Don't worry, we'll fix this."

Carl felt himself being in a state of complete lack of words and just shook his head in disbelief. Then, he inhaled deeply and buried his face in his hands. Allie put an arm around him and leaned in while she rested her head on his shoulder. Her warm personality comforted him, and he found her hand and squeezed it.

"What the hell," he sighed eventually, feeling too crushed to fight for himself, not having the energy or the will to fight Alan right now, even if he should. "He wants me gone that badly? They're going to stand there without a child interviewer." He shook his head again. "I can't believe it. I'm sacked? Never happened before. What am I supposed to do now? I don't know if I can— if I can hand in my resignation. It doesn't feel right. I haven't done anything wrong."

Allie put a hand under his chin and made him look into her determined eyes. "You don't have to do anything for now," she said. "You'll just continue like before. I'm hiring you, at least for now. If Bai doesn't come to his senses, I'll hire you permanently. We'll fix this."

"I'm sorry? What?" He stared at her, and she looked seriously back at him.

"I've told you before; you have the potential to become a great forensic serial killer psychologist. You know that wasn't something I said to make you feel good. Who cares if that's not your exact background? *Could become anything within the field*, remember? I'll teach you what you need to know. I'm a great boss and teacher, and I'd never humiliate you in front of others. If Bai won't come around and see reason, I'll fix special arrangements with Dean. I know he wants you around for those child interviews, and in the end, it will backfire on Bai." Then, she inhaled and looked him directly in his eyes. "I'm sorry, Carl, but you'll probably need to tell me about what you've been through, if this will

148

become permanent, so I don't put you in a rough situation by mistake. We don't have to talk about it now when we're this upset, but some time in the near future."

He couldn't stop staring at her. "You're serious? You're hiring me?"

She gave him a surprised look. "Course I am. Since I started working with you, the thought of hiring someone popped up in my head anyway, and who'd be better for that position than the one who sparked the thought in the first place? And don't worry about money. I'll give you at least what that shithole pays you." She gently nudged his shoulder. "Come now, we need to check this Theo Sullivan. The photos might've arrived already."

She let go of him and went over to her laptop. As he watched her back, a broad smile broke through the shocked mask on his face. He considered himself lucky. He was surrounded by strong, determined women.

Chapter 8

The photos had indeed arrived already. Cheek-to-cheek, they bent over Allie's laptop and studied them in silence. The body was completely hidden in the long tall reeds near the riverbank. It was extremely bloated, and the photos showed how it had burst open. The sign around his neck was washed-out and hard to read, but since they already knew the words, they could discern them. *No one could help.* Allie brought out the photos of Peter Lee. Except that the two victims had landed in different positions, there was no mistaking the same person had killed them.

"Alright, now what?" Carl eventually asked. "What do we do now?"

"Well…" Allie dragged the words out. "Right now, there's not much we can do. We have people out there searching for the rest of the bodies. We know they must be there somewhere, and except for the February victims, we also know in which areas they are. All evidence will go to the lab, obviously, and our work is over."

"But he's not found yet."

"No, but that's not our job. What we do is figuring out if it's a serial killer, what the motive and the trigger are, what kind of person we're looking for, and what kind of victims we're looking for. The rest is, sadly enough, not our job. I mean, sure, if we happened to stumble upon a name, they won't get mad, but usually, we don't."

"But with this one, we don't know his motive yet, and we don't know his trigger."

"I know. You're right, and I hate to admit it, but I'm stuck. I know almost everything else, but not that."

Carl leaned back from the laptop and watched her as she studied the photos with a deep frown on her forehead. "Alright. What do you do when you're stuck?"

She questioningly looked up at him. "What do you mean?"

"You can't just walk around in here like a trapped pheasant, can you? That seems extremely unproductive." She looked caught and a bit sheepish. "Alright, come on," he decided and went to get his jacket.

"Where are we going?"

Carl shrugged. "Don't know. Just somewhere. No, don't bring your laptop. That's just counterproductive. Take your notebook and a pen instead, but put them in your coat or your bag or something, so you don't think about them."

Obligingly, Allie followed his advice, and soon they walked away from the big, gray building, breathing in the fresh spring air.

"It's warmer, right?" Allie turned her face toward the sun and smiled.

"Yeah, maybe. Would be nice to get some warmth again. Been too long without it." With hands in his pockets, he let his feet chose which way to walk and turned in on a pathway that led down to the park behind the FBI-building. They walked in silence for a while until they reached the big lawn just before the obstacle course run. It was a dull place, in Carl's opinion, but it had to do since it would take too long to get to the lush parts of the park. At least, there was some greenery here. They stepped onto the shy, new grass, and he led them toward a faraway bench in the shadow of a couple of birches.

"Alright, tell me something about yourself you usually don't tell people," he asked her when they sat down.

She gave him a curious eye. "Is this your way to releasing 'forensics' block'?"

"Shh, not that now."

"Okay, something about me that I usually don't tell people. Wow, um, thanks for making it easy for me."

He grinned. "You're most welcome."

"Um, okay." She fell silent.

"No, no, don't think, just blurt out something."

"Uh, okay, trees."

"Trees what?"

"What do you mean, 'trees what'?"

"What comes to mind when you think about trees?"

"You want me to be specific? Okay. Um…" She seemed to gather her thoughts for a moment. "Well, there was this tree at our summer retreat when I was a kid. It had fallen sometime, I don't know, some years before I discovered it, 'cause baby saplings were growing up around the tree trunk, twining themselves around it." She started to get lost in memories, Carl could tell, and her body began to relax. "No one knew about this tree except for me, 'cause it was hidden in a, well, I'd like to call it a cave, a green cave of tall birches and junipers and firs. I used to hide there when I'd done something bad, which happened quite often. Or when Mom and Dad, my real dad, that is, argued, which also happened quite often. Or just to get away from things when my family got too much on my nerves, which apparently also happened quite often. I spent a lot of time there." She smiled with something that Carl interpreted as sadness. "It was my best friend back then. Funny, I haven't thought about it in years. It's probably molded now." Her eyes had a faraway look as she, in her mind's eye, saw that place and time when she was a kid. "There were other trees, too," she continued without being prompted. "The elderly couple who my grandma inherited the place from had created a real grotto of lilacs, the pale purple ones, you know, and in the midst, a few dark purple ones. I liked to be there too, but only when the lilacs bloomed. The scent was overwhelming, you know. You got dizzy, and it felt like you were floating. I guess it was like getting high in a way. And then the old apple trees in the orchard. I used to climb them all the way up, and when the apples were ripe, the scent was everywhere; sweet and tart and fresh. They don't have those apples here. *Åkerö* is their name. I haven't tasted them in years." She fell silent, day-dreaming away.

"What other trees do you remember?" Carl's voice was low and gentle, and he watched her face, so bright and soft with memories.

"You know, this place, it was so amazing, there were so many spots where you could hide. I guess hiding was a thing of mine when I was a kid. Behind the main house was a tall pine and fir forest, and the ground was covered in soft white moss and really big boulders. They're called *jättekast* in Swedish, meaning *cast by a giant*, and I climbed them, of course, pretending I was an adventurer." Once again, she fell silent, but he could tell that she was about to lose her concentration. It was time to direct her subconscious toward her consciousness before she lost it.

"So tell me about these people, Allie. Why are they together? And why are they separated?" His voice was still very low and gentle, but he watched her intently. There was a shift in her face, and suddenly her whole body stiffened. Slowly, she turned toward him with wide-opened eyes.

"What did you say?"

"Why are they together, and why are they separated?"

She gasped. "You've got it, Carl! Good God, you've got it! That's why I couldn't see it!" Her cheeks were suddenly flaming red, her eyes gleamed, and without him being prepared for it, she laughingly fell around his neck. "Woot! Whatever you did, it worked! Come! We need to get back!"

She jumped up from the bench, eagerly tugging at his hand. He followed her with a broad grin as they jogged across the lawn.

"Well, go on," he said with his normal voice as they half-ran, "tell me then. Stop teasing me."

"You said it, Carl," she panted over her shoulder. "They separated!"

"Who did? The killer?"

"No, no, he's the child. That's why they live. She, his mom, wanted a divorce. His dad didn't, so he killed her and then committed suicide. He's recreating his own childhood tragedy."

"Oh, my God!" Carl suddenly saw all the pieces of the puzzle come together.

As soon as they got back to the office, Allie brought out all her reports on the table and grabbed some blank sheets of paper and a pen.

"Okay, he must've been around four, five something when it happened. He should have brown hair, 'cause that's what Ariel and Ernie have."

"Hey, wait a minute!" Carl suddenly frowned. "Are you sure you're on the right track?"

She gave him a surprised side-glance. "Yeah, why?"

"Ariel's a girl, and she pointed out ash-blond hair, not brown."

"Oh, yeah, right." She frowned and drummed with the pen on the table. The staccato sounded nervous. "Well, bear with me while I'm thinking aloud for a while, okay?"

"Sure."

"Hrm…" She cleared her throat and tried to find her lost thread. "Okay, um, well, hair can be dyed, but why—" Allie poked about the reports on the table until she found what she was looking for. Once again, she cleared her throat and read out loud, "'*XX experienced a traumatic incident in his early youth, which made him want to regress to a time before this incident. He repressed the trauma since he lived in an environment that was condescending and even frightful of people with psychological problems.*' Yeah, that's the thing. He wanted to get away from this period of his life to the point where he even changed his looks. He didn't have to undergo any surgeries, 'cause he didn't look like a four-year-old for long, but he wanted to get rid of the hair." She paused and looked up at him with a questioning eye.

"Mhm, alright. Not entirely convinced, but go on."

She inhaled and began doodling on the blank sheet. A couple of stickmen appeared. "His dad must've been around twenty years older than his mom. Profession doesn't seem to be important if the men are wealthy-looking, but mom has to be a university student—" Suddenly her phone rang. "What the fuck! Give me a break!" With a frown and a grimace, she answered. "Hello? Yeah, that's me." Suddenly, an

154

overwhelmed expression covered her face. "Um, wow… Uh, okay, but— Well, it's not a good time for that. I need him right now. Is it really necessary to— Can you hold for a moment? Thanks." She turned toward Carl, but the overwhelmed look was gone, and there was a deep frown on her forehead instead as she held her hand over the mouthpiece. "Could you go and get us a couple of, um, I don't know, Frapps or something, please?"

He glanced at their nearly full Frappuccino's on the table but didn't say anything about it. He just nodded and took his leave. Instead of going back to Starbucks, however, he took the short walk to Superfresh and bought a box each of raspberries, blueberries, and strawberries, while he tried to figure out what the hell was going on. It couldn't be Alan. First of all, Alan would never admit that he'd been wrong, and secondly, had it been Alan, he had a distinct feeling Allie would've let him stay around. Maybe it was Dean? Yeah, that sounded more likely. He frowned worriedly. *Please, no more complaints.*

When he came back, he went into the small kitchen area on the first floor to rinse the berries and arrange them in a bowl before returning to the office. As he knocked on the door, it only took a couple of seconds before Allie opened it. The frown on her forehead smoothed out when she saw the minor mountain of berries in his hands, and she smiled delightfully.

"What a great idea, Carl! Much better than buying us yet another Frapp. Come, close the door, we need to talk." With some more butterflies awakening in his stomach and their wings fluttering uncomfortably, he did what she asked. She took a bright red strawberry and bit off the top while studying his face. "Okay, so I got this really weird call from a guy named Armand—"

A piece of raspberry stuck in Carl's throat, and he began coughing violently. Allie quickly got up on her feet and patted his back hard until he managed to stop coughing and catch his breath.

155

"You're kidding me?"

"Yeah, course I am. Honestly, it was Superman, but I didn't think you'd believe me. Oh, come on, Carl, who's this guy? I hate being curious."

Recovering from the initial shock, he chuckled. "Sorry, it just took me by surprise. Armand? Haven't heard from him in ages." He caught a glimpse of Allie's impatient face and continued, "Well, you remember the Project I mentioned earlier today, with Miri and me and Caesar?" She nodded. "Yeah, Armand was our SAC back then, so to say, the Principal Investigator on our team, and Miri's fiancé, but back then his code name was Caesar."

Now, it was Allie's turn to stare at him. "You never told me Miri's a Star Student too," she said eventually, almost accusing. "Or that it was a Star Student case you all worked on. Now, I'm a bit cross. You know how fascinated I am by the Star Students." She crossed her arms and glared at him.

He nearly smiled at how cute she was, but when he saw that she was genuinely upset and not teasing him, he stood up, alarmed, and came around to her chair, pulled her up, and hugged her closely. As he suspected, she exhaled and relaxed in her whole body from the physical contact. He held her a couple of minutes longer than necessary, just because he wanted to prolong the moment of having her soft body in his arms, and she didn't protest.

"I'm sorry, Allie," he mumbled in her silky, vanilla-scented hair. "I'm still working on not being so closed up. Haven't come all the way yet. In the future, I'll let you know."

She exhaled again and put her hands on his face and kissed his lips lightly. When she let him go, he caught her again, and for some reason, which he didn't even want to explain to himself, he deepened the kiss while entwining his hands in her ponytail. Eventually, the kiss ended and aroused he leaned his cheek on her hair. "Damn it, Allie," he mumbled as the guilt hit him. "What the hell am I doing?" He let his arms fall away from her and turned around and went back to his chair. When she didn't move, he looked up at her.

She stood with her arms crossed and glared at him. The color rose on his cheeks. He knew that he deserved that. "I'm sorry. I don't know— I'm sorry."

She continued to glare at him for a moment before she sighed and sat down beside him. When he gave her a guilt-ridden side-glance, he saw that she still had a frown on her forehead.

She caught his gaze. "You know what, Carl? You're a damn tease. Can't you just have sex with me so we can go back to be professional at work?" He stared bewildered at her for a moment, feeling completely speechless. She glared at him again. "It's just sex, Carl, nothing to become so anxious about, and you obviously want it too. It's not just me projecting it."

"I, um—" He cleared his suddenly hoarse voice. "I don't think anyone has ever called me a tease before."

"Well, you are." Restlessly, she drummed her fingers on the tabletop before giving him another side-glance. "I'm not trying to convince you or talk you into something you deep inside don't want, just because your body does. That's not how I work. Okay that you have a different view on sex than I do, which is fine, and that we're not in love with each other, which also is fine, and that your heart is full of Miri, which is as it should be." While she was talking, she never let go of his eyes, and her look was both honest and gentle when she paused for a moment, studying him. "You probably think you're betraying her if you have sex with me." She nodded when he looked away. "I don't, but people usually don't agree with me. Anyway, what I'm trying to say is, having sex with no strings attached can be damn liberating and ease up a tense body, and you're one of the tensest people I've ever met. Usually, I don't even get turned on by people like you who try to hide every damn feeling, but somehow you get to me. So you, my dear, are very special. If you really don't want to, that's fine, but then, please, don't kiss me again. I won't either. It has to be fair."

157

He looked at her, feeling touched deep down in his soul. Without thinking it over, he reached for her fingers and kissed her knuckles with more tenderness than he intended.

"You're right, Allie. I'm not in love with you, but these past days—" He shook his head and blurted it out, "You've managed to sneak into my heart. I think I do like you more than I should. I know I feel a huge tenderness toward you. I've never met anyone else who's as warm and natural as you are, and so generous and caring, and so... just so you."

Her face softened. "You're a very, very special man, Carl. Miri is very lucky." Then, she studied him with something that resembled insecurity, before exhaling and shrugging, obviously putting all eggs in one basket. "Okay, last chance. There's no one at home right now. We can take a couple of hours off, if you want to, and work late instead. If he follows the pattern, which he should, we're not in any real hurry. "

He stared at her, cheeks on fire, while trying to figure out how he had managed to get himself into this situation and if he indeed was displeased with it. Scared, yes, he decided, but not displeased.

Allie's cheeks got blossoming red too when he hesitated, and she turned away and fiddled with her files. Seeing her feeling so awkward and exposed, tugged at his heart. She had nothing to be ashamed of, and he felt like a dog for making her feel that way. His thoughts swirled like leaves on the wind. He had told her the truth. He did feel a deep tenderness for her, a feeling that had snuck up on him somehow during the past days, and she was also right; she wasn't projecting. Maybe she was right about other things too. Maybe he did make too big of a deal out of it. He inhaled and took that scary mental leap.

"Alright."

Her hands stopped in their restless searching, and she turned back toward him with a shocked expression that suddenly turned shy. Apparently, she hadn't thought he would say yes. He leaned in toward her and rested his cheek on hers, feeling terribly nervous. This was something he'd never done before; going to bed with someone he wasn't in love with just because she turned him on, and it had been so long since last time, and he wished that he suddenly didn't feel so guilty about it. Most of all, he wished that life had become different, but this was how it had turned out and—

Allie cupped his face in her hands and watched him closely with a very tender look. "It's okay, Carl. We don't have to."

He inhaled and thought it over for a moment. If he told her no now, he'd probably regret it for a long time. *Might regret this decision too, but she's right. I do want her. I want her badly.* The thought of her naked in his arms made him short of breath, and the thought of having someone who liked him embracing him, kissing him, caring for him, was overwhelming. It was that last thought that tipped the scale. With longing in his heart, he rose and held out his hand toward her. Without any other words, they collected their things and left the office.

All the way home to her place, Carl's mind went on about what a painfully bad idea this was, that what they were about to do was unethical and that it would destroy their friendship, and, most of all, that he was defiling Miriam. Tense and terrified, he sat in the passenger seat without daring to look at Allie. Neither of them spoke a word, and he had a distinct feeling that Allie also had second thoughts about the whole thing.

In the vestibule of the penthouse complex, she greeted the porter with a smile and a name, which Carl forgot the next second, but he managed to greet him casually as well, before following Allie into the elevator. The silence became more and more awkward, and Carl wished that he could just turn around and go back to the office, but he didn't know how to say it without embarrassing both of them even more.

When she unlocked the door, and they stepped into the now empty and quiet apartment, she inhaled deeply and loosened her hair. It fell around her like a golden waterfall.

Then, she turned to him with a smile that was warm and genuine again. "I'll make us something to drink."

He nodded and took off his shoes and jacket. The big windows that let in the harsh afternoon light lured him, and he went over to look at the view. It was breathtaking. It felt as if he could see the whole city from here.

From the kitchen, he could hear Allie clink with some bottles and glasses, and, eventually, she came out with two drinks and handed him one. He took a sip of the sweet-tasting liquor, and his mouth filled with gradually exploding fullness. *Wow, haven't drunk alcohol in years.*

"It's really good."

"Thanks."

He nodded at the view. "Didn't see it last time, but this— It's magnificent."

"Yeah, I know." She sounded awkward again.

He glanced at her, slightly confused. "What?"

She moved uncomfortably beside him, her eyes locked on the view. "It's just, you know—" She fell silent for a second, but then, she sighed. "Well, maybe you don't know how it is, how it feels to invite new people home and know that from now on and forever they'll look at you as 'the rich girl,' or even worse, 'Daddy's little rich girl.' That's why I rarely invite new people over or tell them who my dad is."

Carl put a friendly arm around her shoulders. "For me, you're Allie; doesn't matter if you're rich or poor."

A grateful smile spread over her lips, and she exhaled and leaned into his embrace.

"Thanks." Her voice was low and soft. She took another sip and looked up at him, unexpectedly vulnerable. "It's weird, I can't even remember last time I felt shy, but— I don't know…" She exhaled deeply as if trying to find courage. Her hand was slightly sweaty when she led him into a corridor he hadn't been in before and took him all the way

160

to a door at the end of it. It led into a large, very messy bedroom with clothes and books, pens, and sheets of paper all over the floor, and a huge unmade bed placed on a platform at the far end. In front of it, drapes hung all the way from the ceiling to the floor, moss-green and golden in color. They could easily be pulled together, hiding the bed from sight.

She gave a nervous giggle. "I know, I know, sorry for the mess. I would've cleaned if I'd known."

He shook his head. "Why do you apologize for something that's so obviously you?"

The look she gave him was astounded. "Well, messy isn't exactly looked kindly upon, right, and since you're not the messy type, this must irk you a lot."

He gently pressed her hand. "Don't worry about me. What do some clothes on the floor matter? It's how you are. You're messy. So what?"

She gave him another, more relaxed smile. "Sometimes, you're just way too good for me."

He laughed at her and let his hand caress that lovely, thick hair of hers. "Just trying my best to accept people for who they are."

"Yeah, that's what I mean," she murmured softly. "I like how you touch my hair."

With an affectionate smile of his own, he put their drinks on the desk and let his hands gently tangle her hair. It was heavy and silky and smelled richly of vanilla.

"I like to touch your hair. It's... it's like a golden waterfall."

Her eyes softened. "Aw, Carl, that's beautiful."

Just realizing that his nervousness was gone, he bent down and touched her lips while letting his hands follow her spine down and rest at her lower back. She placed her arms around his neck and pulled him closer. It was like a dance, a sweet, slow dance where they swayed together to some inner music. Unlike the intense and teasing kiss on Saturday, this was a gentle exploration of each other with mutual tenderness and kindness. They didn't talk. There was no need for words. Eventually, they began to undress each other, and Allie was so soft under his hands. He loved her curves and how they felt when he caressed her, and when he kissed her warm naked skin. Her eyes became cloudy, and with a tug of his hand, she brought him to the bed and lay him down on his back. For a long time, they just kissed, long tender kisses, gradually building up tension, but then, he let his hands wander down to her breasts and cupped them, caressed them, and she sighed in pleasure and arched a tiny bit. When she placed her mouth on his neck and let her lips brush him feathery down toward his chest, he closed his eyes. Her tongue touched his nipple, and a sudden electric sensation rushed through his whole body, landing hard in his throbbing loins. He moaned quietly and felt her smile. When her hand unexpectedly caressed him where no one had caressed him for six years, he inhaled sharply at the molten heat that suddenly blazed his already sensitive nerves.

"No," he gasped and managed to take away her hand. "Can't do that now. Too soon. Won't be able to hold it."

"Come," she whispered, suddenly urgent. "I want you."

"I don't have any condoms," he realized, feeling stupid.

With a little smile, she reached over to her bedside table and handed him one while embracing him, caressing him, not giving him time to think or feeling awkward and embarrassed. Then she fell down on her back, pulling him with her, lifting up her knees on each side of him, seizing him, holding him. His heart pounded with a low, heavy beat, feeling her strong, silky thighs around his hips. With her hand, she led him right, and as he sank down inside her, the world turned upside down and into a golden flow of energy that joined them together, and he closed his eyes. For a moment, he didn't want to move; he only wanted to indulge in the heated electricity that pulsed through his body, created by the tightness and the warmth of her. Then, he opened his eyes and looked down into her face. Her eyes were clouded with desire, her breath hot to his chest, and her lips, moist and full, were sensually parted. As he slowly began to move inside her, not being able to resist the ripples of the sensuous force they created together, he let himself lay down on her, feeling her gorgeously full breasts against his skin. Her hands pulled him even closer to her as she moaned and trembled underneath him, creating almost unbearable sweetness.

Breathing heavily, he caught those sensual, moist lips and dove down. Their tongues met, and the taste of her was that of earthy soil on a spring day, full and sweet and filled with myrrh. He let his hands find their way between the mattress and her back, holding her close in his arms as they moved in each other's rhythm, feeling every sensation whirl like tiny tornados in their bodies. Everything else disappeared from his mind, everything but Allie and how she made him feel. When her breaths became faster and turned into quiet, urgent moans, and she met him with more force while her hands moved frantically on his back, he pushed himself deeper, harder inside her, and with a needing cry, she convulsed, dragging him down with her as the world exploded in searing light.

He collapsed on top of her sweaty body, breathing hard.

Smilingly, she kept him in place with her legs. "Don't move," she whispered teasingly. "I like it just where you are right now."

He laughed quietly at her throat and felt her nipples harden against his chest, sending a newborn ripple of desire through his body. With her fingers, she drew lazy swirls and spirals on his back, before moving her hands down, caressing his buttocks while nipping at his throat with her teeth. He sighed in pleasure when his body began to respond to her touch again. He heaved up on his elbow and looked into her happy, teasing eyes for a moment before moving down and taking her nipple into his mouth, caressing the other with his fingers. She inhaled sharply and arched, sending more electricity through his body as he felt himself slowly harden again between her legs.

"I don't know about you," she murmured with a smile, "but I kind of like this idea we had today."

He smiled too and leaned in to kiss the corner of her mouth. "Can't complain, really."

"Good," she whispered at his lips. "Because I have some plans for you tonight."

"Well, technically, you're still the boss, so…"

She chuckled, and a mischievous glint lit in her eyes. "I like your attitude. It's going to take you some places." She squirmed under him and began to sit up. "Come. Let me show you."

Much later, Carl lay sprawled beside Allie on the big, unmade bed while pretending to study the reports on the floor, only dressed in his underwear. To his astonishment, he felt tremendously good, and more than that, somehow, in a way, he couldn't explain, it also felt right, being here like this with her. The sexual tension that had built up between them since Saturday night wasn't gone, but it was soothed, and they were both much more relaxed. For Carl, who hadn't had the pleasure of sex in six years, it felt like his whole body was floating in warm, balmy water, and his mind was calmer than it had been in a very long time. He had pushed the thoughts of Miri as far back in his mind as he possibly could, feeling that if he one day was lucky enough to be forced to answer to her about what he had done together with Allie today, and what he had a slight hope that he might do together with her during the upcoming days, it was a problem for the future. He would gladly take a scene where she got to know that he had had sex with Allie, if he only got her back, but for now, thinking about her and all they'd missed experiencing together, would make him cry, and this was not the right time or place for that. He forced his thoughts away again, before the bad conscious and guilt hit him, as he knew they would eventually.

The room smelled deeply of sex and pizza since they decided that cooking was not on their agenda tonight, and they'd forgotten their leftovers at the office. Carl was very satisfied with the absence of the rest of Allie's housemates as they were away watching Ted on one of his stand-up comedy shows. Obviously, he wouldn't have been able to relax had they been home.

"He's pretty good," Allie said as she sat half-naked and crisscross beside him with a pizza slice in one hand and a Coke in the other. "Hard to guess he's a top-grade university student. Astronomy," she answered his questioning glance. "Doing his Ph.D. right now. And he's starting to make a name out there, locally. He's very appreciated at *The Fox and Hound*, actually, and yeah, it's well deserved. He's funny."

"Won't he be disappointed you're not there?"

"Ted?" She sounded a bit surprised. "Nah, not Ted. Had it been Ardy, whoa, then it'd be a totally different thing."

Carl thought of Ardy's sensitive face and nodded. "Yeah, I see your point."

Allie swallowed the last piece of the slice and drank her coke before reaching for the napkins and wiping her hands and face from grease. Then, she cuddled up beside him and let her lips glide over his back. He closed his eyes at the tingling sensation and let her continue for a while before he rolled around and pulled her up on top of him and kissed her gently, and then not so gently. When she tugged their underwear off, he sent a muddled thought at the reports, and that they should work and that they had had sex for hours, and he was getting sore, but then he didn't think about anything else than her beautifully curvaceous and soft body.

When they looked at the reports next time, they were both completely naked, and darkness had fallen outside the window.

"I have to admit," he said as he skimmed over a report without truly seeing it, "I've never worked like this before. I think I said it already; I can't complain, really."

She laughed and nudged him at his side. "Maybe you'll get used to it."

He grinned and sought out her eyes. "Yeah, maybe I will." With a sweet expression, she found his lips and tasted them teasingly. He put his arms around her and deepened the kiss. Gently they sought out new, different techniques to arouse each other with. Eventually, he mumbled at her cheek, "We'll never be able to get anywhere if we continue like this." He could feel her smile.

"I think we are getting somewhere. Have I told you that I love your kisses? You're one of the best kissers I've ever had the pleasure to enjoy."

"Really?"

"Mhm, really. And don't you even think of leaving tonight. Door's locked, and you don't have your car."

He couldn't suppress a grin. "Is that so?"

"Mhm, that's exactly so."

"Well, if that's the case, then I suggest…" Teasingly, he pretended to reach for a file, but Allie caught his hands and muted him by another kiss.

"Later," she mumbled.

They didn't look at the reports more that night.

Chapter 9

When he woke up, he felt completely relaxed and at ease – and sore. *Oh, God, so damn sore.* Allie sat on the floor with a pen in her mouth, still half-naked, surrounded by reports and scribbled sheets of paper. On the stereo, a more sexually-tense version of *Summer Wine* than the one with Nancy Sinatra played on low volume. As she sat crisscrossed and made notes, her hair hung loose and framed her face, making her look younger and more innocent than she was. *Well, yeah, innocent she's not,* he thought.

As if she felt his gaze, she looked up at him and smiled. "Morning."

"Morning."

"How are you feeling?"

He tried to ignore his heating face and grinned. "Just fine."

She grinned back. "Good. That's what I hoped you'd say." She looked down at her scribbles and sighed. "I wish it were Saturday, so we didn't have to get back to work, but it's time. Take a shower, eat breakfast, and then we'll leave."

"You never told me about Armand," he reminded her as he sat up and put his feet on the floor.

"Oh." A deep frown appeared on her forehead. "Yeah." She looked up at him. "You're sure we're talking about the same person?"

He gave her a surprised look. "What do you mean?"

"You said you respect him tons."

"Yeah, well, I do."

"Really? Okay." She didn't look convinced.

"Come on, Allie, now you're making me curious. What happened? What did he say to you?"

She shook her head and rolled her eyes. "It sometimes happens, especially with older men, that they think they can control me. Alan Bai is a great example, not that he's old, mind you. I mean, he can't be more than thirty-five.

Anyway, apparently, your Armand thought he could command me and that I'd just swoon because he's part of the Faculty. When I didn't, he got, well, cross, I guess."

"Huh, he must've lost his touch. Most women fall for him like rain."

"Well, I'm not 'most women', am I?" she sneered, and Carl smiled amused.

"No, you're certainly not. If you were, I wouldn't be here with you."

The scowl on her forehead smoothed out slightly before it came back with full force.

"Honestly, he was so damn condescending, as if I was going to fall on my knees when he told me he's Faculty, and when I didn't and dared express my honest thought that I might be in bigger need of you than he and your teammates, he hung up on me."

He stared at her. It sounded so far from Caesar's usual professional manners that he had a hard time believing her. "What? No, he didn't, did he?"

She looked sincerely at him. "I kid you not, Carl, he hung up on me, which made me damn angry. I didn't try to piss him off, just having an honest discussion. Can't say he impressed me much. Yeah, okay that we didn't work at all after that yesterday, but I still need you, and he seems to have forgotten that the Star Students have privileges within the FBI, but they're only privileges, not rules set in stone. He can ask me to let you go, but it's my decision, not his."

"Wow." Carl felt a bit overwhelmed. "That must be a first. He's definitely not used to that."

She glared at him, but he could tell that it wasn't him that she wanted to berate. "He'd better become used to it. I'm not dancing to his pipe. And as far as I managed to pry out of him, you were only going to do some research on a dead woman together with your two teammates. No," she hurriedly said when she saw his expression rapidly change and his face losing all blood, "not Miri. Don't worry. I asked."

"You— you asked?" Carl managed to give a weak laugh while he tried to stop trembling, and his heart tried to get back to its regular beat. "Wow, aren't you two going to clash."

"I don't care. If he thinks he can come and demand your presence without even asking if it's okay to let you go— He already has two agents working on his case. He can't leave me without the best profiler I've ever encountered, not in the last burning hours of our case. Well, he definitely needs to think it through again. And speaking of those burning hours, we need to get going. Take that shower and eat something. I'm going to get done too." With that, she rose. "You can use the shower in here; I'll use the main shower. At this point, I don't trust us enough to shower together."

Within the hour, they were back at the office. Allie immediately started to scribble on the whiteboard beside the crime map.

"Okay, I've been thinking. It disturbed me what you said yesterday about Ariel. I can't be sure, of course, since we've only found two out of five children, but as far as I've figured out, our killer thought she was a boy. Short hair, dressed in her provider's son's winter outfit, since it snowed that day and she only had a summer jacket of her own. The killer must've thought, which doesn't surprise me, given the background, that anyone dressed in gender-typical clothes belongs to the sex the color of the clothes suggests."

Carl grimaced but nodded. He'd fought that battle a lot for Sarah, whose favorite color was blue and favorite clothes were jeans and T-shirts, against narrow-minded people of all sorts.

"Sounds likely. I'd like to have an open mind, though, but until we've got further evidence, I think it's the best suggestion we have for now."

"So, we're looking for a case about thirty, forty years old, in which a forty-something-year-old man shoots his twenty-something university student wife to death in front of

169

the eyes of their four-five-year-old son, before taking his own life by jumping off a bridge."

"Mhm, let's concentrate on New York and its surroundings."

She gave him a curious look. "Why?"

"Well, Daddy seems to be the most important person for this man, and all the male victims are from New York; Queens, to be precise. I suggest he was a very dominant man and most likely decided where his family should live."

She smiled broadly. "Yeah, that rings true. Honestly, if it is as we think it is, it's a very curious case. I've never heard of something like it before."

The whole day, they sat at the laptops going through case after case, without finding anything. At four-thirty, Allie stretched and sighed.

"I feel terribly tired and terribly scared. What if I'm wrong?"

A pang of doubt hit him, but he shook his head immediately. *Can't afford to doubt now. It's the only lead we have.*

"I don't think you are. What years have you been going through?"

"Nineteen sixty to nineteen sixty-three. I'm almost at sixty-four now."

"See? Only three years. I've been going through nineteen seventy to nineteen seventy-two. It's a damn high crime rate there during the seventies."

"Okay." She sighed. "I need a break. Since we took the afternoon off yesterday, so to say, I'd suggest we continue on 'til seven. Is that good with you?"

"Yep. Works fine."

"Good. Anyway, I need something. Are you hungry?"

"Yeah, actually."

"Wanna have Chinese takeaway?"

"Sure."

"Okay, I'll get it. Any preferences?"

"Nah, not really."

She nodded and left. Carl sighed. He felt exhausted and just wanted to go home and sleep, but she was right. They needed to keep up. At this point, seeing that they were so close to the next abduction, he would've suggested that they worked until they found it. However, because of them being so tired, the chance was too high that they'd missed the case if they tried that route. *Wouldn't want to work past nine,* he thought unenthusiastically, for once longing for strong hot coffee.

When Allie came back forty minutes later, he could tell that something had happened.

"What?" he asked as she landed a steaming takeaway bowl with rice, vegetables, and chicken in front of him. To his happiness, she had also brought cups of coffee.

"They've found another one. Catherine Nichols. Also Niagara Falls. According to the coroner, she was murdered sometime December to February, so most likely January, since Theo was estimated to have died then. The car was hidden away this time, and they found kid's stuff in it. They're searching for him now, the kid that is."

"Same procedure?"

"Mhm. No question she's one of them. And the media caught up with it."

"It was bound to happen sooner or later. I'm actually surprised it took them this long."

"I guess you're right." She sighed. "Anyway, let's eat and check the photos afterward."

At this point, they just verified that everything checked out on the photos, before continuing with their own search. The atmosphere in the room was more frantic now, and both of them seemed to have gotten more energy. When the clock turned seven, neither of them mentioned it and just carried on. At nine, Carl had just reached the year of seventy-five. He sighed, feeling the exhaustion effectively smothering the energy he'd gotten from the food and coffee.

Allie looked up at him. Her eyes were red, and the color of her face was grayish. "I can't do this anymore tonight. I need to sleep." Her voice was lifeless and dull.

Carl nodded and exhaled. "Yeah, I hear you." He rubbed his eyes, felt them being sandy and sore.

"When do you want to start tomorrow?"

He sighed and said unwillingly, "Hate to say it, but, yeah, as early as possible, I guess."

"Six? Seven?"

Carl grunted. "Yeah, seven?"

She gave him a half-smile. "I hoped you were going to say that."

Quickly, they gathered their work files and took the stairs down. It was chilly outside. Allie shivered, and he put his arm around her. When they reached her car, she turned and threw her arms around him. For a while, they stood just embracing each other, feeling comfort in the other's presence. Then she kissed him longingly.

"See you in the morning, Carl."

"Yeah, sleep tight."

She had just opened her car, and he was on his way toward his own when he heard her cell phone ring.

"Fuck it," he grunted to himself, but stopped in his step and turned around. Allie got out of her car with a distressed bearing and waved toward him. "Fuck it," he mumbled again and went over to her.

"Okay, thanks, Dean. That's great." Her voice sounded exhausted. "They found the boy," she said to him.

"Yeah, thought so."

"I'm not going to look at it until tomorrow. I can't— I can't do anything about it right now anyway. He's dead. No matter what I do, he won't come back..."

"I'm sorry, Allie."

She nodded, her eyes filled with tears. "Yeah, me too."

He hesitated. "You want to sleep alone, or you want to sleep in company?"

The smile on her lips was shadowed, and nearly not a smile at all. "As long as we're just sleeping. I wouldn't mind some company. It's been a little bit too much with all the children..." Her voice trailed away.

"Yeah, I hear you. Here, come. We'll take my car."

"Okay."

At home, he gave her a big T-shirt and an extra toothbrush. Together, they crashed in bed and, loosely embraced, they fell asleep immediately.

When Carl woke up, the time showed five-ten. Allie lay cuddled up in his arms with all the golden hair spread out over his pillow. Even in her sleep, she was beautiful. It felt so nice to have someone to hold in bed again. *If it only had been Miri.* The thought attacked him from nowhere, and to his horror, tears began to run from his eyes. Hurriedly, he went into the bathroom and turned on the shower. He didn't want Allie to hear him cry.

For a while, he sat on the toilet, weeping, with the cold water streaming beside him, but eventually, he forced himself to compose and turned on the warm water for an actual shower.

He felt jaded when he finally got out again as if he hadn't slept at all. Allie had woken up and put some breakfast on the table, still just dressed in his T-shirt. She looked a tiny bit better than yesterday evening, but not by much. She scrutinized him as he came over to the table, and he could tell that she knew he had been crying. He shrugged and gave her a crooked half-smile.

"I like your place, Carl," she said. "It's very cozy."

"Thanks," he said, but it was clear that she knew that he thanked her for not mentioning him losing it in the bathroom, rather than for the compliment of his interior decoration skills.

She looked away with a sigh and rubbed her face. "You know, we're both too exhausted to go anywhere. If it's alright with you, I think we'll just stay and work from here. We don't need the crime map anymore, so it doesn't matter where we are. You've got all the passwords and security questions to the databases and such, right?"

He nodded. "That's an awesome idea, actually. I have to admit that I'm not on top today."

"Not me, either." She sighed again and looked around his minuscule kitchen. Her gaze landed on his tea collection. "By the way, this tea cupboard of yours is awesome— no, it's actually magnificent. I've never seen anything like it except at tea stores."

"Thanks. I'm pretty proud of it."

"I bet. You wanna make some for us?"

"Sure. What do you want?"

"I don't know. Something refreshing to get our minds going, I guess."

"Coming right up."

She curiously watched him when he got to work with the tea. From the cupboard, he chose the black tin jar with gunpowder leaves. In a small bowl, he blended half a teaspoon of that with dried pieces of ginger and about a full teaspoon dried spearmint leaves. Together with a tea infuser each, he put the bowl and a jar of organic honey on the table.

"It's good as it is, but the honey gives it a touch of sweetness and relaxes tense nerves as well."

"Cool." She exhaled tiredly and began to comb through her hair with her fingers and braided it. Eventually, she threw the thick, messy braid over her shoulder and said, "You know what. I've come to a point where I just want this case to end. We have, what, four, five days to catch him before he kidnaps another guy. I hate this stress. I just hate it!"

Carl poured hot water over her infuser and nodded. "Mm, better start with the research again then."

She glared at him, but then she sighed and hid her face in her hands. "I feel that I need to apologize right now if I'm short-tempered today. It's just how I become with too little sleep and too much stress."

"That's fine. Come. It's easier to work on the sofa."

She nodded and took her huge teacup to the living room table before bringing her laptop. Carl brought the big duvet from the bed and placed it over them as they curled up on each side of the sofa with a laptop and a teacup each.

When her cell phone rang, she glared ill-tempered at it before answering. "Yeah? Yeah, hi. No, you're right, I haven't been home, but as you can hear, I'm still alive and kicking. Well, maybe not kicking, since that requires more energy than I have right now. No, I don't know when I'm coming home. Probably tonight, but I haven't dec—" She gave up a frustrated puff. "—Kevin, please. I promise you that I'm in no danger of falling victim to this killer. You can just relax. Yeah, I know. I haven't forgotten. Yeah, I'll ask him later. Don't worry." As she hung up, a huge frown appeared on her forehead. "God, he's touchy." Carl couldn't help chuckling. She glared at him. "What?"

"Nah, nothing." With a smile, he turned his attention toward the files again.

When her cell phone rang at eleven again, he had reached the year of nineteen seventy-seven and begun to get a headache. As she answered, he could clearly hear Dean's distinct voice on the other side.

"Allie, how's it going? Getting somewhere?"

"Hi, Dean. Yeah, we have a good track going, me and Carl."

"Great. Exactly what I want to hear, know what I mean? Care to tell me?"

Allie looked stressed-out. "Sorry, I don't want to say anything yet, but I think we're about to crack it, either today or tomorrow." She inhaled and continued quickly before Dean could say anything, "What I can tell you is that we have a list of men that probably have fallen victim for him. You have paper and a pen?" Dean grunted on the other side, and Allie took it as a yes. "Okay, December-Peter Lee, January-Theo Sullivan, February-Basil Stokes, March-James O'Connor, and April-Ian Field."

175

"Wait a minute, it's one per month? That's what you're saying?"

"Yeah, that's part of his pattern. They're all in their forties, all brown-haired, all from Queens, all abducted around the second in the month."

"Huh! Great job, Allie. Actually, really great job." Dean sounded impressed, and Allie blushed.

"Thanks."

"Found any of the girls yet?"

"No, sorry, he's following a different pattern with them. They're all in their twenties, all university students, but abducted from different states."

"Hm. You'll work on that then, know what I'm saying? Got the photos yet?"

"Yeah, we got them yesterday. It definitely looks like the boy fits the pattern. Did you have a name yet?"

"No, but there's another boy that fits the pattern."

"Another boy?" Allie rubbed her eyes. "Where?"

"Boston."

"Well, that's good. Then we only need to find James O'Connor before Boston's clear. Where was he found?"

"Same wooden area as Siegler. Probably lost his way, according to the PD."

There was a slight pause in which Allie rubbed her face. "What does the coroner say?"

"He froze to death."

"Good God, poor boy," Allie mumbled. A couple of tears fell from her eyes, and she wiped them away with an irritated gesture, but no emotion was heard in her voice. Apparently, she was as good as him at hiding things when she wanted to, Carl reflected. "Okay. Um, Dean, I'd like you to decide if we need to get a warning out in Queens, New York. We're closing in on the time when he usually kidnaps his male victims."

Carl could hear Dean puff on the other side.

"Skip the girls, Allie, know what I mean? Concentrate on getting an identity of the killer instead."

"Yeah, we're working on it."

"Good. Keep me updated."

"Absolutely, I will. Don't worry about it. Thanks, Dean."

"They're working quickly now," Carl commented as she hung up and rubbed her face.

She looked exhausted again. "Yeah, finally."

"I'd say you got your theory right. All the other kids have been boys, eh?"

Allie exhaled and nodded while wiping away a couple of other tears. "Yeah... What year are you on?"

"Seventy-seven. Honestly, I think it's on your side of the line. Don't know why, but I have a feeling I'm too late in time."

"Do you want to check sixty-nine for me then?"

"Sure, I can do that."

The rest of the day, they worked more or less in seclusion, and six hours later, they looked at each other in grim silence.

"You think it happened during the fifties?" Carl eventually asked.

Allie shook her head to mark her lack of knowledge. "I don't know," she said in a dull voice. "Maybe. Or maybe it happened somewhere else and not New York."

He groaned. "Don't say that. If that's the case, we're in so much trouble. We won't find him before next week."

"I know." She fell silent for a couple of seconds as she stared at her screen. "Well," she sighed, "you still have two more years to check during the seventies. I'll start with the fifties. When you're done, you'll help me out."

Carl sighed. "Alright." He checked the time. Five o'clock. "Maybe you should call Kevin and tell him I can't come over tonight anyway. I won't be able to concentrate on games when we're so close to the next date."

Allie nodded and brought up her cell phone and fast-dialed a number. "Hi, it's me. Yeah, sorry, we're just stuck. We need to work 'til we find him. Yeah, we're that close, but

177

damn it! Sure, I'll ask him." She turned toward him. "Next Wednesday if we're done with the case?" He gave her a thumbs-up. "Yeah, that works. No, don't wait up. I probably won't come home tonight." She gave Carl a side-glance, and, out of sheer habit, he made an effort to hide his surprise but shrugged and nodded toward her. "Okay. Kisses." As she hung up, she turned toward him again. "Do you mind?"

"That you stay over?" He smiled at her. "No. Well, at least not as long as we get some proper sleep."

"Yeah, we need that. It was more the time-saving thing I had in mind this time, actually."

He caught the glint in her eyes before she looked down.

"Yeah, right."

"Damn you."

They smiled at each other, and he reached for her hand. "Thanks for staying, Allie."

"Thanks for letting me."

He kissed her hand, but then he sighed again. "Let's get this over and done with."

Another three hours later, he stretched and sighed. "Do you mind if I open the windows? I'd like some fresh air."

"Go ahead. You haven't found anything yet, have you?

"Zero, zilch, zip, nada, nothing."

She smiled at his frustrated voice. "It's probably mean, but I'm happy I'm not the only one feeling frustrated."

He leaned his forehead toward the chilly window glass and breathed in the cold air.

"God, will it never get warm? I mean, seriously."

She got up from the sofa and walked over to him and hugged him from behind. "It might not feel so cold if you put pants on."

He laughed at her and turned around, embraced her with his cheek at her hair. "Look who's talking."

Then, he inhaled sharply as her hands found their way up under his underwear and caressed him gently.

"Do you want a break from work?" she whispered with her lips touching his throat. Her hands pulled him closer to her, still caressing him. The sensation spread through his body like wildfire, and he swallowed hard with a pounding heart and aching abdomen.

"Hrm…"

"We could need a break, just to clear our heads, you know."

"Yeah, right, just to clear our heads. Of course." He swallowed again and felt her smile at his throat. Aroused, he shook his head. "Who are we kidding anyway?" She gasped when he lifted her up, placed her legs around his hips, and turned her around, so she had her back to the wall. He closed the distance between their lips and kissed her deeply, yearningly, while giving in to the dizziness her presence created in his head.

Just then, her cell phone rang.

"Oh, for crying out loud," she panted as she broke free from the kiss. "Wait, let me see. Yeah, it's Dean. Damn it!" Hurriedly, Carl let her down while she tried to catch her breath. "Hello?" She took some steps away so he couldn't hear Dean this time. Instead, he leaned his heated face toward the cold window to calm his rushing pulse. "Yeah, no, I'm fine. What? I don't know. No, I don't have anything for the media right now. Yes, of course, I understand that they want something, but I can't give this away right now. Dean, you of anyone know how sensitive this case is at this moment. I don't want the killer to know that we've figured him out. Yes, we have. We just don't know his name yet. That's what we're searching for right now. Yes, I'm positive that we'll have it either tonight or tomorrow. I don't know, Dean. You're the one who communicates with them. Make something up. I promise that I'll let you know everything as soon as I have his name. It won't take long now. Okay. Okay. Yeah. Bye."

179

Carl turned around when he heard her throw the phone violently into the sofa.

"Media's on him pretty hard, eh?"

She grimaced. "It doesn't look better. Goddamn stress. I don't work well in stress." She sighed and gave him an apologetic look. "Don't forget where we were, okay? I want to explore that part a little more thoroughly later on, but the whip's on our back, alas."

"You're the boss." He had to laugh at himself at the disappointing sting he felt in his chest.

Allie grinned at him and took the few steps back to him to lean in for another kiss. "I definitely do like how that sounds. And yeah, I'm disappointed too. He could've waited another twenty minutes, right?" Carl reddened but laughed at her as they went back to the sofa. "So, are you done with the seventies now?"

"Mhm. Finally."

"Okay. I'm on fifty-two. Start backward, and then we'll meet somewhere in the middle."

At ten p.m., he wanted to throw the damn laptop out of the window. Instead, he put it down on the table and went through a short stretching program to get the frustration out of his body. When he was finished, he felt much better. Allie watched him with an alluring little smile but didn't say anything. He couldn't help feeling a bit turned on. *Good lord, six okay years without sex, and suddenly I can't get enough. Chill out, Carl, you need to chill out.*

Instead of kissing Allie, he went to the kitchen where he poked around in the fridge and took out fruit, cheese and crackers, and the Chinese leftovers which he heated, and brought everything with him to the living room table together with plates and chopsticks.

"You want some?"

"Please."

"Where are you now?"

"Just started on fifty-four."

"Good. I'm almost finished with fifty-eight."

180

She let out a frustrated puff. "Seriously, Carl, we have to be closing in. We have to. If we don't find it— I don't know what to do. God, I promised Dean an answer tomorrow!" Her face got a desperate look.

He exhaled. "Don't think about that now. We'll work through the night if need be."

She nodded but hid her face in her hands. Carl gently rubbed her back. She breathed deeply and seemed to relax, so he went out to the bathroom and came back with some tea tree oil and placed himself behind her.

"Take off your T-shirt," he commanded while smearing the oil in his hands.

Obligingly, she did what he asked, and with long, soothing strokes, he massaged her back, neck, and shoulders until it felt like she was falling asleep. The intense smell awakened his senses, and he felt more alert than he had during these past twenty-four hours.

"Oh, God," she sighed when he finished. "Can I keep you?"

He chuckled and kissed her head. "Maybe for a while."

"Good." She put on his T-shirt again and straightened up. "God, it's almost eleven. This is driving me crazy. I just want to get rid of it."

After eating, Allie changed her position on the sofa to half-laying-down and placed the laptop on her stomach. Carl took away the food before going back to his own spot on the sofa. Stretching out under the duvet, he tangled his legs together with her legs while he continued to scroll through the case files. Time ticked by so damn slowly that it felt like he was stuck in some kind of time loop.

At midnight, Allie nodded off over the laptop. Carl stretched out and sighed. *We've been sitting here for eighteen damn hours! No wonder we're going crazy. I'm so damn fucking tired of this damn fucking shit! Fuck it! I'm not giving up now!*

He let Allie sleep, but straightened up and put his feet on the floor to not follow her example. When he carefully took away the rickety balancing laptop from her stomach, she didn't even move.

Two hours later, he thought about giving up after all. His eyes felt sorer than they had since that night at Kroger's, and he had trouble keeping them open. He had gone through all the case files of nineteen fifty-seven and fifty-six and almost all of the files of fifty-five, and he began to worry. What if they were wrong, after all? It was quite possible. In his mind's eye, he saw himself getting sacked for the second time in one week. He tried to laugh, but it wasn't funny. If they failed, this might indeed be the outcome. Dean had to find some kind of scapegoat to throw to the media, and he and Allie were first in line.

Not willing to give up just yet, Carl stubbornly scrolled down the page again, checking it once more to make sure that he hadn't missed anything. Suddenly, his breath got caught in his throat, and his body became rigid as he stared at the screen with aching eyes. Could it be? Could it really be? He didn't dare to hope.

With trembling fingers, he clicked on the link and skimmed through the text. His heart rate rose to unknown degrees as he sat up straight, suddenly completely awake, and nearly pushed Allie off the sofa.

"Allie! Allie, wake up! Hey, Allie! Come on, wake up!"

"What? What's going on?" She looked at him, dazed and confused.

"I found it! I found it, Allie! Good God, I've actually found it!"

She gasped and sat up, staring at the screen. Then she gave up a whoop and flew up from the sofa, jumping up and down like crazy, and threw herself around him, almost crushing the laptop in the process.

"Oh, my God! Oh, my God! Oh, my God! Carl, you did it! Woot! You did it! You're my hero! I need to call Dean!"

Before he could remind her of the time, she was on the phone with him.

"Dean! We've got it! We've got it! What? Two-thirty? No, I had no idea. Sorry for waking you up, but we found him, Dean! We know who he is now! We have a name! Are you awake enough? Good. Okay, it's Harold Young. Born nineteen fifty-one. Tuesday night, December eighth, nineteen fifty-five, he witnessed his father, Patrick Young, shoot his mother, Jane Young, to death in their car. Patrick Young left Harold in the car together with his dead mother, and a couple of days later, on Thursday, December tenth, he committed suicide by jumping off a bridge. Yes, I know! It's spot on! Totally spot on! I'm so damn happy! Um, I haven't thought that far yet, but tell them what you want, I guess, and that we know who he is. If you don't mind, I'm going to hang up on you now and celebrate with the best partner I've ever worked with. Don't call in the morning if there's nothing really, really important. We've worked nonstop since six o'clock yesterday morning, and we're going to sleep in. Thank you, Dean. Thank you." She hung up with a broad smile. This time, he was prepared and had put away his laptop in anticipation of her attacking him with hugs and kisses. "I'm sorry that I fell asleep," she said eventually. "It doesn't feel fair that you had to work for so long on your own. You should've woken me up."

Carl just smiled and waved away the remark, feeling so lighthearted and happy that he could forgive anything, especially something like that that he hadn't even reacted on. Instead, he grabbed her by her waist and pulled her down toward him and kissed her. She put her hands on his face and deepened the kiss before she began to undress them both.

"Suddenly I don't feel that tired anymore," he mumbled.

"Good, 'cause I have some very dirty plans for you, my dear."

He grinned and let her lead him where she wanted to.

Chapter 10

Exhausted, they slept the whole day until Dean called at two p.m. to let Allie know that the hunt was on. They cuddled up on the sofa under the duvet and turned on the TV to watch the news while they ate breakfast. Harold Young was breaking news. They called him *The Greek Tragedy killer*, a name they both found extremely fitting.

"Ah damn, I wish I had come up with that," Allie said but beamed nonetheless. "It's a great name. Everyone at the *Psychology of the Serial Killer* class will remember it."

Carl couldn't do anything else than agree. "It sticks, that's for sure," he said.

As the news hour continued on, the photo that the journalists had managed to get their hands on eventually came up, and to Carl's excessive satisfaction, it was spot on Ariel's sketch.

Suddenly he heard Allie sob quietly beside him. Surprised, he turned off the TV.

"Hey, what's going on?" he asked in a gentle voice and put an arm around her

"You know he's going to kill himself, right?" Her voice was low and distressed.

Carl frowned. "I hadn't thought that far. You sure?"

She nodded. "He hasn't had any plans for what to do if he got discovered. He'll just panic and either jump from a bridge, like his dad, or let himself get killed by the cops." She sniveled again. "I know people don't get me, but it hurts me so much, thinking about all these broken people…"

Carl hugged her closely. "I do get you, Allie. They were kids once too, and they've been hurt too. If they weren't broken themselves, they wouldn't kill people."

Her face brightened. "Thank you," she whispered.

Eventually, she composed herself, and the rest of the afternoon and evening, they did nothing more than following the hunt on the FBI's encrypted radio channel. Reports were coming in of sightings of Harold Young in Delaware and Virginia. Other witness reports told of him being seen at a motel in Fayetteville, West Virginia, in February, and the local PD sent out people looking under bridges and for abandoned cars in remote areas. Eventually, they reported about finding Basil Stokes' crushed body under the New River Gorge Bridge, under which the search had been concentrated. Carl thought of the bridge he once had seen for himself, and his head spun unpleasantly as the emotion of falling down the seventeen thousand feet to his death occurred to him.

Kevin called at eight and congratulated them on a job well done. At first, Carl thought he wanted to check on Allie and him since it would be most peoples' first reaction if someone they were half in love with suddenly spent several days and nights at another guy's place. However, the sincerity in Kevin's voice convinced Carl that he was genuinely happy about them being successful. Carl had to admit to himself that he didn't get Allie and Kevin's relationship, but since neither of them seemed to be cross in any way, he shrugged and let it be. Not his problem. At least not yet.

The reports dwindled down around that same time, and since Carl and Allie were still exhausted, they crashed into bed and slept.

The next morning, they woke up to the same news as the rest of the country. Harold Young had been located at a motel in Virginia, but when the FBI stormed the room, he had already fled. They did, however, find an unconscious, bound, and gagged man in the room. The FBI channel told the identity; Richard Westman from Roanoke, Virginia.

When Allie heard it, she frowned. "I guess he got stressed out being so close to getting caught that he abandoned his pattern. He must've had someone else in mind originally. It's not even time for the next abduction yet."

They didn't stray far away from the news that day, and Allie decided that they could write their final report at his place as well as at the office. Carl didn't mind.

At ten a.m., her cell phone rang.

"Hello?"

On the other end, Carl could clearly hear a deep, familiar voice that he hadn't heard in two years.

"Dr. Harris? This is Armand from the Faculty. Congratulations on your success in finding the *Greek Tragedy Killer*."

A deep frown appeared on Allie's forehead. "Thanks," she said coolly.

"I'll be happy to take Carl off your hands. He can meet his superior in room three twelve at noon today."

Allie's hand squeezed the phone, and her eyes slit narrowly.

"Mr. Armand. With all due respect, if you give me your contact information, I'll let you know when I don't need Carl anymore. This case is not closed yet."

"This is not acceptable, Dr. Harris—" C began, but Allie interrupted him.

"I'm sorry, Mr. Armand, but acceptable or not, it's still my decision. You told me last time we spoke that you have two other agents working on your case. I don't. My superior, Mr. Dean Henderson of the Homicide Department, expects a final report as soon as possible. Without Carl, I won't be able to deliver it to him in an acceptable time frame."

"Maybe I should talk to your superior, Dr. Harris, and see what he has to say."

Carl saw Allie's face first whiten and then blush in anger. She inhaled, but before she said something she might regret, he gestured at her to give him the phone. She nearly threw it at him and stomped away to the bedroom.

"Hi, C," he said calmly.

"Uh, Cyrus— sorry, Octavius. How are you?" C's voice sounded caught.

"Just fine. What's the rush?"

"Uh, Olwen and Omega need your help with the Suicide Bomber Project at Kroger's."

186

Carl fell silent for a moment. It felt like Caesar had hit him in the head. "Why is that suddenly an FR Project?" he asked eventually.

"Cyrus, I don't have time to go through this on the phone. Just get over here, will you?"

Carl frowned. "Sorry, C, but Allie's my superior now, and she does need me, just as she said. Since you don't want to tell me what it's all about, I doubt it's that urgent. We'll finish the report today or tomorrow."

There was a slight pause before C said in a detached voice, "Is this about Mimi, Cyrus?"

Carl inhaled painfully at the unexpected line. "What do you mean?"

The pause dragged out.

"Nothing."

"Nothing? If there's something about her that I need to know, can you please tell me?"

"It's— nothing."

Carl's eyes narrowed at the sound of Caesar's constrained voice. "Are you still jealous?" he heard himself blurt out, and then he wished he'd bit off his tongue instead. It would definitely have been the smarter move. The phone on the other end went dead in his ear as Caesar hung up on him. Carl exhaled. "Wow... Good job, Carl!"

Allie came out from the bedroom when she saw him put away the phone. "He hung up on you?"

"Yeah, I shouldn't have said that last thing."

She smiled briefly. "You're getting too used to me, I guess."

"Maybe, but not in a bad way."

She smiled again, broader this time, and put her arms around him from behind. Then, she sighed and let go of him while cuddling up on the sofa again.

"I'll let you go on Monday. We should be finished with the report this weekend. I'm pretty sure it's over by then."

"Mm, you're probably right."

187

She gave him a side-glance. "Do you want to tell me what he said?"

"Yeah. He didn't say why, but Kroger's has become a Field Researcher Project."

"What?"

Carl just shook his head. "Sounds crazy, I know. Ah, well, whatever. I'll get to know sooner or later. Let's write this report now."

The day continued on while they tapped away on the keyboards. It was a very intriguing case, now when they had the whole picture. Allie did some research on Harold Young, and what she found suited her first report nicely. After he had become an orphan, Patrick Young's younger sister, Helen Young-Dell, and her family took care of little Harold. From several different records, Allie got to know that Helen Young-Dell was married to a prominent lawyer, Thomas Dell. She was an avid churchgoer and sat on the church committee, as well as in several different charity foundations. She homeschooled her five children, and they grew up to become pillars of the small town of Winthrop, Iowa; a dentist, a veterinarian, two schoolteachers, and a shopkeeper. Harold had broken the pattern by becoming a marine and had been quite successful in that profession. In May last year, he retired with honors. He had never married and did not have any children. Harold's stepfather Thomas Dell had died of old age in late July last year.

"Somewhere in this time frame, between May and November, he must have had a major breakdown," Allie mused. "The structure in his life disappeared, and he felt lost. He should never have quit the marines, but how could he have known? He probably never knew that he had all this hidden inside him. I wonder what set it free; if it was the death of his stepfather?"

Carl nodded in agreement. "Sounds likely. The death of one father closed him; the death of another opened him up. That, plus Thomas Dell probably meant lots of structure for Harold Young as well."

"He was doubly at a loss. Poor man." The shadow fell over Allie's face again. "I honestly don't know what I wish for him; that he's captured and most likely faces the death penalty, or that he commits suicide. The horrible things he's done… People will want him to face capital punishment."

Carl could tell that she didn't agree, nor did he, most likely because they both had grown up in countries that didn't use that practice anymore. It was nothing he wanted to discuss, though. These kinds of topics often ran out of control.

A couple of hours later, they didn't have to worry about the fate of Harold Young anymore. He had been found on Mill Mountain, and when surrounded, he had shot one of the FBI officers to death before being gunned down. Neither Carl nor Allie knew who the officer was, but the devastation that radiated from the FBI radio channel was as thick as an iron bar.

Allie sat slumped on the sofa with a pained appearance. "I didn't see this coming," she said in a low, thick voice, filled with tears. "Sometimes, I'm so damn naïve! Of course, he'd shoot one of them! How would he otherwise be gunned down? I should've warned them that he's dangerous."

"Hey." Carl sat down beside her and pulled her closer until her head rested on his shoulder. "They knew that, Allie. That's why they were so many. It hadn't mattered if you'd told them."

"Are you sure?" She sounded like a child who needed to be comforted that there were no monsters under her bed.

"Absolutely."

"Okay." She inhaled deeply and tried to compose herself. "I know I'm in a terrible mood right now, and not fun to be around, and that I've been occupying your place since Tuesday, and that it's Friday today, but—"

"Shh… You're welcome to stay, Allie. It's just fine having you around here."

"Okay. Thanks. I honestly don't know many who'd say that. Not after this long, and not someone like you who hate the mess I'm making."

Carl entwined his fingers with hers, and couldn't help a small smile from appearing on his lips.

"You know, during these past six years, I've had one person sleeping over here, and that was Miri, about two years ago now, and we weren't even sleeping in the same bed. Having you here, it's nice. I, um, well, I don't feel so lonely, I guess. Your mess, it's nothing I can't live with right now."

Allie looked surprised before snuggling closer into his arms. "You've changed, Carl. You wouldn't have said something like that just a week ago."

"Well, it's no use trying to hide anything from you. I've come to accept that, and, yeah, honestly, I… I miss Miri so damn much, and… and…"

"It's okay, Carl." When she saw his skeptical face, she continued, "No, I mean it, I seriously don't mind being a substitute for Miri. I know that's not all I am for you. I know that we mean something more for each other than we thought we would from the beginning, and for some reason, you and I work really well as FFs. I hadn't expected that." Shocked, he stared at her, and a small mischievous smile managed to break through the tired grief in her face. "Well, isn't that what we are? Good friends, who like to have good sex together?"

"Um, well, yeah, I guess."

"I'd be happy to continue like this, and the day you find Miri, well, then we'll see what happens, right?"

Touched to the core of his soul, he let his fingers stroke her hair. "You seem pretty certain that I will find her," he mumbled, just to have her say that again.

"Of course, I am. Through and through, I'm a born optimist. You just need to start looking for her again."

The strong conviction he heard in her voice made his heart hammer faster. If she thought it was possible, well, maybe it was.

Scared to death, he made himself a promise; *If you're out there somewhere, Miri, I won't stop until I find you, no matter what.*

Chapter 11

Allie went home on Saturday evening after they finally had finished the report, and Carl had to admit that his apartment felt very empty and quiet. *I miss her. I even miss her mess. That must be a first.* He tried to laugh, but instead, he started to weep, not because of Allie not being there, but because he suddenly realized how empty his life was in comparison to the lives of almost everyone else he knew. As usual, his thoughts wandered back to Miri. It was hard to believe that it was only two weeks ago that Kroger's blew up, and his life changed. *I'm so damn tired of thinking 'what if' and 'if only.' It is what it is, and if I want a change, I'm the one in charge.*

He started with calling Caesar, but only reached his answering machine.

"Hi, C, it's Octavius. I'm sorry for saying what I did. There's been a lot of pressure on me lately. It's no excuse, I know, but I'm sorry nonetheless. Anyway, I just called to let you know that we finished the report, and I can start working on the Kroger's Project whenever you want."

When he hung up, he felt much better. The failed conversation with C had been irking his conscience ever since it happened.

The next phone call went to Manda. She was at home, just as he expected her to be.

"Hi, Carl. Nice to hear your voice. How are you doing?"

He could hear that she was worried about him, and instead of it irritating him, as it usually did, he felt cared for. Allie had obviously taught him things he didn't even know that he needed to learn.

"Honestly? Not good, but I'm not walking in the Valley of the Shadow of Death either."

There was a moment of surprised silence on the other side of the line. Yeah, Allie had taught him some things, that's for sure.

"I wish I could invite you over," she said eventually, "but we're going to Mom and Dad early tomorrow morning. They've bought a puppy, the crazy old people."

Carl chuckled softly. Manda's parents were great, even though they hadn't forgiven him for the divorce.

"Yeah, guess I can't compete with that. Had thought of inviting you two to the zoo tomorrow, but maybe next weekend instead?"

"We'll play it by ear, Carl, but I know Sarah's been missing you a lot lately."

"Yeah, I'm sorry. I got involved in the *Greek Tragedy Killer* case. We just finished the report an hour ago. It's been a bit crazy lately."

"You worked on that? Wow! Okay, now I know someone who'll be very proud of her dad tomorrow. I tried to stop her from listening to the news, but she sneaked through to them. Sorry. I know you don't want her to know things like that."

"It is what it is, Mand. I know you're doing your best, and I couldn't wish for a better mom for our daughter than you." The silence on the other side was so deep that he wondered if she'd fainted from the unexpected praise. "Anyway, have a great day tomorrow. What kind of puppy is it, by the way?"

"It's a Havanese," Manda's voice sounded a tad dazed, but she soon recovered. "Dad says it's lovely and follows him around everywhere he goes. My worst fear is that I'll have to either adopt the dog or let Mom and Dad adopt Sarah tomorrow."

They laughed together.

"Sounds great." A thought struck him. "How did her audition go, by the way?"

"She got it."

"She did? That's awesome!"

"I know, right? She's very excited about it. Are you picking her up as you said you should?"

"Can't see why not. If nothing unexpected turns up, nothing will keep me away."

He could hear her smile on the other side of the line.

"Sounds good, Carl. I know she'll be happy."

"Well, kiss her from me, and I'll be in touch during the week."

"Okay, thanks for calling. Take care."

"You too."

He hung up and felt much better. Maybe it wasn't so hard to let other people know what you feel.

He went out into the kitchen and took a couple of tin jars from his tea cupboard. It was way too long ago since he had done something like this just for his own sake. As he blended the spices for the Masala Chai together, memories rose from the first time Miri was here without it being work-related. The atmosphere had been electric between them, and it had surprised him so much that she somehow felt attracted to him. It was something he had never expected. That he felt attracted to her too surprised him even more. In a way, he wished that he'd met Allie before Miri so he would have had an easier time letting her know exactly how much he cared for her. *It is what it is,* he thought again and stirred the milk together with the spices. The scent hit his now sensitive senses, and it felt like a balm on his soul.

He drew a deep breath and let himself relax before walking back to the sofa, where he placed himself under the duvet with the steaming tea and the final report. As he read through it, a feeling of pride spread through his body. It was a great report, and they had been part of catching a serial killer who never would have stopped. That was really something, and Allie's way of understanding these people was both terrifying and downright fantastic. Together they would be able to move mountains. *And that's scary as hell.*

Suddenly his cell phone rang. *Allie again,* he smiled to himself as he answered.

"Yeah?"

"Hi, Carl, Mike Jones here."

The rough voice surprised him momentarily since he had expected Allie's happy voice. Thinking about it, Mike's voice sounded jovial enough, but there was something underneath that Carl couldn't put his finger on.

"Oh, hi, Mike. How's it going?"

"Not bad, not bad. The clearing's pretty much finished, thanks to all the resources helping out. Haven't seen you around in the last weeks. You all good?"

"Yeah, I guess. They required me in the homicide department, so I've been there."

"Is that so? The hom-dep? Something serious?"

Carl glanced at his file on the table. "Yeah, you could say that again."

"Huh. Yeah, I won't ask you about it. Anyway, there was one thing, though. I followed a hunch today and went down to the basement again."

Something in Mike's voice made the hair on Carl's arms suddenly stand up, and a chill running down his spine.

"Yeah?"

"So, I found this ring..."

"A ring?" Carl slowly repeated when Mike hesitated.

"Yeah, just lying there on the floor, gleaming when I looked around with the flashlight. It's a small ring formed as a band of stars, some kind of goldish silver." Carl looked down at his hand, where a small band of stars adorned his little finger. "It's not yours, is it?"

"Um, no." He had to clear his throat.

"Yeah, I had a hunch it wouldn't be." Mike fell silent for a couple of seconds. "You know, I try to keep an open mind. I've seen some weird shit I'd hesitate to tell others about, but I've got a hunch you could tell some stories of your own, am I right?"

"Yeah," Carl said, suddenly hoarse and with a hammering heart.

"Thing is, you see, this ring ain't on its own. There's a small piece of a scarf there too, a red, silky one, matching in color of that coat we found." Mike fell silent again, and Carl

195

held his breath. "Thing is, that scarf, it's, um, stuck, uh, in the air… as if someone's been walking through a door that closed behind and caught the end of the scarf. Know what I mean?"

"Yeah…" Carl's voice was faint.

"Thought you might want to take a look at it."

"Are you around?"

"I can be."

"I'll be right over." As he hung up, a big sweaty mark from the palm of his hand was clearly visible on the cell phone case.

With a feeling of foreboding, Carl drove into the dusk and parked at a public parking lot a couple of blocks away from the Kroger's site and walked the rest of the way. As he closed in, he noticed that the area was still blocked off. This time, there weren't any spectators hovering around. *It's old news already,* he thought with a grimace. There weren't any FBI around either. *Too late in the evening and no more survivors to be found.* The thought felt like a sharp stab to his heart. He couldn't say that he appreciated the scene. It felt too ominous, too much like an unprepared Project, too much like he was going to do something stupid again.

Carl showed his badge to the security guard who stood at the interim gate and got passage immediately. During the two weeks that he'd been absent, the scene had been cleared of all debris that was left. He looked around, astonished. *Amazing. They've been working like crazy.* However, a faint smell of smoke and devastation still lingered in the surroundings. He wondered how many victims and survivors the final count had landed at.

There were no sounds except for the quiet crunch under his feet. A couple of security guards nodded at him as he passed them by on his way to the van. The light that shone through the tiny window comforted him. When he opened the door to the van, the big African-American immediately stood up, and Carl could tell that he felt anxious.

"I came as quickly as I could."

"Yeah, let's go and take a look." Mike led the way out of the van to the now cleared former ground floor where they'd found the crack. The ladder was still standing there, and Mike went down. Carl followed not even a second later. As soon as they hit the basement floor, both men lit their flashlights. Carl stared quietly at the floating piece of Miri's scarf. It really did look as if it was fastened in a slit of a door, just that the door was invisible. His hands became sweaty again, as did his forehead. He let his light play around in the dark room while trying to compose himself.

"Where did you find the ring?" he asked eventually. Mike pointed toward an area not far from where the scarf defied gravity. Then, Mike hauled the ring from his chest pocket and handed it over. Carl's hands trembled slightly as it lay in his palm, glimmering faintly in the flashlight. It felt like a sign of life, and he had to take a couple of deep breaths to not start crying, but he couldn't stop, didn't want to stop, the hope that rose in his heart. When he managed to control himself, he put the ring in his pocket and nodded toward the scarf.

"Have you touched it?"

Mike scoffed. "No way! Who knows what could happen? That's a task for someone braver than me."

Carl moved forward, letting his flashlight shine over the piece of fabric. Shadows played on the wall. He squinted. It looked like— It actually did look like there was a pale, indistinct shadow of a door on the floor.

He pointed. "Do you see that?"

"What? The shadows? Yeah."

"The shadow of the door."

Mike gave him a quick side-glance before looking at the floor more thoroughly. "Huh! What the hell?"

"Do you think we can open it?"

"You wanna go in? What, are you crazy?"

"It's Miri's scarf. It's her ring. This is the only way she could've gotten out of here. She's somewhere on the other side of that door, and I need to find her."

197

Carl took a couple of steps toward where the scarf hung, and it was as if the air around it vibrated. He studied it with mixed feelings of helplessness, anxiety, and determination. *If this is the only way to find her, I have to go in. There's no other option. I've seen things that must be worse than what's behind this door. Right?* Not convinced at all, he pulled vigorously at his hair and continued to stare at the vibrating air. It felt as if the longer he stared, the more solid did the door become. The low gasp from Mike behind him told him that he didn't imagine it. Eventually, the door stood solidly in front of him, looking as normal as any regular, white interior door, except the fact that it levitated one inch above the ground.

Without letting his gaze flinch, Carl said, "Do you have a family, Mike?"

"What?"

"Do you have a family?"

"Why— Yes, my wife and three sons."

"Go home. I don't know if it's possible to get out when you've gotten in, and your family needs you, Mike."

"Yeah? And what about your daughter? She's not as valuable as my sons or she doesn't need you as much as my sons need me? What the hell, Carl! Give me a fucking break!"

Carl drew a shaky breath and felt a tear trying to escape his eye. "That was a bit unfair," he said hoarsely. "Miriam's the person I hope will become my family, but she can't as long as she's in there. If I don't come back, Sarah will always be cared for by her mother, just as she is now."

Mike put a hand on his shoulder. "I'm sorry. This place makes me jittery."

"It's okay. You know, in any case, someone needs to stay behind and inform my Faculty about this – whatever it is – and seal the area, so no one else stumbles in here by mistake. I daren't leave it now. I might not find it again."

Mike grumbled. "Why does what you say now suddenly make sense? Damn it, Carl, I don't want to leave you on your own."

A sudden smile appeared on Carl's face. How come he hadn't noticed before how cared for he was by so many people, or how many people out there who were friends disguised as strangers?

"I hope you know how much I appreciate that, Mike."

"Goddamn, Carl, you and your flowery words. I don't give a shit about how 'appreciated' I am. I give a shit about you going through some damn floating door with whatever is in there."

"I know, but I need to. I need to go in there now before I lose this damn door." Sweat had started to break out on his forehead as he concentrated on keeping the door visible. A thought struck him. "Do you know Sally Oakley?"

"Yeah, she's my superior."

"Good, she's my superior too. Give her a call and let her know what's going on. She's going to come here and help me out, but I need to go in now. I'm starting to lose it."

"Goddamn, Carl! Alright, alright, I'll call her, but then you owe me a damn beer and a fucking explanation."

"Deal on that."

A thought of asking Mike to call Allie to let her know where he went, crossed Carl's mind, but the next second he decided against it. He didn't want her to come looking for him here, and she would. Oh yeah, she definitely would.

With a slightly shaking hand, Carl gripped the flickering doorknob. Surprised at the cool touch, he turned it, and the door opened silently in front of him. His gasp blended with Mike's. Miri's scarf floated slowly down and landed on the threshold. A cool breeze touched his face, and he found himself looking out over a town, an old European kind of a town, which slept silently in the night.

Carl swallowed nervously, while his inner being screamed at him to not do anything stupid, and then he cleared his voice. "Wish me luck, Mike."

"Carl…"

Without acknowledging either Mike's pleading tone or his soul's frantic screaming, he took one step over the threshold, grabbed the scarf on the way, and found himself standing on the top of a high grass-clad hill. When he turned around, the door was gone.

Part Three

what lurks in shadows

Chapter 12

It took some time before she understood that she was conscious. She blinked repeatedly, but it didn't matter; the darkness was compact and intrusive and as thick as tar. Everything hurt, especially her head that felt like it was about to split in two. A pained grimace flashed across her face, and she struggled to free her arm and touch her forehead, to figure out if she had a wound somewhere. She could hear a weird wheezing sound close to her, and it scared her. Where did it come from? She tried to hold her breath to listen, but dust tickled her throat and made her cough. As it did, the wheezing stopped, and she realized that it was her own strained breaths that she had heard. It was harder to breathe than she had ever experienced before. Something heavy lay on top of her chest, pinning her down onto an uneven surface, almost crushing her ribs underneath its weight. With her one free hand, she patted weakly at whatever it was. It felt like cold and damp uneven pieces of concrete. Why was she here? Why was she trapped? It was hard to collect her thoughts.

"He… hello…?" The sound of her voice was unrecognizable; weak, strained, and hoarse, and it didn't reach further than the air above her nose. *I need to get out of this,* she thought when the first sign of panic tickled her spine. She tried to take a deeper breath to calm down, but instead, more dust entered her throat, and she coughed violently.

A low rumble above her made her grasp how dangerous her situation was, but she couldn't stop coughing. Small parts of debris began to rain down on her face. *Stop coughing for everything holy in this world!* As the air disappeared from her lungs, the panic clawed wildly at her. *I'm going to die here!* Without knowing what the hell she was doing, she wiggled from one side to another, still breathlessly coughing without getting any air down her lungs. *I'm going to die here! I'm going to die here!*

202

Bigger pieces of debris came falling down around her. She felt the dull thump when a huge piece just missed the top of her head and landed on her hair. Through the panic, she gained the strength to desperately claw herself away from the rubble one inch at a time. As she moved, so did the broken concrete on top of her, and it started to fall at a faster pace. More dust swirled around and found its way down her throat and nose and into her eyes which teared up. Something hit her hard on her forehead, but she couldn't even groan because of the damn choking. Dizzy and ensnared, she knew that she slowly suffocated to death. The panic rolled over her in wave after wave as she struggled for her life.

Without knowing how, she was suddenly free, and she tumbled down from a big pile of debris so quickly that she didn't have time to protect her face from being scraped by the concrete pieces. She landed hard on the ground and would have lost her breath had she had any. Still choking, she crawled across the floor, away from the dust cloud, and didn't stop until she hit her head on a wall. Gradually, the choking cough stopped, and she could draw breath after desperate breath of air into her aching lungs.

Afterward, she collapsed in an agonizing heap. Tears flowed from her irritated eyes, and she lay motionless on the floor, too weak to move. Her whole body ached, especially her head, which felt on fire, and around her ribcage. Something wet gushed down her face, and gruelingly, she dried it away with her hand. It smelled slightly of iron. Carefully, she located the wound in her head, and although it hurt, she could tell that it wasn't deep. It would stop bleeding soon enough.

She had no idea how long she lay on the floor, cradling her head as she gave in to the alarming pain and the sensation of movement around her. It felt like being stuck in a crazy carousel that sped faster and faster, and it made her nauseous. Waves of hot and cold flushed her face, covered it in a thin layer of sweat, and as the spinning dizziness intensified, her stomach churned, and she vomited violently.

Afterward, she lay on her side, pressing her face toward the cold, damp floor, holding her hands over her aching stomach and ribs. Eventually, the chilliness swaddled her body, making her tremble violently. Her teeth clattered without her being able to stop it. For some time, she lay and listened to the sound. *I did have a coat, didn't I?* The thought felt muddled and slow as if it had a hard time coming through to her. *It doesn't matter. I'm not crawling back there again. I almost died there.*

Slowly, she managed to pull herself up to sitting, feeling the world spin around her again, and a new wave of nausea taking control of her. She moved to the side and vomited again. The disgusting taste of bile in her mouth made her feel even sicker to the stomach, and without being able to hold it, she threw up once more. *God, I need to stop this damn vomiting!*

Sweating from nausea, even as her whole body shook from the cold and the physical strain, she leaned toward the wall and stared out into the pitch-black darkness without seeing anything. *Where am I?* Nothing came to her, nothing at all. She fought harder to remember why she was here – *wherever 'here' is* – but her thoughts were disorganized and her mind as black as the surroundings. A slight touch of fear managed to get through the physical discomfort and made her heart hammer faster. *Why do I feel like this?* Then, the next chilly thought hit her, *Who am I?*

A deep shiver ran down her spine together with slithering fingers of panic. Once again, she breathed deeply to try and calm down. Her throat tickled from the air gushing down to her lungs, but she managed to keep the cough at bay. However, the incipient panic didn't fade. Nervously, she tangled her fingers and tried to think, but the agonizing headache and the dizziness made all thoughts feel weirdly far away and muddled. *Okay, okay... I don't— I don't seem to know who I am right now. I actually don't know my, uh, my name. That's, um, interesting. Do I have anything on me, like a... a wallet or an ID? Something like that?* She let her nervous hands move over her jean pockets but didn't find anything more than some intimate wipes.

The panic continued to rise, and she dug her fingernails into her palms. The short-lived pain only added slightly to the overall aching discomfort. She leaned back toward the damp wall again and closed her eyes. Tears ran down her cheeks without her being able to stop them.

The vile smell of the vomitus found its way into her nose with every deep breath and made her stomach take a new turn. After throwing up once more, she decided to move. With one hand on the wall and the other on the floor, she slowly scooted away from the spot where she'd vomited. Her head throbbed painfully with every movement, and even though she didn't stand up, she had a hard time keeping her balance.

She had no idea how long she had been moving away when her hand suddenly touched a meeting wall. *A corner. Good.* She turned around, and with her back toward the new wall and her head touching the corner, she carefully lay down again, trying to soothe the ache in her head and the whirling sensations born of the physical strain. It was cold and hard, but she welcomed the feeling as it made her focus on something else than the continuous spinning.

As she lay there, looking out into the dark, her mind touched the thought again, as a tongue an aching tooth, *Who am I?* Still nothing. Tears trickled down her cheeks once more. Sniveling, she turned around on her stomach, not giving a damn about how sore it felt, and buried her face in her arms. Exhaustion overwhelmed her, and she drifted off to sleep.

It took a while before she became aware that she was awake. It wasn't until she noticed a cold numbness in her body that made her legs and torso shiver violently, that she slowly realized that she had woken up. With a groan, she pushed herself up to sitting, grimacing at a splitting agony in her head.

"God, it's worse than my migraines," she muttered in a pained voice as she carefully examined her skull. There was a wound on her forehead, but not serious enough to cause this pain. As she acclimatized to the ache in her head, she became aware of dull pain in her ribcage, and tired discomfort in her stomach, not to mention that her whole face and body felt bruised.

"What the hell have I been through?" Nothing came to mind. The headache seemed to take possession of her whole being, making her feel weak and dizzy from the intense pain. She looked around in the overwhelming darkness without being able to see a thing.

"Where am I?" Swallowing hard, she squinted and stared out into the black while carefully holding on to her aching head.

"I don't like it when it's this dark," she mumbled, hating the feeling of being weak and fragile.

She was still uncomfortable in the dark, even though she nowadays managed to sleep with the lights off and without music playing, a progress that she was immensely proud of.

"I'm not letting anything take it away from me," she said in a slightly more determined voice.

For a while, she sat still, trying to adjust herself to the dark, trying to accept the dark.

"Where the hell am I?" she mumbled again. "I can't seem to remember."

Miriam shut her eyes, trying to sense any kind of danger, but didn't feel any imminent threat. There was a smell of vomit in the air, now when she thought about it. Her stomach took a turn and nearly made her retch, and she became aware of a taste of vomitus in her mouth.

"Okay, apparently, I vomited. Not unusual when I'm upset. That's okay. Not fun, but okay. But why am I here? And where is 'here'? What happened to me?"

She leaned her head on her bent knees, hoping that the spinning sensation would calm down. As she forced herself to breathe calmly, she made a new attempt to remember how she ended up here, all the while talking slowly to herself in a low voice and with lots of exhausted, random intervals.

"Okay, let's start from the beginning. It's Friday, right? Yes, should be, should be Friday. Okay, I, um— Andy called, right? Yes, he, um, he called around... what was it? Four a.m.? Something like that anyway. I ate a sandwich in the car, and we, uh, worked the whole day with the, um, the hanged man, right?" The memories of how she and the rest of the Angels investigated the death scene slowly came back to her. "Yes, the hanged man, um, Peter— What's his last name now again? Peter, um, Peter B, something. Um, Braden? No. Bradley? Yes, that's right, Peter Bradley, owner of that jewelry store, um..."

She exhaled frustrated when the name of the store slipped her mind.

"God, it's that well-known store! Um, I know the name! I know I know the name."

It didn't matter how hard she tried; the name didn't surface. With a sigh, she rubbed her cheek and grimaced when she accidentally touched a scrape.

"Whatever," she muttered. "Everyone thought he was a suicide victim, but I— No, wait! Was it me? Uh, no. It was Tam and me who found the rope, um, that had been used to bind his hands. Right? Yes. Okay, good."

Dizzy and exhausted, she massaged her aching temple and closed her eyes, while trying hard to make sense of the images that hovered in her mind. Among them was the image of her boss, the robust, middle-aged, and intelligent man who was such a joy to work under.

"Andy was really happy. Tam, Steph, Linds, and I went to the pub afterward to celebrate. Andy arrived later, didn't he?"

She rubbed her temple again and sighed at the pounding headache that made it so hard to think.

"Yes, Andy came there too after he'd put the evidence at HQ. We're supposed to work with the case tomorrow. Very important case."

Miriam fell silent. It was so hard to remember. As she gently massaged her head, she struggled to recollect her thoughts. They seemed to be so slow and so unwilling to come to her. She thought of the pub again, the cheerful atmosphere, the dim lights, the smell, the happy faces around the table.

"I, um, I stayed longer than I'd planned to originally, but I, um, drank a glass of cider. They have good cider, whatever the place is called now again..."

Exhaling, she put her hands over her eyes. "I should remember the name. We go there all the time," she mumbled but didn't have the energy to try to search for the name.

"Whatever," she muttered again. "Steph teased me as usual, trying to get me to drink more. She always does, just because I'm an FR and don't drink. Except for the cider. Just one cider every time, because it's so good."

Her thumb reached her pinkie to caress the Star Student ring, but it was gone. There was only a cold ghost band around her finger where the ring used to be. She frowned uncertainly.

"Where's my ring?" With another sigh, she tiredly rubbed her eyes, hoping in vain to get rid of the spinning sensation. "Doesn't matter," she muttered, not entirely truthfully. "I won't find it now anyway."

Another sigh heaved her chest, and she rubbed her aching head again, steering back to the memories of her day.

"Okay. Okay, so I was at the pub, um, and then, uh... Yes, then I went home to Carl, and I know— I know how tired I'm going to be tomorrow, but I still wanted to go and see him. I'm... I'm so damn hopeless..."

She blushed, and a reluctant smile broke out on her lips as her stupid heart began to beat faster.

She cleared her throat. "Okay, I was late, but it was on purpose. We've met too often lately. I've been too eager—

Can't let him know—" She puffed, embarrassed again. "It'd be so damn awkward." Then, she frowned. "He probably knows anyway. Can't hide a damn thing from him."

She sighed, scowled, and massaged her head. The memories came easier now.

"He didn't say anything about me being late, and I— it frustrated me a bit. God, I'm silly. Anyway, he was as happy as I was with the turn of events. Not that I should let him know what I'm working with, but— Anyway, I left Carl just before midnight. He's going to see Sarah tomorrow, probably early, but he still didn't ask me to leave. He never does."

Miriam smiled again, a tender smile this time at how appreciated he always made her feel, and her hopeless heart picked up pulse. She cleared her throat once more.

"Okay, so I went home, and I went to bed and I— Hm, well…" The heat covered her whole face this time, and she quickly skipped that part of her memories. "Then what? I don't remember waking up, but I, um, I can't be at home. It doesn't feel like I'm at home. I mean— Of course, it's not my apartment, but— Something must've happened…"

She fell silent, searching for her memories, but it was as if something had erased them completely. Nothing stirred. Nothing came to her. It was as black as the darkness around her. *I went to bed, and then what?* The next thing she remembered was waking up here on the cold floor with a sore body and this agonizing headache that soon was going to drive her crazy. Another thought struck her, and she frowned uneasily. *I haven't been kidnapped, have I? Drugged? Is that why my ring is gone? As proof for me being held captive?* Even though the thought should seem unrealistic, it suddenly felt like a plausible explanation for her memory loss and for why she woke up in this cold, damp darkness.

"I must be in a basement." She frowned again. "But why would anyone kidnap me? It seems improbable. Maybe it has something to do with the case?"

With another frown, she thought it over. It still didn't feel like her theory fit.

"I mean, we've just begun working the case this very day."

Andy had called them in as soon as he got the alarm. On her way to HQ, she had picked up Lindsey, who had told her that Peter Bradley was the famous and prominent jeweler to whom all celebrities turned when they needed something new and unique, so it wasn't at all surprising that Dean Henderson wanted the best DSI team to check out his house. *No, not a house; a mansion.*

As soon as they'd seen the mansion and the hanged man, Andy had squinted suspiciously and said, "*Alright, Angels, if this is a suicide, I'm a grasshopper.*"

It had taken them the whole day to secure the mansion, and even though they knew what great instincts Andy possessed, they all wondered when he was going to turn into a grasshopper. Then, she and Tam had found the rope. It had been hidden in plain sight, in the tool area in the garage, rolled back onto the roll of rope. They had found hair from Peter Bradley's wrists entwined in them.

But it still doesn't make any sense, Miriam thought tiredly. Just because they knew he'd been murdered, they had no clue as to who had done it. There was no reason for the murderer to panic and kidnap an investigator. *I guess I'll get to know sooner or later,* she thought and felt strangely detached from the whole thing.

Exhausted by the effort of thinking, she curled up on the floor and gave in to the spinning sensation. Soon enough, she drifted off to sleep again.

Waking up was a long, slow process.

"God, I'm thirsty," she mumbled. "Maybe someone's been here to give me some food and drink?"

Her body protested as she sat up, and she groaned. The complete lack of light was getting on her nerves, and the damp cold made her body feel numb and sluggish, even as she trembled from it. *I need to move around if I'm not going to freeze to death.* Honestly, she had no idea if she was actually going to freeze to death, but it worried her that she was so numb and slow.

She felt around on the floor, and to her disappointment, she could tell that no one had been here while she was sleeping. There was nothing around her, no food, no drink, no blanket, no potty. As if that particular image was a cue, she felt a very urgent need. *God, I really, really need to pee, like right now! No, no, I have to hold it. Can't do it here where I'm sleeping.*

Shaking from the cold, she helped herself up, swaying unsteadily when the spinning sensation sped up. Trying not to worry about it – *Ha! Aren't you funny?* – she kept her left hand on the wall as she carefully put one foot in front of the other to make sure that she didn't stumble over anything. Eventually, she decided that she'd walked far enough. Urgently, she unbuttoned her jeans, pulled them down her thighs, and crouched, still with her hand on the wall to keep her steady. With a sigh of relief, she could finally let it go, but she grimaced at the sour pain in her bladder.

"God, I hope I'm not catching a urinary infection," she mumbled worriedly. "That'd be so damn typical."

At least she had a few intimate wipes in her pocket so she could clean herself properly. With a relieved sigh at the empty feeling in her bladder, she pulled up her jeans.

Then, she slowly continued to explore the room, one hand at the wall and the other fumbling in the air in front of her. After a few minutes, she found the next corner of the basement. Pleased, Miriam began to get a grasp of the room's dimensions.

A short time later, her feet suddenly hit a piece of stone. She knelt and touched the floor in front of her. *Broken concrete. Lots of them. And big pieces too. That's weird.* She stretched further and felt even more pieces lying around. With a frown, she stretched to the right side of her as well, touching on yet more pieces. *There's so much debris. What the hell happened?* Suddenly, she touched something soft, and, with a gasp, she jerked away. *What the hell was that?* Hesitantly, she fumbled toward it again and felt soft fabric under her hand. The shape was familiar, she realized, and the next second she laughed relieved.

"My bag!" She grabbed it and hung it across her chest while cautiously backing away from the cluttered area. When she reached the corner she'd slept at, she stopped. It felt safe having one wall behind her back and one wall at the side. Then, she turned her attention to her bag. *I should have my cell in here somewhere.* Her hands searched blindly through the interior. Her old, worn copy of *Wuthering Heights* was the first thing they touched. Next were her notebook with a pen attached to it, her purse, an apple, and a chocolate bar – *Oh yay, for good faith!* – her small toiletry bag with more intimate wipes, as well as regular wet wipes, hand sanitizer, deodorant, toothbrush, a tiny hairbrush, a whole pill jar filled with Tylenol 3:s – *God, I really need one of these* – some makeup utilities, and finally her cell phone. With trembling hands, she turned it on. *Let me have some battery left, please, please, please.* It took some time for it to come to life, and the faint white light made her squint. The date on the display showed Sunday, April eighteenth, and it was four-thirty in the morning.

"Sunday? It's Sunday? When the hell did that happen? I've lost a whole fucking day and two nights?" Fear made her shiver even more, and her hands trembled so badly that she almost dropped the phone. She clasped it close to her chest and took some calming breaths before checking the battery.

"Okay, battery's full, that's great," she mumbled. "Now, how about reception?" She stared anxiously at the coverage meter, but it didn't even flicker. *Shit! Shit, shit, shit!* She tried anyway to call first Carl and then her sister, but there was nothing, no tone, not anything.

"*A brokh!*" she cursed in Yiddish.

Maybe if I move around a bit? With the help of the faint light, which she used as a flashlight, she managed to get a slightly better look at her nearest surroundings. It was definitely a concrete floor that she stood on, and a ceiling atop. She walked unsteadily out on the floor, clearly having problems with her balance. That part really began to worry her. Swaying slightly without the support of the wall, she looked around, but the faint light didn't help much. Some eight yards or so from the wall, she saw a huge heap of rubble formed like a slide, and she frowned uncertainly when she noticed her coat being half-buried near the top of it. Watching it quietly in the faint light, she let the kidnapping theory go. When she turned her gaze upwards, she immediately saw something that looked like a sealed crack in the ceiling just above it. *Did I fall from there? Guess I did. Must've lost consciousness, and probably getting a concussion. No wonder I feel so dizzy and unsteady or that I have such a headache. No wonder I vomited. No wonder I can't remember anything.* Silently sighing, she shrugged. Trying to recollect her memories would obviously be in vain.

"Guess I just have to accept that I won't remember anything more," she muttered, feeling annoyed. "Question now is, how the hell do I get out of here?"

She took a couple of steps closer to the rubble but realized that it would be impossible to climb up. The rubble was way too unstable. She wouldn't even be able to get far enough to grab her coat. Instead, she carefully moved around the large pile and found a broken elevator and a narrow slit in the rubble that showed a caved-in staircase. *What the hell happened? An earthquake? That can't be possible. But it looks like something really serious happened.* She frowned again. *I don't get it. I mean, if I'd been somewhere, like the mall or something, there should be other people around, but it's just me. Am I still at Bradley's mansion? Did someone blow it up to hide evidence? That could explain things. It's a big case, after all, probably with ties to people who would lose a lot by getting exposed.*

Her thoughts went to Tam, Andy, Linds, and Steph, wondering if they were buried somewhere above her. A lump formed in her throat at the thought that they might be dead, and she dried away tears that began to trickle from her eyes.

"I don't know anything," she mumbled in a thick voice. "It might be something else completely." Still, her guts agreed with her that it might have been an explosion. Why she couldn't explain, it just felt right.

To steer her thoughts from her maybe dead co-workers, she continued to study the area, pretending not to be severely dizzy. As she did, another thought poked at her, trying to get through to her, and then, it suddenly exploded in her mind in searing light. *How long can I survive here?* She stared at the faintly lit pile of rubble and the sealed crack in the ceiling while shivers of cold fear slowly crept down her spine. Determinedly, she cut off the next thought that tried to crawl into her mind, that there was a possibility that no one knew where she was and that she, in that case, would die alone, slowly starving to death down here, or suffocate if the basement was tightly sealed from the rubble above. Together with the concussion and the cold and the fact that she had nothing at all to drink, it might be a question of just a few days, maybe only hours if the basement indeed was sealed. Even being kidnapped by a moon-batty murderer would be better than being lost and never found. A murderer she could at least have tried to take down and escape from. This place was completely sealed off. There was no way to get out of here. Shaken in her very soul, she went back to the corner, sat down, and turned off her cell phone. It was no use to waste battery on nothing.

Miriam had no idea how long she sat there, staring into the darkness, pained by her endlessly aching head and the constantly spinning sensations. Eventually, she took a Tylenol 3 and swallowed it with the saliva she managed to gather from eating half of the apple. The other half, she put back into her bag for later. She thought that she slept after that, but it was hard to tell. At least the splitting headache calmed down a bit.

The silence started to get to her, as did the darkness. At one time, she thought that she heard low sounds from the rubble, and she sat with wide-open eyes, breathing hard when fear gripped her soul tightly as she visualized how the tentacle monster from Alaska was moving toward her, but nothing ever happened.

When the damp cold made her tremble and shiver to the point of her literally bouncing on the floor, she stood up and made an attempt to go through her *silat* training program to get warm, but lost balance and fell. The headache became even worse after that. With quivering hands, she managed to take out two Tylenol, even though she wasn't supposed to take more than one at a time. Cradling her head, she wasn't in the position to care about the cold floor and curled up in fetal position, moaning in pain. Rocking from one side to another in a futile attempt to cope with the agony, her strained breaths and quiet moaning increased in strength until she wailed, and tears and snot ran down her face. When the pain slowly and, after what felt like an eternity, finally subsided, she fell into an exhausted sleep, still cradling her poor head.

When she woke up, she felt weaker than before she tried her training program, and the headache pounded somewhere underneath the artificial blanket of pain relievers. *Stupid idiot,* she thought listlessly but didn't have the energy to be genuinely angry at herself. Staring into the unforgiving darkness, Miriam tried to think, but her thoughts were hard to catch. They tumbled around from one topic to another without staying long enough for her to be able to focus on any of them.

The intense pain worried her immensely. She didn't know much about concussions except that you weren't supposed to move around, and she didn't have a clue if this kind of pain was normal. *Just stuck between a rock and a hard place,* she thought, feeling the hopelessness trying to take over her. *Can't move around because of the concussion but can't be still because of the risk of freezing to death.*

She fought the fear as hard as she could, but, eventually, the thought that she would indeed die here, overwhelmed her, and she wept. She hugged her knees, embraced herself, and, inconsolable crying, she called out for Carl, for her sister, for her dad and her mom, for Andy and

215

Tam and Linds and Steph, but no one ever answered her. In between the crying, she promised herself that she would meet her fate with dignity and bravery, but then, she trembled with fear again, and the treacherous tears ran down her cheeks. She thought about her past years and how she would re-live them if she had gotten the chance. Instead of working so much, she'd be taking a couple of vacations abroad, going to Crete with her sister as they talked about ever so often. She would have spent even more time with Beth and her beloved nephew Markus, giving him the chance to be himself more often than he could with his parents. She wished that she had broken up with Henry earlier but knew that she wouldn't have been able to do that without Carl pointing her in the right direction. Most of all, she wished that she had been brave enough to tell Carl that she loved him.

"He wouldn't have laughed at me," she cried. "He never does." In her rosy daydream, he held out his arms and embraced her, telling her that he loved her too. She knew very well that he didn't, but staring into the eternal darkness, she preferred her daydreams. They were way better than the waking nightmares that came to her and showed her how much she was going to suffer before she perished.

She tried her phone again, but there was, of course, no reception. It was still April eighteenth, but now it was noon. *It feels like a week,* she thought, feeling empty and detached. Her stomach growled, and she broke off a small piece of the chocolate bar. The sweet taste filled her mouth and made her yearn for more. It didn't help to fill her up at all, but she didn't dare eat everything at once. Who knew when she'd be able to eat something next time? With a test of will, she managed to put the bar back into her bag again.

The seconds turned to minutes turned to hours and dragged on. At nine p.m., she thought that she was going to go crazy if she had to be trapped in this darkness any longer, and desperately she wobbled around the room, once again searching for a way out, but there was none. She wondered how long it would take before she'd become desperate enough to try and climb the pile of rubble. Not yet, but she was definitely heading that way. For now, the increasing pain in her head after that short search made her throw up again, and on unsteady feet, she went back to her corner, took another Tylenol 3 together with the last half of the apple, and hoped that she would fall to sleep. Shaking the pill jar feebly, she thought that there might be enough pills left to commit suicide if she indeed was beginning to starve to death.

"Just as the last solution," she mumbled, fighting the tears and the fear that wanted to break free again. Eventually, someone would come for her, she had to believe that, and when that happened, she could have a major breakdown, but not now. "But it might be wise to cut down on the pills, just in case."

She didn't know how long she had lain curled up on the floor in the pitch-black darkness, or if she had been able to sleep at all when she suddenly thought that she heard someone whisper her name.

"Miriam… Miriam… Wake up, Miriam. Wake up to your dream."

With a gasp, she opened her eyes and saw the room bathe in the moonlight that came from an open door, a door that floated an inch above the ground. Quietly, she stared at the vision in front of her.

Is this a dream?

A peal of dazzling laughter was heard around her, and she tried to get a glimpse of who laughed. No one was around.

It must be a dream.

"Yes, Miriam, this is your dream. Come. We are all waiting for you."

Dazed, she stood up and took a step toward the door, but her foot got caught in her bag. She looked down and picked it up, hung it across her chest again. The moonlight flickered, and she gasped, suddenly afraid that the door would close.

"You need to hurry, Miriam," the voice whispered around her.

"It is a dream, isn't it?" Her voice sounded slow and dazed.

"Yes, Miriam, it is your dream, but you need to hurry before you wake up."

Suddenly, the door began to close, and the moonlight was disappearing, leaving the room even darker and colder and more terrifying than before, leaving her in her grave.

With a shriek, Miriam threw herself toward the door, and, just as it closed, she managed to slip in and fall down on the other side, landing on soft grass.

Chapter 13

Panting for breath, Miriam staggered to her feet and looked around. She stood on a high hill in front of a European looking church with tall spires and windows with stained glass. *Very gothic-looking,* she mused. It seemed like she had exited from the church's enormous portal to wherever she was now. *I wonder if I get back into the basement if I enter the church again?* Just as the thought materialized in her mind, it struck her that she acted as if this was not a dream, but reality. *That's weird...* A cold nudge of uneasiness poked her between her shoulders. *No way, no fucking way! This has to be a dream! It just has to!* But she felt the mild air stroking her face and hair with a touch of spicy fragrance in it, and the salty smell of the sea that stretched out endlessly from the little town at the foot of the hill, blending together with the rich scent of the soil. When she knelt and touched the grass, it felt cool and spiky toward her skin. The hair on her arms suddenly stood up, and a slow chill crawled down her spine and spread its fingers all over her body to the extent that her nipples hurt from being so rigid.

She cautiously rose to her feet again and embraced herself hard while looking around with wide-opened eyes and a rapidly throbbing heart. *It... it feels real... Can it— Can it really be?* She took a deep breath and made a conscious attempt to relax. Her head hurt so much that she squinted and had to hold on to it for a while, but the pain together with the spinning became too much for her. She turned around and vomited violently. There was nothing left in her stomach but bile at this point, but it felt as if she was about to throw up her intestines. After a long time, her stomach finally calmed down, and, sweating profusely, she sank down on the ground, panting for breath, her whole body shaking. Drained, she lay on the grass, cradling her aching head and looked up at the bright full moon in the dark-blue sky until she felt well enough to stand on wobbly legs. When she nearly fell, out of sheer exhaustion, it dawned on her how weak she was, and it worried her immensely.

"Okay," she mumbled. "I need to get moving. I can't stand here all night. The town down there must have somewhere I can sleep and get something to eat, but first…"

With nothing more than sheer will, she forced her feet to move forward to the church portal. She needed to know if it led back to the basement or not. The door handle was cool and smooth to her touch. The portal itself was heavy and resisted her attempt to open it, but, eventually, it gave in and opened. A damp chill welcomed her, and she found herself looking into an old, worn-out church room, almost cathedral-like in its appearance. In the middle of the atrium, numerous slim, deep-orange prayer candles were lit in a huge round ball made from filigree iron. It was beautiful and serene and seemed to lure her toward it. She was only a few steps from it when a feeling of something vile made her stop in her approach, frightened and with heavier, faster breathing.

"Do you want to light a candle, my child?" a soft voice was heard from her left side.

With a slight gasp, she turned her head and saw a figure standing in the dark shadows. A shiver of fear ran down her spine, and hastily, she backed away toward the portico again.

"No… no thanks," she mumbled and hit the door with her back. As she pushed it, a terrifying moment passed in which she thought it wouldn't open, but finally, it gave in, and she stumbled out into the night. As quickly as possible, she began to wobble down the gravel-covered road toward the small town at the foot of the hill. She didn't feel comfortable in churches, never had.

In an attempt to warm herself, she rubbed her arms, wishing she had her coat or her scarf, which probably lay buried in the rubble together with the coat.

The gravel under her feet creaked loudly in the silent night as she closed in on something that seemed to have been a town wall and a city gate once. Now, they lay in ruins, and the big stone blocks adorned the grass-clad moat outside. An old wooden bridge led her over the moat and onto a narrow cobblestone street in between two three-story houses. A couple of gaslights lit up the street and made it look like it belonged in a fairy-tale. *Gaslights? Really? Well, it's quaint, I guess, but it doesn't feel like my dream.*

At this point, she had more or less accepted that whatever it was, it wasn't a dream. None of her dreams had ever been this detailed with smells and sounds, and she had never reflected over the texture in one before either. *It's something else. Some kind of… of… I don't know, different dimension maybe? Or time traveling? I mean, why not? That damn monster in Alaska, for example. It had to have come from somewhere. It just doesn't live somewhere in a house in Bettles, inviting you in for tea when you happen to pass by.*

The sudden thought of tea made her think of Carl again, and she brought out her cell phone and turned it on. The battery wasn't full anymore, but with nervous excitement, she saw that it had reception. The date was weird, though, she noticed with a slight frown. It showed April twentieth and eight p.m. when it had been the eighteenth and nine p.m. not long ago. She shrugged uncomfortably and fast-dialed Carl. When the tone went through, she held her breath. It felt like her heart was going to hammer itself out of her chest in anxiety.

"Yeah?" The sound of his melodic voice made shivers of happiness and love run through her body, and her eyes became moist. She leaned in toward the phone as if she could lean into him that way. Her cheeks blossomed and she smiled broadly and relieved.

"Carl! It's me!" Her own voice sounded light and happy as a lark's trill.

"Hello?"

Her bright smile died away. "Carl? Can you hear me?"

"Hello?"

"It's me, Carl, it's Miri. It's wonderful to hear your voice."

"Miri?"

"Yes! Wow, finally. God, I thought you couldn't hear me." She heard him breathe on the other end of the line. "Carl? Can you hear me?" She listened again to his breaths, and a treacherous tear fell down her cheek. "Oh, God, he can't hear me," she mumbled, devastated. "Damn it!" She sniveled and wiped away the tears before she inhaled and tried again, "Can you hear me, Carl? It's me, Miri."

The click let her know that he had hung up on her. Slowly, she took the phone from her ear and stared at it while more tears wetted her cheeks. Resolutely, she dialed the number again, but this time, the line was busy before it suddenly broke, and no tone went through. When she checked the cell, the reception was dead.

"Damn it," she whispered. Then, she took a deep breath and wiped away the tears with an irritated gesture. "Well, I got through once," she said and made a serious effort to sound hopeful. "That means I can get through again." For now, she turned it off, though. It worried her that the battery had lost so much power since she looked at it last time. "I can't have it dying on me," she mumbled pleadingly.

When she put it back in the bag again, the thought hit her that this might have been her life's biggest mistake, going through that door. What if she could never come back, what if she was trapped here? Alive, yes, but never get to see Carl again, never talk with him again, never hear him laugh or feel his hand on her arm. What if she never got her life back? She would lose everything; her parents, Beth and Ted and Markus, her job, everything that was important to her. The breath stuck painfully in her chest, and she swallowed hard to get control over herself, but then, the tears came. Hyperventilating, she sank down on the cobblestones and leaned toward a house wall, burying her face in her hands.

She didn't sit there long before her anger finally awoke. With resentful gestures, she dried her eyes and pulled herself to her feet again.

"No, Miri, this is not acceptable! I'm not going to give in to this nonsense! I haven't even been here an hour yet, and I'm already giving up my life? No way! I'm going to find somewhere to sleep, a motel or something, and something to eat, and then I'm going to find a way out of here. I'm NOT giving up!"

Determined, she continued to stagger through the quietly sleeping town while trying to think about something mundane that wouldn't trigger her already exhausted being. One of the courses she'd taken at the Western Shore University came to mind, the one about city planning. As she put together what she had seen from the hill and what she experienced while wandering around in it, she thought that this seemed to be one of the medieval European towns that haphazardly grew up around a commercial spot. The narrow streets meandered between houses and through open spaces with large stone wells in their midst. She walked up one street, across an open place, and down another street, and so on, over and over until she felt out of control. At least she always knew relatively well where she was, since her sense of direction hadn't failed her. Her sense of time, however, lacked logic in every aspect, not that that was very surprising.

Miriam had no clue about how long she had muddled around when she stopped at a tiny plaza and sat down on a stone bench while trying to recollect her thoughts. Squinting from the headache, she studied her surroundings, but they didn't differ from any of the other ones she'd walked through. *This is so weird,* she thought. *I swear that the town didn't look this big from the church grounds, but I must've wandered around here for hours.* She refused to check the cell phone, though. *I can't use it as my watch. I'll need it later. I need to get through to Carl. It has to work sooner or later.*

Something else that made her contemplate the town was the lack of people. Sure, it was in the middle of the night, but she'd never experienced a city without any kind of nightlife around. *At least there should be some prostitutes somewhere and people out in shady businesses, right?* She broke off another piece of her chocolate bar while she looked around, trying to decide which way to go next. The sweet taste made her close her eyes for a moment while she chewed slowly on it, trying to make it last longer. When she swallowed, she opened her eyes again. *Okay, try to think logically for once, Miri. Not your strongest suit, but at least you can give it a try.* Without thinking about it, she broke another piece of the bar and put it in her mouth. *How would Carl have approached it? He would've said,* "If I'd been a motel owner, where would I've put up my motel?" She tried to remember the layout of the town from the view at the top of the hill. It had been placed like a necklace at the edge of the mound and followed it around at least halfway before it turned away and stretched out toward the water. It was bean-shaped, she remembered now. "Well, I guess it would be logical to set up something near the water if this is a seaport."

Determined and filled with new energy, she rose from the bench and headed in the direction of the water. This street was broader than the others, she noticed, as she walked down a street seemingly leading toward the port, and it had a main street feeling, even though there were no stores around, at least none she could discern.

The salty smell of water had become stronger when she finally caught a glance of a sign hanging from the wall at the side of a door. A large window spread a warm yellow light onto the street. Miriam gave up a feeble cheer and hurried her steps, but the damn dizziness almost made her fall. Slowing down, she concentrated on keeping herself as steady on her feet as she could, which didn't say much. As she came closer, she could make out the words *The Wicked Merchant* on the worn-out wooden sign. A once brightly painted image of a peddler with a mask and a big sack from which he pulled out something that wasn't at all recognizable disturbed her. With a slight frown and a sudden bad feeling about the whole place, she hesitantly opened the door and stepped in. It wasn't as if she had much to choose from right now.

A short man with a pale, scrawny face and shiny black hair slicked back from his forehead stood at the back of the wall behind an old-fashioned-looking counter, viewing her void of surprise. He rather looked as if he expected her. Miriam felt an unexpected tightness in her chest, for no apparent reason, and when the man beamed at her, her breaths became shallow. There was something with his slightly round eyes that she didn't like. They had a silvery tinge to the black, making them resemble the eyes of a raven, and they looked— She couldn't put her finger on it. Excited? Maybe.

"Splendid night to be out traveling… Miriam. Did you enjoy the moonlight?"

Staring at him, she felt even more uncomfortable for every passing moment. *How does he know my name?*

"Um…" She took a deep breath to compose herself, and then a movement in the left corner of her eye caught her off guard. An old, wrinkled man in a likewise old, wrinkled suit, sat comfortably at a table with a big pint of beer in front of him. Miriam tensed. *How did I not see him when I came in?* He blinked mischievously at her after letting his gaze deliberately wander up and down her body. Miriam blushed awkwardly and looked away.

"Isn't she a sweetheart?" he said with a surprisingly pleasant voice to the night porter, who grinned and nodded in agreement.

"She sure is." The night porter cocked his head and let his gaze pierce her. Miriam cringed. "You want a room, yes?"

"Um…" No, she did not want a room at this place, but she needed somewhere to sleep that wasn't outside on the street. "How much is it?"

"Just a piece of your soul." The night porter laughed when he saw her suspicious and somewhat frightened expression, a dazzling kind of a laugh that made her shudder uneasily. "Of course not, dear. For you, it's only five dollars."

"Five dollars?" Her voice sounded skeptical, but the man continued to watch her with his head slightly tilted. Miriam looked wearily at the old embellished cash machine on the counter. "You don't take cards, do you?" she asked.

"It depends on what cards they are, sugar doll," the night porter grinned. "One of you naked as Queen of Hearts would surely suffice."

Miriam blinked, and a wave of heat slowly covered her face.

The elderly man in the corner chuckled. "I don't think she's that kind of a girl," he said.

"More's the pity," the night porter replied without letting his gaze off her.

Miriam wished that she dared to leave this place and find somewhere else, but somehow, she doubted there was anywhere else. Reluctantly, she opened her bag and brought out her wallet. Surely, she must have some cash there. Regardless of her uneasiness, a wave of relief went through her when she found not just one, but three five-dollar bills and a twenty. She gave one of the fives to the night porter who held it up to the gas lamp and studied it thoroughly.

"Haven't seen one of these before, Matthew," he said.

The old man smiled. "Time passes unnoticeable here," he said, and Miriam stared at him, trying to hide her apprehension.

The cash machine clanked loudly when the night porter put the bill away. Then he grabbed a large key from the wooden shelf.

"Number six will do," he said. "That's a nice room for a nice lady."

As she cautiously followed him up a half-stair, she could feel the old man's stare as piercing needles behind her back, and she cringed again.

The lion-colored carpet in the corridor matched the flowery tapestry on the walls and effectively silenced their steps. Gas lamps lit up their way and cast strange shadows all around. It didn't take long before the little man stopped at a richly adorned door with the number six in golden metal – *Brass?* – placed on the side of it. As the door opened, he bowed elegantly toward her and said, without leaving her face with his gaze, "You are hungry, are you not? There's a hunger in your eyes. I will come with a tray immediately." He bowed again and left her.

Miriam waited until he disappeared from the corridor before she took the key out of the keyhole and stepped into a large room. As she closed the door behind her and locked it, she finally felt as if she could start breathing again.

Turning around, she looked at the room, and some of her anxiousness melted away. It was large with an old-fashioned feeling to it, just like the rest of the place. With a sigh of relief, her eyes set on the big bed. A bed after all this time on a cold, damp floor. Gas lamps on the wall instead of impenetrable darkness. Food that was soon to arrive when she had had nothing but an apple and a chocolate bar to eat before. She was inside a warm place, and she had a key in her hand. For now, this was enough. For now, she didn't ask for much more. *Except being home. God, I wish I were home instead.* With a grimace, she let the thoughts of home go. She wasn't home yet, but as soon as she had rest and eat a bit, and the damn headache and dizziness were under control, nothing was going to stop her from finding her way home again. With satisfaction, she studied the two big armchairs at the window. When the slimy man had brought her some food, she would drag one of them in front of the door. She wasn't keen on waking up to some nasty surprise in the middle of the night, and she trusted neither of the two men in the foyer.

It knocked on the door, and when she opened it, a huge tray with food and drink was placed on a serving trolley. Suspiciously, she looked for the porter, but he was nowhere in sight. Her gaze wandered back to the tray. The smell was heavenly, and Miriam felt her mouth water. She lifted it up – *God, it's heavy* – and, staggering, she carefully carried it to the table at the window, so she didn't spill anything, before wobbling back and locking the door again. Then, she took one of the armchairs and, grunting at its weight, she pushed it all the way to the door and placed it so the door couldn't open even if someone tried. Pleased with herself, she went back to the other armchair. As she sat down and hungrily looked at the food, a small voice in her head told her to be cautious. *Are you sure this isn't like Persephone in Hades, Miri? You eat and then you can never leave?*

"Oh, for crying out loud," she muttered and put a big piece of bread in her mouth, followed by some tasty, well-spiced stew. The wine was deep red and went very well with the food. Ravenously, she wolfed every single bit down and drank all the wine. With the bread, she even wiped the sauce from the bowl, something she was taught from home to never do. When she was finished, she felt pleasantly full and sleepy, but before she went to bed, she visited the bathroom.

It was big and luxuriously and dominated by an enormous bathtub on lion-feet. It was placed on a soft cream-colored rug that hugged her feet. She looked longingly at the tub. Yes, she wanted a bath; no, she needed a bath, yearned for a bath, for being clean, in a way she hadn't yearned for something since— Well… She blushed. *Since I was with Carl last time.*

As the bathtub slowly filled, she delightfully looked through the many beautiful glass bottles with bubble bath products and chose a transparent one with an intricate pattern that gave away a rich scent of vanilla. Pouring some of the whiskey-colored liquid into the water, it just touched the surface, but the deep scent immediately rose with the steam and made her smile. Then she saw herself in the mirror, and the smile disappeared.

"Oh— My— God…"

Her face was covered by a gray layer of dust, streamed by relatively clear parts where tears had run down her cheeks. Her right side was plastered with dried blood that originated from a cut on her forehead. With an uneasy frown, she closely studied the wound. *When did I get that? When I fell from the ceiling? Yes, probably.* She looked gaunt and stressed out and ready to drop, with large, dark smudges under her eyes. Her usually wavy hair lay slicked to her head, coated with dust and sweat.

"Wow… Do I need that bath, or what?" she mumbled. "Almost wish I had a camera so that every time I feel ugly, I'll just look at the photo and feel on top of the world again."

She turned away from the depressing sight and undressed. Her clothes were in the same bad shape as her face.

"Wonder if they have a washing machine around?" But she knew that she wouldn't ask. Just the thought of the slimy night porter made her cringe. Instead, she pulled all her clothes into the big washing basin and covered them with hot water and soap. The water immediately turned grayish-brown in color and she grimaced disgustedly. She had to scrub them three times before the water came out clear and she could hang them over the edge of the basin. At that point, the room was foggy from the hot steam, and with a deep sigh, she lowered herself into the filled bathtub and closed her eyes, enjoying every second. Her limbs floated, surfaced by the well-scented bubbles, and warmth spread throughout her chilled-to-the-bones body. She didn't even move until the water was lukewarm rather than hot and then she massaged her hair and head with more well-scented products. When she accidentally touched the wound in her head, a flash of pain made her inhale sharply and whimper. It had not healed properly yet. She was probably in need of some stitches, but since that clearly was not possible, she would have to live with a scar. She shrugged indifferently. *It's just another one to the collection. No big deal. At least not as long as it doesn't fester.* Eventually, she climbed out of the water and wrapped herself in a thick, soft bath towel. *This place is amazing. Too bad it's something weird with it, but since I don't have a choice, I'm going to enjoy the ride.* Feeling better about that decision, she smiled at her image in the mirror and went to get her toiletry bag. Now, she was doubly grateful that she always brought her own toothbrush with her.

After brushing her teeth, she checked the wound again. As far as she could tell, it looked good and clean. With a sigh of relief, she went out of the steaming bathroom and curled up in the big, soft bed. She almost disappeared amongst the many pillows and the thick duvet, and within seconds, she slept.

She didn't know how long she had slept when she woke up by a low, creaky sound. Not surprised to see the doorknob slowly turning, she sat up in bed. Instead of being afraid, she welcomed the anger that rose inside her. If that slimy man thought that he could try and take advantage of something he saw as vulnerability, he'd better think again. Even in this state, she was dangerous, especially toward people who just saw a short, slim woman and not a well-trained body. Getting up, she moved lithely toward the table and picked up the dinnerware knife and put it in position. It wasn't much, but she doubted that he was as trained in self-defense and martial arts as she was.

That she was standing there naked didn't bother her either, to her surprise. The thought struck her that she, just a couple of years ago, would almost rather have been murdered than been seen without clothes. For a second, she allowed herself to shake her head in self-disgust before she once again felt proud of how she had changed.

The doorknob wrestled again, harder this time, but the door was tightly locked as well as blocked by the chair and didn't give in. Just to be sure that whoever was on the other side would get a surprise should he manage to get in after all, she closed in toward the door and placed herself at the sidewall with the knife ready. The minutes ticked by, but the doorknob remained still. Miriam smiled grimly and went back to bed, extremely satisfied with herself. Soon enough, she fell asleep again, still holding the knife in a loose grip.

Next time she woke up, she felt much better, well-rested and energetic. Even the dizziness was gone, though the headache was still present. Food, sleep, and a clean body did wonders as usual. She trotted off to the bathroom, relieved herself, washed, and checked her clothes. Still not completely dry, but she shrugged and put them on anyway. When she pulled the heavy curtains from the window in her room, it surprised her to see that it was night again. *Why, I must have slept around the clock. No wonder I'm so awake.* Suddenly feeling a bit amiss, she checked the surroundings outside the window. The view showed her a small cobblestone-clad courtyard with a lone birch, a stone bench, and a water fountain. The full moon shone over the tree and weaved strange-looking patterns over the ground.

"Now what?" she mumbled. Her plan had been to examine the town and its surroundings in the hope of finding a way home again, but she wasn't very keen on doing that when it was dark outside. Feeling a bit restless, she pulled the draperies together again and went over to grab her cell phone. When it turned on, she stared at the battery meter. *Almost empty? What the hell?* At least, she had reception again. Nervously, she fast-dialed Carl. A signal went through before she heard Carl's voice on the other side. Her heart beat faster and, as usual, just hearing his melodic voice so close to her made her warm inside and gave her a pleasant weight in her lower abdomen.

"Yeah?"

"Carl, can you hear me? It's me, Miri."

"What the hell's going on? Miri? Is it you? I can't hear anything. Just damn static. Miri?"

"Yes, it's me. Oh, for all good in the world, please hear me. I'm sorry. I don't know where I am. I'm somewhere else, somewhere… in another realm or time or something like that, I think. God, it feels crazy just saying it. I don't even know how I can reach you like this."

"Damn it. I'm going to hang up now. Miri, if it's you, please call again right now, alright?"

"Alright, alright, I'll do that. Just hang on to me, okay?"

As soon as she heard Carl's phone click in her ear, she hung up and redialed. No tone went through. She took the cell from her ear and stared at it. It was dead.

"No way! No fucking way! You have to be fucking kidding me!" Anger rose fiercely inside her, but she bit it back and tried to turn it on again. Nothing. "You fucking piece of fucking shit!" she yelled at it, and without thinking, she hurled it violently into the wall. As it hit, it cracked and fell on the floor in two parts. She stared at it, breathing heavily in the silence that followed.

"Oh, damn," she mumbled devastated. Then the tears came. She slid down onto the floor and leaned her back toward the bed. "You fucking idiot!" she sobbed with her face hid on her bent knees. "You damn fucking idiot! Why did you have to break it? Was it really necessary? Can't you just think before you do something?" With a falsely cheerful voice, she said mockingly through the tears, "Hey, I know, I'll throw it into the wall. That's a great idea."

She sobbed again, thinking about the wasted chances to contact Carl again, to contact anyone again. Not that she knew how they'd be able to find her even if she managed to let them know what happened, but if there had ever been a chance, she'd definitely blown it now.

Eventually, she composed herself and dried her tears with the back of her hand. She shuffled over the floor, grabbed the phone and checked it. Maybe it wasn't that broke? Maybe she'd be able to fix it? She was good with her hands, good at fixing things.

"Goddammit," she mumbled again when she saw the pieces. It was an old cell phone, of the type where you pulled up the earpiece from the mouthpiece, and it had completely broken at the hinges. There was no way to repair it. She tossed them away again, but without any strength in the pitch.

Then, she drew a deep breath and struggled to calm down.

"Okay, I'm an idiot. That's okay. It might be a problem, but it's okay. I just have to remember that there's no problem without a solution, and I'm not going to sit here like a damn princess. I'm going to find my way out on my own, just as I planned anyway. I got in, so there must be a way to get out."

She went to the bathroom and washed her face with ice-cold water. It didn't make her feel better, but at least the damn tears stopped falling. Glancing at the cell phone parts, she sniveled and grimaced, but took them and put them into her bag. It didn't feel right to leave them in the room. The phone had been a loyal companion to her during the last three years, after all.

When she opened the door to the corridor, she found the trolley there again with a tray full of breakfast food. She stared at it. The tea was still steaming.

"Why do they give me breakfast in the middle of the night? What a weird place this is."

She wasn't hungry but took a couple of mouthfuls of the tea and put the scones and the apple in her bag for later. The carpet in the hallway silenced her steps as effectively as before, but as she quietly opened the ornate door to the foyer, all her hopes of sneaking away unseen were spoiled.

"Good morning, Miriam," the night porter said with a smile that rubbed her the wrong way.

"Um, morning? It's still night, right?"

She heard a chuckle behind her, and when she turned around, old Matthew was sitting in his corner with a pint of beer, peering at her with a mischievous glance in his eyes. Like last time, she hadn't seen him when she stepped in. She stared uncomfortably at him, wondering if the concussion had made her less perceptive.

"Oh my, you're just a baby, aren't you?"

Miriam frowned at him but didn't care to answer. The two men made her seriously tense and insecure. When she turned toward the night porter again, she gasped startled as he suddenly stood face to face with her. *When did he get so close?*

233

I didn't even hear him. She took an involuntary step back, and he showed her his pearl white teeth in something that resembled a smile.

"You smell nice, Miriam. May I offer you something to drink before you leave? A glass of wine? Or the little green fairy, maybe?"

"Um, no… No thanks…"

Quickly, she backed away toward the main entrance. As she hurried out, Matthew's chuckle followed her, but it got abruptly cut off when the heavy door closed behind her.

In a rush, since she wanted to get away from *The Wicked Merchant* as fast as possible, she headed down the street that she suspected would take her to the port. The moonlight tried to brighten the dark areas between the gaslights but didn't succeed. Looking at the shadows, Miriam got an eerie feeling that the darkness was alive, that it was lurking, and only waited for the right moment to pounce. She tried a chuckle at her vivid imagination, but it fell flat. *Been in too many strange Projects to just laugh it off,* she thought with another cautious glance at the deep pools of darkness in between the gaslights. So far, nothing moved.

Just like the previous night, there was no one in sight, only her and her echoing steps. She found it strange and uncanny, and as she apprehensively looked around to make sure that she was truly alone, it struck her that there were no lights at all in any of the windows around her. *Isn't that odd?* She tried to remember what the time had been before she threw the phone into the wall, but she'd been so excited to have reception, that she hadn't paid attention. *Stupid beginner mistake,* she grumbled.

Decidedly, she went to the closest house at her right and tried to look through the window with its beautifully ornated panes. It was dark inside, and she couldn't discern anything, so she knocked hard on the door. *I don't care if I wake them up. I need some directions, and they can't all be as distrustful as the night porter.* She waited for a couple of minutes, but no one seemed to wake up.

With a troubled frown, Miriam went to the neighbor's house. The low staircase that led to the front door held large pots with blooming pale tulips. No one answered her knocks here either, and she couldn't hear any sounds or see any lights from inside.

Puzzled, she walked down the street at a slow pace while studying the houses. They were all built from bricks in different colors, and none were higher than three stories. Between two of the houses to her right was an alley. Curiously, she looked into it. It rose steeply into the dark shadows before it made an abrupt right turn. There were a couple of doors close to the turn. As she pondered the likelihood of anyone answering them, she suddenly got an uneasy feeling of something dangerous lurking somewhere in the dark. Immediately, she backed away and quickened her steps. Instead, she approached a house way further down the main street. When no one answered her decisive knocks, she stared at the old wooden door in front of her with its large and rusty iron fittings, before cautiously trying the handle. As the door silently opened up in front of her, she found that she wasn't as surprised as she should have been. In front of her was a gloomy and empty hallway, and to the left, a doorway opened to a dark room, but she couldn't distinguish any features in it. Intimidated by the dark and feeling like a coward, Miriam closed the door without stepping inside. Then, she crossed the street and tried another thick wooden door. It also opened without a sound. This time, she looked into an empty kitchen. There was no furniture and no wood in the open fireplace. The floor looked worn out as if it had been trodden by many feet during the years.

Thoughtfully, she went to the neighbor. That door too opened to an empty and unfurnished apartment. As she stood on the threshold, looking at the bare walls and floors, it dawned on her that the reason no one was around was that she was walking in a dead town. A sudden shiver ran down her spine.

Why is there a functional inn here when no people are around? The question made the hair on her arms standing straight up, and she wasn't sure if she wanted an answer.

For a moment certain that someone was there, watching her, Miriam looked over her shoulder again, but of course, the street was empty. *I wish I had my gun,* she thought, but it was safely put away in her closet at home together with her FBI uniform. Carefully, she took a step back and off the threshold, painfully missing the relative safety the gun provided. As the door closed behind her, she hurried down the street, wanting to get away from the dark, quietly staring windows as quickly as possible.

Within a few minutes, the street opened to the harbor, and like the rest of the town, it was empty and abandoned. No boats, no ships, no cargo, no nothing. Miriam shuddered but walked all the way to the edge and looked down into the black water. It had the same lonely feeling as everything else around here. Viewing the dark and foreboding sea, she saw an island on the far right, with a castle built on it. To her surprise, flickering lights shone through a narrow window in one of the towers. It wasn't close enough for her to discern any people inside, but at least the castle looked more alive than anything else she had seen here, well, except for the inn. She stared at it with an uncertain frown. *Huh, maybe I'm wrong about the town being abandoned, after all?* Once more, she looked around, but nothing moved. The whole town felt empty and abandoned. *There's something here that I'm missing.*

"There must be some kind of logic, some kind of pattern to it all," she mumbled. "I've met people or seen signs of life at three places, at the church on the hill, in the Inn, and now over at the castle. None of them are private places, not directly anyway." She frowned. "It doesn't make any sense. If that were the pattern, the streets would be crowded with people."

As she continued to watch the flickering light in the window, she experienced the same bad feeling as the church and the inn had given her. With a slight shiver, she turned her to walk away from the castle, but suddenly, she got an unexpected sensation that it tried to lure her back, and she reluctantly looked over her shoulder. Gasping at the sight, she stared at the castle and its suddenly lit up windows, and thought that she could hear music. In her mind's eye, the tones came to her like physical waves. Wide-eyed and with a hammering heart, she turned her back to it once again, trying to ignore the malicious tendrils that seemed to reach out to her, and hurried away along the harbor's edge. The worst thing was that there was a small part of her who wanted to give in to the music and the lights, and go… *dancing…* The word popped up in her head together with an image of her in a shimmering ball gown, swaying together with someone in a mask. For a moment, she slowed down her steps and turned around. *What the hell, Miriam!* she thought alarmed. *What are you doing?* Even though the bewildered thought broke part of the attraction, she found herself taking a step toward the castle.

"No," she said sternly and took another step. The music was stronger now, and she walked two more steps toward the lit castle. With a strength of will, she dug her nails hard into the palms of her hands. Grimacing at the pain, she clenched her fists even harder and managed to turn around. Bent, as if struggling against a strong wind, she walked away, step by difficult step.

When she thought that she wouldn't have the strength to walk away, after all, the lure suddenly lost its attraction, and she could finally stop. Whatever had caused the temptation had entirely lost its grip over her. Slowly, she released her fists and looked at the dents from her nails in her palms, shaking her head at the sight. *At least they're not bleeding.* Her limbs trembled after the effort, and she had to sit down at a nearby bench. She wiped away the sweat that covered her face and tried to get her labored breath under control.

For a time, Miriam sat and watched the dark water that lay in front of her. Blank like a mirror, it clearly reflected the stars and the full moon. Then, in the corner of her eye, the castle's lights began to die out, one after the other. Alarmed, she stood, but she didn't have the courage to look straight at the castle for fear of it trying to lure her toward it again. Instead, she abruptly turned her back to it and hurried along the harbor's edge toward the other end.

As she continued on and nothing else happened, the fear soon subsided and gave way for fascination. She looked around to try to figure out the layout of the seaside area. Apparently, the harbor was natural, since she couldn't see any breakwater structures anywhere. The ground around the port was covered with setts rather than cobblestones, which made it easier on the feet, and the old brick houses were taller than the ones she'd seen last night on her winding way through the town. The roofs were beautifully decorated in a way that reminded her of medieval crenelations. She tried a few of the large wooden doors, and some of them opened up to what seemed to have been storage spaces for the ships' cargo, while others seemed to have been stores and inns, while yet others looked like they had served as living quarters. All the houses she looked into were bare and abandoned without recent traces of people.

It was clear that the port followed the whole town's seaside from beginning to end, and just as she experienced the night before, it seemed longer to walk than it looked like it would be.

"It must be some kind of optic illusion—" She caught herself as an intriguing thought struck her. "Well, things might not follow the same physical laws here as I'm used to." As the words left her lips, they suddenly felt heavy and seemed to, in her mind's eye, fall to the ground with a dense thump, and she stopped dead in her tracks.

"If there are no physical laws here?" Her heart hammered in her chest at the possibilities that opened if that was the case. "No, wait, let me think."

Slowly, she began to walk again while trying hard to think outside the box.

"There has to be some kind of physical laws here. Otherwise, everything would just float around, but maybe—" She abruptly stopped talking as a near-impossible thought hit her. "Maybe they're bendable?" With a skeptical chuckle, she said, "There's only one way to figure it out, I guess."

With nervously pounding heart and sweaty palms, she thought about the inn. Nothing happened.

"Maybe I'm not thinking hard enough?" She inhaled anxiously and closed her eyes. *What am I doing? I'm so damn crazy.* Despite that, she continued to concentrate on the sign and the door to the inn, trying to see all the details of the scene in her mind's eye; the brown brick wall with its many cracks and the heavy, dark-brown wooden door with its high threshold, its black and twisted metal handle, and the large ornate keyhole, but nothing happened, nothing stirred. She sighed, let go of the picture, and opened her eyes. For half a second, she couldn't understand what she saw, but the next moment she nearly fainted when it hit her that she was standing only a couple of inches from the door to *The Wicked Merchant.*

Miriam chuckled nervously, and with frantic movements, she rubbed her arms hard where the hair stood up. Her heart hammered like crazy in her chest, and the breaths rasped and ached on their way through her throat.

"Um, okay… That was quicker than walking…" She recognized the hysteria that hid somewhere under the joking tone. She leaned toward the uneven wall, and as she slid down to crouching, she hid her face in her arms and inhaled deeply. *I'm not going to lose it. I'm NOT going to lose it! Everything's fine, Miri. Everything's just fine.*

"Except that I suddenly can teleport." *Wrong thing to say, Miri. Just shut up!* She bit her tongue to try to stop the hysterical laughter from breaking through but failed. The laugh found its way out of her, first low, like a giggle, only to rise in tone and hysteria, and soon she shrieked with laughter while tears flowed from her eyes. Desperately, she hit her head hard into the wall to let the pain take over. She hit it

239

again and again, and finally, the laugh faded away. Something wet flowed down the back of her skull to her neck, but she didn't care. She just cradled together while rocking herself back and forth, giving in to the searing pain in her head.

Chapter 14

Miriam didn't know how long she sat outside the inn, rocking, swaying, and crying before the hysteria slowly disappeared, and she could stagger to her feet. Her body shivered and trembled. It felt limp and boneless. Not yet able to control her ragged breaths, she struggled with the heavy door and wobbled into the inn. The night porter and Matthew smiled at her, and there was something about those smiles that made her think about sharp pikes hidden just beneath the surface of turbid water.

Looking down at her feet, she refused to acknowledge them. She passed them by as quickly as she could and slammed the door to the corridor behind her back. As soon as she came into her room, she locked the door and pushed the chair in front of it again. Then, she went straight to bed without undressing or even checking the head wound. She thought that sleep would be immediate, but her head hurt too much. Instead, she squirmed back and forth, trying to find a position that didn't pain her, but it was impossible.

Whimpering, she stopped trying and sat up in the bed, holding on to her head with unsteady hands. *I should check the wound,* she thought listlessly. *Then, I can sit at the window and watch the dawn break. Eventually, I'll be so tired that I'll fall asleep.*

The floor was cool to her feet, soothing in a way, but as soon as she stood up, the whole room began swaying wildly, and sudden waves of nausea washed over her. Cold and sweaty at the same time, she staggered toward the bathroom, trying to hold the urge to vomit until she reached the toilet. She nearly made it. Just as she reached for the bathroom door, she projectile vomited over and over again until she thought that she was going to throw up her intestines. The dizziness in her head only got worse, and when the last heaving went through her body, she collapsed in a heap and fell into darkness.

She woke up gradually, feeling completely out of touch with her body. The thick duvet embraced her, and the pillow let her head rest gently. It hurt badly, but not as painful as before she vomited. Speaking of vomiting, she sniffed the air like a dog but couldn't smell other than clean linen.

Confused, Miriam frowned, and a sharp flash of pain shot through her temple. She grimaced and groaned weakly. Then, she opened her eyes and squinted at the lit light in the room. The gas lamps seemed to sway gently back and forth on the wall. Her head spun, making her slightly nauseous again, and she closed her eyes. This time, the dizziness disappeared quicker than before, and when she once again opened her eyes, the lamps still danced, but not as much.

In an attempt to not move her head, she only glanced toward the bathroom door and scowled in disbelief. There was no vomitus neither on the floor, the wall, nor the door. It was shiningly clean. *That's weird,* she began but gave a mental shrug. *Everything's weird here.*

Then, she made another attempt to glance toward the door leading to the corridor without moving her head. It was hard and her eyes watered by the strain. It didn't look like the chair had been moved. She must have cleaned everything up herself. She let out a deep sigh and relaxed. *Okay, I've suffered from another minor memory loss. Great. How long was I gone this time?* She had no way of checking that. *Well, at least I still know where I am. Maybe I should take it a bit easy for a few hours.* Her mind shied away from the memory of her teleporting from the harbor to the inn. *So, I remember that. Why, thank you,* she thought sarcastically. *No wonder I reacted so strongly.* She sighed again and squirmed around to find a better position, but the slightest movement made her head sear in pain. Eventually, she just lay still with closed eyes, hoping to drift off to sleep.

The rest of the day or night or whatever it was, she spent half-sleeping. When she had to visit the bathroom, her skull felt like it was going to split in two. Carefully holding on to her head, and with painfully squinting eyes, she took one shaky step at a time. It worried her that she still was in such agony. *Is it because of the wounds combined with the concussion, or because of the teleportation, or all put together?* She wasn't sure. When she was done using the toilet, she brought out her little mirror from the toiletry bag. Holding it at the back of her head, she found an angle where she could see the wound in the mirror in front of her. The first thing that struck her was that her hair was a damn mess, hard, slippery, and nearly unbendable as it was smeared with blood that hadn't yet dried. *God, there's so much blood. Not surprising, though. There's always lots of blood coming from head wounds, right? But still...* Carefully she parted the strings of hair and exposed the wound. She stared at it in silence. It was worse than she thought; bigger and meatier. The blood didn't worry her, but the risk of infection did. *How the hell did I manage to bang my head so hard? I didn't think— It didn't feel like— This is insane. I am insane! I can't continue like this. I need to get a grip on myself.*

"I need to clean it..." She hated how weak and feeble her voice sounded and cleared her throat. "Can't see the damage properly." Yes, that sounded better. She took another staggering step toward the bathtub and held on to the edge, all the while she filled the tub with cool water. When it was deep enough, she took the unopened olive oil soap bar that she found amongst all the other products, inhaled deeply, and put her whole head down. It hurt, but she concentrated on what she needed to do. While ignoring the discomfort, she rubbed the soap gently over the wound. The pain flashed through her head like a spear, but she continued stubbornly. She would rather take this pain here and now than an infection that she couldn't treat. She only hoped that it wasn't too late. When she ran out of breath, she surfaced just long enough to get new air down her lungs before continuing. As the dizziness got worse, she stopped and surfaced. It had to be enough now. She couldn't risk falling unconscious into the tub and drown. The water was reddish in color. She grimaced and let the water out. Then, she carefully dabbed the area with a clean towel and looked at it again. A whoosh of relief came through her mouth as she saw it clearly now. *A couple of stitches wouldn't hurt, but it'll heal, and there are no infected areas so far. Thanks to all good and holy things for that. I only wish I had gauze or something.* She didn't think that she had any, but checked her toiletry bag, nonetheless. When her fingers touched the pill jar with Tylenol 3s, she brought it out and stared at it.

"God, am I stupid, or what?" Hurriedly she opened it and swallowed a pill. She couldn't wait to put a wall between her nerve endings and the searing pain. However, there were no gauzes and no Band-Aids. *When I get back, that's the first thing I'll do, buy some and put them in here.* She drank more water and wobbled back to the bed, where she stopped and stared at the made bed with its fresh and clean bed linen. The armchair was still at the door, and this time she knew that she hadn't changed the linen. *I guess that if I can teleport, the hotel cleaner would be able to do so too,* she concluded with a sigh. Not able to worry about it, she crawled into bed and flopped down on her stomach. Soon enough, the artificial wall built up, and she could finally fall asleep painlessly.

If Miriam could trust her inner clock – which she grumpily had to admit that she couldn't – she spent the next seventy-two hours in her room, recuperating. Thanks to her Tylenol pills, she managed to keep the pain at bay. With the aching discomfort gone, she was able to clean the wound properly and also sleep a lot. To hasten the healing process, she decided that she needed to eat more. Thus, she ate everything that was served, but even so, she never seemed to become quite full.

She didn't want to think about the teleporting or the strange town until she had the strength to do something about them. To keep her thoughts from the recent disturbing events, she read and re-read *Wuthering Heights*. However, even though she loved the book, it wasn't the best story to read at a place like this. It didn't make her think about a normal life and a normal world. *From now on, I'm just going to carry happy-go-lucky novels in my bag,* she decided. Therefore, she spent quite some time planning what book would be the best choice for a situation like this and had some fun writing lists in her ever-present notebook. Eventually, she came to the reluctant decision that *Cold Comfort Farm* would be a splendid choice. Not only was it fun and lighthearted; it also reminded her of Carl. Frowning at the list, she felt the longing for him as something painfully ridiculous, especially now, seeing as her independence had become so important to her. After berating herself over and over for her silly need of his company, she decided that she had had enough of self-loathing and let it go. In the calmness that followed, a revelation hit her. *I can be independent and still long for him,* she thought, wide-eyed, and the thought resonated deep within her. *Independence doesn't mean solitude. It doesn't mean that I cannot accept help if I need it. It doesn't mean that I need to do everything on my own.* Then, another thought hit her, *He wouldn't want me to be dependent on him anyway, but that doesn't mean that he wouldn't be there for me if I really needed him. I mean, I don't try to steer him through life, but I would definitely lend him a hand if he were about to fall off a rooftop. Accepting a hand every now and then doesn't take my independence away.* The sudden revelation made her feel both lighthearted and serene. For hours after this, she found herself going back to these thoughts again and again, and finally finding the balance she knew that she had lacked during the past years. *No, not years,* she realized. *My whole life...*

Now, when she for the first time ever felt so in touch with her inner self, she couldn't wait to get back to her own world and set things right with the rest of her life. The possibilities she saw in front of her were suddenly endless, and she couldn't stop smiling at the prospects. It annoyed her immensely that she lacked the physical strength to find a way home. Therefore, she doubled her efforts to regain her health.

On the fifth day after her breakdown, Miriam finally felt strong enough to make an attempt. She woke up to another night with the same beautiful full moon shining over the small courtyard outside her window, and unexpectedly, she reflected over the fact that it was still full moon after so many nights and that she had never seen even a glimpse of daylight since she came here.

"Okay, just another weird thing going on with this place," she muttered. "If I can teleport, why would it be any stranger that it's always night here, or always full moon?" She glared at the slip of sky that she saw over the rooftops around the courtyard.

"I'm tired of this place. I want to go home. Now."

Nothing happened, but she didn't expect it to, seeing as she didn't focus at all on her apartment. During her recovery, she'd come to the conclusion that the extreme agony in her head had been a combination of the initial concussion, the teleporting, and the wall-hitting, and if she reacted so violently on traveling less than a mile within the same dimension, then she definitely did not want to try to teleport between dimensions.

"I'd become a vegetable, I swear. Can't risk that. There has to be another way out."

Resolutely, she packed her bag, including the loyal dinnerware knife, hung it across her chest, and stepped out of the room. The night porter and Matthew were still in the foyer, and she greeted them coldly before heading out.

As the door was about to close behind her, she heard Matthew say, "She'll come around," and Night Porter answer, "Yes. Time is our friend, not hers."

Wide-eyed, she turned around and stared at the now-closed door as shiver after shiver covered her body.

"I need to get out of here," she mumbled and hurried down the street toward the harbor. "I don't have a minute to spare." The statement resonated deeply within her, and with her hair standing on end, she hasted her steps even more to the point that she was on the brink of running.

Even so, she couldn't help but focus on the surroundings of her previous walk here. There was the house with the adorned windowpanes. There was the low staircase with the pale tulips blooming in large pots on each side. *How can they still be alive?* She shook her head. *Anything seems possible here.* There was the alley that rose steeply before it abruptly turned left into darkness. It seemed even more dangerous this night than when she last had looked into it, and she kept as far away as possible when passing.

When she finally reached the harbor, she panted from the run, and the dull headache she still suffered from began to increase.

"Okay, no more running," she mumbled and held a hand at her aching temple.

She avoided looking at the dark castle where it loomed on its island, afraid that she wouldn't have the strength to withstand its luring this time. With her back toward it, she followed the edge of the harbor toward the spot from where she had teleported and continued past it. She would first explore the harbor side, she decided, and then see where some of the winding streets and alleys would lead her. It made sense, she thought, that she felt a need to get to know the town better before she tried any other kind of mind-bending trick.

"I just don't want to mess anything up, especially not myself. And I don't care what they say. Time is on my side. I'll check the town tonight, and if I feel that it will work, I'm out of here." She felt much better after she said it out loud, as if the resistance made her more self-confident.

There wasn't much to see in the harbor. It ended where the broken town wall began. Miriam stood where the main gate had once been and looked out over the overgrown, lonely road that stretched between patches of grass and bare ground. She didn't know why, but she had a distinct feeling that it didn't lead anywhere, and it made her hesitant to even step out on it. The wind played lightly with the high grass, and that was the only sound around. There were no crickets, no night birds, nothing. Not even the water murmured. *It's so lonely.* A deep feeling of this place being lost even in memories and dreams made her throat ache, and she almost wept. *What happened here? Where did all the people go?* In her mind's eye, she saw the town in daylight with people milling around, carts coming through the town gates with wares to sell, ships rocking gently in the harbor while the seamen shouted at each other. *Where did they all go?* she thought again and wiped away a tear that snuck down her cheek. Then, she took a deep breath and shrugged. *It has nothing to do with me.*

She turned her back on the road and followed the main street in between three-story houses. The cobblestones under her feet were slightly uneven and had her walking slower than she liked. *Not that I'm in any kind of hurry, but it's not like I'm out sight-seeing. I mean, it's a bit too ominous a place for that.* She chuckled quietly at the thought even as she cautiously kept watch for anything that could be a threat.

Soon, she reached a large plaza that once must have served as a marketplace. Just like all the other smaller plazas she had passed, large buildings surrounded this one, but these structures had a more administrative feeling to them than the others had had. In the midst was a large stone well. *The vendors probably put up their wares around it,* Miriam thought and walked over to it and looked down. The moon shone in the black water, and a metal bucket hung on a chain at the side, gleaming in the dark as if it invited her to take a sip.

"No, no," she mumbled, "I'm not going to drink from it. I'm not that stupid."

Suddenly, a strong sensation struck her of someone watching her. With her breath stuck in her throat, she turned around. Her eyes darted this way and that, trying to see anything in the many shadows around the plaza, but all was still. *Doesn't mean someone's not there.* Sweat trickled down her spine as she stood on edge, waiting. *I can't just stand here,* she decided. *I'm way too exposed.* She looked the way she'd come, but the thought of going near the castle again made her shiver from bad omens. However, several alleyways led away from the plaza. She counted to eight. One of them seemed less dark than the others. It was located to her right, in between a large building with columns in front of the portico, and a smaller building without any ornaments.

Just as she was about to step away from the well, a flickering of light at the building with the columns caught her attention for a split second, before it died out and left the building dark again. Caught in her step, Miriam studied it with rapidly beating heart and sweaty hands, but she didn't receive any bad vibes from it. *No good vibes either,* she mused, *just neutral.*

Uncertain of what to do, she stood in her place, trying to decide. *It would be stupid going over there,* she thought. *Nothing good has ever come from this town.* She bit her lip. *On the other hand, can it be the way out? Or, maybe it's someone else who's stuck here? Someone who's as cautious of this place as I am?* At this distance, she couldn't be sure, but she thought that the huge doors stood open. It was darker at the opening than it should be would they be closed.

Slowly and on guard, she moved across the plaza toward the wide stairs that led up to the portico and the large entrance. Something stirred on top of the stairs. With her breath caught in her throat, Miriam stopped dead and stared into the dark with wide-opened eyes. *Is it a trap, after all?* She frowned anxiously. *Can very well be.*

For a few seconds, everything seemed to be still, but then, a shadowy figure freed itself from the darkness. Gracefully, it glided into the building through the doors, confirming Miriam's suspicion that they stood open, and a warm light suddenly emanated from the opening, illuminating the wooden doors, making them gleam in a golden hue. *I really thought it was a dead town, after all,* she thought apprehensively. *This is bad – really, really bad. If I can't even trust my own instincts anymore, how the hell will I ever be able to get home?*

Hesitant and watchful, she continued on. The stairs were higher and wider than they had looked from afar, and she had to take larger steps to get up than she had expected to. Before she reached the highest step, she panted heavily, and her legs trembled from exhaustion. It worried her a lot. The physical trauma that she'd been through during the past days must have taken a tougher toll on her body than she had thought. *Can't be helped,* she thought determinedly. *I'm going home as soon as possible anyway. Hopefully, this is the way out.* It didn't feel like it was, but there might be something in there that could help her find it. *Or kill me. Or drive me insane,* she thought with clenched teeth.

As she approached the enormous doors, she felt naked and vulnerable without her gun. With a sense of ridicule, she grabbed her dinnerware knife and held it in position as she quickly looked into the building, FBI-style. Strange mild light floated heavily over book-filled shelves, but nothing stirred. The shadowy figure was nowhere to be seen. Wise from experience, Miriam knew that it didn't mean it wasn't there, but she didn't sense it either, and that should mean more. *If I can trust my instincts, which I seemingly can't.*

Then, she became aware of her surroundings. In awe, she looked around the beautiful, fairy-tale-like library. With its warm brown stone floor, stained-glass dome ceiling, and painted wall panels; lush green with medieval hunting scenes, it surely didn't resemble any kind of library she was used to. The closest shelves were placed directly at the entrance without any kind of logical structure to them. It was as if someone had just tossed them randomly into the huge dome-like space without caring about pretense. She couldn't see any reception area and no checkout desk from where she stood. *Maybe it's not a public library? Am I to step inside someone's private residence?* Maybe, but she decided that she needed answers more than caution. She took a couple of hesitant steps into the enormous building, still on guard, but she couldn't sense anyone around. It felt empty, and yet, it was the first thing here that felt truly alive. Suspiciously, she squinted at the thought but shrugged and continued, half expecting the large doors to slam shut behind her, but nothing happened.

The first shelf was only a couple of yards in, and she approached it carefully while keeping her eyes on her surroundings. She didn't want to be taken by surprise by anyone. Despite that, she touched the wooden shelf without being able to restrain herself. It was lustrous and golden in color and adorned with beautiful floral and geometrical patterns, and the texture was smooth and soft under her fingers, like silk. Miriam leaned her cheek toward the glossy surface and closed her eyes, indulging in the smoothness of the wood and the slight mustiness of the old books combined with a faint scent of vanilla and the full-bodied smell of grass that always seemed to linger in old antique stores. Smiling at the well-known sensation that embraced her, she reached out and let her hand glide over the packed row of books. She caressed them gently before choosing one and taking it from the shelf. When she opened her eyes and looked at the cover, the thick leather-bound book didn't have a title. Struggling with keeping the knife in place without damaging the book, she managed to open it, but to her astonishment, she didn't recognize the alphabet. She closed it, put it back, and took another one. Same kinds of letters in that one, as in the next three she took from the shelf. *Well, nothing else is normal around here, so why did I think they'd use a Latin alphabet? Too bad, though. It would've been nice having something new to read.*

With a sigh, she reluctantly turned away from the shelves. It was no use looking at books that you couldn't read.

Instead, she searched through the library to try and find the shadowy figure, but no one was around on the lower level, so Miriam began to ascend the stairs. The grand helical staircases that adorned the walls at opposite sides of the library were architectural marvels with their iron-wrought railings and ruby-glass inlays. She felt like a queen walking up to the large circular balcony that stretched around the downstairs library like a necklace. *Or I would've, had I had a ball gown or something,* she thought with a slight smirk. For a moment, the air shifted and gave her a sudden sense of layers of fabric wooshing around her legs. Immediately, she stopped and looked down at her body, only to see her regular jeans and shirt.

"I could've sworn…" she began but shook her head. "Whatever," she muttered.

251

The important part was to find the person who might be lurking around, not experimenting with this realm's physical laws, even though it was tempting.

"I can do that in the safety of my hotel room, close to a bed and a toilet, should I need them – if I'm going back, that is."

As she continued on and reached the highest step, the huge multi-colored glass dome stretched out above her, showering her in a faint light from the moon overhead. She couldn't resist rising to her toes to try and touch the glass. It was way too high up, of course, but she let her hands bathe in the light and watched how the different colors played on her skin. Delightful, she turned her attention to the rest of the balcony, and let her gaze wander over the many sofa groups that stood around, haphazardly thrown out onto the floor, just as the shelves on the main floor. It looked chaotic but inviting. She wouldn't have minded spending some time reading here. However, she couldn't see anyone else around, so she leaned toward the balustrade and looked down. From where she stood, she had a perfect view of the whole library, but she couldn't see a living soul anywhere.

"I must have missed the person going out," Miriam mumbled to herself, sulking a bit. With a sigh, she turned her back to the balustrade. "I guess it doesn't matter," she concluded. "If he or she is hostile, I'm rid of him or her, and if not, well, I'm pretty good at solving puzzles. I can find my way out of here without anyone's help."

As she pondered her next move, she looked back at the rd, velvety sofas and the beautifully ornated tables. In the middle of the balcony, not far from where Miriam stood, was an enormous fireplace. It, too, had ruby-glass inlays in an intricate pattern.

"It must look beautiful when lit." She could just imagine the sparkle from the red glass. The next moment, the dry wood in the insert suddenly burst into flames. Miriam gasped and took an involuntary step to the side, finding only air where she put down her foot. With a sharp intake of breath, she managed to grab hold of the railing to stabilize herself. As her eyes darted to the staircase that was much closer than she had thought, the fire went out. Sweat wetted her armpits, and her heart hammered hard in her chest.

High time to get out of here, she thought and rushed down the stairs, terrified that the doors would be closed and that she had walked into a trap after all. To her enormous relief, they still stood ajar, and she hurried out into the night. She didn't stop until she reached the houses on the opposite side of the plaza.

For a while, she stood with her back against a cold stone wall, trying to catch her breath, while watching the doors to the library. Nothing happened, and no one was in sight.

Okay, good. Now move, please. Get out of here. After cautiously looking around the empty plaza, she decided to walk a street in a direction she hadn't tried yet, hoping that it would take her someplace from where she could reach her own world. As she began walking, she became aware of a thought that hovered just outside her reach. *It's something I know. Something that might help me getting back... God! What is it?* She stopped again and buried her face in her hands, trying to think. *I know there's something I've overlooked. What is it?* Frustrated, she rubbed her eyes, and suddenly an image of the church on the hill popped up in her mind.

"Yes! That's it!" she exclaimed. "I never investigated it properly. I can't believe it just slipped my mind like that." Looking around, she tried to orient herself.

"I came from there, so the harbor must be over there, which means that the inn is—"

Suddenly, a loud bang from the library doors made her jolt. She dashed around with the dinnerware knife in a hard, tense grip. Gasping, and with her heart hammering in her dry throat, she struggled to make sense of what it was she saw, but she couldn't wrap her mind around it. The plaza was filled with a compact, floating darkness. Whatever it was, it clearly didn't have any good intentions, and the hair on Miriam's arms stood straight up in fear.

Move, Miriam. You need to move. Now! Move, damn it!

With feet that didn't want to react to her inner screams, she desperately fought with herself to back away, but her whole body was petrified. Her limbs simply refused to respond to her frantic attempts. The darkness began to stir and separate, and with a shock, she realized that it wasn't compact darkness, it were shadows standing there, watching her. The malevolence that radiated from them seemed to take on physical form and began to reach out to her as smoky, see-through tendrils. She stared at them and how they slowly floated in the air toward her, conscious as if they could sense her, smell her. A clawing feeling of terror grabbed her deep in her stomach and made her nauseous. Her breaths became heavier, and it was hard to get enough air into her aching lungs. Every time she blinked it looked as if the shadows had moved closer. A scream wanted to tear its way out of her but got captured in her dry and clenched throat. Her face was clammy with cold sweat, and she tried hard not to blink.

Move, you idiot! Move!

Finally, her feet jerked, and she managed to take a step back, but her foot twisted underneath her as she stepped on some loose cobblestones, and she lost her balance and fell. The knife slipped from her hand and bounced away somewhere, disappearing into the shadows. Without losing any time, she sprang up, prepared to run, but no one was there anymore.

Panting in fear, she attempted to look around in all directions simultaneously while trying to get away from the plaza without it seeming as if she was running. She had a distinct feeling that it would be a bad idea to run. Her heart hammered wildly in her throat, and then a door to her left suddenly opened without a sound, like a wide gap that wanted to swallow her whole, and something moved inside.

Miriam hastened her steps, not running yet, but almost, as she couldn't control her pace, and then something stirred behind her, tugged hard at her hair. She gasped, and all her self-control disappeared, and she ran. A sense of excitement and anticipation built up in the air, and it made her skin crawl.

Another door opened in front and to her right, and something came out from the opening. It looked like a mist, greenish-grayish in color. Abruptly, she turned into another, narrower street. When it made a sharp left turn, she found herself in front of a house flanked by two other buildings.

Trapped.

Gasping in dread, she turned around only to see the mist slowly but deliberately floating toward her. Behind her, the three doors opened, and when she turned toward them, even more mist floated out. Panicking, she closed her eyes hard and thought of her room, of the big bed in the middle with its white well-scented sheets, the lion-colored armchairs, and the small round table with its long cloth in the same color as the chairs. She thought of her bag sitting on the table and of the steady wall lamps in their frosted glass shades. She visualized so hard that her head began to pound and sweat broke out on her face. Blood trickled down her neck from the head wound.

After an eternity without anything happening, she cautiously opened her eyes. Everything in the hotel room swayed and twirled around her, but her relief was so great that she sobbed. When she lifted her foot to take a step toward her bed, she lost her balance and fell. She didn't faint this time, nor did she vomit, but it was close. Little by little, she managed to crawl up her bed and slump into it, panting and wheezing while her heart hammered irregularly in her chest. *Can't... do... this... again... can't...* Even with her eyes closed, she could feel everything twirl as if the bed was caught on a crazy merry-go-round. The pain in her head was so intense this time that it made her cry, and she lay curled up in a fetal position cradling it.

Time flies.

Time stands still.

Time works differently.

And Time loses its meaning.

It started slowly with only a few shadows, but soon they were all there, standing outside her window. They didn't try to come in. They didn't move. They just stood there, pressed together, silently watching the closed curtains; the whole courtyard filled with shadows, silently waiting for her to come out. She didn't know why they were so present in her mind. Sometimes it felt as if the green-gray mist had physically crawled inside her head through the open wound.

She cried a lot. Sometimes she spoke quietly to them from behind the curtains. Sometimes she begged them to disappear. Sometimes she yelled at them to get the hell out of there. Sometimes she just hid under the bed.

It happened that she knew her own name, but as time gently stroked its fingers over her mind, it was harder to recollect, and it lost its meaning. It happened that she found herself muttering that time wasn't on her side after all, and she had a feeling that she should know what she meant by it, but she didn't.

Sometimes she knew that she was losing it. At those rare moments, she cried and screamed and banged her forehead on the wall, hitting herself in the face, and bit her wrists until the skin broke because she didn't dare to leave her room to find a way out. She promised herself to keep the sneaking insanity at bay and rattled frantically about everything she knew about herself to keep a sliver of her mind sane, to continue to know who she was. At other times, she stared at the reflection in the mirror and wondered who she was looking at and why that person had so many bruises on her face.

The presence of the other guests in the inn had begun to make themselves known to her, and she sometimes felt how they stood outside her door, whispering to each other. That whisper came to her like tiny mice paw-prints in her mind. Sometimes she yelled at them to go away. At those times, the whispers stopped long enough for her to be able to curl up in fetal position and sleep.

Every now and again, when she woke up, a new tray of food was placed on the table. She never saw anyone enter, and the chair was always in the same place in front of the door. She didn't eat. Somehow that food made her even more aware of the shadows and the whispers. She had stopped showering too after the water that came out of the showerhead turned into tears and whispered to her about their losses.

This time when she woke up, she lay in bed and stared up at the ceiling, followed the cracks with her gaze until it seemed as if they became aware of her and stared back. Whimpering, she turned around and curled up into fetal position again, hugging herself. Eventually, her heartbeat calmed down, and she wondered what had happened and why she had been afraid. Slowly, she sat up on the bed and looked around the room. It was empty, but the usual tray stood with steaming food in a bowl on the table. She frowned at it. The way the tray was placed on the table disturbed her. It didn't align with either the wall or the chair. Fidgety in her whole body, she stood up and went over to it, studying it thoroughly. No, it didn't align.

"It has to align," she muttered and fiddled with it. "It has to align if the door shall open…" More and more exasperated, she tried out different placements to make it look like it was part of the room. As she became even more aggravated by her inability to align it properly, she pushed the food tray aside with a low wail. A bag she hadn't noticed fell on the floor, and its contents poured out. She looked at the things as if in a dream, and slowly, she crouched to study them closer. It felt as if she should recognize them. Amongst the clutter was one thing that seemed to call out to her. What was it called now again? The word had slipped her mind, but her hands caressed the pieces of it, and a vision that seemed brighter and clearer than the whispers and the shadows, appeared in front of her, watching her with sad eyes.

"Hi, Carl," she smiled at him. "I've missed you. Where were you? I've been looking for you." The vision disappeared without saying anything, and she inhaled stuttering. "No! Please, don't go. Don't leave me here."

Tears fell silently from her eyes, but somehow, she felt cleaner, clearer than she had for— how long? She didn't know. Too long. She inhaled shakily again and stood up, straighter in her back and more determined than in a long time. With a piercing gaze, she turned to the window and opened the curtains. The presence out there didn't have any power over her anymore. They were mere shadows. They had lost everything, and that was what they wanted her to do too. She was not going to let them get to her. She was not going to hide in here anymore. She was going home.

The full moon shone on the courtyard. In silence, she watched it being empty. All the shadows were gone. Some of the mist in her head cleared away, and instead of pulling the curtains together, she let them hang open. Once again, she crouched at her things on the floor and started to put them back in her bag. As she worked, she talked to herself with a deliberately clear and calm voice.

"I am Miriam Glukel Goldblum. I am thirty-one years old. My birthday is on September twelfth. I will turn thirty-two. My sister is Bethany Bluma Miller. She is thirty-six years old. She is married to Ted Miller. Their son is Markus. He has just turned twelve. I was at his party. I gave him a camera so he can photograph wildlife. My mother is Mathilde Goldblum, and my father is Jakob Goldblum. They are both sixty-seven years old. They were both babies when my grandparents fled France in nineteen forty-three. They all love me very much." As she continued talking calmly to herself, she went into the bathroom and packed her toiletry bag as well. When she returned to the bedroom, her gaze fell on the tray, and in silent astonishment, she saw how it aligned with the wall and the chair in a perfect triangle. A slow chill crept down her spine before she turned her back at it, pushed the chair in front of the door aside and left the room without looking back.

Even as she passed Night Porter and Matthew in the foyer, she talked aloud, counting out her few living relatives and their ages, where they came from, what pets they had, if any, and what their names were, before going on to those of her relatives that had perished in the concentration camps during the war. As far back as she could remember, their names had been imprinted in her mind. *So many, they were so many. I remember that. I remember them.* The more she talked, the more of her and of herself came back to her.

As she walked down the empty street toward the harbor, she began to recite the *Tanakh*. The *Tanakh* had been such an important part of her childhood. It had often been recited at home and at the synagogue. Once, she knew all the *Tanakh* by heart, but that was a long time ago. Nowadays, she wasn't very good at it, but she remembered that she had a friend, once close, but now distant, with whom she had had many philosophical discussions about it. *And so many disagreements. It was silly how much we didn't agree upon. I remember that too. And that he called me an* apikoros. *God, he made me so angry, and I refused to talk to him for months after that. But he was right, I became an unbeliever eventually. What was his name now again? A something... Andre? No, Ardy. Ardy Meier.* She smiled triumphantly as the name came to her, and with that the image of his sensitive face with glasses and dark hair. Her parents had hoped that she would marry him, but neither she nor he liked that idea. Her mom had been especially disappointed when Miriam frankly told her that she was neither in love with him nor would she like to have him raise any children with her. She couldn't help grinning at the

259

memory of how shocked her mom had been and how amused her dad had looked.

Pleased with herself that she remembered so much, she recited the text passages of the *Tanakh* that she still recalled. As always, it was the poetry of the *Shir Hashirim* that came to mind. She started out with the first chapter but skipped the first line about Solomon and went directly to the part she liked.

"'*Let him kiss me with the kisses of his mouth, for your love is better than wine.*' I love that part. It's so beautiful and so true," she mumbled. She skipped a couple of other lines. "I like this one too, '*Draw me, we will run after you; the king brought me to his chambers. We will rejoice and be glad in you. We will recall your love more fragrant than wine; they have loved you sincerely.*'" Even though the lines didn't describe anything chaste, they managed to sound so sweet and innocent. "And these ones, '*A bundle of myrrh is my beloved to me; between my breasts he shall lie. A cluster of henna-flowers is my beloved to me, in the vineyards of Ein-Gedi.*'"

She remembered Ardy's face as she recited those lines for him when she was seventeen and he was nineteen, and their parents were at their worst. His face had been as red as a beetroot, and she had been bad enough to point it out. She couldn't help laughing at the memory, and the shadows seemed to pull even further away.

"That's right!" she shouted, suddenly angry. It felt good to be angry. It felt clean. "I'm not afraid of you anymore. You can't claim me!"

Abruptly, their presence was gone from her mind, completely gone, for the first time since forever, and the harbor opened up in front of her. Still reciting, too afraid to let go of the tiny sliver of sanity that she had left, she walked along the harbor until she could see the broken town wall. She sat down on a stone bench from which she could see the whole harbor from one end to the other. For once, she didn't feel frightened being outside of her room.

"*I am a rose of Sharon, a rose of the valleys,*" she mumbled, reciting lines from chapter two. "'*As a rose among the*

*thorns, so is my beloved among the daughters. As an apple tree among
the trees of the forest, so is my beloved among the sons; in his shade I
delighted and sat, and his fruit was sweet to my palate.* "

Afraid to shut her eyes, she fell silent and followed
the strong instinct that told her that Carl was the key, that her
love for him would help her find her way out of here. First,
she concentrated on him, on the different expressions his
eyes showed her when they were together; the happy one, the
amused, the sincere, and the mischievous, and above all, the
always present reserved air that kept her from coming too
close, which told her that he didn't have the same feelings for
her as she had for him, that even though he enjoyed her
company as a friend, it was all she would ever be to him.
Sometimes, it felt as if she didn't have any pride left at all,
that she continued to make a fool out of herself, and that he
just felt sorry for her, but none of that mattered. As long as
she was allowed in his presence, she would be happy.

That last thing was a lie, of course. If she was
completely honest with herself, she knew perfectly well that
she wanted more than friendship, more than the occasional
tug at her arm, much more than that. Even though she
sometimes cried because of him and the unrequited feelings
she nursed, she knew that she would greedily collect every
crumb he threw at her.

*No, this is not the right approach. I'll never get home thinking
like this. I could as well be thinking about my mother and hope for
something good to happen.*

Sighing, she steered away from the thoughts of her
misplaced love and concentrated on a physical place that she
might be able to reach, even from here.

She thought of his apartment, and of the warm colors
that always made her feel so happy and welcome every time
she visited his home. She thought of the many bookcases that
stood wherever there was room, filled with books in so many
different languages. He had told her once that he had read
them all. That still amazed her. She thought of the huge
coffee-colored sofa and the many Arabic wall art and rugs

that worked so well together, that were friends with each other, and of the potted plants and the standing candelabras that he always lit when dusk broke, and how the colors, the light, and the incense created a magical atmosphere.

She thought of the many hours they had spent there together, and of the conversations they had enjoyed there when they explored what they liked and what they didn't like, what they agreed upon and what they didn't agree upon, and how easy it was to talk with him and respect him and how easy it was to also receive his respect. *Sometimes he respects me a little too much,* she thought grumblingly.

Quickly, she focused her thoughts on all the different variations of teas he had treated her during the past two years, and all the meals they had cooked together in the small, but cozy and well-planned kitchen, and how they had shared not only the food but also their own perception of the food, at either the freestanding kitchen island or in the living room.

She thought of—

Something stirred in the corner of her eye. She gasped, and her mind quivered. Anxiously, she began to recite again in a trembling voice, "*'My beloved raised his voice and said to me, 'Arise, my beloved, my fair one, and come away. For behold, the winter has passed; the rain is over and gone.'*" The shivers of her mind calmed down and still reciting, she dared to turn her head and look at what had happened. At first, she couldn't see anything that was different. It was just a feeling that something had changed.

"*'Until the sun spreads, and the shadows flee, go around—'*" The words stopped abruptly as she finally saw what was new. There was a bridge further down the harbor's edge that hadn't been there before. It stretched high above the water to a point where she lost track of it. Hesitantly, she rose and took a couple of steps toward it. This could be the way home. It could also be a trap, but if she didn't try, she'd never know.

"I think it's my way home," she mumbled, but then she shook her head. "No, it is my way home. I know it is my way home." The more she repeated it, the more she believed in it, and it seemed as if the bridge got stronger and heavier, sturdier by her conviction.

With light-hearted steps, she went closer, but suddenly, there was a presence so strong and alive, so thick behind her. She gasped, and stopped dead, but didn't dare to turn around and look. It was so close, whatever it was. It was too close. Tears of terror and panic fell from her eyes, but she couldn't move. Her limbs were locked in place, and no matter how hard she struggled, how loudly she screamed in her mind to GET MOVING, she couldn't move. It was even difficult to breathe. Shivering in her whole body, she closed her eyes, waiting for the presence to come closer and when the hand touched her shoulder, she collapsed.

Part Four

where no sun shines

Chapter 15

Instead of the door that he came through, there was a European-looking church located in its place. Carl cleared his throat and tugged nervously at the scarf. The church's shadow loomed over him. It gave him an extremely bad feeling, making him hesitate even at the thought of going in. *Alright, just a peek to see what's inside.*

He doubted that it would be the basement. It would be too easy. He hung Miri's scarf around his neck and thought that he could smell her perfume on it underneath the distinct smell of wet concrete. The weak whiff of Miri that emerged from it calmed him down, but it also made his heart beat extra hard with hesitant hope and warmed his body with anticipation.

He cleared his throat again and concentrated on the big door. It was heavier than he thought it would be, and he just poked his head inside to take a quick look around. When he saw a regular church with no people, he immediately went back out.

"Yeah, too easy, indeed. So, now what? Shall I wait for Olwen, or shall I search for Miri?"

The longing to start looking for her immediately was so strong that it felt like a physical need in his body, but he had been reckless so many times before, and who knew what could lay in waiting for unaware travelers?"

In the church's shadow, Carl walked to the edge of the hill. Without knowing what to feel or think, he looked out over the small town below. It was situated at the seashore and resembled a bean in shape. He had a hard time to wrap his mind around this. What was it? Where was it? Had he stepped into another dimension, or had he managed to go back in time? He tried to recall the history lessons from his Star Student years and had a feeling that the town that lay sleeping in the moonlight didn't resemble any European town during any era. There were things missing, as far as he could

265

see anyway, like an execution place, for example. He wasn't sure that was a good sign, though. *This place feels like someone made it up.* A tiny ripple caressed his back, and suddenly, he shuddered violently.

Not allowing the bad omens to take control of him, he studied the little town more closely. Just as with the door in the basement, he had a feeling that the air trembled around its edges. He frowned uneasily.

"I hope it won't collapse right in front of me."

He stared at the town and tried to see the vibrations, but every time he looked directly at them, they disappeared, unlike the clearly visible vibrations around the door in the basement. "No, I don't think it'll collapse." He tried to sound convinced and self-assured but failed.

How long would it take for Olwen to get to Kroger's? An hour? He didn't know how far away she lived, and then there was the matter of how long it would take for her to open the damn door — if it was still there.

"Alright, she'll get max two hours. If she's not here by then, I'll go on my own."

Satisfied with his decision, he sat down on the grass and continued to try to figure out the town. It gave him the sense of a fairy-tale town in a dark fantasy story, the one in which you knew something bad would happen, and you never had any idea of what went on behind your back.

He moved uncomfortably on the ground and took out his cell phone to check the time. Ten sixteen. To his disbelief, he did have some reception, lousy reception, of course, but still. With trembling fingers, he fast-dialed Miri, but no tone was heard, and no one picked up the receiver. He glared at the phone and put it down again.

Restlessly, he stood up and walked around the church while studying its architecture. It was long since he visited Europe, and even though he wasn't religious, he appreciated the beauty the churches provided the European cities. This church, however, did not radiate any of the serene magnificence he was used to, but malicious intensity. The strangest thing was that he somehow recognized it from somewhere. Carl shook his head. At this point, he couldn't put his finger on it. He checked his cell phone again. Ten twenty-eight. It was going to be a long wait.

To make the time go quicker and to keep his mind from nagging at the thought of the malicious feeling of both the church and the town, he started to sing with a low voice, beginning with *Here Comes the Sun* with The Beatles, a song that seemed very inappropriate at this place, which in an odd way amused him, and went on to *Kbar Chway* with Darine Hadchiti. He had a melodic voice, nothing special, but he enjoyed the way it sounded when it blended together with his favorite music. Soon enough, though, his voice wavered and broke. It felt as if it disturbed even the air, and that he lured some kind of presence to the church, the kind of presence that you definitely did not want to have around.

Nervously, he once more walked around the church to get rid of the ill omen feeling. Three rounds later, he checked his cell phone again. It showed ten fifty-five. *Just a little bit more than an hour now. Damn waiting.* To calm himself down, he developed three different Zen-like patterns that he walked over and over. After every finished pattern, he checked his cell and phoned Miri without any result.

It felt like he was walking in some kind of time-jelly, in which he didn't manage to get anywhere no matter how hard he tried. He was into his twenty-seventh damn pattern walking when the door to the church suddenly opened and Olwen and Omega stepped out. As the door closed behind them, they stopped, flabbergasted, and stared at the view. To Carl's relief, they seemed to come well prepared with large backpacks and Olwen's doctor's bag. *Good thinking. Miri might need medical attention if we find her.* He frowned and corrected himself. *No, not 'if' – 'when.' When we find her.*

From his point of view, the two women exited directly from the inner of the church, and he couldn't see the basement behind them. It took them a couple of seconds before they noticed him approaching them.

Omega's kind face lit up with a smile. "There you are," she said. "We weren't sure what to expect."

"Yeah, no wonder." As he turned to face Olwen, he immediately realized how displeased she was with him. "Olwen," he nodded toward her, silently wondering what the hell he had done now.

"Good to see that you're finally working," she said sarcastically.

Carl blinked and stared at her. "I'm sorry?"

"We needed you, Octavius. The report writing on the serial killer case was not a priority. Our Project was, and you just ignored us."

Carl exhaled slowly and bit his tongue to not slip any angry words. Instead, he chose his words carefully while thinking about the absurd in the circumstances, having to answer to his P.I. about his work performance while standing in another kind of fucking dimension.

"I'm sorry if this is how you perceived the situation, Olwen. When Armand called, he didn't explain anything. It was hard to come to a correct decision without the facts. At the point when he called, Allie and I had hardly slept at all in forty-eight hours, and we were really pressed to finish that report. If I had gotten any kind of information about the Project, I might have decided differently."

Olwen stared at him. "I'm sorry?" she said. "It's a Project. Armand isn't entitled to explain anything to you on the phone. You come to our aid when we call on you."

In silence, Carl looked back at her, and for the first time, he placed himself in her shoes.

"You're right," he admitted eventually, as he thought of how irritated he would have been had the roles been reversed. "It won't happen again."

With a short nod, she said, "Good." Then, she looked around and seemed to have composed herself quicker than he had. "I'm happy to see that you found the gate. We've been searching for it."

"You have?"

The sudden flash of gloating didn't fit her sweet-looking face well, but Carl kept a neutral expression. It amazed him how tired he was of keeping up his disinterested appearance, but this was how Olwen and Omega knew him, and he wasn't keen on changing it here and now. There was enough friction between them as it was. He glanced at Omega. As usual, she kept quiet and let Olwen do the talking, but he could clearly see her concern about the whole situation.

"Yes. We finally got to know that she wanted to destroy the portal and that's why she bombed Kroger's. She'd been trapped in here with her baby, and the baby died."

"Alright. Can you give me some details, like who 'she' is?"

"Her name's Florence Tyler. She got identified shortly after her head was found. When Andy and his team combed through her apartment, they found her diary in which she had written down her experiences and her motives for bombing Kroger's. Andy turned the case over to the Faculty, and Armand handed it over to us. We've been searching for this portal for some days now."

"Huh."

Omega broke in with her gentle voice. "Jones told us that Ophelia is trapped in here."

Carl nodded. "That's what we think, yes."

"I'm not pleased that you involved him, Octavius," Olwen snapped.

Carl bit his tongue and said in his usual expressionless tone, "He was the one who alerted me."

Olwen frowned, and he wished that she could stop trying to frame him. Eventually, she would only embarrass herself in front of Omega and lose trustworthiness.

In an attempt to steer her thoughts away from the recent events in the every-day-world, he nodded at the little town at the bottom of the hill.

"I haven't looked for her yet. I wanted to wait for you."

Omega let up her voice again. "Where do you think she is?"

He was about to shrug but held back. "I don't know." Then, he glanced at Olwen's irritated face. *Why the hell is she so damn annoyed? It's not only because of me. There's another reason that makes her tick like this.* "Did Florence Tyler write anything in her diary, like landmarks and such?"

"She described a harbor, that's all."

"Um, and that the town is hard to find a way through," Omega added timidly.

Carl nodded. It didn't surprise him. Most medieval towns were a maze, and he doubted that this one would be any different, even though the city planning might be artificial.

Then, he gave the women a glance and took a couple of steps toward the gravel-covered road to see if they would follow him. He yearned to start looking for Miri now. To his relief, they immediately walked up to him.

"Florence Tyler obviously found a way out of here," he said. "Did she describe how?"

Olwen frowned again, but this time, it was an intrigued frown coming from thinking through a problem.

"She mentions it, but it's not like a building kit from Ikea." Omega giggled at her side, but Olwen ignored her. Instead, she gave him a side-glance. "The journal's very fragmented and hard to read. You can clearly tell that she's struggling with reality."

Carl was careful not to show anything of the worried pang that hit him hard in his stomach. Miriam had been here for two weeks. How long time had Florence spent here?

"Does she say anything about how long she was here?" he asked, casually.

Olwen shook her head. "Nothing at all, and she was never reported missing either. Apparently, she was very lonely. No close relatives or friends. No records of who the father is either."

They walked in silence for a while. Olwen didn't seem keen on giving him more information at the moment, and he was too anxious to find Miri to coax her. He recalled that she had said something about a baby, but he didn't want to ask. He had had enough of dead children.

Soon, they stood in front of an old wooden bridge that would take them over a moat and through the town gate. Carl continued to lead the way. As long as Olwen didn't protest, he was going to use his male dominance for once. It wouldn't make him more popular in Olwen's eyes, and he might regret it later, but right now, he didn't care. The only thing he cared about was finding Miri. *What if she's gone mad? No, stop it. Stop it right there! She's going to be fine.*

As soon as they entered the town, Carl led the way to the left. During the time he had waited for them to arrive, he'd had plenty of opportunities to imprint the layout of the town in his mind. The fastest way to get to the harbor would probably be to follow the town wall.

No one talked as they walked through the quiet, empty streets, but he had a feeling that something stirred around them. *Probably the damn vibrations,* he thought, trying to calm the anxiety that wanted to take over him. It irked him that he was so nervous and so on edge. It wasn't how he usually behaved during Research Projects. *On the other hand, I wouldn't call this my average RP.* The explanation didn't feel right, though. Upon a closer look, it was more like these nervous sensations were forced upon him and wanted him to lose control over himself. Glancing at the other two, Carl realized that they, too, were on edge, both sharing an expression of extreme tenseness. *Guess I'm proven right,* he thought grimly.

Without stopping in his tracks, he said as casually as he could, "This place, I think it's trying to force sensations of anxiety on us. I feel more nervous than I should be, like I'm a nine-tailed cat in a room filled with doors swinging in the draft."

271

Omega giggled again, and it sounded more relaxed than he expected. Even Olwen forced out a smile. The rest of the walk was more composed and calmer, as if their combined presence was harder to penetrate now that they were aware of what might be going on. *What a damn, scary place this is if that's the case, if it's forcefully trying to make people go mad.* Again, he shied away from the thought of how Miri might have been affected after two weeks. *I should've tried harder to find her from the beginning. I should've known something was wrong as soon as I climbed down into the damn basement.* He clenched his teeth hard. *Yeah, you're doing a great job putting all the blame on yourself, Carl. Stop trying to win all the points in 'Who's the best martyr?'.*

The cobblestone streets meandered on in what felt like an endless walk in one of those stupid corn mazes his parents took him to when he was a kid, and the longer it took them to reach the harbor, the more present the anxiety became again. Carl had to consciously force himself to calm down and breathe easier.

Finally, the street they followed ended at a once-stately town gate that now lay in ruins. If they were to continue to the right, they'd step right onto the dock. They exchanged relieved looks, and in silent agreement, they walked onto the broad waterfront. Then, Omega suddenly stopped dead and grabbed a hold on Carl's arm.

"Octavius!" She pointed at something in front of them. At first, he didn't catch what she was seeing, but then— Was it? Could it be?

"Miri." The name came out as a soft breath. His cheeks blossomed, and his heart hammered. She was sitting on a stone bench some hundred yards away, looking out over the water.

For a couple of seconds, he stood as if frozen. It was as if he was afraid that what he saw wasn't real. For so long, had he thought her dead, and there… There she was. His face felt numb from the shock of actually seeing her sitting over there, and it wasn't until this moment that he realized that he hadn't believed they would find her, that he hadn't believed in his own theory.

Omega smiled openly. "Come on. Let's go."

Just as they were about to continue on, Miri stood up and took a couple of steps in their direction, clearly without noticing them, but then, she froze.

Omega gasped. "What the hell is that?" Her voice trembled slightly.

Carl followed her gaze and let out a sharp gasp too. Some kind of greenish-gray fog crawled on the ground toward Miriam. It looked as if she was aware of it. Her stance was that of a deer in headlight.

"Move, Miri!" he shouted, but the words fell dead in front of him. Without another word, he started to run and heard the footsteps of the others behind him. The fog reached Miriam, who stood still as a damn statue, and to Carl's horror, it rose behind her, forming into a humanoid shape. He didn't know that he could run this fast, but it felt like he was flying down the dock. It didn't help. He wasn't fast enough. The fog raised an arm-like limb and put it on Miriam's shoulder. The next second, Miriam fell on the ground while the fog became more compact. It crouched over her lifeless body and laid a now solid hand on top of Miriam's head, and even from this distance, Carl could hear a sickening slurping sound.

A gunshot disturbed the otherwise completely silent town, and the gush of the bullet was too close to his shoulder to be comfortable. It didn't seem as the figure was hit, but the slurping stopped, and the humanoid fog stood and turned toward them. As Carl closed in on Miri, the fog floated away some ten yards or so but continued to keep them under surveillance. At this point, he didn't care about the fog as long as it kept away.

Finally, he reached her and fell at her side, checking her pulse before he had even managed to land properly on his feet. Olwen and Omega ran past him, trying to close in on the humanoid, but it floated away even more. Olwen shot at it again without any results. He didn't care. Trembling, he touched Miri's cold, clammy face. Her weak, irregular breathing worried him. She was clearly in deep shock. Somewhere far away, Olwen shouted, "Don't follow it, Omega, it's trying to lure us somewhere. Let's stick together."

"Miri," he mumbled. "Don't die on me! We're here now. We'll manage together, as we always do." He checked her body to see if there was anything, clothes or belt or something else that restricted her, but her clothes hung loosely on her body as if she'd lost more weight than she could handle, and she didn't wear any belt. When he saw a heavily bleeding head wound, he swore quietly. While checking his pockets for something, anything, to use as pressure, he tried to remember his first aid, but it was a couple of years since he took the course last time. *I'll improvise. I'm good at that.* When he didn't find anything in his pockets, except her ring, he took off his jacket and her scarf that was still draped around his neck, and wrapped them around her, trying to keep her warm, before taking off his T-shirt. He folded it neatly, put it on the wound, and let her head do the pressure. Then he placed her feet high in his lap to hopefully help reduce the shock. *Or is it better to place her in recovery position?* He couldn't remember.

It worried him immensely that she had so many bruises in different stages on her face. Some were yellow and old, and some were purple and new. He took her hands and caressed them. They were so damn cold. To his shock, her wrists were full of bite marks. Reluctantly, he pulled up the sweater's arms and saw her skin covered in bruises and bite marks.

"What the hell have you been through, Miri?" Tears burned his eyes and blurred his sight. "I came as quickly as I could." Anxiously, he stopped talking. Suddenly afraid that she might be able to hear him, he decided to put on his composed and reassuring persona. It wouldn't help her if he was upset and anguished. He wiped away his tears and took a calming breath. "Don't worry, *albi*, it's all good, it's all going to be fine." He looked around, trying to see Olwen and Omega, but they were gone somewhere. In his mind, he swore but didn't let anything else but calmness radiate from him. His hands revealed him, though, as they trembled when he placed her Star Student ring on her finger. It felt better seeing it in its right spot, and tenderly, he brought her hand up to his cheek, leaned into it slightly. It was cold to his touch, and he clasped it in his own hands, trying to warm it.

When he estimated that fifteen minutes had passed, he checked her head wound again. To his relief, the pressure seemed to have helped. It didn't bleed anymore. "That's great news, *habibti*. You're going to be just fine. We just need you to get warmer." He draped his jacket tighter around her, but it didn't help much. She needed a blanket or two, and she needed a doctor. Where the hell had Olwen and Omega gone? He needed them here, not chasing some damn fog monster. *Priorities, teammates. Come on now. Please!* He couldn't do anything but wait and hold her hands and talk to her. His legs fell asleep, but he refused to move her.

Eventually, he heard footsteps approaching, and when he looked up, Olwen and Omega came toward him, looking grim. *Finally.*

When Olwen crouched beside Miri and looked her over, he said in a voice not as steady as he had wished, "She has a bad head wound and lots of bruises everywhere and some minor scrapes. I managed to stop the bleeding, but she needs to be checked out."

Olwen nodded. "We found an inn of some sort. It's open."

He stared at her. "An inn? Really? I thought this place was, well, abandoned."

"Me too. We shouldn't move her, but there's no other choice. She needs to get warm and have that wound looked after. Let's carry her there. Octavius, you take her upper body, Omega, you take the mid-part, and I take the feet. Omega, your job is to stabilize her. I'll count the pace."

Miriam was lighter than he thought she would be, but she became heavier the longer it took them to get to the place. Soon enough, they were all panting. Eventually, they reached the inn. Olwen, being the closest, opened the door, and they went in. The foyer they stepped into was old-fashioned-looking, and behind the counter stood a short man, beaming at them.

"Welcome, welcome. Lovely to get new guests. Oh, poor, poor Miriam. She shouldn't have tried to leave. Come, I'll show you to her room."

Without finding the breath to answer him, they carried her up a few steps and into a corridor where they stopped outside an adorned door with the number six on the side. The man opened it, and they carried Miriam to a big bed and lay her down. Carl immediately put the thick duvet on top of her and listened with only half an ear to the conversation between Olwen and the man.

"You want a room of your own, yes? And the lovely young lady too, I'm sure. Carl, I assume you will sleep here."

He jerked his head up in surprise by the use of his name and met the bland little smile on the porter's lips.

"What?"

"Well, if you insist, there's a nice room for you too, but your friend would be quite sad. She is so very fond of you."

"If you could be so kind, I'd prefer my own room," he said coolly.

The slimy man chuckled. "Of course, of course." Then he turned to Olwen. "Ma'am, if you could follow me?"

She made an irritated gesture. "It has to wait. If you'll excuse me, I need to check on my co-worker here, so she doesn't die on us."

A secretive smile played on the porter's lips. "Ah, no need to worry. The air here is so very, very healthy. She'll come around in no time, but suit yourselves. I'll be back shortly."

As soon as the door closed behind him, they all shared a glance.

"What the hell was that?" Omega said eventually but shrugged. "Whatever. I'll fix some boiling water and see if they have any gauze and such."

"Good thinking. We need more than I brought with me," Olwen said as Omega rose. The younger woman nodded and went out the door. As soon as it closed behind her, Olwen gave Carl a short side-glance as she started to unbutton Miri's jeans. "Could you help, please? We need to get her properly warm. These damn jeans are wet."

"Um... Alright..." He cringed but came over to her and tried to help her with slightly fumbling hands. It felt extremely awkward, taking off Miriam's clothes. This was not the situation he had daydreamt about when it came to undressing her.

"You haven't been here before, have you, Octavius?"

He gave her a quick uneasy look. "What? No. Why?"

"He called you Carl. How did he know your name?"

He scowled uncertainly. "Um, I don't know. Maybe... Maybe Ophelia talked about me?"

"Maybe." The silence was uncomfortable and stretched out longer than he liked, but he was careful to put on his neutral mask, and as usual, his face didn't show anything he felt. Eventually, Olwen gave him another side-glance that, for some reason, was hard to interpret. "Are you on real-name-basis, you two?"

He squirmed uneasily and couldn't hinder another damn blush. "Um, yes, but only as friends." He bit his tongue at the revealing slip, but of course, it was too late.

She raised an eyebrow. "Mm," she said. "I thought the porter might be right. Someone should sleep in here, and if you two are such good friends, it would be best if you were here when she wakes up."

"Um, alright." It sounded reasonable enough, he guessed, since Miriam had been alone here for so long, but there was something in Olwen's voice that he couldn't place,

277

something that made him feel uncomfortable and embarrassed, as if he'd been caught naked somewhere he shouldn't be naked at.

They finally managed to get Miriam's jeans off, and when Olwen, without any further ado, grabbed Miri's underwear and tugged them off, Carl quickly turned his back on the two of them and took the jeans into the bathroom. It seemed as if she had wet herself when she went unconscious. He decided to wash them later after Olwen and Omega had left him alone with her. There was no reason to embarrass Miriam when she woke up. His heart made a happy little leap at the thought of her coming back to life. It felt so good to think '*when*,' and not '*if*.'

When he came back out to the bedroom, Omega was there with a bowl of hot water and some clean pieces of fabric. The two women had taken off the rest of Miriam's clothes, and Olwen concentrated on the many wounds on her body. Shocked at the sight of the many injuries, and awkward from seeing Miri naked and vulnerable, Carl left the room, taking all the dirty clothes with him into the bathroom and began washing them. While he was at it, he washed his own blood-soaked T-shirt as well, but it was clear that it never would get rid of all the blood. He shrugged. It was only a T-shirt.

He hung the clean clothes wherever there was room and peeked out. Omega and Olwen sat in the two armchairs at the window and ate some tasty smelling food. His stomach rumbled and he realized that he hadn't eaten since the early dinner together with Allie.

"Come, eat something," Omega said and offered him a plate. "It's really good."

"Thanks."

Finding nowhere to sit, he ate while standing up. Omega was right, it was really good. He gave Miriam a look. She lay on her stomach, covered by the duvet, with a large bandage around her head. Her skin was pale, but she breathed calmly.

"Is she better?"

Olwen nodded and gave Miriam a clinical glance. "Mhm. I don't know what's going on with this place and its so-called 'healthy air,' but she'll live, and she'll wake up. Maybe tonight. Maybe tomorrow. Her whole body is covered in bruises and bite marks and minor scrapes, but nothing terribly serious." The relief was so great that he felt himself relax in his whole body. "She's way too thin, though, on the border of starved, and quite dehydrated. When she wakes up, she needs to drink."

"I'll tend to that."

Olwen nodded and found an unopened water bottle in her bag. "Here. Let her drink this in intervals." He took it and put it on the bedside table. "And speaking of sleeping, I'm really tired too. Omega and I got a room each further down, twelve and fourteen, if you need us. For now, though, we should all try to hit the sack." She gave him a penetrating look, and it felt like she'd caught him with his fingers in a cookie jar. "That goes for you too, Octavius. Don't try to be heroic and sleep in the chair. They're not that comfortable. Oh, come on!" she said irritated when he hesitated. "It's a big bed, and she needs some warmth and comfort from a friend when she wakes up."

"Alright, alright." He ran his hand through his hair several times and felt like he would say anything at this point to make her stop.

"Good." She stood and yawned before she took her bag and the big tray out with her.

When the door closed behind her, Omega winked at him and whispered, "There's an extra blanket and a pillow in the drawer. You don't have to do as she says, you know. She's still mad at you and tries to make you feel uncomfortable. She always does things like that. Don't worry. It'll pass."

The relief that went through him made him smile back at her. "Thanks."

As soon as Omega left, Carl checked the drawer and found a soft, cozy blanket and a pillow. He locked the door and put the two big wing chairs together beside the bed, crawled up in them, and fell asleep immediately.

Chapter 16

Carl didn't feel like he'd slept at all when a knock on the door woke him up. He grunted, feeling sore in his whole body. It irked him, admitting that Olwen had been right, but the chairs weren't comfortable after all.

As he opened his eyes, he saw Miriam lying in the same position as before. She was still unconscious. He frowned worriedly, but then the knock came again louder this time. He struggled up from the chairs and opened the door. Olwen and Omega stood there looking astonishingly fresh and awake, but Olwen scowled when she saw his tired face.

"Let me guess," she said as she went inside, noticing the two armchairs with a disapproving look, "you slept in the chairs after all." When she turned that gaze toward him, he felt as ashamed as a berated schoolboy, but then anger rose inside him. She had no right to command him to sleep in the bed. It was as if she enjoyed the somewhat dirty thought of him beside a naked, unconscious Miriam. He glared at Olwen, who returned his gaze with a stern look. "You're not very good at taking orders, Octavius. I'll soon need you awake enough to be able to function, and if I read you correctly in between the lines, you didn't sleep much at all during that serial killer case or during the first days at Kroger's. Am I right?"

When she continued to glare at him, the berated-schoolboy-feeling came back with full force. Damn it that she had to be right about that too.

"Um, yes."

"Mm. I'm serious, Octavius. You need to sleep. This place gets to all of us, me too, I admit. I need you as my second-in-command, and you can't take on that role if you're continuing like this. If it disturbs you so much lying in the same bed as a friend, then maybe you can sleep head to toe with her. That's quite chaste."

"Um, yeah, I guess…" He felt stupid. Maybe he interpreted her wrong. He tugged at his hair. Nowadays, exhaustion seemed to be as big a part of him as his red hair, and he didn't feel that he could trust what he read in people anymore.

"Good. Matter settled then." Satisfied, Olwen turned toward Miriam and started to check on her.

Omega shrugged at him with a crooked smile, and Carl gave her half of a smile back, before going over to the other side of the bed to watch Olwen work. Under all those bruises, Miri still looked pale, but she was breathing calmly, and when he gently touched her cheek, it was cool, but not clammy anymore.

"She's sleeping," Olwen said at last. "She's not unconscious anymore. That's great news. Her head wound looks good too. The stitches look fine—"

He stared at her. "You stitched her?"

"Of course, I did. The wound's deep. I don't know what she did, but it's been healing and interrupted and re-opened several times. I don't think it was deep originally, but— Something else happened. Maybe it was that fog thing—"

"God, I totally forgot about that!" Carl ran his hand through his hair, feeling like an idiot.

Olwen glared at him and crossed her arms over her chest. "You need to sleep. You need to focus. Go to my room. I'll stay here with her." He stubbornly shook his head and got another glare as an answer. "When Ophelia's strong enough for us to leave, you'll be alert and focused. Otherwise, this will be your last RP. Do you understand?"

Wide-eyed, he stared at her, but she was deadly serious. He swallowed hard and acknowledged her. "Yes, I do."

"Good."

Omega gasped beside Olwen. "She's awake!"

They both turned and looked at Miriam. Her eyes were cloudy and clearly confused, but she struggled to turn around. Olwen and Omega helped her while Carl kneeled beside the bed and took her hand. A pained grimace flashed over her face when her head wound touched the pillow. Immediately, Olwen's and Omega's hands were there, letting her sit up. Miriam swayed and leaned her face down in her lap, but lost balance and fell back on the bed on her side.

"No," Olwen said, "she's too weak. Let her lie for now, on her side, if that's how she prefers it."

Omega nodded, and together, they tried to make it comfortable for her.

Carl took her hand again, and she opened her eyes and looked at him. "Hey, Miri." His voice was hoarse and near tears. Embarrassed, he cleared his throat.

With a few steps, Olwen came around the bed and kneeled beside Carl. He let go of Miri's hand and moved a bit to give Olwen more room.

"How do you feel, Miriam?" Olwen asked, clearly using her real name to not confuse her even more.

Miriam didn't answer, just stared at them. Then she closed her eyes, and tears began to trickle down her face.

Carl gently wiped them away. "It's alright, Miri. We're here with you. Everything's fine."

She fumbled weakly with her hand, obviously trying to grasp his. He took it and caressed it calmly.

"Miriam?" Olwen's stern voice had a touch of empathy in it. "Can you look at me a couple of moments? I'm just going to check your eyes." She brought a small flashlight from her doctor's bag. With another pained grimace, Miriam moved her head on the pillow and opened her eyes. "Good girl," Olwen mumbled and shone the light into one eye at a time. Then, she turned off the light with a relieved expression. "You're okay, sweetheart. Do you want something for the pain?"

"Yes, please…" Miriam's voice was faint and weak.

Carl squeezed his arm behind Miriam's back and helped her to sit up again. She was limp and heavy and swayed lightly, clearly dizzy, but she swallowed the pill Olwen handed her, and drank eagerly of the water before she sank back into the bed on her side. He draped the duvet over her again, didn't want her to get cold.

Olwen leaned forward and looked her in the face. "Miriam?" When Miri nodded, she continued, "This will take away the pain and most likely help you fall asleep as well. Carl will be here with you. You're not going to be alone. Okay, baby?" She nodded again, and Olwen looked up at him. "It's hard to say for sure, but I can't see any hemorrhage or large swelling in her brain. The pupil test isn't that accurate, but it's the best we have right now. Without proper equipment, I can't see if she has any minor swelling. Hopefully, she just needs to recuperate. We'll need to give her at least a couple of days before we leave."

"Alright."

"She's probably going to sleep for a while now. Those codeine pills are quite strong pain relievers, and she's exhausted. I'll come back later to check on her and give her one more."

Carl nodded. Olwen took her bag and gave Omega a commanding glance. The two women went out the door, but Omega peaked back in immediately.

"There's breakfast here for you, Octo. Do you want me to take it in?"

Carl managed to grin at the weird pet name she just made up, and she winked at him.

"Yes, please," he said, and when she came back with a tray full of savory food, he eyed it eagerly and added, "Thank you."

With a sweet look at him and a "Sleep tight," she left the room.

Not long after, Miri's hand fell out of his grip, showing him that she was asleep again. He tucked it in under the duvet before sitting down at the table, indulging in the warm, newly baked bread with honey, and the somewhat spicy tea. After eating until he couldn't possibly eat anything more, he left the tray on the trolley outside the door. As he sat down on the bed and watched Miri sleep, he felt so blessed to have her here, alive, that tears found their way down his cheeks, even though he was smiling. Gently, he caressed her dirty hair. He found a spot on her face that wasn't bruised and hesitantly put his cheek there. Her breath ruffled his hair, and his heart vaulted. Then, he hesitated once more, before doing as Olwen had suggested and placed his pillow at the foot-end, curling up under the extra blanket. Feeling the weight beside him, that was Miri, made him fall asleep with his heart filled with amazement.

Hours later, he woke up, more alert and focused than in a long while. The weight beside him in the bed was unfamiliar, but his heart took a leap at the feeling of having Miriam so close to him. Immediately, he sat up and checked on her. She was still asleep, but she looked healthier, and her face had more color, well, at the places where the bruises weren't dominating anyway. He held her hand for a while before using the facilities and taking a long shower. His T-shirt had finally dried, even though the big spot of blood made him grimace. He was just done when he recognized Olwen's specific knock on the door. When he unlocked, the two women surprised him by carrying a third armchair into the room.

"We need to work," Omega explained when she saw his raised eyebrows.

"And you need to sit," Olwen filled in. "Good," she said after giving him a look. "I'm happy you've slept well."

Both women put files and notebooks on the table, and then Olwen checked on Miriam again.

She gave a satisfied nod. "She's coming around quicker than I anticipated. That's great. Anyway, we need to fill you in on this Project." They sat down at the table, and Omega handed him an unused notebook and a pen while Olwen continued, "I guess I wasn't very clear with you yesterday. I'm sorry."

Carl waved away the remark. "No worries."

"Okay. I didn't bring Florence's diary. It's mostly just lots of rambles that are hard to interpret, but what I've managed to figure out is that she accidentally stepped through a portal when being at Kroger's with her baby, Jasmin, and came here. At least, I guess it's here. It seems unlikely to find two portals to two different dimensions in one place, but then again, I'm no expert. She talks a lot about shadow people, and from what we saw, I think we know what they look like." They all nodded. "Jasmin died in here. After what I've figured out, the shadow people ate her." A cold chill ran down Carl's spine, but he didn't show anything. "I guess that's what was going on with Ophelia yesterday. We were all lucky that we arrived when we did." Omega nodded, and with his soul filled with terror, Carl stretched out for Miri's hand and held it hard. "Our assignment was to find the portal and seal it. I mean, how many people have walked through that portal throughout the years without anyone knowing?" She made a short pause, and dread struck him at the unexpected thought. "The statistics we checked showed a higher rate of disappearances in the area around Kroger's than is normal." Another shiver ran down his spine, but he managed to keep a calm appearance. "But when Jones called and told us that you'd gone in, things changed. Armand wasn't pleased."

When she gave him a penetrating look, his face burnt in embarrassment, and in his mind, he could clearly hear C's irritated voice saying, "*Again, Cyrus? You went in on your own – again?*".

Eventually, Olwen continued, "He asked us to do some research around here, so Omega and I have been out and checked the surroundings." Her voice changed slightly and became livelier. "It's quite fascinating actually. I haven't worked out what's going on here, but the distance, for example, is, well, I don't know how to explain it—"

"Bendable," Miriam said faintly behind them.

Immediately, they all turned around and saw her watching them. Carl's heart hammered like crazy as he

286

bounced up from the chair and sat down on the bed beside her.

She smiled at him with some light back in her eyes. "Hi, Carl."

"Hi, Miri. It's nice to see you." His voice was soft, and he couldn't stop beaming at her.

"It's great to see you." She let her gaze include Omega and Olwen. "To see all of you."

"How do you feel?" Olwen asked as she came around the bed and picked up her bag.

"I... I'm not... sure..."

Carl glanced at Olwen, but she kept her professional facade focused on Miri.

"Can I take a look?"

"Yes, of course."

Olwen used the flashlight again and was apparently satisfied with what she saw. While she checked the rest of the wounds and scrapes and listened to Miri's heart and treated the head wound, she asked, "What happened to your head, sweetie?"

Miri frowned uncertainly and seemed to try to gather her thoughts, but eventually, she slowly said, "I... I hit it, I think. I don't really remember... It's, um, it's a blur..."

"Okay, don't worry about it. It might come back to you. Anything else you remember? Like all these bite marks and bruises?"

"Um, bite marks?"

The uncertainty in Miriam's voice got a tinge of alarm, and Olwen changed the subject.

"It's alright, baby. It's nothing major. I wondered, though, when you said 'bendable,' what did you mean by that'?"

Miriam's face suddenly got an expression of pure anxiety, and she mumbled something in a low voice. Carl thought that it sounded like a poem, but he wasn't sure. Instead of showing anyone how worried it made him, he put on his reassuring mask and continued to caress her hand.

"Miriam?" Olwen said again.

"Um… Spikenard and saffron, calamus and cinnamon, with all frankincense trees, myrrh and aloes, with all the chief spices," she rambled in a low voice, and her eyes looked desperate and wild.

Olwen frowned. She seemed worried, Carl thought with a pang. "Okay, Miriam. I'm going to give you something for the pain that most likely will make you sleepy as well, seeing as how exhausted you are."

Miriam's head jerked, and she stopped mumbling. "No! No, please. I'm— I'm fine! I, uh, I really don't need to sleep. I, um, I can just lie here and listen to what you're talking about." Her grip on Carl's hand was so hard and tight that it began to hurt, and the frown on Olwen's forehead grew even deeper.

"I'm not sure this is the best topic for you right now. Sorry, Miriam, but you need to rest. You're not well enough yet to take part in any RP. Here, take this pill now. Since I'm your doctor at the moment, you need to do what I say."

"Okay…" She closed her eyes, and a tear escaped. She didn't wipe it off, so Carl did it for her. Then, he looked up at Olwen, but she concentrated on getting a codeine pill out of the jar. Miriam took it obligingly and drank some more water to swallow it down. Olwen watched her with a concerned frown but didn't say anything. Instead, she placed her doctor's bag at the door before joining Omega, who looked through the files at the table. Carl continued to hold Miriam's hand until she fell asleep again. He sighed and glanced at Olwen, who fiddled around with things at the table in an attempt to look busy.

"She's sleeping."

"Good. I was hoping she would."

"So, what's going on, Olwen? Is she— Has she become… mentally ill?"

Olwen exhaled and threw a glance at the sleeping woman.

"I'm not a psychologist."

"No, but you're still a doctor, even if you're not working as one right now. Surely, you've gone through some basic courses in mental illness, just to be able to recognize it."

Olwen sighed and gave him a straight look. "Yes, I've done that, but it's too early to say anything. She's rambling, and she has a minor memory loss, but it could be a way for her to hide from memories that are too frightening to face right now. But you know this as well as I do. You don't need my evaluation."

Omega let up her melodic voice. "We'll have to help her feeling so safe and secure that she doesn't need to hide."

Olwen nodded. "You're right. I wish we could try and get home with her, but—"

"But what?" Carl asked when she hesitated.

"Well, do you know the way home?"

It felt like she had hit him. *Of course, we don't know it. I should've been prepared for that.*

Omega frowned nervously. "Olwen, you said something before, about how Florence did it."

"Mm. She's written about it in her diary, but I don't understand it yet. I'm working on it." When Carl was about to ask her what was written, she held up her hand to quiet him. "I can't put my finger on it. It's all over the text, not a single paragraph or something straightforward like that."

Carl sighed and tugged at his hair, wishing Olwen could adopt Allie's attitude of information sharing.

"Yeah, would've been too simple, eh?" he said instead.

For some reason, his words made Omega giggle. It was a sparkling giggle, so contagious that he felt a tug at the corners of his mouth, and Olwen's face softened as well.

When the giggle faded away, she looked cheerfully at them. "We're going to make it. Don't ask me why or how, but I just know we're going to make it."

She said it with such confidence and optimism that the gloomy atmosphere somehow shivered, and unexpectedly, Carl felt a tiny vibration lightly tugging at him.

It was such a familiar sensation that he turned around to see if there was a portal behind him.

Just then, it knocked on the door, and the feeling disappeared. Olwen frowned and got up. Outside, Night Porter stood with a big tray in his hands, and an oily smirk playing on his lips.

"What do you want?" Olwen sneered, and Carl felt a vague worry inside him. Omega seemed to shrink where she sat at the table, and her cheerful expression disappeared.

"Tsk, tsk, what a rude greeting, sweetheart, when I'm only here to serve. I wanted to give my appreciated guests some food, some extra special food today, no less, since you are, in fact, appreciated."

Olwen's back was stiff, but she accepted the tray from the porter, shut the door in his face with her foot, and came back to the table. As Carl and Omega cleaned the table from papers, notebooks and pens, the whiff of the food swirled around them.

"Mm, it does smell delicious," Omega said with a new smile on her face as she helped Olwen with the food.

"Hm," Olwen grunted with a sour voice.

When they sat down to eat, Omega picked up the lost thread. "Where were we now again?"

Carl didn't know why, but suddenly, a heavy anxiousness hit him.

Olwen frowned as if she had to think about it. "Mm... Yes, you asked about Ophelia," she answered eventually and turned to Carl. *Was that really what we talked about?* He tried to think, but Olwen continued, and the weird feeling in his gut disappeared, "No, as I said, I'm not a psychologist, and I think that your evaluation probably is as good as mine." She gave him a straight look. "Honestly, I'd say that you're probably better at evaluating her than I am since you're actually trained in psychology, which I am not."

He nodded. "Fair enough." When he looked over his shoulder at the quietly sleeping Miriam and saw all her bruises and wounds again, it made him want to cry. "How long do you think she'll sleep?"

"Impossible to say. They're pain relievers, not sleeping pills, even though they're probably helping her relax right now. She'll sleep as long as she needs, I'd say, but she'll most likely need another pill after she wakes up. That head wound of hers must hurt like hell, and sleep will only be good for her."

He nodded again. "Now what?"

"Armand gave me specific instructions that we need to research this place for the Faculty. From now on, that's a task for Omega and me. Your place is to be here with Ophelia. I don't dare to leave her alone. Who knows if that fog monster made some connection with her and come here looking for her? Drugged like this, she'll be totally helpless."

A sinking feeling of fear dug its claws deep into him, and illogically, he longed for his gun. He swallowed and admitted to himself that he suddenly was afraid. *Wow, progress, Carl. Maybe, this time, you won't make a damn fool out of yourself, just to prove that you're so damn tough.*

"Alright, and where are you going to start?"

"I want to start with this inn tonight. I mean, we've already checked the town, even if not in all that much detail, but what I want to know is if we're the only humans trapped here. Are there other 'guests'? How big is this inn?"

"Don't separate, whatever you do otherwise, alright?"

Olwen stared at him. Then her appearance turned from unbelieving to arrogant. "Do I teach you your job, Octavius? We're not stupid."

Omega giggled, and Olwen gave her an affectionate glance.

Embarrassed, Carl looked away. "I deserved that, eh? Sorry."

To his surprise, they smiled, and Omega winked kindly at him. "You're just worried and concerned and tired, Octo. We get it, and we understand."

Olwen nodded, and the arrogant air was gone. "She's right, you know. You look like you could use some more sleep while we're away. We'll come knocking when we're back."

He exhaled and felt that they indeed had a point. His eyes were sore, and it was as if a fog had taken up residence in his head. He grimaced. *Bad reference, Carl, really bad reference.*

"Yeah, I'll try that. I'm not on top."

"Mm. It shows."

"Why, thank you." Even though his tone was somewhat sarcastic, he smiled to show that he wasn't mad at her, and she gave him a genuine smile back. It felt good having that old camaraderie returning to them. It was as if they began to remember what it was like being a team.

Chapter 17

As soon as they left, Carl brought the big tray to the trolley outside the door. As he left it there, he looked at it with squinting eyes. He could swear that it was something he should remember about it, something that eluded him, something he couldn't put his finger on, but nothing came to him. While shaking his head at the annoying feeling, he went inside the room and locked the door. Whatever it was, it would come back to him sooner or later. He glanced toward the bed and the unmoving Miriam while trying to pretend that he didn't stall for time. If he was to be totally honest with himself, he had to admit that he didn't understand why he felt so uncomfortable with the situation. *It's Miri, for crying out loud. We're great friends, we've spent numerous hours together, we know almost all there is to know about each other, and I'm in love with her. Why the hell do I feel like this?* It wasn't only because she hadn't been able to give him any kind of consent for sleeping at her side or that it felt like he was taking advantage of her vulnerability now when she was injured and unconscious and naked, even if he logically knew that he did nothing of the sort. Yet, it was something else that irked him.

"I should be happy, damn it…"

As he thought about it, there was no doubt that he was happy somewhere deep inside; happy that she was alive, that he was with her, that he might get a second chance after all.

"I don't even believe in second chances, and still, here it is, hitting me on the head…"

A faint smile managed to appear on his lips, and he sat down beside her, letting his hand brush away the hair from her face.

"I am happy, *albi*, I really am. It's all the other things that make me restless and nervous, just like a damn nine-tailed cat. This whole place, this… this realm… and the slimy night porter who has some kind of agenda, I swear he has,

293

and that fog monster that tried to, you know, eat you, and all your bruises and wounds and... and the way you talk... Just because your team-name's Ophelia, doesn't mean you have to turn into her, okay, *albí*?" His hand followed the duvet down to her waist, half embracing her. She breathed calmly, and the movement underneath his hand felt good and comforting. With a deep breath, he changed the subject. "You know, there's so much that has happened while you were away, Miri, and it's hard to believe—" He shook his head and tried another angle. "You know, until I told Allie about you and how weird I thought it was that you weren't in the basement, everyone was so certain that you were gone, and I could see in their eyes how they pitied me for not giving up on you, and somewhere down the line... I think I did give up on you. God, I'm so sorry, Miri, I'm so very sorry..." He exhaled and wiped away a couple of tears. "And now... It's like I don't understand that you're truly here with me, that this is real. It's more like a dream, and I'm afraid I'll wake up in my bed at home, and... and you'll be dead, buried somewhere where it's cold and dark, and I'll be alone again... and this second chance will be gone forever..." His voice cracked, and he wiped away more tears that persisted in falling from his eyes. "And you'll probably get mad at me for worrying so much about you. I know that you can manage on your own, heck, you've managed this place on your own for two damn weeks, and, God, do you have my respect for that, but sometimes, you know, I need you, and I do worry about you, because I need you, and because you mean so much to me." He fell silent again as a thought struck him. "I guess it all ends up with one thing; I'm not in control. That's it, eh? I'm not in control. Yep, that rings true." He sighed and tugged at his hair. "Better try to get in control, then, don't you think? And the best thing to do to get in control is to sleep and get rested. If I'm really honest, I think that even though you might feel awkward about me sleeping beside you, you'd probably rather want me to be rested than sleeping on those damn chairs again and not knowing what I'm doing out of sheer exhaustion, not to mention losing my job." For a moment, he frowned. "Can't believe I'm facing the risk of getting sacked for the third time in a damn week," he muttered to himself. As if the thought of his everyday life was a cue, an image of Sarah showed up in his mind, and he swore quietly, while vigorously rubbing his neck. "Goddamn, what day is it?" Fumbling with getting his cell out of his pocket, he continued to swear to himself, feeling the powerlessness of not being able to keep his promises to the most important person in his life. When he finally got it out, he stared at the dead cell in silence for a moment, before he made a disheartened gestured and put it down again. "It might not be Friday yet," he mumbled and continued, despite knowing better, "Maybe we'll get home before then."

With a sigh, he stood up, trying to shove the thoughts of Sarah's upcoming disappointment out of his mind, and went around to the other side of the bed where he stopped uncertainly. *Um, jeans or no jeans tonight?* Irritated he shook his head. "God, I'm so damn silly. Just take the damn jeans off. Or do you want them so dirty that they'll walk by themselves? She's sleeping, for crying out loud."

Resolutely, he unbuttoned the jeans before taking them off and hesitantly sniffing them. A disgusted grimace appeared on his face. *Oh God, this is truly revolting. Anyone could tell that I've worn them constantly for at least three days and nights.* Sighing, he took them into the bathroom to wash them. When he finally could hang them up to dry, he felt so exhausted that even his overambitious mind was quiet. On unsteady feet, he went to bed, head to toe with her, with at least a couple of inches between them. It felt so damn good to place his head on the pillow and pull the soft blanket all the way up to his chin, that he sighed with pleasure and closed his eyes.

When the key turned in the keyhole, and the doorknob rattled, Carl wasn't even aware of being awake. On edge, he sat up and looked at the open door, seeing a naked foot disappear as someone just turned to the left outside in the corridor. He frowned, feeling disoriented. Then, he turned to look beside him in the bed. It was empty. Waves of cold and heat flashed through his body, and his heart pounded like crazy as he threw the blanket off him and rushed out into the corridor. At the end of it, someone turned right around the corner and disappeared.

"Miri?"

As he ran after her, he passed rooms number twelve and fourteen, banging on the doors to get Olwen's and Omega's attention, if they were there, but when he turned around the corner and saw an empty staircase, he decided that he couldn't wait for them. Afraid to lose Miriam, he rushed up the stairs and landed in a new corridor that seemed to be empty, but he couldn't be sure since it ended in shadows. *Where the hell did she go?* For a moment he stood unmoving, swearing quietly, before running all the way to the end of the corridor, only to find that it was a dead-end, with a door leading to room number twenty. When he knocked on the door, it silently opened in front of him.

As he struggled to discern something, anything, in the compact darkness inside, an ominous feeling sneaked up on him. Unconsciously, his hand went down to the absent gun holster in his jeans. He frowned. Something was wrong, but he couldn't put his finger on what.

Suddenly, footsteps pattered from inside the room, and a door opened and closed in the compact darkness. *Goddamn, I can't see a damn thing in there, but whoever is in there can see me as clear as a beacon with this light behind me.*

"Miri? Are you in there?"

The door inside, probably the bathroom door, opened again, and a singsong voice reached him.

"Spikenard and saffron, calamus and cinnamon, with all frankincense trees, myrrh and aloes..."

"Miri? Can you come out here, please?"

The bathroom door closed. Anxiousness began to creep through Carl's body as if he was standing on an anthill. He didn't want to go in on his own. He'd done that mistake so many times before and it had always led him and others to so much damn trouble. Not to mention that he didn't trust this place one bit. It might not even be her in there, just someone who wanted to lure him by pretending it was her. *I need a weapon of some sort. Doesn't matter what.* He searched his jeans pockets but couldn't find anything. The feeling of something being wrong came over him again.

"Miri? You'll have to come out here, 'cause I'm not going in."

A malevolent giggle was heard just a couple of steps in front of him, making him gasp and involuntarily back away.

"Coward..." The whisper slithered like a snake toward him, and for a split second, a tiny green snake was seen as it swiftly slid out from the darkness and disappeared behind him.

He took a step to the side and put his back against the wall, FBI-style, and checked the corridor, but the snake wasn't there to be seen anymore. *I hope it's not venomous.*

"Carl is a coward; Carl is a coward..." The singsong voice was closer to the door now, and even though he was still scared, he couldn't help laughing. The voice silenced abruptly as if surprised.

"You think that'll make me bite? You think I'm a ten-year-old? Oh, come on! Go and hide somewhere if you can't come up with something better than that."

The door suddenly slammed shut with a bang that made him jolt. Carl exhaled sharply and wiped his forehead. *Alright, most likely not in there.* Worriedly, he looked after the snake, but couldn't see it. On light feet, he moved toward door eighteen. Before trying the handle, he glanced over his shoulder to make sure that door twenty was still closed. *Don't trust this place. Not one bit.*

The door swung open, revealing a brightly lit room. Without stepping in, he studied the room closely from the doorway. It looked much like Miri's room, with a large old-fashioned bed, and a table with two armchairs. The bathroom door was open and showed a flowery wallpaper. Everything seemed uninhabited. There was nothing out of the ordinary to be seen here.

As he stood outside the door without even touching the threshold, Carl gave a wry half-smile. *Wow, C would be so proud. He'd say I've finally learned my lesson.* The smile faded away. *Yeah, proud indeed. It only took me three stupid mistakes to learn it.*

Then, he frowned. Something moved inside the bathroom and a shadow appeared on the floor at the ajar door. He squinted. The shadow looked weird, as if it belonged to a humanoid, but not actually to a human. *Is it the fog monster from the dock?* His throat dried up at the thought, and when something tentacle-like reached around the doorpost, he nearly fainted by sheer terror as the strong déjà vu caught him in its grip. He wanted to pull away, to close the door, but some disturbed, perverted part of him couldn't look away, and then something was seen in the doorway. At first, he couldn't comprehend what it was he saw, something short and distorted and blackish-red. The proportions were all wrong. It stumbled out on legs that lacked both feet and shins, swaying and flailing to keep balance. The long arms ended in blackened stumps and helped the upper body to keep straight as it determinedly dragged itself over the floor. There was nothing left of the head, only damaged pieces of a bag that hung around the neck.

In a flash, Carl realized what it was, and wave after wave of nauseated terror crashed through his body, hit him so hard that he stumbled as he jerkily moved backward from the door on legs that had turned to water. His heart pounded so loudly, drowning out all other sounds, as the remains of the guard he had doomed to the fire shambled toward him.

Suddenly, he moved into something soft. He gasped and spun around and looked into Ned's ruptured eyes. At that moment, Carl lost control over his bladder.

A smile formed around the big, blue tongue hanging out from Ned's mouth. "Going somewhere, Nero?"

Carl couldn't answer. He just continued to move back toward the staircase with stiff, jerky movements and painfully shallow breaths. God, he was crazy who came here alone, looking for Miriam, who obviously wasn't here. *It was a ruse all along. I swear she's still in the room, unprotected from whatever wanted me out of the way.*

Ned talked again, "Don't go, Nero. We have some unfinished businesses to take care of first."

Despite knowing better, Carl mumbled with a throat as dry as a desert, "No, we don't." When he saw Ned's eyes gleam, he knew he'd made a mistake. To his horror, his old P.I. seemed to become more solid, more physical. On itching, watery legs, he took another step backward, away from the apparition.

"You have to help us. It's so painful. It's still burning. Can't you see?"

In between the pieces of Ned's cracked skin, Carl saw the fire burning. Desperately he fought the urge to give in to the terror, to close his eyes and curl together on the floor, screaming and wailing and crying. *I won't. Not this time. Not ever again.*

He cleared his throat. "You're not real, Ned."

"This pain is. God, this pain is!"

"No, you're not real. I don't believe in you."

It took all his might, all his willpower to not collapse, but slowly, Carl turned his back on Ned and took the steps down to the first floor. He managed to keep his eyes focused on the corridor in front of him and not turning back to take one last look. This time, when he passed doors twelve and fourteen, he didn't knock. Who knew what kind of things hid in there, preparing to get him, to try their best to drive him out of his mind? Even as he closed in on the now shut door to Miri's room, he refused to look back, refused to acknowledge the things this place attempted to scare him with.

With a deep breath, he turned the doorknob, suddenly afraid that the door would be locked, but it swung open without any resistance. When he cautiously peeked in, he saw two people in the bed. The person beside Miriam looked exactly like him. The hair on his arms stood up. *I didn't expect this,* Carl thought with pounding heart and painfully shallow breaths.

His doppelganger caressed Miriam's naked body. She moved restlessly in her sleep and moaned, but it sounded more painful than anything else. With a grimace, she touched her head wound. Carl's doppelganger sat up in the bed and pulled the duvet back over her. He looked affectionately at her when Miriam opened her eyes, but Carl could tell that it was a mask. Whoever tried to look like him didn't care a rotten apple about her.

"How's it going, sweetheart?" Carl's doppelganger asked, and the voice sounded exactly like Carl's.

A light layer of sweat moistened his forehead. Who was this guy?

Miri gave Carl-in-bed a tired smile. "It hurts, but that was expected, right?"

"I guess. You've got a bad thing going on there.

"I shouldn't have banged my head so hard into the wall, but I couldn't stop laughing."

Wide-eyed and stunned, Carl watched the scene from the doorway. He saw himself reach out his hand and caress Miri's cheek.

"Yeah, you got a little crazy at the end, didn't you, sweetie?" The smile froze on Miriam's lips, and she stared silently at the doppelganger. "But I'm here now," Carl-in-bed said jovially. "You can just relax and take it easy. I'm going to fix everything. We'll start with this, I think. Best recipe old Uncle Pete ever recommended." With eager hands, the impersonator cupped her face and leaned in to kiss her.

"No!" Carl yelled as a sinking knowledge spread inside him that a kiss in consent would create irreparable damage to Miriam's mind, but no one seemed to hear him. He stared in disbelief at the word when it took physical form and silently fell to the floor where it shone inflamed for a

300

moment before burning into the hardwood planks. Trying desperately to move, but realizing that he couldn't, Carl fought invisible chains to no avail. Miri was blossoming red on her face and watched Carl-in-bed with eyes wide-open as he closed in on her, but just as he was about to put his lips on hers, she frowned and turned her head toward the door, looking straight at Carl without seeing him.

"I… I don't know," she mumbled. "It doesn't feel right."

"Oh, come on, honey, you know you want to. I've seen it in your eyes."

The frown got deeper, and suspiciously, she looked back at the impersonator. "You're not Carl, are you?"

Carl-in-bed sat up with a surprised look on his face, but then he grinned pleased, and his appearance changed into Night Porter.

"I can't fool you, it seems, my heart's queen. My deepest respect to you." Night Porter glanced at Carl. "To both of you. You've proven stronger than I suspected initially. Interesting. Well, time is on my side. I'll take my leave for now." With a smile, he snapped his fingers.

There was a knock on the door, and Carl moved tiredly in bed, shoving the pillow over his head, but the hard knock came again. He sighed as he recognized it as Olwen's characteristic and determined knocks. When he sat up, everything swirled around him, and he had to lean his head in between his knees to get in control of it.

"Octavius?" he heard his P.I.'s voice from the other side of the door. "Are you there?"

"Coming…"

He put his bare feet on the floor and stood up, swaying slightly as he took the few steps to the door and turned the key. Olwen marched in with Omega in tow. Carl closed the door behind them and turned around, realizing that they were staring at his bare legs. A blush crept up his face, even as the thought struck him, *It wasn't real after all. It had to be a dream since I had the jeans on, but, damn, did it feel real…*

301

"Um, I, uh, washed them. I—" He gestured vaguely toward the bathroom as he briskly went in and grabbed them. They were more wet than damp, but he struggled to get them on anyway while grimacing at the uncomfortable feeling.

When he came out, Olwen was doing her usual check-up on Miriam, and Omega sat curled up in one of the armchairs with a steaming cup of tea in her hands. Her face had a grayish tinge that worried him. Sitting down in the middle chair, Carl grabbed a cup of tea of his own from the tray on the table.

"How are you?"

Omega exhaled and took a sip, grimacing at the heat. "Well…" She exhaled again and took another sip as if stalling for time. "Let's say like this; I want to go home."

"That bad, eh?"

The raw expression in her eyes when she looked at him, scared him.

"This house never ends, Octo. It just goes on and on and on. For a while, I didn't think we'd find our way back, and the dimensions are so weird and… and… stairs that stop in the middle with nothing that connects to them. Rooms where you go in and realize that you're walking upside down on the ceiling, and when you realize that, you're damned, you fall and can't get out because the door is placed at the ceiling. You must convince yourself that you're a fly on a wall and can walk like one. I… I actually saw— I saw Olwen transform into a… a… fly…"

Her hands trembled, and the tea rippled in the mug. She brought it to her mouth and took a large gulp as if the heat could burn the images from her mind. Carl sat quietly staring at her, and goosebumps appeared all over his body.

Olwen packed her things and closed her bag before taking a seat in the last chair. He could tell that she listened closely with a grim look that never left her face.

Omega sighed and cradled the mug as if it was a teddy bear. "And… and… Honestly, Octo, I have no idea how many rooms and corridors we went through, how many stairs we climbed, how many elevators that tried to lure us into them, how many lost people we found, completely insane—"

"Three, Omega. There were only three."

She turned her head violently at Olwen. "Three are too many!" Olwen kept her mouth shut and glanced at the younger woman. "And then this part that Olwen says didn't happen—"

"Because it did not happen."

Omega didn't seem to listen. "She made a deal with Night Porter."

A sinking feeling grabbed Carl's abdomen, and he stared wildly at Olwen, who looked angry.

"No, I didn't. It would never occur to me to do something stupid like that."

Omega continued to talk as if Olwen hadn't said a word. "I knew we would find our way back eventually. I just knew it in my heart, Octo, even though there were times that I doubted it in my head, but Olwen didn't believe—"

"We were lost, Omega, totally lost. You admitted it too. You said your sense of direction didn't work."

"Losing my sense of direction isn't the same as not finding one's way back again. We just needed to keep on looking."

Olwen exhaled frustrated.

"What's this about Night Porter, Omega?" Carl asked with a surprisingly composed voice that seemed to calm Omega.

"We were in a ditch, like from World War I. Don't ask me how we managed to get there. We opened a door and just slid down a muddy slope into this ditch. I admit, at the time, it seemed quite hopeless, but I'm sure there was a way out. I mean, if I can transform into a fly, I swear I can find a damn door that leads out of there.

"Seems logical, yeah."

"I was just about to start looking for one, but then, suddenly, Night Porter showed up from nowhere, I mean literally from nowhere! One second it was just Olwen and me, next he stood behind her back, smirking at me as if we shared some funny secret."

Olwen shook her head but didn't say anything.

"What happened then?" Carl asked, still with a calm voice, but his heart hammered so hard in his chest that it created a pounding headache. Omega exhaled and drank the rest of the tea in one gulp.

"I'm not sure," she said at last. "It was as if I became trapped somehow, in— I don't know! A glass cube or something. I could see everything, but not move or hear. It disappeared just when Olwen and Night Porter shook hands, and he said, 'Good deal, sweetheart, a very good deal for the both of us.'"

"I would never do something like that, Omega," Olwen said tiredly, but Omega continued to look down into her cup.

"And then this door opened at the end of the ditch that led back to our corridor here. It hadn't been there before."

"That's not even a good deal!" Olwen snapped frustrated. "A good deal would be to get us all back home, not open a damn door to this corridor here! I might have struck a deal with him if that was the outcome, but this? It makes no sense."

Silence fell hard in the room, and Carl watched the two women sitting in their chairs with clenched teeth, avoiding each other's eyes.

Eventually, he sighed and let his hand nervously comb through his hair. "There were weird things going on here, too, while you were gone." Both of them looked at him, and he thought Olwen seemed relieved to not have the focus on her anymore. "I don't know if it was real or not. In this… dream… or whatever it was, I had jeans on me, even though I'd just washed them and gone to sleep without them, so—" He sighed and ran his hand through his hair once more. He hadn't planned on talking about it, but, whatever. "I woke up by the door opening and Mi— Ophelia wasn't in the bed. I went up and saw her, or at least someone, disappear around the corner at the end of the corridor. When I followed her up, she was gone. I opened a couple of doors and encountered... things... but they disappeared, and I went back here and found Night Porter trying to— I don't know, drive Mir— Ophelia insane, I think. And then, you knocked on the door, and I woke up."

Olwen sighed and rubbed her eyes. "We need to get home before we do something incredibly stupid. This place is toying with us, and we're starting to lose perspective."

Omega nodded tiredly. "Yes, I agree." Olwen shot her a dark look, but she continued without acknowledging it, "How is she? When can she start walking?"

A grimace appeared on Olwen's face. "Better, but not good. The head wound starts to heal, but optimally she'd need a couple of weeks in bed. We don't have that time, obviously. She should start coming around any moment now, and then we'll just ask her, I guess, and hope she'll be coherent."

"Um..." Carl tugged nervously at his hair, and they watched him inquiring. "She's... quite dirty. Do you think— Could you maybe give her a shower when she wakes up?"

Omega's face softened as she looked at him. "Of course, we can. Right, Olwen?"

Olwen shrugged. "Why not. It's not like we have anything else to do, except sleeping."

Restlessly, she walked around in the room, seemingly unable to sit still while Omega and Carl sat at the table. Omega's face slowly got its normal color back, and soon, it was as if the things she had been through just ran off her like rain on an oiled boat.

"What's the first thing you're going to do when you get home, Octo?"

He couldn't help smiling at the unexpected question. "Change clothes, definitely."

She laughed at him. "You're not used to being out in the field, right, wearing the same clothes for weeks?"

Smitten by her sudden good mood, Carl put on a playfully frightened look. "No way! Not this dandy."

Omega laughed again, and her eyes glittered. "Come on, you're not a dandy, not from what I've seen of you in the field. No one as good as you could be a dandy."

He felt touched but just smiled at her. "Not swell enough? I have to show up in my silk shirt and cravat one fine day, I hear."

"And trousers," Omega grinned, and he laughed out loud.

"Going to hear that a lot, eh?"

"You bet."

"And what about you? What's your plan?"

"Mm…" Her face got a longing expression. "Yeah, I do have some plans…"

"Sounds promising." Just as the words slipped out of his mouth, he felt a familiar tug in his mind, as if a tiny vibration appeared behind him, and he turned around to see if he could discern it. A faint glimmer shimmied in the air, but before he could focus on it, there was a knock on the door, and the feeling and the vibration disappeared as if they had never been there.

"What is it now?" Olwen growled and went to the door. A new tray of food was placed on the trolley outside, and she grabbed it, slammed the door with her foot, and brought it in.

"We're going to be fat as Christmas pigs if this continues," Carl muttered. He glanced at Miriam, and with a sudden leap of his heart, he realized that she was watching him. Immediately, he rose from the chair and took her hand as he placed himself beside her.

"She's awake, Olwen," Omega said urgently.

Briskly, Olwen went over to Carl's side and knelt. Miriam let her gaze fall on Olwen.

"How are you doing, Miriam?"

"I… I'm thirsty…" Her voice sounded cracked and dry.

306

Omega immediately approached her with a water bottle in hand, and she grabbed it thankfully. Carl and Olwen helped her sit up and held her as she swayed slightly before managing to get the dizziness under control. In just a couple of moments, she emptied the bottle.

"Thank you," she said weakly.

"Do you want to eat something?" Olwen asked, but Miriam shied away from the question and shook her head. "You need to eat, Miriam."

When Miriam stubbornly shook her head, a strong wave of relief flowed through Carl. *She's Alright. She's going to be fine.*

Olwen frowned. "Fine. Let me look at your eyes, and if you're feeling okay, we'll give you a shower."

For some reason, Miriam shied away from that too, before she inhaled and seemed to relax. "Are you going to be in there with me?"

"Yes, we will," Olwen said and glared at her as to challenge her to disagree. "You're not to be alone when you're this dizzy."

"Okay," she said meekly, but Carl thought that she looked relieved.

Within a few minutes, Olwen and Omega helped Miriam into the bathroom, and he heard the shower. Looking at the bed, he wished for some new bed linen, but he refused to go out and ask for them. As he stood there scowling at the bed, there was a new knock on the door, and he answered hesitantly. On the trolley, lay an organized pile of freshly clean bed linen. Carl frowned but took them with him and started to undo the bed.

I hate this place. Nothing is as it should. Nothing goes according to plan. Everything here is out to get you.

"What plans, Carl?"

With a slight gasp, he turned around at the unfamiliar voice, but no one was there.

"What the hell?"

307

"Tell me. I might be able to help you." The voice was behind him again, and Carl spun around with the dirty sheets tightly cradled at his chest, but of course, no one was there.

"Fuck off!"

"Tsk, tsk, language."

This time, he recognized Night Porter's voice. His heart pounded hard in his chest, but he put on an uninterested and nonchalant appearance and went about making the bed. He was not going to be lured into another trap, and there was a trap hidden in the amused voice. Soon the presence disappeared, and he breathed easier again.

When he was done making the bed, he put the dirty laundry at the door, nicely folded. It felt good, doing something as ordinary as folding. It helped him recollect his thoughts and calm down.

The door to the bathroom opened and let out steaming air that smelled of vanilla. Olwen and Omega led a very pale but clean Miriam, dressed in a large towel, to the bed. She looked exhausted. *She won't be able to leave tonight. Damn it.* As Omega draped the duvet around her and took the towel back to the bathroom, Olwen came over to him where he stood at the door.

"We'll give it a try tomorrow," she said. "Miriam agrees with me that it might be worth a little bit of extra effort to try and find a way home."

"Alright." He wasn't so sure about it, but then again, he wasn't a doctor, and he wouldn't argue about it. He wanted to get home too much for that.

Omega joined them at the door, and Olwen gave her a stern look. "Omega, shall we take another tour around the town? It will be the last chance we have."

"We can do that," the younger woman agreed.

"Don't teleport," Miriam said from the bed.

They all looked silently at each other and then at Miriam's pale, tense face.

"I'm sorry, Miriam, what did you say?"

"Don't teleport. It's going to hurt you." Tears fell down her cheeks, and she began to tremble. She closed her eyes, and with a painful expression, she said, "Always have somewhere to run. Don't get trapped. Don't teleport."

Carl drew his hand through his hair several times, and Olwen and Omega looked bewildered.

"Don't worry, Miriam," Omega said in a kind voice, and she went back to the bed, bent down and hugged the shivering woman. "We won't."

Miriam opened her eyes again and stared wildly at Omega, who took a cautious step back, but Miri's hand shot out from under the duvet and captured the other woman's arm.

"Promise me," she demanded.

"Sure, I promise," Omega said in a scared tone.

Miriam exhaled and let her arm go. Rapidly, Omega moved closer to the door.

"Then it's all good," Miriam mumbled.

With a deep frown, Olwen stared at her before turning toward Carl, giving him one of the codeine pills.

"She needs one of these to help with the pain. She needs to drink more too. Understood?" He nodded at the underlying meaning, agreeing with her that Miri needed more rest, much more rest. "Good. We'll let you know when we're back."

Chapter 18

When Olwen and Omega left the room, Carl shuffled the dirty laundry out into the corridor before taking out the untouched tray with food. None of them seemed interested in eating anymore. They just needed to get home now. The longing for normal was so strong in him that he wanted to cry or scream. Instead, he closed the door and reached for the key to lock it. To his surprise, it wasn't in the keyhole anymore. He frowned uncertainly and opened the door. It wasn't in the keyhole on that side either. *Where the hell did it go? I thought I left it there.* He checked his pockets, but it wasn't there either. *What the hell?*

Suddenly a tentative hand was placed on his arm. With a slight gasp, he spun around. Miri stood just behind him with the duvet around her. With her pale, gaunt cheeks and enormous eyes, she looked so vulnerable that he just wanted to hug her, but he braced himself. He didn't want her to feel awkward when she was only dressed in that duvet.

"Carl… Can you stay a little longer? I… I don't want to be alone…"

"Course I can, Miri. That was the plan." His voice was very soft, and she seemed to relax slightly.

She let go of his arm, and he stepped into the room again, closed the door to the empty corridor behind him. Then he stared in disbelief at the key in the keyhole. With trembling hands, he turned the key and locked the door. He wished that it had more than one lock, more like three or four, but it would probably not help even if there were forty locks. He had to bite his tongue to not laugh. Tired and scared, he rubbed his face. *God, this place is getting to me.*

Miriam curled up in the big bed with her back toward the wall and closed her eyes, hugging her knees. A couple of seconds went by while Carl watched her sitting there without moving before he said, "Do you want your clothes, Miri? They're clean."

She didn't answer, so he went to the drawer and grabbed them. With them neatly folded in his arms, he placed himself at the end of the bed, feeling insecure.

For a short time, they sat in silence.

Then, she said without opening her eyes, "Is it real, Carl? Are you really here? You're not... one of all those images anymore, are you? I think you're you. You feel like you now, but— I've been wrong before."

A flash of anguish rushed through Carl's heart. He reached over and placed his hand on hers. She wrapped her fingers tightly around his, and he tried to put all the warmth and reassurance he could into his voice.

"I am really here, Miri, and this is real."

She didn't answer, but a lone tear fell from her eye. With an aching heart, he moved up into the bed and placed himself beside her, easing his arm around her back. She leaned into him with a shaky breath and rested her head on his shoulder. He embraced her gently and let his cheek rest on her head. Her hair was damp and smelled of vanilla.

In a low voice, he said, "We've been here for some time now, Miri. You've been unconscious, and you've slept a lot, but you're not alone anymore. You won't have to face this place on your own from now on. We're here. I'm here."

More tears fell from her eyes, and he dried them away. She put her hand on top of his, made it stay on her cheek, and he caressed her cheek line with his thumb. A deep sigh made her body relax even more. He closed his eyes, let himself become even more aware of her in his arms, her smell, her touch, her bare skin under his hands, and he sighed content. Without thinking, he snuggled in closer to her.

When he started to talk again, he surprised himself. "I've been looking for you so long, Miri," he mumbled into her hair. "When we didn't find you under the rubble, I tried to convince myself that I was just looking for a shadow, that I couldn't accept you were dead, but I never stopped trying to find you."

As the words left his lips, he realized that it was the truth after all. Another tear fell on his hand, and he hugged her harder. Her body was so thin. Even with the thick duvet around her, he could feel how much weight she'd lost.

"I'm not a shadow, Carl! I'm not a shadow! Please, don't say that."

He cursed himself for letting that particular word slip and caressed her shoulder calmingly. "I'm sorry, Miri, wrong word."

"It's so hard to understand." Her voice was so low and exhausted that he nearly didn't hear what she said. "I don't know how long I've been here. It's always night, and time ceases to exist. And it's so empty and silent. The only ones I've spoken to are the old man and the night porter. When I'm out, I sometimes see... shadows... but no real people. I... I thought I had lost my mind and was committed— Are you sure this is real?"

His heart ached when he heard how broken she sounded. He turned her face gently toward his.

"Look at me, Miri." She opened her tear-filled eyes and looked at him. "I swear to you that this is real. I swear to you that you are not committed. This is not just happening in your head, and as soon as you're feeling better, we're leaving this place; you, me, Omega, and Olwen, and we're going home."

"Olwen said that, but— Do you think we can go home?"

He nodded. "Yeah. I do."

She looked at him as if she hadn't heard. Instead, she closed her eyes and buried her face in her hands.

"I'm so tired," she mumbled. "So tired..." She sat in silence, breathing hard. Carl held her tightly, caressed her neck and her back with long, smooth strokes, and slowly, she composed herself. She looked up at him with her dark eyes that shimmered with tears. "Would you mind— Can you— I'd like to—" She didn't find the words, and more tears fell. He tenderly dried them away.

312

"Everything's alright, Miri. You can ask me whatever you want."

She looked at him with anguished, desperate eyes, and his heart ached. "Can you sleep here tonight? Beside me? Please? I… I need you…"

He hoped that he managed to hide his surprise. "Uh… Sure, I can, Miri."

"And hold me? Please?"

She sounded so small and so lost that holding her until she felt better was the only thing he wanted to do.

"As long as you like."

A deep, relieved sigh heaved her chest. "Thank you. Thank you so much."

The thought of sleeping beside her while she was naked made him short of breath, and he loathed himself for it. Grabbing her clothes again, he held them out to her.

"Um, do you want your clothes? Olwen said that you needed to drink. And… and here's the pill…"

She stared at him in silence for a moment before she obligingly took her T-shirt and underwear and put them on while he looked another way. Then, she drank the whole bottle of water, but she didn't take the pill. Carl put it back into his pocket again. He couldn't make himself to force her to take it. She fumbled with the duvet, and he helped her. Together they curled up under it, and she turned on her side, facing him. Her head rested on his lower arm, and he embraced her with the other. Not knowing what to think, he felt Miri easing her knee in between his legs and hugging him hard, getting as close to him as she possibly could. After that, she shut her eyes and breathed deeply, seemingly falling asleep immediately.

Carl, on the other hand, felt tense and overwhelmed by suddenly and so unexpectedly having Miriam so close to him. *Like a stamp,* he thought with some of his old amusement, and then she snuggled in yet more in his arms, and he found it difficult to breathe. Stiff and uncomfortable in his whole body, he swallowed hard, and his heart rate rose.

Alright, breathe now. You're allowed to breathe. He took a deep, shaky breath and then another one until he managed to relax. Then, he looked down at her pale face with the dark bags under her eyes shading in black, and all the bruises that painted her face in yellow, green and purple, and an ocean of empathy struck him. Affectionately, he caressed her tousled brown hair before closing his eyes too. Even though he thought it impossible, he soon drifted off to sleep.

He didn't know how long they had slept when he woke by a knock on the door. Miri was still sleeping in his arms, her thin body so close to his, and his heart overflowed with tenderness. A strand of hair lay over her mouth and moved slightly by every breath. Careful to not wake her up, he moved it away from her face. The knock came again, a bit harder this time. Quickly, he untangled from the embrace, went up from the bed and unlocked the door. Olwen stood outside with an exaggerated expression of calm on her face. *Alright, what went wrong?*

"Just wanted to let you know that we're back," she said and tried to sound casual, but didn't succeed. She avoided his penetrating look and tried to look over his shoulder. "How is she?"

"Still sleeping," he said in a low voice and let her off the hook. Olwen peeked in at Miri's half-dressed body that was almost covered by the duvet. As they watched her, she moaned anxiously and began to toss and turn in her sleep. Concerned, Carl frowned. Not caring about what Olwen would think, he hurried over to the bed and wrapped the duvet around her again. With soothing movements, he stroked her neck and shoulders until she gradually calmed down. When he looked up, Olwen was still waiting at the door, her whole stance worried. With a last glance at Miriam, Carl sighed, stood up, and walked back to his P.I. Feeling the anxiety throbbing hard in his body, he let his hand comb through his hair several times before he could speak.

"She's not good, Olwen. We need to get her out of here. She's… she's not sure we're really here with her, or… or that we're real."

Olwen's eyes widened. "Shit. I knew it was bad, but that bad? Damn it."

"Yeah. And she didn't want to take the pill. Sorry, but I didn't want to force her."

Olwen shrugged it away. "Don't worry about it. As long as she's sleeping, she's all good. She should be eating too, she's way too thin, but I can't force her. At least she's drinking." She exhaled deeply. "Alright. Let her sleep 'til she wakes, and if she's able to walk by then, even if it's wobbly, well, then I say we'll get the hell out of here. We're three that can help her if she needs it. After all, she'll probably recuperate faster if she's at home, feeling safe and relaxed." She paused and frowned before giving him an honest look. "Omega and I are staying in our rooms from now. It's too dangerous out there, too many of those shadow people, and— They're trying to herd us somewhere, trap us, just like Ophelia hinted at." Carl's eyes widened. "I don't think we should go anywhere without you and Ophelia from now on. We need to stick together."

He exhaled. "Appreciated. I'd prefer not to have to go looking for you two as well. We're not in that great shape."

She gave him a faint smile. "Just make sure that you get some more sleep too. Remember that Ophelia will be mainly your responsibility when we get out of here, so you need to be alert. You're the one she trusts the most."

"Alright."

She nodded and took a step away, but changed her mind and turned toward him with a demeanor that, to his surprise, was clearly defiant.

"Carl," she began, and it astounded him that she used his real name. "I'm sorry that I treated you the way I did when we first came here. I've meant to apologize to you for some time now, but I've never found the right moment." She

315

exhaled and continued while looking him straight in the eyes, "It's not a nice trait I have, and I've been fighting it for as long as I remember, but sometimes— Well, I can get extremely grumpy sometimes, and it lasts longer than I wish for, and— Sometimes, I can't control my need for petty revenge, like—" She paused and shied away with her gaze, noticeably embarrassed. "Well, like trying to force you to sleep in the same bed as Ophelia. It was very unprofessional, it was not my place and not my business, and I'm very sorry." Before he could say anything, she looked back at him again, with hard-blushing cheeks, but when she continued, it was in a less tense voice, "I do need you as my second-in-command, Octavius. Omega is a great team member, and she's great at keeping the spirit up, but she's never going to become a good leader. You already are. I never told you, but you did impress me immensely when we were in Bettles, and I think it'd been fair if you'd become the head of our team back then, but— Well, eventually, I'm sure you will be." She inhaled and stared him rigidly in his eyes. "Since we're soon leaving, there are a couple of things I want you to have in mind." She waited until he nodded. "It's extremely important that you follow my orders in front of the others, even… even when it's my petty revenge talking. I can't have a rebellion in a situation like this, from any of you, especially now, when Omega—" She hesitated. "I'm sure you know what I mean."

He nodded again, filled with respect for her. If he were completely honest, he wasn't sure if he'd be able to do the same had the situation been reversed.

"I'm sorry too for creating the situation, Olwen, and I promise I won't do it again."

She relaxed, and suddenly she gave him a genuine smile. "You're fine. We'll manage to become a great team if we just communicate. Just kick me next time, because it will be a next time." With a nod, she turned and walked back to the end of the corridor.

Carl grinned and watched her enter her room before he closed and locked his door again. He went back to bed

316

much more relieved than only a few minutes ago, and giddy at the thought of leaving. As a second-in-command – even for a very small group – he'd be able to make a difference. Olwen did the best she could, but she wasn't flexible, and when it came to communicating— No, he didn't have to point out the obvious.

When he wriggled down under the duvet, Miri fumbled after him in her sleep. In an attempt to soothe her, he put his arms around her once more. She immediately relaxed, and her breathing calmed down. Olwen was right, he realized with surprise. Miri did trust him, and it touched him that she relied on him so completely.

It made him genuinely happy to feel the warmth of her body next to his. Shyly, he leaned his cheek at a spot on her head that didn't seem to have any wounds, and she sighed contentedly while curling up yet closer to him. Feeling that huge tenderness toward her again, he embraced her a little tighter. He found it hard to comprehend just how lucky he was. Again, he went over it in his head; she was alive. She was not lying buried somewhere in the dark and cold. She was warm, she was here, she was breathing calmly on his chest, and her arm was draped around his waist. *Allie was right,* he thought with some surprise. *I do love her. When did that happen?*

"I love you, Miri. I love you so much," he mumbled into her hair, and it felt so good, so true, to say it. For a while, he lay indulging in these unusual feelings of happiness and love and wonder, before he reluctantly heeded Olwen's advice, closed his eyes, and tried to sleep.

Next time he opened his eyes, he looked right into hers. They seemed to be brighter and clearer, more awake, saner, and she even smiled at him. He realized that they were holding hands under the duvet, and his heart skipped a beat.

"Hi." He cleared his voice.

"Hi."

"Did you sleep well?"

She nodded. "I did. Thank you." She lowered her eyes. "I'm sorry for... for before. I... didn't really know what I was saying."

Once again, his heart overflowed with empathy for her apparent awkwardness. "Shh, no need to apologize."

She didn't look up, but a heavy blush colored her pale cheeks bright red.

"But making you sleep here... Asking you to... to hold me... I feel— It's a bit, um, assertive..."

Carl couldn't help smiling, and he fondled her fingers. Her cheeks turned even brighter red if that was at all possible.

"Assertive?"

"Mhm..."

Gently, he loosened his hands from hers and put his arms around her, moving her closer to his body. With his free hand, he caressed her hair.

"I didn't mind," he said quietly with his lips almost touching her hair. When she tensed slightly, he loosened his embrace so she could turn away if she wanted. Instead, she put a tentative hand on his chest.

"Oh, um, okay... Good," she said nervously but didn't move. Her hand felt hot through his T-shirt. For a while, they just lay there, cautiously, feeling each other breathe. Carl's heart hammered like crazy, and second thoughts vaulted over each other in his mind. *What the hell, Carl. What the hell are you doing? She's injured, for crying out loud. She has a big, damn hole in her head. She hasn't been eating for days. She's bruised. She's exhausted. And what do you do? You're longing for intimacy, Carl. God, you're disgusting!* Without being able to help it, he continued to berate himself. *First of all, you shouldn't think about it at all. Secondly, it's an extreme situation, and she might confuse gratefulness of someone, anyone, being here with her, with desire. Thirdly, even if she would want to be intimate, which honestly isn't likely, it's way too early. She needs time for herself, time to heal.* As he struggled to calm down, other thoughts snuck up on him, made him relax, and helped him to not be so unfair toward himself. *I'm holding her in my arms. Honestly, that's enough. For now, it's actually all I want, to feel her close to me.* He turned his head and looked at her, trying to say something about it, but she met his probing glance with a shy glance.

"I'm not good at this," she mumbled, and his heart melted.

"I'm— Neither am I."

"Carl..." Her voice was a soft whisper, and her lips parted slightly. All second thoughts, all concerns, all anxiety flew right out of his mind. All he wanted to do was to kiss those lips so badly. Slowly, and with hard-beating heart, he moved his hand to her cheek and caressed her gently, giving her space to move away if she wanted. When she didn't, he closed in on her, so their noses almost touched. Her dark-brown eyes didn't leave his gaze for a second.

"Do you mind?" he whispered.

She shook her head slightly and lifted her mouth toward him. In wonder, his lips touched hers. They were so gentle, so warm, and so eager. He sighed softly. *Finally... finally...* Slowly, they grazed each other's lips, feeling the warm exchange of breath, but soon they began to explore and gently taste each other. Carl couldn't let go of the overwhelming feeling of wonder that she seemingly wanted to kiss him. He had never truly dared to hope, but now she let the tip of her tongue caress his lips, and with the blood pulsating in his ears, he met hers with his own. Her hand caressed his cheek, followed his neck down to his shoulders, and moved down his chest. When she found her way in under his T-shirt and touched his skin, he inhaled sharply and closed his eyes for a moment, concentrating on the tingling sensation her fingers created in his body. When he opened his eyes and sought out her lips again, meeting her tongue, the electricity in his body made him tremble. Without thinking, he moved his hand to her breast, cupping it in his hand – *So perfect.* – and she let out a quiet moan into his mouth that nearly drove him out of his mind. His breaths became heavy when he found her nipple. At his touch, she jerked toward him, and her hands found his buttocks. She pressed herself hard toward him and spread her legs apart for him. He moaned too, and urgently, he wanted to get rid of the clothes that were in the way. He wanted to caress, to kiss, to see, and to have her naked in his arms.

"Wait, wait," he panted, couldn't believe what he was doing.

"What?" Her gaze was cloudy and yearning, and her hands were on his jeans, trying to unbutton them. Taking them off him was one of the hardest things he had ever done. He brought them up toward his lips and kissed them longingly. She sighed and pressed herself toward him, putting her leg over his hip, almost driving him over the edge. Her lips glided over his neck. He gave up a shaky breath, wanting nothing more than continue. Instead, he clasped his hands gently around her face. She suddenly watched him with some concern.

Still breathing heavily, he tried to formulate words. "Miri, I... I don't want to take advantage of you."

A disbelieving expression spread over her face, and she moved her leg and hands off him as if she got burnt.

He felt like an idiot and tried to get the words out without making things worse. "You're hurt, and maybe still in shock, and... and this place... I mean, this place, Miri! Is this really what you want? Here? With me? I mean— With me?"

She turned away from him, but not quickly enough to hide the hurt and the embarrassment shining in her eyes as she struggled to sit up. He put an insecure hand on her waist, not hard enough to hinder her if she really wanted to move away, but she stopped.

"Goddamn, Miri, I'm so bad at this. I feel like a jerk." She suddenly inhaled shakily, and a tear fell on his arm. Devastated, he ran a hand through his hair. "Miri, I'm sorry, I... I would never want to hurt you."

"It's okay, Carl, it doesn't matter. I know you don't want something more with me." Her voice was distressed and filled with embarrassment. "I just don't understand why we suddenly, you know, if there's nothing to it. I... I thought—

For a moment, I thought that you actually wanted me. God, I'm such a damn fool!"

"Wait— what?"

"Whatever. I already said too much. I'm just so damn tired of making a fool out of myself all the damn time. All the damn, fucking time!"

He felt like a fool himself and fought an urge to tug at his hair again.

"Miri," he said insecurely, "you're not a fool. You're— you're the best person I know and I— I don't know what you mean with 'something more.' I don't know— I... I do want—" As he inhaled, he felt her tense under his hand, but at this point, he could as well burn all the bridges. "I do want you, Miri. I— I want you. I... I do want you in my life..."

The sudden silence stretched out, but he didn't dare to move. It felt like an eternity went by before she looked up at him in disbelief.

"You want me?"

"Yes, I do. I do want you. Goddamn, Miri, I want you naked in my arms, for crying out loud! I've longed for you for years!"

Blossoming red in her face, she stared at him as if she couldn't believe what he said. "But why— Why did you stop?"

He trailed a finger over her cheek. "I... I was afraid— I am afraid. It's not the best of times. You're still so hurt, so weak, and... and this place!"

She shook her head, and he couldn't interpret what he read from her face.

"I don't care where we are. And yes, I might be hurt, but— Do I still look like someone who can't decide on my own, who need someone to make my decisions for me? You taught me that, Carl, that the decision is mine. You taught me that I can decide on my own. Don't take that away from me now."

Shame hit him like a landslide, and he hid his face in his hands, rubbed his eyes hard. His cheeks burnt, and for a moment, he didn't dare look at her, but she deserved that he did.

With a deep breath, he took her hands and looked her straight in the eyes. "You're right. I'm sorry, and I mean it from the bottom of my heart. Honestly, I'm so ashamed right now, so I might go and hide under the bed for a while."

A faint smile touched her lips, and her face softened. "Don't hide under the bed, Carl. There's no need. I'm right here."

He smiled shakily back at her. "That you are."

With trembling hands and shallow breaths, he brought up her hand to his mouth, let his lips touch her open palm, and gave her a shy butterfly kiss. She shivered, and he closed the distance between them. When he touched her lips with all the tenderness and respect he felt for her, she tensed. At the subtle signal, he tensed too, still uncertain of what she really wanted. Tentative, but without daring to stop, in case it was yet another misunderstanding from his side, he let his tongue cautiously ease in between her lips and meet hers again. She trembled violently, and suddenly, without him being prepared for it, she embraced him so wildly that he lost balance and fell backward on the bed. She followed him down and kissed him desperately. It felt like he was drowning in waves of furious intensity.

Without knowing what he was doing anymore, he grabbed her by her shoulders and deepened the kiss even more, closing his eyes, indulging in the taste of her. She took his hands and pulled them up under her T-shirt, and placed them over her breasts. Her nipples were hard at his palms, and she moaned loudly when he caressed her. The sound aroused him so much that he nearly lost it. Her T-shirt was still in the damn way. Frustrated, he fought with it, trying to get it off, and he thought there was a faint rip as it finally came off. He didn't care. She was almost naked at last. Feeling dizzy at the sight of her and unable to resist, he

322

stroked her breasts and moved closer until he finally could take a nipple between his lips.

She gasped and moved restlessly on him. The heat between their bodies was unbearable, but there was still too much fabric in the way. Wanting everything at once, he let his tongue eagerly glide over her breast and grazed the nipple with his teeth while pressing himself hard toward her and moving his hands fervently over her buttocks. With her eyes shut, she gave up a half-cry, pushing his hands away before jerkily moving off him. Her hard panting blended together with his as she grabbed his jeans and desperately tried to unbutton them again, giving up frustrated groans when her fingers slipped. Impatiently, he tugged them off, and she straddled him, tearing her underwear to the side when failing to remove them quickly enough. When her hand enclosed him and led him into her, his deep, raw moan blended with her cry, and he couldn't hold it any longer, couldn't be soft and tender. He thrust himself deep inside her again and again, and she gave up another cry before her body convulsed, and she fell on top of him, wildly quivering. He didn't know how he managed to think, but he pulled out of her just in time, going under in frenzied waves while holding her close, close to his body.

Then, they lay panting, embracing each other.

Chapter 19

Miri soon fell asleep again, softly snuggled up in his arms. She glided into sleep, relaxed, and even though she looked exhausted, her appearance was calm and content, satisfied. *She's still too weak.* But he had learned his lesson. It was her decision. *Her body, her decision.* A touch of that intense shame hit him again. He couldn't believe that he had fallen so deeply into the trap. He had been so certain that he respected her, but when it truly mattered, he had once again taken away her choice and her voice, believing that he knew what was best for her. He felt like a hypocrite. From now on, he promised himself, he would do everything he could to never fall into that trap again.

Lovingly, he let his fingers lightly touch her face, her lips, her unruly hair. He marveled over how much she obviously wanted this, needed this, in a way that had taken him utterly by surprise. *Is she... is she in love with me?* The possibility that she might be made him jittery and giddy and wondrous.

Of course, he knew that she had had some kind of feelings for him during the past two years. *I'd have to be a stone to not notice that,* he thought, but she had never shown him any kind of invitation beyond friendship, more like the opposite; she had always kept a distance, never touched him, never even placed a hand on his arm. She had never taken any initiative, and he had definitely not wanted to push her.

Even if he wanted to, he couldn't hide from the fact that she and Caesar had had a serious relationship going on for four years, and that C had loved her so much that he even proposed to her. That the relationship wasn't impeccable didn't matter. The love between them had been genuine. That C had tried his best to force Miriam into a mold that suited him but not her might have been a problem a year ago, but not any longer. Her own personality was so strong that she had managed to break free, and Carl had to admit that it was his own fear of rejection that had kept him back. It had kept him from even trying. It had made him hide behind an image of himself as the knight on a white horse who chivalrously let her decide her own pace.

He sighed and rubbed his eyes but decided to let all that go. It was in the past now. He wasn't going to dwell on it anymore. *I've got my second chance, for crying out loud. It's all new now, all blank unwritten sheets. And if she wants me, if she truly wants me in her life, and this isn't a grateful projection…*

Feeling torn between uncertainty and hope and wonder, he didn't dare to finish the thought. Instead, he looked down at her calm face. Even in her sleep, her features were strong, he mused. Solemnly, he kissed her on the forehead, touched the corner of her mouth with his lips, and with that wondrous feeling in his heart, he leaned his cheek on hers.

Her strength shouldn't amaze him, but it did. To survive this place alone for two weeks required strength of such kind that it was almost frightening. If he were completely honest, he wasn't sure if he himself would be able to do it. Everything here was created with one sole purpose; to drive you insane. To further weaken your mind, you were faced with the real, terrifying possibility of being stuck here for the rest of your existence, if you couldn't figure out how to get home, and if that wasn't enough, you could add the physical and mental shock of teleporting. *Did you really do that, Miri? Did you teleport? That's— That's amazing! You'll have to have a damn strong mind to overcome all that without going completely insane.* And, obviously, she wasn't completely insane. Scarred, probably, but not out of her mind. She'd most likely cracked soon enough, he mused, if they'd arrived much later, but now, they'd been able to help her find a mental base to stand on, and he had a feeling that she was on her way to healing.

He let a hand stroke her stomach and her sides, finding it hard to believe that he was allowed to touch her.

"I don't think you know how long I've wanted to do this," he murmured. "I can't— I really can't believe that you're lying here like this with me. I just wish we were home." when he thought of her lying in his bed like this, completely naked, a pleasant shock spread through his body. Dwelling on the thought, his hand found its way to her chest and cupped her breast. Gently, he caressed her nipple with his thumb. She didn't even move.

"You're so tired…" The tenderness in his voice astonished him. It was hard, but he moved his hand to her hair instead and kissed her again. Even with all the bruises, he thought her beautiful.

"We'll soon be home, *habibti*, and then maybe… maybe you want to be…" His voice trailed away. He had no idea what she wanted to be. What did he want her to be? His girlfriend or his fiancée, or… or his wife? Mother to their children? *Whoa, aren't you speeding things up here?* Still, the image of her, pregnant in the last trimester, was absolutely beautiful.

"Alright, cut it off now." He tried to sound stern, but his voice was soft and longing, and his hand caressed her stomach again. "Just play it by ear, take it easy, don't rush anything. It's perfect just the way it is."

He cupped her breast again, let his hand rest around its softness, and eventually, he drifted off to sleep. Even as he let the dreams catch him, the strong and wondrous sensations of having her in his arms caressed his soul.

And somewhere along the way, everything changed.

There was laughter around him, teasing laughter, as if he were a boy again, and all the kids in school taunted him. Then, the laughter stopped, and to his dread, he realized that he wasn't in school; he was in the barn in Bettles, and all the children around him were both dead and alive. In anticipation, they waited for the barn doors to open. They milled around him, smiling eagerly, and with terrifying clarity, Carl knew that they herded him toward the sacrificial table. No! he screamed and tried to flee, but their hands were so strong, and they pushed him even harder toward the table. Someone stood barely visible in the dark shadows behind it, holding a huge silver knife in one hand. It glimmered with a dull reflection in the faint light. The children forced him down onto the table, all their small hands touching his body, and he screamed in anger, panic, and fear, mostly in fear, as he desperately struggled to break free. Then, the person with the knife stepped out of the shadows and looked down at him with a joyous smile. Carl, what a pleasant surprise. I was wondering when you were going to join the party. *And with an elegant thrust, Night Porter cut his throat.*

"Carl? Carl, please, wake up. Please." Miriam's voice was so close to him. Still half in his dream, he fumbled for her, and she let herself be embraced. Her hands caressed his face, dried away the tears from his cheeks, and he held her hard. She lay chest to chest with him and whispered words he couldn't hear through the sound of his wildly throbbing heart, but eventually, he calmed down and breathed easier. He dried his eyes with one hand and refused to let Miri go with the other.

"Oh, wow," he exhaled. "What a bad dream!"

"And it's not over yet," she said concerned.

He shivered violently and looked up at her. "What do you mean?"

"I'm sorry, Carl."

With an elegant thrust, she slit his throat.

Panting desperately, he opened his eyes. Miri lay in his arms, sleeping. She didn't seem to have moved since he fell asleep. *Am I still dreaming?* His heart pounded so hard that it felt like it was going to hammer its way out of his chest. The image of his heart violently bursting out of his chest materialized in front of his eyes. He shied away from it. *No! No more scary thoughts! I don't want it to actually happen—* A loud banging on the window made him jolt violently, and a half-choked scream found its way out of his throat. The curtains in front of the window shimmied, and he grabbed Miri's arm hard for comfort, but it was so cold and stiff. Something was wrong. His whole body froze in terrifying foreboding, and he couldn't breathe. Slowly and hesitantly, he glanced down at her face. It was bluish in color, and a thin membrane covered her open eyes. With a shriek, he pushed her away and tried to get up from the bed. She rolled over onto her stomach and lay still. Blood covered her whole back and the bed. It pulsed out of her head wound as if something fought to push itself out from her head. With a loud crack, Miri's skull split into two pieces and something – no, someone stood in front of him, covered in blood. Shallow, rasping breaths forced themselves through his throat, the shock locking his chest so hard that it was painful to breathe, and in paralyzing horror, he stared at the humanoid in front of him. It resembled Miri, but a disproportioned and malevolent Miri.

"Hello, Carl. I'm Athena." The creature smiled hungrily and leaned in toward him.

Terror made his body feel like water, too weak to be able to move. He just lay there, waiting inertly for her to reach him, and too late, he realized that she was going to kiss him. He wanted to scream, to desperately crawl away, but his throat and limbs were locked.

With a swift move, the creature eased down on him, straddled him. She held him in place with legs thick and strong as timber. With a hungry look in her eyes, she pressed her mouth hard and greedily toward his, and Miri's blood was forced into his mouth with her tongue. He was suffocating, and he tried to scream but couldn't. The tongue invaded him. He struggled fiercely to get free, but she held him in an unbreakable grip around his throat that made him choke. Flailing wildly with his arms, he fought desperately to break her grip, to no avail. She moved her free hand down to his groin and grabbed him hard. As the pain seared through his lower abdomen, he gasped in anguish. The touch was rough as her hand jerked him up and down. To his horror and shame, he turned rigid in her hand, and with a triumphant look on her face, she forced him violently inside her. *It's burning! It's burning! Oh, God!*

He screamed in agony, struggled to get away, to push her off him, but she was too strong. Wildly, she thrust herself on him, moaning and crying out in yearning until he thought

328

that he was going to disappear inside her. Tears of pain, shame, and helplessness flowed from his eyes when he ejaculated. The creature quivered in pleasure and forced him even deeper inside her.

As the orgasm went through her in wave after wave, she collapsed on top of him, smothering him, while she stuttered in pleasure, "You're going to have a baby, Carl."

He cried when he woke up. Inconsolable, he put his arms over his face and cried hysterically, gasping for breath.

"Carl?" Miriam's voice sounded sleepy as she moved beside him and put a warm hand on his arm. He jerked and couldn't stop a half-scream.

"Carl?" The sleepiness in her voice was gone, and she sounded worried. "What's going on?"

He didn't dare to look at her in case she wasn't going to be herself, or if she was going to be dead, no matter that she talked and moved, and his breaths were ragged, almost hyperventilating.

"You're scaring me. Please, Carl, look at me. Tell me what's wrong. Please."

He couldn't move his arms from his face, he couldn't move at all, the only thing he could do was to cry and try to breathe.

Miriam's hands were on his chest, rubbing him calmly, and she continued to rub him as she leaned in and put her cheek on him, warming him. "It's okay, Carl, it's going to be okay. Whatever it is, I promise you, it's going to be okay." Her voice was a soothing murmur, and slowly, his breathing began to calm down. "It's all good, *neshomeleh*, it's all good. I'm here with you, I'm right here with you."

That word? He didn't think he would dream that word. It sounded Yiddish, and he had no idea what it meant. Slowly and with a wildly beating heart, he lowered his arms and managed to look at her. *She's bruised, she wasn't bruised in the other dreams.*

"M... Miri...?" His voice was unrecognizable, and she took his hands in hers and kissed them, caressed them.

"I'm right here, *neshomeleh*, I'm right here."

Still terrified, he looked around the room. It looked as it had when they went to bed. No quivering curtains, no blood on the bed.

"Can... can you... can you turn around...?"

At the sound of his shivering voice, she frowned worriedly but did what he asked. The gauze covered the head wound, and it looked good. It didn't bleed, and it didn't pulsate. Hesitating, he reached for her hand, but as soon as he touched it, he jerked away. What if she wasn't Miri when she looked at him again?

When she turned around, her bruised face was sculpted in worry and uneasiness. Several minutes had passed. Maybe he could trust that this was the reality and not another dream? He reached for her hand again, and she held on to his in both of hers.

"Tell... tell me something that I don't know. Please?"

At first, she looked at him concerned, as if he might be slightly insane, but obligingly, she thought through the request. "Um, Alexander the Great undid the Gordian Knot at Gordium in Phrygia?"

He almost laughed. "I knew that," he said in a calmer tone. "Tell me something about you that I don't know."

"About me? Now?" She looked baffled at him, but he nodded vigorously. "Um, okay." She thought it through for a moment. "I don't think I've told you this because I'm ashamed of it." She laughed reluctantly. "As a child, I loathed how connected Beth was with animals. It was like she understood them and could speak to them. I wanted to do that too, but I've never had that gift. I used to tease her all the time by calling her Snow White. She hated it, which made it even funnier. I didn't stop until she tried to color her hair red and got a spanking by mom. We can't watch that movie anymore."

Carl chuckled a little, even though he felt sorry for Beth. He wasn't sure, but it didn't seem like he was dreaming anymore. He inhaled deeply and rubbed his eyes, but the tension in his body refused to go away. When he cautiously looked up at Miriam, he expected her to have turned into something else, but she was just sitting there, holding his hand in hers, watching him worriedly.

"Thanks," he said and tried to give her a reassuring smile, but the frown on her forehead deepened and told him that he failed with calming her down.

"Are you sure you're okay, Carl?"

"Not really," he said and saw her surprise. That's right; she wasn't used to him telling the truth about his feelings. He squirmed awkwardly. *I need to continue being honest about myself. The macho-thing doesn't work anymore.* As he met her worried gaze, he decided to accept this as reality. It felt more real than the other awakenings had.

He inhaled deeply. "I… I had such bad dreams, but I don't want to— I don't want to talk about them, not here, and honestly, I don't dare sleeping here again." He looked around the room, wondering if the shadows were listening. "This place, it's just escalating." When Miri followed his gaze and shuddered, he continued, "How are you feeling? Do you think you could walk for a while?"

She nodded. "If it means that we're going home, yes, absolutely. I'll walk until I can't, and then I'll walk some more."

He caressed her hands and looked sincerely at her. "You're amazing, Miri."

With a faint blush, she looked down at their entwined hands. He wanted to tell her how beautiful she was and how much he loved her and how proud he was of her, but he didn't dare to do that here anymore. This place sucked up all emotions it could find and fed on them.

With some help from her, Carl managed to sit up on the bed and put his feet on the floor. That's when he realized that he was still naked from the waist down. Awkwardly, he looked for his pants and underwear. When Miri handed him them with a sly little smile, an image of Athena riding him flashed before his eyes. It made him feel dirty and unclean, and less worthy than he knew that he was. Determinedly, he pushed the image and the feelings away. They belonged in a dream and had absolutely nothing to do with Miriam.

"Um, thanks," he said and had to clear his throat.

She grinned at him. It was more like a shadow of a grin, he thought, but at least she seemed to have a much better grasp of reality than before they went to sleep.

Tense and jumpy, he went around the room and gathered their things, careful to always have Miriam in sight. It took her longer to put on her T-shirt, jeans, and shoes than it should have, he noticed with concern, but when she rose and came toward him with a loving smile and took his hands, he only saw how she beamed. *Does she know that she looks like she's in love?* Then, the question popped back into his mind, on the brink of hope, *Is she?*

"You're beautiful, Miri," he said quietly and caressed her fingers.

She heaved up on tiptoe and brushed her lips toward his. His heart fluttered.

"You're beautiful too, Carl," she said with a touch of shyness when she let go.

Wide-eyed, he stared at her. *Beautiful?* Had someone ever called him that before? He didn't think so, not even Manda, and they had a child together.

Once again, his thoughts skirted the boundaries of the Athena-dream. Immediately, he shied away, but couldn't stop the intense feeling of shame and guilt. The sensation of being deeply unclean ate away at him. *I'm NOT giving in to you,* he thought tenaciously to the dream character, and with a deep, stubborn breath, he pushed the feelings away.

Miriam unlocked the door and stepped out into the corridor. Nervously, she checked both sides of the corridor.

"Which room?"

"Over there."

He tugged her hand, and she followed him like a frightened shadow. At number twelve, he knocked on the door, and Omega opened immediately. As soon as Miri walked in, she embraced Omega hard and got a warm hug in return.

"Happy to see you awake and on your feet, sweetheart," the young F.R. said.

"I'm so happy to see you too, both of you," Miri said emotionally and acknowledged Olwen, who sat crisscross on the big, disheveled bed. "You don't know how happy I am."

Carl met Olwen's inquiring gaze over Miriam's shoulder and made a tiny 'so-so' gesture.

His P.I. nodded and hopped off the bed. "Are you prepared to find the way home now, Ophelia?" she asked.

"Yes," Miri said with emphasis, "I've never been more prepared than now."

Satisfied, Olwen nodded. "Good. Let's go then – if everyone's been to the potty."

She smiled broadly. The others laughed at her, and some of the tension melted away. *Good try,* Carl thought and managed to give her an appreciative look. She winked at him before waving them all out of the room.

As soon as they entered the corridor, Miriam fumbled for his hand. He took it and held on tight. When he gazed at her, she looked frightened and tired already, and her eyes were like black holes in the pale face. It was high time to shove away his own feelings of discomfort and fear, and help Miri keeping her feet on the ground. Carl squeezed her hand harder to try to give her some confidence. He was happy when she squeezed his hand right back.

Night Porter beamed at them when they stepped into the foyer, and Carl thought that the slimy man's gaze lingered a bit longer on him as if he knew everything that had happened. He managed to not squirm and met Night Porter's gaze with a bland expression. Something – *disappointment?* – flashed over the porter's face.

"You're not leaving already, are you?"

Miriam stiffened beside Carl, and he calmly stroke his thumb over her hand.

"Just wanted to take a look at the sights, sir. I haven't had the chance to see them yet, but Miriam's well enough now to show them." Carl kept his thoughts sternly on the narrow meandering streets that they'd walked on their way here, and after a piercing look into Carl's eyes, the broad grin returned to Night Porter's lips.

"Ah, I see. Well, if you happen to pass by, I know that there's a masquerade at the castle tonight, and I happen to have some masks here. They wouldn't notice if you slipped in for a while."

A masquerade? Is he mad? The night porter looked expectantly at them, so Carl pulled out all his acting skills and beamed toward the despicable and scary man. "A masquerade? Really? What a great idea! We'd love to do that," he said sincerely.

Miri's hand jerked, but he caressed it calmingly. The porter dived down behind the counter and came up with four beautifully decorated masks gleaming with jewels.

Carl raised his eyebrows. "Magnificent."

"They are, aren't they?" The porter petted them fondly before handing them to him.

For some reason, Carl felt right out disgusted touching them and had to hinder a strong impulse of throwing them on the floor, but his face showed nothing of this. Instead, he continued to beam toward the man. When he saw an anticipative gleam in Night Porter's eyes, Carl knew that he was right. This was clearly another trap.

"We'll let you know everything about the masquerade later," he said excitedly. "This will be so much fun."

The porter smiled back at him, and Carl got an image in his head of a hovering snake.

"I wish you the most… thrilling… time tonight."

"Thank you." Carl's cheeks hurt from all the smiling when he looked at the others. "Let's go, ladies," he said in a joyful tone., but they all stared at him as if he was crazy. *Come on now, don't leave me hanging here. We need to convince him that we're going to have a fabulous time.*

They didn't seem to get his cue, so he quickly led them out of the inn before the porter got suspicious. For a few blocks, they walked in silence. When they couldn't see the inn's sign anymore, Miriam anxiously stopped and turned toward him.

"We're not going to the castle, right?" she asked in a small, frightened voice.

"Of course not," Carl reassured her. "We're going home."

Omega laughed relieved beside him. "You convinced me in there," she admitted. "I thought you'd lost your mind."

Even though what she said wasn't funny, he couldn't help laughing too, and soon they were all laughing. He wondered if anyone else heard the hysterical undertone in it. However, when the laughter died away, the mood among them seemed brighter, to Carl's relief.

"Alright," Olwen said briskly, "You remember I told you about Florence's diary and notes. I couldn't put my finger on what she tried to say, but I think I might've figured it out now." They all looked expectantly at her. "I can't be sure, but it seems as she concentrated on a specific place that had a special meaning for her, and that's what drew her back. I thought maybe you could do the same thing, Ophelia. At least it's worth a try. If it doesn't work, we'll figure out something else."

Miri nodded thoughtfully. "I can't explain it, but that resonates with me. Last thing I remember before I woke up and saw you around my bed, um, yesterday?" She frowned confused. "No, not yesterday. Um, whenever..." For a moment, she seemed to have lost the thread, but then, she started over again. "Something strange happened when I sat at the harbor looking out over the water, just thinking about being, um, uh, home. And then, I suddenly saw a bridge that hadn't been there before. I was just going to explore it when, uh, when—"

335

She shied away from the last memories before her collapse at the harbor. Carl couldn't blame her, but there was something else. He studied her fiercely blushing face. *No, Miri, you didn't think about home, you thought about somewhere else. It doesn't matter. I trust you wherever you want to lead us.*

"Huh," Omega said. "Strange, indeed, but then again, it sure suits this place as hand in glove. Well, let's see if the bridge is still there, shall we?"

Olwen nodded. "Great, Ophelia. You lead for now. By the way," she glanced at Carl's hand, "you might want to put those away somewhere."

"Hm? What?" He looked down at the masks in his hand and couldn't stop staring at them. *How could I've forgotten about these?* The repulsive feeling returned with full force, and he dropped them where he stood and desperately dried his hand on his jeans. The others stared at him.

"They feel disgusting, like dipping your hand in a pot of leprosy," he tried to explain.

Sounds of disgust were heard around him.

"Octo!" Omega protested, and he shrugged half-apologetic.

"Sorry."

"Alright," Olwen said. "Let's go. Ophelia?"

Miriam took the lead, still hanging on to his hand as if she never wanted to let go. The half-lit, half-foggy streets lay quiet and empty, ominous and yet sad, Carl thought. *It's like they've been abandoned but persist in searching for the people who once lived here.*

Their footsteps sounded muddled, and the air was damp. It didn't take long before they once again stood at the harbor where they had found Miri.

A relieved smile broke out on her tired face, and she pointed. "Look! It's there! Let's go!"

Briskly, they followed the harbor all the way to its end. A large masonry-like structure seemed to wait for them with a ladder showing them the way up.

336

Miriam watched it skeptically but shrugged. "Okay, here goes," she mumbled as she let go of Carl's hand and began to climb.

Immediately, he missed the nearness her touch had given him but shrugged too and tried the ladder. It seemed sturdy enough. He waited until she had reached the top until he started to climb. Soon, he was up there with her, and she turned to him, looking cheerful. *She's happy that we're finally doing something, that we're on our way home. I knew she didn't need much encouragement to find her strength again. She's wonderful.* Then, he saw the bridge and raised his eyebrows. It wasn't broader than four feet, it lacked railing, and he couldn't discern the other end.

"Well," Omega said, stepping up beside him. "This'll be interesting."

"Yeah."

"Are you afraid of heights?"

He shook his head. "No, I'm happy to say. You?"

She grimaced. "A tiny bit."

"A tiny bit?" Olwen echoed from behind them. "You're a ranger!"

"But I'm not flawless. Not to worry, though. I'll manage it. I've trained a lot to overcome situations like this one."

Miri stepped up to the younger woman and put a gentle hand on her shoulder. "Do you want us to find another way?"

Carl stared at her, couldn't believe that she even now, in this state, managed to think of others before thinking of herself. *She's so amazingly strong. And she doesn't even realize it.*

Omega didn't even ponder the question for a second before answering. "No. Let's not confuse this place. You think of your home, Pheli, and we'll get to where we're supposed to be."

"Okay."

Miri stepped up to the bridge and inhaled deeply before carefully putting her foot on the stone, testing it. When she found it sturdy enough, she began to walk.

Carl hurried up behind her and felt Omega's presence behind his back. Sternly refusing to look down, he concentrated on following Miri's straight posture, positively surprised by her determined stance and how quickly she led them over the bridge without hesitating or stumbling. She didn't even flail her arms to keep her balance. Behind him, he could hear Omega's suppressed breathing. It sounded harsh and on the edge of panic. He wished that he could turn around and hold her hand, comfort her, but there was no room to navigate on the narrow bridge.

Twenty minutes later, they finally reached the other end. When Carl's feet touched the solid ground, his legs felt all wobbly, and he wiped away cold sweat from his forehead. As he slowly started to breathe normally again, he had to admit that just because he wasn't afraid of heights, didn't mean that he felt comfortable walking on a stick thirty miles up in the air.

Violently shaking, Omega collapsed on the rocky surface and hyperventilated. Her face shone from a thin layer of sweat. Worriedly, they kneeled beside her, but she waved dismissively with her hand.

"Just… just need a couple… a couple of minutes…" She put her arm over her face and continued to breathe heavily.

Carl didn't feel that he knew her well enough to dare to comfort her physically, but Olwen reached for her hand, and Miri stroked her arm calmingly. A few minutes later, she began to calm down and breathe normally again. She lowered her arm and looked at them.

"Wow, that was bad," she puffed. "And I mean, really, really bad. Probably the worst height I've ever encountered." She chuckled faintly. "Lieutenant Russell would be so damn proud of me. Too bad he's not here." She took another deep breath and managed to get up on her feet, facing the bridge determinedly. "Yeah, this bridge will haunt me in my nightmares, but I crossed it, I beat it, and I survived. Now, let's move on."

They all stood up and looked around. Behind them, the town began to disappear in fog. As they observed it, the fog thickened. At first, Carl couldn't understand what was going on, but goosebumps appeared on his arms when the fog began to shape into a giant uneven bubble. It floated over the bridge toward them at a slow but determined pace.

"I've got a bad feeling about this," Omega mumbled with a touch of fear in her voice.

Miri frowned uncertainly, but then she closed her eyes hard, her face taking on a concentrated expression. Suddenly, Olwen and Omega gasped, and Carl turned around just in time to see the bridge fade away and disappear with the fog falling into the water while transforming into an enormous mist-like squid. Miriam staggered, and he managed to catch her before she fell to the ground. She breathed hard and leaned heavily on him. Worriedly, he tried to keep her on her feet. When he looked back at Omega and Olwen, it was clear to him that both of them struggled to remain composed. Omega's clasped hands trembled violently, and Olwen crossed her arms tightly over her chest. They glanced at each other, before turning toward Miriam, watching her with an apprehensive expression, but neither of them uttered a word. Carl pulled Miri even closer into his arms as if his embrace could wipe away the fear that lingered around them in the damp air. Suddenly, something wet dripped on his hand. *Damn it!*

"Olwen?"

"Yes?"

"Can you come and take a look at this, please?"

She seemed relieved to get something else to focus on, and the fear in her face leveled out as she closed in on them. Omega trotted after her with a gray tone on her face that made her look sick.

Carl held Miriam closely to his chest and pointed to her head.

Olwen looked as if a revelation hit her. "So, this is how it re-opens all the time. That's no good. Let me take a look at those stitches again. Omega, can you give me my bag?"

Omega nodded and took the few steps back to where they had rested. As she grabbed the bag, she hesitantly looked down to where the squid had fallen, and her appearance turned terrified and dizzy. On unsteady feet, she came back and handed Olwen her bag. Carl caught her gaze.

"It's still down there," she said hoarsely. "I don't know why it doesn't, you know, dissolve. It should just, you know, become fog again, right?"

Carl stared at her. "What— what does it do?"

Omega got a fearful look in her eyes. "S... swimming around and staring at me. Just, you know, staring at me..."

The thought of the fog as a living being, a dangerous living being, terrified him immensely. "Okay." He cleared his throat that suddenly had turned dry. "Good thing we're leaving."

"Yeah. I... I have a thing against, you know, tentacles." She embraced herself hard and rubbed her arms.

Olwen listened to them with a deep frown on her forehead, before bringing out the flashlight and removing the gauze.

"Mm," she mumbled, concentrating on the wound again. "At least one has broken. I can't do anything about it here, more than put on another gauze to stop the bleeding. Omega?"

"Yeah?"

"Can you hold the flashlight for me?"

"Yeah, sure."

She seemed relieved by getting something to do, and it surprised Carl that Olwen was so clear-sighted that she gave the younger woman a task to concentrate on, instead of worrying about the squid. *Well, she's been a team leader for a long*

340

time. You can't go around being a leader for several years without learning some basic psychology.

The whole time Olwen worked with her wound, Miri stood unmoving in his arms, but her breathing was shallow and pained.

Eventually, Olwen took a step back and reached for the flashlight. "It's all done, sweetheart," she said as she turned it off and put it into her bag again. Miri turned around and faced Olwen, who looked back at her with a serious appearance. "Try not to do whatever it is you're doing again, if it's not necessary, Ophelia. We need you, we want to keep you alive, and we don't want you to turn into a vegetable. Okay?" Miriam nodded, her face exhausted and pale again. Carl could sense the concern radiating from all of them as they watched her. "Do you need a break?" Olwen asked.

She shook her head. "I just want to get home. And I want to get away from anywhere that squid-thing can get to us."

Omega looked extremely relieved and gave Miri a grateful glance.

"Okay," Olwen agreed. "Where do we go from here?"

They turned their backs to the fog-covered town and studied the scenery ahead. A flat, sandy terrain lay in front of them, weirdly lit up from somewhere. It was as if the light physically floated on top of the ground, Carl thought. Except for it being a grayish beige surface, dry and dead, the landscape in front of him was one very familiar, the endless grass plains outside of his childhood's Edmonton.

Miriam inhaled and fumbled for his hand. He took it in a calm grasp. Then, something stirred on their left. A winding staircase rose up, slowly and majestic, some fifty yards from where they were standing. A shiver ran down Carl's spine, and he could hear the faint gasp from Olwen and Omega.

Miriam stopped concentrating and nodded toward it. "That way."

341

Olwen exhaled deeply and seemed to force herself to relax. "Okay, you lead," she said calmly, and Carl thought that he was the only one who heard the slight shiver in her voice, but there was nothing he could do for her at this time. *She wouldn't let me,* he thought regretfully.

Miriam began walking with his hand in a firm grip. Her stance wasn't brisk anymore, he noticed worriedly, but he had to trust that she was able to do this without breaking.

Just as with the bridge, the staircase was narrow and lacked railing. As he squinted at it, followed it with his gaze as it spiraled up in the darkness and disappeared out of sight, a thought suddenly struck him from out of the blue. He gave Miriam a furtive side-glance. Her face and the way she carried herself showed all the signs that she was exhausted and only managed by mere will. *It has to do with how strained her mind is. I bet all my apples it'd been broader, safer, had she done this the very first day. Bet my apples it would've had a damn railing too.* He had a feeling – a bad, terrifying feeling – that everything she created would become even narrower and more dangerous the longer it took them to find the right way out.

Miriam studied the staircase with eyes that were mere slits. Carl thought he saw a flash of doubt on her face, and that scared him more than anything else. Shrugging, she put her foot on the first step. She climbed with slow, tired movements. The stairs were so steep that she needed both hands to hold on to the steps above her. As he climbed behind her, he could hear her strained breathing clearly. The higher up they went, the more often did she need to rest. She cowered on the step, hiding her head in her arms. Every time she crouched, he calmly stroked her ankles, which were the only parts of her body he could reach. It worried him that she was so extremely exhausted and that she apparently tapped into the last reserves of energy already. It didn't take long before the damn gauze bled through. He glared worriedly at the blood that trickled down from under it. *She can't do this for too long. I hope we're out soon, or at least that we can find someplace to rest properly.*

It felt as if they had climbed for an eternity in the weird half-lit darkness when they finally reached a narrow plateau without a railing. Not even hesitating, Miri stumbled over it to the short end and looked down. Carl took a couple of uncertain steps toward her before stopping, nauseated by the vast emptiness around this floating stone they stood on. It scared him, seeing Miriam at the edge of it, swaying slightly, without anything to hold on to.

Then, a quiet sobbing reached him from behind. He looked over his shoulder and saw Omega laying down on the platform, crawling together like a hedgehog, clearly trying to not fall off. Tears flowed from her eyes, and her face was completely ashen. Olwen sat down beside her and embraced the younger woman's wildly trembling body as hard as she possibly could. Behind them, the stairs vanished in the air, and there was nothing left that could hold this plateau in place.

Sudden dizziness hit him, and he closed his eyes, trying to calm down. *Zen... Think Zen...* Slowly, he regained control over his breathing and could open his eyes again. When he turned around, Miriam concentrated again, and from nowhere, a door appeared in front of her, hovering a couple of inches above the floating stone, visible in the gloom like a beacon. The relief was so strong that a teary lump formed in Carl's throat. His hopes that it would lead out to the Kroger's basement crumbled when she opened it, and it showed a corridor brightly lit by wall lamps. At least it had steady walls, and it didn't look like the corridors at the inn. He couldn't wait to get in there, getting away from the open space around him.

Miriam stepped into the doorway and leaned heavily on the door to keep it open, rubbing her face.

Carl frowned. Something was wrong with it. At first, he couldn't grasp what it was, but suddenly it dawned on him; the corridor was only visible inside the door frame. On the outside, the door was still hovering unattached to anything. He swallowed hard and trembled when vertigo hit him with full force. He had no idea how long he stood there, quivering, sweating, and on the edge of panic, fighting to get a grip on himself.

Behind him, Olwen said in a soothing voice, "Come on, Omega, you can do this. It's only a few steps to that corridor."

"I'm going to fall! I know I'm going to fall!" Omega's voice was high-pitched and frantic.

Grateful to have something to concentrate on, Carl turned toward them. Omega kept her eyes tightly shut, and her face was ash gray. She held onto Olwen with a fierce grip, like someone who was about to drown and in desperation drowned the person helping her.

"No, you're not," he said, surprised by his calm tone, and took the few steps back to her. Then, he realized that he was way too close to the edge and that he couldn't spot the ground from here. His head began to spin again, and he closed his eyes. *No, stop it! I need to get back in control. I can't let this win over me.* He needed to ignore the seemingly bottomless pit that waited for them only a couple of inches away, needed to stop thinking about what would happen if any of them took one wrong step.

I can do it.

With a deep, calm breath, he opened his eyes again. Refusing to look down, he stretched out his hand toward the terrified woman, while putting all the reassurance he could muster in his voice.

"Omega, look at me." He waited for a second, but she had her eyes tightly shut and didn't respond. "Omega. Look at me," he said, sharper this time. At last, she squinted at him. In a softer voice, he said, "We're here for you; we're going to help you. Here, take my hand. Olwen's going to take your other hand, and we'll be with you every step of the way."

He could tell that she didn't believe him, but despite that, she tried to reach his hand.

"That's good," Olwen mumbled. "That's a good girl."

344

Quivering, Omega grabbed his hand. Carl suppressed a grimace when she held on so hard that it hurt. She was stronger than she looked. As she began to rise, she wobbled wildly, and in sheer terror, he felt himself losing balance. Olwen reacted before he knew it. She grabbed Omega hard under her armpit and him around his arm, giving them the support they needed. Carl's heart pounded violently, and sweat covered his face. Together, they stood in a tight circle, breathing heavily while holding on to each other, concentrating hard on not swaying and lose balance again.

"Just holding her hand won't work, Octavius," Olwen said after a moment, her voice strained and hoarse. "You need to get in closer when we're walking. Hold your right arm around her back and your left arm under her armpit. We need to keep the balance, whatever we do otherwise." He nodded, not trusting his own voice, and while they slowly and carefully straightened out into a single line with Omega in the middle, he followed her instructions. "Good, Octavius. Omega, you keep your eyes on Ophelia. She's holding the door for you. It's only fifteen steps toward it. Let's count, okay? One…"

Together they counted, Omega in a violently shaking voice, her eyes sternly set on Miri and the door. It took them ten minutes to get Omega all the way to the corridor, but finally, Miriam was able to reach her and pull her inside. Together they stumbled and fell on the floor, backs toward the safe wall. Miriam closed the door and glided down too.

Olwen chuckled faintly and hugged the crying, quivering Omega hard. "That's probably the worst thing I've ever done," she admitted in a trembling voice. "You were so brave, Omega, so brave."

Carl nodded weakly, shivering uncontrollably in his whole body. "No wonder you're a ranger," he managed to say, his voice hoarse and on the brink of cracking. "God, facing this all the time, I'd go crazy."

In the midst of all the crying, Omega managed to laugh. "You're both crazy," she sniveled. "And I love you.

You too, Pheli, I love you too. You're the best team I've ever worked with."

"You've never worked with another team," Olwen said with an unsteady smile, and all of them laughed on the edge of hysteria.

After wiping her sweaty face, Olwen took off her backpack and found bread and apples that she handed out. They hummed appreciatively at the sight, and then they concentrated on eating, even though they had a hard time getting the food down.

After she swallowed the last piece, Omega rubbed her eyes and exhaled. "Are we— Are we going to face more of these heights, Pheli?"

Miriam scooted over to her and hugged her closely. "I wish I knew," she mumbled. "I don't think so, I have a feeling we're pretty close, but I don't know how close, or what's going to lie between us and our world."

Omega exhaled again. "Okay. I'm going to be brave."

"You already are."

Omega looked grateful and hugged Miri again. "Thanks," she mumbled.

"Since we're already taking a break, I want to take a look at that wound of yours again," Olwen broke in.

"Sure." Miriam obligingly turned her back toward Olwen, who was already digging out things from her doctor's bag. As she took away the blood-soaked gauze, the big meaty wound made Carl queasy in a way he hadn't experienced since his first Project. He swallowed hard and placed his sweaty face between his knees and concentrated on breathing, terrified to hear a cracking sound from Miri's skull.

"Mm, okay. It's not as bad as I thought. Only one of the stitches broke. There's still a lot of bleeding going on, but nothing you can't handle."

"Good," Miri mumbled.

"Yeah, as long as we keep it clean, it should heal properly as soon as it gets a chance." As Carl finally managed to compose himself and look up, Olwen placed the new gauze on the wound. "It will scar pretty badly, though," she said, but Miriam shrugged indifferently.

"Whatever."

Olwen, Omega, and Carl all smiled at each other over her head, and Olwen embraced her fondly.

"I hope you all know how lucky I feel having you three in our team. We're one hell of a good one."

For a little while longer, they enjoyed their silent camaraderie before they felt well enough to continue down the narrow corridor that stretched straight ahead. Even though it was brightly lit, they couldn't see the end of it. In the beginning, they all marched briskly with the unaired hope that they soon were going to find their way out, but nothing changed. The corridor went on and on, looking the same no matter how far they thought they went. Carl thought that they might have walked for hours. His feet hurt, and his legs felt wobbly from all the physical strain. The never-changing view of the corridor in front of them made him dizzy and slightly nauseous. No one talked. Stubbornly, they struggled on. Miriam stumbled in front of him, clearly exhausted again, but when he put a hand on her arm, the look she gave him over her shoulder warned him to intervene, and he took away his hand, let her struggle on as she wanted to. At least the gauze was clean. *Her body, her decision,* he thought again, more hesitantly this time, as he watched her haggard stance. *But if she's hurting herself, there's no way I'm not stepping in. She can't break herself out of sheer stubbornness.*

Eventually, when even the thought of taking one more step made him want to cry, and Miriam's pace was more of a persistent wobble than anything else, Olwen called for a stop. When they turned toward each other, they all looked beyond exhausted and on the edge of breaking, even though it was clear to him that Olwen tried to hide her own anxiety and weariness from them.

"I think we need to rest," she said fatigued and slurred on the words. "I don't know about you, but it feels like we've been walking for days."

Without any more hassle, they lay down in the narrow corridor, trying to make it as comfortable as possible. Carl took off his jacket and placed it under his head. With his back to the wall, trying to ignore the hard stone floor underneath his shoulder, he held out his arm toward Miri. She didn't even hesitate before laying down with her back toward him, and he embraced her softly while snuggling in at her shoulder. Regarding the hard surface and last night's – *or whenever it was* – terrifying nightmares, he didn't think he'd be able to sleep, but within minutes, he drifted away into a dreamless slumber.

When he woke up, Olwen was already awake. She sat leaning toward the opposite wall with her arms resting on her bent knees. She seemed to be taking a moment to just be herself for once. There was no strain on her face, no commanding-officer-look, just a woman in her late thirties with softness characterizing her. She would most likely not take it positively being caught in this position, so he closed his eyes again and left her to her privacy.

The next time he woke up was because someone was nudging him repeatedly.

"Hm?" He squeezed at the bright light and saw a silhouette in front of his eyes.

"We're soon leaving," Olwen said. "I have a bread piece left. Do you want it?"

"Um…" He yawned and sat up while rubbing his eyes. "Yes, please."

He took the offered bread. Olwen looked less strained and exhausted than she had yesterday – *or whenever it was*. Further away, Omega and Miri sat together. They talked in low voices while eating. The atmosphere was overall more relaxed than before they slept.

"How are you feeling?" he asked his P.I., and Olwen couldn't hide her surprise.

"You're not supposed to ask things like that, you know," she said seriously, and he met her on her own terms.

"A second-in-command is allowed to check on his Principal Investigator to see if she's alright and hanging in there properly. And she's allowed to give him an honest answer."

An unexpected smile touched Olwen's lips and even reached her eyes. "Well, if that's the case... I'm doing alright. Better now after some sleep. I'm a bit surprised, to tell the truth, because I had a hard time keeping myself together yesterday."

He nodded. "Yeah, I feel it too. It's like the air is easier to breathe, eh? Not so heavy, not pressing down on our minds."

Olwen looked astonished at his words. "You're right," she said in a brighter tone. "I hope that means we're closing in on our world. I wouldn't mind getting home, taking a proper shower, eating a proper meal, and sleeping in a proper bed."

"I hear you. So, what's the plan for the rest of the day? Just keep on walking?"

She grimaced. "Pretty much. My cell stopped working some days ago, and I have no clue about time or anything, but we'll walk 'til we collapse again, then we'll sleep and eat and walk again."

He nodded. "Yeah, figured."

With a wry smile, she said, "When I get home, I'll put on my wristwatch. Hopefully, it's more reliable than the cell." As an afterthought, she added, "Not that I plan on coming back here."

He shuddered. "No, never again, if I can help it."

For a second, their eyes met in an understanding they had never shared before, but then, Olwen exhaled and seemed to shake off bad thoughts, and the moment of understanding was gone.

"We've all relieved ourselves over there." She pointed to a place further back in the corridor in the direction they came from.

"Good, I'll follow your example then."

He swallowed the last piece of bread and wished he had something to drink. Miriam smiled at him when he came over to her and Omega, and, despite the presence of the others, he leaned down and touched her lips softly. Behind him, he could hear Omega's soft, "Aww…" and when he let Miri go, she was smiling, but under all the bruises, a sudden blush could be clearly seen.

As soon as he had relieved himself and come back, Olwen put on her backpack and looked demandingly at them.

"Okay, team, let's go."

The 'day' dragged on as they walked the endless corridor hour after hour after endless hour, and too soon, they lost control over the direction. Eventually, Carl felt so dizzy that he sneaked out a pen from his jacket and drew an arrow on the wall, pointing at the direction they headed toward.

"Good thinking, Octavius," he heard Olwen's low and tired voice from behind.

"It feels like we're just walking at the same spot all the time, don't you think?" Omega asked on edge.

Miri stopped and turned around, exhausted and worried. "Do you think that's what we're doing?" Her voice sounded strained. "I mean, I don't have a feeling we're moving forward either. I… I don't know why. I thought we were close."

A worried expression spread over Olwen's face, which she quickly hid by sitting down and digging in her backpack again until she got out four survival bars.

"Let's take a break, okay." Omega and Miri eagerly wrapped off the packaging, but Olwen waved at Carl to take a couple of steps away. "Okay, so this worries me," she said with a frown when they had moved away far enough for the others to not overhear. "I know I told her not to use that, um, silly word; 'power' again, but we need to get out of here. I trust her instincts. If she says we're not moving forward, we're probably not. Maybe she needs to do whatever she does again. What do you think? Any suggestions?"

Carl sighed and tugged tiredly at his hair while glancing back at Miri, feeling too numb to come up with any other ideas. Nothing popped up, not a single suggestion.

"That's the only solution I can see," he said eventually. "I don't want her to do it either, but— The thing is, this here; this... place.... is her creation. I'm afraid we're going to confuse whatever 'this' is if anyone else of us would try to concentrate on a place important to us, and I have a distinct feeling that could be bad." He fell silent a moment and saw Olwen's strained face. "I'm not making any sense, eh?"

She sighed. "On the contrary, Octavius, I think you're perfectly right." She looked at the other two women who patiently waited for them to return. "Okay. She has to try." Determined, Olwen walked back to the women. "Ophelia, you have to make a new try to think about your home. If you say we're not moving, then we'll need you to make us move. Understood?"

Miriam paled but nodded. "O... okay. Um..." She hesitated for a moment as if she thought something through, before glancing at him. "Carl?"

"Yeah?"

From being so pale, the fierce blush created more of a contrast than it would have otherwise.

"Um, I'm a bit tired. I need you to, um, to hold me for a while so I can concentrate. I, uh, I'm afraid that I'd fall otherwise."

He felt embarrassed, as well, at what could be read between the lines, but took the steps toward her and embraced her. She hid her face at his chest and stood completely still. As the minutes ticked by and nothing happened, he closed his eyes too and held her tighter, trying to give her some of his strength – not that there was a lot of it left. Her body began to tremble, and suddenly, the damn blood trickled down on his hands again, but he ignored it and continued to hold on to her. When Omega gasped behind them, he knew it had worked. He opened his eyes and saw a

351

couple of staircases some yards in front of them, of the kind he thought could be found at a doctor's office.

"It worked, Miri," he mumbled, but she continued to tremble, and suddenly, she staggered and lost balance. Carefully, he put her down on the floor, and she slumped into a heap. Olwen hurried over with her doctor's bag and started to check on her, flashing her light in Miri's eyes, and changing the blood-soaked gauze again.

"She's not unconscious, but she needs to rest for a while."

"Alright," he said and remembered how to breathe again. He slumped down on the floor with his back toward the wall and pulled Miriam up onto his lap, let her rest her head on him instead of on the hard floor, and then they waited. Soothingly, he let his fingers trail through her hair. Omega took advantage of the break and curled together on the floor like a ball, falling asleep immediately. Shortly after, Olwen followed her example, and in a couple of minutes, he found himself being the only one awake. The minutes passed by, but he couldn't say how long time they waited. Every now and then, he dozed off but woke up with a start every time his head glided down to his chest. After a while, he decided to force himself to stay awake instead.

With a deep sigh, he rubbed his eyes that felt red and irritated from sleep deprivation and looked at his sleeping teammates. Their calm snoozing made him think of home, home as in his parents' farm just outside Edmonton, and the endless prairie where the wind made the grass dance under the never-ending sky. In a low voice, he began to sing a Lebanese lullaby that his aunt Shukriyya had used to sing to him when he was a boy. It always calmed him and the sensation of his aunt's hands lovingly combing through his hair came back to him, just as soothing as it used to be back then.

When the song faded out, Miri softly said, "That was so beautiful, Carl."

He looked down at her with a loving smile and saw her eyes glitter with tears. "Welcome back, *albi*. You made it. Look." He pointed at the stairs, and she stared silently at them. With a deep breath, she closed her eyes, but before he could ask her to not concentrate on anything at all, she opened them again and beamed at him.

"I think we're almost there, Carl. I actually think we're almost home."

A shimmering glint of hope lit in his heart. "God, I hope so. Let's wake the others."

Within a few minutes, Miri took the lead up the stairs. These ones did have railings, even though they were as narrow as everything else she created. Omega's deep sigh of relief led to some friendly laughter, but Carl sympathized fully with her by now. If he never again had to experience a height, it would still be too soon.

As he tiredly trailed after Miriam, he saw how she unexpectedly got more energy in her steps, and there was a desperate, hopeful tug in his heart. *Is it true? Are we that close? Please, say we're that close. Please, please, please...*

After climbing five steep stories, they landed on a platform large enough to hold all of them. A plain-looking door hovered a couple of inches in the air in front of them.

Miriam beamed at them. "This is it! I'm sure this is it!"

"Well, go on then, Pheli! Don't make us wait any longer!" Omega's voice trembled.

Carl didn't dare to hope, even though he did. He held his breath as Miriam turned the doorknob.

The door opened to a living room bathing in moonlight. Between the brightly lit staircase and the moonlit living room was a thin, vibrating boundary. Seeing the boundary made Carl feel the difference in the atmosphere between this dimension and the one they were looking in at. For a couple of seconds, they stood silently as if they didn't believe what they saw, but as on cue, they moved simultaneously, trying to push themselves into this wonderfully every-day-feeling room. Within seconds, they stood in the moonlight, looking around while the gateway silently disappeared behind them.

Carl couldn't help smiling as he recognized himself. "Huh," he said and gave Miriam an amused look.

She blushed ferociously and looked away, trying to hide her embarrassment by searching for the light switch. The next moment, the room bathed in light.

Relieved and cheerful, Omega viewed the small, inviting apartment. "Nice place, Pheli. I love the colors."

Carl thought that Miri was about to faint from mortification, but before he could come to the rescue, Olwen did it for him.

"Thanks for leading us home, Ophelia. No offense, but please don't offer anything to eat or drink. I just want to get home to my place and collapse in my own bed."

Omega nodded. "Collapsing sounds like the best idea ever." She hugged Miri hard. "Take care now. Sleep a lot." Turned toward Olwen, she asked, "When do we meet again?"

Olwen looked caught, but then she laughed. "I have no idea what day it is, but let's say two days after today if that's not a weekend. We need some serious rest. If it's a weekend, we'll meet on Monday, eight hundred sharp at the F.R. office at HQ."

"Sounds great."

Olwen dug down into her doctor's bag. "Mm, Ophelia, here, take these pills. You'll probably want to have them for the pain, right?" Miriam nodded. "If you notice any kind of infection before I get to see you again, go directly to Dr. Bernard."

"I will," Miri said, sounding beyond exhausted.

"It shouldn't be any problems as long as you rest. I'll call Andrew Gorlois in the morning and let him know the news and that you need a break from work a couple of weeks until you've recuperated. Armand will probably request your presence in the RP until it's properly solved as well, but that's his table."

Miri nodded, and Olwen and Omega moved toward the front door with her trotting after them. Carl went out into the kitchen, where he put on a kettle. It was best if she got some time to compose herself before he said anything. It touched him, though, it touched him deeply, that she had led them back home to his place.

Part Five

balm for the soul

Chapter 20

Ten minutes later, he took the two hot steaming mugs of chai out to the living room but stopped immediately. Miri lay on the sofa, curled up in a heap, sleeping soundly. She had been crying.

Aww, sweetheart... This last thing was too much for you.

Carefully, he placed the mugs on the table and went into his minuscule bedroom, where he got an extra duvet from the closet. After putting on a new cover that smelled freshly of clean linen, he tucked her in. She didn't even move. He sat down on the floor on the opposite side of the table and watched her tenderly while he drank the wonderful chai and felt his muscles begin to relax. They were home. Being home had never felt this good before. He couldn't stop smiling. And she had led them straight home to him. That made him almost, almost certain that she had stronger feelings for him than he had ever dared to hope, but if he knew her well enough, she was going to try to sneak out when she woke up, probably feeling too embarrassed to know how to handle the situation. An idea struck him, and he went to get his sketchpad and pens and started drawing. When he was finished, he ripped off the sheet and taped it up on the front door before taking a step back, studying it critically.

It only said, 'Please stay,' and underneath was a stickman with wavy brown hair looking at another stickman with red hair who held out its hands toward the first one. Maybe a bit overly sentimental and romantic, but he wanted the message to be clear. He knew how difficult she had to grasp the right signals.

Satisfied, he cleaned up the tea mugs, looking longingly at his bed, but decided that he wanted to be clean before he slept. It felt like something from the other realm was sticking to his skin. After a long, hot shower, the apartment oozed of vanilla. He put on clean underwear and sprawled out in bed. The bed linen smelled fresh and crispy. Before he knew it, he fell asleep.

A hard knock on the front door woke him up. Feeling dazed, he squinted against the afternoon sun that shone abundantly through the window. Sun! What bliss after that eternity in half-darkness. Before he could get up, he heard the front door open, mumbling voices, the door close, and then, was that the smell of pizza? His stomach growled violently, and he shoved the duvet aside and draped a morning gown around him. Miri stood in the kitchen and placed pizza slices, coleslaw, and garlic bread on plates, only dressed in one of his oversized T-shirts that nearly reached down to her bare knees. His heart melted at the sight of her, looking so at home. Smilingly, he strode out to her and casually put his arm around her waist and landed a gentle kiss on her hair. It was damp and smelled of his shampoo. When she turned around with a bright smile of her own, she looked happier, more energetic and less haunted than she had only a few hours ago.

"Good morning, beautiful."

Her demeanor softened. "Good morning, Carl." She winked teasingly at him. "Or should I say, 'Good afternoon'? It's five p.m."

"Five? Wow. But you know what? I couldn't have woken up to a better day. You're here – and you've ordered our special pizza."

"You noticed?" She beamed at him.

"Course I did. It's the first meal we had together here."

Their eyes locked together, and then Carl's stomach growled again. Miri giggled.

He grinned. "Let's eat. I think I'm hungry."

They brought everything out to the living room table, and for a while, they were too occupied eating to talk. It tasted wonderful. It tasted real. Within minutes they had wolfed down everything there was, and Carl felt satisfactorily full. He carried the dishes back to the kitchen and came out with a new toothbrush still in its package.

"Here. You'll probably want this."

"Oh, God, I owe you. Thanks."

She jumped up from the sofa and went into the bathroom. He could hear her turn on the water and brush her teeth. As soon as she came out, he went in and brushed his teeth too. Pizza was sometimes heavenly to eat, but it left much to wish for regarding fresh breath.

Miri had curled up under the duvet in one of the corners of the sofa, and he sat down in the other corner. As soon as he did, he realized the mistake. The small space between them suddenly felt like miles. For once, he had no idea what to say, and an awkward silence fell.

It's Miri, for crying out loud! We can talk about everything nowadays. Come on! Say something, Carl! Nothing came to him.

It struck him that the atmosphere between them felt like the early days when they loathed each other's guts, except that this time, the silence and the awkwardness weren't deliberate from his side. He felt sillier and sillier the longer the silence stretched out. Miri's face turned red, and she moved uneasily on the sofa. He cleared his throat. She glanced at him.

"Oh, whatever!" he said when the silence grew too thick to stand. "Please, come here." He held out his hand toward her. Obligingly, she scooted over to him, and he put his arm around her. She tensed but relaxed marginally again.

"This is better," he mumbled, and she nodded, leaning on his shoulder while her hand shyly searched for his. When she found it, she let out a nearly soundless sigh and squeezed it gently. For a little while, they sat there, listening to each other's breaths. It should feel right, but it didn't. Something was wrong, Carl knew, but he couldn't figure out what it was, so he waited, more on edge than he'd been with her for a long time.

"I was—" she said eventually but stopped herself.

"What?"

She inhaled and sat up again, released her hand, and began fiddling with the hem of the T-shirt instead. There was a frown on her forehead.

"I was wondering—This might sound stupid, but I— I really need to know…"

"Know what?" he asked nervously when she fell silent again.

'She kept her eyes lowered. Then, she inhaled as if to gather courage, and he had to stop himself from squirming as the nervousness built inside him.

"I have to admit that I— I wasn't paying attention to everything you said."

"Um, alright. That's okay."

"Just let me try and finish! This is hard as it is without you interrupting me all the time."

With anxious fingers, he combed through his hair, tugged at the strands. "Sorry…"

She glared at him, but he could tell that the sudden outburst came from anxiety rather than from her being angry with him. *That's a relief. I think.*

She took a deep breath, and then the words tumbled out of her. "I thought you said, 'I want you in my life' back there."

"Um, yeah, I did." He sounded scared, and he cleared his throat. She still didn't look at him, and it made him so damn nervous. Uneasily, he tugged at his hair.

"What did you mean?" she asked. "I mean, really? What did you really mean by that? Surely you didn't mean what it sounds like."

He sat very still, feeling insecure and vulnerable. The silence stretched out as he wanted her to look at him, wanted to read her, but she didn't, and he couldn't. He inhaled deeply. *Alright, burn the damn bridge.*

"I… I don't understand, Miri. Um… What I meant is— I meant that I—" He exhaled, and his forehead became moist. *Come on now. Burn the damn bridge! Just burn it!* "I've been in love with you for two years, Miri, and I… I would like you

360

to, well, um, become a bigger part of my life than you have
been…"

She didn't move. Once again, the silence stretched
out. Her frown seemed to deepen. Realizing he had stopped
breathing, he forced himself to relax. She finally glanced at
him, but her face was disbelieving and the pain he felt when
his heart slowly began to crack made his eyes water.

"Really, Carl? Is that really what you meant?"

At the tone of her voice, he wanted to give up. She
didn't love him. Why did he ever think she would? With a
voice on the edge of breaking, he managed to say, "I… I
don't know how to say it more clearly. I'm in love with you."
He couldn't understand why she still had that frustratingly
disbelieving expression.

"If that's really true, why haven't you said anything,
showed anything?"

For once, it was impossible to read anything out of
her voice. He swallowed nervously and tugged helplessly at
his hair again.

"What do you want, Miriam? Do you want me on my
knees? I can do that."

She just stared quietly at him with those big, dark
eyes. How could they become so closed, so impossible to
read? He sighed, thinking about brightly burning bridges and
how he left his self-respect on the other shore, and suddenly
anger rose in him.

He glared furiously at her. "You want to know why I
haven't said anything?" he snarled, and with regret, he saw
her eyes widen and her body tense, but he couldn't stop the
words from tumbling out. "Let me see. There were some
events that happened two years back. You left Caesar, for
example. That was a damn important decision from your side.
Yes, I was in love with you at that point. No, I didn't say
anything then because you had no need of another person
stepping in, taking C's place, someone that could continue to
hold your hands. You needed to find your own damn feet!
You needed to learn how to walk on those damn feet by

yourself." He glared at her and saw that her eyes were moist with tears on the brink of spilling, and his anger vanished. In a calmer voice, he continued, "Goddamn, Miri, I didn't want to push you. I wanted you to take your time, after Caesar, to find your strength and self-confidence again. Not getting involved with another man when you needed to find yourself first. And then, um, I was afraid. It's never pleasant being rejected" A couple of tears trickled down her cheeks, but he didn't dare to dry them. "I'm sorry." He sighed and rubbed his eyes, trying to distance himself from the devastating defeat that crushed him. "I'm so very sorry. I shouldn't have said anything. Just forget everything. I... I would still want to be friends with you, but I understand if you don't... if you don't want to—"

Her hand was suddenly on his leg. It burnt through the thin fabric of his morning gown.

Her voice was filled with regret. "No, don't say that, Carl. I shouldn't have pushed you so far. It wasn't fair. I was just so afraid."

He swallowed another sigh and glanced at her. There were so many feelings swirling around on her face now; astonishment, sadness, happiness, regret, and he couldn't figure her out.

Then a soft smile appeared on her lips, and her eyes shone. "You are a wonderful man, Carl."

He felt his feelings enjoying a tour at the biggest, badassest roller-coaster ever invented, and he stared at her, confused and bewildered. "Um, what?"

"You're so caring. You always think of others first. You probably don't even know how hard it is to read you."

"Um, alright." He tugged at his hair, let his nervous fingers tangle the strands, and didn't know if he could start to breathe yet, or in which direction she was heading. "What have I missed?"

She took his hands in hers while looking him seriously in the eyes. The touch was gentle, and his heart jumped a beat.

"I didn't think you cared about me that way. You never gave me the slightest signal. You were so distant all the time. How was I to know? I was so scared to be rejected that I never dared to show you… that I'm in love with you too."

"What?" he exhaled, feeling his heart-rate speed from zero to three hundred in one second. His face heated, and he couldn't tear his gaze from her. "Are you? Are you truly?"

She nodded. "I've been in love with you for a long time, Carl. A year and a half, at least. Maybe even since we went looking for Her Child and Margery Phillips. At least, I became attracted to you back then." Miri gave up a little laughter that sounded embarrassed. "My sister knew long before I did."

"Beth?" he croaked.

"And when— when you said that back there, and kissed me, touched me— God, I wanted you so badly, but I… I wasn't sure what you really felt for me, I mean, really felt for me, and I— I was afraid that I misunderstood something because I wanted you to say— Really wanted you to mean that you have feelings for me, not only that you wanted to… to have me."

Suddenly he remembered to breathe again. "You're in love with me?" he beamed, and she laughed.

"I'm in love with you."

Smiling, but feeling like crying, he lifted her hands and kissed them. "Oh, God! You're in love with me! I'm in love with you too, Miri."

Her whole demeanor spoke of pure happiness. Unable to sit still, she rose from the sofa and twirled around, her arms in the air.

"I can't believe it!" she laughed. "It's so amazing!" She stopped and held out her hands to him. "Come, I want to hold you."

Carl stood and took her hands, and she drew him in toward her. His heart rate had to hit orbit at any time now, he thought. Seeing her like this was alluring. It was intoxicating. They stood together, so close. The warm gush from her

363

breath on his throat when she kissed him made him shudder, and the sensation spread throughout his whole body.

Miri took a step back. Her face was glowing with the same astonishment he felt. When their lips met, it was like they had never kissed before. Lingering, she let go of him, and before he was prepared, she took off the T-shirt and stood naked in front of him. It felt like she had kicked him in the stomach. It was hard to breathe, and he couldn't take his eyes off her.

"Do you want to make love to me, Carl?" she whispered softly.

His throat tightened, and he couldn't answer. So many mixed feelings rushed through his body and mind, making him dizzy, but then, two complicated emotions rose from the spinning whirlpool. The first was sheer desire combined with such powerful love that it terrified him. The second was based on the deplorable memories of Athena. The images of how she controlled and used him filled him with devastating self-disgust, and he couldn't rid himself of the helplessness and the vulnerability she forced upon him. He hated it, but he felt broken. *It wasn't real. It was just a dream!* It didn't matter. It felt real.

He watched Miriam standing there naked, willing to give and take, to love him, but most importantly, to respect him. With a deep inhale and exhale, he determinedly pushed Athena to the back of his mind. He would never let her win over him. He would never allow her to crush him or make him feel worthless. Most of all, he was definitely not going to allow her to rip his soul and self-respect apart. She was not going to make him a victim.

Solemnly, he took the few steps toward Miri and embraced her hard. Her body was warm and soft underneath his hands, and he breathed in her special scent. She smiled when she kissed his neck and ripples of desire flowed throw him. Then, she took his hand and led him into the bedroom.

***

It was much later. Dusk had set, and long shadows covered the room with intimate softness. With her face turned toward him, avoiding the head wound, Miri lay sprawled out on her back, calmly sleeping. Her face looked so peaceful. Carl resisted a strong wish to caress her. Instead, he took advantage of the fact that he could study her closely without her feeling embarrassed.

He loved her high cheekbones and her slightly eagle-formed nose. They gave her face character instead of being traditionally pretty. His gaze moved down to her full lips, slightly parted, and he wanted to kiss them again, but didn't. She needed her sleep. She had so much to recuperate, even though her feeling loved most likely helped the process immensely. During the few hours they had been home, she had become happier and more energized, and it strengthened his suspicions that the other dimension tried to drain people of their energy and their lives.

With a grimace, he steered his thoughts away and continued to watch her. Her slender neck led his gaze down to her shoulders and her chest. He had to admit that her breasts fascinated him. They were small enough to fit into his hands, and that aroused him beyond belief. He cleared his throat and let his gaze quickly wander further down, over her fit, but way too skinny stomach, over her vulva with the generous amount of hair, and her strong, muscular legs. She had numerous scars over her body. One was especially frightening, something that looked like a huge and jagged bite mark on her left thigh. *Whatever gave her that must nearly have killed her,* he thought and wondered what had happened.

He knew that he shouldn't compare, but it was hard not to. Her appearance was as far from both Amanda's and Allie's as was possible. Manda was tall, almost taller than he, with long blond hair and amazingly green eyes, which she enhanced with her glasses' frames in the same color, and her body was generous with beautiful curves. Allie resembled her physically in many ways, he suddenly realized, even though her exuberant personality made her glimmer from within in a way he had never experienced with anyone else. Miri, on the other hand, was short, slim and physically fit, wisp-like, with light-brown unruly hair that begged to be touched, and those large dark-brown eyes he felt like he could lose himself in. Then he shook his head. *It doesn't matter how any of them look,* he thought. What did matter was that all three of them possessed this extraordinary inner strength and iron will that drew him to them like a moth to a candle.

Lovingly, he tucked her in under the duvet, and she sighed in her sleep and turned toward him on her side. To have her here, beside him, in his bed at home… He had yearned for this moment for so long now that he felt solemn. It felt right in a way his life hadn't felt for years. *I don't feel lonely anymore.*

He kissed the tip of her nose lightly and rested his cheek on her hair that he loved so much. Then, he turned on his back and looked up at the ceiling. They should start calling people. Beth and her parents needed to know. Allie was probably worried. There might be others. Manda would be happy, he knew that, and she probably wondered why he hadn't called about that zoo-trip he'd talked about. Hopefully, she wouldn't be too angry with him for what she probably saw as negligence toward Sarah from his side. It felt so weird to be back in the ordinary world with ordinary things to worry about. Weird, but relieving. *What date is it, by the way?* It felt as if they'd been gone for months. A worried frown appeared on his forehead. *It can't be months. Can it?* The very thought that it could have been months made him sweaty and nauseated.

Careful not to wake Miri, he left the bed and headed for his laptop in the living room. While he waited for it to start, he went back into the bedroom to put on his morning gown before lighting the candles in the living room. They flickered happily when he opened the window to let in some air. For a few moments, he stood there, watching the night-lit city, and felt the love for it, for being so alive. Even at this distance, he could sense the pulse of it. The air that found its way in held a mild scent of spring. Smiling, he went back to the laptop. Time showed ten forty-nine p.m., and it was Thursday, May thirteenth. They'd been gone for two weeks. Two weeks!

"At least it's not two years," he mumbled, and with a flash of terror, he glanced at the year on the screen. A huge relief filled him. "No, not two years." Checking the time again, he fiddled with the phone. "Whatever. She's probably awake." Resolutely, he dialed Allie.

"Carl!" she exclaimed as soon as she heard who it was. "I've been so worried! Where have you been? I tried to press Armand for info, but he wouldn't say anything to me, even though I knew he knew."

"I'm sorry you've been worried, Allie," he said regretfully. "I couldn't tell you before I went—"

"Course you couldn't, if it was a Star Student case," she interrupted. "I get that."

"It's been some weird, crazy days. Long story short, we've found her."

The pause on the other end was almost too short for him to notice.

"Miri? You found Miri?"

"Yeah."

"And she's…?" Her voice was torn between fear and eagerness to know.

"She's alive."

She exhaled relieved. "Oh, my God, Carl, I'm so happy for you! So very happy! How is she?"

"Quite traumatized and injured, but she's alive. That's the important thing."

"And?"

"'And' what?"

"Oh, come on, you know! Just tell me before I go mad out of curiosity, have you told her?" When he laughed happily, he could sense her smiling on the other end. "Oh, my God! Oh, Carl! These are the best news I've gotten today! I think I'm going to cry— Yep, here they come, the tears."

367

She sniveled and laughed at the same time. "Okay, you enjoy your weekend now."

"I will. I definitely will."

Again, he could hear her smile. "You'd better. By the way, I have some news for you too."

"What's that?" he asked when she drew out on it.

Her chuckle had a tinge of schadenfreude. "Alan Bai is under investigation for his decision to fire you."

"What?" he exclaimed, hardly believing his ears.

"Yep. You're supposed to meet with Jeremy Kane this upcoming Wednesday and leave your report. Meanwhile, you're hanging between chairs, so to say. Mr. Kane has given you full permission to continue your Star Student investigation until the committee has come to a decision, but you're not supposed to work with either the interview group or me right now."

"Are we talking about the Jeremy Kane? Head of the whole Behavioral Science Unit?" Carl asked, feeling slightly dizzy.

"That's the same."

Anxiously, Carl tugged at his hair. "Um, whoa! Talking about making me nervous here, Allie."

"Sorry, but you know it wasn't fair. I had to do something about it. He can't go around trying to get people sacked just because he takes something personally. That's not professional, and that's not how it's supposed to work around here. His mistake was to have a witness to the whole scene. Anyway, your task is to write a report about what happened. You know, the usual, what led up to it, his request and behavior, and what you responded, and e-mail it to Mr. Kane before you meet him. His secretary has probably already sent you an e-mail about all the details you need to know. There will be an interview with you as well. Until then, you and I are not supposed to talk, just to let you know."

Completely bewildered, Carl tried to get things straight in his mind. "Wait a minute! I need a pen and paper.

You said Wednesday. That's what, the nineteenth? Do you have a time?"

"At his office, that's all I know, but I'm sure you have all the details in your e-mail."

He puffed nervously and entwined some strands of hair between his fingers. "How am I supposed to sleep now?" He almost whined, but Allie just laughed.

"You're not supposed to be sleeping, Carl, you're supposed to have fun with your girl. So, shush now, hang up, and we'll talk after the nineteenth."

"Yes, ma'am, I will." Smilingly, he hung up on her. When he turned around, Miri stood sleepily in the doorway to the bedroom with his T-shirt on. He took the few steps toward her and hugged her hard. She yawned and hugged him back.

"Sorry. Who were you talking to?"

"My eventual new boss."

The sleepiness in her eyes gave way to curiosity. "Your new boss? What happened to the old one?"

"I got sacked."

She stared at him in disbelief. "What? What do you mean, you got sacked?"

"Long story, but I was working on a serial killer case when Alan came in and said that I'd disgraced the unit and that he couldn't trust me to do my work properly."

He watched her while she digested the news.

"Wait a minute, I need to sit down." She went back into the bedroom and sat down on the bed. "I don't get it. He sacked you? What the hell? You're the best they have! What did you do? I can't see you do anything that would lead to that."

"I threw up and fainted when I found a burnt victim while searching for you at Kroger's."

She stared at him, confused, clearly torn between feeling indignant for his sake, and distressed and caring. She shook her head and got rid of the confused look, before taking his hand.

"I'm so sorry that you had to go through that." Her voice was gentle, and he leaned in to kiss her nose. She wiggled around until he kissed her mouth instead. For a moment, they lost themselves in the sensation, but then, she broke free.

"Sorry," he mumbled with a sweet smile. "I got a bit side-tracked. You were going to say?"

"I still don't get it. He sacked you because of that?" When Carl nodded, she continued, "That's just bizarre. I mean, it happens to everyone. I did worse than throwing up and faint the first time I saw a person who died horribly." Curiosity peaked, but before he could ask, she continued, "Okay, so he sacked you. What happened then? Who's your new boss? Aren't you FBI anymore? God, it feels like I've been gone a year. You're sure it's not been a year?"

He chuckled and kissed her knuckles. "No, not a year, love. About a month."

She stared at him with a harrowed look in her eyes. "I was at that place a whole month?" She shuddered and paled. "No wonder I was going crazy." She fell silent a few seconds before she urgently looked at him again. "Come on, tell me now! I'm so curious I'm going crazy anyway. Who's your new boss?"

It fascinated him that she well-nigh used the same words to express herself as Allie had.

"Maybe new boss. I'll know after the nineteenth. You know Dean Henderson at the homicide, right?" She nodded. "Well, while I was clearing debris at Kroger's—"

"Hold on for a moment." The confused expression on Miri's face returned. "You keep talking about Kroger's. What's going on with Kroger's?"

A sinking feeling made him cold all over, and he watched her silently.

She moved uncomfortably on the bed. "Okay, um, why are you looking at me like that?" Carl pulled a hand through his hair, and Miri's eyes widened slightly. "Oh, wow, it's that bad? Please, tell me."

He nearly glared at her. *'That bad,' eh? I need to stop that damn hair pulling.* With a deep inhalation, he tried to relax. There was no reason for him to snap at her just because he was anxious.

"Um," he began, stalling for time. "You never told me how you came to that place."

Obviously ill at ease, she glared at him too. "You're not playing fair, Carl. I asked first."

He took her hand, trying to calm them both. "I know. I'm sorry. I just need to know how much you remember. Please?"

"How... how much I remember? I— I don't remember anything after I left you that Friday, probably because of a concussion." She stared at him, suddenly horrified. "Oh, God! Was that where I was? At Kroger's? And something happened? A fire? I thought I was at Bradley's mansion. I know I thought they might've blown up the mansion to hide evidence. It seemed to fit. But that means that Tam, Andy, Steph, and Linds are safe, right?"

"Oh, uh, yeah, they're alive."

She sighed deeply of relief. "Thank you. Thank you, all good things in this world. That's been hanging over me a lot, that they might be dead." In a calmer voice, she said, "Please, tell me now. I need to know."

He scowled nervously, trying to figure out the right angle to approach the event, and was about to tug at his hair again, but managed to restrain himself this time.

"Um, alright. April seventeenth is now considered our own Nine Eleven. You're right about it being an explosion. Kroger's behind your place blew up. I'm not sure about the last victim report, but— Well, you were there." He watched her shocked face. "You don't remember it."

She shook her head. "But," she said slowly, clearly trying to wrap her mind around this new piece of information. "No other people were there. It was just me. If I was at Kroger's and it exploded, there must've been more people around."

371

Carl inhaled and held her hand gently. "Um, Miri… Well, now that you're back— You'll probably hear about it sooner or later anyway, so—" He paused and searched for words.

"Hear about what? Carl, don't do this to me. Just spit it out. I can take it."

"Alright. Um, spit it out… Um, you're considered a hero." He felt so anxious that it nearly made him laugh to see her looking so shocked and perplexed, but he suppressed it. Instead, he took her other hand and caressed it too. "You saved a lot of people, Miri. You saw the person who bombed Kroger's and warned the whole store. Thanks to you, about three-fourths of all the people in the store survived. Without you, there would've been maybe one survivor out of twenty."

She stared at him with her mouth half-opened. Suddenly, she hid her face in her hands. "No, I can't— I can't take that," she mumbled. "That's too much. I'm not a hero. I can't have done that."

He watched her for a moment before he went up to get his box with the newspaper clippings. When he came back to the bed, she glanced at him, looking completely dazed.

"Here," he said and gave her the paper with her photo on the front page. *FBI-HERO!* the headline screamed. Miri didn't even take the clipping. She just stared at it in silence, before her face suddenly turned white. With one swift move, she went up from the bed and out into the bathroom. He could hear her vomiting.

"Wow, you handled that one great," he muttered and put the paper back in the box and placed it in the closet again before walking to the bathroom. The door was open, and Miri sat on the floor by the toilet, sweaty and trembling.

"Hey," he said gently and sat down on the floor at the threshold. She managed to give him a faint smile. "Sorry about that. I could've played it smoother, eh?"

Even though she'd just thrown up, she managed to chuckle lightly. "Maybe, but I asked quite demandingly, didn't I?"

"I guess you did."

They smiled at each other, and Carl could almost see the golden threads they weaved between them. *We belong together. Never saw that one coming.*

Miri heaved herself up, flushed the toilet, put down the lid, and washed herself thoroughly before turning toward him.

"I'm not going to have a lot of secrets being with you, am I?" He felt a broad smile play on his lips and shrugged. She smiled back and gestured at him. "You're in the way, Carl. I need to pee, and I prefer to at least do that alone."

He chuckled lightly and went back into the bedroom. A couple of minutes later, she came back, looking fresh and collected again.

"Okay, tell me the rest now," she said as she sat on the bed, leaning toward the wall.

"Alright, do you want to see the rest of the clippings?"

"No, not about me, about you and Alan Bai."

"Oh. Yeah, alright. Well…" He tried to recollect his thoughts. "Um, I got called in for a child victim interview. Turned out she'd witnessed a woman being shot by a serial killer. Dean sent my report to Allie Harris—"

"Wait a minute, I know that name." Miri frowned, searching her memories. "Yes, she's that renowned specialist, right?"

"Yeah, and she liked my reports and wanted me to work with her on this case, and when Alan came in and actually sacked me in front of her, she sort of hired me, and now she's reported him to Jeremy Kane. You can't get higher up than JK." Without thinking, he combed through his hair with his hand.

Miri stared at him. "He sacked you in front of her? What the hell, Carl! He's supposed to be a profiler and

373

behaves like that? What an idiot!" She shook her head with a disgusted look. "But I know you've not been terribly pleased working under him. Is she better? She sounds better."

A burning blush covered his face, and she looked surprised at him while he moved awkwardly on the bed. He had hoped to get more time before getting to this particular scene. Not that all the time in the world would make it easier.

Miri frowned uncertainly. "What? What did I say?"

He inhaled and tugged at his hair. "Um, well, yeah, she's a better boss, to answer your question, but, she, uh, also kissed me. And, um, asked me to, uh, to stay over at her place. Eventually, I… I did…"

For a moment, she stared at him, dumbstruck, before composing herself. "Um, okay… Well, she has good taste." Now it was his turn to stare at her. She looked him sincerely in the eyes. "Do I have a reason to be jealous?"

For a second, he sat speechless, before tenderly placing his hands around her face. "You… Wow! Miriam Goldblum, you're the most wonderful woman I've ever met. I'm sorry that I ever was afraid that you were going to cry or yell at me when you got to know. No, Miri, you have no reason to be jealous. Allie is a fun, damn sexy woman, and totally unpredictable, but she's not you."

She looked amused. "And what about me? Am I a fun, damn sexy woman too?"

He leaned in and kissed her slowly. When their lips parted, he asked in a hoarse voice, "Do you want me to show you just how damn sexy I think you are?"

**

They slept late that morning and didn't come around until noon. While eating leftover pizza for breakfast, since his fridge had turned into *The Swamp of Eternal Stench* again, Miri said what he had thought about the evening before.

"I should call Mom and Dad, and Beth and Ted. If everyone thought I blew up at Kroger's, they're probably trying to convince the rabbi to hold a memorial service for me. Mom will get a minor shock hearing my voice. God, what a mess."

He took her hand. "Do you want me to call? I can smoothen the way a bit."

A broad, teasing smile lit up her face. *God, she's beautiful.*

"Yeah, you're good at that."

He tried to look hurt, but couldn't keep the mask, and laughed at her.

"Haven't impressed you much lately, eh?"

She grinned and kissed his hands but continued with a more serious look. "It's not a bad idea, though. You call and tell them I'm alive, and then, I'll talk with them."

"Alright. Let's do it immediately. They've been waiting for this call too long as it is."

She nodded, and they went out to the living room where she dialed the number on the stationary telephone. Nervously, he waited for Mathilde or Jakob Goldblum to answer and felt his hands perspire. He'd never met Miriam's parents or talked to them, and now he was going to tell them that their daughter, whom they thought dead, was alive. At least it wasn't the other way around, thank goodness. He hoped Miri was right in thinking that they'd manage to take the news without getting a heart attack.

"Goldblum." The voice on the other end of the line was familiar.

"Beth?"

Miriam's face lit up with a bright smile, and she jumped up and down beside him in excitement.

"Yes, this is she. Who is this?" Beth's voice was tired and sad, without the amount of energy that it usually carried.

"Um, sorry, it's Carl Hansen, FBI, you know?"

"Oh, Carl. Hi. I've been trying to get a hold of you. I know you're not Jewish, but you might want to come to our *Kaddish* for Miriam anyway."

"Um..." He pulled a hand through his hair.

375

"It's a mourning prayer. It's planned for next Saturday, the twenty-second. Then it'll be just over a month since she died. There won't be a regular funeral since there's no... no body, but our rabbi has agreed upon a *Kaddish* by now."

"Beth..." This didn't work the way he had planned.

"If you don't want to, it's okay, but I thought that since you two were quite close, well, you should at least get invited. Henry will be there too. You know Henry, right?"

He took a deep breath. *I'm quite good at burning bridges nowadays.*

"Beth. We've found her." The silence on the other side was deep. "Beth?" Miriam waved at him to give her the phone, but he held up his hand. "Beth, are you there?"

"Y... yes..."

"Are you okay?"

"You... you found her? Is... is she... is she..."

"She's alive, Beth. She's right here beside me, and she wants to talk to you." Relieved, he handed Miri the phone, and she cleared her throat nervously.

"Beth, *zisseh neshomeh.*" Even from here, Carl heard the deep sobbing on the other side of the line. "Beth. *Zissele, zissele...*" Tears began to fall from Miri's eyes. "It's okay, Beth, I'm okay. It's all good, *zissele*, it's all good."

The crying faded away as if Beth dropped the phone. Another voice was heard. "Hello?"

"Ted, it's me, it's Miriam." Once again, the silence was compact. Beth's deep crying could be heard somewhere far away. "Ted?"

"Is... is it really you?"

In the midst of her tears, Miri laughed. "Yes, Ted, it really is me."

"Good God, Miriam, Miriam... Matty! Jake! Come here! It's Miriam! She's alive! She's alive. Good God!"

Another voice was heard, an elderly trembling voice, "Miriam, *beybi?*"

"*Mame.*"

376

The voice nearly broke into tears when Mathilde Goldblum sternly said, "Miriam Glukel Goldblum, you come home immediately now."

Miriam smiled broadly. "Yes, *mame*."

"I expect you to be here within the hour."

"I will, *mame*. I love you." She hung up and looked smilingly at Carl through the tears. "Nothing else was expected, really. Are you coming?"

He swallowed nervously at the thought of meeting Miriam's whole family at the same time, without more time to prepare himself, but the focus wouldn't be on him, thank goodness.

"I'd love to."

She raised her eyebrows at him, and her appearance touched on the skeptical. "Really? Mom's a bit… special. She likes to get her way, and when she's gotten an idea into her head, it's stuck there for an eternity. And she'll get ideas about you, most likely big ideas. Just so you're prepared."

He swallowed again, and his hands became sweaty. "Well… Eventually, I'd like to meet them anyway. I mean, if you're not going to treat me like Bertha in *Jane Eyre*, of course."

She laughed and put her arms around him, embraced him lovingly. "Never."

He placed his hands gently on her face to avoid hurting her, and their lips met longingly.

"And what about you?" he mumbled. "What kind of ideas do you have?"

Her lips smiled under his. "Mm, I might have one or another of my own."

His heart beat faster, and he had to remember to breathe again. "Is that so?"

"Are you going to run away now?"

He heard the serious and scared tone in her voice that she tried to hide behind casual joking, and he smiled a little. *She'll have to practice a lot if she's going to get away with something like that.*

"Run away? I've just found you, Miri. I'm going to hang on to you as long as you want me to."

"That… that might be a while…"

"That's fine by me. We've got some catching up to do, don't you think?"

"Um, is that, uh, is that—" She inhaled deeply and mumbled, "Okay, who said I'm too old to learn how to burn bridges?"

"I'm quite a good bridge burner, myself, if I'm allowed to brag."

She smiled broadly at his throat. "Brag as much as you want." She inhaled again and held on tightly to him, hiding her face at his chest. A couple of seconds went by.

"Is it a big bridge?"

She laughed heartily, and he kissed her on her head, feeling giddy and jittery, and happy and solemn, all at once.

"Enormous." Another moment went by. "Okay, here goes." This time, she exhaled, and when she finally looked up at him, she looked strained and nearly petrified. "Do you want to burn bridges together with me for the rest of our lives, Carl?"

He looked her lovingly in her eyes. "Yes, I do, Miri. Which one do you want to start with?"

"What about… 'I love you'?"

With burning cheeks, he caressed her hands. "I love you, Miri. I've loved you for a long time."

"Do you? Have you? Have you really?" she breathed, her eyes on the edge of believing him.

"I have, but it required a catastrophe to make me understand that."

He saw her taking the step over the edge, and her eyes filled with tears.

"I love you too, Carl. I wish I'd told you that before."

"Shh, no need for that. It's all good now."

She nodded and smiled through the tears. "It's all good."

Chapter 21

About an hour later, they parked the car in the back lane leading up to the garage of the classy house where Miri's parents lived. They hadn't even gotten out before the front door opened and everyone rushed out to meet them. As Carl slowly stepped out of the car and casually leaned toward it, pleased with hovering in the background, Miriam hurried out. With tears flowing freely, she embraced the wisplike elderly woman with the gray hair in a loose bun, before turning toward a slender old man with a straight back and piercing blue eyes.

"*Mame. Tate.*"

"Miriam, *HaY'Karah.*"

"*Oy*, Miriam, your face, your head! Look at you, *zissele*. And you're so thin. *Oy, oy!*" Mathilde's hands fluttered like anxious butterflies over Miriam's body. Even though she tried hard, she couldn't hold back her tears. Miri took her mother's hands and held them still while leaning in cheek to cheek.

"I'm fine, *mame*. It looks worse than it is. Promise. The doctor says I'll be fine in no time." She kissed Mathilde's wrinkled cheek and turned toward Jakob. He embraced her hard without saying anything, leaning his cheek on her head, closing his eyes, breathing solemnly. Carl could see the old man's body relax and his face soften, like a layer of grief washed away from him. It was clear that the bond between father and daughter was stronger than that between mother and daughter. Not that the love was less strong between Miri and Mathilde, he mused, but there wasn't a lot of understanding going on between them.

When Jakob finally let her go, Beth pushed herself between them and hugged Miri tightly, sobbing hard, her face gaunt and pale under all the black hair. Miri stroked her hair and mumbled things he couldn't hear. A bit behind them, a man and a boy stood, radiating happiness, waiting for their

379

turn. At long last, Beth stopped hugging her, and Miri reached out for the other ones.

"Ted, Markus."

They both entered the little circle of love and hugged her hard.

"I knew it wouldn't be easy for Death to take you away, Miriam," Ted said with a smile and a snivel. "You're too damn stubborn."

As Miriam laughed and Carl grinned where he stood leaning on the car, Mathilde gave up a shocked gasp, but Jakob put a calming hand on her arm, and she didn't say anything. As Markus shyly put his arms around her, Carl could hear him say in a low voice, "We've missed you, Luce and me."

"And I've missed you too, so much, so very, very much." Miri's voice was thick when she tenderly embraced her nephew.

Suddenly, a voice was heard from the other side of the well-tended hedge that separated the two neighbors from each other, "Matty? Is that Miriam? Is it?"

Everyone turned around toward the slender lady who stood with her cell phone in her hand. Carl frowned. Had she just taken a photo of them?

"Miriam, you remember Patty Smith, right?" Mathilde said, caught off-guard.

Carl could see that Miriam, in fact, did not remember the classy-looking lady, but she smiled politely and went over to take her hand. As she came closer, Patty Smith brought up her cell phone and took a photo of Miriam's face. Miri stopped dead in her track, and a wave of strong, unexpected anger rose inside Carl. With determined steps, he closed in on the lady while bringing out his FBI-badge. When she saw him coming at her, she looked surprised and worried.

"Carl Hansen, FBI. I'm here to escort Miriam Goldblum to her parents. Please, hand me your phone. You do not have any rights to take photos of a lead witness in an investigation." She paled and gave him the phone without any protests. Quickly, he checked it. She had managed to take thirteen photos of the family reunion. In fuming anger, he deleted them all before handing it back to her. "Next time you ask for consent."

Her face was dead-white, and she looked down. "Yes, sir."

He looked at Miri. She was still half-gaping in shock.

"Agent Goldblum?" Her head jerked back as she focused on him. "Let's ask your parents if we can go inside."

She nodded and turned her back to the lady. Just as he was about to follow her, he caught the furious expression on Patty Smith's face. *Damn, this could mean trouble.* He couldn't feel any regret for acting the way he had, even though he had lied to the woman and could get in serious predicaments for it.

Jakob had already started to urge everyone in, and when Carl came up on the veranda as the last person, Jakob put a gnarled hand on his arm.

"Thank you," he said.

"My pleasure."

As soon as they came into the living room, Mathilde nervously touched Miriam's hair and shoulders with those butterfly hands of hers.

"I'm sorry, *zissele*, I didn't know—"

"Don't worry, *mame*, of course, you couldn't know. No harm done."

Mathilde's eyes sought him out. "Maybe you could introduce us to your friend, who helped you out so nicely?"

"Um, yeah, sorry." A blush covered Miriam's face as she closed in on him. "This is Carl. He's my co-worker and… and my boyfriend."

She fumbled for his hand, and he took it calmly. The silence that followed was almost palpable. Then, Beth's quietly radiating face smiled, and she came over and hugged them both.

"Finally! Good God, you finally came to your senses. It only took, what, two years? There's no doubt about it, you

381

belong together. I don't think I've ever met two people as stubborn as you two, like ever."

Miriam laughed, and Carl glanced at her, feeling his heart soar. *You're so beautiful, habibti, so beautiful.* He longed to kiss her again, but maybe not here. In the corner of his eye, he noticed Mathilde standing with crossed arms, looking disapproving, and Carl's heart just about stopped beating.

"Boyfriend? Don't be silly, Miriam. You can't have boyfriends at your age. You're not a *maidel* anymore." Miriam grinned, and Mathilde came up to him and embraced him. "Welcome to the family, Carl, *aydem.*"

Another fierce blush hit Miriam's face, and the rest of the family laughed heartily at her. Carl looked around, slightly confused and bewildered.

Beth winked at him and grinned. "Mom just wedded you two, that's all."

"Oh, hush, child. I'm old. Let me have my illusions."

Miri sought out Carl's eyes with a questioning glance, and he nodded with a terrified smile.

"*Mame?* Instead of a *Kaddish,* would you like to plan for a wedding?"

Apparently, she dropped a bomb, and he felt bad for how amusing he thought it was, with the deafening silence as a result. Mathilde looked dazed, but Jakob took the few steps toward them and pressed Carl's hand hard with a kind smile in his eyes.

"It will be our pleasure. Carl, welcome, most welcome."

He gave the older man a genuine smile. "Thank you, Mr. Goldblum."

"Just call me Jake. Everyone else does."

"Alright. Thank you, Jake."

Miriam nudged at Mathilde. "*Mame,* stop it. You're acting as if I told you I've been elected President. It can't be that surprising I want to get married at last, or—" A mischievous grin bloomed on her lips. "Is it that someone wants to marry me that make you look like this? Don't give Carl second thoughts here."

"Not possible, Miri," he said, and she turned with blushing cheeks and beamed at him.

"Do you see why I love him?" Everyone laughed, and suddenly that hole of silence got plugged in when all of them began to talk at once. Ted came to shake his hand too.

"It'll take a while to get accustomed to this bunch, but I promise you, it's worth it."

Eventually, Miri, Beth, and Mathilde went out into the kitchen while talking about wedding ceremonies, and the men looked silently at each other. It was apparent that all of them were feeling left out.

"Never understood this need to plan everything without the other half of the couple," Ted said, and Jake chuckled quietly. Carl didn't feel like getting involved in a discussion about gender and wedding planning. Instead, he turned toward the boy who sat quietly on the sofa beside him.

"So, Markus, Miri tells me that you want to become a veterinarian?"

His sensitive and intelligent face lit up. "She talked about that? Wow. Did she tell you about Luce?"

"She did. I actually met him once, just after she got him."

"So, you were there, at the crime scene? That's so cool."

Carl avoided the question. During the past two years, all the planted memories from that specific crime scene had disappeared, and the only thing left was a gray void.

"I don't know much about canaries," he said instead. "The only birds we had on the farm when I grew up were hens and ducks."

Markus got a longing tone in his voice. "You lived on a farm? Where?"

"Alberta, Canada."

"You're Canadian? That's pretty cool too. We went to Niagara Falls last summer, but I've never been to Alberta. I wish we could live on a farm too. I love pigs. They're so intelligent and funny. Did you have pigs?"

"Yeah, we did. I actually did have a pet pig. I called him Wilbur after *Charlotte's Web*, you know? I taught him tricks, like 'play dead,' 'roll around,' things like that."

Markus laughed. "That's so cool."

"So, you like pigs. I guess you're fond of all kinds of animals, eh, if you're going to be a veterinarian?"

"Yeah, I am. My dream is to open a sanctuary for mistreated animals one day. As it is now, I volunteer at the shelter at West Mingan every second Saturday. It's a no-kill shelter. I couldn't stand it if it wasn't."

In the corner of his eye, Carl saw the surprised look on Ted's face. Apparently, Markus rarely talked about this.

"That's a great dream and an important job," he said sincerely, and Markus gave him a shy smile.

A knock on the door got all of them to look up.

Ted heaved himself up from the sofa. "You sit, Jake, I'll get it." He was back only a moment later and turned toward Carl, looking dazed. "There's a bunch of journalists out there. They want to talk with Miriam."

"What?" Carl exclaimed.

Ted shrugged. "I don't know. Someone must've called them."

Jake frowned. "Patty Smith."

Yeah, probably. Damn it. Knew she meant trouble.

Markus' face lit up with excitement. "I'll go and get her."

He jumped up from the sofa and rushed into the kitchen. The next moment, all the women were milling around in the living room. Miriam looked tired already, and she had a deep frown on her forehead.

"Journalists? Is it because of what you told me yesterday?"

"Most likely. Can't think of any other reason."

"I don't want to talk to them. Do you think I should?"

Carl's own frown deepened as he thought of this unnecessary complication of the situation. He pulled a hand through his hair and sighed wearily.

"They're going to write about you anyway, but if you play along, they'll write nice things."

Miri sighed too and nodded. Together with Matty and Jake, and Beth, Ted and Markus, they stepped out onto the front porch. *Oh, for crying out loud, it had to be a whole army of journalists, eh,* Carl thought as he looked out over a sea of people with cameras, film cameras, microphones, and recorders. As soon as the journalists saw them coming out, a wave of excitement crashed over them and they pointed with all their devices toward the family, and camera flashes went off. All of them began throwing out questions at the same time. With another sigh, Carl composed himself, stepped in front of the family and held up his hand. The journalists quieted down at this familiar cue.

"Alright, guys. This will be a five-minute-long interview. Agent Goldblum is still convalescent and needs to rest. We'll take one question at a time. Who wants to start?"

A burly man in the front row raised his hand a millisecond before the rest. Carl pointed at him.

"Bill Hynes from *The Esquire.*"

"Bill," Carl acknowledged him.

"Agent Goldblum, did you know two hundred and six people owe you their lives?"

Miri blinked astounded and squirmed beside him. A few seconds passed before she let up her tired voice. "Mr. Hynes, I wouldn't say they owe me their lives; I would say they took their lives into their own hands and did the best they could with it. Some made it out in time, others tried, but got trapped."

Great answer, Miri.

He pointed at a classily dressed woman in the second row with a man holding a film camera beside her.

"Samantha Goodwill, *Channel One News.*"

"Samantha."

385

"You're injured, Agent Goldblum. What happened to you? And how did you survive?"

Miri tensed beside him and took a deep breath. "When the explosion hit, I fell into an unused part of a basement and got trapped. I got some bruises, a concussion, and some head wounds. The doctors say I will be fine. I managed to survive because I had apples and chocolate to eat."

A woman further back in the row waved with her microphone. Carl pointed at her.

"Candace Williams, *The Morning Sun*.

"Candace."

"Is there anything you would like to say to the relatives of those who didn't make it?"

What the fuck? What kind of idiot question is that?

Miriam trembled, and her breathing was suddenly shallow, but he avoided touching her. He knew that everyone in the sea of journalists would see that immediately.

"Miss Williams, there's nothing I can say that will ever console those who lost a loved one that day."

Carl breathed easier. *You're great at this, Miri. Wow.*

"Alright, last question." He pointed at a well-dressed man in the second row.

"Harold Peters, *The Globe and Mail*."

The Globe and Mail? What the hell are they doing here?
"Harold."

"April seventeenth had a great impact on the world and sparked an intense debate about national security. As being a victim, how would you relate to that debate?"

Miriam frowned. "Mr. Peters, I'd like to stress that I'm not a victim anymore, and security can only protect a country's citizens to a certain point."

"Thank you very much, everyone."

"And you are?" a journalist in the front row asked.

"Carl Hansen, FBI."

"Carl Hansen?" another journalist broke in. "You're the one involved with finding *The Greek Tragedy Killer*, right?"

He stared at the journalist for a split second. *How the hell do they know that?*

"That's correct, together with Special Agent in Charge Allie Harris."

"So, what's your connection to Agent Goldblum?" the first one asked.

"I'm just escorting her to her family."

"Carl." Mathilde's voice was disapproving. Facing the camera, she said, "Carl has just asked if he can marry my daughter."

Oh, for CRYING OUT LOUD! A wave of excitement went through the crowd again. Miriam looked devastated where she stood beside Mathilde.

"Mom!"

"Yes, *HaY'Karah?*"

"They didn't need to know that."

"Of course, they did, *neshomeleh*. It's a beautiful ending to a tragedy. It shows people that even in the darkest of hours, there's still light, still hope. And I'm proud to welcome Carl to our family. He's done so much good for both us and others."

Even though she fought against them, tears trickled down Miri's cheeks, mostly out of embarrassment, but also out of love for her mom. Mathilde smiled toward her and kissed her cheek.

"Mrs. Goldblum, when will the wedding be?"

"That is still to be decided."

Well, Carl thought and gave up a quiet sigh. *It won't be more official than this. Wow... Just wow...* In his mind's eye, a parade of people walked by who he had wanted to tell the news personally, but now would get to see it on TV. His family in Canada, Allie, Caesar, Manda, Sarah— *Oh, for heaven's sake, I have to call Sarah before she sneaks by to check out the news tonight. Damn it! Damn it!*

"Alright, guys," he said in a strained voice, "Agent Goldblum is still convalescent, and she needs some rest and to be with her family."

"Can we have a kiss, please?"

For a moment, he stared unbelievingly at them and swore some really, really bad words in his head. Of course, they wanted to see a damn kiss! Miriam moved in toward him. Her face showed clear signs of exhaustion. In her eyes, he could read her silent thoughts, and he agreed with her. *Yeah, just give them what they want, pet them the right way, and then they'll leave us the hell alone – at least for a while.* As she nervously stepped into his arms, he tried to let go of his anger and hide his own anxiety, and smiled encouraging at her.

"Burning bridges, remember?" he whispered at her, and a smile broke out on her lips. He leaned in and softly kissed that smile while the cameras flashed around them. It was still sweet, even with all the audience, but... He broke the kiss and stood up, holding Miri around her back to stabilize her.

"Alright, guys, time's up. She really needs to rest now."

"Sure thing, Carl. Agent Goldblum. Mrs. Goldblum. And congratulations." The mood amongst the journalists was happy and excited. Maybe Mathilde did the right thing after all, but he knew he would have a hard time forgiving her. *Wow, what a great start to my relationship with my mother-in-law.* As quickly as possible, they retreated into the house.

Beth glared at Mathilde with arms crossed over her chest. "Seriously, mom. That was not necessary."

"Beth," Miriam broke in with tears in her eyes, looking exhausted. "It's okay. Don't— Don't fight. I can't take fighting right now. It's done, and it's over."

She collapsed on the sofa, and Carl sat down at her side and took her hand. "Shall we go home? You're exhausted."

She nodded. "Yeah, I need to sleep, but let's wait for ten minutes until we're sure everyone's left."

"Alright. I need to call Sarah."

Miri's eyes widened, and she put her hand in front of her mouth. "Oh, Carl—"

"It is what it is." He turned toward the others, still fighting with the anger. "If you'll excuse me, I need to call my daughter."

At this point, he didn't care that he left a sea of awkward silence behind him as he stepped into the kitchen and pulled out his cell phone. *Thank goodness I remembered to charge it.* One signal went through, two, three. He was just about to hang up when Manda answered.

"Carl! Where have you been? I've tried to get a hold of you for two weeks!" She sounded angry, as he had anticipated.

"I know, Manda, I'm sorry. I've been— We've found Miriam."

There was a silence at the other end.

"You found her? Is she—"

"She's alive, Manda."

"Oh, thank goodness for that," she exhaled, the anger immediately gone. "How injured is she?"

"Lots of bruises, some quite serious head wounds, but they'll heal, some dehydration and signs of starving, but the doctor says she'll be recovering."

"That's great news. You must be so happy."

"I am. Um... We're... we're getting married."

"What?" Her voice went from shock to sheer joy for his sake. "Oh, Carl, I'm so very happy for you. I wish you were here so I could hug you! Congratulations."

Warmth flowed through him at her blessing, and a smile finally broke out on his lips. "Thank you, Mand. It means a lot to me that you approve."

"Don't be silly, Carl. How long have I told you that she's good for you?"

He chuckled lightly. "A year now." Then, he inhaled, anxious again. "Problem is, I wanted to tell you, and especially Sarah, in person, but— The media hooked up on it, and it will be on the news tonight. I need to talk to her."

There was a slight pause. "Sure. Wait a minute." He could hear her walk and then her voice, "Sarah, it's Daddy.

389

He's got some news for you." The rustling sound of the phone changing hands was louder than he thought was comfortable, but then Sarah's serious voice was in his ear.

"Hi, Daddy."

"Hi, Peanut. How are you doing?"

"I'm fine. Grandma and Grandpa have a puppy."

"Yeah, I heard. That's awesome, eh?"

"Aha. When are you coming to see me? I have my first theater class tonight." As he slapped his hand on his forehead at his forgetfulness, she said, "You forgot, didn't you?" The disappointment in her voice made his heart cringe. In the background, he heard Manda say, "Honey, your dad has just come home from a difficult case. He won't make it in time. He'll pick you up next week instead."

"Okay."

"I'd like to come tomorrow if your mom hasn't decided anything else." He could hear her brighten on the other side of the line.

"Okay, she hasn't. What time are you coming?"

"Um, I don't know? Three? Is that good?"

"Mom? Can Dad come over at three tomorrow?" There was another slight pause in which Manda's voice sounded further away, saying something he couldn't discern. "Mom says yes if I still want it after you've told me the news. What news, Daddy?"

"Um…" He pulled his hand vigorously through his hair. "We've found Miri, Peanut, and she's alive, and… and…"

"Are you marrying her?"

"Um…"

"Because if you are, I think that's great. You shouldn't be alone anymore."

He had to dry a tear that unexpectedly found its way down his cheek.

"I love you, Peanut."

"I know. Are you marrying her?"

"Yes, I am."

"Good. So, is she coming with you tomorrow?"

"I hope so. I think so."

"Good. Okay, Dad. I'll see you tomorrow. Say hi to Miri."

"I will. And have fun tonight."

"Of course."

He smiled at her nonchalant tone that hid her true feelings, and his voice got even warmer. "Good. Bye, Peanut."

She hung up on him, and his heart danced with pride and joy. She was the best, most special and fantastic little girl he knew.

"Why do you call her 'Peanut'?" Markus asked behind him. Still beaming, he turned around.

"Because she looked like a peanut when she was a baby."

Markus, smitten by Carl's happy demeanor, smiled back. "How old is she? What's her real name?"

"She's nine, and her name's Sarah. Here, I have a photo of her."

To Carl's surprise, Markus took the phone and studied the picture of Sarah closely.

"She looks smart," he remarked.

"She is. She reminds me of you, actually."

Markus glanced his way to see if Carl was serious and when the boy saw that he was, he looked happy.

"I like smart people. You can talk with them, and they understand. Can I meet her someday?"

"Sure. If it's not your volunteer Saturday tomorrow and your family doesn't have any plans, you can come and meet her."

Markus gave him another glance. "You remember my volunteer Saturday? Wow!"

Carl gave him a surprised look. "Of course, I do. We talked about it."

"That doesn't— Some people – adults – they don't really care."

The faint sound of experienced neglect in the boy's voice touched his heart.

Carl looked him sincerely in the eyes. "Well, you know what, Markus? I do."

A short moment of silence fell as Markus considered his words thoroughly, and then, Carl saw a shadow outside the door in the corner of his eye. Ted peeked in on them, but Markus didn't notice.

"I think you do. I'll ask Mom and Dad if I can come."

When he turned around and went out to the living room again, Ted had already disappeared. Carl frowned. *What the hell is going on?* He shrugged uneasily. Sometimes it was way too easy to read things that weren't there because it was your job to find the things that were. When you witnessed so much brutality all the time, you got extra sensitive. It was probably nothing more than a father worried about his introvert son, but he would keep his eyes open, just in case.

Chapter 22

Miri slept in the passenger seat on their way home to Carl's apartment. Her face was pale again, and she seemed to have lost everything she'd gained in the form of energy since they came back from Night Porter's realm. The dark smudges under her eyes were back as well, and she had held on to her head when he first started the car. Carl suspected the pain had returned with full force. *No wonder. I'm more surprised she hasn't complained about it earlier.*

They had left a slightly quieter family than had greeted them, and he had clearly seen Mathilde's flashes of doubt when she thought about the interview. He might be bad, but he hadn't tried to comfort her. There was one type of people that irked him, and that was the kind who thought their way was the only right one. He thought Mathilde would place in that category, but he might be wrong. Time would tell, he guessed, as it usually did. He also had a feeling that Mathilde would get her fair share of scolding as soon as they left. Beth had looked furious and only been seconds from exploding.

At least they'd agreed on Markus and Miri coming with him to meet Sarah tomorrow. Carl had a strong feeling that Sarah and Markus would get along just swell. They were both serious, introvert kids, and Sarah behaved older than her age, which probably would suit Markus just fine. He liked Markus. In a way, the boy reminded him of himself at that age, not a lot of friends, but with a vision and a need for a future that separated him from all the other students in his class, and a way of observing people rather than communicating with them. Yeah, unlike today, tomorrow would be a good day.

When they were almost at home, Carl swung by the nearby supermarket. If he could avoid it, he'd rather not eat pizza for breakfast tomorrow. He just went in and out to get the basics, while letting Miri sleep. He didn't want to drag her

393

into another store before he knew more about how traumatized she was. His wife-to-be… A soft smile lit up his face at this unexpected turn of event. *I'm so grateful. I've never been a huge believer in second chances, and I promise I'll take care of this chance and nurture it until it blooms and beyond.* Thinking about blooming, he also bought a new package of condoms, since he wasn't sure of how old the other ones were and if they still were protective. *I certainly hope they are. It's way too early for both of us. I mean, we've just been a couple for a few hours. Miri needs to take care of herself first, and honestly, I have no idea about how she would feel about a pregnancy.* His heart fluttered. There was so much new to discover about his wife-to-be. *My-wife-to-be. I like the sound of that.*

She was still sleeping when he came out of the store and drove the last minutes home. When he nudged her, she slowly woke up, smiling faintly at him. The stagger when she got out of the car was nearly unnoticeable, but he casually put his arm around her as they took the slow-moving elevator up to the apartment.

"Did you stop to buy food?" she asked surprised when she saw him carrying the fabric bags he'd bought as well.

"Mhm."

"God, I didn't even notice. Wow, I'm tired." She fell silent for a while and waited until they got into his apartment. "I'm sorry about everything. It turned out worse than I expected."

"I think your sister had a thing or two to tell your mom when we left."

Miriam giggled. "God, I shouldn't laugh at it, but boy, does she deserve it. Ah, well, we'll have to see the wretched misery just to know how to meet people's reactions afterward."

"You were great, by the way, Miri. If you didn't have a career already, I'm sure anyone would like to hire you as their spokesperson."

She looked astounded at the praise. "You really think so?" she asked as she helped him clear out his *Swamp of Eternal Stench* that definitely lived up to its name this time.

"Yeah, no doubt. You even found good and respectful answers to the questions that irked you."

"It was that obvious?"

"For me, yeah. I don't know about them. But I think you made a great impression amongst them. They seemed happy, not frustrated when they left. I hate to admit it, but your mom might've been on to something after all. It did give them extra glazing on top of the cake."

"Wedding cake," Miri smiled.

He looked up at her from the other side of the fridge door. "Are you happy, Miri?"

"Very. Happier than in many, many years."

He closed the door and took her in his arms. "Me too. Sarah— Sarah said she's happy we're getting married because I won't be lonely anymore."

"Aww..."

"And it's true. I don't feel lonely with you. You're... you're just perfect for me." He paused and thought about it for a second. "Never thought I would ever say something like this the first time we met," he admitted.

She squirmed and laughed embarrassed. "Oh, God, Carl! Why do you have to bring up that horrible moment?"

He placed his finger under her chin and made her meet his gaze. "Because you never know what you might find if you don't start looking."

She smiled, suddenly shy, but closed in on him, shortened the distance between their lips and tasted him gently. Flashes of electricity ran through his body, and his hands followed her spine down until he caressed her buttocks. He loved the feeling of them under his hands, fit and soft at the same time. She exhaled, and the gush of her breath on his lips was irresistible. He let his hands wander up her sides, in under her T-shirt, and she drew a sharp breath as he caressed her breasts. The fabric of her bra that almost let him touch her skin made the sensation even stronger. Teasingly, he avoided her sensitive nipples, and breathing heavier, she pressed her body hard toward him, made him gasp for breath.

"Carl, you tease," she murmured, and the sound of her voice, so raspy and needy, sent jolts down his body.

"I know, I'm bad," he breathed at her throat and nipped at her skin with his teeth. She moaned and pushed her hips toward him. His heart beat faster, and he closed his eyes for a second.

"I... I want you!" Her voice was tinted with a slight need, and the desire shot needles of pleasure all through his body and concentrated in the hot spot in his lower abdomen. Still, he continued his slow exploration of her body, unbuttoning her shirt and moving his hands over her shoulders and arms, kissing the little hollow where her shoulder and her neck met. She breathed in, shakily, and closed her eyes. The tip of her tongue wetted her lips, and he caught it with his own lips. The taste of her was earthy and full and nearly drove him out of his senses. He let go, and she sighed. Instead, he let his lips follow her neckline down, over her breasts and almost, almost touching her nipples. She moaned, low and raw, and her body trembled, but he wanted her to feel more, take more. Slowly, he caressed her stomach with his lips while unbuttoning her jeans before pulling them down. She trembled even more but tried to catch her breath, slow it down. He smiled and placed his hands on her buttocks again, moved her hips toward him and kissed her vulva through the plain cotton in her underwear. She jerked, almost in shock.

"Oh God, don't do this to me! No! No, don't stop."

Her raspy voice made the world spin around him. He breathed heavier, faster, but managed to keep control over himself. Slowly, he pulled her underwear down and touched her gently. The curls were moist and she trembled under his hand. She whimpered when he let go. The sound nearly drove him over the edge.

As he stood up and feverishly unbuttoned his own jeans, he watched her flushed face, her softly parted lips and her muddled gaze. He closed his mouth on hers as he lifted her up onto the smooth wooden surface of the kitchen counter, and as he slid into her and the world vaulted, he murmured, "You're so beautiful, Miri, so beautiful."

Her breaths were ragged, but she smiled at him, caressed his face. "You're beautiful too, Carl, and you make me feel beautiful."

For a moment, they were still, unmoving, feeling the sensations of the intimate nearness; she enclosing him, he filling her. The moment she moved in to kiss him, he gasped at the unbearably sweet sensations that filled him, and he closed his eyes shortly before opening them again and looking into her loving face as their lips met.

"I want to undress you, Carl," Miriam whispered and tugged at his shirt while starting to unbutton it. "I want to see the whole of you naked."

The words made him tremble, and as she took off his shirt, he unhooked her bra and caressed her breasts, touched her nipples. She moaned and shut her eyes, hanging on to his shoulders, pressing herself toward him, and their heavy breaths blended together. She put her legs around his waist and writhed on him, making him slowly lose his mind.

"I love you, Miri," he breathed raggedly.

"I love you," she moaned.

The release came quickly, and they hung on to each other as if drowning. When their breaths started to calm down, she laughed quietly.

"I don't think I'll ever see your kitchen the same way again."

He chuckled and embraced her even more, snuggled into that little hollow at her neck that seemed to be meant for him. "In time, I'm sure we'll say that about everything."

She hummed pleasantly. "You're giving me ideas here."

At the tone of her voice, he grinned. "I certainly hope so."

She hummed again, but then she moved him out of the way and jumped down, picked up her clothes, and while looking him all over, she started to dress again

"What?"

"I just do like you naked, is all."

Even though a sudden shyness hit him, he laughed at her. "I guess we're even then."

She smiled mischievously and pulled the T-shirt over her head.

"I'm also hungry," she said, her head still buried in the fabric. When she pulled out from the neckband, her gaze went toward the bags with food. "What did you buy?" With more energy than before, she went through the bags and brought out the grilled chicken, the cherry tomatoes, the potato salad, and the bread. "Mm, I do love you."

He grinned and put on his own clothes. After thoroughly washing his hands with soap, he carried plates and cutlery to the living room. Soon, they sat on the sofa, indulging in food.

"How's your head?" he asked eventually.

"Not good, to be honest," she said with a grimace. "I've been thinking about taking one of those codeine pills, but— I don't like losing control over myself like that."

He took her hand and squeezed it. "It's okay, Miri. I think you should. You need to relax properly so you can start healing, but if you really don't want to, well, it's your decision."

She smiled and squeezed back. "I might take one tonight, and if I don't feel better on Monday, I might go and see Dr. Bernard." She checked the time. "Here goes. Are you prepared?"

"No, but I'll never be prepared for this, so shoot, I guess."

She turned on the TV just in time for the news introduction. He wasn't surprised that they had managed to make it to the first place.

"For one family today," the news anchor started, "life changed drastically for the second time in a month. Cassandra Riley has the story."

As the news clip started with a shaky amateur video showing the actual explosion of Kroger's, Miriam watched wide-eyed and held Carl's hand so hard that it hurt. He put his arm around her, and she leaned into his embrace.

"April seventeenth," the voice-over said, "changed the lives of fifty-eight families when one woman, Florence Tyler, decided to take her own life and bring as many people as possible into death with her." The clip continued by showing the chaotic aftermath with all personnel milling around, moving debris, and carrying away lifeless bodies. "Thanks to another woman, Miriam Goldblum, a brave FBI-officer who happened to discover the home-made bombs while shopping for groceries after her shift and warned all the customers and staff in the store, the number of the survivors reached two hundred and six."

Carl glanced at Miriam as she gawked at the description and placed her hand at her left temple, shaking her head in disbelief. The clip changed to the young butcher Carl had met that first horrible night. It was from an interview he'd seen before. The young man was covered in dust and blood and stared right into the camera with a shocked, distant expression.

"She came running through the doors, waving her badge, screaming 'Get out, get out, there's a bomb in the store.' We all started to run, and she was right behind me and then— Then, everything went black…"

Another news clip showed up, one Carl hadn't seen before, of a ceremony. The camera zoomed in on Miriam's parents standing on a stage, crying, and holding a blue and golden pillow where a medal rested. Carl hugged Miri closer when tears silently trickled down her cheeks. "Last Saturday,

Miriam Goldblum posthumously earned the *FBI Medal of Valor* for exceptional bravery. It was handed to her parents during one of the most prestigious ceremonies amongst the Federal Bureau of Investigation."

"This is absolutely crazy," Miri mumbled and touched her temple again. "Absolutely crazy…"

The voice-over continued as a photo of a happily smiling Miriam in her FBI-jacket filled the screen, "Until today, no one doubted her death, even though her body hadn't been found." The photo faded out, and footage of Miriam's parents' house showed up. It continued to a close-up on Miriam's exhausted, gaunt, and bruised face with all the numerous wounds on her forehead. Her calm but tired voice was clearly heard, "When the explosion hit, I fell into an unused part of a basement and got trapped. I got some bruises, a concussion, and some head wounds. The doctors say I will be fine. I managed to survive because I had apples and chocolate to eat."

The camera zoomed in on Mathilde's and Jakob's radiating faces as they stood holding hands half a step behind Miri. The voice-over continued, "When asked about how she felt having so many people owing her their lives, her answer was humble." Once again, Miriam's bruised and exhausted face was in focus. "I wouldn't say they owe me their lives; I would say they took their lives into their own hands and did the best they could with it. Some made it out in time, others tried, but got trapped." The camera panned away to Candace Williams, who asked her stupid question again. "Is there anything you would like to say to the relatives of those who didn't make it?" When the camera zoomed back to Miriam, it looked as if she was near tears. "Miss Williams, there is nothing I can say that will ever console those who lost a loved one that day."

The somber voice-over turned up a notch and sounded over-joyed. "As if this wasn't the best news the Goldblum family could get today, there was even more to celebrate. Mrs. Mathilde Goldblum let us know that FBI-officer Carl Hansen, who earned his fame participating in the reveal of the identity and the capture of *The Greek Tragedy Killer* two weeks ago, has special plans regarding Miriam Goldblum." As the camera zoomed in on Mathilde's joyful demeanor, Carl rubbed his face and squirmed on the sofa. "Carl has just asked if he can marry my daughter." There was a clip to Carl and Miriam embracing, both smiling as if they weren't even aware of the crowd, and then the kiss, while another voice-over was heard; Mathilde's quietly happy voice, "It's a beautiful ending to a tragedy. It shows people that even in the darkest of hours, there is still light, still hope."

The camera zoomed out, capturing the whole family on the porch, but suddenly, Miri gasped beside him and dug her nails hard into Carl's hand, as the camera for a moment landed on a familiar person standing at the edge of the crowd, smiling secretly at the camera, looking directly at them where they sat on the sofa. Night Porter.

They sat as if frozen while the TV flitted on in front of their shocked eyes. The news anchor smiled broadly at her co-anchor.

"It's a beautiful story, don't you think, Andrew?"

"Indeed, Helen. You could say that partners in crime become partners in love."

"Such a wonderful ending. We have to wish them happiness in their marriage. And now on to the undergoing investigation of the political scandal in the Mayor of Westbury's office. Matthew Strong has that story."

Jerkily, Carl found the remote control and turned off the TV. At that moment, his cell phone rang. Still in shock, he managed to answer.

"Y... yeah...?"

"Did you see that, Octavius? Did you see him?" Olwen's usually calm voice was on the brink of breaking.

"Y... yeah..."

"How the fucking hell did he come here? How the fucking HELL did he come HERE?"

"I— I—"

401

"We need to stop this! We need to shut off that fucking portal! We need to check if it's still around in the basement, if there's one in Florence's apartment, and most importantly, you must check Ophelia's apartment. She led us right in there, she opened a damn, fucking portal in her damn apartment!"

It felt as if she had kicked him hard in the stomach. For a second, he bent over, nauseous, before he managed to compose himself, and with a terrified look around, he tried to find any kind of vibrations.

"Do you hear me, Octavius?"

"I— I do hear you."

"We'll meet tomorrow, ten a.m. sharp at the main library downtown. Armand says he has some ideas. I'll talk to him and then— Then, we'll close that damn dimension."

Chapter 23

Carl hadn't yet managed to put down his cell phone when the landline phone rang. He didn't even care to check it. It was probably just one or another of friends, family, or colleagues who wanted to congratulate them. There would be some calls like that from now on, he believed, but it was more important to find out whether there were vibrations in his apartment, rather than spending time receiving sweet blessings. *Damn it, I kind of looked forward to them.*

He cleared his voice, trying to stop it from shaking. "Miri, Olwen said we need to check if there's a portal here, if the door we came out of is— If it's still around."

She stared at him as if struck by lightning, but then she got up from the sofa, clearly unaware of how she held her hand at her temple and started to scrutinize the opening to his bedroom. Meanwhile, the answering machine buzzed and went on.

"Hi, Carl. It's me, Allie." He couldn't figure out why, but her voice sounded strained. Then again, he might be wrong, seeing the mood he was in. "That was the sweetest, cutest thing I've seen in a long time, and you're right, she's fabulous, suits you perfectly. I'm very, very happy for you two. I'm also impressed by how well you managed to hide how much everything ticked you off, both of you. Well done." There was a long pause, and Carl frowned. Something was wrong.

"Wow," Miri muttered from the doorway. "She must be really good if she saw that. I didn't see it, and I knew about it."

"Here's the thing, though," Allie's voice finally continued. "I mean, you know I'm prone to the dramatic, right, Carl? But as far as I know, which might be the key here, I might not know, but let's pretend I know, okay?"

Carl stopped searching and stared at the answering machine. *What the hell's going on, Allie?*

403

Miri came up to him with a frown. Somehow, she had caught on to the tense strain in Allie's voice.

"Okay, I know what you're thinking, stop babbling and get to the point, right?" They heard her inhale. "So, I'm prone to the dramatic, but I'm not prone to seeing things that aren't there. As far as I know." There was a slight pause, and Miri's eyes were wide-opened and anxious. "Kevin and Laurie might be standing outside my door laughing their pants off right now, but... but I don't think so..." Another slight pause occurred before she continued, this time with the strain in her voice clearly detectable. "I know I can trust you, Carl, so please, please tell me if that scary Joker guy at the end was real, 'cause... 'cause Kevin and Laurie say they didn't see him."

With a pounding heart and dry mouth, Carl managed to move his feet the few steps to the phone and pick it up.

"Allie?" He put on the loudspeaker so Miri could hear her too.

A relieved whoosh was heard. "God, I'm so happy you picked up."

"Are you sure they didn't see him? They didn't just look away at that moment? They're not just kidding you?"

"I don't think so. They seemed genuinely surprised when I commented on him."

"What did they say?"

"Uh, well, I said, 'That guy really looks like the Joker, don't you think?' and they said 'What guy?' and I said "The one in the end, the smiling one who looked right into the camera' and both of them stared at me as if I was crazy, and then Laurie asked if I'd bumped my head today, 'cause there wasn't any guy there, and Kevin told me to stop pulling their legs. But you saw him, I hear it in your voice. So at least I'm not crazy. Well, at least not if this phone call doesn't only happen in my head right now. That might be a possibility, of course."

"Allie, are you sure they aren't messing with you?"

"Normally, I would say they were completely honest and serious, but now? I honestly don't know. I'm… I'm shaken…"

Carl shuddered and stared at Miriam. Her eyes were enormous and appeared black in contrast to her pale face.

With an urgent look at him, she said, "Tell her to come over here. I don't think we should have this conversation over the phone."

"Miri?" Allie's voice sounded frightened.

"Yes?"

"I might risk Carl's career if I do that."

Allie paused, and then Miri said something Carl never thought she'd say, "Only if anyone gets to know about it, right?" The silence stretched out, but eventually, Miri took Carl's hand and continued, "You know, mom might've done the right thing after all. I mean, they talked about you like you're popular, both on the news and during the interview. Even if Jeremy Kane would get to know about you two breaching the agreement of not seeing each other or talking to each other, I don't think he can sack you right now. I might be wrong, but I have a feeling she should be here. But I'm torn, you're right too; you do have too much to lose if this gets out."

He sighed and let his hand tangle his hair. *Burn the damn bridges.* "It might be best if you come over anyway, Allie."

"Okay, thanks."

She immediately hung up on him, and he put back the phone at its place while looking at Miriam with a worried frown.

"I've never heard her sounding frightened before."

"Do you think it's true that her friends didn't see him?"

"You tell me, but Allie's never been wrong about reading people before, and these are her closest friends. She'd notice if they'd tried to pull off some practical joke on her, and I've met both Kevin and Laurie. They don't seem to be the kind of people that would do such a thing."

Miri shivered visibly, and he went over to her and embraced her hard, wanting to both give and take comfort. With a calming inhale and exhale, she tried to compose herself before turning toward the doorway between the living room and the bedroom. She began walking toward it but stopped before getting halfway. Instead, she turned her back to it as if she wasn't ready to discover that the damn portal might exist in his apartment.

"You know, in a strange way, I look forward to meeting her, to see what she's like. I mean, with… with Henry, I was always so prone to jealousy, but I don't feel jealous now. I hope that's a good sign."

Carl tried to adjust to the sudden change of topic. It struck him as weird to have this talk now, but she clearly needed something else to focus on.

Trying to redirect his thoughts, he paused for a second, looking for words. "Don't take this as if I'm looking down on the relationship you had with him because I'm not. You really loved each other, but Miri, you were very sealed-in, very, uh, protected, and I think the jealousy came from the insecurity you felt."

She was quiet longer than he expected, with her gaze on the floor, but eventually, she sighed and looked up at him.

"I don't know. I have a hard time seeing him clearly, or rather, him and me clearly. It's not that I love him anymore—" Apparently, she caught herself and gave up a short and quiet laugh. "I mean— God, that would be awkward, to say the least." She looked sincerely at him. "I'm ashamed to admit it, and I've never— I've never said it out loud, but after we broke up, I never longed for him. I never wanted him back. Not once. All I felt was a huge relief and that— That made me ashamed of myself, as if I cheated, as if I faked the love I thought I felt for him." She fell silent again, lost in thoughts, and he reflected on how brave she was, managing to admit something like that. He caressed her hand,

406

and she gave him a faint smile. "Anyway, why are we standing here like two morons talking relationships when we're supposed to look for a portal to another dimension?"

He managed a chuckle since she hoped for one, but when he thought about the possible catastrophe on its way to happening, it died away. "Just to let you know, um, Allie's very physical, very much hugging and kissing and such, but she's like that toward anyone she likes."

"Okay." Miriam's voice was tired again, and when she turned around, her stance was slumped as she walked to the threshold.

Carl watched her back and tugged at his hair. *It's been a too long, too emotional day. She should sleep, not work, not strain her mind again. And after all these events today, she's going to meet the woman I slept with when she was away. What a damn clusterfuck.*

He went over to her, and side by side, they studied the threshold, almost touching each other's shoulder, but there was a small, insecure gap in between them. He didn't know what to say to make it better, so he kept quiet. Instead, they searched for the vibrations they both knew were there. Now, when he thought about it, he could feel it, like an electrical sphere around the doorway.

"Do you feel it too?" he asked, and she nodded. "Can you see it?"

"No, but it's there. It doesn't have the same sensation as the inn or the castle. I don't think it's bad right now. It just, you know, is."

He nodded. "Yeah." Then, he glanced uneasily at her. "The castle? Were you there?"

She shivered violently and touched her temple again. "No, no. It sent out such bad vibes. I didn't even go close to it."

"Good." Then, he surprised them both. "I love you, Miri. Never forget it."

Apparently caught off guard, she gave him a baffled look that immediately turned to relief, before embracing him.

407

"Thank you," she mumbled. "I needed to hear that now." A moment later, she looked up at him. "Shall we make some Masala Chai while we're waiting for Allie? I mean—" She glanced at the doorway. "I don't plan on opening it, so there's not much else we can do right now."

"That's a great idea."

Half an hour later, they sat shoulder to shoulder on the sofa, taking comfort in the physical nearness, while sipping the tea. On the table, an untouched mug with steaming Masala Chai waited for Allie. When there was a knock on the door, Carl went to open it, trembling from the stress levels that pulsated in his body. *Please, please, please, let this work out smoothly...* As he suspected, she immediately embraced him and lightly kissed his cheek.

"Nice seeing you again, Carl." She gave him a penetrating look. "But you don't look as happy as I thought you would."

He laughed, but it was void of humor. "You wouldn't be very happy either after going through what we've been through. Come, I want you to meet Miri." To his surprise, even now, during this strained moment, his heart soared in his chest, and a broad, genuine smile played on his lips as he brought her into the living room to meet his wife-to-be. Nervously, Miri stood up and held out her hand to Allie, but Allie just ignored it and embraced her in a long, warm hug. Carl couldn't help but feel amused when Miri astonished glanced at him over Allie's shoulder. He just smiled and shrugged. *It's Allie. What can I say?* Eventually, Miri's slightly stiff body relaxed, and Allie let go of her, wiping away a couple of tears.

"I'm sorry. You probably think I'm nuts, hugging you like this and crying, but Carl has talked so much about you. It feels like I know you. I know I don't, but still, that's how it feels, and I'm so very, very happy that you're alive. And I'm so happy that you're getting married. Wow, look at me, crying again." She sniveled, and Miri's somewhat dazed expression softened, and a smile replaced it.

"I thought he was exaggerating when he said you hug a lot."

Allie burst out laughing. "Hugging a lot is probably an understatement. I do it all the time. Kissing too. And touching. That's just how I am, but I don't do it to people who feel uncomfortable about it, so if you don't like it, I'll stop."

"No, don't stop. If it's you, then it's how you're supposed to be, and that's okay."

Allie beamed at her, but then she saw the extra tea mug on the table.

"That's for me? Aw, thanks." She sat down, and Miri joined her. Carl kept in the background, watching how they bonded, feeling so blessed by having these two amazing women in his life. Then, Allie sought him out. "Why are you sitting over there? Come here and sit with us instead."

Obligingly, he scooted over before stopping at the opposite side of the table.

Allie turned serious again. "Okay, I wish we could just have a nice evening together, getting to know each other and such, but you look like you need to sleep, Miri. I'm sorry, I know it's none of my business, but I'd be sad if you were awake just because of me."

Miri smiled at her, and Carl could see that she was getting as charmed of Allie and her straightforwardness as he was, and a wave of relief went through his body, and finally made him relax. *It might still work out.*

"You're right. I am very tired. It's been a long day."

"A long month, I'm sure."

"Yes, that too…"

Allie took her hand and caressed it, and Miri got that astounded look on her face again.

Allie smiled at her. "Sorry, it might take some time to get used to me." Then, she included Carl in the conversation. "Okay, so what's going on with that man in the news? You both saw him, right?" She looked at Miriam, who nodded, pale and shaken again.

"Yes."

"So, who is he? Why did I see him, but Kevin and Laurie said they didn't?" She turned toward Carl with an anxious appearance. "This isn't some kind of weird practical joke, is it? You haven't ganged up on me together with Kevin and Laurie, have you?"

Carl could hear the strain in her voice again under the joking facade, and he leaned over and took her hand, caressed it. A flash of surprise fluttered over Miri's face, but in the next second, she seemed to come to the conclusion that it was him comforting a friend, not him comforting a lover, and she relaxed again. The relief was so huge that he nearly cried. Instead, he took a deep breath and looked Allie seriously in the eyes.

"We would never do something like that, Allie."

She inhaled and nodded, joined his and Miri's hands together with hers. "In a way, I kind of hoped it was a practical joke, even if it would mean an end to our friendship. I can't handle practical jokes. They're too mean. But if it isn't a joke, then the only other conclusion I could come up with is too scary to even think about, but I need to know."

Miri and Carl shared a look, and he could clearly see that she thought they should tell her. *Why?*

As if she could read his mind, she said, "I don't know why, Carl, but what scares me is that if we're only a few who saw him, why is she one of us? I heard Olwen when she called. She saw him, but that didn't surprise me. After all, she was there. She met him too. We've all met him, we've talked to him, but Allie hasn't. She has no connection to that place. Why has she been chosen to see him?"

A cold shiver ran down his spine at her specific words. *'Chosen'? For fuck's sake, it rings true,* he thought, startled.

"What place?" Allie's voice sounded scared, and they both looked at her, weighed her.

Carl pulled at his hair and came to a decision, probably a mad decision, but it felt as if the choice had already been made for them.

"Let's show her."

Miriam stared at him. "Are you crazy? I'm not going in there again!"

"No, no, not going in. Just show her, you know, the vibrations."

She shook her head skeptically. "We couldn't even see them this time."

"Hey, come on! I'm sitting right here. Talk to me, please."

Carl looked at Allie and caressed her hand again. "Come. We'll show you."

He stood up and pulled her toward the bedroom.

She got a suspicious look on her face. "What kind of 'vibrations' are we talking about here? I mean, I'm all for a threesome one fine day, but I'd like to be part of the planning, okay?"

Carl stopped dead, and his face turned hot and red. Miriam giggled nervously behind them.

"Um…" *God, the images…* "Um, I wasn't talking about sex, Allie."

"Okay, good. It would've been really weird and out of character if you did. So, what are you talking about?"

He rubbed his neck vigorously. "Um… Alright… Just stand here. Close your eyes."

She gave him another suspicious glance before doing as he asked. "I swear you're pulling a damn joke on me."

"No, we're not. I promise you, Allie, it's not a joke. God, I wish it was a damn joke!"

For some reason, his sudden outburst made her relax, and she took a deep breath. "Okay, I'm having my eyes shut. Now, what?"

"Just breathe and feel."

"Feel what?"

"Shh… Quiet now."

To his immense relief, she stood still and kept silent. Carl tried to make himself relax but couldn't get away from the hunch that this might be a huge mistake. As the silence

411

stretched out, he could clearly feel the damn vibrations, and Miri's strained expression told him that she could too.

A curious look spread over Allie's face, and eventually, she said, "What is it?"

"It's a door."

"I guess you're not talking about the bedroom door, right?"

"Right."

"Okay, can I open my eyes now?"

"Yeah."

As she did, she squinted and focused on the doorway, and suddenly, a couple of shimmering vibrations were seen.

"NO!" Both Miri and Carl shouted at her, and Allie gave up a faint shriek, jolted, and lost her concentration. The vibrations disappeared.

Carl's whole body felt like it turned to liquid. Trembling, he slid down on the floor with his back toward the wall.

"Oh, God, that was close."

"Too close," Miriam agreed faintly and hugged herself hard.

Bewildered, Allie looked back and forth between them. "Okay... Not a practical joke... What is it?"

"It's a door, a portal to another dimension," Carl said feebly, leaning his head toward the wall and glanced at her.

She laughed nervously. "Yeah, right..." When neither Miri nor Carl laughed with her, she fell silent and watched them with huge, scared eyes. "You're not kidding." Carl shook his head. Jerkily, she turned back toward the door but took a couple of steps away from it. "How... how is it possible? It... it wasn't here before, was it?"

"No. Miriam opened it when we finally managed to get out of there."

Allie looked haunted and stared at Miriam. "That's... that's why he couldn't find you, why you were gone from Kroger's. When I saw the news, it— It didn't ring true. I knew they'd found the place you fell into. You've been in... in another, uh, dimension for... for a whole month?"

Miri nodded, and a couple of tears found their way from her eyes. She dried them with an irritated gesture and exhaled. "The Night Porter— You call him The Joker. He comes from there. He... he tends to a hotel in a dead town there. It sounds— I know it sounds crazy, and I— I was going crazy, but it really exists."

"Okay, okay... I... I need to sit down. Um, do you have some more of that tea?"

"Great idea." Carl heaved himself up on unsteady legs and went out to the kitchen. Leaning his forehead on the cupboard, he concentrated on the blending of the tea and wished that he could relax. The soft mumblings from Allie and Miri, where they sat talking on the sofa, reached him, and when he came out with a full kettle of Masala Chai, Allie leaned back on the sofa, her face pale and her eyes frightened and wide-opened. She looked at them.

"Is this— Is this what you're really doing? The Star Students, I mean? Weird things?"

"Yeah."

"Okay. And... And... There are enough weird things going on out there that you need a whole damn university for it?"

"Well, um, I guess you could say that," Carl agreed. "Just keep in mind that for the Star Student program, they're only taking in one student per year, with a few exceptions. For all the other students, it's as normal a university as you can attend anywhere."

"Okay. Sorry, probably bad manners and all that, but, um, do you have— Do you have any proof?"

"Um..." Carl tried to think about something but couldn't come up with anything. "We're sending all things back to the Faculty when we're done, reports, evidence, the lot."

"I have something," Miriam said and stood up, starting to unbutton her jeans. For once, Allie didn't say

413

anything about sex, which felt like a relief. When Miri pulled down the jeans, she turned and showed them the huge, jagged bite mark on her left thigh. Allie gasped.

"I've always wondered how you got that, Miri," Carl said in a low voice.

"You've never asked."

"No, I thought you'd tell me when you were ready for it."

She gave him a tender smile. "Well, I guess I kind of am now." She looked down at it, traced it with her index finger. "It happened when I was on my first Research Assistant position with the FRs from M, so nine years ago now. It was such a— Such a weird Project..." Her voice trailed away for a moment. "Yeah, weird, to say the least. I won't go into any details, but it led us to a— Well, it was like, you know, a kind of ruin in West Virginia, an old factory, and this ruin, it went deep down underground, floor after floor after floor. It never ended. We never got to the bottom. It was crazy, and, God, I was so damn scared. We were looking for a group of people who we suspected was involved in cannibalism, but we were totally unprepared for what we met." Her face lost its softness and became grim, while her finger continued to trace the scar around and around. "I don't know which floor we were on when they surrounded us. One moment we were all alone, and the next—" She shuddered, lost in memories. "They— They didn't look entirely human. I mean, they, um, they were humanoid, looking exactly like ordinary people, except for these, um, these mouths— No, not mouths; jaws. Jaws they somehow unhinged. Kind of— Kind of like snakes." She paused. Her forehead shone from sweat and her eyes had a faraway expression as she looked back into the haunting memories. "To this day, I can't get a grasp of what really happened. It's just memory flashes in my mind of these... these creatures who surrounded us and tried to eat us. I guess we were lucky. Morley lost his leg, but none of us died."

414

Silence fell, and she pulled up her jeans and buttoned them.

"What... what did you do to the place?" Allie asked with a faint voice.

"We bombed it. Honestly, I don't think we managed to kill any of them, and I'm quite sure they found another way out eventually. It was a stupid solution."

She sighed and placed herself on the sofa again, looking exhausted.

Allie squirmed next to her, glancing at Carl. "Um, that scar you have... the one on your back... You told me it's classif—"

At that moment, the embarrassment exploded in Carl's body, and he just wanted a huge hole to open up underneath him. His face burned with mortification, and he didn't dare to look at Miri. Clearly, it struck Allie too as soon as the words left her mouth.

She got blossoming red in her face and rubbed her eyes vigorously. "Oh, God! Why do I always speak before I think? I'm so sorry." She looked absolutely devastated as she turned to Miri. "I— It's, um..."

For some reason that Carl couldn't comprehend, Miri smiled. It was a weak, tired smile, but genuinely sweet.

"He told me. It's okay. We didn't have a relationship going on at that time, and even if we had, I wouldn't say anything about it. You both thought I was dead, for crying out loud." Then her smile got broader and a bit teasing. "And as I told him, I think you have good taste."

Allie squirmed again, even though a shadow of a smile played on her lips. "Well, I— Thank you." She fell silent for a moment. "I... I guess I should go home. You... you need to sleep, and it's getting way too late, but, um..."

Miri caught Carl's eyes with a questioning gaze, and even though he felt awkward, he nodded.

"You can sleep here, Allie," she said.

Allie inhaled deeply. "Okay, thanks. You're absolutely crazy, but... Thanks. I'm usually not this squeamish, but—"

415

Miri leaned in and embraced the younger woman hard.

"It's not every day you get to know that the reality doesn't look like you've always thought it did."

Allie took another deep stuttering breath, and, suddenly, Carl realized she was crying. He came over and placed himself at Allie's other side, putting his arms around both women. Together, they sat embracing each other for a long while.

Chapter 24

They ended up sleeping in his bed all three of them since Allie was so shaken. She couldn't stop trembling, and even though she claimed to not be miserable, tears kept trickling from her eyes. As Carl lay in the middle between Miri and Allie with an arm around both of them, he had to admit that this was another one of all the new situations he never thought he'd find himself in, and he felt more awkward than he had been in a long time. At least Miri had taken one of the codeine pills so she could sleep without pain, and her arm and head lay flopped over him while she was breathing calmly on his chest. That she took the pill showed him both how much pain she was in, but also how much she trusted him, seeing as Allie was there, and his love and respect for her went as deep and wide as the ocean. The difference between Miri's calm breathing and Allie's trembling body and shallow breaths couldn't be bigger.

"Do you want something so you can sleep?" he asked, eventually. "I have some Xanax I take when I get a panic attack. It would help you."

She lay quiet a moment. "You get panic attacks?"

"Sometimes."

"Do you... do you mind if I ask why?"

He sighed and moved a tiny bit, not that he could move a lot, squeezed in as he was.

"Well... My last RP in N ended badly, to say the least. As did my last RP in C."

"What happened?"

He glanced at her but couldn't discern her face in the dark.

"Well... The N-one is the Project Alan mentioned, so I was going to tell you eventually anyway. We— My FRT, uh, that stands for Field Research Team, and mine was the N-team. We and the supporting team, U, got caught, and... and..." He inhaled, trying to keep the emotional distance.

"Long story short, we were going to be executed by being burnt at the stake, and I saw all of them burn."

"Oh… my… God… Oh, my God!" Her voice was shocked, and she embraced him harder, trying to give him comfort, even though she herself was in bigger need of it. He leaned his head toward her and caressed her shoulder to show her how much he appreciated it.

"The other RP, in C— I honestly don't think you'd believe it."

"After today?" She laughed shakily. "I guess I'd believe anything, even Santa coming after you with a chainsaw."

"Well, at least Santa looks human."

She froze for a moment, before deliberately forcing herself to relax. "Okay, now you scare me even more."

"I'm sorry."

A couple of longer moments went by before she sighed and moved around a bit. "Goddamn, I shouldn't have asked. I'll probably regret it, but you have to tell me. Otherwise, I'll make up so many scary stories in my head, and I'll never know if they're scarier than yours or not."

He sighed again. "Alright. It was the RP I told you about in which I got to take over the team, remember?" She nodded. "I can't go in on the details, but it was a— It was a family sacrificing children to a monster. Thing is, this monster was real." She lay stiff beside him, breathing with short, strained breaths. "I don't remember much of the last moments, only glimpses of chaos. It came there. We were completely unprepared for it. I mean, we didn't even think it existed. We never even talked about that possibility, which is just insane, in hindsight. Anyway…" He squirmed and exhaled, thinking about those last nightmarish images. "It was huge… enormous… and… and it had tentacles, like an octopus, only more. The last thing I remember is, it lifted me up in the air, sucking out my blood from my neck. There's still a scar. Don't know if you've seen it."

Allie's unsteady fingers searched for the scar, and he moved his head to the left and exposed it to her. She touched the big smooth and perfectly circular mark, before quickly moving her fingers away. Again, her breaths were shallow and shaking.

Carl gave her time to try to comprehend, and eventually, she said in a small, scared voice, "How... how do you survive? I mean, mentally? How... how do you do it?"

"What other option is there? Either you survive, or you let them win. I won't let them win." He paused for a second. "But the last one, it almost won. I was catatonic weeks afterward, but thanks to Miri and Sarah, I managed to fight it somehow. But I won't lie to you. There are many who don't make it through. Either they die, or they get committed. That's how you change teams and code names. Your own team gets destroyed, and you survive, and you get a new FRT, one that lost a member or two and needs to get filled up."

"Can you— Can you quit? Or retire? Or something? Or are you in until the point of no return?"

"We can ask to quit. Usually, they, the Faculty, grant us that wish, at least nowadays, because the worst thing that can happen during an RP is to have someone with you who doesn't want to be there. That's when it gets out of control, and you lose people you wouldn't lose otherwise." The image of Nigel and his chain-smoking showed up in his mind. Regretfully, he pushed it aside and continued, "After you've quit, you can go on to other professions, or continue in your side-profession, like the FBI, or become a teacher at Western Shore. All of the teachers there are former Star Students and Field Researchers." He fell silent for a couple of seconds. "I was hoping Miri and I could take a break for a couple of years, have a family, but I don't know if it will be that way now."

"What... what do you mean?"

Carl exhaled and embraced the sleeping Miri tighter, stroke her over her back. "How do you stop entities from another dimension?" he asked in a low voice. "How do you

419

close a portal to that dimension? How do you get rid of the one standing right here in your own room? The things we saw in there— You can die there. Or go insane. And now one of those entities is out in our world, apparently on a mission aimed toward us. These portals, you can open them to anywhere that's special to you if you concentrate hard enough. How can we hinder Night Porter to go where he wants, and now when he's out here in our world, what kind of power does he have? What can he do to us and to others? Honestly, Allie, I don't see a happy ending to this anymore."

"But… but you said you won't give up; you won't let them win!"

"And I won't. If I have the tools and the knowledge, there's not a chance in hell that I'll stop trying, but— Sometimes, your own will and determination aren't enough. What I think I'm most afraid of is if it comes to a choice between saving Miri, but going under myself, or get out on my own and leaving someone behind— Well, it isn't even a choice." He thought about it for a moment. "She'd be so angry if she heard what I said." To his surprise, he managed to laugh. It was a loving little laugh that seemed to brighten the heavy atmosphere in the room, but then they both lay in their own thoughts for a while.

Eventually, Allie said in a soft voice, "You're so special, Carl. If you didn't have Miri, and I— Well, it seems to be the night for confessions. If I wasn't in love with Kevin, I might be tempted to try something serious with you. And that's the simple truth."

A soft smile spread on his lips, and he turned his head and touched her temple with the tip of his nose. "You already know you have a place in my heart, Allie, a big place, and most likely always will. If nothing else works out the way we want in the future, well, who knows? But I have a feeling that we both would be happier if things do work out the way we hope for."

She nodded and traced her finger gently down his cheek. When it touched his lips, he kissed it lightly. She

420

grazed his lips a moment before moving her hand, and he continued, feeling that it was important to say this, "And you know, you and Kevin will be a fabulous couple. Just give him a chance to tell you what he feels for you because it's a lot."

He could sense her smile and noticed that she had finally stopped trembling.

"The advantages of having a profiler as your friend. I bet you knew all along what I feel for him too."

He chuckled quietly and caressed her shoulder. They lay in friendly silence for a while before Carl suppressed a yawn. "What do you say, shall we try to sleep, or do you want to talk some more?"

"I… I don't think I can sleep. Maybe I should take one of your damn pills after all. I feel like my world suddenly is upside down."

"It's because it is upside down. There's a jar in the drawer in the bedside table beside you. Take one. It will help you relax. You might feel a bit muddled tomorrow, but if that's no problem, I think you should take one. Your decision, of course."

She nodded and turned around, fiddled with the things in the drawer until she found it.

"You don't have any other jars, right? So, I don't take the wrong one?"

"No, that's the only one. You brought your tea, eh?"

"Mhm, yeah, good idea."

He could hear her unscrew the lid and the faint rattle when the pills got shaken out. When she sat up to swallow, he used the time to get some blood back in his arm, before she lay down and embraced him again, her head resting on his shoulder. Within twenty minutes, she was sleeping.

Carl lay staring up at the ceiling for a while, astounded by the fact that he had two beautiful, loving, and caring women sleeping in his arms. *Drugged, beautiful women,* he thought and couldn't help an amused smile from appearing on his lips. Without context, it sounded so very wrong.

Miri and Allie breathed calmly, and it was an incredible feeling holding them like this, like all three belonged together. *It's also damn uncomfortable,* he thought and tried to move to a better position, but it was hopeless. Eventually, he gave up with a sigh and closed his eyes, hoping that sleep would come to him, nonetheless.

At seven a.m., he stopped trying and squirmed out of bed. Out in the living room, he went through one of his short programs to try to get some feeling back into his arms. Afterward, he checked in on the women again, and they had curled together in the middle of the bed, casually side by side with their arms draped around each other. There was a sweet tug at his heart when he saw how the golden blond and the golden brown entangled on the bed. *It's weird. It feels like I love them both.* He shook his head in astonishment, before moving his concentration to the portal again and taking a reluctant look at the vibrations. They were still there, but as faint as they had been before they got to know about them. *Well, at least we seem to be able to live a normal life so far, even with the portal here. That's good.*

Feeling weary from the lack of sleep, he yawned but decided to do something productive with his time rather than watch TV. Therefore, he went into the kitchen where he brought out the ingredients to sweet-tasting scones that Sonia and Simon had taught him when they were Star Students together. The scones were easy and quick to bake and usually made eyes glitter, and after these past twenty-four hours, both women could use it. While the scones were in the oven, he used the time to take a quick shower.

Both Miri and Allie were still sleeping when he came into the bedroom to put on clean clothes. He checked the time. Eight fifteen. He had to try to wake them up soon if they were going to make it to the library at ten. *And what are we going to do with Allie? I doubt Olwen will be pleased about this, but what could we do? Leave her in the dark with Night Porter targeting her for some obscure reason?* He sighed. *Well, I'll take the blame and the responsibility, as always. I'm kind of used to it nowadays, and I'm not going to let Allie face Night Porter on her own. That's just not fair.*

Feeling better for having decided, he continued to put the breakfast items on the living room table. The scones came out perfect and smelled delicious. He cut a few into halves and buttered them. Together with the raspberries and the strawberries and the large glasses with orange juice, it all looked like something from a magazine. With the scent of warm, newly baked bread swirling around him, he went into the bedroom to wake the women up. He sat down on the bed between them and nudged them gently. It took some time, but eventually, they began to stretch and yawn and look up at him with squinted eyes.

He smiled at them. "Good morning, beautiful ladies."

Allie flopped over on her stomach and put a pillow over her head and mumbled something incoherently. He laughed at her. Then, he leaned over and kissed Miri amiably. Her lips were warm and soft under his, and he wished they'd be able to do something more than just amiable kissing, but yeah, he didn't feel ready for something like a threesome, probably never would. Just the thought of it made him squirm awkwardly. *God, why did she have to say something like that? I'll never get the images out of my head now.*

Miri smiled at him and caressed his hands. She looked better, less pained.

"How are you feeling? How's your head?"

"Better, I think. Not yet stressed-out, so no bad headache yet." She nudged Allie gently on her back. "What about this one? How are you feeling, sweetie?"

Allie crawled out from under the pillow and squinted at her. "Carl gave me a pill so I could sleep and told me I'd feel mushy in the morning, but he didn't tell me how mushy. God, I'm never taking pills again, I swear!"

"Yeah, sorry about that. You'll feel better in a couple of hours. Promise." He looked them over and decided that some breadcrumbs on the sheet wouldn't hurt for once. "Don't move. I'll get breakfast."

He placed everything on a big tray and got his reward in the form of those glittering eyes he had hoped to see when he came back with it.

Miri looked up at him with a soft appearance. "Did you bake this, Carl?"

"Yeah."

"You're amazing."

Allie pouted. "I never get fresh-baked scones in bed at home. You might have to share more mornings like this with me."

It felt good, no, it felt great to hear Miri laugh and see that nudge she gave Allie on the shoulder without any kind of jealousy, just sheer satisfaction of the company. It struck him that they all felt natural together, and it amazed him and made him happy at the same time. Allie beamed at Miri in turn and kissed her cheek, before grabbing one of the scones. They all followed her example.

"Alright," Carl said when the plates were empty. "We need to figure out a couple of things for today. Miri and I are supposed to meet Olwen at the library downtown at ten. That's in an hour, so, yeah, time's ticking. We need to leave in half an hour. She said Armand might have some ideas. If this means Armand saw Night Porter too, I don't know. What worries me is you, Allie. You're neither a Field Researcher nor a field agent, and if Night Porter has some kind of agenda with you, well, I'd like to have you around. Not that I know what Miri and I could do to protect you, but at least you wouldn't be alone if something would happen."

Allie nodded with her eyes big and scared again, and Miri looked worried.

"But you must have plans of your own, don't you?" she asked Allie.

"For today? Not really. We talked about the movies, but nothing's decided."

"Miri? What do you think?"

"I think you're right. I want to know what Olwen has to say, but I think you need to be around, Allie, just in case. I'd never forgive myself if something happened to you."

Allie smiled relieved and obviously tried not to cry when she fell Miriam around the neck, kissed her cheek, and hugged her hard. Miri hugged her back.

"I can't believe how amazing you are," she sniveled suppressed at Miriam's throat. "I mean, I'm just crashing into your lives here, when you two have so much to catch up on. Don't think I don't understand that."

Miri stroked Allie's fabulous hair and smiled a little. "Don't worry about that. We've caught up on quite a lot already, and I prefer to think we have a whole life in front of us in which we can continue catching up."

Touched deep down in his soul, Carl closed the distance and embraced them both. Then he checked the time again. "Sorry, hate to be the time dictator, but we need to get moving."

It merely took them twenty-five minutes to get ready, even though they only had one bathroom, and they were just five minutes late when they arrived at the main library downtown.

Just as they were going to step out of the car, Carl turned to Allie in the back seat. "Olwen won't be happy you're around. She's the P.I., the Principal Investigator of the team and has problems being flexible. Unplanned things stress her out."

"Okay." Allie nodded. "Good to know."

"And we're not supposed to talk about FR business with others either," Miriam filled in. "So, she's probably going to fret about that too."

"Okay. I'll be quiet and keep to the background."

Yeah, right, Carl thought but didn't say anything.

They stepped out into the chilly spring air and walked up to the large library doors. Olwen was already waiting for them in the lobby, nervously pacing back and forth and checking her wristwatch every few seconds. When she saw them, she looked relieved, but only a second later, her gaze landed on Allie, who trotted after them. Carl got an impression of a storm cloud covering her face.

"Who's this?" was the first thing that came out of her mouth.

"This is Allie Harris, Special Agent in the Behavioral Department on the psyche of serial killers, and my previous SAC." That's when it hit him. *God, how could I've forgotten we're not supposed to be seen together? Oh, fuck, what have I done? My career is gone. It's over.*

"What's she doing here?"

He tried to recollect his thoughts. *One thing at a time. Just one thing at a time.* "Night Porter has reached out to her."

Olwen stared at him. "What?"

He turned to Allie, trying to get a moment to compose himself. "Tell her."

"Um, okay... I was with my friends yesterday evening and watched the news clip about Miri and Carl, and at the end, I saw, um, him..." Olwen nodded impatiently. "Um, my friends didn't."

"Didn't what?"

"They didn't see him."

Olwen stared at her. "What do you mean they didn't see him? He was right there in focus. How could they not see him?"

"He wasn't there for them. I saw him as clearly as I see you, but for my friends, the news clip ended with Miri and Carl kissing."

Olwen stared at her, clearly torn between believing her and thinking Allie was pulling her leg.

"That seems improbable," she said, eventually.

"Just as improbable as him being there at all?" Miri asked quietly. Olwen shifted focus to her, and Miri continued, "She needs us, Olwen. Night Porter wants something from her. She's not an FR, and she's not a field agent. We might not know how to protect her, but at least she's not going to

426

be alone. And she could see and interact with the vibrations in the portal."

Olwen's head jerked back to Allie, and she stared at her with a penetrating glance. "I don't care that you're a SAC. This is my team, and you follow my lead. Do you understand?"

"Yes, I do."

"Octavius is second-in-command. You follow his lead if I'm not around."

"Yes."

"And if he's not there, you follow Ophelia, and lastly, if it's only you and Omega around, you do what she says."

"Who are Ophelia and Omega?"

"I'm Ophelia," Miri said. "Where's Omega?"

A worried expression flashed momentarily over Olwen's face before it disappeared, and she looked stern again. "She didn't answer her phone yesterday."

A worried pang hit Carl as he glanced at Miri and saw her frown.

"Maybe we should check her out, just to see if she's okay?" she said, but Olwen made a dismissive gesture.

"We don't have time to drive all the way to Quenora Meadows right now. We need to concentrate on this first, and if she doesn't call back during the day, we'll check on her. I don't see why she would be in any danger."

Carl and Miri glanced at each other. *I have to talk to her. Can't do it in front of the others, though, especially not when Allie's around.*

He cleared his throat, and Olwen glared at him. "What did Armand say? Why are we here?" he asked, and she relaxed.

"He talked about urban legends." She glared at Allie, who put up her hands in a defensive gesture and walked away a bit. Miri frowned and crossed her arms over her chest.

Olwen lowered her voice. "This portal has to have been around for ages. The records show that disappearances have occurred there in larger quantities than at other places,

427

ever since law enforcement started to keep records." She paused and they could clearly see how worried she was. "I wish Omega was here. She's the one with the records."

Carl gave Miri a look and a small gesture with his head toward Allie. She nodded and trotted away. Olwen glared at him.

"Olwen, we need to check her out," he whispered urgently as soon as Miri was out of earshot and before she could berate him for taking the lead. "We can't just ignore something as serious as her not answering her phone, not while we're on an RP, and especially not with Night Porter around. Anything could've happened. You know that too." Olwen looked down with two red spots forming on her cheeks. Carl pulled a hand through his hair. "This isn't about you. It's about our safety. I wouldn't have brought Allie if I had thought it'd be safe for her to be home at her own place. Now, I think she's in danger, that we all are in danger, and you tell us that Omega doesn't answer her phone. How many times have you called?"

"Five."

He stared at her. "Five? Since eight p.m. yesterday?"

"Yes."

"What about email, messenger? You've tried that?" She nodded but avoided his gaze. "For crying out loud! I'm your second-in-command, remember? You have to communicate with me. If you don't, we won't make it. I can't go around blindly, trying to guess what you're up to."

She finally looked up at him, defiantly. "I know I'm not a great leader, Octavius, but I'm doing my best."

He stared at her. "Just communicate with me, alright. And talk with me about any big decisions before announcing them. I'm here to help you, but I can't if you're shutting me out."

Reluctantly, she glanced at him and asked in a grudging voice, "So, what do you want to do?"

"I want to check on Omega. We'll call her, and if she doesn't answer, we need to go to her."

"But what about—" She made a vague gesture toward the bookshelves.

"People are more important than books. If Omega's fine, we'll go back later today or tomorrow."

Olwen sighed and looked defeated. He didn't like seeing her like that. She wasn't a bad leader, just bad at communicating, and he wasn't sure if he managed to get that part through to her.

"You miss Oona, don't you?"

She gave him a surprised glance, but then, she nodded. "I do. She was hopeless, questioned every single step, but she made me a better leader. Without her, I feel lost, off the track."

"I'm sorry."

"Yes, I think you are." She fell silent. "Let's do what you suggest. You don't want us to split up, do you?" He shook his head. "No, I thought so. So, what about Miss Harris? Is it true that her friends didn't see him? The Night Porter?" Carl nodded, and Olwen sighed. "Would it be alright if she went with me in my car? I'd like to talk to her."

"I can't see why not."

"Good. Let me just call Omega again, okay?" She brought up her cell phone and dialed the number. Carl could hear the signals go through and then an answering machine. Olwen shut it off. "Okay, let's go."

Chapter 25

As they went out to their cars, Carl couldn't help feeling relieved that Allie was going with Olwen. He didn't need another damn situation to worry about.

As soon as they sat down and put on their seatbelts, Miri looked at him. "Hey, what's wrong?"

He sighed and pulled a hand through his hair. "I forgot I'm not supposed to talk with Allie or meet her, and here I'm driving her around, coming to a meeting with Olwen with her; Olwen, who definitely won't bend the truth for me if it comes to that. My career is gone because I'm stupid."

She stared at him. "*A brokh!* I didn't think either." She put a hand on his arm when he started the car and followed Olwen. "We have to tell the truth in that case, that she was in danger from a suspect in our RP, and this was the only way to protect her."

Carl brightened, and he gave her an appreciative side-glance. "That might actually work. Oh, wow, you're the best, Miri. If I weren't driving, I'd kiss you." She grinned at him and moved in and kissed his neck. The touch of her lips made him shiver and inhale sharply. The wheel quivered slightly in his hands. "Whoa, do you want me to crash the car?"

Still smiling, she put her hand on his thigh and let it rest there while turning her body slightly, so she didn't have to lean the back of her head toward the headpiece.

"So, what's going on between you and Olwen?" she asked eventually, and he frowned.

"Well…" he dragged on, wondering where the boundaries went for what was acceptable to talk about in a relationship, and what was not. *No details,* he thought, *the rest must be fine.* "She has a hard time communicating. She just, you know, does things without discussing them with me. That might've been okay if she hadn't made me her second-in-command, but I need to know what the hell she's up to.

430

Can't risk someone getting hurt or dying because of bad communication."

She watched him drive for a while, but then, she said thoughtfully, "It's weird. We've known each other for more than three years now, we've been friends for two, and we're getting married, but we've never talked about the RPs we've been through."

He felt surprised. "Never thought about that," he said and fell silent.

After a few moments, she said, "Do I read you right when I say that you want to talk about this some other day?"

He gave her an amused side-glance before turning serious again. "Yeah, maybe it's not the right place for it now. I'm too jittery, too distracted. I want some calm around me, someplace where you can hug me when I cry." She leaned in and placed her head on his shoulder, and he continued, "On the other hand, you should know about them, and now that you've opened this can of worms, I'd like to hear about yours too. I mean, knowing more about what we've been through over the years will probably make us understand some things better."

"But at a time when we can cry and hug. Yes. There will be a lot of that." A sudden flash of sadness and regret was seen on her face.

Carl placed a hand on her leg and squeezed it gently before taking the wheel properly again.

It wasn't that long of a drive to Quenora Meadows, a mere forty minutes. Carl hadn't been there before. It was a nice, newly built middle-class area with a focus on nature and young families. *Does Omega have a family?* he suddenly wondered as he followed Olwen through the lush areas, dotted with play parks and spray parks, off-leash areas, and picnic sites. Omega was the one in the team he knew the least about. She was the youngest and the shyest of all the members in O. She never spoke about herself. It struck him that he didn't even know her real name. *I should have asked more about her, should have gotten to know her better. It's my damn job to keep people together.*

His fingers drummed restlessly on the wheel while waiting at a stoplight. Miri watched the scenery and sat in her own thoughts. They've spent numerous silent drives like this during the past three and a half years, but Carl preferred this kind of silence, the friendly one, over the tense one they used to experience up until Alaska. *Mostly my fault,* he admitted, feeling stupid. *I really enjoyed making her feel awkward back then. Mature, Carl, very mature.* It dawned on him that they would probably never talk much while driving. They weren't accustomed to it. *I don't mind. There's no need to fill the silence with sounds all the time. Just being together, enjoying the company, is enough.* He took her hand and caressed it, and she turned her head and smiled at him. *I love you, Miri.* Her eyes told him that she loved him too, and he felt so blessed, so lucky.

Olwen turned into a small residential area where three-story brick buildings surrounded a little park and a playground. When they parked and stepped out of the cars, Carl noticed how battered Allie looked. *Wow, Olwen must have been hard on her. That wasn't necessary.* He felt a sliver of anger when Olwen glared at him. *Again? What did I do this time?* Without a word, his P.I. marched to the entrance with the number thirty-two above it and determinedly strode up the stairs to the highest floor while the rest of them trailed after her. Carl noticed how Allie kept to the background and how Miri took her arm, encouraging her. *Well, at least they're getting along. That's more than I expected.*

To the side of the left door, a sweet handmade sign hung with the name *Pieretta Aretha Williams* written in calligraphy in the middle of a blooming garland. Olwen knocked hard on the door, and then they waited. Nothing was heard from inside, and Olwen knocked again. With a frown, she tried the door handle, and the door slid open without a sound. Before Carl even had the chance to react, she went in.

"Omega?"

Oh, for crying out loud!

"Olwen!" he hissed behind her, but she didn't seem to notice. *I can't work like this. I can't! It's not possible. She's supposed to be professional. Why isn't she?* He loosened the gun in his belt, just in case, and went in after her. She had already gone through the small apartment and approached a closed door. He hurried up beside her and put a hand on her shoulder. She glared at him and shook it off.

"What the hell are you doing?" he hissed at her. "You can't just run your own race. You're supposed to be professional, for crying out loud. Is this how you behave amongst the SWATs? I doubt it."

She glared angrily at him. "I am professional. There's nothing here. You should be able to feel it in the air if you knew what you were looking for. Your way of doing things is not the only way. Stop being so patronizing, Octavius."

"Patr—" He exhaled sharply and tried hard to calm down. "We need to talk about this later."

She just gave him a cold look and opened the door. Omega lay naked on the big unmade bed, seemingly sleeping. Suddenly overcome by awkwardness and embarrassment, Carl looked away, pretending that he studied the surroundings instead. The room had an intense musk-like scent, and it seemed as if Omega was either very messy, unusual for a former Star Student, or that she had had rough company.

He backed out and turned to Miriam. "Can you check the room for me, please? I don't want to embarrass her."

"Sure."

They changed places, and still fuming about being called 'patronizing,' he stomped away and checked the rest of the apartment. At first glance, he couldn't see anything out of the ordinary, but he admitted that he wasn't concentrated. Someone was in the shower, and he refused to stomp in there when everything seemed to be alright. In the background, he heard the mumbling voices of his teammates, but Allie stood

433

alone by the front door, looking uncomfortable. He went over to her.

"I'm going to the car. Are you coming, or do you want to wait for the others?"

She puffed. "Of course, I'm coming. You can slice the air in here like bread."

"I can't believe she called me 'patronizing,'" he said when they sat in the car. He turned to her. "Honestly, Allie, am I patronizing?"

"I don't think so, but Olwen feels inferior to you, and since you two can't communicate properly, you probably stand out as patronizing to her."

He tugged hard at his hair. "I'm trying to respect her, but she refuses to involve me, to involve any us, as if being a leader excludes discussing the situation with the rest of us. I have no choice. I have to call her out on it. She calls me her second-in-command, but that's just a title to keep me happy. It doesn't work like that. And what the hell was all this about 'feeling the air'? She's a SWAT team leader, for crying out loud! SWATs don't 'feel the air'; SWATs go in with their guns ready if there's the slightest chance of it being a hostile situation." He puffed frustrated. "I won't be able to work with her like this. Eventually, she's going to kill us by sheer stupidity. I'm not going through that again. One time was enough, thank you very much."

Allie stared at him with slightly wide-opened eyes. "Um, you know you're burning your bridges here, right?"

"I'm getting used to that," he muttered under his breath.

"Carl," she said, clearly concerned, and put her hand on his arm, "you have too much to lose for that. Don't try to talk to her today. Arrange a meeting at a time when nothing's at stake and talk it through then. Get someone you both trust as a mediator, if you want to. Just don't do it today."

He drew a deep breath and took her hand, caressed it slightly while trying to get his tense body to relax.

"Thank you. You're right, of course. I'll go up there again, clench my teeth and pretend everything's fine."

With a sigh, he ran his hand through his hair, but composed himself and got out of the car just in time to see Olwen and Miri step out of the front door. When Olwen saw him, a slightly gloating look flashed over her face. Carl clenched his teeth and put on his old emotionless mask. He didn't like it anymore, he realized, but gave a mental shrug at it all.

"She's fine, except a little embarrassed that we came in on her tête-a-tête, and she's promised to have her cell on next time."

"Good, that's what we wanted to hear, eh?"

She seemed a little disappointed that he didn't take the hook, but continued, "It's too late to go to the library now, and since the archive is closed tomorrow, we'll meet there on Monday eight-hundred sharp."

"Sounds good."

He watched her go back to her car and drive away before taking off his mask. Sighing, he put his hands in his jean pockets. Allie came out to them.

"What a damn mess," he muttered, and Miri put an arm around him. She looked worried.

"I don't know if it's alright," she said in a low voice and glanced around. "Come, let's go sit in the car."

They all did as she asked, and when in the seat, she turned and faced them both. "There was so much booze and joints in her bedroom it was enough for a whole party."

"Really?" Carl raised his eyebrows in surprise.

"What's wrong with that?" Allie asked.

"We're almost brainwashed as Star Students to never use any kind of artificial stimuli," Miri explained. "I've never met a Star Student who drinks or smokes."

"Huh," Allie said thoughtfully. "It does make sense, I guess. It must be very tempting to drown all the weird stuff in liquor and such."

435

The thought of Nigel and his ill-fated habit of smoking came to mind, but Carl shied away from it and steered his focus back to Omega again.

"How was she?" he asked.

Miri shook her head. "I don't know. She seemed intoxicated, dazed, which isn't surprising, but— I don't know her well enough to say if it's out of character for her to indulge in sex, booze, and drugs. Olwen didn't react on it."

"Yeah, Olwen should know, I guess," Carl said with a frown.

"It's just that— It didn't feel right, but maybe I'm naïve. Just because no other FR I've met does things like that, doesn't mean there aren't any at all doing it." She puffed. "I don't know. I might exaggerate things. On the other hand, she's not a Star Student."

Carl gave her a questioning glance. "What do you mean?"

"She told me when we were in Alaska that she started out as a ranger, and at some point, she got involved in some strange stuff, so she took the intermediate course, you know, the one that's only a year. Harder to brainwash people then."

"Huh, I had no idea. Yeah, that might explain things." Carl restlessly drummed his fingers at his legs.

"What do you want to do?" Allie asked. "Do you want to go in again, without Olwen?"

Carl rubbed his face. "No, I don't think that's a good idea. I don't want to piss her off even more. Did she seem close to passing out to you, Miri? Omega, I mean, not Olwen."

She shook her head. "No. And I saw no signs of a portal."

He sighed. "Alright. Let's go and pick up Markus and Sarah and think about this on Monday." Carl gave Allie an apologetic look. "I'm sorry for all this, and right now, I'm a bit confused about the whole situation. You might not be in danger. I honestly don't know."

She winced. "This might be everyday stuff for you guys, but I'm not sure I'm out of the gravy yet. If you don't mind me hanging on to you a little while longer, I'm not complaining."

"I don't mind. Miri?"

"I'm fine with it too."

"Alright." He started the car for the hour-long drive to pick up the children.

Taking Sarah and Markus for a picnic at the lake was like a balm for the soul. It finally felt like they could relax again. Carl was overjoyed to see how Sarah managed to bond with Markus. She usually didn't care for other children, especially not about those who didn't pay attention to what she called 'the important things in the world,' but Markus shared the same kind of vision as she did, and while other children ran around screaming and playing soccer and tag, they sat calmly on the jetty, talking seriously while feeding the birds.

Miri's eyes shone. "I wish Beth and Ted were here," she said in a low voice. "They're always so worried about Markus, that he's so introvert and serious, but just look at him."

"He needs the right person to connect with, that's all," Allie said. "Do you know how much it irks me when people start treating introvert kids as if it's something wrong with them? No offense to your sister and brother-in-law, but it really isn't that hard."

Miri just smiled. "No offense taken. I've often thought the same, but you know, they're both extremely outgoing and don't get Markus' need for silence and space to think. Instead, they exhaust him by taking him to every single birthday party they can, or the amusement parks or the skating rink or the waterpark, things like that, where there are a lot of people, instead of just go with the flow and let him communicate with the world at his own pace."

"That's really sad."

"It is sad. I usually try to give him a break when I can. You know, go bird watching in nature, things like that, where he doesn't have to talk or be forced to connect with people or feel forced to look happy for his parents' sake." She gave Allie a curious look. "But you strike me as a very outgoing person. Aren't you?"

"In a way, I guess, but only with the right people. I can be very awkward around people I can't tune in on. I mean, just because I can read others, doesn't mean I can interact with them in a great way."

"Hm, that must be hard sometimes, right?"

"I don't know. Once I thought so, yes, but now, I don't care anymore. I don't spend energy on people who don't like me. It's no use."

Miri looked at the children again. "It's interesting how priorities have changed from when we were kids, at least for me. It was always so important for me to be part of the cool girls, so I changed myself to be like them, and when we quit high school, we promised to always keep in touch. After that summer, I never heard from them again, but I saw them hanging out together every once in a while. It was as if I never existed for them." Allie squeezed her arm comfortingly, and Miri continued, "No, it's okay, I'm not sad about it. I actually think it was a good eye-opener, you know, because it taught me that real friends are different. They accept you as you are instead of trying to make you change, so this is what I try to help Markus with, accepting himself for who he is and being proud of who he is, not striving for something that might not be true just to fit in."

"That's a great lesson."

Miri laughed quietly. "It would be if I could learn it myself. I still fall into pits in the road sometimes, but they get fewer and fewer. When I'm eighty, I might even walk on a smooth and leveled street."

Allie chuckled. "And then you might miss all the bumps and pits."

"Maybe."

The women smiled at each other. Carl lay quietly stretched out on the picnic blanket and watched the sky while pretending not to be listening to them talking.

"I don't know," Allie said thoughtfully, "the bumps and the pits, they're really annoying when they happen, but when you've managed to leave them behind, I find that you actually needed them. I don't know if I want to get rid of them completely. Life would probably be damn boring without them, and I'd most likely miss all the opportunities of making a fool out of myself, especially since I'm so good at it."

Miri chuckled, and then they sat quietly for a while until Sarah and Markus came back to them.

"How's it going?" Carl asked when Sarah daintily sat down beside him.

"Good. Can we have some more grapes, please?"

"Sure, go ahead."

"I might have changed my mind, Daddy."

"How's that?"

"I might become an officer in the animal police service instead."

"Oh?"

"Yes. I think it's a good decision to save innocent animals from cruel people."

"It is a very good decision, I agree. Don't you think you'd feel very upset about it, though?"

"Maybe, but I'd be more upset if I didn't help them at all. Can I take all the grapes?"

"Nah, here, take these. That should be enough to feed the ducks with."

"Okay. Thanks, Dad."

"You're welcome. Oh, and we'll need to leave in half an hour, to get Markus home in time."

"Okay. Can he come over some other time?"

"You'll have to ask Miri."

Miri smiled at her. "Absolutely. I'm happy you like each other."

"He's my best friend now."

"That's great, Sarah. You'll have to come and visit his place too one day."

"Okay, if Mom and Dad say I can."

"Of course, you can." Carl ruffled her hair, and she trotted off with the grapes.

"She's awesome," Allie quietly said and looked at her with a sad smile.

Carl wondered why but didn't want to ask. It might be too personal to share at this point.

"I think so," he slightly teased instead. "But I might be biased."

Miri chuckled and nudged him with her sock-clad foot. "You're allowed to be biased."

He grinned at her and took the opportunity to tickle her sole. Laughingly, she squirmed and tried to get away from him, and then Allie's fingers were at his waist, mercilessly tickling him until he let go of Miri.

Twenty minutes later, they gathered everything together, called out for the children, and left the park. Sarah held Carl's hand while chatting away with Markus. Carl looked down at her and felt his heart overflow with love. This was what he wanted out of life, this quiet love that was his relationship with his family; the every-day-life, the bedtime rituals with the storybook reading, the breakfast, the dropping off and picking up at school, the cuddles in front of the TV, and the easy talk about what had happened during the day. Maybe if he and Miri moved closer to where Manda and Sarah lived, they could do this. It was something to think about later, to talk about later, after the RP was over.

When they parked outside Amanda's house, Miri and Markus followed Sarah to the door together with Carl. It felt important to him that Manda got the chance to meet them, now when they were going to become such a huge part of his life.

When Manda opened with a genuine smile, she immediately took Miri's hand in hers and shook it hard.

"I'm so happy to finally meet you, Miriam," she said warmly. "Or should I say Miri? What do you prefer?"

"Miri's good," Miriam smiled back, clearly charmed. "And it's nice meeting you too. Sarah's such a sweet kid. We had a great time, didn't we, Markus?" The boy nodded shyly and took half a step back, but Manda took his hand in hers and shook it.

"It's nice meeting you too, Markus, and I can tell that Sarah had a great time. Did you too?"

"I did. Thank you for asking."

Sarah tugged at Manda's arm. "Mom, I want to go home to Markus one day. He has a canary whose name's Luce. Did you know that means light in Italian?"

"I did. That's a beautiful name on a canary. We'll talk about visiting Markus later, but now you have to say good night. It's dinner and bedtime."

Sarah nodded and shook Markus' hand. "Bye, Markus."

"Bye, Sarah. Bye, Mrs. Hansen."

Carl saw how awkward Manda became before she composed herself and gave the boy a friendly smile. "It's Miss Dreyfus, but you can call me Amanda, Markus."

"Okay, sorry." Markus' slender shoulders tensed, and he took a step back until he was obscured by Miri. Carl watched with surprise how the boy perceived Manda's feelings, but Manda didn't notice Markus' reaction. She smiled at them again, ushered Sarah indoors, and closed the door.

Carl put on his casual look instead of the frown that wanted to take its place. If Markus were this good at reading other people, he wouldn't want the boy to think he'd done anything wrong.

When they came back to the car, Miri changed place with Allie and sat with Markus in the back all the way home to Beth and Ted.

It was nine p.m. when they finally were back home at Carl's apartment again. For a while, Carl fought against the

441

sleepiness before it dawned on him that he didn't have to play the host any longer. Miri and Allie were as familiar with the place as he was at this point. A huge satisfaction filled him.

"I didn't sleep well last night, so I'm going to bed. Do what you want, eat what you want, sleep where you want, but try not to wake me, please."

Miri closed in on him and kissed him longer than he had expected.

Then, she smiled, nose to nose with him. "Sleep well."

Allie gave him the usual light kiss on his cheek and a quick hug, before ushering him into the bedroom.

"Sleep tight. I'm closing the door, so I can talk more to your fiancée without you listening." He smiled, caught, and she laughed at him. "Yeah, I noticed."

She closed the door, and he fell into bed. At ease in his whole body, he soon drifted off to sleep.

Part Six

thin lines

Chapter 26

They spent Sunday just relaxing. After a slow morning, since Miri and Allie had talked the whole night through, they took a ride to Lincoln Spring Park. It was as Carl suspected, Miri had never been there before. It was a lovely day, one of those that get to be a shining pearl on life's necklace. They walked around hand in hand, all three of them, fed the birds and the squirrels, played around in the nooks and crannies, got lost amongst the magical beauty of the park, and they laughed a lot.

When they followed Allie to her penthouse complex in the evening and turned down an offer to come in and say hi to her roommates, there was a shimmer of happiness around them, and they lingered just a little longer than necessary while saying goodbye, but eventually, Carl and Miri left her and walked back to the car. They went to the little Arabian restaurant on the outskirts of the dock district that was their favorite and enjoyed the fabulous food and the excellent service before taking a stroll at the seaside, holding hands, stopping every once in a while, to hug and kiss and teasingly touch. At home, they ended the day in bed, longing for each other as they had throughout the whole weekend.

The morning after, when they woke up to *Bohren & der Club of Gore*, spring had turned to winter again. Through the window, Carl stared at the single snowflakes that drifted down through the air.

"It's the seventeenth of May!" Miri exclaimed beside him. "Have you ever seen snow in May before?"

He knew it was a rhetorical question but couldn't help answering it anyway. "Yeah, as in June, July and August, and all the other months of the year. That's Albertan weather for you," he said when she stared at him. "The only thing you can be sure of when it comes to the weather in Alberta is that you can't be sure of it."

She laughed at him and nudged him on the shoulder. "You have to show me your famous Alberta one fine day."

Hit by the thought, he smiled at her. "Why not? We can take a road trip there sometime during the summer. There's actually a lot to see that's not just prairie. You'd love Banff and Drumheller. And we can bring Sarah and Markus too if you want to. I think Markus would be fascinated by Drumheller. Dinosaur country, you know."

"Really? Yes, he'd love that. It's a great idea, Carl." She tiptoed and gave him a sweet kiss. "Let's get ready. I don't want to stress today if we can avoid it."

He nodded, and, soon enough, they were on their way to the library. Olwen was waiting for them at the same spot as last time, but this morning she looked less angry and stressed-out, which was a relief.

"Omega called," she said after greeting them. "She doesn't feel good, so she's staying home today, but she e-mailed us the reports. We can look at them later."

Yeah, no wonder she doesn't feel good if she's been partying the whole weekend, Carl thought and saw an insecure frown appear on Miri's forehead. Apparently, she found the situation as unusual as he did.

"So, what do you expect us to find?" he asked, steering his away thoughts from Omega's odd behavior.

Olwen thought through the question. "I'm not sure," she admitted, "but I like the idea of urban legends. There's often a grain of truth in them. Maybe we can find anything about those portals and how to close them. At least it's a starting point, especially since the Faculty doesn't have any information about this at all. They're quite interested in our findings."

She fell silent as they closed in on the reception, and a tall, lean librarian looked them over.

"Yes, how can I help you?" he asked with the kind of low voice that still managed to bear through to the audience.

Olwen brought out her badge. "We'd like to get access to the old archive."

The librarian glanced at the badge before looking up at her again. "Only one person at a time is allowed in the old archive," he said.

Olwen nodded. "I'll go. I've been there before and know the system."

The librarian took out a ledger and grabbed a pen. "Name, please."

"Sally Oakley-Wittinger."

Miri stiffened beside Carl, and he himself was completely baffled.

"Address?"

"First Rowan Road."

Without his long training, Carl wouldn't be able to keep his chin up, but mentally it hit the floor.

"Ah, yes, that's right. I have the postal code right here. You can wait here, for now, Dr. Oakley-Wittinger. I'll just get the key."

As Olwen nodded and turned back at them, Carl glanced at Miri's dumbstruck face. She looked as shocked as he felt.

"Um, Wittinger...?" she asked hesitantly, and a soft, loving smile appeared on Olwen's face.

"Yes. Henry and I are married."

Carl didn't think Olwen noticed the slight pause before Miri spoke again, "Um, wow... Congratulations..."

"Thanks," she radiated.

"How long...?"

Olwen laughed like a woman very much in love. "It was unexpected, I'll give you that, but since our first meeting we shared this attraction between us; you know, he's intelligent and well-versed and experienced, and when we came back from the second RP in Alaska, we started dating, and we got married in December that year. He simply couldn't wait."

Before Miriam could answer, quick steps were heard behind them, and the librarian showed up again with a large key in his hand.

"Dr. Oakley-Wittinger, if you'd please come with me."

Olwen immediately stood up, and still smiling, she followed the librarian through a door behind the desk. Carl looked at Miriam, worried about what he would see. She was watching the door through which Olwen had disappeared, looking dazed, as if someone had pulled a car wreck over her head. Silence fell hard, and Carl resisted an urge to pull at his hair.

"Um, wow…" she said again. "That was unexpected." For once, he had no idea what to say. Eventually, the stiff and shocked expression disappeared. She turned her head toward him and gave up a short, unbelieving laugh, devoid of humor. He'd never heard that kind of a laugh from her before.

"Okay," she said slowly as if she were searching for words. "I guess he didn't have any obligation to let me know, but— What the hell?" She shook her head in disbelief. "They married, what, five months after they met? Four months after he asked me? What the hell?"

Carl could only shake his head too, totally bewildered.

She exhaled deeply. "I hope they're happy," she said in earnest. Surprised, Carl looked at her, and she shrugged with a slight grimace. "Clearly, a marriage between him and me would've been a huge mistake, him longing for Olwen and me longing for you, and why not wish him happiness? I mean, it seems as if neither one of us loved each other; I mean, really loved each other, even though we thought we did." Then, she frowned. "But I never thought he'd be such a coward to not let me know. Okay that he didn't invite me to the wedding, that would've been awkward, but— What the hell?" Another thought seemed to hit her because the frown grew even deeper and two angry red spots appeared on her cheeks. "And apparently she doesn't know about me. I mean, seriously? We spent four years together before they even knew about each other and his wife doesn't know about me?" She fell silent a couple of seconds, still scowling. "I think I need to take him down from that pedestal I placed him on."

447

For a while, she stood silent, staring out at nothing before the red spots on her cheeks disappeared, and her frown smoothed out. To Carl's surprise, she smiled openly at him as she focused on him again. "Wow, I feel— I feel relieved. I'm finally free from him, from the guilty feelings I've always nurtured for telling him no." She laughed again, happily this time. "I feel great! Come, let's go and check those reports."

Seemingly closing that chapter inescapably, she took his hand and led him over to the study area, while he tried to adjust to her sudden flip in emotions.

Well, he thought, watching her pleased and relaxed face as she sat down at one of the computers and brought up her work e-mail, *maybe it wasn't sudden, maybe she just needed to get rid of the guilt.* However, he did find it strange. He'd been certain that C genuinely loved Miri. Another thought struck him, hit him hard in the guts. *Oh, God, I hope he didn't marry 'second-best.'* Mentally, he hit his head hard against a wall. *Of course, he did. That'd be just in line with how he is. Can't take rejection and needs to get an ego-boost and a petty revenge toward Miri. Not telling her about it is part of it too. I bet he didn't even try to straighten things out with her first. God, what a damn mess!* Pulling at his hair, he took a deep breath, trying to shake it all off. *Ah, well, he's not involved with us anymore other than being our team's contact, but he has no reason to talk to us. All his communication goes via Olwen.*

Turning on his laptop, he located the report Omega had sent them. It was quite lengthy and showed disturbing patterns of disappearances.

Eventually, Miri tapped on her screen with a pen. "It's interesting to see the development here. I don't know if you've read this yet, but just before it became Kroger's in ninety-three, it was a game arcade. I checked it out, and it was forced to close within two years because three teenagers at different times disappeared while visiting. The owner was questioned by the police but got released since they couldn't find anything on him, but it leaked, and he couldn't keep it running. Poor guy. It'd be interesting to see the floor plan over that arcade, don't you think?"

Appreciatively, he nodded at her. "Mhm. The portal must've been placed so people somehow had access to it. If I remember the floor plan over Kroger's correctly, it must've been placed just at the customer's washroom."

"Huh." She looked thoughtful. "I've used it a couple of times, but never felt any vibrations. I wonder what activates it."

He gave her a curious look. "Huh, activates it? That's an intriguing idea. How did you activate it?"

Uncertain, she frowned and seemed to shy away from the question. "I... I don't remember. That's weird..."

At this sign of distress, Carl took her hand. "Didn't you say that you had a minor memory loss? A concussion? Not surprising you don't recall it."

Relieved, she said, "Yes, you're probably right." Then, the frown returned. "But it's an important question. It has to be activated somehow. Otherwise, it'd be open to everyone, and we can clearly establish it isn't. Just look at the one at home, for example." The word 'home' tugged at his heartstrings and brought a smile to his lips. "Oops, Freudian slip, I guess," she grinned, and he leaned in for a tender kiss.

"It was a good slip," he murmured at her lips and felt her smile. Then, she put a light hand on his chest, and he reluctantly pulled away. "Yeah, you're right," he agreed.

"As I was going to say, the portal at home—" They smiled at each other, and Carl squeezed her hand. "We can walk through it without anything happening. We know it's there, and we can feel the vibrations if we concentrate on them, but it doesn't do anything, it doesn't even send out any vibes. It's almost like it's sleeping, or waiting, or something."

He focused on the second word. "Waiting? For what?"

"I don't know. The right person?"

For some reason, that resonated with him, and a shiver ran down his spine.

"It feels right, doesn't it?" she asked.

He nodded. "Yeah," he said hoarsely. "But what is the 'right' person? Who is it?"

"I don't know."

Carl leaned back in the chair and drummed his fingers on the table. "Let's approach it from another angle. Us."

She gave him a curious glance. "Okay?"

"Yeah. Um, I'll try to keep a straight line here." For a moment, he recollected his thoughts. "When Kroger's blew up, you were under huge emotional stress and physical pain and shock, obviously locked in at the same place as the portal. It wouldn't surprise me if it reacted to those strong emotions."

An expression of sudden insight flashed over Miri's face. "Yes, that sounds likely, thinking about how the whole dimension tries to drain you."

"It would be interesting to know if Florence Tyler suffered from depression or something," he mused. "And the teenagers."

"I remember teenager-years," Miriam said and shuddered. "Horrible. So much anguish."

"Yeah, me too." He grimaced and let go of the thought of himself as an insecure, pimpled teenager. "I never told you how I managed to find out where you were," he said instead.

Wide-eyed, she placed a hand at her temple. "God, I'm stupid. I never even reflected on how you all suddenly stood around my bed when I woke up."

"Well, not very surprising, eh, given the circumstances." She didn't seem to hear him as she shook her head in self-disgust and rolled her eyes. Resolutely, he took her hands and gave her a serious look. "Don't do that, Miri. Be kind to yourself. You have to give yourself a break sometimes."

Her lips parted in surprise as she let out a sigh and relaxed. "Thank you for not making me feel stupid," she mumbled.

Touched and sad at the same time, he caressed her hands. "Never. I would never do that. I believe in you, Miriam. I believe in your thoughts and instincts. You're good at what you're doing. Honestly, you're very good. Why do you think Andy wanted you as an angel? You know he only takes in the very best. Don't try to make yourself believe otherwise. Don't belittle yourself."

To his surprise, her eyes suddenly flooded. She pulled her hands away and hid her face. Her shoulders quivered as she cried quietly. Slightly puzzled, he embraced her to give her comfort.

Eventually, she composed herself and inhaled deeply. "No one has ever said anything like that to me," she mumbled as she dried away the tears. "Not once."

"Well," he smiled, hiding his sudden anger at C for never encouraging her. "I guess it was time then."

She chuckled softly and kissed his fingers. "No wonder I love you."

Solemnly, he touched her face. "And I love you. I think we're good for each other."

"Yes, we are."

As they smiled at each other, Carl had a feeling that there weren't any obstacles between them anymore, and whatever would happen in the future in the form of emotional morasses, they'd be able to overcome them. *I never felt like this for Manda,* he thought with some surprise. *Never. No wonder we didn't manage to keep our marriage together.*

Still holding his hand, she said, "You were going to tell me how you found me."

"Um, yeah, right," he said and tried to get on the right track again. "Mike— He's a SWAT officer who helped me look for you. He was the one who figured out where you were. We found the basement where you fell down, and your coat stuck in the rubble. It's actually waiting for you at home now. So, we knew you'd been there, but we couldn't understand where you'd gone." As he thought of those horrible days, the old terror of losing her welled up inside

451

him again and he embraced her forcefully. "I'll never be able to describe how it felt when I thought I'd lost you forever, Miri," he whispered and fought to hold back the tears. She held him close, while soothingly stroking his hair, and he managed to calm down. "I wish there were other words I could use to tell you how much you mean to me, Miri," he said, "but there are none I know of."

"I know." Her voice was hoarse. "I know. There are so many feelings inside me, and I can't— I can't tell you about them, just hope that you'll see them."

"I see them."

"Good," she said with a trembling smile. "That's a start."

Carl took a deep breath and caressed her hands. "You know," he said, "for two weeks I thought you were gone, that there was no hope, but then, Mike called me one evening and told me he'd found your ring and your scarf in the basement. I went there, and the scarf was floating in the air, trapped between our world and Night Porter's. That's how I knew."

Miri squirmed uneasily on the chair. "But, weren't they there before when you found my coat?" He shook his head and saw the same apprehension on her face as he felt. "But that doesn't make any sense," she said with a touch of anxiousness in her voice. "Did he— The Night Porter, did he try to lure you there?"

"That could be the case, yes."

"But Mike didn't come with you, did he?"

"No, I asked him to stay and call Olwen, because I couldn't hold on to the portal. It almost closed on me."

"And Olwen and Omega obviously managed to open it." She stared at him with a skeptical look as if she didn't believe in what she was about to say, "Do you think— Does he— Does Night Porter try to make us connect other people to his realm?"

He stared at her as a cold shiver ran down his spine. "I have no idea. It's a thought, a possibility."

She puffed anxiously. "If that's the case, Carl, we have a huge problem."

"Yeah, I know."

"No, no, I mean if his realm is actually spreading through us, like a virus, we can't tell anyone about it, because we might start a process that connects people to his dimension and makes it easier for them to find the portals, or the portals to find them, but... but if we don't tell them or ask them, we have no idea if they've already encountered anything from there." Speechless, Carl stared at her, and she shook her head. "I'm rambling. I'm sorry."

He shivered violently as the scenario she just described suddenly seemed very plausible after what they'd been through in the Night Porter's realm.

"If we're running down that alley," he continued her thought, "then maybe just the fact that they spend some time in our company one afternoon might be enough to connect them to that place."

"Okay, okay, let's calm down. We don't know anything. We might exaggerate this threat a lot. We're good at exaggerating."

A faint laugh found its way out of him, and he ran his hand through his hair several times. "Yes, we are," he agreed, hoping that it was the case, but was terribly frightened about what would happen would she be right. "And now what?" he asked.

"What?"

Slightly irritated, he gestured at the laptop. "Why are we going through these files anyway? We know the portal's been there since ages back. That's not important in any other way than to establish a pattern."

"You're right. We need to know if Olwen's found anything yet and if she has something else for us to dig into."

Carl gave her a tentative side-glance. "You do know that what we're trying to do most likely is in vain?"

Miri looked down at her hands. Then she said in a low voice, "I was hoping you weren't going to say that, but of course it's in vain. Anyone can open a damn portal from that side if they want to. I'm sure I could open a portal from anywhere here to that place by now, too, because I know how to tune in on those vibrations. I mean, Carl, those vibrations, they're not bound to a specific place, they just are."

He stared at her. The plain certainty in her voice made goosebumps appear on his skin, and he had to rub his arms to get rid of them.

Her face got a faraway look as she continued, "It's just physics. You need to understand the laws, and then you can do what you want within the boundary of those laws. But you have to pay the price. There's always a price."

"Um, Miri? You're scaring me."

"Hmm?" The faraway look slowly disappeared. "Sorry, I was just thinking." She stood up and gave him a normal look, but when his cell phone rang, he jolted.

"God!" he exclaimed and hurried to answer while Miriam, erased her search history, logged out, and gathered their things. "Yeah?"

"Carl?" Allie's voice was just a whisper, and she sounded frightened. "Um, I need to ask you… I'm hiding in the bathroom at the office. Olwen's really scary. She doesn't seem to be herself. She's standing outside with some damn masks in her hand and wants me to come with her to a damn masquerade party. What the hell's going on?" For a moment, he couldn't breathe, the terror gripped his soul too hard. "Carl? Goddammit! Answer me!"

"Um…" He let his hand rest in his hair and felt completely blank.

At the other end of the line, Allie gasped. "Oh God, she's coming in."

In the background, Carl heard a voice that could be Olwen's talking in a sing-song-like tone, but it was hard to discern the words as Allie's hard breaths just about drenched them.

Finally, he managed to get his own voice to work. "Allie, whatever you do, don't go with her! We're on our way. We're coming to you."

He hung up, and Miri stared at him with big, scared eyes.

"What's going on?"

As he pulled her along toward the reception, he said in a trembling voice, "Olwen's trying to take Allie to a masquerade—"

"What?"

He didn't want to say anything more as they were in earshot of the reception.

A woman with black hair framing her face looked up at them. "How can I help you?"

"We need to talk to Sally Oakley-Wittinger. She's visiting the old archives. Please."

The librarian shook her head. "Sorry, there's no one in the archives now. It doesn't open until noon today."

Miri's hand jerked in his. "But— We came here with her. She... she went there together with the other librarian."

The woman frowned at them, on the brink of becoming worried. "What other librarian?"

"The tall one, the... the tall man; slender with pale skin, black hair and blue eyes, and a star tattoo on his left temple. Long face, eagle-formed nose, thin lips, high cheekbones. He... he has a silver ring in the form of a snake on his left index finger. He was dressed in black trousers, gray shirt with silver snake buttons, black jacket, and black dress shoes," Miri said, and Carl glanced at her in awe. He had completely missed those details.

"Um, I'm sorry, Miss, but we don't have anyone working here that matches that description."

"Could you please check the ledger for us?" Carl interposed and managed to sound casual.

The librarian gave him a glance and reached for the ledger, traced her finger down to the end. "What was the name?"

"Sally Oakley-Wittinger."

"No, sorry. The last entry I have is from Saturday afternoon, and that's another name."

Miri and Carl looked at each other in terrified silence.

"We... we need to go," Carl said, feeling as if his head were spinning.

Miriam nodded with eyes big and scared.

Without even trying to pretend that everything was fine, they turned around and ran out of the doors to the parking lot and their car.

Chapter 27

Before he started the car, Carl handed Miri his cell phone.

"Call Omega. We need her. I don't care how hungover she is. She'll move her damn ass over here now!"

Miri nodded, and with trembling fingers, she went through his phone book as he bustled the car out of the parking lot and out on the street.

"She doesn't answer."

"Fuck! Try again. See if she has a damn landline. Anything."

Then, he concentrated on the road and on driving as fast as he could without risking a damn accident.

"She has a landline, but it's just a busy signal."

"Oh, for crying out loud," he muttered and passed by a white truck. When he was safely in front of it, he said, "She's never struck me as a person who doesn't take her duties seriously. She's a damn ranger, for crying out loud! She'd be sacked if she did things like this!"

"I know, but..." Her voice trailed away. "I'll just keep on trying."

They reached the FBI complex only fifteen minutes later, and without even caring about grabbing their bags, they ran as fast as they could up to the third floor, taking the stairs in double steps. First, they checked the women's washroom. It was empty. Then they busted into Allie's office and stopped dead when Allie looked up at them with an amused smile as she sat at the table with her laptop.

"Wow, you must've missed me," she said and winked, but the next second, her smile disappeared. "What's going on?"

"You called," Carl managed to say.

When Allie just looked confused, Miri grabbed Carl's arm and held on hard. He stared at Allie and squinted suspiciously.

457

She stood up and came over to them with a deep frown on her forehead. "When?"

"Half an hour ago. You said you hid in the bathroom here and that Olwen was going to take you somewhere."

"Um, okay. That's weird." She looked concerned. "I haven't seen Olwen since Saturday, and I haven't called you."

For a while, they stood silent and stared at each other. Carl's chest felt tight, and his breathing was shallow.

"Is this," Miriam said eventually in a voice that wasn't entirely steady. "Is this—"

Suddenly, Carl's phone rang, and all of them jolted.

"Yeah?" he answered quickly.

"Octavius, where the hell are you?" Olwen's voice was stressed-out and on the brink of anger.

"Um, where are you?"

"What the hell do you mean? I'm at the library. You have to tell me if you're going somewhere, you can't just run away on your own, remember? Communicating, remember?"

"Um, we'll be with you in half an hour. Don't go anywhere." He hung up on her before she could answer and ran his hand through his hair, staring wildly at Miriam, who looked frightened.

"She's... she's at the library."

"What? But— She can't be. The librarian—" She fell silent, looking pale and uncertain.

Allie put calming hands on them and asked in a collected voice, "Okay, guys, why can't she be at the library?"

Carl exhaled, feeling completely bewildered. "I— She—"

Miriam took a deep breath and managed to compose herself. "Okay. When we got there this morning, she was taken to the archives by a librarian. Forty minutes ago, you called and said that Olwen was trying to force you somewhere. Another librarian said that the archives are closed until noon, and no one was there, and no one matching the description of the first librarian worked there, and no one was entered into the ledger, so we came here

458

looking for you, and now you're here, and Olwen's at the library."

Allie's eyes squinted, and she swallowed audibly, clearly troubled. "Um, okay, this wasn't really what I expected when I first started to work with you, Carl, but you sure make life more interesting."

Both of them managed to laugh, even though it didn't sound great. Then, Allie surprised them by returning to her desk and packing up her things. Carl and Miriam exchanged looks, and Miriam shrugged at his unaired question. Carl sighed. *Yeah, I agree. She's part of this now, whether she wants to or not.* Then another thought struck him. *I wonder if we were lured away from Olwen, or if we were supposed to come here and get Allie. Whatever reason, we went right into the trap. Mission accomplished.* He exhaled slowly and pulled a trembling hand through his hair.

"I'm just working on my book anyway, I can take today off," Allie said when she came back to them.

Carl gave her a piercing glance. Under that cheerful attitude, she was pale and frightened. He placed a comforting hand on her arm, and she gave him a grateful smile that shivered faintly.

After getting to the car, they sat in deep silence the whole way back to the library. Carl had no idea what to say. The thoughts swirled around in his mind like nervous birds, but he refused to catch any of them. Stubbornly, he tried his best to create radio silence in his head.

In the back seat, Miriam had taken Allie's hand as if to comfort her. One thought stopped long enough for him to see it clearly; she had become more sensitive to other people's feelings since her time in Night Porter's dimension. That scared him too. How much had their staying there influenced them in ways they didn't yet know of? With an uneasy shrug, he let the thought go.

As soon as they stopped in the library's parking lot, they left their things in the car and hurried to the entrance. Olwen was pacing back and forth just inside the doors with an angry look that clearly didn't get better when she saw Allie.

459

"Is she part of our team now?" she asked sharply when they stopped in front of her. "Let's give her a name, shall we? Let's see, yes, I know. Odette. That has a nice ring to it." The sarcasm was clear, and an awkward expression spread over Allie's face as she looked away, not wanting to meet Olwen's glare.

Miriam glanced tiredly at Olwen without saying anything.

Carl couldn't help tugging at his hair, but he closed in on her and moved her away a bit. "Olwen, we don't have time for this now. Something's happened."

Her angry appearance slowly became worried. "What?"

He inhaled and told the crazy story once more. As he talked, he studied her thoroughly. She looked confused and disbelieving. He couldn't blame her.

"Before we left," he continued, "we did try to get a hold of you, but another librarian told us that the archives don't open until noon on Mondays, and that you weren't in the ledger and that the librarian we met in the morning doesn't work here. We got worried and went over to HQ, where we found Allie, who hadn't called us."

"She must be lying," Olwen said decisively.

Carl suppressed a frustrated sigh. "She's not lying, Olwen. Trust me. She's scared. And even if she would lie for some obscure reason, how would you explain the librarian?"

She scowled, touching on irritated again. "I, um, I don't know."

"Did something happen down there?"

"No."

"Olwen, I hate to ask you, but— Did you make a deal with Night Porter?"

"No! I already told you!"

He watched her thoroughly. She looked frustrated and scared and out of control. There was no sign of her lying. If she'd made a deal, she didn't remember. He swallowed his own frustration and looked down the corridor toward the check-out area.

"Alright. I want to speak to the librarian. I want to know why she lied to us."

Olwen nodded and went with him. As they closed in on the information desk, Carl stared grumpily at the librarian they had met in the morning. He was talking quietly with another visitor, before standing up and leading the man toward a couple of shelves. The two agents waited patiently for him to return, even though Carl mostly wanted to interrupt the librarian and get going. Instead, he put on his expressionless mask and thought about Zen.

After a few minutes, the librarian returned and came over to them. "How can I help you?"

This time, Carl noticed the star tattoo and the snake buttons on his shirt. With the dyed black hair, he matched the stereotype of a sophisticated grown-up goth.

"Earlier today, I spoke with a female librarian, mid-thirties, black hair, slim, dressed in a black skirt and blue blouse. I would like to talk to her again, please."

The younger man gave him a puzzled stare back. "I'm sorry, sir, are you sure about that description? We do have some women working here, but none of them have black hair. Only Doreen is here today, but she's blond and in her fifties. She should be over at the history section sorting books if you want to talk to her."

"And what's your name?"

A worried frown appeared on the man's face as he looked Carl over, but the voice was pleasant when he brought out his library ID. It was clear that he had no intention of getting in trouble with the FBI.

"Greg Gardner."

"Thank you for your time, Greg," Carl said and walked toward the history section with Olwen in tow. "I just want to ask her too," he said to her, feeling irritated, scared, and out of control.

461

Olwen nodded, obviously still confused. Soon enough, they saw a woman matching the description.

"Doreen?" Carl asked when they closed in on her, and she looked up from the books on her trolley with a friendly appearance.

"Yes. How can I help you?"

"Hi. I was just curious. I met another librarian today, a woman in her mid-thirties with black hair, black skirt and blue blouse, slim, and I'd like to speak with her again. Do you know who I mean?"

She smiled at him. "Sorry, you must have mistaken a visitor for a librarian. That happens sometimes."

"Oh, alright, then. And the librarian at the front?"

"Greg?"

"That's right. Is he new here? I haven't seen him before."

"Hm, he's been here, what is it now...? Since before Christmas, I'd say. Very meticulous, very knowledgeable, especially when it comes to the archive. He spends most of the time helping people out there."

"Alright. Well, thank you for your time then."

He took a step to walk away, but she stopped him. "So, is there anything I can help you with?"

"No, not really. I was just curious about a thing the other lady said. Nothing important."

Amusement flashed over Doreen's face, and she nodded knowingly. "Well, good luck in finding her."

The unexpected hint took Carl by surprise, but he managed to put on a friendly air of his own and take his leave.

"So, now what?" he puffed, slightly frustrated, on their way back.

"May I come with a suggestion?"

He gave Olwen a surprised glance, but she just looked worn out and worried. "Of course," he said, slightly irked that she asked for permission.

"Let's go home to Omega. We need to discuss this in private, and she needs to be in on it. I can accept that she's not feeling well enough to go anywhere, but she should definitely be in on a briefing as important as this one." She fell silent a couple of seconds before she continued, "I don't like the direction this Project is moving in."

Carl nodded and couldn't agree more. "Sounds good. Did you find anything in the archives, by the way?"

She didn't answer, and when he looked at her, she had a faraway expression as if she thought about something else. Carl shrugged and let her be.

This time, Allie went in his car. Since the phone call, he refused to let her and Olwen be on their own together, not that he said that out loud, of course. He didn't have to undermine Olwen's authority more than he already had. A tiny sting of guilt hit him. There had to be a better way of communicating, but he couldn't figure out what that would be. They never managed to meet. They just talked past each other and got irritated and confused while doing it.

As soon as they got into their cars, Olwen took the lead, and Carl followed her.

They drove a while in silence before Miriam asked from the back, "She didn't work there, did she?"

"Nope."

"But he did?"

"Yeah. I even got to see his ID, and another librarian confirmed it."

"Damn it. I can't believe we got so fooled."

"Hate to say it, but I think it was the difference in appearance that did it," Carl admitted and scowled. "She looked more like a librarian than what he did."

Miriam blushed. "Now, I'm embarrassed," she muttered.

"Yeah, you and me both." Carl gave the women a look in the rear-view mirror. "You're awfully quiet, Allie."

"I— Yeah, I guess. I don't know what to think, honestly."

"Fair enough."

"Welcome to the club, sweetie," Miri said with a faint smile.

Allie frowned nervously. "She wasn't serious, right, about me joining your team?"

Miriam shrugged to show her ignorance. "I don't know. Probably not, but I've never been able to figure her out."

Carl shook his head slightly. "Right now, I'd say she doesn't know herself. She's pretty confused. As are we all. We'll see during the briefing how she treats you. It's not usual procedure taking in new members like this. I haven't heard of anyone who hasn't been placed on a team by the Faculty, and Olwen's pretty stuck to the book."

In the mirror, he saw Miriam turn to Allie with a flash of curiosity in her face. "Are you really interested in joining us? Because if you are, there's an intermediate course, you know, that you could take at Western Shore. The one Omega took."

"Uh, yeah, I don't know... Just seeing how I feel about all this, of all the weird stuff you told me about, all the danger... I don't think I'd be able to quit the booze, to tell the truth, and then I'm going to be the one responsible for everyone's death, I swear. Nice future prospects. Can't think of anything better, really." Carl chuckled, and Miriam smiled broadly. Allie grimaced. "I can't even see the fun in it. I'm serious, you know. Not that I'm an alcoholic, mind you, just not brainwashed."

For some reason, that made Miri laugh out loud, and Carl couldn't help grinning. When Allie glared at them, Miriam leaned in and kissed Allie's cheek, to Carl's huge surprise.

"You're such a sweetheart, Allie. Usually, it helps to laugh at it. There's not much else to do, honestly."

A deep sigh heaved Allie's chest, and she leaned into Miriam's shoulder and rested her head there while Miri held her arm around her. Carl struggled to keep a straight face but seeing them cuddle in the back truly surprised him. He had never seen Miriam as the cuddly type before, but maybe Allie brought it out of her, and she felt self-confident enough to answer to Allie's warm personality. Whatever brought it out, he was happy about it. She would blossom by having a friend, other than her sister.

The rest of the drive continued in silence. Allie and Miri sat close to each other and watched the traffic go by while he held his concentration on the road, content to be the one driving, so he had something to focus his mind on, rather than the weird events this morning. He followed Olwen's car through the quiet neighborhood of Quenora Meadows and parked beside her at the guest parking lot in front of the apartment complex.

Olwen nodded at them, and they followed her up the stairs to the third floor and knocked on the door. As they waited for Omega to open, Carl looked at the handmade sign. *Pieretta Aretha Williams,* enclosed with flower garlands. *It's sweet. Not what you'd think a ranger would put on her door, but it suits her.*

As the seconds went by, Olwen frowned and knocked again. A slight touch of worry caressed Carl's mind, and he could feel how the atmosphere changed amongst them when no one answered the door. *Something's wrong.*

As if she could read his mind, Olwen looked up at him. "Something's wrong," she said in a low voice.

He nodded and grabbed his gun. Behind him, he heard Miriam lock and load her gun.

As Olwen prepared her own, she turned to Allie with a professional appearance. "You don't have a gun, right?" When Allie shook her head with wide-opened frightened eyes and pale face, Olwen nodded. "You keep to the back. Don't engage in anything. Understood?"

"Yes, ma'am."

"Octavius, you're back-up, Ophelia and I go in first."

They nodded and changed places. Miriam stepped up to the left side of the doorway, and Carl took some steps

465

back while Olwen kept her place to the right. Frightened, Allie moved to the side and hid in the corner.

Olwen checked them, and they gave her the signal. Carl tried the door. It opened, and Carl got a glimpse of the hallway before he moved back. Olwen and Miriam went in, silently as shadows. As always in a hostile situation, Carl's senses were overloaded. It was as if he was aware of everything and when he silently followed his team-mates, he was prepared for anything.

The air inside was stale and smelled dirty. It was as if nothing had drawn breath inside for a long time. The worry for Omega was still there, but Carl distanced himself from it to be able to concentrate. Olwen pointed military-style toward the open kitchen. Miriam nodded and checked it, made the okay sign and came back to Olwen, who checked the bathroom where the door stood open. With a slight shake of her head, she let them know it was empty. Instead, she pointed toward the closed bedroom door. Together, they moved in and got into position. When Carl opened the door and moved back to let the women in, a combined bittersweet smell of blood and vinegar hit them. He heard Miriam gasp and both women put the safety back on their guns and hurried in. A quick glance showed him Omega still lying naked on the bed, but this time, there was blood around her. *God, is she dead?* No one else was in the room. Olwen determinedly turned toward him and threw her car keys to him. Reflexively, he caught them one-handed.

"Get Odette to find my emergency bag in the trunk. Now! Not a second to lose!"

Hurriedly, he went out to the stairway and waved at Allie with the keys in hand. "We need Olwen's doctor's bag. It's in the trunk. Now!"

She nodded, immediately realizing the urgency as she took the keys and flew down the stairs. Carl rushed into the bedroom again and stopped dead, trying to take in the scene to see where he could help the best. Olwen was methodically doing artificial respiration on Omega, and Miri was on the cell.

"—overdose and vaginal trauma. Olwen says she has Naloxone, and she's doing AR right now. No cardiac arrest, just no breathing. No, no idea how long. We just arrived. At least she's still alive. Okay. Good." She put down the phone just as Allie came rushing in, panting heavily, with the bag in a hard grip. "They're here in forty minutes," Miri said to Olwen.

"Should be enough. Who knows AR?" Olwen asked in between blowing air down Omega's lungs.

"I'll do it. I took the course in January last time," Miri said.

As Miri took over, Allie handed the bag to Olwen, who opened it and found a small bottle, a syringe, and a large unopened needle.

"Don't just stand there, Octavius. Go and get thick towels and warm water. I need to check her as soon as I've given her this."

"Yeah…"

He waddled through the mess on the floor toward the closets, found some clean towels and put them on the bed, avoiding the big spot of blood, before he went out into the kitchen. After a bit of rummaging around, he grabbed a big plastic bowl from a cupboard and filled it with warm water. When he came back, Miri was still AR:ing Omega, while Olwen slowly inserted the, in Carl's opinion, gigantic needle in Omega's upper arm. As he put down the bowl of water, Allie tugged at his shirt.

"Yeah?"

Pale and with enormous eyes, she handed him some Polaroid photos. He gave her a questioning glance before looking at them. The breath stuck in his throat as shivers of cold fear ran down his spine, and his body began to tremble. On the photos, a lifeless, seemingly unconscious Omega lay on her stomach while Night Porter was standing behind her and, smiling toward the camera, thrusting himself into her.

467

He met Allie's frightened look again, and she cleared her voice.

"There are more. Look."

She pointed to the floor, where hundreds of photos covered it. Carl hadn't even realized that he'd stepped on them when he went to get the towels. Reluctantly, he bent down and took up another one.

Behind him, Miri said with a relieved voice, "She's breathing."

"Great. We'll have about forty minutes. Can you help me down here, please?"

"Of course."

This photo was another one with Night Porter, but on this one, Omega was still conscious, having a look of horror and excruciating pain on her face. Carl exhaled shakily, his stomach a hard core of terror and compassion. Helplessly, he tugged at his hair.

"Let's just gather them, eh?" he muttered in a hoarse voice and brought out a couple of latex gloves from his jacket and handed her a pair.

Allie nodded and together they began putting the photos into piles on the drawer, trying not to look at them.

Chapter 28

They didn't have time to brief Olwen or Miriam before team B arrived. Dr. Bernard had brought both of his nurses with him; the red-haired sister Blaise who never smiled, and the lighthearted sister Banafshe who always wore a *hijab*. Together, they brought the still unconscious Omega down to their ambulance and drove away, sirens on, the whole thing taking less than ten minutes.

"I wish I could follow them," Olwen said in a low voice, continuing to look after the disappearing ambulance as Allie and Miri went inside the apartment building again, Miri with her CSI bag in a firm grip. "We've been on the same team for four years, and all this— It's my fault."

"Olwen—"

"No, Octavius, don't say it. It is my fault. It was far more important for me to show you that you were wrong than to make sure that she actually was okay when we found her on Saturday. I mean, yes, I know she smokes sometimes, and drinks, but never… never injecting heroin… God…" A couple of tears found their way down her cheeks.

"It might not have been Omega who did it, Olwen," Carl said in a tense voice. She wiped away the tears and glanced up at him. "Allie found photos. Night Porter's been here."

"What…?"

"You'd better see them, but— They're pretty gruesome."

Without saying anything more, Carl went over to his car and brought out his own CSI bag, surprised but pleased to see that Olwen waited for him before they headed up to Omega's apartment again. Allie and Miri had taken the photos and spread them out on the kitchen table. They stood watching them with strained faces. Olwen closed in, put on the latex gloves Miriam handed her, and took up a photo. Her face paled, and she gave him a quiet look.

"Was it… was it him… all along? Was he here when we were here?"

Carl exhaled, hoping with all his being that she was wrong, but thought reluctantly about the person who had been in the shower. "I couldn't tell. We've to see if we can find any traces from another guy. If not…" His voice trailed away, and he shuddered violently at the terrifying thought of Omega being trapped with Night Porter since Friday.

Olwen rubbed her pale face, looking more nauseated than he had ever seen her.

"That might explain the injuries she had," she mumbled in a thick voice, near tears. "I… I guess he's not human…"

Silence fell hard in the room, and no one looked at each other.

Eventually, Miriam cleared her voice. "There are dates on the photos," she said hoarsely.

"Okay." Olwen exhaled, seemingly calming down, but her trembling hands betrayed her. When she talked again, her voice was a mere shadow of the commanding-officer-voice she usually used, "Odette, sorry to put you on this, but you and I need to go through the photos while Ophelia and Octavius check the apartment for other evidence."

Allie paled even more, most likely of being called Odette and suddenly being part of the team. Having to look at the gruesome photos clearly didn't help. She didn't protest, however. Miri and Carl glanced at each other but left them and went into the bedroom. Carl was careful not to close the door. It seemed improbable that something would happen between Olwen and Allie when they were all together, but he wanted to play it safe.

"Where do you want to start?" he asked, and Miriam looked around.

"Let's take some photos. Then, we'll do the bed, take samples, put things in e-bags as usual, and proceed from the bed in a circle movement."

470

He nodded, and she brought out her camera, taking photos while he put on new latex gloves. When she put away the camera, they concentrated on the bed. The investigation was pretty straightforward, in Carl's opinion. There was only one big spot of blood, which suggested that Omega hadn't even moved since she started to bleed. There was no semen and no other obvious spots of bodily fluids.

Carl tried to distance himself from the images on the photos that insisted on coming back to him. The worst thing was that they triggered the sickening dream-memories of Athena's lustful, triumphant face above him, and the pain and the powerlessness she made him feel. Trembling, he forced the images away. He wouldn't be able to work properly if he let the feelings take over.

It took them forty minutes to go through everything in the bedroom. When they were finished, they checked the rest of the apartment before returning to Olwen and Allie, who were still placing the photos in order. The work was about halfway done, and both women looked pale and nauseous.

As Carl and Miriam stepped into the kitchen, Olwen put down the photos she held with a relieved expression she apparently wasn't even aware of. "Anything?"

"Well," Miri said. "There are no drugs at all. Nothing to show what they used, no needles, no powder, no butts, nothing. There's no semen either and no condoms. Have to check the garbage, but I don't expect to find anything. There are those bottles of alcohol beside her bed, of course, but no glasses. I couldn't say for sure, but they don't seem to have been touched since we were here on Saturday. No diaries, no notes, no phone books, no cell phone. Her laptop has a password I can't figure out."

Olwen sighed. "Okay. Let's just hope she'll be coherent when she wakes up, but—" She looked down at the photos. When she talked again, her voice was on the edge of cracking. "If she's in her right mind, it's a miracle..."

471

"Earliest photo we've found so far is from Friday," Allie added in a distant and emotionless voice that Carl hadn't heard before. "Night Porter's in it. He's in all of them."

"Who holds the camera?" Miri asked. "And where is the camera?"

They all looked at her, surprised at the words.

Carl cleared his voice, suddenly overcome by an unexpected thought. "Does he need a camera? Are we sure all of this actually happened?" The three women stared at him, disbelievingly, frightened, and angry, and he held up his hands in a defensive gesture. "I'm asking because I could swear it was Allie who called me today, but it wasn't. I'm asking because we all saw Night Porter on the news on Saturday, but Allie's friends didn't. He doesn't need a fucking camera. These dates can be as real as Santa. I don't even remember seeing the dates on the first photos we looked at. Allie?" She shook her head, slowly and wide-eyed in beginning fear. When Olwen opened her mouth, he held up his hand toward her. He wanted to finish his thoughts before she could accuse him of anything. "I know, the injuries are real. He raped her, no doubt about it. I'm not questioning that. I'm questioning how tricked we're right now. How come we managed to arrive just in time to save her life? She didn't breathe. Had we arrived ten minutes later, she'd be dead, and she was definitely not in a state to clean the drugs away." Once again, silence fell heavily in the room. Carl began to feel frustrated. "Do you think this was just a coincidence? I don't. Coincidences don't happen in our job." Miriam gave him a meaningful glance, and he squirmed, remembering a certain conversation they had had in his car two years ago. "I've changed my mind, Miri," he said, trying to sound dignified, but couldn't look her in the eyes.

"You... you think he was here when we arrived?" Allie asked faintly.

"I don't know. Maybe."

"I haven't felt any portals anywhere," Miri said, but Carl just shrugged.

472

"Does he need any? The portals might be for humans. As Olwen said, he's probably not human."

"So, what the hell does he want from us, Octavius? Is he just playing with us? And why us?"

Carl ran his hand through his hair and exhaled. "I have no clue. Because we got away?"

"If he's as powerful as you suggest, then we didn't get away. He let us go," Miri said in a tired voice.

"But why?" Olwen asked again.

Miri looked down at her hands. "We talked about it at the library." She exhaled. "Maybe we're spreading this to people."

"What... what do you mean, 'spreading'?" Allie sounded frightened.

Miriam took another deep breath and continued to stare at her hands. "Spreading it like a virus. Maybe we make people aware of these vibrations, somehow make it easier for people to tune in to them and get to the other realm. The shadow people who live there, they feed on humans. Maybe they need more."

Both Allie and Olwen stared at Miriam, and then Olwen shivered violently. "If this is the true reason, then we only have one choice."

"What's that?" Carl asked.

As she looked at him, all color disappeared from her face, and her eyes were like black holes with a faraway look in them. "Go in there and never come back out again."

This time, the silence was as heavy as a falling axe, but then Allie threw her hands up in the air, photos forgotten, and they tossed up to slowly float down to the floor.

"No way! No fucking way! I'm not going in there, and I'm fucking not going in there to never come out again. No fucking way. This is just *jävla idiotier! Jävla helvetesidiotier!* You're out of your fucking mind!"

"Olwen, you can't be serious," Miriam said determinedly. "I'm not going in there again."

Olwen ignored them and looked urgently at Carl with an obsessive expression that worried him. "I'm serious. You know that's the only solution."

"Olwen…" He paused and exhaled, running his hand through his hair several times, trying to figure out what to say. "You can't demand something like that. At this point, it's only speculations, and you know it. He's not human, for crying out loud! How can we possibly understand how he thinks? How can we even try to begin to understand that goddamn realm?"

"I mean it, Octavius. If what we're doing is spreading it to people around us, we must go. Otherwise, others will suffer and die."

"Please, Olwen, just stop it. Just… just stop it and think. We're not the only ones who've been there, and we know other people have managed to get out. It's very honorable of you wanting to sacrifice ourselves to save others, but we're not going to be able to stop this anyway if it's really what's going on. Or do you think that we're going to gather Dr. Bernard, sisters Banafshe and Blaise, my daughter, my ex-wife, Miri's whole family, all of Allie's roommates, Caesar, and to go even further, my daughter's classmates and their families, my ex-wife's friends and co-workers, all the others that people we've been in contact with have been in contact with in turn, and bring them with us, creating a whole colony of humans at the inn? You know that's impossible. If we're spreading something, it's already too late."

Olwen stared at him, and then, she blinked and looked disoriented. Something in that look gave fuel to the suspicious feelings that poked their ugly heads up, and he squinted at her.

"Um… sorry…" She rubbed her eyes. "I'm just tired."

"So, now what?" Miri asked before he could say anything.

474

Olwen glanced at her, apparently trying to get her thoughts in order. "I have to think about it," she said eventually. "For now, let's treat it as an ordinary Project. I know it's not, but let's just put the photos together, and then we'll break for today. I'm sure we'll come up with something."

"So, no more self-sacrificing thoughts, eh, Olwen?" Carl casually said and kept a probing eye on her.

She gave him a surprised look that turned insecure, but the next second she scowled and didn't answer. The suspicion grew even stronger, but he didn't push her. It was probably not the right time or place, and she might not even remember what they had just talked about. He exhaled slowly and tried to let go of all uncertain thoughts and instead concentrate on the task before them.

For the next half an hour, all of them sorted the photos in piles according to date and time without trying to look at them. The silence around the table was tense and uncomfortable, but the things on their minds were even more uncomfortable, and nothing they wanted to talk about right now.

As soon as everything was in order and placed in e-bags, Olwen put them in her bag together with the samples Carl and Miri had gathered. Before they left, Miri checked the kitchen garbage just to be sure she hadn't missed anything but found nothing of interest. In the hallway, Olwen checked Omega's purse where she found a key. Then she ushered them out and locked the door.

When they reached the cars, Olwen said, "I'll take these to HQ, and then, we'll meet tomorrow in room three-six at eight-hundred sharp. I'd like to have you there too, Odette. It seems as you're part of this team now."

Allie shuddered violently, but before any of them could respond, Olwen turned her back on them and got into her car.

When she drove away, Carl exhaled and tugged at his hair. "I wonder if those samples will ever get to the lab," he muttered.

Flabbergasted, Miri turned toward him, but Allie just nodded.

"Yeah," she said. "I don't think she'll even remember this afternoon."

"What do you mean?" Miri demanded.

They looked at her.

"There's something wrong with her, Miri," Carl said with a worried frown. "It might have been a big mistake letting her go, but what can we do? We can't restrain her." Miri scowled at him, and it dawned on him that she didn't know, that neither of them knew. "When we were at the inn before you regained consciousness properly, Olwen and Omega went on a... on a research expedition, I think they called it, and according to Omega, Olwen made a deal with Night Porter, but she doesn't remember it."

With eyes wide-opened, Miri stared at him. "You're kidding, right?"

He shook his head. "I wish I did."

"I don't know her well," Allie said, looking deeply troubled, "but when she rambled about us going in there and not letting the thought go, there was a slight, um, shift in her personality, not very apparent, but still there, and afterward, she didn't seem to know what Carl meant when he said that thing about self-sacrifice." She gave him a look. "You did that on purpose, right?"

"Yeah."

"Mm, thought so."

Miriam rubbed her face and exhaled. "Is she going to force us in there again? It seems irrational. I mean, we were already there. To let us all leave and then let her take us back— Why?"

"I have no idea, but—" He gave Allie a glance. "I might be wrong, but Allie might be important somehow. On the other hand, why use us to connect you to that realm?

He'd probably be able to do that himself if he wanted." He sighed. "Honestly, everything seems very farfetched right now."

Allie puffed and gestured irritated with her hands. "But why me? What's so special about me?"

"If I knew we wouldn't be in this mess, eh? Miri, you have any idea?"

Nervously, she shook her head. "No. Can we go home now? I feel too exposed standing here talking about Night Porter." A shiver ran through her body, and Allie put an arm around her. In a slightly calmer voice, she asked, "Do you want to come home with us, Allie?" She turned to Carl. "That's okay, right?"

He nodded. "Sure. If you want to."

Allie looked uncomfortable. "I wouldn't mind during ordinary circumstances, but— I need to get back to my own life, you know, even if I'm afraid. I don't know if I can accept that Night Porter has some kind of weird, hidden agenda against me. Do you— Do you really think you've spread something to me that I, in turn, will spread to the others at home? I mean, it does sound crazy."

Carl managed a smile devoid of humor. "I know. And I understand. Can't speak for any of you, but I'm quite confused and don't have a clue about anything right now."

"I... I think I want to go home. I can't let this dictate my life."

"Yeah, I hear you. Come on, let's go."

They took the same seats in the car as on the way to Quenora Meadows. While driving, a crazy, probably stupid, and maybe even dangerous idea crossed Carl's mind. He tried to argue against it, but it wouldn't give in. Eventually, he sighed and looked at the quiet women in the rear-view mirror.

"Allie?"

"Yeah?"

"You don't really believe in all this, do you?" She looked caught. "I don't blame you." In the mirror, he glanced at Miriam. "I want to take her to Kroger's."

477

"What?" both of them exclaimed.

Meeting Allie's wide-open eyes in the mirror, he said, "It's probably a stupid thing to do, but you won't be able to get it if you don't see it yourself. Not going in," he hurriedly said when Miri paled. "Just open the damn portal and show her the view. I mean, seriously, Allie, we can't work with you if you think we're nutbags, and in the end, you'll drift away from us as friends because you think we're crazy."

In the mirror, he saw Miri nod thoughtfully, and Allie looked more nervous and scared than he'd seen her since Saturday. Neither of them said anything, though, so he took it as an affirmative.

Fifteen minutes later, he parked in the restricted area.

"You want to come, Miri, or you want to stay in the car?"

"I, um, I'm coming."

"Alright."

He knew she wouldn't take it kindly that he'd keep an eye on her, but he wasn't sure what kind of trauma she still suffered from. On the other hand, he had nursed the thought for a while now, that it might be good for her seeing this place again, to face the nightmares and overcome them, and this might be as good an opportunity as any other one, maybe even better, since the focus wasn't on her. When he covertly glanced at her, he noticed how pale she still was, but her determined expression eased his heart.

Together, they went to the gate and showed their badges to the security guard, who let them in without any questions. Miri's eyes were wide and dazed as she looked around the once familiar place, but no memories seemed to show up in her mind. Allie kept her hands in her pockets, and her whole body was tense and strained. One part of him felt guilty for doing this to the two women in his life that meant the most to him, but if he didn't, he knew he would lose Allie tonight. It was as clear as crystal. *I can't risk that. She's too important to me. I have no idea when she became this important, but I can't stand the thought of losing her.*

The stepladder stood at its place. They climbed down, and Miriam shuddered violently when her feet touched the floor. He followed her gaze as she looked around, seeking out different spots, spots he suddenly realized that Cutie had marked for them. For a short moment, he embraced her and tried to ease her mind, but since he didn't want to prolong their visit here more than necessary, he soon let her go. Instead, he walked across the floor to the place where he had felt the vibrations last time. Allie and Miri took some steps closer to each other, seeking comfort in one another. Carl felt their gaze as they stood together, watching him in silence.

For a while, he stood unmoving, trying to feel, rather than think. It didn't take long until the vibrations made themselves known to him, to his extreme relief. *God, I'm crazy, feeling relieved. It would be better if they were gone.* He took a deep breath and concentrated on them. It seemed to go quicker than last time – *maybe I know more about what I'm doing now –* and that was not reassuring. Within a couple of minutes, the plain white door hovered in front of them.

Allie's heavy and scared breathing was clearly heard behind him, and he felt like a jerk. Despite that, he opened the door, sweaty and trembling from concentrating, and there it was; the town lay silent and ominous and sad at the foot of the hill. With her face white as a sheet, Allie stumbled toward it with Miri's hand in a hard grasp. Shaking uncontrollably, she put her hand on the door. For a while, she stood there, breathing tightly, taking in the view with eyes big and frightened. Eventually, she composed herself, and with a reluctant expression, she let her hand move through the portal. Almost falling, she bent down on her knees and grabbed a handful of gravel from the other side. At that point, Carl saw how the door began to sway violently, and without thinking, he grabbed her arm and pulled her back. The next second there was nothing there for them to see anymore.

Chapter 29

They let Allie off at her car at HQ and saw her take her leave, quiet and withdrawn.

"I wish she'd followed us," Miriam said with a worried tang in her voice when she got into the front seat.

"Yeah…" Carl sighed, and the guilt hit him hard. "It probably was a really bad, stupid idea, showing her that. Sometimes, I'm not sure where the line goes, where to stop. I… I just don't want to lose her." Regret made his chest tighten. "Maybe I'll lose her anyway now," he mumbled.

Miri took his hand and leaned in to kiss him lightly, but instead, he put his arms around her and prolonged the kiss, deepened it, trying to make all the confused, regretful feelings disappear. It felt good and pure to kiss her, to feel her loving presence, and gradually he calmed down. All the positive energies she radiated overruled the feeling from Omega's apartment that constantly forced itself upon him with its horrifying events. Once again, he shoved them away and concentrated on Miriam and the love she awoke inside him.

When they let go of the kiss, Miri trailed a finger over his cheek. "You know, I don't think it was stupid. I think you're right. She needed to see it, to really understand in her heart that we're not crazy." She turned silent, but he could tell that she wasn't done yet. In a thoughtful voice, she continued, "I don't want us to lose her either. She's like no one else I've met. Sometimes, she feels like a minor sun. She'll need time to think and to accept, but then I hope she'll come back to us." Suddenly, she gave him a probing glance. "And knowing you, it might even have been your intention taking me there too." He felt himself looking caught, and her smile was tender and trembling. "I love you, Carl. Thank you for doing that. It wasn't as hard as I thought it would be."

He cleared his voice, feeling his cheeks heat from the overpowering emotions inside him. "I love you too, Miri."

They kissed again, and finally, he managed to ease off, to shut away from the day's horrible events, and concentrate fully on Miri. Her lips were so soft and willing under his, and her hand on his thigh was warm and sent trickles of sweet sensations through his body that landed in a glowing point in his lower abdomen. The thought struck him that the parking lot at FBI headquarters might not be the best place to try to seduce his wife-to-be, but made a mental shrug, smiled at her lips and let his hands find their way in under her shirt, enjoying feeling like a teenager.

She laughed and squirmed away. "Carl!"

"What?"

"We're at HQ."

"That we are." He tugged teasingly at her shirt, and she laughed again as she leaned into him, letting him touch her. She closed her eyes, and he heard her breathing change slightly. With slowly pounding heart, he caught that breath with his lips. When her hand touched him over his jeans and caressed him gently and teasingly, he had trouble breathing as thousands of small tingling needles of pleasure concentrated at the spot under her hand. She gave him a sexy smile that increased the heavy sensation in his jeans, as she continued to caress him.

"What do you say about dinner out, a nice walk home, and then…" She paused with a mischievous gleam in her eyes.

"Then what?" he teased, slightly hoarse, seeing her in bed naked and wild in his mind's eye.

She winked and smiled playfully back at him. "I think we can come up with something."

"I don't have any better plans," he mumbled as he stole another long, deep kiss before he started the car.

They parked at home, and hand in hand, they walked through the chilly May afternoon to a nearby Indonesian restaurant that was another favorite of theirs. It was nice, taking a pause from all the gruesome details of the Project, and just revel in their own, newfound love for each other.

481

When they sat down, surrounded by the rich aroma from the kitchen, the waiter immediately approached them. As soon as they had ordered, they shut everything else out from their own little bubble of reality. Under the table, they tangled their feet together. On the table, they tangled their hands.

"So, where do you want us to live?" Carl asked when the food arrived. When Miriam gave him an inquiring glance, he continued with a touch of loving lightheartedness in his voice, "I mean, my apartment is nice and such, but it might become small eventually."

A fierce blush covered her face as she suddenly understood what he was talking about, and she laughed on the brink of being embarrassed.

"Aren't you rushing headlong?"

"Well," he smiled and caressed her hands. "That's usually what becoming a couple and getting married ends in, sooner or later. Not necessarily that way, of course, but I wouldn't mind. On the contrary." He paused for a moment, watching her red cheeks. "Would you? Mind, I mean?"

The embarrassment gave way to shyness, and she lowered her eyes, before looking up again, solemnly caressing his cheek. "I can't believe how lucky I am."

He felt a deep and sweet tug at his heartstrings as he looked into her soft, loving eyes. "But you want to wait for a while." She nodded. "So do I. There's no need to rush anything, but it can be a good thought to have in the back of our minds, eh, that we might not want to keep two apartments and that we eventually might want to get something bigger."

She nodded again. "To tell the truth, I don't mind getting rid of my apartment. I— I don't feel comfortable there, haven't since, you know, those eggs ended up there."

"Mm, yeah, I remember. That was a weird, scary thing." He turned her left hand and looked at the wide scar, caressed it gently. "Sometimes I wonder what happens with the items we send back to the Faculty, and then I get this scene popping up in my mind, you know, from *Indiana Jones*, of the guy in the end placing the ark together with all the other weird boxed stuff."

Miriam laughed out loud. "God, now I'll always see that scene before me when I think of the eggs."

Carl chuckled. "Not a bad one to have in mind, honestly. Quite liberating, I think." He looked at her with a smile and kissed her hand, feeling anticipation emanating in his body. He'd been waiting for a moment like this for some time now. "You know, there was something else I've been thinking about."

"What's that?"

"Well, when this Project is over, how about we take a long vacation? You show me Crete, and I show you India, and then maybe a short visit to Egypt."

Her eyes suddenly looked like stars, bright and shiny. "Yes! When do we leave?"

He laughed happily. "October? November? That should give us enough time to fix everything with work and the Faculty, and with your apartment."

She nodded, her whole face radiating. "I like that. A lot. It's a good plan. Oh, the things we'll do! I can't wait!" She jumped on the seat by sheer excitement, and he had to laugh at her and at their shared enthusiasm and delight.

"Miri, you and I... God, we're going to have the best vacation ever. I can't wait to do this together with you. I want to start looking for flights right now."

She beamed at him. "You know, I've meant to ask you, but there hasn't been enough time. I prepared mom and Beth that we might not want a big wedding, just our two families. They weren't happy about seeing a big, three-day-long celebration go, but I reminded them it's about you and me, not about them, and with a small one, we can actually get married just before we leave, say the first week in October. It would be beautiful with a fall wedding. Maybe we can have it in Lincoln Spring Park? It doesn't have to be very traditional or religious. What do you think?"

A broad smile appeared on his lips, and his heart pounded faster in amazement as he thought of how well she understood him.

"I think I love you, future Mrs. Hansen."

Happily, she leaned forward and touched his lips with hers. "I like the sound of that," she whispered.

"Me too," he mumbled at her cheek and stole another kiss. Then, a thought struck him. "Or do you want me to take your name? I wouldn't mind. Carl Goldblum has a nice ring to it too."

Miriam stared at him with astonishment painted over her face. "Would you— Would you really do that?"

He gave her a surprised look. "Sure, I would. It's your name, Miri, and you mean the world to me."

Her eyes got moist. "Oh, Carl, you're just amazing, do you know that?" She laughed quietly. "Mom would get a heart attack." Carl laughed with her and with a solid grip of his hand on her cheek, she tilted her head. "What about a compromise? Isn't that what marriage is about after all, compromises?"

He nodded with a touched smile. "Which combination do you like the most?"

She thought it over with a sweet smile of her own. "Goldblum-Hansen, I think. That works with both our names and it has a nice rhythm."

"Alright, Carl and Miriam Goldblum-Hansen it is."

They beamed at each other.

"Shall we go home?" Miri asked, and the color on her cheeks deepened.

Carl cleared his voice. "Yeah, I think it's a great idea. By the way, you might want these." He brought out his extra door keys and put them in her hand. "Just to let you know that it's your home too."

She stared at the keys in her hand, before looking up at him, overwhelmed. Without being able to say anything, she grabbed his hands and placed them on her cheeks, and he caressed her gently. For a while, they sat silently at the table, and he was astonished by how this small gesture had moved her so deeply. Eventually, she composed herself, and beaming, she refused to let him pay, and they walked out of the restaurant, hand in hand.

A trickling rain had begun, replacing the short-lived snow from the morning, and a warm gushy wind blew around them, tangling their hair. Miri turned her face toward the darkening sky. Raindrops fell on her cheeks and gave her wet freckles.

"I love this weather," she said dreamingly. "It's not polite."

A feeling of sadness gripped his heart at the fact that she had gone through life without being able to show her true emotions even amongst people who claimed they loved her. With a squeeze of her hand, he promised himself that he would try to respect every kind of emotion she had.

Instead of hurrying, as the other people around them, they walked slowly, enjoying the escalating rain and the wind in their faces. When they reached his apartment complex and got into the elevator, they were soaked. Determinedly, and with a certain gleam in her eyes Miri pushed him into the corner, taking advantage of the slow-moving elevator as she put her arms around his neck and, tip-toeing, began to kiss him; passionate, lingering kisses that made him dizzy and longing to finally take off those wet clothes. When the elevator at long last arrived at the right level, they stepped out, laughing breathlessly. Then, they stopped dead.

With tears running down her cheeks, Allie sat on the floor outside the door, hugging her knees. All Carl's thoughts of being naked together with Miri in bed disappeared as they both hurried over to her and knelt, embracing her.

"Can— Can I come in?" she asked in a small, cracked voice.

"Of course, you can, Allie. You should've called. How long have you been here?"

"Doesn't matter," she sobbed.

"Goddammit, Allie, it matters! Come."

He helped her up while Miriam unlocked the door and grabbed Allie's bag and laptop. Without being able to stop herself, Allie embraced him hard and cried inconsolably into his wet jacket. Soothingly, he stroked her over her back and leaned his cheek on her head while catching Miri's glance.

"Could you make some tea, please?" he asked, and she nodded with sympathy written all over her face.

Yeah, we've both been there, feeling so damn alone and scared in a world that doesn't make sense anymore.

"Hey, Allie, let's go in, shall we? It's cozier inside," he said in a low, soft voice, and she nodded but refused to let go of his hand, so he kept his arm around her. She kicked off her shoes while still holding on to him with a desperate grip, and he did the same. It took a little longer to twist himself out of his wet jacket, but, eventually, it lay on the floor together with their shoes. As they passed the doorway to the kitchen, Miriam glanced compassionately at them as she prepared a teapot with Masala Chai.

As soon as they sat down on the sofa, Allie embraced him with full force again, and he let her rest on his chest while holding her gently and stroking her hair. Her whole body trembled, and her tears wet his shirt. It didn't take long before Miriam came out with the teapot and three big mugs. She sat down on the sofa beside them and hugged Allie from behind.

"Hey, sweetie, I'm happy you came back."

Allie let go of Carl with shuddering breaths and turned around and embraced Miriam instead.

"I didn't want to, but I had nowhere else to go," she cried. "I tried to go home, but I couldn't be there. How can I possibly act normally toward them again? They haven't seen what I've seen! Goddammit! Did you have to show me that? Did you?"

Carl let his hands stroke her back. "Allie…"

With eyes suddenly fuming in anger, she turned around toward him again. "*Helvete! Helvetes jävla helvete!* I'm so damn mad at you, Carl! So damn, fucking mad!"

486

She hit him on his chest repeatedly. The blows weren't hard, but felt uncomfortable, nonetheless. Instead of holding her hands to stop her, he put his arms around her to comfort her, but she shook him off. Her face flared red with rage when she stared at him, and then she suddenly attacked him; her open mouth pressed hard and demandingly on his, while her tongue violently invaded his mouth. Her body clung forcefully to his while her hands ferociously pressed his head toward hers. It felt as if she wanted to swallow him whole.

His eyes opened wide in shock. Without being aware of what he did, he struggled to push her away without succeeding. In his mind, Athena was laughing at him, and over Allie's shoulder, Miri stared at them in disbelief. As suddenly as she attacked him, she let him go, panting heavily while gawking at him with a devastated look in her eyes, before hiding her face in her hands, crying again.

Carl and Miri shared a silent, stunned look over her head. Trembling, he combed through his hair several times while watching Allie sitting crouched on the sofa, crying inconsolably, with her long hair loose, hiding her from them.

Calm down, Carl, he managed to think. *It's Allie, not Athena, and she's beside herself. You did this to her. She's not to blame. She doesn't know what she's doing, for crying out loud. She would never hurt me intentionally.* He took a couple of deep breaths, and the trembling in his body began to calm down, as did his racing heart. The seconds went by slowly.

Suddenly, Miri slid down on the floor in front of Allie, gently prying the other woman's stiff hands from her face. Eventually, Allie let go. She lifted her head to look at Miri, but her expression was raw, naked, and exposed.

"Allie," Miri said with a very soft voice. "It's okay."

"How can you even say that?" Allie's voice was thick with tears. "I'm kissing your fiancé, and I want him to touch me. How can you say it's okay?"

"Because it is." When Allie continued to cry and just shook her head, Miri looked annoyed. "Allie, seriously, knock it off," she said sharply.

Allie's head jerked up. Unsure, she stared at Miriam's irritated face.

Miri met Allie's gaze on the edge of anger. "Why does everyone try to victimize me all the damn time?" she asked in a heated tone. "Is it some kind of special presence I have, something I radiate? I'm not a damn porcelain doll! I can make my own decisions. I don't need anyone to make them for me. Neither of you has ever asked me how I feel about you two. You both just presume that I'm going to fret about it. Why would I be more prudish than you? Because I look like the girl next door? God, I'm so damn tired of being told what to think! Maybe I think it's sexy seeing you kiss! Maybe I want to see you touch! Maybe it turns me on! Maybe I want some adventure in my life too!"

Shocked, Carl stared at her. Her face was flushed from anger, and she panted heavily. Everything happened too fast, and he didn't have time to grasp what was going on.

Allie had stopped crying, and she looked at Miri, stunned, but slowly the expression gave way to wonder. Hesitantly, she raised her hand and placed it on Miri's cheek. Then, she leaned in and put her forehead on Miri's, so they were almost nose-to-nose. Anxiously, Carl swallowed hard and didn't know where to look. Were they truly going to kiss? How had they managed to come to this?

While he tried to make sense of the situation, Allie slowly and gently let her lips touch Miri's, and Miri opened up to her, nipped at Allie's lower, full lip. Allie closed her eyes and deepened the kiss. With intensely pounding pulse, but speechless from disbelief, Carl watched them taste each other. Miri's cheeks were still flushed, and her eyes dimmed before she closed them. She put her hands around Allie's shoulders as she raised up on her knees to close the distance between them, and Allie's hand, seemingly unconsciously, searched for Miri's breast. When she finally touched her, Miri moaned quietly. Carl's breaths shortened as a heatwave shot through his body and made him hard. Just as slowly as they had started, they separated and looked at each other, smiling,

488

breathing heavily, Allie still with tears glistening on her cheeks.

"That was nice," she said in a calmer voice, and Carl could hear the mild teasing. Apparently, Miri could too because she laughed.

"I thought so too," she admitted with a shy, but self-satisfied smile.

"First time?"

"Since I was ten, yes."

"Ten doesn't count," Allie smiled.

"Probably not," Miriam agreed.

"Want to try again?"

"Mhm."

This time, they were more confident when they met. Miri cupped Allie's face, Allie held Miri around her back and found the way in under her shirt, moving her hands gently over Miri's bare skin. Their tongues met again, and Carl found it hard to breathe. It didn't feel right to look, but he couldn't make himself look away. When Allie's hands moved around toward Miri's breasts and cupped them, caressing them, they all breathed harder, and Miri suddenly decided to take off her shirt. Carl stared at her hands as she unbuttoned it, showing her naked skin without feeling awkward, and a sweet, yearning ache spread in his body, made his pulse beat even faster. As soon as the shirt fell open in front of her, Allie broke the kiss and let her tongue glide down to the thin cotton of the bra, teasingly licking her at the edges while gently caressing her with her hands.

With a pleased sigh, Miri turned her head and saw him watching them. At first, she looked caught, but the next second, her eyes got a mischievous glint. She took his hand and pulled him in toward her mouth and kissed him, slowly, longingly. Her tongue tasted of both her and Allie. Muddled, he wondered how he could taste that, but he could. Smoothly, she squirmed out of Allie's embrace and stood up, squeezed herself in between Carl's back and the sofa, pressed herself against him. Her breasts caressed his back, and when her teeth grazed his neck, he inhaled sharply and closed his eyes for a moment. Allie's hands touched his thighs and sensually moved them up over his loins, in under his shirt while she leaned in toward his lips but didn't touch them. This time, she waited for his consent. The warm air on his lips from her hard, passionate breaths, together with Miri's nipping kisses on his neck, and their bodies pressing against him, almost drove him crazy.

Without thinking, he closed in on Allie and touched her lips. It felt as if she melted under him. Her breaths were so warm, her lips so soft and her tongue so eager. *I've missed her kisses,* he thought, dazed. Then, her fingers touched his nipples, and he jerked with a harsh breath. Both women giggled in an expectant tone that made him blush before they met over his shoulder and kissed each other again, long, slow kisses. Miri's fingers started to unbutton his shirt, and he turned his head and kissed her exposed neck. She shuddered and smiled; her lips pressed toward Allie's.

It seemed as if none of them dared to talk to not break the spell they suddenly were under. Carl's shirt was open, and Miri's fingers tangled with Allie's as they caressed his nipples, and he moaned. Allie broke the kiss and leaned down, took the closest nipple between her lips and licked it. *Oh, God...* His hands seemed to work on their own as he tugged off Allie's shirt and she straddled him, letting her bra fall to the floor. With trembling hands, he caressed her full, soft breasts and took first one and then the other in his mouth, licking, slowly sucking, and she moaned and moved on top of him, making the sweet, throbbing ache in his loins almost unbearable.

Miri's voice was deeply aroused when she said, "Let's go into the bedroom. There's more space there."

She squirmed out from behind him, and while she walked, she unbuttoned her jeans and wiggled out of them. Her underwear and bra fell to the floor, and completely naked, she kneeled on the bed, waiting for them.

There wasn't a lot of sleep that night. Sometime around four a.m., they cuddled up together under the duvet, naked, satisfied, calm, and happy, and slept for two hours before the CD-alarm went off. Still muddled from lack of sleep, Carl turned it off.

"Why do we always do things like this when it's a workday the day after?" he muttered.

Allie laughed quietly on his right side, and Miri smiled where she lay on his left.

"Sounds like there's a story behind those words," she teased, and Carl couldn't help but blush.

He leaned down and kissed first Miri and then Allie before he stumbled up and into the bathroom for a well-deserved shower.

Chapter 30

They managed to be at HQ at eight-fifteen, hollow-eyed and yawning. Olwen paced back and forth in the briefing room with her constantly worried expression painted on her face. She looked rather relieved when they stepped inside, but then she scrutinized them.

"Have you been up all night? Seriously! I need you on top, not muddled by sleep deprivation…" Her voice trailed away as she stared at something on Carl's neck.

Awkwardly, he put his hand there but couldn't feel anything weird. Her gaze wandered to Allie and Miriam, who tried too hard at looking innocent.

Olwen got blushing red in her face and turned her back to them. "Anyway, not my business, is it?" she muttered, still with her back at them.

They shared a look, and both women had a hard time hiding a smile as they glanced at Carl's neck. *What the hell?*

"What?" he mouthed, and they both laughed at him in almost complete silence to not gain Olwen's attention.

Miri leaned in and whispered in his ear, "You have love bites all over."

His hand flew up again and covered his throat as he blushed violently. "No…" He glanced accusingly at them. "You could've said something, for crying out loud."

Allie grinned. "Sorry, didn't see it. Must've been too tired."

Miri took pity on him. "You must have extra clothes in your locker, Carl. Go down and change."

He nodded relieved, thinking about the bottle-green turtleneck shirt he saw in there last time he looked.

"I'm just, um, going to—" He pointed vaguely at the door when Olwen glared at him, and with a sense of embarrassed relief, he slipped through the door, still holding his hand protectively over the bites. Now when they'd

492

pointed them out, he could feel how tender he was, and his cheeks burnt with embarrassment that Olwen had seen it.

Fifteen minutes later, he was back with the shirt hiding his bruised neck. After seeing himself in a mirror, he couldn't believe that he hadn't noticed the love bites back home. *Next time I'm checking it.* He blushed heavily at the thought of a next time, but cleared his voice, pushed the thoughts to the back of his mind and concentrated on Olwen instead.

"Heard anything from Bernard?" he asked in an elaborated neutral voice.

She glared at him without meeting his eyes, but looked away and exhaled, clearly thinking about Omega. "She's awake, but she doesn't talk. Dr. Bernard says she's going to be fine, physically, and that she's not addicted. As far as he could tell, it was her first time. No needle marks, nothing. I've filed a report blaming Night Porter. We don't want to lose a good FR."

They all nodded.

"So, now what?" asked Miriam. "Where do we go from here? I know you want to try and close the portals, but I don't know if it's possible."

Olwen gave her a tired look. "Why do you say that?"

"Because these vibrations that open the portals are everywhere around us. Some are just more powerful than others, and as far as Carl and I've been able to figure it out, anyway, they react to people's trauma or strong, negative feelings. If I concentrate, I can feel them around me all the time. I guess it's because I'm aware of them now in another way than I was before."

"That's horrible," Allie mumbled beside him.

Carl glanced at her. As he suspected, she was quite pale.

Olwen looked at Miriam, clearly worn-out. "I know you're all on first-name basis, but please, can we use the FR-names? It makes it easier for me."

493

Miriam looked embarrassed. "Yes, sorry," she mumbled.

"What about me?" Allie asked bluntly. "You're treating me as if I'm part of your team, but first of all, I haven't attended the Star Student program, and secondly, you haven't even asked me if I want to be a part of this."

"You're right," Olwen agreed. "I've come to the conclusion that you've seen so much of this Project by now that you're more or less part of our team anyway. Like this, we can keep an eye on you if Night Porter indeed has an agenda against you. You won't be alone. If anything happened to you and I had a chance to prevent it, but didn't... I never would be able to forgive myself. It's only for this Project."

Allie nodded slowly. "Makes sense. Could you inform my supervisor, Dean Henderson at homicide, about this?"

"Absolutely. I'll do it directly after this briefing."

"Thank you... Olwen."

She got a rare smile back. "My pleasure, Odette." Olwen looked at Carl. "I understand you have a meeting with Jeremy Kane tomorrow at ten?" He nodded. "Do you need some references? I'd be happy to provide you with one if you want me to."

Pleasant surprise flashed through him, and he smiled genuinely at her. "Thank you, Olwen. I don't know yet, but if he asks, I'll refer to you."

She nodded and looked them over. "Okay. Anything else that needs briefing, but doesn't have anything to do with the Project?" They all shook their heads. "Okay. When I spoke with Armand, our task was to close the portal at Kroger's. Now, there's a portal at your apartment, as well, Ophelia, and maybe in Florence Tyler's, and you tell us it might not be possible to close them."

Allie looked confused. "But what about the portal at Carl's, um, sorry, Octavius' place?"

Miriam looked embarrassed again. "It's, um, it's the same. Um, I, uh, didn't lead us home to me. I... I don't like my apartment very much anymore." Apparently unaware of it, she rubbed the scar in her hand.

"Oh, okay." Allie looked slightly confused but swallowed the questions she had.

There was a frown on Olwen's forehead as she leaned toward the table. "So, there's one portal at Kroger's we know of, maybe one at Florence Tyler's place, and one confirmed at Octavius' apartment? None at yours? Is that correct?"

"Yes."

"And you don't think we're able to close them?"

"Not… not really. I mean, the vibrations will always be there, and the portal will be dormant until someone whose feelings correlate to Night Porter's realm comes close. At least that's my theory."

Olwen nodded thoughtfully. "Mhm. It sounds plausible." She sighed again. "Well, I don't know what to do then, except write a report to the Faculty and let them take it from here." She looked down at her notebook on the table, resigned and worried.

None of them spoke a word, and Carl tugged at his hair.

Suddenly, there was a shift in Olwen's demeanor, and when she looked up at Miriam, it was with a new light in her eyes. "Or, do you think that *you* could close it, Ophelia? You seem to be in tune with them. Can you §convince the portal to disappear?"

Miriam looked dumbstruck. "I don't know. Maybe. I haven't thought about it that way before."

With a broad smile, Olwen straightened up. "Okay, I'll just talk with Mr. Henderson, and then we'll give it a try at Kroger's. Meet me at the main entrance. I'll be with you shortly."

Not daring to hope, they looked wide-eyed at each other as Olwen exited.

"Can it— Can it be that easy?" Allie asked with a skeptical tone in her voice.

Miriam smiled affectionately at her but touched the head wound that had finally healed enough to be covered by pink skin.

"I wouldn't call it easy, but it'd be worth it. I doubt it would stop Night Porter, but at least people wouldn't step into his realm by accident anymore."

Allie exhaled. "That would be a great achievement, Miri. Wow, I hope it works."

"Mm, me too."

Together, they took the stairs down to the main entrance and stepped outside, basked in the sunshine that for once held some warmth.

Olwen joined them within twenty minutes. "It's all clear," she smiled at Allie. "He was a bit surprised and then a bit worried, but he didn't have any objections."

"Thank you," Allie said again, but Olwen just waved the remark away.

"Let's take my car," she said. "I don't want any of us to be on our own."

Carl took the seat beside her while Allie and Miriam occupied the back.

As soon as they started driving, Carl turned toward her. "Did you find anything useful at the library yesterday?" he casually asked and watched her closely. Immediately, a faraway expression covered her face, and this time, she didn't even seem to be aware of him asking. He glared at her. *Damn great defense mechanism. She'll never know about it.*

He tugged at his hair and looked out of the window instead. They would probably never get to know what had happened at the library. Maybe she was a walking catastrophe waiting to happen, but there didn't seem to be any way of finding out. No one spoke during the ride. Everyone sat silently in their own thoughts.

To Carl's concern, Olwen appeared withdrawn all the way to Kroger's. They parked outside the cordoning, and it wasn't until Olwen opened the trunk and brought out her doctor's bag that the withdrawn air disappeared. Hastily, she

496

ushered them along. They showed their badges to the security guard and were immediately let in. With determined steps, Olwen headed toward the basement.

Carl glanced at Miri's closed face. "Are you nervous?" he asked, but bit his tongue. *Stupid question. Of course, she is.*

Miri nodded. "Not so much for trying to close the portal," she said, "but I don't want the wound to re-open again. I'm tired of being injured all the time."

"The wound in your head?" Allie quietly asked at her other side. When Miri nodded again, she continued with a worried frown, "Did you get it because you tuned into the vibrations? I thought you got it during the explosion."

"I… don't remember… It's all a blur, the memories…"

Carl and Allie glanced at Miriam's somewhat clenched face, and Allie changed the subject. "So, you said you live close. Can we see your apartment from here?"

"Mm…" She looked around and pointed to a medium-high apartment complex, painted in white. "Mine's on the other side, though."

"Finished sight-seeing?" Olwen bitingly asked as they approached her, and Miriam blushed, embarrassed.

Carl glared at Olwen, but she didn't take notice. Instead, she hurried down into the basement. *Yeah, she and C might suit each other like hand in glove, seeing as how much they both enjoy bossing people around and embarrassing them under the pretense of lecturing them.*

The women climbed down the ladder and Carl followed them. Olwen had lit her flashlight, and the narrow light shone on the cracked walls. Alarmed, he discovered that he could see the vibrations this time, faintly golden in color. He frowned worriedly. *My fault, I swear. Shouldn't have opened it yesterday.* He scoffed when he realized what he was thinking. *Yeah, would you rather have had Allie walking out of your life? You know you'd open it again if you could re-live that part.*

"Ophelia, do your thing." Olwen's voice sounded more demanding and frantic than Carl thought necessary.

497

He scowled again. It was what they were here for, after all.

Miriam looked pale. "Um… Okay… I need some calm around me, I think." The anxiety emanated from her in waves.

Carl wanted to take her in his arms to calm her down, but with Olwen watching, it might give a signal that Miri was weak, and that was the last thing she needed right now.

"Can you… can you all move a couple of steps back, please?" Miriam said. "I… I need some space…"

They did as she asked, and when everything was quiet around her, she hesitantly walked up to the shimmering vibrations. For a few seconds, she stood and watched them before she reached out her hand and placed it inside the vibrations. Somehow, Carl thought that he could see them sway happily and welcoming around her hand, and the sight made goosebumps appear all over his body.

Inhaling, Miriam closed her eyes and stretched her arms to the sides, like a T. As Carl watched, the vibrations spread out along her body. She moved her arms inwards as if hugging them, and they were dancing in her embrace. She breathed slowly, calmly, looking as if she ventured into some sort of trance. For a while, nothing happened. Miri stood there, breathing deeply, with her arms creating a circle in front of her. The thought that she soon had to feel the strain of holding them up like that touched Carl's mind, but she didn't seem bothered by it. Then, something happened. At first, he couldn't point out what was changing, but soon he saw how the vibrations began to calm down in her embrace, and slowly changing color from faint golden to deep bluish-green, like the ocean. Gradually, he became aware of a slight humming sound that began to disappear, and he realized that it had been there the whole time, but it had been so in tune with him that he hadn't even noticed it.

In a slow movement, she embraced the vibrations even tighter to her chest, and it looked like they shifted together, clustered, and became thinner until they finally disappeared together with the humming sound, and everything was still and quiet and calm.

Some seconds went by as Carl tried to comprehend what had happened. Suddenly, Miriam stumbled. Before he was even aware of it, he was at her side, holding her up. She was limp in his arms, and even though she was so petite, he had problems keeping her unconscious body upright. *Doesn't matter. I really don't want to put her down on the floor.*

Allie hurried up to them, clearly overwhelmed, and helped him holding her.

"Is she bleeding?" he asked in a strained voice.

Allie took a quick look. "Yes, a lot."

"Damn it!" Carl exclaimed. "Olwen, we need you!" There was no answer. He made an attempt to look over Miri's head, but couldn't see her. "Olwen?" When he still didn't get an answer, he frowned irritated. "What's she doing, Allie?"

Allie stopped trying to stem the bleeding and looked at the side. She gave a harsh gasp. "She's collapsed!"

"What? Damn it! Alright, I'll move around, you put Miri on my back, and I'll carry her up. You check Olwen."

"Are you sure you can get her up?"

"I have to try."

Allie nodded, and with mutual effort, they managed to get Miri up on Carl's back without her falling off. With one hand holding Miri in place, he tried the ladder. *God, Allie's right; this won't work. And what the hell happened to Olwen?*

After a couple of attempts, he had to admit defeat. It wouldn't work. She was too limp. Even though he loathed the thought of putting her down on the floor, he had no other choice. As soon as he got her down in a recovery position, he took off his jacket and put it under her head. It bled badly. *I hate this head wound! I just hate it!*

Quickly, he went over to Allie, who was trying to wake up Olwen without succeeding.

"I don't know," she said in an anxious voice. "I have no idea why she's not responding."

He kneeled and checked Olwen's pulse. It seemed normal. The color of her face was normal, as well. She breathed. Her body temperature wasn't off.

He shrugged and hauled out his cell phone. "Here, call Dr. Bernard. Tell him it's FRT O, and we need him here ASAP."

Allie nodded and climbed up to get some reception, while Carl grabbed Olwen's doctor's bag and hurried over to Miriam again. He rummaged around until he found a piece of gauze, opened it, and gently pressed it toward the head wound. In the background, he heard Allie's surprisingly calm voice explaining the situation to Bernard. The gauze bled through quickly, and he unwrapped another one.

Allie came down and handed him his phone before checking on Olwen again.

"I can't do anything more for her," she said after a couple of minutes and crouched by Miri's side. "I've put her in the recovery position. Dr. Bernard will be here within half an hour, he promised."

"Good."

"How bad is it?"

"If it's following the pattern, it shouldn't be bad. It's just some kind of sign that she's too strained. Olwen wasn't terribly worried before."

"Okay."

"We need to put some pressure on it, though, to stop the damn bleeding. Let's put her on her back and let her head do the pressure. It worked last time." Together, they managed to turn Miriam around without any major commotion.

"Good thinking," Allie said. "It's not my forte, this healing-people-thing."

In the midst of everything, Carl managed to laugh. "I have a feeling I'm doing something wrong here too. Don't really remember the last first aid course I took…" His voice trailed away as he worriedly watched Miri's pale face. "You know what?" he said as a sudden thought struck him. Allie shook her head. "You're pretty good at healing people's feelings, in my opinion, and that's something very special, don't you think?"

She put her hand on his. "Thank you," she said simply, and he squeezed her hand. She looked at where the vibrations had been. "Did you see what she did?" Her voice was astounded.

"I think so."

"She closed the portal, I'm sure. She's amazing, Carl."

A soft, loving smile appeared on his lips. "I know."

"I don't know if I'd be able to do something like that."

"You haven't been forced to try yet. Hopefully, you won't."

"Yeah, you're right. It was just so amazing to see how she handled it. It was as if she, I don't know, lullabied them to sleep."

"That's a nice way of describing it," he smiled and caressed Miri's cool cheek. "Can you check on Olwen again, please? I don't want her to suddenly die on us or something."

"You think she could?" The anxious tone was back in her voice as she stood up and walked over to Olwen.

"Seems unlikely, but—" He fell silent.

"But, indeed. No, she's still fine. Can't feel any fever, pulse seems normal, she breathes. Weird, don't you think?"

"Did you see her collapse, Allie?"

She came back to him again. "No. She was behind me."

He grimaced. "Wish I knew what's going on—" He stopped himself. "I've said that a lot lately, haven't I?"

Allie embraced his arm, trying to comfort him. For a while, they sat in silence, worriedly keeping watch over Miri and Olwen.

Eventually, Dr. Bernard climbed down to the basement with sisters Blaise and Banafshe in tow. His hair had turned white during the past two years, but his eyes were as kind as always, and the deeper laugh-lines suggested that he still found things to laugh about in life. He greeted Carl as an old friend, as usual, even though they only met when Carl needed to be stitched up in one way or another, and amiably shook Allie's hand. Then, he turned his attention to Miriam and Olwen.

"I need to take her in," he said after checking Miriam's head wound. "I don't like the way it looks. What did she do?"

"Um, I'm not sure," Carl said awkwardly, even though it wasn't entirely a lie.

"Of course not." Dr. Bernard winked at him and knelt at Olwen's side. "Seems like she's in some kind of coma," he said after a while and glanced at Carl. "Guess you don't know what she did, either."

Carl tugged at his hair. "I don't. After we tried to help Miriam, she was just lying there. Neither of us noticed when she collapsed."

Dr. Bernard rubbed his chin. "Interesting. Well, let's get them on their way. They won't get any better by lying around here."

Twenty minutes later, both Miriam and Olwen had been taken away.

"What do you mean, I can't come?" Carl asked edgily, trying to hide the frustrated tone in his voice, but failed.

"Carl, my little clinic is full of your teammates. You're just going to be in the way. I promise I'll let you know when she's awake."

"Even if it's in the middle of the night?"

Dr. Bernard gave him an amused look. "You know she won't let me call you then."

Carl puffed frustrated and ran his hand through his hair, knowing he was right.

Dr. Bernard placed a friendly hand on his shoulder. "I'll call you as soon as she's awake. I'll let you know when Sally's waking up, as well. And, if you want some advice, Carl, you and your teammate here look like you could use some sleep."

"Yeah, I know," Carl muttered. Then, Dr. Bernard surprised him by reaching for his hand and shake it.

"Congratulations on your upcoming marriage, Carl. You've made a splendid choice, and she's going to give you a hell of a ride."

"She already does," he replied, feeling a weird sense of pride.

"Of course, she does. All great women do. Now, if you'll excuse me, I'm going to make sure she won't let you wait too long for that ride to begin again."

When he got into his car and drove away, Allie smiled. "What a sweetheart he is."

"Goddamn!" Carl suddenly exclaimed.

"What?"

"I don't have my car."

"Oh, shoot! Well, no big deal. We'll take a taxi to your place. My car's still there. If you don't mind me staying, I'll drive you to Dr. Bernard when Miri's awake."

"Thanks. You want to eat something first, or you want to make pasta at home?"

"Pasta sounds great." She gave him a look. "You're cross."

"Yeah. I wouldn't have been in the way."

She smiled half-teasingly. "I think you would've. You love her too much to not be in the way." Carl muttered something foul under his breath, but she didn't let that stop her from putting her arm supportively around him. "Let's call that taxi now."

Chapter 31

Carl knew that he was silly, but he felt trapped, like an animal in a cage. He should be happy, feeling safe knowing Miri was in good hands and finally getting proper care, but he just wanted to be there with her, sitting at her side, holding her hand, just— just be there, goddammit! Instead, he sat on the sofa in his living room, trying to compose a damn report to the Faculty.

Eventually, Allie closed the lid of her laptop, placed it on the table, and turned toward him, slightly frustrated.

"What?" he snapped.

"You're huffing and puffing and pulling your damn hair and checking the damn time every effing minute. She's not going through labor, you know."

He glared at her. "No, if she were, I wouldn't be here. How the hell can I be in the way if I'm just sitting beside her damn bed? It's been five hours! She should be awake by now!"

Allie sighed. "I don't think you have to worry. From what you've told me about Dr. Bernard, it makes me quite certain she's in great hands. He promised to call you, and he will."

"Goddamn!"

"You want to take a walk?"

"A walk? Why?"

"To think about something else, of course. Or we can have sex. We have consent now. Or we can catch a movie. Just something else. You're driving me crazy going on like this."

He felt like throwing the stupid laptop out of the window, but instead, he just shoved it on the table and tried to calm down.

"I don't want to go anywhere," he muttered grumpily, feeling silly.

Allie rolled her eyes at him. "I assume he has your cell phone number, right? And we don't need to go far, just around the block or something."

"Yeah… I don't know…"

She exhaled frustrated. "Okay, let me give you a blowjob, then."

His head jerked up, and he stared at her. "Allie! Goddammit!"

"Finally, a reaction. Put on your shoes. I don't care what you say. You need to do something."

Grumpily, he did as she said, muttering under his breath the whole time.

She took his arm as they left the building and walked down the street. The wind was chilly and brisk again, and the afternoon sun was bleak and distant.

Carl breathed deeply and felt some of the irritation melt away.

"Thanks," he said, still ill-tempered, even though he tried to hide it. When she laughed at him, he wondered why he still bothered. It wasn't as if she couldn't read him like a damn book anyway.

They walked in silence for a while, looking through windows at the different stores.

When they passed a Starbucks, Allie tugged at his arm. "Coffee? Or tea? Something to warm you up with anyway, I think."

"Alright."

They went in. The line wasn't terribly long, and soon they enjoyed hot coffee as they continued to walk down the street, turning toward the small Ellerslie Park. They had it more or less on their own, except for a few people who were walking their dogs. The weather did not lure out many people today.

"Okay, so now when I'm part of your team," Allie said as they sat down on a bench, watching a few ducks swimming in the pond, "are your cases still classified? I'm still curious about that scar on your back, you know."

505

"They're called Projects, not cases," he said meticulously, and she rolled her eyes, but a smile played on her lips. It soon died away, and she shuddered.

"You two, you have so many scars. It's frightening."

"Yeah, I guess we have."

"So, can you tell me?"

He thought about it for a moment, before shrugging. "Sure. It was one of all the numerous times when I was stupid."

"Hey, come on! Don't try to make me believe that."

A reluctant smile forced its way out on his lips, and with his arm around her shoulders, he squeezed her tighter.

"I'm not indulging in some kind of misleading misery here. Just ask Miriam or Caesar. I still can't believe he kept me after that incident."

"So, what happened? Come on, you're just making me beg you."

He laughed at her and placed a kiss on her temple. "Sorry, it's just hard to talk about, because I was so damn stupid. Probably shouldn't have been in that RP from the beginning. It was too early."

"RP, that's Research Project, right?"

"Yeah. Anyway, I got transferred to C in January of that year. They'd lost Cecilia during the previous Project and had an open spot. Miri and Cecilia were quite close, as I understand it, and she was naturally very upset and grieving."

"And you had just been through that horrifying execution, right?" He nodded and managed to suppress a shiver. "I can see why you clashed."

"Yeah, it was a pretty bad start. Terrible start, actually. Anyway, we only met a couple of times, until May that year when C called us and briefed us on a Project here in town. Close to home. Great." Carl fell silent for a moment. "It was a murder case the local PD got stuck on. Too weird. Nothing made sense. Lots of different victims all over the city and no pattern, except all of them were ripped apart. Looked like an animal had done it, but it had to be a damn huge animal in that case, and no zoologist could identify the claw- and bite marks. It was all over the news, and the Chief of Police was damn near getting his retirement way too early. You probably heard about all of that, right?"

Allie nodded. "I was in my last year as a Ph.D. candidate and didn't have time to engage in it. What I did hear made me dismiss it since it wasn't presented as a serial killer case, more like 'the monster animal.' It didn't fit, you know."

"Yeah."

"Of course, I was curious, but I wrote my thesis."

"Mm, bet that takes a lot of time."

She laughed heartily. "You can say that again. Well, go on then," she nudged him when silence fell once more.

"It's a long story, lots of weird turns, but we managed to rule out some things after a couple of weeks, and we were closing in on the perpetrator. Miri and I had had one of our numerous stalemates, and I was angry. This was at the beginning of June, so quite warm."

"Mm, not like now," Allie said, and he became aware of her slightly shivering.

"Are you cold? We can go home."

"As long as you don't forget this story."

"Don't worry, I won't forget it." He gave up a humorless chuckle and guessed she could hear the bitterness at the bottom of it because she embraced him affectionately.

It only took them ten minutes of brisk walking before they were sitting on the sofa in Carl's apartment, warming up with a cup of tea each.

"Okay, so you and Miri had argued. What happened next?"

Carl sighed and tugged at his hair before realizing what he was doing and placed his hand onto his lap.

"This is the part I don't like to think about," he mumbled and looked down at his hands.

Allie scooted over to him and leaned into his chest. With a tender touch, she placed his arms around her before stretching out on the sofa, tangling her legs with his. It was comforting, and he rested his cheek on her head for a moment before he sighed again and continued, "Yeah, stupid indeed. Miri made me so damn angry. I don't even remember what she said, but God, did she touch my nerves! So, I decided I was going to show her that I wasn't a newbie." He shook his head in self-disgust, and Allie kissed his hands. "We had found the area where we thought he operated from, but C was hesitant of going in before we knew more. I don't know what I was thinking. I mean, C was a great leader back then, before the Alaska Project, and I trusted him a lot, looked up to him as I haven't with any other team leader, not even Ned. Despite that, I went in on my own with only my gun, my knife, and my rifle."

"You… you went in on your own…? Against something that had killed so many people?"

Carl smiled harshly. "Now you know why I don't like to think about it."

There was a slightly astounded pause before Allie said, "I guess you found it."

"Yeah… It had its lair somewhere deep down in the sewers. I had a map that I followed and a headlight I used until the last ten minutes. I'm a pretty good sniper, so I thought I'd sneak up on him and put a bullet in his head. Simplicity at its best. It didn't really work out that way." He moved uncomfortably on the sofa as his pulse raced and his breaths got shallower. A thin layer of sweat broke out on his face. Allie kissed his hands again before she placed them on her breasts. He looked down at her, feeling slightly confused. "Uh, what?"

"Just distracting you, so you don't get lost in those memories. You're getting pretty upset."

"Yeah, I guess…" He inhaled deeply and caressed her breasts. "It seems to work," he said with a wry smile when he felt calmer by the nearness and her warmth.

She snuggled in at his neck, placing her hands over his. "Good. What happened then?"

"Well…" He exhaled and saw the scene in his mind's eye; the burning fire in the barrel, the latest victim lying tossed in a heap on the floor, completely unrecognizable, and the creature sitting beside it, enjoying the victim's arm as a meal. "It was the first time I saw something that wasn't human. I knew other teams had met non-human entities before, but I always thought the stories were exaggerated. You know, kind of like when you're at summer camp and the leaders tell you ghost stories you know aren't real." Allie nodded. Her body was tense in his arms, and it was not from arousal. Her hands held his in a cramped grip. "Who needs distraction now, eh?" he mumbled at her head and caressed her soothingly again.

She took a deep breath and laughed shakily while trying to force herself to relax without succeeding. "Kiss me, please?" she asked in a small voice, and he obliged her, feeling the need for distancing himself from the memories too. When they let go, she exhaled and fell back down on his chest, but kept his hands firmly in place. "Okay, you can go on now."

"Are you sure you want to hear the rest? It's pretty gruesome."

"Probably not, but karma's a bitch, and I asked for it."

"Alright." He tried to recollect his thoughts. "Um, so this, uh, this creature was sitting by a barrel with a fire burning, chewing away on an arm—" Allie shuddered and tensed again, and without thinking, he caressed her as he started to get lost in the memories after all. "He, if it was a he, had a…. a head formed like a… a combination of a… a dog and a human, with a muzzle and pointy ears, but human forehead and eyes. God, I must have made a sound or something because the… the thing looks up and sees me, and then, um, it drops the damn arm and starts coming toward me, and I, uh, I can't get my damn muscles to move. I'm, uh, I'm just standing there, rifle in hand, head in clear sight, and—I—can't—move." Allie let out a painful moan, and Carl realized that he had clasped her breasts in a hard grip. "God! Oh, my God, I'm sorry, Allie!" Hurriedly, he let go and sat up before touching her gently again, trying to make sure she was fine.

She laughed breathlessly. "It's okay. There were layers in between. No harm done."

Awkwardly, he placed his hands on her shoulders instead. "I'm still ashamed. God… Never intended to hurt you—"

"Shh, I know that. It's okay. Promise." Determinedly, she placed his hands on her breasts again. "See? No problem. Go on now. Get it over with."

He nodded and swallowed. This time, he tried to stay in the present when he continued talking. "I think what saved me was that it went for the rifle first. When he took it and threw it away, I saw the claws; huge, scary claws, and I knew how all the people had died. I finally managed to get my feet moving. First, I just staggered backward, you know, couldn't get myself to turn my back on it, but then, I finally realized I needed to do that if I was to get away."

"And that's when he grabbed you?" Allie's voice was faint on the brink of trembling.

Very aware of what he was doing, he caressed her gently and kissed her temple. "No. I'm quite sure I'd be able to get away at this point, if, uh, if I hadn't decided I needed to shoot it." Allie groaned, and now, he could laugh at it. "Yeah, I know. Not my smartest move ever." He fell silent and leaned his cheek on her silky hair for a moment. "So, I turn around, and he's actually some feet away, so I grab my gun, and I shoot it, and I hit it in the shoulder. He yells… God, that sound…" Carl shivered. "And I empty my mag, and he falls—"

"He falls?"

"Yeah. I want to make sure he's dead, so I walk toward it—"

"Carl!"

"Told you I was stupid."

"I know, but seriously?"

He chuckled at her disappointed tone. "Ruining your dream about the white knight, am I?"

"Ruining it? God, I'm devastated." She smiled at his throat and kissed him lightly.

He couldn't help laughing at her, and the atmosphere in the room wasn't as dark anymore. Then, the laughter died away, and Carl looked back into his memories, feeling the agony and unbelievable pain once more.

When he started to talk again, his voice was strained. "So, I stand there, touching it with my foot, when another one puts those claws into my back." Allie gasped. "Never thought there could be more than one. It never crossed my mind. Not once." He exhaled and moved around a little. "At that point, I was still kind of conscious. It held me with its claws deep into my back and dragged me over the floor. God, the pain..." His voice trailed away, and in the silence, Allie's strained breaths were clearly heard. "It's weird how much pain you can take... more than you believe yourself capable of... before you go under."

Allie moved and turned around, kneeled in front of him, and put her hands on his face. Her eyes were moist and pained for his sake. His heart made an extra beat.

"Carl, you don't have to talk about it if you don't want to. I— I didn't realize—"

With a tender gesture, he put his finger on her lips. "It's alright, sweetie. It's alright. It's long ago now."

She kissed his finger before moving it away without letting go of his hand. "Three years. Not that long."

An affectionate smile appeared on his lips. "Long enough."

Hesitantly, she leaned in and kissed him before slanting back again, watching him seriously. "How did you get away? I mean, obviously, you did."

"Well, at that point, I'd lost consciousness since long, but Miri got one of these urges to apologize. She used to get them quite often before, very annoying, honestly, but she was so damn insecure back then. Anyway, when she didn't get a hold of me, she got suspicious for some reason – she's got great instincts, always had – and told C I was missing. They found my gear gone and concluded I was a stupid twit that needed to be rescued."

"Good for you," Allie mumbled and caressed his hand.

"Yeah, I was very lucky. Apparently, the creature was just going to start to eat me when they arrived. They shot it and delivered me to Dr. Bernard, who stitched those claw marks."

He fell silent and thought about the aftermath, how C had given him a scolding he had never received either before or after from anyone, and how those creatures mysteriously had disappeared from the sewers. Miri and C had searched the tunnels without finding any trace of them, so either there were more of them who had moved the two dead ones – *if they were dead* – or they had just vanished. Whatever the case, they were never found again, but the killings had stopped – or at least no bodies had been found indicating these kinds of creatures were still active.

"And you believe I want to become part of the team with all these stories?" She shook her head with a slightly sad smile. "Not what I thought Star Students did. Why do you continue? I mean, seriously? Why do you do it?"

"To protect people. It's like the old device but taken a step further. Without us, there are more monsters out there, both human and non-human ones. We can at least try to make a difference. For me personally, I'm thinking a lot about Sarah, and it scares the hell out of me knowing what's lurking out there, knowing she could walk into one of these nightmares any day."

"Okay, that makes sense." She gave him a long, thoughtful look. "You know, even though what you did was really stupid, I kind of respect you for it."

"Really?" He laughed. "Why?"

"Because you're brave. Maybe Miri was the trigger that made you do it, but deep inside, I think you wanted to stop it, that it frustrated you Caesar held back."

Carl smiled, feeling touched, and took a strand of her hair between his fingers. "I think you're projecting, but I won't say it, 'cause it's really flattering and gives more fuel to my white-knight-delusion," he said, gently teasing her.

Her laughter was unexpectedly amused. "I just think you're brave, is all, whatever made you do it." She leaned in and gave him a light kiss on his mouth before moving away. "I'm getting hungry and tirederer. I want to eat and sleep. What about you? You want some more pasta?"

"'Tirederer'?" He laughed kindly, stretched, and stood up, holding out his hand toward her. "Let's fix it together."

They ate and went to bed early and slept loosely tangled together. Allie seemed to be having a good sleep, deep and calm, but Carl tossed and turned, waking up every now and then, checking the time, wondering why he hadn't heard anything from Dr. Bernard. He decided that if he hadn't gotten a phone call after his meeting with Jeremy Kane, he would go there, no matter what Bernard said. He needed to know, goddammit! *She can't be so injured it's dangerous, can she? She's not dying on me, right? Of course, she's not dying. Goddamn, stop it! Just stop it!*

Eventually, he gave up, caught a book he hadn't read for ages, and spent the rest of the night reading, just to have something to focus on. When the CD-alarm went off, he still felt this anxious energy bouncing around in his body, but his mind felt muddled and distant. *Great day to meet the head-zilla on. Just a great day... He'll think I'm on drugs or something, I swear.*

Allie read his emotions correctly, as usual, and adjusted to his mood by being calm and supportive. As they drove, she tried to re-direct his thoughts from the upcoming meeting and talked about the roleplaying game he still hadn't created a character for, but he had a sense that she somehow didn't feel as enthusiastic about the game as she had when they first met. He should probably ask why, but he couldn't focus.

Eventually, she gave him a penetrating look, and with a light kiss and a squeeze of his hand, she said, "Okay, I'm quiet from now on, so you don't get irritated."

"I'm just so, you know, jittery."

"No wonder. He'll be used to it, though. Everyone's jittery when they're meeting with him. And if you tell him Miri's injured, he'll get the picture. I'm sure it'll work out well in the end. I mean, who likes Alan Bai anyway?"

"His wife, I hope."

She giggled. "He's married? Oh, God..."

Although the butterflies in his stomach made him somewhat nauseous, he couldn't help laughing at her. "For seven years and they do have two kids together. He's very proud of their achievements."

"Well, good for him, I guess." She parked outside the minor FBI building where all the big shots had their offices. "I'll wait for you in the foyer."

A feeling of gratitude spread in his heart, and he kissed her gently. "Thank you. You're great support, you know that?"

To his surprise, she blushed and shied away with her gaze before composing herself. "Go now. Can't be late, you know."

He smiled, left the car, went in and over to the receptionist.

"Good morning. My name's Carl Hansen. I have a meeting with Mr. Jeremy Kane at ten today."

The elderly lady gave him a friendly nod. "He's waiting for you, Agent Hansen. Take the elevator to the third floor, turn right, and it's the second door on your left from there."

"Thank you."

The butterflies fluttered lively in his abdomen when he went over to the elevator. It opened immediately, and he stepped in. There was no mirror in there. *Damn it!* Nervously, he dragged his comb through his hair and pulled the turtleneck higher up to make sure none of the love bites showed. That's all he had time to do before the elevator stopped and he stepped out, following the receptionist's directions.

The door to Mr. Kane's office stood open and before knocking, Carl took a quick look inside. The room was tidy and held several potted plants, making it look quite inviting. The fit man at the desk was in his sixties with steel-gray hair and glasses with a thick frame.

"Come in, Carl." Apparently, he was also a great observer, Carl thought as he stepped in. Jeremy Kane stood up, came around the desk, and vigorously shook his hand. "Thank you for coming. Please, take a seat."

As Carl did what he asked, Jeremy Kane closed the door and sat down at the desk again. For a couple of seconds, they studied each other, and seeing the intelligent gaze that obviously didn't miss anything, Carl was once again thankful for the turtleneck shirt and that it was still chilly enough for him to wear it.

"I got your report, but I'd be grateful if you could explain the events in your own words."

Not a man who wastes time. Good to know. He decided that a short explanation was more in line with Mr. Kane's personality than a long flowery one.

"Yes, sir. I cleared debris at Kroger's when I found a victim who had been burnt to death. Some years ago— I'm sure you know that I've seen people being burned alive. Usually, I can compose myself if I know this is what I'm going to meet, but I didn't know. It took me by surprise. I lost consciousness for a short time and vomited afterward. Mike Jones from SWAT helped me away from the site. A week later, Agent Bai let me know he had gotten complaints about my behavior and said he couldn't keep me on as a profiler."

"Mhm. Is this something that happens regularly, that you get complaints?"

"No, sir."

"So, this was the first time?"

"Yes, sir."

Mr. Kane took a sheet of paper and looked through it. "Agent Alan Bai told me that your work performance has been slipping during the past six months."

A sudden shock hit Carl at Kane's words, but it immediately gave way to anger. He carefully composed himself and kept his mouth shut to not say anything that could tip the scale to his disadvantage.

Mr. Kane glanced at him. "Would you agree with that statement?"

"No, sir."

"And has he given you any reason to think you might be asked to hand in your resignation?"

"No, sir, on the contrary."

"Please, tell me."

"As late as the day I interviewed Ariel Wing, that was April twentieth, Agent Bai called me and told me he was very pleased with my performance and its leading to my involvement in *The Greek Tragedy Killer*-case."

"As I understand it, you were requested by Dr. Allie Harris to participate in this particular case. Is that correct?"

"Yes, sir."

"Did you know her before this case?"

"No, sir."

"So, you would say she would be objective when it comes to this particular investigation?"

Carl managed to not squint in suspicion. There was a trap here somewhere. "I, uh, I hope so, sir."

"Mhm. And you managed to solve this case together."

"Yes, sir."

"Was there any friction between you and Dr. Harris during this time?"

Carl tried desperately to keep a neutral face and met Mr. Kane's scrutinizing gaze with an honest look of his own. "No, sir."

"Would you say that Dr. Harris is objective when it comes to Agent Bai?"

Carl swallowed nervously. It would be impossible to answer that question honestly without her losing all credibility. "I… don't know how much they've been associating, sir."

"That was not the question, Carl. Would you say that Dr. Harris is objective when it comes to Agent Bai?"

"I… I hope so, sir."

Mr. Kane gave him a piercing glance, and Carl forced himself to not squirm on the chair.

"Are you in a relationship with Dr. Harris, Carl?"

It felt as if a stone had hit him in the head. For a moment, he stared at Mr. Kane. With a deep intake of breath, he tugged at his hair, immediately realizing that he practically admitted their relationship by this gesture. "Is that of importance for this investigation, sir?" he asked to stall for time.

Jeremy Kane was not fooled by this as he put down his paper and gave him a neutral look. "I've heard implications that Dr. Harris might not be objective as a witness to this incident between you and Agent Bai because of her recent intimate relationship with you."

"I'm sorry?" *Who the hell said that? No one could've known about it. God, don't tell me Alan has spied on me?* He let the suspicion go with some effort but felt distressed by the nagging thought.

"Would you agree?"

"No, sir. I don't think Dr. Harris would try to steer an investigation in favor of someone."

"Consciously."

Carl kept quiet.

After a last penetrating look at him, Mr. Kane brought out another sheet of paper, but it was clear that

517

Allie's statement held little validation now. "I've been led to believe that Agent Bai was stressed out during the weeks of the Kroger's incident. Would you agree?"

Alright, tread carefully now.

"Agent Bai is a profiler, sir, and not used to handling a situation like the one at Kroger's."

"That is a 'yes,' I take it?"

"He probably felt out of control in that situation, yes."

"In your personal opinion, could his stress levels have affected his judgment of the incident with you?"

"That is possible, sir."

"But you don't agree."

"I— My personal opinion is that Agent Bai's stress levels could've had an impact on his judgment, but I couldn't say how high of an impact."

A faint smile touched Jeremy Kane's lips. "In your opinion, how did Agent Bai manage the first days of Kroger's?"

"I, uh, I'm not sure, sir."

"How come?

"He, uh, wasn't around a lot, at least not when I was there. The very first night, he worked with interviewing the surviving witnesses on site before they were transported to South Side Hospital where Sharon Wilkes and David Miller took over."

"And what were your orders during that night, Carl?"

He couldn't hinder an awkward blush covering his face. This was going south so quickly it wasn't even funny. "Agent Bai wanted me to join Ms. Wilkes and Mr. Miller at South Side Hospital."

"But you didn't. Why is that?"

"I... I wanted to find my co-worker, Special Agent Miriam Goldblum, who had been at the store during the bombing, sir."

"So, you refused to follow a direct order, is that correct, Carl?"

"I... I... Yes, that is correct, sir."

"Mhm." After another penetrating glance, Mr. Kane took up a new sheet of paper.

Carl wished he could wipe away the sweat from his forehead, but he didn't dare.

Still looking at the sheet of paper he held in his hands, Mr. Kane said, "I've been led to understand that Agent Bai has problems leading a unit, and an opinion that Agent Bai might not be suited for a management position has been expressed. What is your personal take on that?"

Kane looked up at him, and Carl tried hard to not show how surprised the question made him, but he had a distinct feeling that he failed. He couldn't suppress the curiosity of who had said that.

"I think there is some truth in that, sir."

"Why is that?"

His pulse raised and he had to take a deep breath before answering. "I don't want to put Agent Bai in any bad light, sir."

Mr. Kane put down the papers on the table in front of him and looked him straight in the eyes with a severe expression. "This is an important investigation, Carl, in which I must come to a decision about an employee's suitability of continuing as a Special Agent in Charge. It's especially important since the line of your work, together with the work of the CSI units, is the base of any investigation. If Agent Bai has wrongfully asked you to hand in your resignation, I need to know that. I've asked your colleagues the same question, and they answered honestly. Now, I need you to do the same. Is that clear?"

Carl swallowed and nodded. "It is clear, sir. I'd say that Agent Bai's talents might be better used in a full-time profiler position where he can concentrate on what he's truly good at instead of using his time as a manager, a position that he, in my opinion, is not suited for."

"And why would you say that he's not suited for a management position?"

Carl exhaled and rubbed his neck.

"Your honest opinion, Carl," Jeremy Kane reminded him.

Carl nodded. "Agent Bai seems to be very concerned about appearance, about how he and his unit look in other people's eyes. In my honest opinion, that concern takes away his focus from what he is supposed to do, and it has consequences for our unit's work performance. He also doesn't respect or acknowledge Ms. Wilkes' talents."

"Isn't she good at what she's doing?"

"On the contrary, sir, she's a great profiler, one of the best I've met."

"So, why would you say that Agent Bai doesn't respect her talents?"

Carl inhaled and decided to burn that bridge too. "Because Agent Bai doesn't respect women, sir."

Jeremy Kane gave him a long look, which Carl did his best to meet without shying away.

"Is there anything else you'd like to comment on when it comes to Agent Bai's capacity as a Special Agent in Charge?" Kane asked eventually.

"Only that he's not very good at handling people or perceiving situations, even though he's an excellent profiler, sir."

"Mhm. I'd like to ask you how you perceived the situation in which Agent Bai asked you to hand in your resignation."

Carl swallowed nervously. "I— I'd say that he was very displeased, sir."

"Because of your behavior on the site or your behavior at HQ? He told me that you had used, mm, 'vulgar' words."

Awkwardly, Carl shied away from his gaze. "I did, sir."

"Did you think it was necessary in that situation?"

Carl frowned at the memory. "Honestly, sir, I was too baffled and later too angry to choose my words properly. I might've used other words had I been prepared."

"Mhm. Did you hand in your resignation?"

"No, sir."

"Why?"

"It didn't feel right, sir. I didn't feel that I'd done something wrong."

"It seems that there's a tendency for disobedience from your side, Carl. Would you agree with that?"

Carl tugged at his hair and exhaled, feeling that what he said now could have a deeper impact on the decision than the other answers. "I—" He fell silent, searching for the right words. Mr. Kane watched him steadily. "Sometimes, when I get upset about a situation, especially a situation where someone seemingly on purpose tries to make me lose control, I lose my perspective. Under those circumstances, it happens that I do disobey an order."

"Mhm." Jeremy Kane picked up another sheet of paper, his face an unreadable mask. Carl felt the sweat as a thin layer on his face and neck and longed for a Kleenex. "You have good testimonials from Mr. Dean Henderson. He says that you take your work very seriously. Would you agree?"

"Yes, sir. I do."

"I also have people who say that you might take your work too seriously. They imply that you might not know when it is time to stop. Does that sound familiar to you?"

"I— Yes, I want to go home knowing I've done a job well, sir, that I've done the utmost and the best of the situation. If that means I might stretch my limit, it's something I must live with, but I, um, I wouldn't want it to irritate people or to have it impair my work performance."

"It might be something you need to think about in the future, Carl, that sleep is necessary for good progress at work."

"Yes, sir."

521

There was a slight pause in which Mr. Kane fiddled with his papers and seemed to try to come to a decision of some sort.

Eventually, he put down the report and looked Carl straight in the eyes. "I thought you'd like to know that Officer Michael Jones says it never was his intention to give an impression of complaint against you and that he's sorry this is the way it got perceived. He was worried about your condition, given your previous experiences, and asked Agent Bai if there was something else you could do. Would that be something in line with Officer Jones' personality, in your opinion?"

Finally, everything made sense! Carl couldn't help smiling, and his eyes became moist. "Yes, sir."

"Did you know that it was Officer Jones who had talked with Agent Bai, Carl?"

"No, sir, I didn't." Then, he frowned. "But it doesn't make sense, sir," he blurted out.

Jeremy Kane gave him an intrigued look. "Why is that?"

Carl squirmed uncomfortably on the chair. "Well, I'm sorry, sir, but I had my collapse on Monday the nineteenth, and I was away from Kroger's from the twentieth. Agent Bai didn't ask for my resignation until the Monday after. Officer Jones wouldn't have had any reason to talk to Agent Bai if I wasn't on-site. Why did he wait a whole week before he talked to me? In my opinion, he seemed to just have heard it."

There was an appreciative smile on Mr. Kane's lips. "Agent Bai explained to me that he hadn't listened to his answering machine at work for some time." In his mind, Carl hit his head against a wall. *God, what a stupid thing to admit!* "I think I have everything I need now. Do you have any questions for me, Carl?"

"How long will it take for the verdict to be reached, sir?"

"Not long now. Sometime this week. On Tuesday next week at the latest."

"Thank you, sir."

"You're welcome. It was nice meeting you, Carl, and I hope I'll see you again in a couple of days."

He stood up, and Carl followed the cue and shook Jeremy Kane's hand. Just then, there was a determined knock on the door.

"Yes?" Mr. Kane said and let Carl's hand go with an apologetic smile.

The door opened and Night Porter came in, dressed in a suit. The shock of seeing him here hit Carl violently in his stomach. A sinking sensation in his body made his head spin, and it felt as if he were going to faint. His body turned cold and weak, and his breathing was suddenly shallow.

"Message for you, sir," Night Porter said in his oily voice and handed Mr. Kane an envelope.

"Thank you, Samuel. Maybe you could escort Agent Hansen to the elevator."

"My pleasure, sir." Night Porter gave Carl an amused look. "If you come with me, sir."

Dazed, Carl realized that he didn't have a choice. Jeremy Kane had already turned his back on them and sat down at the desk with a faraway expression.

With a deep breath, Carl took a step over the threshold and saw with another shock that he was standing in Miri's room at the inn. Night Porter stood at the window, smiling at him. The full moon shone in on the floor and created mesmerizing patterns that tried to ensnare him.

"Welcome back, Carl. I've missed you."

Fear clawed in his stomach and made him shiver, and his throat burned with bile. The realization that he was here on his own, without the safety of his team pushed him to the brink of throwing up. He swallowed hard and took a couple of deep breaths to try to gain some control over his body.

"What— What am I doing here? What do you want with me?" His voice was strained, cracked.

A satisfied and almost thrilled look appeared on Night Porter's face as if he was the cat, and Carl was the mouse. "Oh, nothing in particular. Just having a chat with one of my favorite guests. As I said, I've missed you."

The underlying tone in the porter's voice sounded sinister and made Carl weak and nauseous again. Desperately, he struggled to get a grip on himself.

The clear pit-coal eyes that never let their gaze leave his were excited under the pretended earnest. "You left so quickly. I was very disappointed. You didn't even go to the masquerade ball as you promised." Night Porter tilted his head and looked expectantly at him. "Never promise anything here that you don't have any intention of keeping, Carl. That is very bad manners. Almost naughty, I'd say. Something that might need to be, well, punished even."

Carl paled, and his throat dried as waves of fear crashed over him.

Night Porter smiled broadly. "But what am I saying? Would this be a way to treat an old friend? Of course not. I just wanted to have a little chat and catch up on things. Glad to see you're doing well, Carl. Thank you for stopping by. I'm sure we'll see more of each other as time passes." He made a tiny gesture with his hand, and the door to the corridor opened silently, but the view was that of the foyer at HQ, and Carl could see Allie sitting with her laptop in the waiting area. With pounding heart and steps he tried hard to keep casual, he closed in on the door, fearing it would shut in his face.

Just as he put his hand on the cold door handle, Night Porter said in a rich, purring voice behind him, "You can't always keep an eye on the golden queen, Carl. Enjoy her as long as you can."

Chapter 32

As Carl stepped out into the foyer from the elevator, he felt weirdly dizzy and nauseous. *Wow, that interview must've been more stressful and intense than I thought, but he was exceptionally good. I usually don't get this caught. No wonder he's the head of the department. Anyway, it's finally over and done with. Now, I can concentrate on Miri.* As an afterthought, a small voice whispered in his head, *And Allie. Don't forget Allie.* He frowned, feeling oddly insecure and suddenly worried as if he needed to protect her. For a moment, he stood still, trying to catch that elusive sensation and turn it into something comprehensible, but when Allie looked up, saw him and waved, the sensation disappeared. He shook his head and walked over to her.

"How did it go? You look quite mushy."

He took her arm. "Let's talk in the car."

She shot him a worried glance. "Okay." As soon as they got into the car, Allie turned to him on the brink of being upset. "It didn't work out?"

He pulled his hair. "Honestly, I have no idea. It felt relatively alright at the end of the interview, but he's got a damn good poker face."

"So why are you looking so grim?"

"Except me looking like a damn fool during the whole thing? Well, the biggest issue is that your witness report doesn't have validation anymore because someone saw us together and told Kane we're having a thing going."

Surprised and appalled, she looked at him with slightly wide-open eyes. "Oh, damn it! And suddenly, I'm partial, right?" He nodded. Anger flashed across her face. "I hate gossipers! Just hate them!"

"Well, at this point, he's probably trying anything to put the blame somewhere else."

She gave him a long look. "You think it was Alan Bai?" she asked in a much calmer voice, but it was tinted with disdain.

"Who else would care enough to find out? We kissed at work, what, twice? Once in the briefing room and once in the parking lot late in the evening. Sharon might've worked late, but she'd never been able to restrain herself from teasing me. David wouldn't have said anything to Kane. Dean might, of course."

Allie shook her head. "If someone saw us, it must've been in the parking lot, and he usually doesn't work that late, at least not at the office. He's like you and takes his work home."

Carl scowled. "It shouldn't matter who said it, but it does. I feel spied on." He exhaled and tugged at his hair. "Whatever. He'd told Kane my work performance had gone down the past six months too."

"Seriously!" She was mad again, but her angry face smoothed out immediately. "But that won't fly. I'm pretty sure Dean would speak in your favor if he were asked."

"He was, and he did, and it seemed quite well received. Ah, well, I'm to know sometime this week, or on Tuesday at the latest, but, at this point, I'm not very hopeful. My disobeying Alan's orders came up. Twice. That doesn't look good."

Allie put a comforting arm around him. "Let's not dwell on it. Just guessing won't get us anywhere. We don't know what the others said, and what I said doesn't matter anymore. Let's go and check on Miri instead."

He nodded gratefully, and she started the car. As they drove, Carl went over the interview again and again in his mind, and for each time, it seemed worse than it had the time before, but he couldn't let it be. There was something else too that nagged at him, but he couldn't put his finger on what. It was something that had happened at the end of the interview. Whatever it was, not grasping it was about to drive him crazy.

When Allie stopped in front of Dr. Bernard's combined house and clinic, he sighed relieved and waited impatiently for Allie to park before he opened the door and stepped out. Allie came hurrying after him and grabbed his arm.

As they stepped into the clinic, Sister Blaise met them, serious looking as usual.

"Are you here for Pieretta or Sally or Miriam?" she asked in her emotionless, professional voice.

"Miriam primarily, but the other ones too."

Sister Blaise nodded. "I'll see if Dr. Bernard can see you now."

"Thanks, Blaise. How is she? Miriam, I mean?"

She just gave him a quiet look that made Carl ashen and feel sick to his stomach.

"I'll see if Dr. Bernard can see you," she said again and left them.

Allie tugged at his arm. "Don't look like that, Carl. She must be alright. Carl? Please?"

He couldn't answer. There was a daze in his head, and the lump in his throat would make him cry if he said anything. *She's dead.* He could hear Dr. Bernard's rapid footsteps as they approached in the corridor. *He never hurries.* When he came out to the small waiting room, his face was serious, and he came over and touched Carl's arm. *He never touches like that.*

"Carl." With a greeting nod, he turned toward Allie. "Allie. Come. Let's go to my office and talk."

Carl felt like a robot when he tried to get his feet to move, and Allie held his arm tightly as they followed Dr. Bernard. He showed them the chairs in front of the desk and sat down himself.

First, he fiddled with the pencil in front of him, but then he looked up at Carl. "Did you get my message?" he asked. Carl shook his head without being able to say anything. "Ah, I was afraid so." He paused and looked them over. "We had to execute a surgical debridement yesterday. She had a minor sandpit in her head."

"A sandpit?" Allie frowned, and Carl noticed that she held his hand.

"Yes, most likely from the Kroger's incident. The tissue around had started to become infected, and it could have become very bad hadn't we discovered it."

"Is she— Is she—" Carl couldn't say anything else, and Allie squeezed his hand.

"She's not in a critical condition, and it will not cause any brain damage since it hadn't reached the brain. For being a head injury, it's straightforward and easily fixed. For now, she's sleeping. She needs to rest, but I think she'll come around pretty soon. Maybe even tomorrow." He gave Carl a sympathetic look. "There's no need to worry, Carl. We got to her in time. Here." When Bernard handed him a box of tissues, Carl realized that he was crying silently.

"Can we see her?" Allie asked.

"A couple of minutes."

"And what about Olwen and Omega?"

"Olwen's still in a coma. We did a CAT scan on her and are awaiting the results. We won't know more until then. Omega's awake, but she doesn't talk. She's not at the clinic anymore. She needs psychological help to get over the rape, which honestly is one of the most brutal I've ever encountered, and we cannot give her the help she needs here." He stood up. "Come. Let's go see Miriam."

With a weird combination of anxiety and calmness, Carl followed Dr. Bernard. Allie held his arm, and it felt comforting in a way that nearly made him weep again. When Dr. Bernard opened a door and showed him into a tiny sickroom, Carl's throat clutched, and new tears fell. Miriam lay on her stomach with her head resting on the side. The back of her head was shaved, and gauze was neatly taped to the exposed area. Even though her face held some color and her breathing was calm, seeing her like this was heartbreaking. She looked so vulnerable without her hair.

Carl stepped in and kneeled by the bed, took her hand in his and kissed it, feeling that he had done this too many times during the past weeks.

"Hey, Miri," he mumbled since he didn't want the others to hear. "I miss you at home." With a deep breath, he made an effort to sound cheerful. "You did it, you know. You closed the portal. No more people will stumble in there anymore." Dr. Bernard waved at him from the doorway. "Need to go. Bernard is chasing me out, but he says you might come home tomorrow." He placed a gentle kiss on her temple and mumbled, "I love you, Miri."

When he left the room, he felt totally exhausted.

Dr. Bernard glanced at him. "When's the last time you slept properly?" Carl shrugged, feeling too drained to answer. "Go home, Carl. I'll give you a couple of sleeping pills. Take one early this evening, and I want you to take tomorrow off from work. Doctor's orders. I'll give you a doctor's note too."

Carl nodded and let himself be led out to the waiting area. Allie held his arm in a steady grip and glanced at him with a worried frown but didn't say anything. As soon as Doctor Bernard came back, he handed Carl the note and a jar of pills.

"Here, there are five pills in here; just enough to give you proper sleep a couple of days. They'll make you a little groggy, but won't cause any dependence, so they're safe to take this week. I would suggest you take them relatively early every evening, so your body has the chance to go through the artificial sleep and enter into natural sleep before your alarm goes off in the morning."

He nodded again, and Allie tugged at his arm. "Okay, I'll drive you home. Thank you, doctor."

"My pleasure, my lady," he said with a kind smile and raised an invisible hat for her. Her smile back was flirty, Carl noticed before she dragged him out to the car.

"I didn't understand how exhausted you are," she said in a worried tone when they sat in the car again.

He just sighed and shook his head. It felt like too much effort to even speak. With another worried frown, she started the car and drove him home.

As soon as she got him into the apartment and forced him to sit on the sofa, she said, "I'm going to run some errands, but I'll be back soon enough. Just try to take it easy, okay? Don't cook anything. I'll get you something when I'm out. Is it okay if I take your keys so I can get in again?"

He nodded and sank back into the sofa, putting his arm over his face, and he wasn't even sure that he heard her leave.

When he woke up again, the sun was beginning to set, and a heavenly aroma reached him from the kitchen. Breathing calmly, he realized that he felt more relaxed than before he fell asleep, and the exhausted brain fog had disappeared. He scooted up to half-sitting, noticing the duvet Allie had placed on him, and a sweet tug yanked at his heartstrings. Looking toward the kitchen, he saw Allie at the stove, stirring something together in a big pot. It was strange how the sight of her made his heart overflow. She wasn't Miri, but she was Allie, and she had definitely taken a big part of his heart in her hands, without any signs of giving it back.

He smiled tenderly as he watched her rummaging around in his kitchen. *Honestly, I don't mind. She makes me happy, and it feels good having her here. No,* he corrected himself, *it feels great. It feels as if she belongs here too.* While he sat there, observing her as she sang quietly to herself while working, it dawned on him that the sensation in his heart was a tender love. With eyes wide-open and pulse suddenly speeding up, he realized something else. *It's not just that I love her, I... I love her a lot, and I've done that for some time, I think. I don't know why I feel so damn weirded out about it, or why I keep fighting it. One fine day I have to stop fighting it and just accept that this is how it is. Maybe... maybe that day is today...*

With slight dizziness that gradually disappeared, he pushed himself up from the sofa and went out to her in the kitchen, coming up from behind and putting his arms around her. She stopped singing and turned around in his arms with a worried frown that smoothened out when she saw his smiling face.

"You look better! Do you feel better?"

"Yeah, a little. What are you making? It smells heavenly."

A happy smile of her own broke out on her lips. "*Boeuf Bourguignon*. Dad's recipe. Lots of meat and veggies that'll get your blood going, and some wine and bouillon and spices. You'll love it. Promise."

"Yeah, I believe you. Can I help you with something?"

Allie gave him another sweet smile. "You're so awesome. It's just about finished, but if you want to cut the baguette and take out the butter and cheese, go ahead."

He raised his eyebrows. "Wow, you're going big tonight."

"Well, you're worth it, I'd say. Just wish Miri was here too, but as soon as we can, I say we'll celebrate in style all three of us."

"Sounds like a great plan," he mumbled and placed a gentle kiss on her temple, before doing what she asked.

She took the plates and scooped up generous portions of stew and rice and placed them on the kitchen island together with a bottle of non-alcoholic red wine that she apparently had bought just for tonight. Suspiciously, he squinted at her, and she looked away.

"It's nothing." The tone was slightly defensive. "Just food and wine." When he raised his eyebrows, she couldn't hinder a blush, but said in a nonchalant voice, "Come on, I don't have to buy take-out and coke every single time we're together. I like cooking, and I'm pretty good at it."

"Mhm," he said, not at all convinced that that was the entire motive but dropped it. As she sat down and gestured to him to start eating, he had to admit she was right. It was pretty damn good. *No, take away 'pretty.' It's damn good. Best thing I've had in a long time, honestly.*

"Did you like it?"

"Yeah, it's amazing and so much better than take-out. Thank you for doing this."

531

She grinned at him and kicked him lightly on his shin. "Told you."

They laughed together, and then they concentrated on eating, while he, being curious, asked her about her cooking interest.

"Guess it goes back to my complete lack of tasty food as a kid," she smiled lightheartedly. "Mom and Anders, that's my real dad, hated cooking, so me and Aggie and our brother Andy, lived on store-bought blood pudding and spongy fish balls." She laughed heartily at his terrified look. "Yeah, fish balls are yucky, but blood pudding isn't that bad if you eat it with lingonberry sauce. Most kids love it."

"Not convinced," he smiled at her.

She smiled back. "Can't help you with that, sorry. You just have to take my word for it."

"Mhm, alright."

"It wasn't until we came here, and Dad, Leo, cooked all these fabulous dinners for us that we realized food could taste great. He's a great cook, and he taught Andy and me a lot, and now Andy's in chef school."

"He must've been a great influence on you, your stepdad," Carl remarked.

Allie's face got a loving expression. "Yeah, he's awesome. He's not only my dad, but he's also my best friend, and he always has time for me."

Carl clasped her hand, and she smiled at him.

Sooner than he thought, his plate was empty, and he felt full and satisfied and more relaxed than he'd been for a while now. *Well, since yesterday morning, anyway,* he corrected himself.

"Wow, that was awesome."

Allie radiated. He tried to glance at her, covertly, but of course, she noticed.

"What?"

With a shrug, he casually leaned back in the chair and put on a lighthearted demeanor, not that it was hard doing so in her company.

"I just have a feeling there's more to this than you who like cooking, but if you don't want to talk about it, I won't probe."

Once again, a rare blush covered her cheeks, and she scowled, reached for a piece of bread and began shoving it around in the sauce on her plate. After a few seconds, she dropped the bread, sighed, and leaned back in her chair.

She avoided his gaze while looking slightly awkward. "Well, I might try to bribe you is all."

He stared at her, utterly surprised, and sat up straight again. "Um, what? What do you mean 'bribe' me? Why on earth would you need that for?"

The blush got deeper, and to his concern, she looked even more awkward, almost teary-eyed.

"I just— I made a new try going home today, and well— It still doesn't work."

He leaned over and took her hand in a kind grip. "You feel out of touch with Kevin?"

"Not just him. All of them. I look at them and how they live their lives, not knowing what's going on. I mean, really going on. They have no clue people like you and Miri, and Olwen and Omega are out there fighting for them, getting injured for them, losing your mind for them – dying for them – so that they can keep on living their everyday life like that…" Her voice trailed away, and now, he could hear the tears in it.

He caressed her hand gently. "But, Allie, that's why we do it."

"But there are so many people out there who just— They just waste their lives on, I don't know, nothing, while you get hurt protecting them."

"I don't think that's how we see it. And it doesn't matter what they do with their lives. Even if they never get off their sofas, they still don't deserve getting eaten by monsters, or disappear into another dimension, or getting sacrificed by crazy people."

Now the tears trickled down her cheeks. "I don't know what to do, Carl. I… I feel so damn lost… My life doesn't fit me anymore. I— I feel kicked out of my own home, and the only place I can go to where someone understands is here. You and Miri, you understand, and I— I feel like I'm taking up so much space here – and I wasn't even going to talk about it tonight. Damn it!"

"And then you try to bribe me so you can stay for a while?" She nodded and sniveled, and he dried the tears from her cheek with a tender touch. "Allie, you don't have to bribe me. Stay for as long as you want. I don't think Miri would mind when she comes home. She likes you a lot." He looked into her tear-filled eyes. "I'd say you're at a crossroad now where you have to decide what you want to do. You know so much now, more than you should, and it's hard knowing this much, because, well, either you try to forget and go on the same way you lived before, or you become one of us. I wouldn't think less of you if you chose the first option."

"But I would," she sniveled.

"You don't have to decide tonight, Allie."

A deep trembling sigh found its way out of her, and she wiped away some late tears with a weary gesture. "Thing is, I think the decision has already been made. I— I can't see myself going back playing roleplaying games every week when I know that you and Miri might fight some damn, scary monster, so I can be safe. That glove doesn't fit that well. The scale tips over to the other side."

Carl kissed her hands. "Then, you'll become one of us and continue to play roleplaying games when you can. Being a Field Researcher doesn't have to exclude the fun, light things in life, you know. If it does, then you go under, 'cause that's when you lose your mind or get careless because you're so damn nervous and have nothing to live for anymore. Don't do what Miri and I did, Allie. Don't shut people out. Don't become lonely."

A shaky smile played on her lips, and she dried her eyes. "How can you be so good to me, Carl? Sometimes, I'm terribly afraid that I'm falling in love with you."

There was a sweet and surprising tug at his heart, and he gave her a tender, loving smile.

"Well…" He dragged it out but decided he could as well burn this bridge too. "Sometimes, most times, I don't understand how I can love both you and Miri at the same time. It doesn't make sense, but that's how I feel. I've been struggling with it for some time now, but you just won't let me go." He shrugged lightheartedly and caressed her hands, feeling fine with letting her know.

Her eyes opened wide. "Do you— Do you love me?"

The smile on his lips became teasing. "You're a profiler, and really, really good at it too. You should know." He had to laugh at her as she sat on the other side of the kitchen island, looking as if someone had hit her over the head. "Come on, Allie. I've told you before you're holding a piece of my heart. It can't be this sudden."

"Yeah… No… But…" She shook her head as if trying to get rid of a daze. Then she hopped down from the chair and came around to him, kissing him vigorously. He closed his eyes, getting lost in the feeling of her soft lips and her tongue. When she let him go, her eyes were close to his and overflowing with feelings.

"No one ever said that to me before. No one," she whispered.

With intense feelings of tenderness and love, he placed his hands on her face and looked her solemnly into her eyes. "I love you, Allie."

"Can you say it again?"

He smiled. "I love you, Allie."

A deep sigh heaved her chest, and she looked solemn too as she traced his cheek with her finger.

"It's crazy. How can you love me? I'm not steady. I'm not wife material. I'm just, you know, butterflying around."

"Allie…" His smile became sad. "You're wonderfully warm and generous and optimistic and funny and honest. You're lovable because you're you. Who cares about wife material? What is that anyway? Do you think I'm marrying Miri because I think she's wife material?" Allie looked embarrassed and shied away from his gaze. "No, sweetie, don't be embarrassed. I just never thought you were insecure when it comes to your own value. Don't let all these conservative people out there get to you. They're wrong."

She looked back and smiled again, a bit shaky, but genuinely warm. "You're making me feel very special, Carl."

"Well, you should, because you are."

She leaned in and kissed him again, a tender kiss that continued on and became longer, more intense and passionate, before slowly letting him go.

She looked him in the eyes, still a bit insecure. "Do you want to make love with me?"

An electric thrill rushed through his body when it hit him that she had never used those words before, and he traced a finger over her lips. "I do."

With breathing that suddenly became heavier, she took his hands and led him into the bedroom; plates still on the table, dishes not washed, food still out, and it didn't bother him at all.

The next morning, Carl woke up late, around nine, he saw when he squinted at the alarm clock. He felt groggy from the pill, as Dr. Bernard had predicted, but he had slept well, and most importantly, he hadn't slept alone. He never wanted to sleep alone again. From the living room, he heard the rattle from the keyboard on Allie's laptop, and he lay there in bed, enjoying the sounds of another living being in his life while dozing off again. Today, he wasn't going to get up if he could avoid it.

When she came in around eleven, he realized he had fallen asleep again.

"Hey there," she smiled at him as he squinted up at her. Casually, she leaned on his naked chest, kissing him sweetly.

"Mm, hey there," he mumbled contentedly and tangled his fingers in her gorgeous hair while enjoying the natural feeling that radiated between them. "How's it going?"

"Really good, actually. I'm getting along great with the text now, for some reason."

"What are you writing? You said a book, eh?"

"Yeah, it's a take on serial killers and triggers, hopefully through an angle that is somewhat new. We'll see. I'm only on chapter two, so far. I've planned fifteen." She gave him a look. "Kane called. I heard him on the answering machine. He wants to meet you on Monday at ten."

Anxiousness filled him. He exhaled and was just about to tug at his hair, but Allie caught his hand and kissed it.

With another deep breath, he shrugged and managed to relax. "Alright. Glad it's decided, but I'm not going to think about it over the weekend. Did Bernard call?"

"No, not yet."

He nodded. "I must've been so tired yesterday. Now, I'm only happy that she's fine, but yesterday…"

Allie squeezed his hand. "I don't think I've ever seen you so exhausted, Carl. No wonder you reacted so strongly. I'm happy you got those sleeping pills."

"Yeah, me too. Honestly, I'm not going to do anything today, just lying here, taking it easy, maybe reading, but not working, not even filing the report to the Faculty."

"Good." She nodded in approval. "We've got lots of food from yesterday, so we're not going to starve. And I've cleaned everything up."

He smiled lovingly at her, touched by her efforts. "Thank you for staying. It means a lot to me. And thanks for everything."

To his surprise, she blushed heavily, and then, she glanced at him, a smile lurking in the corner of her lips.

"It means a lot that I can."

Quickly untangling herself from his embrace, she rose from the bed and went out into the living room. He looked after her with squinting eyes and thought about some cues she'd unintentionally given him during the past few days, and it suddenly dawned on him that she actually was on the brink of falling in love with him, if she hadn't already. As he watched her golden head being bent over her laptop, he carefully investigated his own feelings. He'd never expected that, he mused. She'd never seemed interested in anything more than friendship and sex before. *Maybe she surprised herself too?* And he himself seemed to have skipped the whole falling-in-love-stage and gone directly from friendship to love. It was a bit weird, but he slowly became aware of how wonderfully blessed he felt. The thought of Miri came to him. Yes, they had all done things together that they enjoyed, but it didn't mean that the two women were also falling in love with each other. Maybe it would come, and if it didn't... He shrugged. *Nothing I need to think about today.*

Suddenly, it hit him that the extreme situation with Night Porter most likely pushed their boundaries so much further away than it would have done during normal circumstances. Carl highly doubted that this development of their relationships would have happened had they been in a perfectly normal everyday-life-state. He could readily admit that both he and Miri would have been too conservative for such a liaison. *So, in a way, I have a lot to be thankful to Night Porter for. How insane isn't that?* He shook his head and chuckled quietly at the absurdity of the thought. Even worse was that if Night Porter knew about it, he would probably be as amused as Carl. *Oh, he knows. No doubt about it. He definitely knows.*

His thoughts wandered back to Allie again. He had to take Kevin into consideration, as well. It was undeniable that the two of them had very strong feelings for each other. On the other hand, if he could love two women, why wouldn't she be able to love two men? Maybe this wasn't even his problem. Maybe Kevin and Allie were fine with her having two separate relationships. Maybe he was overthinking things. *Yeah, that has never happened before,* he thought sarcastically. *Maybe it's time to just go with the flow, letting things solve themselves for once, as long as they don't need a nudge.*

He continued watching her working, her concentrated appearance, her flowing hair, the warmth and generosity that painted her face in a beautiful light, and he was filled with amazement that she had opened her heart so much to him that she had fallen in love with him. Somewhere in his gentle study of her, he fell asleep again.

The next time he woke up was because someone was kissing him. He squinted and looked into Miriam's pleased eyes.

With a gasp, he opened his eyes fully. "Miri!" Forcefully, he embraced her, and she smiled happily. "When did you get home?"

"About an hour ago. Dr. Bernard drove me."

"God, I'm so happy to see you!" He didn't want to let her go from his embrace, but he had to make sure that she was fine. "How are you? How's your head? When did you wake up?"

She laughed at him and leaned in to kiss him once more, a lingering kiss that awoke all nerve endings in his body.

"I'm actually feeling much better now," she said when she looked at him again. Tenderly, she caressed his chest, and the touch sent trickles of sweet sensations through his body. He suddenly noticed that he was still completely naked, but the expected feeling of shame over him and Allie didn't show up. Instead, it was wonderfully liberating that they seemed to be able to accept that they had something fabulous and special going on between the three of them.

"It hurts, of course," she continued, "but it's a cleaner ache than before. I get it now; how bad it really was. And I woke up this morning, but Dr. Bernard wanted to take a couple of tests before I was allowed to go home. And how are you? Allie said you've been pretty worn out."

"Don't worry about me. I just need some sleep. And I'm fine now that you're finally at home." He took her in his arms again, snuggled in at her cheek, breathing in her special Miri-scent, kissing her temple. "I'm so happy to have you home again, Miri. So happy," he mumbled, and she took his face in her hands and looked at him with rosy cheeks and smiling eyes.

"I'm happy too." Lingering, she kissed him again before her expression changed, and she sighed. "And I would be even happier if everything could turn out fine for everyone, for once."

"Did you get to see Olwen?"

Miriam shook her head. "No, she's still out, and Dr. Bernard is waiting for the CAT scan results. It's all so weird." She glanced at him. "You know, ever since Dr. Bernard told me about her, I've been thinking—"

"What?" he worriedly asked when she fell silent.

"I'm wondering if she somehow was tuned in on the portal when I closed it and if that was what caused it. I mean, why would she otherwise collapse like that?"

Cold inside, Carl stared at her, thinking about the damage that could have been done to Olwen's mind if that was the case.

Vexed, he cleared his voice. "Yeah, sounds likely," he muttered and rubbed his eyes. "Goddammit! I just hate this Project!"

"We're going to come out fine on the other side, Carl." Miri's voice was clear and determined, and he was happy to hear that conviction. "We always do, even if we always collect some more scars on the way."

The bad feeling didn't disappear, but it weakened as they laughed together. Once again, he snuggled into her arms. With a pleased sigh, she let her head rest on his shoulder, and for a while, they just lay together, enjoying each other's presence.

Soon, Allie poked her head into the room, and when she saw that they were awake, she came in and snuggled close to Carl on his other side. Miriam's face brightened, and she leaned over and gave Allie a kiss on the mouth, which Allie willingly returned and made a little bit deeper. Seeing the golden brown and the golden blond tangle together in front of him made Carl's heart skip a beat, and the thought that they all belonged together came to him again. *Just go with the flow. We don't have to do anything else right now, just go with the flow.* When the women's lips parted, they smiled at each other.

"You know, Allie," Miri said thoughtfully and took Allie's hand in hers, "my very traditional upbringing is screaming in horror of what we do together and how we feel about each other, but you know, I really don't give a damn. We're great together. It feels like, don't laugh now—" Allie shook her head. "It feels like we belong together."

Instead of laughing, Allie looked like a cat that bathed in cream as she held her arm loosely over Carl's chest and casually leaned on him. Miri, on the other hand, gave her an amused look and laughed at her. Somewhere during that laugh, Allie's expression changed, and she affectionately caressed Miri's cheek.

"You're right, Miri," she said solemnly. "I feel that too. I love you two deeply, which I wasn't expecting to do, and I love being with you. I wish I could stay, but tonight, I'm going home. Carl said something yesterday that's really important, and I realized I have some relationships to repair at home."

"That's okay, Allie. That won't take anything away from us."

Allie smiled relieved and leaned in for another, longer kiss. "Thank you," she mumbled. "Thank you for understanding."

541

Part Seven

endgame

Chapter 33

After spending the rest of the day in bed, they ate Allie's fantastic *Boeuf Bourguignon* when the sun started to set, and Allie left afterward, looking hopeful and determined. Carl had a feeling that she was going to rock some people's world this evening.

"So, what did you say to her yesterday?" Miriam curiously asked after the door closed behind her.

"That she shouldn't distance herself from her friends, just because they don't know what she knows now."

"Mm, great advice." She took his hand and stepped into his embrace. "Is she going to become an FR?"

"Yeah, I think so. She said she couldn't stand knowing these things now and not doing anything about it."

"I know the feeling," Miri mumbled and sighed. "Sometimes, I wish I could let it go, though."

"Well, we can for tonight. What do you want to do? Talk? Watch a movie? Take a walk? Read a book? Sleep?"

"Make love."

He grinned. "I can put that on the list too."

"It is the list. I want to make love with you, and I want to sleep really, really close to you. I've been so lonely without you, Carl."

"I'm happy to hear that," he mumbled into her hair. "I've been lonely without you too. I mean, I love Allie. Honestly, I love her a lot." When he looked her straight in the eyes to see her reaction, she just smiled and nodded.

"I know. And she's in love with you. We talked about it when you were sleeping."

He stared at her, speechless. Her eyes carried a calm self-confidence that he had never seen in her before, a knowledge that he loved her too, that she was special to him, that she was loveable in her own right.

With a gentle touch on his cheek, she continued, "You know, it doesn't take anything away from me." She

543

winked mischievously. "On the contrary, I'm quite pleased with the situation."

Even though her words suddenly made him shy, he couldn't help but laugh wholeheartedly. When the laughter faded, he turned solemn and cupped her face, feeling the love for her as a combination of a wildfire and the tranquil, endless sky. "I just wanted you to know that— It's just that— With you, I feel perfectly whole. I want to have you near me. I need you in my life. You— You are the missing piece."

Without a word, she hugged him hard as if she never wanted to let him go.

They didn't have much energy for something long or adventurous, but that wasn't what they wanted either. They just wanted to be near each other, feeling the tenderness, the softness, and the love, and they fell asleep loosely embraced, completely relaxed and calm.

Since Miriam was on sick leave and Carl wasn't allowed to join any of his work teams yet, they slept in. It was as if they were already on vacation. They lay in bed, talking, cuddling, laughing, went up at eleven to eat breakfast and went back to bed again. Miriam slept for a while. The head wound felt better, she assured him, but it still pained her. He read a book. At around three, they had managed to get up and eat some lunch, just toasts with lots of cheese, ham, and tomatoes, and a simple salad on the side, when Carl's phone rang.

He recognized Allie's phone number on the display window and smiled affectionately. "Hi, Allie! How's it going?"

"Carl?" Allie's voice was just a whisper, and she sounded frightened. He frowned uncertainly, feeling his heart rate speed up. "Um, I need to ask you… I'm hiding in the bathroom at the office. Olwen's really scary. She doesn't seem to be herself. She's standing outside with some damn masks in her hand and wants me to come with her to a damn masquerade party. What the hell's going on?" For a moment, he couldn't breathe; the déjà vu and the terror gripped his soul too hard. "Carl? Goddammit! Answer me!"

"Um…" He let his hand rest in his hair and felt completely blank.

At the other end of the line, Allie gasped. "Oh God, she's coming in."

In the background, he heard the same sing-song-like voice that could be Olwen's, but just like last time, it was hard to discern the words as Allie's hard breaths just about drenched them. Somewhere a memory stirred, a voice that purred in his mind; *you can't keep an eye on the golden queen all the time, Carl…*

He felt nauseous but tried to compose himself, and finally, he managed to get his own voice to work. It sounded panicked, but at least he managed to talk. "Goddamn, Allie, whatever you do, don't go with her! She's taking you to Night Porter! We're coming to you. We're leaving right now!" He hung up, and Miri stared at him with big, scared eyes. "Same— It's the same phone call! Allie in the washroom, and Olwen—" Quickly, he found the number to Dr. Bernard in the phone book. When Bernard answered, a wave of relief gushed through him. "Olwen— Is she—"

"Carl?" He could hear the answer in the doctor's out-of-control voice.

"Is she gone?"

"Banafshe checked on her ten minutes ago, and she's not here anymore. None of us have seen her walk away. CAT scan came back, Carl, and she— She shouldn't be able to… to…" Bernard's voice trailed away.

"I know where she is. I need to go."

"Carl—"

"Need to go, doc." He hung up.

Miriam had already gone into the bedroom to put on clothes, and he followed her, scrambled some clothes together before joining Miriam at the front door.

"I checked the stove," she said in a deliberately calm and collected voice. "It's off. And I put the food in the fridge." She didn't say, 'Who knows when we'll come back,' but she didn't have to. He could see the laconic question in her eyes.

"Great. Thanks."

Together, they rushed down the stairs instead of waiting for the slow-moving elevator. That's when he recalled his car was at HQ.

"Fuck! Where's your car, Miri? It's not here, eh? I— I don't remember."

"At home. I haven't— I haven't needed it."

"Taxi. Can't believe—" As he dialed the cab company, he couldn't stop the nervous pacing back and forth outside the entrance. "Alright, they'll be here in ten." He phoned Allie again, but he was immediately directed to her answering machine that let him know that she couldn't pick up the phone at the moment. The sense of powerlessness grew so strong within him that he had problems keeping his temper under control.

"What did you mean with the Night Porter-thing, Carl?" Miriam asked anxiously, and he inhaled deeply, trying hard to calm down.

"I, uh, I don't really know, but I keep hearing his voice in my head, telling me that I can't protect her. I— I have a feeling there's something I should remember, but I can't!"

She stared at him, frightened. "It's, um, it's like with Olwen, right? She couldn't remember making a deal with him."

He stopped his pacing and stared at her. His heart hammered with fear as the truth of her words hit him. "I— I certainly hope I haven't been that stupid…"

Miriam exhaled. "It seems unlikely that you would."

Helplessly, he rubbed his face and ran his hands through his hair. "I can't be sure. How the hell can I be sure with my track record? Fuck! What a fucking mess!"

Miri went up to him and embraced him hard. "Don't think like that, Carl," she mumbled in his ear. "It's what he

546

wants. He wants to make you doubt yourself. Don't let him get to you."

He exhaled and hugged her close, taking comfort in her nearness. A taxi turned into the quiet street and pulled up in front of them. Hurriedly, they took their place in the backseat.

"FBI headquarters, please," Carl said in a calm and collected voice while hiding his true feelings. Sometimes, his mask was a great asset. No one who didn't know him well would be able to tell that his inside was in total turmoil.

Miri looked at him and took his hand. Apparently, she had learned to read him by now. It felt damn good. He didn't want to be able to hide anything from her anymore, even though he knew perfectly well that he would be able to fool her if he truly tried.

The driver was a quiet sort, to Carl's immense relief, since he couldn't take any light chatter at this point.

As soon as the driver parked outside HQ's entrance, they paid and rushed in. Just like last time, they took the stairs, running like crazy. First, they checked Allie's office, just to make sure she wasn't there like she had been the other day, but today it was empty. Her laptop stood on the table in sleep mode surrounded by notebooks and several books on serial killers, and her bag stood half-opened the floor, spilling out pens, a make-up bag, and a green batik scarf.

Hurriedly, they left and busted into the women's washroom. It was also empty. Carl ran a hand through his hair and banged his other hand hard against the wall. Miri crouched at one of the booths.

"Is this her cell?" she asked and pointed at a cell phone that lay abandoned on the floor. With alarm, he recognized the case and nodded, feeling tears in his eyes that he furiously blinked away.

"Yeah..."

"Okay, what do we do?"

He took a deep breath and cleared his voice. "Can you feel any vibrations in here?"

She didn't even have to concentrate much. "There," she said and pointed toward a place just in front of the frosted window.

"Great," he muttered as the faint vibrations made themselves known to him. He glared at them and tugged hard at his hair. "Alright, I'll try to contact Olwen. Who knows, she might answer."

He didn't disagree with her skeptical appearance, but he had to try. Not a single signal went through. He stared at the phone in silence before exhaling, feeling snared in choices that weren't choices.

Reluctantly, he glanced at Miriam and loathed himself for what he was about to say. "There's one more person we should try to contact."

"Who's that?"

"Henry."

She stared at him. "Carl…"

Without being able to stop himself, he combed through his hair over and over again, feeling the soft strands of hair in between his fingers. However, the gesture didn't calm him down as much as it used to. "I— I know, but— She's his wife, and he's still Faculty and our contact. He needs to know."

She exhaled, looking tired and aloof again. "I don't like it, but I guess you're right." With another sigh, she rubbed her face. "He's just going to try to take over," she muttered.

With a deep scowl, he nodded. "Probably. It's what he's used to doing with us. He doesn't know we've changed." He grimaced at the perspective but shrugged. "We'll see what happens. I don't want to fight him if I don't have to. He used to be a great team leader, Miri."

"But that was before all emotional chaos, Carl. As soon as you and I started to communicate, he got totally— Whatever."

He took the short steps toward her and clasped her hand. "No, it's not 'whatever.' It matters. Your opinion matters, Miri. Don't forget that." She tried to smile, but her face was clouded. "Honestly? I don't want to do this either, but what other choice do we have?"

"Go in and find them on our own."

"Yeah, that's the plan, but we can't go in without letting him know his wife disappeared." Carl paused and looked at her distressed appearance. "Do you really think he'd want to come with us if he gets to know?"

The cloud disappeared from her face, and she looked relieved. "No, I don't. He's too old. And I've never heard of Faculty members going on RPs themselves. Isn't that breach of contract or something?"

Carl breathed easier, thinking about that particular paragraph he had forgotten about. "Yeah, you're right. They're only there for guidance." Another thought struck him, and he grimaced again.

"What?" Miri worriedly asked.

"I just realized— Goddammit! I need to call him anyway. He's the only one who can save my career by now." The laugh that escaped him was completely void of humor. "Wow, isn't that ironic?"

Miriam frowned uncertainly. "What do you mean?"

"I told you, didn't I, that I have a meeting on Monday with Jeremy Kane? If I don't show up, it won't matter what decision he's made, it's going to be over."

"Oh, shoot, I remember!" She looked devastated.

Ill-tempered, Carl glared at the happily dancing vibrations at the window. "I don't think we'll be able to make it back in time. We have to go in now, we can't wait, and who knows when or if we'll be back again." He shrugged and dialed the number. "Whatever. I can't think about that now," he muttered.

A couple of signals went through before Henry answered, and the sound of his warm voice made Carl's heart hammer faster in sheer nervousness. He put on the loudspeaker so Miri could hear too.

"Hi, C." He was impressed by how calm he managed to sound. There was a minor pause on the other end.

"Octavius." Henry didn't sound overly happy, Carl reflected and swallowed uneasily.

"Yeah. Um, we, uh, we have a slight problem…"

"What's that?"

Carl inhaled and decided that he couldn't make this sound good whatever he said. "It seems as if Olwen has abducted Allie and taken her into that other dimension we found," he blurted out. At his side, Miri giggled apprehensively. The silence stretched out. "Um, C?"

"I don't want to hear such idiotic things, Octavius." The voice on the other end was final. "Are you trying to be funny? You should know better."

"I'm not trying to be funny."

"Olwen's in a coma, Octavius. Surely, you know that. What are you up to?"

Oh, great, this is going so great. Why the hell hasn't Bernard called him?

"Just listen to me, C. Allie— Uh, Odette— Uh, Dr. Harris called me around three and told me Olwen was trying to take her away somewhere. We called Dr. Bernard, and he told us Olwen was missing. When we came here ten minutes ago, none of them were here, and we see traces of a portal."

Another silence stretched out.

"Dr. Bernard hasn't called me, Octavius," Caesar finally said. "It's improbable he wouldn't let me know she's woken up."

"I'm deadly serious, C. If you don't believe me, call him."

After yet another pause, Caesar said, clearly irritated, "Where's 'here'?"

"The women's washroom on the third floor at HQ."

"I'll be there in half an hour."

"C—" Carl stared at the phone when the signal let him know that Caesar had hung up on him. "Oh, great!" He

550

had a terrifying feeling that all his plans were just about to go up in smoke.

Miri sighed. "Whatever. I won't die from it. Let's go to Superfresh while we're waiting." When he stared at her, she shrugged. "We'll need things; food, rubbing alcohol, compresses, things like that." She touched the head wound carefully. "This time, I want to be prepared."

He nodded, and they left the washroom.

When they came back an hour later, Caesar stood in the corridor outside the washroom, looking nervous. As soon as Miri saw him, she straightened her back and held her head high. It gladdened Carl immensely that she didn't reach for his hand as he had been afraid she would, and that she wanted to face the situation as a strong, independent person.

Caesar straightened up as well when he saw them approaching and he attempted to put on a calm expression. He hadn't aged much, Carl thought. There was still more black in his hair than silver, and the look in his blue eyes was as piercing as he remembered.

"Been out shopping?" Caesar said when he saw the fabric bag in Carl's hand as if it wasn't two years since they last met.

"Yeah."

C nodded and glanced at Miri without meeting her gaze. "Ophelia," he said.

"Henry."

Carl could see him flinch at the cool, collected tone and the use of his real name.

Caesar inhaled. "I hear congratulations are in order," he said reluctantly.

"Thank you," Miri said, still in that cool, detached voice. "And to you and Olwen. I heard about your marriage last week. Otherwise, I would've congratulated the two of you long ago."

Caesar flinched again. "Um, thanks. It was, um, a quick decision."

"So, I heard. Shall we switch over to business, maybe? Time's ticking, and I don't want either Allie or Olwen to be in there longer than necessary."

Behind his quiet and composed mask, Carl couldn't help but cheer her on. *You rock, Miri! Goddamn, you're great!*

When Caesar nodded, slightly dazed by her calm, commanding behavior, she continued, "First of all, you need to contact Jeremy Kane and change the date for Carl's meeting with him on Monday. We might not be able to get back by then. Time runs differently there." C gave her a baffled look that she seriously returned. When he didn't say anything or made any gesture that he was going to make the call, she continued, "I'd appreciate it if you could call immediately since you're Faculty and we don't want to forget about it."

Caesar opened his mouth, but not a sound came through. Miriam just watched him steadily.

He avoided her gaze and frowned. "Um, of course."

He fiddled with his cell phone, and after going through the phone book, he dialed the number. When the receiver was picked up, a voice was heard on the other end of the line, but no words could be discerned at this distance.

"Mr. Kane, sir. This is Armand from the Faculty. Yes, that's right. I understand you have a meeting with Special Agent Carl Hansen on Monday, is that correct? Yes, good. As you know, Agent Hansen is also one of the Star Students here at the FBI, and I will need to send him on a Research Project today. We don't know how long that will take. Most likely several days. Yes, that would be appreciated. Thank you very much for your understanding, sir, and I apologize for any inconvenience. Yes, yes, of course. He's right here. Thank you."

Scowling, Caesar handed Carl the phone, and, suddenly finding it hard to breathe, Carl took it with slightly sweaty hands.

"Sir?"

The calm, professional voice at the other end of the line had a warmer tone than he remembered. "Carl, I wanted to let you know in person the decision that has been made, but since it won't be possible before Monday, as Armand has let me understand, there's no reason for you to go around feeling anxious about it. As soon as you come back from your Research Project, I want you to report to Agent David Miller, who is now Special Agent in Charge of the interview group."

A warm wave of relief rushed through Carl's body, and he smiled broadly toward Miriam, whose face, in turn, got a quietly glowing expression.

"I will, sir. Thank you, sir."

"You're welcome, Carl. It's been a pleasure."

Still smiling, he hung up, and Miriam embraced him forcefully.

"Woohoo!" she laughed and twirled around with him. "You made it! I'm so happy!" Without warning, she leaned in and kissed him vigorously. It felt extremely awkward being kissed in front of Caesar. Carl's face burnt with embarrassment, but he didn't want her to feel stupid, and hesitantly kissed her back. When she let go of him, her gaze suddenly fell upon Caesar, and she tensed in her whole body. Carl had a feeling that she, for a moment, had forgotten about C. Her radiant expression immediately disappeared at her former lover's stern, unforgiving appearance.

Carl handed C's phone back to him, and Miriam regained her composure.

In a voice completely detached from emotions, she said, "Thank you, Henry. Now that that's been dealt with, I'm going to show you the portal."

She opened the door to the washroom and went in, back straight and head held high, while Caesar bewildered stared after her.

"After you, C," Carl said, smiling broadly at Miri's powerful appearance and at the great news.

Caesar gave him a stunned look. "What have you done with her?"

553

"Me? I haven't done a thing. She's done it all by herself, and I'm damn proud of her. Come, let's go in."

Carl passed him and held up the door to where Miriam was waiting. Caesar took a couple of uncertain steps into the room and looked around, clearly trying to compose himself.

As soon as the door closed behind them, Miriam let up her cool, collected voice again. "We found Allie's phone on the floor," she said and pointed to it. When Caesar nodded, she stepped close to the frosted window. "If you look here," she said and concentrated on the barely noticeable vibrations. Within seconds, the air shimmered visibly and began to form into a door. Immediately, Miriam let go of the portal, and it faded back into nothing. With a faint grimace, she carefully touched the gauze, but to Carl's immense relief, no blood seeped through.

Caesar didn't seem to notice the minor intermezzo as he stared at the remnants of the portal and gaped flabbergasted.

Eventually, Miriam continued in a slightly pained voice, "This is the portal through which Olwen brought Allie. It leads to the other dimension."

"But... but why?" Caesar's voice was baffled. Apparently, he didn't understand the severity of the situation. Miri glanced at Carl, but he wanted her to go on, keeping up her fabulous momentum, so he kept quiet.

"Omega told us that Olwen made a deal with an entity from that dimension, and now, when she was in the coma, it might have been able to communicate directly with her. It probably did something to her, like taking control of her mind or something similar. She wouldn't do something like this otherwise."

At her words, a slightly grayish nuance spread across Caesar's face.

"How are you feeling, C?" Carl asked, concerned, and took a step toward him.

"How would you feel if your wife suddenly disappeared into another dimension?" C sneered back, and Carl stopped dead in his track. It felt as if he'd been kicked in the stomach.

Furious, Miriam clenched her fists. "Shut up, Henry!" she snarled. "Just shut up! He knows. That's why he asked. Because he's concerned about you."

Caesar looked regretful. "I'm sorry," he mumbled and put a hand over his eyes.

"It's okay, C," Carl said, feeling for the older man, but Caesar didn't acknowledge him.

Silence fell over the room a couple of moments before Caesar inhaled and composed himself. "Shall we go in or do we need something else than what you have?"

"We?" Carl asked, shocked, and with a bad feeling spreading through his body.

With a straightened back and a somewhat pained appearance, Caesar looked him over. "She's my wife. You went in after Miriam, why wouldn't I go in after Sally?"

Carl shrugged, feeling awkward. "You're also Faculty. You don't do RPs anymore. Isn't that breach of contract?"

Caesar glared at him, and Carl had a feeling that he had hit a nerve.

"That's none of your business. You have absolutely nothing to say about this, Octavius. I'm your superior. You do what I say."

Carl raised his hands in defense. "If you say so," he muttered. "Just remember that of all of us, Miri has the most knowledge and experience with the place. She was there a whole month. You'll need her advice."

Caesar didn't acknowledge that either, just looked him over with a cold glare. "Is there anything else we need?" he asked again, his voice distant and reserved.

Deliberately, Carl turned toward Miriam with a questioning look, but she turned away from C with her arms crossed over her chest, and understandable and justified anger painted over her face. Carl sighed quietly. Not because of her, her reaction was completely rational, but because of how easily this situation could become even worse.

"Miri?"

"I'd like to pick up some knives and guns," she responded without acknowledging Caesar in turn. "And a backpack each, first aid, some strong pain relievers, maybe morphine if we can get it, a couple of blankets if anyone goes into shock."

He nodded but didn't want to step on C's toes. *If it's this important for him to take the lead, well, then let him.*

As if he hadn't heard her, C turned his back to them and left the washroom. Carl stared unbelievingly at the closing door, before tugging at his hair. Then, he walked up to Miriam and took her hands.

"You're awesome. Don't let him get to you."

"He might get to me," she said with a strained smile, "but I won't let him walk all over me."

"Good. How's your head? I saw you grimace."

"It's actually not that bad. It hurts, but it hasn't started to bleed yet."

Relieved, he caressed her hands. "Hopefully, it was the sand that caused it before."

She nodded, but Carl thought that she looked tired.

With a deep intake of breath, she said, "Let's go. I want this over and done with."

He nodded, and they exited the washroom. where Caesar waited for them.

Once more, he addressed Carl without even looking at Miriam. "Where's Omega?"

Carl and Miri shared a surprised glance. *Why hasn't Olwen let him know?* Carl thought and cleared his voice, "What do you mean, C? You know she's committed, eh?"

Caesar made a dismissive gesture with his hand. "Don't lie to me, Octavius. Where is she?"

Anger spread through him like wildfire, and this time, he couldn't hold it back. With a cold look, he stared Caesar straight in the eyes. "I'm not lying, C," he said in a low, dangerous voice that surprised him too. "This is the second time you've implied that I do. Seriously, you do not want to go there with me." Caesar flinched and looked away. After a short pause, Carl continued in a more normal tone, "Last time we saw her, she laid on her bed, intoxicated by alcohol and drugs, raped until she lost consciousness by the same entity who tricked Olwen. She was taken to Bernard's on Monday, but she's committed now. She needs professional psychiatric help getting over the trauma, which he can't give her."

Disbelievingly, Caesar stared at him. "Omega doesn't take stimuli," he said at last. "I know her."

Carl stared back at him, but before he could say anything, Miriam upset broke in, "She was raped, Henry! Why do you care about the fucking heroin?"

There was a slight twitch in Caesar's face, but then, he looked grumpy again.

"Maybe you don't know her that well after all," Carl said, failing with hiding the sarcasm, and got a tired glare back. He scowled at Caesar's indifferent expression. "And maybe, just maybe, you should care less about the heroin and more about her wellbeing and mental health, just as Miri suggested."

"She's alright, I suppose," he said and gave a slight shrug. Carl just stared at him. *What the hell's wrong with him?*

"How can she be alright, Henry? She's been raped!" Miri's voice was high-pitched in anger. "A fucking entity raped her! She's suffering from physical and mental trauma, for crying out loud! Can you show any damn emotion about that?"

With his eyes still on Carl, Caesar said, "She must have been intoxicated by that entity you talk about. She wouldn't do it herself. I know her."

Carl threw out his arms in an unbelieving gesture and kept quiet.

Miri exhaled audibly, trying hard to compose herself. "Henry, I'm standing right here. Talk to me. Talk – to – me!

Don't act as if I'm not here or not important or too dumb to understand what you're saying."

Caesar's eyes drifted toward her and then back to Carl again, who fought intensely with himself to not lose control over his temper and show how angry he was. *What the hell is wrong with him? He used to have more compassion than this!* He couldn't understand how it could be more important for Caesar that Omega had taken drugs than that she'd been raped. And his behavior toward Miriam? It was appalling by any standard. How could he treat her with such disrespect? Was it all just a petty revenge? Was he still hurt by her rejection?

At this point, it was impossible to be objective, and Carl had no idea if what he read from the older man was correct or not. He wished passionately that he could stand up more for Miriam, but if he did, C would still not gain any respect for her, only for him. No matter how much he hated it, she had to do it herself.

As if she read his mind, Miriam suddenly took one furious step toward Caesar and poked him hard in the chest. Clearly surprised, C took a step back toward the wall. Miriam's face was flushed, and her eyes squinted in rage.

"You're obviously my superior at work, Henry," she snarled, "but don't you dare treat me this way. You might know me as someone who never has the guts to speak my opinion or to question you, but I have changed. I'm not that insecure little girl anymore, and I demand that you treat me with respect. Otherwise, I swear I'll take you there and leave you. If this is some kind of revenge against me for turning you down, then respect me enough to tell me that, or at least respect Olwen that much. She doesn't even know about me, about you and me. How can you treat her that way? How can you treat yourself that way? Don't you have any respect for yourself?"

As she pierced Caesar to the wall with her furious stare, Carl felt so proud of her that he could break. *Finally! Goddamn, I knew you could do it!*

Miriam and Caesar stared at each other in silence, but eventually, she turned away with a disgusted look on her face. "Whatever. You're not worthy of my respect either, and don't expect me to do what you say. I won't obey your orders, but you'd better stick close to me if you want to come back here again."

With her back toward them, she stiffly marched to the elevator and pressed the button. Carl gave Caesar a hugely disappointed look before joining Miriam. To Carl's surprise, Caesar slowly followed them. Seemingly, his love for Olwen was stronger than his humiliation. That gave him at least one good mark, even if he failed all the other ones.

When the doors opened, and they stepped into the elevator, the silence was so heavy that they could have cut it with a knife. Miriam leaned toward the wall with her arms crossed over her chest, looking withdrawn. Caesar impassively watched the doors, and Carl had to suppress a burning impulse to kick him hard. *Breathe, Carl, just breathe. Nothing will be better if you lose your temper.*

When the elevator stopped at the first basement level, Caesar took the lead toward the depot, but when they stepped inside, Miriam passed him, and without looking at Caesar, she began gathering things together on a table.

"Carl, can you check out these things for me, please?"

"Sure."

He grabbed an unused inventory list and started to write down the gears while Caesar closed in and began to fill the three large backpacks Miriam brought to the table. Instinctively, they fell into their old habits from when they were Team C, Carl noticed with some fascination. Miri organized what was going into the backpacks with meticulous detail, Carl checked the items off the list, and C packed them. Within twenty minutes, they were all done, and Miri turned toward them, even though she didn't directly acknowledge Caesar.

"I suggest we dress in uniform," she said. "We'll need to be able to move unimpeded and maybe also blend into the dark."

"Alright," Carl agreed and glanced at C, who stood silent and sulking beside him. At least he didn't disagree with them, which was a relief.

Instead of going to the women's changing room to put on her own uniform, Miriam looked for a fitting uniform at the depot. Carl frowned confused, but didn't want to leave her alone with Caesar, whom he knew didn't have one, being a pathologist. Quickly, he found a new uniform for himself as well and saw Caesar search for one too. Miri looked like she didn't care a rotten apple about if they saw her naked since she changed in full sight without moving away.

Carl's frown deepened when he saw Caesar furtively watching her but didn't say anything. He guessed this was a power test from Miri's side aimed toward C, and he didn't want to raise even more tension by calling it out. *I should, shouldn't I? Fuck this damn situation!* Trying hard to calm down, he looked away but felt hugely ashamed for doing it, for not standing up for her. *It's not as if he hasn't seen her naked before,* he tried to justify his behavior.

Once again, he glared at C, who just pulled up his pants, still covertly looking at Miriam, who took a longer time than usual putting on her clothes. With her upper body still naked, she leaned down to tie her shoes, her butt in the air, a sexy pin-up stance that most likely was deliberate. *But it's not him watching her that irks me, it's the damn hypocrisy,* he thought with clenched teeth, glaring at Caesar who didn't notice. *He refuses to respect her as a person, but he can look at her damn naked body. She proved her point, alright.*

When he had dressed, and Miriam finally had put on her bra and a T-shirt, Carl passed Caesar, who still had some clothing to put on. Without planning on doing so, he stopped in front of him, trying to catch his attention. When C surprised looked at him, Carl gave him a long, harsh stare, arms tightly crossed over his chest, and had the immense satisfaction of seeing C look away, caught and embarrassed. It felt damn good.

Back at the table, Carl chose one of the backpacks. He felt much better and less angry now, after having had the guts to call C out on his behavior. As he put it on, he was satisfied that it wasn't as heavy as he'd been afraid of and that it was well-packed weight-wise. Miri soon came over to him and put on her own backpack. Carl clasped her hand in his, and she gave him a grateful smile. It might not be the time or the place, but at this point, he didn't care anymore. With a gentle hand at her waist, he leaned in and kissed her lovingly. It could be the last time he did it because he wasn't going to make that mistake again in there. She opened up to him, and when he reluctantly let her go, they were both smiling at each other, and he could tell that she felt better and more relaxed, as did he.

"I'm so proud of you, Miri," he breathed into her ear and got a sweet kiss back.

Caesar passed them on his way to the door, and Carl got a glimpse of his inflexible, stubborn face. He sighed, feeling slightly guilty, but followed him out.

As they took the elevator up to the third floor again, Miri said, "I could've opened a portal down there, but I don't want to have too many places from where people can stumble in. Since there's already one in the washroom, we'd better use that one."

"Sounds reasonable," Carl nodded. "We've got to come back here later and close it. I don't want to be responsible for the whole female staff suddenly disappearing."

Miri laughed at him, but Caesar just stared at the elevator doors with crossed arms and an unforgiving expression. Carl glanced at him with something that resembled resignation. *How the hell is this going to work? I can't believe how damn stubborn he is, how he just won't give it a break. And he presses all my damn buttons at once. That takes some skill. Sooner or later, I'm going to lose my temper if this goes on. And Miri just wants to*

561

show him that she can dominate him. God, what a damn clusterfuck. What a damn, fucking mess! We're going to die in there, just because we can't work together anymore. I wish he could stay behind and let us do this, but apparently, he can't be less of a 'white knight' than what he thinks I was when I went in. Stupid man. It's not a damn competition!

He regretted that he had ever seen this side of C. All the deep respect he once had had for him had crumbled and died.

As soon as the elevator stopped and the doors opened, Caesar strode out toward the women's washroom. Both Miri and Carl had to increase their speed to keep up. When they burst into the washroom, an employee who just washed her hands turned around and gave up a little gasp when she saw the two men in full gear. With a frightened look at them, she backed out as quickly as she could. Miri checked the other booths, but they were empty. She picked up Allie's cell phone that someone had placed on the mirror shelf and put it in her chest pocket. Then, she placed herself in front of the barely visible vibrations.

"Okay, here goes…"

She inhaled and concentrated, and immediately, the air danced happily in front of her. Within seconds, a steady door hovered an inch above the ground. *Wow, that went fast. She definitely knows what she's doing now.* That thought didn't calm him down; on the contrary, it scared the hell out of him. At least no blood seeped through the gauze this time either, to his huge relief.

She glanced over her shoulder, and he nodded at her, hoping that she couldn't see how frightened he was. She nodded back, turned toward the door again, and opened it.

Chapter 34

Carl and Caesar followed Miriam over the threshold and out of the church on top of the steep hill. The small town lay silent and dark at the bottom, just as Carl remembered it.

Miri looked astounded. "Weird," she mumbled.

Carl stepped up to her, trying to remain calm. Just breathing the air in this place made him feel fidgety.

She turned to him. "I'd totally forgotten this was the place where I entered last time," she said.

An anxious feeling stirred in his chest. "I, um, didn't remember it either," he said and tried hard to keep his voice under control.

"Did you enter through the church, too?"

"Yeah, as did Olwen and Omega."

"And now us three again. Interesting, don't you think?"

"Well…" A nervous laugh broke out of him. "I don't know if that's the word I'd use. More like 'eerie' or 'uncanny,' in my opinion."

She smiled at him and took his hand. The warm touch comforted him. "Let me guess, physics wasn't your favorite subject in school?"

"Correct."

The sound of something heavy crashing to the ground behind them made them turn around. Caesar sat on the grass with his head between the knees, heavily breathing. Miriam scowled and crossed her arms over her chest without any sign of going near him, which wasn't at all surprising.

"Hey, C, what's going on?" Carl nonchalantly said as he took the few steps toward the older man and crouched beside him. Putting a hand on his shoulder would go beyond what he could bring himself to do, though. Caesar waved dismissively toward him, and Carl shrugged and stood up again. It seemed as if he hadn't truly believed in all this. *Well, now you do, don't you? Welcome to the realm that drives you crazy, you old bastard.*

Miriam held Allie's phone in her hands with a gentle, loving expression, and the sight filled Carl with hope.

When she noticed that he looked at her, she pointed toward a spot out of the harbor. "I think she's over there. Probably at the castle."

He stared at her while goosebumps covered his skin. "Can you— Can you feel her?"

"Mhm."

"Alright… Um, good…."

While he watched her, her face slowly succumbed to the faraway expression, which he recognized all too well now. He'd seen it on Olwen's face many times lately, and he was quite sure that he wore it at times himself.

As if asleep, Miriam raised her hand and drew a line in the air with her finger, and for a moment, Carl thought that he could see a sprinkle of light trailing after it. Wide-eyed, he stared at the air, but the trail had disappeared.

"There's a line between the church and the castle and the inn," Miriam explained dreamily, "like a triangle, with the library in the middle. Can you see it?"

He turned his gaze from where he'd seen the faint light and looked out over the town. "Um, no."

"You have to concentrate."

"Um, that's fine. I, um, I trust you."

For a moment, she watched the harbor in silence before she turned her blank look at him. "Are you scared, Carl?"

He had to swallow to moisten his dry throat. "Yeah."

"Okay."

Void of emotions, like she wore a mask, she put Allie's phone in her pocket and continued to watch the harbor. Terrified, Carl thought that she looked like her soul had left her. He stared at her emotionless face, and a tiny ripple of fear ran through him. *She's somewhere else in her mind, and I'm losing her. I can't fail her again. I can't! I need to hold onto her somehow.* Suddenly, it dawned on him; *She's way too familiar with this place, and she's changing. She's letting it into her mind, and she's becoming a part of it.*

The terror made him ice-cold and dried out his mouth. He had to force himself to walk over to her and take her hand. With a gush of relief, it was warm to his touch, and the faraway look began to disappear when she turned her head and lovingly viewed him.

With a deep intake of breath, Carl cupped her face and looked her seriously in the eyes. "You have to fight this place, Miri," he said with emphasis. "Don't let it take you. Don't try any shortcuts, regardless of how tempting they might be. We'll do it the hard way, and we'll do it together. Never go on your own, even if it means you'll go with Caesar."

With a light sigh, she nodded. "I'll try." Not satisfied, Carl continued to demandingly watch her. For a second, she looked away before meeting his gaze again. "I'll do my very best," she said, "but you might have to remind me at times. This realm, I have a connection with it now. I— I kind of understand it…"

A slow, cold shiver ran down his spine. "That's what scares me," he whispered.

Seemingly oblivious to the disturbing atmosphere in this realm, Miriam leaned in and pressed her lips toward his. *I wasn't going to kiss her here,* he thought, acutely aware of the unsettling air, but couldn't help but return the kiss. Her lips were warm and tender, and the tip of her tongue on his lower lip still sent trickles of heat through his body. When she slowly broke the kiss and looked at him again, she was completely herself. Inhaling deeply in relief, he embraced her hard.

"I understand what you're saying, Carl." Her whisper was warm at his throat. "You might have to be my anchor here. I'm starting to find this place way too fascinating for my own good."

"I can see that. It's frightening."

She didn't answer, just hugged him even closer. Behind her, Caesar struggled to his feet. Carl let go of Miriam, but she took his hand in a firm grip.

"I meant what I said," she said, deadly serious. "You'll need to be my anchor. I'm going to hold on to you as much as I can."

"Alright. I'm fine with that. More than fine."

Her hand squeezed his, and together, they walked over to Caesar. His face was pale, and the shocked look in his eyes made Carl apprehensive. *He'll get a grip of himself soon enough,* he tried to reassure himself. *C never loses his footing for too long.*

Finally, Caesar acknowledged Miriam. "You were here for a month?"

"Yes."

"Can you— Can you tell me about it?"

Her calm expression helped him relax, which in turn helped Carl ease off a bit. Once more, he realized that the mere atmosphere here tried to press people down and make them feel more anxious than they were. The image of the nervous nine-tailed cat popped up in his mind again.

"It's always night here," Miriam said in the cool and distant tone she used toward Caesar now. "The town down there, it's a dead town, but there are beacons in it, beacons of malevolence; the church here, the inn where I stayed, and the castle where I think Allie and Olwen are. They connect somehow, but I haven't figured out how yet. I do have a feeling they're important to how this realm works, though." She paused, and an intrigued frown formed on her forehead. With an anxious tug at his heart, Carl pressed her hand, and Miriam looked up at him with a sweet smile, before continuing. "There are shadow people around, but I've never seen them anywhere outside the city walls. They feed on you, on your energy, and they can kill you. You can teleport between places, but it will hurt you physically and mentally. It is way too easy to lose yourself here."

Caesar exhaled and let his glance trail over the view and back to her again. "I'm, um, I'm sorry."

Miriam didn't answer, she just continued to watch him calmly, and eventually, he couldn't keep his gaze on her and looked away.

"I can't accept that," she said calmly. "It's not even a real apology."

Caesar clearly struggled with himself. "I'm sorry if I treated you badly or disrespectfully," he said at last with a touch of defiance in his voice.

She waited for something more, but he didn't give her what she hoped for. At last, she shrugged. "You know what, Henry? It doesn't matter. It did once, but not any longer. It's sad that it had to come to this, but—" She shrugged again with a detached expression. "This is probably all you're capable of, so I accept that you can't give me anything else, but when we get out of here, please transfer our team to another Faculty member. Or at least me. I'd be grateful if you could transfer Carl together with me. If you promise to do that, I promise to try to only remember the good things we had together when I think about you."

Caesar flinched, but then, his shoulders sloped, and he looked old and beaten. "I promise," he said in a tired voice. "You and— You and Carl."

"Thank you." The look she gave him was honest but indifferent. "I meant what I said before, Henry. You must keep close to me if you want to be sure to get back home. Distance here is an illusion." She fell silent, and a touch of that quiet look appeared on her face. "Actually, most things here are an illusion." She focused on Caesar again. "If we get separated, and you can't find us, you can open a portal of your own if you concentrate hard enough on a place you love, but it has a price."

"And what's that?"

Miriam shrugged indifferently. "It depends. It's different for different people, but you always leave a piece of your soul here."

At her words, cold shivers ran down Carl's body, but she calmly caressed his hand, and he could breathe again. *She's my anchor too, but God, does she scare me.*

He cleared his throat. "Can we start looking for them now, please? I want to spend as little time here as possible."

When Miriam sought out Caesar's eyes, he nodded at her. "You lead. You know this place."

A faint smile played on her lips at the long-awaited acknowledgment, and she took the lead. Together, they walked the gravel-covered road down the hill and left the looming church behind.

When they reached the crumbled town wall, Miriam stopped and hesitated.

"What?" asked Carl worriedly and craned his neck as he tried to look at everything around them at once.

Caesar caught on to the anxious atmosphere and fiddled with the knife in his belt with a deep scowl on his forehead.

"I— I don't know…" She looked up into the air as if sensing something he couldn't. "There's so much activity going on. I don't know if it's safe to go through the town."

Carl continued to look around, feeling like the nine-tailed cat again, but couldn't see anything and he refused to open himself to whatever it was she could sense. *One of us needs to keep our feet on the ground.* Instead, he gripped her hand even harder, and she squeezed back.

"Shall we go around, or is that dangerous?"

"Everything here's dangerous," she said in the distant voice that scared him so much. Decidedly, he turned her around and kissed her harder than he planned, but this place truly got to him. It terrified him to his bones.

She violently plopped back into herself, and shocked, she stared at him. Immediately, he broke the kiss, and something in the atmosphere felt disappointed and on the brink of anger. He crouched involuntarily and looked around but couldn't see anything. Despite that, he decided to stick to his initial decision and avoid kissing her from now on.

568

"Sorry," he mumbled, trying desperately to ignore the presence around them. Her fingers trailed over her aching lips, and a pang of guilt hit him. "Didn't mean to hurt you."

She squeezed his hand comfortingly. "I know." She let her gaze fall over the dark and shadowed surroundings. The moonlight shining over the landscape didn't brighten it, it only made the dark feel even darker. "Um, yes, maybe going around. It could be dangerous too, but the feeling of danger isn't as strong as when I think about going through." She scowled and looked over her shoulder toward the town gate. "There's something waiting for us."

Carl shivered and had to try hard to remain composed. "Where?"

A concentrated frown appeared on her face as she searched for whatever it was she felt in the atmosphere.

"It's moving toward us, and it comes from several directions, but the moat is clear."

He squinted suspiciously at it. "A trap?"

"Maybe. Possibly. Can't say, actually."

His hand combed through his hair before he was even aware of it. Then, he shrugged. "Alright, let's go."

She nodded, and with Caesar behind them, they jumped down from the bridge into the dry moat, avoiding the big blocks that had fallen from the damaged wall. The thick, high grass reached all the way up to their thighs and had a strange dry and oily feeling, like an old mink skin used for car-washing. A disgusted grimace flashed across Carl's face as he tried to avoid touching it. *Anything can hide in here*, he thought and looked around. Just then, a sense hit him hard of something vile awakening in the grass and becoming aware of them. With rapid pulse, Carl loosened the knife from his belt, preferring the sharp weapon instead of the gun this time since a gunshot could attract the other beings Miriam had talked about. Behind him, Caesar unsheathed his knife too. Without letting go of Carl's hand, Miriam grabbed her knife and crouched into FBI-stance, and as a result, almost disappeared in the high vegetation.

The grass swished at their legs when they carefully moved forward while trying to keep an eye in all directions. The wall on their right side rushed past them, going from visible to a blur, but Carl had no idea how long time had passed before he became aware of it.

Stopping dead, he tugged at Miriam's hand. "You're not taking any shortcuts, are you?"

"Hmm?" Her face was blank again.

"Goddamn, Miri," he hissed quietly. "You need to stop this! You need to focus on being in yourself, not floating around somewhere in the sensations of this place. Please?"

She looked up at him, but her eyes were shadowed. "Sorry…"

Frustration boiled in his body. "No! I don't want your apologies; I want you to keep your mind in place."

Caesar moved uncomfortably at their back and stepped up beside them. He looked over Miriam's head to Carl. "What keeps her grounded?"

Carl sighed wearily. "Physical contact, it seems."

There was a twitch at the corners of Caesar's mouth, but without hesitating, he moved the knife from his right hand to his left. "Sheath your knife," he ordered Miriam, and with her face still blank, she obliged. When Caesar firmly grabbed Miriam's free hand, she winced as if surprised, but not even a second later, she exhaled, clearly back in herself again. For a moment, she stared at Caesar's hand holding hers but didn't try to pull away. Without a word, she began walking, and this time, the wall kept the same speed as they did. Carl gave up a relieved sigh.

A waiting sensation hovered around them, but he couldn't discern anything moving, even though he too had a strong feeling that something was out there. Whatever it was that closed in on them from behind and the sides, it effectively shut off their retreat and left the front open. *Herding us,* Carl thought with clenched teeth, feeling his hands getting sweaty. *They— it— whatever it is, wants us to go this way. I bet it would get very angry if we tried to go back.* Something hissed quietly behind him as to confirm his suspicions and he jolted. Caesar turned around with squinting eyes, clearly afraid. Carl's mouth dried up. Caesar was never afraid, never. *Great, just great. We're such a steady, calm team.*

Miriam looked at him. "Don't think about them. They won't do anything as long as we're going in the right direction." *And what damn direction is that?* "The castle," Miriam absentmindedly answered.

Bewildered, Carl stared at her, but she concentrated on the moat before them. *Did I say that out loud?* No one answered him this time. His forehead was moist, even in this cool air, and his heart hammered faster than usual.

He tugged at her hand and felt almost like a child. "Can we go now? If this is the end, I want to get there as quickly as possible. This damn waiting gets to me, and I'm going to be a wreck before long."

She searched in the air again, sucked in the sensations that whirled around her, that he now could see whirling around her, as if she attracted them, as if she was a light and all those sensations were fireflies. Openmouthed, he stared at the phenomenon. *What's happening to her? No wonder she can't keep grounded.*

"It's not the end, Carl. It's something else."

"Oh, great," he muttered but managed to close his mouth and shut up.

"Carl's right, Miriam," Caesar said in a clearly constrained voice. "If I'm assessing the situation correctly, there's something here that fatigues us and drains our mental resilience, or buffer, if you'd like. The longer we stay, the more fatigued we'll be. When we get to where this entity wants us, we're not going to be able to resist whatever it is we're meeting there. We need to get going. Now."

To Carl's surprise, Miriam nodded without any kind of resentment. It should make him pleased that the team was more stable. Instead, it worried him. It didn't feel like she was in touch with her own feelings.

"You're right," she said and started to stride toward the collapsed town gate, which they could see from here.

Carl had to lengthen his steps to keep up. He kept a suspicious eye on the wall, but it wasn't moving. Within what only felt like ten minutes, she led them out of the moat. They crossed the cobblestone street in front of the town gate and followed the stairs down to the dock. There, her steady walk slowed down until she stopped completely and focused on something further down. Following her gaze, Carl saw a bridge he hadn't noticed last time, leading from the dock out over the water. It looked like a simple wooden suspension bridge hanging in thick chains from a massive stone construction.

"Simplicity for the king, jewels for the jester," Miriam whispered beside him.

Carl glanced at her in desperation, and Caesar scowled at him.

"I don't care what you do, but you've got to get her grounded. We need her." While talking, Caesar sheathed his knife and placed himself behind her. He forced her backpack off and began to massage her shoulders with vigorous movements.

Carl nodded and stepped up in front of Miriam. The expression in her eyes was so distant. She looked like she was somewhere else in her mind, like it was only her body that stood in front of him. *An empty shell, that's what she looks like,* he thought distraught.

Cupping his hands around her face, he let his thumbs caress her cheeks and continue up through her hair, combing it gently through his fingers. Her eyes flickered, but to his horror, he could see the visions play on her irises.

Desperately, he leaned his cheek at her temple and whispered softly in her ear, hoping that she couldn't hear the touch of anguish in his voice, "Miri— Please, come back to me. I need you."

He withdrew from her and looked at her. The muscles in her face twitched. It was clear that she fought hard to take control over herself, but the visions were stronger and smothered her will.

Suddenly, an idea struck him, and he brought out a chocolate bar from his jacket. The sight of this everyday object brought in a heavy sensation of reality from the outside world and from Superfresh with its stressed-out customers and the staff who just longed to go home. It was as if the atmosphere around them twisted in disgust and hesitantly withdrew. With trembling hands, Carl ripped open the wrapping and broke the chocolate in pieces.

"Here, eat this." He held up a small piece to her mouth. As if in a trance, she took it and began to chew. A tiny string of saliva trickled from the corner of her mouth, and he wiped it away, giving her a new piece of chocolate as soon as she swallowed. Something happened in her eyes. The visions faded, and when she looked at him and actually saw him, his throat clasped, and he had to wipe his eyes.

"Can I have some more, please?" Her voice sounded feeble and hoarse.

"Eat as much as you want. We have lots."

When she'd eaten the whole bar, she glared over her shoulder and caught Caesar's hand in hers.

"Thanks. I'm okay now." Her voice was stronger and once again cool toward Caesar.

The sound of it made Carl breathe easier. She was here. She was herself.

Caesar let her go, unsheathed his knife, and took a step to the side. With his tense shoulders and quick glances around, C looked apprehensive, and the hand that held the knife tightened and relaxed and tightened again.

Miriam inhaled deeply and rubbed her face. "There are so many—so many people here," she mumbled. "There are so many stories they want to share. They're crowding me..." She closed her eyes and let the tip of her tongue taste the air. "I've always wondered where they went," she continued. "I know now. They told me. Their empty bodies are all inside the castle. The rest of them, their souls, their shadows, are out here, searching for living people like us to consume." Urgently, she grabbed his hands. Her eyes were frightened when she looked at him. "I think— no, I'm sure— I know that if I go in there, it'll be extremely difficult for me to get out. I will need you, both of you, to keep me in myself. Do whatever it takes." She glanced regretfully at Caesar. "I understand if you don't want to help me, Henry."

The anxious expression on C's face suddenly changed as a furious flare flashed across it. Seemingly without thinking, he shook his fist at her. With a startled gasp, Miriam took an instinctive step back.

C glared viciously at her while clenching his fists at his sides until they whitened. The knife trembled in his grip. "What the hell do you think I am? A monster?" When Miri stared at Caesar with half-open mouth and shook her head slightly, realization dawned on him. Disgust covered his face. "You think I'm going to beat you!" He glanced at his knife. "Or stab you?"

"N… no…"

"Damn right, I'm not!" Forcefully, he threw the knife on the ground and it clattered away a few feet.

"C, calm down, okay?" Carl said alarmed. "You can't afford losing it, not here."

Caesar breathed heavily, his eyes flaring as he continued to stare at Miriam. "You think I'm jealous, don't you?"

"Um…" Miriam swallowed hard and shied away with her gaze, before looking up again with tears in her eyes.

"You're right," he snarled. "Of course, you're right! I am jealous! Have been for years! Ever since you turned me down, I've regretted not trying harder to keep you! Once, you looked at me as you look at him now!" He gave Carl a poisonous glare before turning back to her again. "I could've kept you if I'd tried, you know. You were always really easy to sway, but even back then, he was so much on your mind, it was embarrassing. Why would I want someone who longed for another man's arms around her? I have more pride than

574

that." Half in shock at C's outburst, Carl stared at him, realizing that his former P.I. couldn't stop the words that came tumbling out of him, that the words had been growing poisonous inside him for two years, and now, in this malevolent environment, the strain on his mind broke the dam. "Sally was there; she was willing enough, more than willing. Yes, I admit, it might've been a mistake marrying her when I loved you so much, but who the hell cares? She gives me exactly what I want, except for being you, and seeing how you are now, I'm happy you're not mine anymore. He can keep you." Another venomous glare found its way to Carl for a second, before turning back to Miriam. "Apparently, he likes you like this. Swaggering around. Nose up in the air. Sitting on a blasted pedestal, looking down on everyone else! And the way you're behaving now with all the touching, all the smooching? Where the hell's your decency?" Not expecting an answer, C continued, "Yes, I admit; I can't stand seeing him kiss you! I – can't – stand – it! Do you do it just to rub it in? Am I worth so little in your eyes? Even if I am, do you really think I want you to lose your mind? No, I don't! Do I want you to die? Fucking hell, no! Do I want to leave you here? NO! No! So – just – shut – up!"

They stared at each other, Caesar with fuming eyes, and Miriam shocked with tears running down her cheeks. For a moment, Carl stared at Caesar in complete distress, but with some difficulty, he managed to compose himself. He tugged at Miriam's limp hand and handed her the backpack. His whole body trembled from the shock.

"Alright," he muttered hoarsely. "You're definitely grounded now." With a lop-sided glare at C, he continued, trying to sound calm and reasonable, but couldn't keep the resentment out of his voice, "We're supposed to work as a team, with respect for each other, C, and you just broke every damn rule. I don't care one rotten apple about how you feel when it comes to us. That's not important. Not here, not now. You were the one who wanted in on this RP. It's too late to back out now, so from now on, you keep your personal opinions to yourself." He paused, feeling his pulse beat hard, and watched C, who stared down at the ground with two fiercely red spots on his cheeks. "I need to know, are you going to work with us? I don't want to leave you on your own, but you know as well as I do that we're going to die here if we're not cooperating, and I'd rather leave you than risk all our lives, including your wife's."

The silence dragged out, but finally, Caesar reluctantly looked up at him, and his voice was bested when he said, "I'm— I'm sorry. I— I really am. I shouldn't have said all that. I— I don't know..."

Carl shook his head. "No, you're right. You shouldn't have said that, but I'm not the one you should apologize to."

Caesar inhaled and turned his gaze toward Miriam, with a distressed look in his eyes. "I'm sorry, Mimi. I— I don't know what came over me. It's— It's been hanging over me for so long. I— I just lost it..."

Still looking dazed and beaten with tears glittering on her cheeks, Miriam stared at C without saying anything. It was as if she had lost all her self-confidence in one violent blow. The anger boiled hot in Carl when he saw how defeated she looked, and the temptation to leave Caesar behind was so strong that he had to mentally restrain himself to not do it. *I've never hated anyone, but this? Goddamn!* He took some deep breaths, trying to clear his head from the intense resentment. *No, I'm not going to start hating anyone now. It's not worth it. She's not beaten. She's going to find her self-confidence again. I know that. She's stronger than him, and that's what he can't take.*

"You have to make your choice now, C," he said in a cold, detached voice. "Are you going to stay here, or are you going to work with us as a team?"

Reluctantly, Caesar turned his gaze toward him again. "I'm... I'm going to work with you."

Carl exhaled deeply, still feeling his body trembling as he struggled to let go of his antipathy.

"Alright," he said calmer. "Let's move then. We can't waste any more time." Turned to Miriam, he said, with a

576

gentle touch of her hand, "I promise to do whatever it takes to get you out of the castle sane and in one piece, Miri. Whatever it takes."

"Thank you," she mumbled in a crushed and defeated voice.

Seeing and hearing her like this was like a stab in his heart. He wanted to embrace her, showing her all the love he felt for her, letting her know that she was a fabulous person, worthy of everything good coming her way, but it wasn't the right time. She would only withdraw from him now. With a test of will, he avoided the venomous looks he wanted to shoot at Caesar. Instead, he took Miriam's hand and began to walk. After C picked up his knife, he grabbed her other hand, but she jerked and pulled away from him as if she couldn't stand him touching her. *No wonder. Stupid, fucking idiot! If he does something like this ever again, I swear I'm going to leave him here without any qualms. I don't care what would happen to him. He can go fuck himself!*

The silence was deeply strained as they continued forward toward the suspension bridge. Concerned, Carl kept a look at Miriam. Even though her face was blank and devoid of any kind of feelings, she seemed to keep the visions at bay, to his enormous relief. In a way, it didn't matter what kept her grounded right now, as long as it wasn't another devastating downfall. *You need to fight it, albi. As long as you do, it's all good.*

When they closed in on the bridge, they became aware of a familiar figure who stood in the shadows of the huge bridge tower, waiting for them. Seeing Miriam straightening up and defiantly glaring at the entity, made Carl take a deep breath of relief.

"Welcome," Night Porter said and smiled secretively at them when they approached him. "It's a wonderful night, don't you think?"

Carl refused to answer, and Miriam looked away. *Yeah, we've learned our lesson. Don't talk to him. Don't let him into our minds. Don't let him get a grip on us. Don't play his game.*

"What kind of a clown is this?" Caesar asked brusquely.

A mockingly sad expression appeared on Night Porter's face. "Aw, Henry, the words. You're hurting my feelings. But I survive. Your darling Miriam might not."

"She's – not – my – darling!"

Night Porter grinned at him. "Living in denial, are we? I can see right through you, Henry, all the way into your dirty secrets, and aren't you such a sweet little liar."

Anger turned the older man's face as white as a sheet. "Go to hell!" he snarled.

With a hearty laugh, Night Porter bent over in amusement. "Oh, dear, you have no idea, but I'd be more than happy to show you." He pointed at the bridge. "It's straight ahead and to the right." Caesar glared infuriatingly at him and got an amused look back. "No? I thought that was the way you were heading, the way your darling Mimi was leading you."

"Leave her out of this," Caesar growled.

Night Porter grinned expectantly. "I can't. She's already one of us."

With his body turning to water out of sheer terror, Carl spun toward Miriam. Seeing her furious face, staring at Night Porter, made his legs feel wobbly from the enormous relief that filled him, and he had to fight to keep himself on his feet. *Not entranced. Not that much under his influence. Not gone.*

When Caesar talked again, she even rolled her eyes slightly at him. "Where's Sally? What have you done to her?"

Night Porter grinned, and there was a triumphant gleam in his eyes.

"Sally, oh, determined, obstinate Sally… I don't have her anymore. She's under the spell of someone else."

"Who?"

"I can't tell you without spoiling the surprise, now can I?"

Miriam looked distressed as she glared at Caesar, and Carl thought that she must be the better person of the two of them since she actually stopped C from going down with Night Porter, which he didn't.

"Why are you listening to him? He'll just wrap you around his finger. You're doing exactly what he wants. Let's go instead."

The laugh trilled like dark pearls in the air when Night Porter turned his attention toward Miriam. Carl shivered violently as the sound penetrated his ears. With a grimace, he placed a hand on his temple.

Instead of meeting Night Porter's eyes, Miriam deliberately turned her head, looking out over the murky water, something that seemed to make Night Porter even more amused.

Caesar scowled darkly at everyone, and before Carl had the chance to interrupt, he sneered at Miriam, "I can handle myself."

Miriam shied away at his tone, and Carl tugged desperately at his hair. "C," he said, almost pleadingly.

Night Porter interrupted them with an oily smile. "No, no, no, don't argue. Are you going to make it easy for me?"

Suddenly united against him, they looked back at him, and he laughed again. Then, he tilted his head and watched them intently with his clear pit-coal eyes, obviously pleased with the situation. Silence fell, and Night Porter's eyes filled up Carl's whole vision. With a sudden dread in his heart, he jerked his gaze away from him, terrified at how easy it was to fall into Night Porter's many traps.

He cleared his voice, trying to take control of the situation. "Let's go. We're just wasting our time."

Caesar and Miriam blinked confused at him as if they had just woken up.

"Oh, but you'll need these," Night Porter said benevolently. "You won't gain entrance otherwise." He held up his empty hands, but the next second, three jewel-glittering masks appeared. The moonlight made the gems twinkle like tiny stars, making Carl faintly dizzy.

Night Porter held out the masks at them, but suddenly, as if reading each other's minds, they said with one voice, "Simplicity for the king, jewels for the jester."

There was a shift in Night Porter's eyes as if they surprised him, and with a quick gesture, he threw the masks into the water. Silently, they disappeared into the dark.

"Fine. Go in. Be kings. But you might have preferred being jesters."

Chapter 35

Ignoring Night Porter's sarcastic grin, Carl. Miriam, and Caesar turned their back on him. The conversation left Carl extremely anxious. *What does it mean, 'kings and jesters'? Does it mean anything at all? Do I need to remember it later? And what the hell does it mean that Olwen's under someone else's spell? Who's spell? Allie's? That doesn't make any sense at all!*

Cautiously, they walked through the oppressive bridge tower onto the rickety bridge, trying hard to keep their balance on the swaying planks. The dark chain links holding the bridge in place were as big and thick as a man's arm, stretching up and disappearing in the shadows of the stone construction far above them.

Carl glanced at Miriam and Caesar, noticing how they kept as long a distance to each other as possible. Neither of them held hands, which he clearly understood, but— *I need to make this work. It's my damn job. As soon as we get out of here, we don't have to see him ever again, but for now, we must be able to work with him. We must, or we're going to fail. It's that simple.* Out of the corner of his eye, he saw the sensations swirling around, trying to close in on Miriam. Desperately, he tugged at his hair and casually said the first thing that popped into his head, "Alright, Miri, I've been wondering, what was your favorite subject in school, except for physics?"

Both Miriam and Caesar stared at him as if he was crazy, but the next second, understanding dawned in Caesar's eyes, and he nodded, reluctantly, but appreciatively. Miriam, on the other hand, looked as if she wasn't sure that she had grasped what he had said.

"You want to ask me that now?" she asked disbelievingly, and he was happy to hear the stronger tone in her voice. Clearly, she was fighting the visions, rather than giving in to them. He couldn't help but smile lovingly at her.

"Why not? It's as good a time now as any other."

She rolled her eyes at him and said, "I care to disagree."

The next second, an insecure expression spread doubt across her face, and she lowered her gaze, seemingly thinking the question over. It ticked him off that she wanted to oblige him, as she had Caesar back then, even though he knew why she reacted like this now. It would take some time and some work before she would stop feeling this crushed, and to downright refuse something he asked of her now was more than she could handle. Without being able to stop himself, he sent a vicious gaze at Caesar's profile.

"English and history," she said eventually, in a hesitant tone. Clearly, it vexed her, talking about everyday things with C walking beside her, and he regretted asking.

"What was the name of your teachers?" Caesar asked immediately without grasping her mood. *Or he just doesn't care. I don't know which is worse.*

With a suspicious glance toward them both, Miriam kept her silence. C grabbed her hand and tugged it. She jerked, but C kept his firm grip, and she exhaled, sounding distressed. Squinting in anger at his former P.I.s behavior, Carl was just about to say something when Miriam gave up.

"Mrs. Elmwood in English and Mr. Dunbruigh in history," she muttered hesitantly.

Carl caressed her hand, but she ignored him, probably out of sheer self-preservation. He guessed that she desperately tried to get back on her feet and that she needed to distance herself, even from him. *That's okay. Totally unnecessary turn of events, but if she needs to indulge in her own space, I won't stomp in on it.*

"What was special about them?" Caesar continued obliviously.

Miriam gave him another weary glance, and when she talked again, the words seemed to slip out of her without her having any control over them. "Not many students appreciated them because they were so demanding."

Her voice sounded exhausted, Carl thought and gave her a worried look. Her face was gaunt, and there were dark smudges under her eyes. Concerned, he covertly checked the gauze, but it was still nicely white, to his relief.

"That's it, Mimi?" Caesar asked. She shook her head but kept her silence. "Mimi?" When she still didn't say anything, Caesar scowled and pulled hard at her hand.

Carl glared at him. "It's okay if she doesn't want to talk about it."

"I... I can tell you... if you... if you're really interested, Carl," she said, and that she managed to take an initiative at this point, gladdened him immensely.

"I'd love to hear it," he said sincerely.

C scowled at him over her head. He didn't care.

In a drained voice, she said, "I learned so much from them. Mrs. Elmwood was also our drama teacher, and when she recited the classics, it was— it just took my breath away." Losing herself in the memories, some kind of emotion finally tinted her voice. "Mr. Dunbruigh always managed to make history come alive for me, made me understand that even people who lived thousands of years ago were like you and me. It was hard for me to grasp before I got him as a teacher. Sometimes we got assignments where we had to try and imagine what historical people were thinking. I especially remember the one about Augustus. '*What did Emperor Augustus think when he got the news about the defeat in the Teutoburg Forest?*'"

"What a great way of making history come alive." The sincerity in Carl's voice made her actually look at him. He caressed her hand and this time, she caressed him back. Without giving her any time to reflect on the sensations that still tried to get to her, he continued, "What did you answer?"

"That he couldn't think. He was too devastated. Then, everything started to sink in; all the men he had lost; the worst defeat he had ever faced. Sometimes, I wonder if he ever thought about the families that stood without their husbands and fathers and brothers, or if he only saw the numbers. And then, he butted his head against the wall and shouted the famous words, '*Quintilius Varus, give me back my legions!*'"

As they talked, they had managed to cross half the bridge without her going into a trance, and the everyday topic kept the swirling sensations away from her, but Carl could see them clearly. They were spinning around, weaving golden streaks in the darkness beyond the bridge, wanting to get to her, but keeping a fair distance.

"Tell me about the Minoans," he asked while keeping an eye on the streaks. "What did Mr. Dunbruigh say about them?"

He could see that she knew what they tried to do and that it vexed her. "Oh, come on, Carl, stop it already. I don't want to talk about that here."

Hearing her irritated voice made him oddly happy. It meant she didn't try to oblige him all the way, and that even though C had done his best to strike her down, she started to get back on her feet. *Good. Good for you, Miri. You're so damn awesome, so damn special, and I love you so very, very much.*

"You can tell me about the Minoans. Is it something special you find fascinating?" Caesar said and was rewarded with a sour face.

"Sure," she muttered, "I can tell you. You're so very interested. Always been."

"Please?"

Miriam shrugged and gave up, letting herself fall into her old submissive behavior toward him. *She doesn't have much energy left to fight him anymore, and he just doesn't get it. He's so damn determined to crush her so he can remold her into the form he likes. Does he do that with Olwen too? I highly doubt it.*

"Linear A and B."

"Why?" Caesar asked.

She gave him an annoyed glance. "You should know that at least. Did you forget, or did you never pay attention in the first place, or are you just trying to make me think about something else except this here right now?" The sudden outburst made Caesar hesitate. "You never paid attention, did you?"

"I did pay attention," he protested, "but it was six years ago. Don't try to tell me you remember every detail of what I told you when we first started dating."

"I do remember," she mumbled with a sad look in her eyes.

Caesar gave her a skeptical look. "Really?" She didn't answer. "What were my favorite subjects in school then?"

"Biology."

"And?"

"Chemistry."

"Huh."

She sighed tiredly. "I don't know why it still feels important to me that you believe me." There was a slight pause, in which Carl took the opportunity to hold on to her hand with both of his. Then, she inhaled and continued, "When you were in high school, you managed to make a gas that evacuated the whole school, and you got suspended for a month."

Even in this situation, and with all the angry feelings inside him, Carl suddenly gave a short laugh at the image that popped up in his mind.

"Did you do that, C?" he asked, having a hard time seeing the always meticulous Caesar do something like that.

The annoying self-awareness disappeared for a moment from Caesar's face, and he grinned sheepishly.

"Yes, I did. And it was on purpose too, just to show Mr. Evans that I was better than him in chemistry. That's why I got suspended for so long."

Yeah, okay, that makes sense. You haven't changed all that much, have you?

The rest of the walk over the bridge was tread in silence, which felt like a relief. The whirling sensations came closer, but Miriam looked at them with a deep frown on her forehead, and – as if they were sentient beings – they seemed to hesitate.

As the bridge turned right, for no good reason at all, the castle loomed over them, crushing them under its shadow. Seemingly unaware of his actions, Caesar hunched while suspiciously squinting at it, and there was a touch of discomfort and anxiousness in his appearance. Miriam's face, on the other hand, closed again, and her eyes watched the shut doors at the end of the bridge with an emotionless gaze. She didn't respond to his squeeze this time, but at least she wasn't entranced.

He, himself, found the towering castle being the center of the anxiety that forced itself upon them. Even though he knew what was happening by now, he couldn't control his body's reaction to it. Somewhat curious, he noticed how his heart rate sped up to an almost unknown rate, as his hands, armpits, and face perspired excessively, and his breathing became shallow.

All the way toward the entrance, Carl thought about Zen and fought to drive the anxiety out of his body and mind without succeeding. It struck him that walking toward the enormous doors was like walking toward the mouth of a sleeping giant.

When they finally came to the end of the bridge and stepped down onto the unmoving ground, their legs shook from the long, unsteady walk. While catching their breaths, Carl studied the entrance in front of them. The upper edge of the doors disappeared into the shadows far overhead.

Carl nervously cleared his throat but put on his reassuring mask and the calm leader voice that accompanied it. "From now on, we have no idea what we're going to face, but it doesn't matter as long as we stay together. We're a team, and we're going to stay a team. We won't separate, we'll keep holding hands. Where one goes, everyone goes. I don't want to hear any kind of negative word about any of us from this point on. I won't have our own disagreements kill us. Do you understand?"

Miriam nodded. "Yes. I promise."

He caressed her hand and finally got a tug back.

"C?"

"Of course. That goes without saying."

Carl sighed quietly as he had to accept that this was the best answer he would get from C.

"Good. Our objective is to find Allie and Olwen, nothing else. When we've done that, you open a portal to my place, Miri, since there's already one in there. Again, always remember to communicate, always remember to respect each other. That goes for all three of us. Any questions?"

"Who leads?" Caesar asked.

"Miriam. She can feel where Allie is, and she knows how to open the portals, but if I come with an order, I want both of you to follow it. Can you agree to that?"

They nodded, and a wave of relief filled him. Maybe it would still work. Maybe they would still be able to get through this together. *Yeah, and maybe pigs really do fly...*

Miriam turned to Caesar. Overjoyed, Carl noticed she could look at C with some self-respect again.

"Do you have anything belonging to Olwen I can have for now? I need to know if she's in the same place as Allie."

"Um..." C fiddled with the wedding ring, but Miriam shook her head.

"No, that one's more for you."

"Um, then I don't have anything..." A flash of shame passed over his face, and his gaze shied away.

"Okay, we'll have to try without anything then."

On her own initiative, she took Caesar's hand again, but then, she hesitated. Turning toward Carl, she had a raw look in her eyes. She wanted something from him, and he thought he understood what. He glared at C, who frowned with something that resembled insecurity.

"What?"

"Can you turn around, please?"

"Why?"

Carl scowled. *Why do you have to question every damn thing? Well, suit yourself.*

587

"I'm going to kiss my fiancée."

"Oh, um…" Embarrassed, C half-turned away and let go of Miriam's hand as if it burnt him.

Miri let out a relieved sigh as she closed in on him, tiptoed to reach up. Carl embraced her lovingly. Her body was warm and familiar in his arms. Closing his eyes, he met her lips, and the physical sensations that hit him were as strong and clean as always. This time, he couldn't sense any presence around them, enjoying their physical contact. When she let him go, she smiled and looked like she used to, and just because he could, because she seemed to be so *her*, so natural and self-confident, and so much in love, he stole another kiss.

"I think she's grounded enough now," Caesar interrupted them, and even though his voice clearly was pained, it also held a surprising hint of amusement and even a touch of freedom. Carl glanced at him. C watched them with a sad and resigned appearance, but somewhere in his wistful eyes, Carl also read determination.

Caesar caught his glance, and gave him a crooked half-smile, finally free of jealousy. "I want to find Sally now and get out of here. Is there anything else we need to resolve before going in?"

"No, I think we're fine," Carl answered with a slightly strained half-smile of his own, silently acknowledging Caesar's accomplishment. Both of them nodded at him, showing that they were as ready as they would ever be.

With a deep breath, Carl faced the entrance, grabbed the huge handles, and opened the doors. It occurred to him that he might step into the last moments of his life, but he immediately let go of the thought. If that was to be the case, so be it. He couldn't dwell on it now, not if he were going to be able to lead the other two. He didn't have a choice anyway. Turning around, leaving Allie and Olwen here, was not a choice.

Silently, the doors opened to an enormous hall. The white marble plates on the floor faintly mirrored the multitude of lit candelabras, like faraway blinking stars. Throughout the corridor, within regular, even spacing, several Night Porters stood watching them, all wearing different kinds of smiles, all of them unpleasant. Miriam and Caesar gasped beside him as they stared at the sight. Perspiring from mere bewilderment, Carl counted to twenty versions of him. This time, he was dressed as a butler and held trays of glasses containing golden liquid in his hands, offering them something to wet their dry throats with.

At the very thought of something to drink, Carl suddenly felt it as if his whole being was suffering from severe dehydration. His tongue was swollen, and there wasn't even a trace of saliva in his mouth. The terrifying memory of the execution overwhelmed him, and without being able to stop it, his body began to tremble.

At Carl's reaction, all the Night Porters turned their heads toward him. A grin appeared on their faces as they slowly changed appearance, clawing their way into his memories and copied the bald woman in red, down to the bullet hole in her heart. Miriam and Caesar both jolted and gasped. Desperately trying to keep back the tears at the sight, Carl forced himself to look at all of them, one at a time.

I'm not giving in to you. I didn't give in to her. I will NEVER give in! Staring at them defiantly, he dried his eyes and took a deep breath. *You won't break me. I don't care what you're throwing at me. You won't break me.* At the far end, two of the cult leaders transformed back into Night Porter as they reached for the closed doors that ended the hall. When the huge doors opened yet another version of Night Porter strode in toward them.

"Whatever you do," Carl whispered urgently in a voice cracked by the lack of saliva, "don't eat or drink anything and don't interact with anyone here. I have a feeling it'd be really bad news for us."

Hesitantly, Caesar nodded and put down his hand again. It worried Carl immensely that C had reached out to one of the cult leaders and her tray of glasses. *For crying out loud, C, you've got to be stronger than that. Come on now, I know you can do it.*

Transfixed, Miriam watched the approaching Night Porter.

"Miri?" Carl anxiously said. "Did you hear what I said?"

"Yes… Yes, I did." With some effort, she managed to look away and glance up at him with a haunted appearance that tugged at his heart. "I won't."

He caressed her hand and got a faint squeeze back.

"Good. Let's go and meet him. Let's take some initiative." A couple of words Allie had said the first day they met came back to him. "We have to own the scene."

"'Own the scene,'" Caesar mumbled. "Yes, we need to own the scene. That's what kings do."

For some reason, the sentence made Carl shiver, and he glanced worriedly at the older man, but C looked as resolute as Carl remembered from other RPs. Inhaling deeply, shrugging it off, he hoped that C wouldn't give them any other surprises down the line. *Take one catastrophe at a time, that's all you can do.* He desperately needed to tug at his hair but couldn't, seeing as both his hands were occupied. Instead, he took a tighter grip of his knife. It felt almost as good, even though it didn't relieve all his tension.

Determinedly, they walked toward the approaching Night Porter while Carl continuously squeezed Miri's hand to help her remember that she wasn't alone here.

As they closed in on him, he seemed to stand taller than before, looming over them, like the church on the hill. At the thought, Carl frowned uneasily. *What church?* Somehow, it seemed important that he remembered what church he was thinking of, but he'd seen so many. It was impossible to figure out which one it was that materialized in the outskirts of his mind.

Night Porter interrupted his thoughts with a sweeping, elegant bow. "Welcome, Kings. Welcome, Queen of my Heart. Your audience is waiting."

Without acknowledging him, they passed him by and continued into an enormous ballroom. Hesitantly, they stopped, silently trying to take in what lay before them.

In the air inside the empty room, a vibrating tone quivered with an excruciating high-pitched sound, faintly visible as dark streaks overhead. It resonated with them, made their bodies tremble. Their hearts hammered hard together with its pulse.

"This is the core," Miriam finally said in a pained voice.

Shaken, Carl nodded. To step inside, into the suffocating streaks, seemed impossible.

In the mirrors that covered the walls, they saw themselves standing in the doorway like three small dots in a huge, overwhelming landscape, simply dressed in black, their gaze staring bewildered and pained at their surroundings.

Suddenly, there was a shift in the mirrors. The air in front of their reflections shimmied, and slowly, almost painfully so, human shapes took form. They filled up the whole room, taking physical form before their eyes. Hundreds of masked people dressed in old-fashioned gowns and dress coats waited eagerly for them where nothing had existed only a moment ago.

Everything glittered with jewels, from the masks to the clothes and the jewelry that hung heavily around necks and wrists, in ears and hair and on fingers. The intense glittering created reflections in the large mirrors, and Carl began to feel dizzy from all the dancing colors.

As the crowd moved toward the walls, a walkway opened up in front of the agents, leading to a podium that hadn't been there a minute ago. Five simple wooden thrones that didn't look like they belonged in here waited for them. Strangely enough, the middle throne was placed slightly higher than the other four, on a podium of its own. Carl swallowed hard, feeling a trap opening in front of them.

As if their feet had a life of their own, they moved forward with jerky movements, but slowly, as if they were walking in jelly.

Carl tried to discern Allie and Olwen in the anticipatory crowd, but it was impossible. *Why are we doing Night Porter's bidding?* he thought anxiously as they approached the podium. *We can't play his game. If we're playing, we're losing. It's as simple as that.*

"Where are they, Miri?" he asked urgently in a low voice.

He had a terrifying feeling that something extremely bad would happen if they went up on the podium and sat down on the thrones. Miriam stopped and closed her eyes for a moment. At the sudden disturbance, the crowd began to whisper. They sounded hungry. Wide-eyed in beginning terror, Carl let his gaze move over them. They were writhing where they stood, moving restlessly from one foot to the other, wanting to get going, but something hindered them for now. *Oh, God! This is bad. They're not going to eat us, are they?* Sweat trickled down his forehead, but he put on a calm appearance. He caught Caesar's gaze, and the older man looked distressed and frightened.

"We can't fight all these people, Carl. They're too many."

"I know. We need to come up with something quickly. I don't like the look of those thrones. Don't ask me why."

"They're on the second floor," Miri said in a dreamy kind of voice.

He glanced at her, but to his relief, she was just concentrating.

She let C's hand go and pointed up behind the thrones. "Somewhere in that direction. At least I can feel Allie, but there's a faint glimpse of something warm beside her, which I think could be Olwen."

"Alright, take C's hand now." As she did what he said, he asked, "Can anyone see a staircase or something?"

592

As they craned their necks to be able to see something beyond the crowd, the whispers became louder, angrier, and there was a more intense and impatient movement rolling through the audience, but something seemed to hold them back, and to Carl's enormous relief, the masked people continued to stand still at their place.

"If we're going to do something," Caesar said frantically with a stiff face, "we need to do it quickly. Thrones or stairs?"

"I can't see the damn stairs!"

"Thrones then. We'll probably be able to see the stairs from up there."

Carl nodded, even though it felt like a huge mistake going up there. When he looked over his shoulder as they started their slow pace again, the crowd had closed in on them and effectively shut them off from the entrance. *Herding us.* At the gigantic doors that now were closed, the triumphantly smiling Night Porter towered over the mob.

The thoughts tumbled wildly in Carl's mind. *We're the kings and the queen in his game. Why does that make me think of Greece?* He concentrated on the images that hovered on the outskirts of his mind, trying to make them come to him. *There was a ritual, a ceremony... A king and a queen for a day. What did they do with kings and queens for a day in Ancient Greece? Did they eat them for a prosperous year? Did they exile them? Execute them? I don't remember.*

As if he could read Carl's thoughts, Night Porter gave him an intimate smile, and suddenly, the man held a large silver knife in one of his hands, and a bleeding rose in the other. Carl gasped as a sensation of excruciating fear somehow forced itself into his mind, twisting around to make as much damage as possible.

Jerkily, he looked forward again, his head pounding with intense pain. "No, we can't go up there!" he panted, out of breath in lingering terror. "We need to get out of this room! Miri, show us. Now!" When she didn't answer, he glanced at her and saw her blank face staring out at nothing, her eyes filled with tiny flickering stars. *Damn it! No time, goddammit! No time!* "Goddamn, C, let's break through!"

"Which way?"

Own the scene, damn it! Just own the goddamn scene! Without thinking, he chose.

"To the right."

They took the crowd completely by surprise when they suddenly broke through to the right with Miriam being dragged after them by her hands. Clothes rustled over Carl's body when he forced himself through the hollow shells of people that had once lived. Their skin felt like dried snakeskin when he accidentally touched them.

With a grimace, he waved his knife in front of him to make the masked people quicker move out of the way. The whispers grew in strength behind them, and he recognized the hissing sound from the moat. *God, we're so boned, we're so damn boned!*

They were finally through, but there wasn't any exit here, only the mirrors in which they could see their own frightened faces, pale, with wide-opened eyes and panting breaths, except Miriam's face which was shadowed and dreamy with streaks of light surrounding her.

"Now what?" Caesar asked in a voice marked with dread.

Own the scene, goddammit! Own the fucking scene! Desperately, Carl looked around. There was absolutely nothing here that could help them. There was nowhere to go, except back to where the hungry masks slowly and eagerly closed in on them from all sides. The whispers weren't angry anymore, only expectant and yearning, hungry.

Ignoring the pain in his head that physically pressed him to the floor, Carl tried to calm down enough to catch the thoughts that wildly fluttered in his mind. He inhaled deeply and closed his eyes, fiercely searching for inspiration. As a spear of light, a vision came through his muddled thoughts, and he gave up a terrified laugh. *It's crazy, but it might work.*

Laws of physics are bendable. Wasn't that what she said? Bendable. I have to believe that it'll work, I have to!

"Turn around, C. Close your eyes. Back up toward the mirror. Hold Miri tight."

"Carl—"

"Just do what I say, goddammit!" Carl realized he yelled at him, but to his immense relief, C was finally quiet, doing what he was told.

With a deep breath, he followed Caesar around, faced the mob that now was so close that they could touch them. Their fingers were old and dry as parchment on his skin when they eagerly caressed his face, and their breaths were warm and smelled like sewers. It made him gag. *How the hell am I supposed to concentrate now? Goddamn, they're going to rip us apart, eat us, and suck up our energy. No, don't think about that. Think— Think about summer. Think about the pond, like a mirror.*

He closed his eyes and struggled to shut off the hissing whispers in front of him and ignore the clawing fingers on his body. While he walked backward toward the mirror with a tight grip on Miri's hand, he imagined himself lazily swimming in green, cool water. The image built up quickly in his mind. *It's summer. I'm thirteen years old. My cousin Haniyya and I are swimming in the pond at the farm. I call her Han Solo, 'cause she's just as reckless as him. She's so proud of that name that she always plays the daredevil when I'm around. Haniyya is only nine, but she's a better swimmer than I am. She's like an otter, and she loves pinching my toes under the water. It makes her laugh so hard when I panic, which I do every time. But now, we're just lying on our backs, looking up at the sky. It's one of those warm, warm summer days. It's probably around thirty degrees, and the pond's our rescue. There's not a single cloud in the sky, and the colour is so amazingly blue. The water is clear as a mirror and easy to move in. It feels like silk surrounding me...*

When the hissing slowly disappeared, Carl realized that he had forgotten about it. When it was completely gone, he opened his eyes. They stood in a corridor facing a wall. With a pounding heart, aching head, and wide-open mouth, he stared at the wall, couldn't believe what he saw. Jerkily, he turned his head and looked at Caesar who still had his eyes shut. Sweat drops ran down the older man's tightly closed face. Then, he looked at Miri, who now hung slumped between them with her head down. No one else was in sight.

"You can open your eyes now, C," he croaked and didn't recognize his own voice. A strong taste of iron in his mouth made him grimace.

As Caesar opened his eyes, his face was struck with amazement and streaked with fear. "What did you do?" he whispered and glanced at him, then the amazed look became worried. "You're bleeding."

"What?"

"You're bleeding." With his free hand, Caesar pointed at his nose, and Carl patted it with his hand. Bright red blood covered it immediately.

"Damn," Carl said and became aware of how muddled his voice sounded.

Caesar pulled out a gauze pad from a pocket, ripped it open and handed it to him.

"Thanks," Carl mumbled. "I think I need to sit down for a moment."

Caesar nodded, and together, they managed to make Miriam sit down on the floor too. Since he couldn't hold her hand now, Carl placed himself shoulder to shoulder with her. Her body felt limp beside him.

"Can you try to give her some chocolate?" he asked and pinched the bridge of his nose as hard as he could.

Caesar searched his pockets and got out another gauze pad and a chocolate bar. "You're bleeding through quickly," he remarked and gave him the new gauze.

"Yeah… Probably a bad idea doing that thing, but I couldn't come up with anything else." His voice was even more muddled now. It sounded thick, and the blood tasted heavily of iron in his throat. It bled too much for him to be able to lean his head backward. The blood that flowed down his throat made him gag and made him feel like he was drowning. Instead, he placed his head between his knees and continued to pinch the bridge of the nose as hard as he could. It had to stop bleeding eventually.

"It seems to have worked, whatever it was you did." Caesar broke the bar in pieces and put one at Miriam's mouth. "Here, Mimi, eat something." There was a slight pause. "Come now, you need to eat." After yet another pause, Caesar said, "She doesn't take it. I probably need to force her to eat it."

"Whatever it takes, remember?" Carl mumbled. "Force her, hug her, kiss her, slap her... Whatever it takes..."

"Kiss her? You can't be serious."

"I don't know..." Carl felt lightheaded, and everything was spinning around him.

"No, I'll leave that to you. My kissing-Miriam-days are over since long, and it's time to understand that and let them go. Besides, I swear Sally would step in at just the wrong moment. One angry woman at a time is hard enough to handle."

"Do you have another gauze?" Carl managed to ask. He could hear the faint rustle when Caesar took out another one from its package.

"How are you feeling?"

"Dizzy..."

"Here, let me take a look." Caesar's hands were suddenly placed around his face and pulled his head up. "You're bleeding a lot. We need to stop it."

"Miri..."

"No. She can wait, but you need to get that bleeding under control."

"Dangerous?"

"Not really, but you'll get weak if you lose too much. Take off the backpack."

As soon as he did, Caesar squeezed himself in between the wall and Carl's back. He put one firm hand on Carl's forehead and leaned him into his broad chest while

597

grabbing around Carl's nose bridge, pinching so hard that tears were forced out of his eyes. Carl groaned in pain.

"Don't worry," C said reassuringly. "It'll stop in a minute or so."

After what felt like eons, the grip around his nose finally stopped, and Caesar scooted away. His warm hands were placed on Carl's face again and lifted it up, and his blue eyes examined him closely.

"You're fine now," he said eventually, and added, "I wouldn't do that thing again, though."

"Agreed. Thanks." With trembling hands, Carl searched for the package of wet wipes in the backpack's pocket and started to clean himself up. *So much blood…*

As if the physical contact with Carl had given him some courage to touch Miri, Caesar took off her backpack and placed himself behind her back too, leaning her head toward his chest and tried to feed her the chocolate. At first, it didn't have any effect, but when Caesar closed her mouth around the piece by holding her chin up, the sweet taste seemed to reach her, and she chewed slowly and mechanically. As a nestling, she gaped for more, still with her eyes closed. After two full chocolate bars, she opened her eyes. They looked shadowed, and she seemed to have a problem focusing.

Carl took her hand and kissed it. She turned her head toward him, and when she saw him, she fell into his lap and closed her eyes again.

He caressed her hair. "How are you feeling, *habibti*?"

"Tired," she mumbled. "Where are we?"

"I don't know. Probably still in the castle. Can you feel Allie and Olwen?"

After a slight pause, she nodded. "Up there. Closer now."

"Good. How's your head wound?"

With slow movements, she patted the gauze. "Seems fine," she mumbled, and he could breathe easier again. Maybe it was that damn sand that had been the problem all the time.

598

He kissed her forehead. "I know you're tired, but we probably should get going before they, um, you know who, can find us again."

A deep sigh heaved her body, but she didn't disagree.

Carl glanced at Caesar. "Can you help her up?"

"Of course. Fascinating. I never thought I'd ever be the one in the best shape out of us three. I have to indulge in the feeling as long as I can since it won't last."

He smiled kindly at them for the first time since they met, and it was so nice to see that sympathetic expression again that tears formed in Carl's eyes. Embarrassed, he suppressed them, but let a broad smile break out on his lips.

"Yeah? It's not over yet, old man."

Caesar scoffed. "You make me feel as if I'm looking for my cane."

When he stood up and reached for Miriam, Carl took his hand and squeezed it. Caesar looked surprised at him.

"You've been missed, C. Just saying."

A faint flush covered Caesar's cheeks as he understood what Carl meant. To Carl's surprise, C returned the squeeze before loosening his hand to help Miriam up. She hung slumped in his arms. C glanced worriedly down at her.

"We need to do something with her. She can't function like this."

Carl heaved himself up with a tired sigh. He had to admit that his legs felt wobbly, but it was nothing he couldn't handle. Then, he looked at Miriam.

"I don't know what more I can do," he mumbled distressed, but closed in on her, embraced her, and put her head on his shoulder.

"Whatever it takes, remember?" Caesar said. "Pretend I'm not here and work some of your magic on her. We need her."

Carl gave Caesar a lop-sided look. "There are some things I won't do here and now."

"I didn't say you should."

A slow blush covered his face, and to hide his embarrassment, he cupped Miriam's face in his hands, leaned in and placed his mouth at her ear. With a quiet voice, he started to sing the Lebanese lullaby she liked, while being careful to push out his breaths on the bare skin of her throat. Goosebumps appeared on her skin and she shivered slightly.

When the song ended, she stood up without much help from Caesar, and Carl began to speak to her in Arabic. It was easier, less embarrassing, to say what he felt for her in a language C didn't understand. He could tell that she was listening closely to him, and maybe she could understand the context through the gentle, loving tone he used. Eventually, he just leaned his head on her shoulder, feeling exhausted.

Her hands embraced him, and he could feel her smile. "That was beautiful, Carl," she whispered tenderly. "I don't think anyone has ever said something like that to me before."

He stiffened slightly. "Um, did you— did you understand what I said?"

"Of course, I did."

He swallowed awkwardly. *Did I say all that in English? I thought— God, I'm a mess!*

"Um, good," he mumbled. "I meant it, every single word."

She embraced him hard, smiling at his throat. He decided to push the awkwardness to the side. It didn't have any place here.

"Do you feel better now?" he asked. "Can you continue?"

She nodded. "I think so. Do you have any more chocolate? And maybe something to drink."

Caesar opened his backpack. After a bit rummaging around in it, he handed her three chocolate bars and a bottle of water. With a content sigh, she devoured everything. Afterward, she even had some color on her face.

"Here," Caesar said and gave him some chocolate and water as well. "You need some energy too. And don't worry;

I truly didn't understand a word of what you said. I've never been good at Arabic."

Carl stared bewildered at him and then at Miriam, who smiled quietly at him with rosy cheeks.

This place… We need to get out of here.

Chapter 36

Being at the end of the corridor, Carl, Miriam, and Caesar faced a long shadowy hallway. It seemed to be constructed like one of the numerous hidden servant corridors that winded through every respectful castle. Still holding hands, they moved at a slow pace. Caesar was vigorously in the lead this time, and with Miriam in the middle, more awake than she had been since they entered the castle, Carl felt like he trampled in mud. Every step was grueling, and his legs shook. Every now and then, he touched his sore nose to make sure it hadn't started to bleed again. A faint ache throbbed quietly behind his ears, and even though he tried, he couldn't get rid of the annoying tunnel vision. *I'm not going to be of much help if it comes to a fight,* he thought with a sigh *So, I'll just pretend everything is going to be bright and shiny and happy-go-lucky from now on.* An indistinct voice in the back of his head laughed at him.

When they turned around a corner, a steep stairway waited for them.

"Good," Caesar said and sounded virtually cheerful.

Exhausted, Carl watched the steepness. The mere thought of climbing it was overwhelming. *Just have to grind it out. Everything will eventually end. It's just a matter of time.* He clenched his teeth and concentrated on one step at a time when they appeared in front of him. Time ceased to exist. The only thing that mattered was his trembling, aching legs that had to defeat the next step, and the next, and the next. When there suddenly weren't any more steps to climb, he curled up in a heap on the floor while everything was spinning around him. A couple of warm hands traveled over his shoulders and face.

"Henry, he's bleeding! There's so much blood!"

"Move, Mimi. I'll take care of it. It's nothing serious."

"Are you sure?"

"Just move."

There was a shift between light and darkness, and then, a couple of strong hands pulled him up to sitting. He was leaning into a broad chest. A piercing pain soared through the dizziness, and he gasped.

"Easy now, Carl. Don't struggle. We need to get it under control."

"I'm here, Carl. It's okay, everything's okay."

A warm hand caressed him calmingly, and he leaned into the two different experiences that blended together; the pain in his nose and the warmth around his hands.

"Is he okay?"

"He's just exhausted. I should've thought about it being too much with the physical strain on top of the first bleeding."

"He bled before? Why didn't either of you tell me?"

"You're not in a position where you need more strain on your mind, Mimi."

"I don't care. If I'd known, I could've checked him."

"Maybe, but we decided differently. I'm sorry if it irks you."

"Everything here irks me. I just want to get home, right now. Carl needs to get home. He needs to rest."

"Don't— Don't open anything here, Mimi. Please. We haven't found Sally yet."

"Does she matter that much to you?"

There was a slight pause before Caesar said in a low voice, "That wasn't fair, Mimi. I wouldn't have married her if I didn't care for her."

"Okay, good. I wanted to hear you say it. It felt important that you could admit it to me. How is he?"

After a baffled silence, Caesar sighed and said, "There's a broken blood vessel high up in his nose. It's nothing serious, at least not now, but it can be if it continues to open up. Eventually, if it doesn't stop, it has to be burnt, but for now, it just needs some pressure to stop the bleeding. He needs to relax and stop any physical strain, so it can heal properly."

603

"That's not possible here."

"I know. We'll have to check on him every now and then. I'm going to put gauze up his nose. That'll help."

For a while, no one talked. C kept his fingers hard around Carl's nose, and the pain pulsed in his head.

When Caesar spoke again, his voice sounded slightly calculated to Carl's ears, "If he gets to be your responsibility, Mimi, can you take it upon yourself to keep an eye on him, to make sure he doesn't start to bleed again?"

Apparently, Miri didn't hear the tone, as she readily agreed. "Yes, absolutely."

Even in his dizziness, Carl couldn't help feeling slightly admiring. *You old fox. You're such a clever old fox. Don't worry, I'm going to play my part.*

Eventually, Caesar let go of Carl's nose and carefully eased up the gauze to prevent any more bleeding. Carl grimaced at the uncomfortable feeling but didn't protest. Caesar let him lean toward him again to regain his strength while Miri gently touched him.

"I'm going to clean your face to get rid of the blood. How are you feeling?"

Carl struggled to sit up, but groaned quietly and fell back on Caesar's chest.

"Could be better," he muttered. "But I'm tough, you know. Just need to relax a couple of minutes." He squinted to see her reaction and felt guilty when she worriedly bit her lip. *God, I'm bad,* he thought and decided against his own judgment to let her know that he was going to be okay. "It's alright, honestly. I'm fine."

She looked far from convinced, and he could tell that she now thought that he only tried to calm her down. He didn't have the energy to reassure her. Instead, he caressed her hand and closed his eyes, letting it all be.

For a while, they sat in silence, and Carl thought that he had fallen asleep. Then, as if far away, he heard C nervously clear his throat, and slowly, he became aware of his surroundings again.

"Mimi, I, um, I wanted to take this opportunity to apologize."

Surprised, at the words, Carl wondered what went on in C's mind. There was something else, something ulterior, that he couldn't put his finger on. He thought that C probably wanted Miri to say something, but she didn't. Without making any sign to show that he was awake, Carl continued to listen. *Yeah, I know, bad manners. I don't care. He's up to something, and I need to know what.*

"I… I was angry," C continued at length. "I, uh, have been angry for a long time now, since before Alaska." Caesar paused again, but Miriam kept quiet. "You could have told me you dated him, you know, when you rejected me."

"I didn't." Miri's voice sounded exhausted.

"What do you mean, you didn't?"

"I didn't date him."

"You didn't? Of course, you did. Don't lie to me."

In the stunned silence that followed, anger rose in Carl at Caesar's words, and he had to fight with himself to be able to continue to pretend that he was sleeping.

Miri sounded sad when she finally answered. "I've never lied to you, Henry."

There was a new pause before C said, "But… but why didn't you want to marry me if you didn't date him?"

Miri exhaled tiredly. "Henry… I told you back then. I needed to learn how to stand on my own feet without any man holding my hand. That included Carl. And I've learned it now, on my own, but apparently, you don't like me like this. That's okay. I didn't do it for your sake. I didn't do it for Carl either. I did it for my sake because I needed it."

"But—"

"But what?"

"I don't understand. I gave you everything, Mimi, everything, and it still wasn't enough."

"No, Henry, you closed me in. You protected me. You made me into something I'm not. Everyone loathed me, you know that. Conrad hated me, but he never said anything to you because I was 'Caesar's girl.' Cindy never trusted me to do a good job because I was so insecure. Cecilia pitied me. She liked me, but she pitied the girl I was. I thought I was a grown-up woman, Henry, but you kept me being a little girl, because you liked me like that, and I let you do it because I adored you."

"I— I didn't protect you. I let you go on all the RPs. You were in on all the danger. By Pete, you were hurt so many times!"

"That's not what I'm talking about."

"I don't— I don't understand."

Miriam sighed deeply. "Is it important to you that you understand, Henry? I can tell you, but you might not like it."

"But what about Carl?" he asked as if he hadn't heard the last thing she said.

"What about him?" Carl could hear the slightly irritated tone that crept closer to the surface.

"Ever since he joined us, you hated him. All the arguments the two of you had, all the tears you cried over him, all the times you told me how angry he made you... Was it just a show?"

"Henry..."

"What?"

"No, it was not a show, but when you were with your mom when she lay dying, we needed to find a way to work together without you as a mediator, and as soon as we tried, really tried, we found common ground and eventually common respect."

"In bed." Caesar's voice was poisonous.

The silence that followed was long and tense. Carl continued with his relaxed breathing, trying desperately to not give away that he was listening.

"Is that the catch?" Miriam asked eventually. Her voice was very close to anger. "You want to know when I had sex with Carl for the first time? You do, don't you?"

"I—"

"Three weeks ago."

"I— Wait, what?"

"You heard me."

"But, Alaska?"

"Please, Henry. Please, can you just let this go? We didn't date back then. We've never dated the way you're thinking. If Kroger's hadn't happened, we'd probably not be dating at all."

"But— I know you two had something going on back then. It was obvious. Don't lie to me, Mimi. I... I need to know the truth."

Miriam's anger finally broke free. "I told you, I've never lied to you! Why can't you ever listen to what I'm saying? We – didn't – have – anything – going on, as you think of it." She exhaled frustrated, before continuing in a slightly calmer voice, "I did start to feel attracted to him around that time, that's true, but it wasn't until after Kroger's, that I got to know that he was attracted to me too. Seriously, Henry, you know how good he is when it comes to hiding his feelings. Yes, I can usually see what's going on inside him now, but only because he doesn't hide it from me anymore. But, back then— Do you really think I would've known if he felt something for me back then? He says he started to, but I never saw it. Never! Do you know how much that irks me? I've missed so damn much!" Her upset voice bit off the last word. For a few moments, Miri's heavy and angry breathing was the only sound, but clearly, she tried to calm down. However, when C kept quiet, she impatiently said, "I don't know what you want from me, Henry. A timeline? Let's see, first kiss, three weeks ago. First—"

"It's— It's— No, I— I don't want to know."

"Are you sure? I honestly don't know if I believe you. Maybe it's my turn to call you a liar? No, I won't call you out on it. I'll just give you all the details."

"Cut— Cut it, Mimi. You don't have to react this way."

"No? You're the one bringing it up. You say you want to apologize. That's fine. Thank you. Appreciated. But it's not

607

what this is about, is it? You want to know if I cheated on you. I didn't. Never have. I mean, seriously, Henry. Instead of going around being angry at me these two years, you could have just asked me."

The pause was longer and calmer this time as if Caesar thought it all through. Then, he exhaled so deeply that Carl's head fell down at the side. Surprised, Carl jerked and gasped, but C caught him in time.

"Don't wake him up," Miri said, and her tone told him that she frowned. "He needs to rest."

He could feel them both looking at him. Even though it was awkward, he continued to pretend to sleep. This was definitely not the right time to 'wake up.'

At length, Caesar said, "He's still sleeping."

"Good."

C took another deep breath, and his chest heaved under Carl's head. "I, um, feel, uh, dumb… stupid… Can you— Can you forgive me?"

For the first time ever, Carl heard honest regret in Caesar's voice.

At first, Miriam didn't answer, but after a while, she sighed. "I'll try. I'll give it an honest try."

"Thank you."

"I'm tired, Henry. I'm going to rest for a while."

"Okay."

Carl could hear her take the blanket and wrap it around herself on the floor before silence fell. Caesar's chest continued to heave from regretful sighs and deep breaths, but eventually, he seemed to calm down. Soon after, Carl fell asleep too, feeling a relief so deep that he could cry.

He didn't know how long he had been out when Caesar nudged him. "Hmm?"

"It's time to move on. We can't wait any longer."

Carl immediately jerked up, but his head began to spin again. Feeling dizzy, he leaned forward and let his head rest between his knees. The movement pulled the gauze from his nose. It was soaked with blood, but to his relief, it had finally coagulated.

"God, I must've dozed off," he mumbled. "Sorry."

"You needed it."

"I guess, but it doesn't feel good." He rubbed his eyes and exhaled, trying to get his thoughts together. "You're right," he said, "we need to move on." He looked around. Miri lay on the floor, sleeping. "How is she?"

"Steadier."

Carl smiled. "Good." Reluctantly, he gave Caesar an admiring side-glance. "You're such a bad man, C, making her care for me, so she has something to focus her mind on."

Caesar looked caught, but chuckled. "Just do your thing. It'll keep her grounded."

"Don't worry. I will."

With a grunt, Carl stood, and even though his legs felt wobbly, some energy had returned to his body. While reaching for an ER survival bar in his pocket, he studied the surroundings. His stomach growled at the thought of food as he ripped open the bar, broke it into a chewable piece, and devoured it. As usual, it didn't taste much, but at least he didn't feel ravenous anymore. He resealed the bag and put it back into his pocket.

Caesar woke Miri, and to Carl's relief, she was in complete control of herself. *Alright, I have to apologize to her later, but for now, I need to get those acting skills going.* Leaning heavily on the wall, he rubbed his temple, seemingly absentmindedly, as he studied the corridor in front of them. There wasn't much to see. The stone floor was dirty and obviously well used, and the dull white color of the walls was flaking. The corridor itself was lit up by an undetermined light. It should unsettle him that he couldn't find a source to it, but at this point, something as vague as not finding a light source didn't even make him flinch. Some twenty yards further down, the corridor turned right.

Miri came over to him. It was obvious that she tried to hide her worry for him, but as usual, he could see right through her. With a feeble smile, he touched her cheek. She leaned into his hand and looked him steadily in the eyes, a lot calmer than before. The talk with Caesar had obviously been good for her and helped her get back on her feet again.

"Hi, *habibti*. Slept well?"

"Relatively, I guess. How about you? How are you feeling?"

As he shied away with his eyes, he tried to suppress a genuine blush as he was about to lie to her. To his surprise, he found that he couldn't.

Moving his feet awkwardly, he mumbled, "Um, fine… I'm fine. Shall we go?"

She gave him a piercing gaze. Even though she didn't look convinced, she reluctantly nodded. "Yes, Allie's still quite close, and Olwen too, but I can't sense her as well."

A worried pang hit him, but he brushed it away. "At least she's there. Same order as before? C in the lead, then you, and me as the anchor?"

"Sure," Caesar said. "You shouldn't lead now anyway."

"I could do it. I'm not that out," Carl protested, but even to him, it sounded half-hearted.

Caesar gave him a long look, and Miri scowled as she worriedly let her gaze travel between the two men.

Eventually, Carl looked down and pulled a hand through his hair. "Whatever," he muttered.

Miri grabbed their hands with a determined expression. "Okay, let's get going. You need to get out of here."

Torn between satisfaction that he hadn't lied to her and guilt that he had wanted to, Carl followed her as they began to walk. As soon as they rounded the corner, they saw a plain-looking door a couple of yards down the corridor.

"They're in there," Miri said with conviction.

Carl's heart began to beat faster, and his hands perspired. Finally, they were going to find Allie! Finally, they were going to go home! Then, he frowned suspiciously.

Something wasn't right. *It can't be this simple. It seems improbable, just walking in and getting them. I swear Night Porter has some plans for us and plenty of traps for us to fall into. God, I hate this game!*

With a deep intake of breath, he decided that it didn't matter what traps lay before them. They would overcome them, just as they had with all the other traps.

"Alright. Let's go in and get them," he said in his calm, casual leader voice that hid his worries.

Eagerly, Caesar tugged them with him as he closed in and opened the door. As soon as he did, the corridor changed. It crawled out, spread across the floor, and became lighter and brighter, enclosing them. Carl had to squint at the brightness, but couldn't discern anything. The sound of a child's happy laughter reached them from within the light. *What the hell?* Gradually, he got his sight back in time to see a streaked calico cat casually coming toward him and brush against his legs, a perfectly normal cat, except that it had nine exceptionally long tails. Slightly weirded out, Carl gasped and took a step back, but the cat followed him, marked him with its face. A toddler with copper-red hair and shining blue eyes tottered after it with his hands stretched out, trying to catch one of those long tails that nervously whisked around the room.

Carl got a sudden urge to throw up. *Where the hell did that cat come from?* he thought, sweaty and nauseous. *It's the same cat, my cat, that I had in my mind before, and now it's here, alive. Did I make it come alive? How?*

With difficulty, he tore his gaze away, let the cat continue to cuddle his legs – *at least it seems friendly enough* – and looked around. On a throne at the far end of the room sat a naked and masked bald woman, caressing herself. At her feet, covered by her golden hair, Allie lay in a heap, crouched and unmoving. Carl gasped in anguish when he saw her. *God, what happened to her? She's— She's not dead? She can't be. It's Allie, for crying out loud. She can't die!* That's when the thought hit him. *That's why she's here! She's so vibrant and vivid. They need her! They need her energy and her love of life.*

She was robed in a luminous red dress that flowed around her in an invisible wind. Caesar moved slowly toward the throne and the naked woman, shock radiating from his face. Jerkily, Carl managed to take a step forward, dragging Miriam with him toward Allie, when suddenly someone sensually embraced him from behind, and a deep, purring voice whispered in his ear, "Do you like what you see, Carl? Anything in here can be yours. You just have to reach out for it."

The hair on his body stood up in painful knots, and his breath stuttered as he recognized the voice. Athena moved around him, slithering like a snake, and let her long, protracted tongue glide over his neck and throat, licking away the dried blood. It was as if he had turned to stone. He couldn't move a muscle, a limb, as his dream stood in front of him, forcefully thrusting itself into his mind, trying to shatter it. Unwanted tears trickled down his cheeks, and his whole body trembled as he desperately fought to stay sane. *You are... not... welcome... here... You are not... welcome... here... You...*

"C— Carl?" Miri's frightened voice came from far away.

A hungry smile played on Athena's lips as she turned around, facing the woman she resembled. "Mother," she purred.

Wide-eyed, Miriam took a cautious step back without seeing the toddler crawling on the floor right behind her. Dread filled Carl, and he managed to tear away from the paralyzing sensation of drowning inside himself.

"Miri, watch out!"

Still walking, she turned her head to look behind her but stumbled over the child. With a muffled scream and flailing arms, she fell backward over him, hitting the back of her head hard on the marble floor. The crack sounded loud, too loud, just as it had when Oona died. Violently shivering and hyperventilating, Carl stared at her, unable to move, as shock penetrated his body, making it cold as ice. She lay still

612

with her eyes glassy and open, blood slowly covering the floor around her head. *Miri! Oh, God, no! No!* With a high-pitched yowl, the cat thrust its claws deep into his leg, and finally, he could move. With limbs that felt as if they didn't belong to him, he moved jerkily, wanting to get to her, but Athena danced into his path.

"You are not welcome here," he hissed at the abomination, tears cracking his voice, and she pouted while her eyes glittered with amusement. Smoothly gliding toward him, her naked body pulsated in crimson, and he was on the brink of throwing up. Without thinking, he unsheathed his knife and held it up against her with trembling hands. "You're not welcome here. You're nothing but a dream. You don't have any kind of power over me. I discarded you long ago."

She smiled malevolently at him. "Oh, Carl. You don't understand. You are in my realm now. It is you who don't have any power here."

She closed in on him until the edge of the knife pressed against her skin. The seconds passed by slowly as they locked eyes. The cold and dark amusement in her gaze scared him. Suddenly, she grabbed his hands tightly, forced him to hold them still while she slowly pressed herself onto the knife with an aroused look on her face. In sickening terror, he tore himself away. With the knife's handle in a steady grip, she pulled it out from her stomach, licked the blood from the blade and held it out to him, handle first.

"Do it again," she whispered in her full, deep voice. It sent trickles of disgust down his body.

He jerked back a couple of steps. A movement to his right caught his eye, and the red-haired toddler stood there looking at him with his thumb in his mouth and the dead cat hanging by its neck from his hand.

Athena purred again. "Have you seen what an accomplished son you have made? I call him Herakles."

In terror, Carl stared at the child who met his eyes with a blank face and held up the cat toward him.

"Daddy's cat," the child mumbled around the thumb, cradling the dead, limp body in his arms, before laying down on the floor. Closing his eyes, the boy fell asleep.

Violently shivering and filled with shock and grief, Carl stared at the scene. A dead cat he never knew, the light and hope of his life maybe dead at the throne, and his wife-to-be slowly turning pale on the floor.

Athena danced around him again, curving, winding, laughing, and to keep her in focus, he forced himself to move too until he felt Miri's soft body with his foot. With a watchful eye on Athena, who now kept her distance, concentrating on licking the knife, he crouched and lifted Miri up in his arms. Her weight made him stagger. She was dreadfully cold, and her head slumped back over his shoulder. He knew that she was dead, but he was not going to leave her here.

With strained breaths and a throbbing headache, Carl panted heavily by the effort of carrying Miriam. Step after arduous step, he backed toward the throne where Caesar huddled together with Olwen. Something wet dripped onto his hands and he realized that he bled again, but it didn't matter. Nothing mattered anymore, except opening a portal and get them all the hell out of here before anyone else died or went mad.

Finally, he closed in on them. Athena was occupied at the far end of the room, so he tore his watchful gaze from her for a few moments. Allie lay lifelessly on the floor, but she was breathing. An unexpected tug in his heart made him understand how right he was about her being his light and his hope. Caesar had removed the blanket from his backpack and wrapped it around Olwen. With a faint feeling of surprise, Carl noticed the tears that ran down Caesar's cheeks.

"I can't take the damn mask away, Carl. I can't take it away," he sobbed.

After checking that Athena hadn't moved, he dared to take his gaze off her again and stole a glance at the masked woman who silently sat on the throne, playing with her fingers as if she created a spider web.

"What do you mean, 'can't take it away'?" he panted with effort, his voice muddled by blood and tears. "It's not glued on her, is it?"

"I don't know. It doesn't even feel like a mask. It's like it's part of her face."

Shiver after violent shiver ran down Carl's spine, and he stared at Olwen with wide-opened eyes. "Goddamn," he whispered. "We need to get out of here."

"How?" Caesar looked up at him, anger and fear and sorrow flashed over his face. "There are no doors here anymore, and you're bleeding again and Mimi's unconscious. How the hell are you planning on getting us out?"

"I don't care if I'm bleeding to death," Carl gurgled, almost swallowing the blood that ran from his nose down his throat, feeling like his own death was going to be a very likely outcome of this, but it didn't matter anymore, not with Miri dead. "Take Olwen down from there, put her in your lap. I'm going to place Allie and Miri together and then— Just hold us."

He gurgled again, found it hard to breathe, and nearly panicked. He spit blood on the floor before gently laying Miriam down beside the throne. Her eyes were still open and glassy, and her skin was so cold, so pale. When Caesar pulled Olwen down into his lap, cradling her in his arms, he glanced at Miri, and his eyes opened up wide as shock painted his face gray.

A wail found its way out of him. "No... No! NO! She can't be dead! She— She can't be dead!"

Carl didn't answer, only dragged her up in Caesar's lap, trying not to think, and went to get Allie. She was cool in his arms, unconscious, with a pale face and dark shadows under her eyes. Tears had dried on her cheeks, leaving visible stripes of the mascara she sometimes used. She breathed shallowly, deep in shock. A movement on the floor caught his attention. Athena was dancing again in a curving, slithering motion, one moment a woman, the next a snake, and then a dark shadow. She caught his gaze, and an ecstatic smile broke out on her lips.

"There's nowhere to hide, Carl," she whispered in his mind. "We're part of you now. We'll always find you. Run, my love, and see how far you get before I catch you and devour you."

Cold fingers of tremor grabbed him by his gut, but he shook them off. There wasn't any time to give in to the terror now. Instead, he turned his back to her, grabbed Allie around her waist, and carried her over to the inconsolable crying Caesar, where he placed her on top of Miri. Kneeling, he put his arms around all of them, feeling Caesar's fingers touching his waist. He closed his eyes. Athena was laughing, and he could feel her presence in his head, how she twirled around them, closer and closer.

He thought about his own apartment and the smell, the atmosphere, the colors, but it didn't work. It didn't feel like home anymore. Tears trickled from his eyes, and he sniveled quietly as he leaned his head on Allie's chest and tried again.

Athena's hands caressed his shoulders, and he felt her breath on his ear. "You're such a bore, Carl. Let's do it again."

Carl flinched as he stood outside the plain-looking door, holding Miriam's hand hard in his. *Why does it feel like I've been here before?* He shook his head to get rid of the weird, tingling sensation in his mind.

"You're sure this is the place?"

Miriam nodded, and she looked pale again, the shadows under her eyes darker than they were just a minute ago. He watched her worriedly and caressed her hand. As she craned her neck, studying the door with a slightly anxious expression, he suddenly saw a small spot of bright red blood on the gauze at the back of her head. Without raising any alarm, he studied it for a few moments, but it didn't seem to

616

spread. *Looks okay enough, I guess, but I better keep an eye on it, so it doesn't bleed through.*

"Alright. Let's go in and get them," he said in his calm, casual leader voice that hid his worries.

Caesar tugged them with him as he eagerly approached and opened the door. As soon as he did, the corridor changed. It bolted up into a dome with its roof made out of stained glass, bathing the room in soft red light. In the middle, a raised platform was placed with an ornate golden throne on it, and a naked, masked woman without hair slept casually in it. Carl frowned as he stared at the somewhat familiar person. *Is that Olwen?* She looked so different without her hair, without her clothes, so vulnerable, even with the mask that covered half of her face. At her feet, another woman lay sleeping on her stomach, her face turned away from them. Her golden hair spread out, covered her naked body. *Allie. Why are they naked?* He shrugged uneasily, trying to let go of the bad feeling. What did it matter that they were naked? They were here, and they were alive. The relief and the love inside him when he looked at Allie were so great he had to dry away tears that uninvited fell from his eyes.

Caesar, on the other hand, looked shocked as he slowly moved toward the throne and the naked women. Miriam hurriedly followed him. She crouched by Allie's lifeless body and moved the hair away from her face, so she could kiss her gently.

Carl squinted. It felt as if they were off the script somehow. *What script?* With suspicion rising inside him, he turned around, looking for hidden traps, but he couldn't discern anything in the red shadows. A child's happy laughter came from inside the shadows. *What the hell?*

A toddler with copper-red hair and shining blue eyes tottered after it with his hands stretched out, trying to catch one of those long tails that nervously whisked around the room.

A streaked calico cat came casually tripping toward him and brushed against his legs. It was a perfectly normal cat, except that it had nine extremely long tails. Slightly weirded out, Carl gasped and took a step back, but the cat followed him, marked him with its face. *It seems friendly enough.* A toddler with copper-red hair and shining blue eyes tottered after it with his hands outstretched, clearly trying to catch one of those long tails that nervously whisked around the room. Carl got a sudden urge to throw up. *Where the hell did that cat come from?* he thought, sweaty and nauseous. *It's— It's definitely the same cat I had in my mind before, the... the copy of my Tardis from when I was a teenager, and now she's here, alive. Did I make it come alive? How?*

With difficulty, he tore his gaze away, let the cat cuddle his legs, and continued to look around. *I have to find the trap before it closes around us.* He didn't know why it didn't surprise him when the trap sensually embraced him from behind, and a deep, purring voice whispered in his ear, "Do you like what you see, Carl? Anything in here can be yours. You just have to reach out and grab it."

"It's not much to see, Athena," he said in a deliberately calm voice, even though he trembled in his very soul. The images of her on top of him, forcing him inside her, nearly smothered him and made his breath shallow and hurting.

She laughed at him. Slithering like a snake, she moved around him and let her long, protracted tongue glide over his neck and throat, as she licked away the dried blood.

"It's the pleasures, Carl," she whispered. "Eternity of pleasures. You like that. I know. I've seen you, you and Mother, at the Inn before I was born, in your bed at home, in the kitchen. And you and the golden queen, indulging in each other everywhere, never getting enough. Here you can have them both."

Even as the hair stood up in painful knots all over him and her voice sent trickles of disgust down his body as she whispered about things that were private, he tried to keep calm, tried to sound nonchalant. "I can have both at home, too, if I want. I don't need to stay here for that." When she looked angry and confused, he smiled venomously at her. "Oh, you missed that, didn't you? How sloppy." Then, his fake smile faded away. "You don't have anything I need or want. You can't tempt me. You're just disgusting."

The confused and angry look disappeared. She smiled secretively at him and reached out for his body. Hurriedly, he took a step back, almost stumbling in his urge to get away from her, with a terrifying feeling that he would go insane if she touched him again.

Her voice followed him, wrapped itself around him, tried to snare him. "Show me, then, Carl. Show me what you can do. Don't just talk. Look, you have so many to enjoy here, who all yearn for you. I might take you again too, just for fun, for old memories sake. Poor Herakles is so lonely and needs a sister to take delight in. That cat of yours is not enough. He always kills it. A shame, don't you think? Come here. Let me take those clothes off. Make another child with me."

Hot and cold alternately, and shivering of nauseous terror, Carl stepped back once more. He didn't dare to leave her hungry face with his gaze, but he had a feeling that he closed in on the others. Suddenly, he stumbled over a couple of legs and fell backward, flailing desperately with his arms. Landing heavily, he lost his breath.

In the next moment, Allie clung desperately to his throat, suffocating him. "I can't find a way home, Carl. I've tried, I've tried so hard. There's nowhere to go, nowhere to hide. I just want to go home! I want to go home," she cried into his shoulder.

Her arms were solid like iron bars around his throat, and he couldn't breathe. Struggling and choking, he frantically tried to get a grip on her to loosen her arms so he could get some air down his aching lungs.

Athena closed in on him and in his panic, he reached out to her. He could hear her laughing, but it sounded as if it came from far away.

"Now, you want me? I'm not that easy."

Suddenly, her demeanor changed as she looked at something behind them. She frowned and lost interest in them. The next moment, Allie screamed in agonizing pain, and her hands let go of his throat. Air finally gushed down the sore and aching passage.

Panting, Carl fell to the floor and realized that he bled profoundly again. Behind him, Allie's violent sobbing of despair and anguish made him cringe in compassion, but he couldn't do anything but cough and breathe and give in to the pain. He turned on his side, giving the blood from his nose another outlet than down his throat. In front of him, a wall-covering mirror showed him his own sickly pale face with eyes squinted in pain and big bruised smudges under them, and the swollen, bleeding nose. However, it was what went on behind him that really terrified him. Chaos unfolded, like an old film, unsteady and jumpy. Staring into the mirror, fear smothered him, clawed his stomach, and ripped him apart. Right behind his back, Allie sat crouched, arms around herself, rocking back and forth, her eyes empty sockets and blood like tears on her cheeks.

"Oh, my God, Allie!" He managed to push himself up and crawl over to her, taking her in his arms, crying helplessly. "What did she do to you? God, what did she do?" His voice was cracked and muddled, and blood ran from his nose down on her head, creating a red crown around her hair. Wildly trembling, he cradled her with one arm and pinched the bridge of his nose with the other hand.

In the mirror, another catastrophe rolled out before his eyes. Caesar and Miriam worked desperately to remove the mask from Olwen on the throne, without seeing the mask she held behind C's back. With a sly smile, Olwen quickly pulled it over Caesar's head before he even knew what happened. As soon as it was placed over his face and he looked through it, something changed. Carl couldn't put a finger on it, but something in C's gaze, something in his demeanor, was wrong. He let go of Olwen and stood up, back straight, while the mask stiffened in an unforgiving expression.

Miriam looked up at him, scowling, and said something, but no sounds were heard. A deep silence seemed to have replaced everything, even the sound of his own pained breaths. Without even looking at her, C shot out his fist and hit Miriam hard in her face. As she stumbled back with her hands on her cheek and her face painted in a pained, frightened grimace, Carl fought to push Allie to the side and get over to Miriam, but she clung desperately to him, weighing him down. Terror, anger, and confusion battled inside him.

"What the hell are you doing?" he shouted to C, but his voice fell dead in front of him, and no one acknowledged him.

With a silver knife in her hand, Olwen stood up from the throne. Carl's mouth dried up, and his heartbeat picked up speed. Sweat covered his face as he desperately tried to push Allie down on the floor, but she was too strong. He struggled ferociously but to no avail.

"I need to go to her!" he yelled at her, but she didn't hear him either.

In the mirror, Miriam stared in disbelief when C grabbed her hair and lifted her up to her feet. In agonizing pain, she screamed when he let her dangle in her hair an inch above the floor, but no sounds came through. With an anticipatory smile, Olwen closed in on them. As she raised her hand, C let Miri's feet touch the floor, and with a fast, strong strike, Olwen decapitated her. The knife went through her throat and neck as through butter. Miri's body stood by itself half of a second before it understood it was dead and collapsed in a heap at Olwen's and C's feet. Grinning, C raised Miri's head high in the air with one hand and grabbed Olwen with the other, kissing her violently. Together, they turned around and took their seats on the two thrones. Miri's head with wide-open eyes and mouth was put on a velvety pillow on top of a pedestal between them.

In shock, Carl sat unmoving on the floor with Allie continuing to cling to him. His feelings could not have caught up with what he had witnessed, because he didn't feel anything. It was all emptiness inside him as if a switch had been turned off.

Suddenly, Athena appeared and strode to the middle of the room. Scowling, and with arms crossed over her chest, she looked around. "Where are you?" she said in an annoyed tone. Night Porter stepped out from behind the thrones with an amused smile playing on his lips. She glared at him. "This is my realm. You're not allowed to play with my people. Get out. You're just destroying things."

"As you command, fair lady," he said and took a bow, still smiling, as if he had just granted a favorite daughter a wish, and then, he was gone.

Athena glanced at Carl, the scowl deep on her forehead. "I don't care for broken toys," she hissed. "Again."

Carl flinched as he stood outside the plain door holding Miriam's hand hard in his. *Why does it feel like I've been here before?* He shook his head to get rid of the weird, tingling sensation in his mind.

"You're sure this is the place?"

Miriam nodded, and she looked pale again, the shadows under her eyes were darker and deeper than they had been just a minute ago. He watched her worriedly and caressed her hand. As she craned her neck, studying the door with a slightly anxious demeanor, he suddenly saw a small spot of bright red blood on the gauze at the back of her head. Without raising any alarm, he studied it for a few moments, but it didn't seem to spread. *Looks okay enough, I guess, but I better keep an eye on it, so it doesn't bleed through.* With a yet deeper frown, he noticed the narrow sliver of blood across her throat. *When did she get that? It looks like someone tried to cut her throat.* With a gentle touch, he traced his finger below the thin wound. She jerked and looked at him with big, frightened eyes.

"What's this, Miri? Have you cut yourself?"

She swallowed hard and shook her head as tears trickled down her cheeks. "I… I don't know," she whispered, insecurely. "It hurts…"

"Let's clean it before we go in, alright?"

She nodded, and while he brought up a packaged wet wipe from his pocket, he glanced at C, who sternly looked at the door. Two red spots flamed on his cheeks. Squinting in sudden suspicion, Carl stared at him, fighting to get rid of the ridiculous thought that C had cut her. *For crying out loud, Carl! He would never do anything like that. That's just crazy.* His heart pounded hard in terror as he thought of the possibility of going insane at this place. *I'm not going crazy, am I? I haven't let Night Porter into my mind, have I? I feel— I don't know, so damn shaken for some reason. More than I should.* He inhaled deeply, feeling his body tremble for no good reason at all. *Goddamn, when I start doubting myself, then we're really in trouble. We need to get out of here.* Determinedly, he pushed the thought from his mind and concentrated on cleaning the wound. Miri grimaced in slight pain but kept still.

"It's not deep, more like a scrape," he said when the blood was removed and he could study it closer.

"Good," she mumbled, and he leaned in and kissed her tenderly.

"I love you," he whispered in her ear after he let her soft lips go, and she smiled shakily.

"I love you too," she mouthed, and warmth radiated throughout his body.

"Let's go in and get them so we can go home," he said, and she nodded.

"Finally." Caesar exhaled relieved before tugging them with him as he eagerly opened the door. As soon as he did, the corridor changed. The walls disappeared, and a cold mist closed in on them. A large field of hard, spiky grass stretched as far away in all directions as they could see, disappearing into the mist.

"Where are we?" Miriam whispered. Her voice was frightened again.

Carl frowned uncertainly. This wasn't what he had expected. Not that he knew exactly what he'd expected. Nothing should surprise him here.

"I— I don't know."

Out of the mist, a bald woman came strolling toward them, only dressed in a glittering mask. The multicolored sparkles created tiny light arrows that hurt his eyes and made him feel dizzy. *Olwen?* She held a thin golden chain loosely in her hand. It dragged behind her and ended in a jeweled collar placed around the neck of Allie as if Olwen was walking her obedient dog.

In shock, Carl stared at Allie's emotionally broken face, and his heart crumbled. She shouldn't look like that, not Allie. She was the one with all the bright, shining life inside her, but now her face was pale and distant, lifeless.

Tears fell down his cheeks as he hurried over to her with Miri closely behind. Together, they embraced Allie hard. Carl's hands tangled her hair, caressed her soothingly over her neck, and felt the damn collar under his hands. There had to be a way of opening it. He couldn't stand seeing her trapped and broken like this. His hands moved nervously around it, trying to find a lock, but there wasn't any.

Behind him, he heard C's weak, shocked voice. "Sal?" When Carl stole a glance her way, the mask on Olwen's face was void of emotions, and she didn't say anything. "Sal, what are you doing?"

In the silence that followed, Miriam took Carl's hands in hers and held them over the collar. "Think about us," she said in a low voice. "Think about how we feel together, how we belong together. We love her, Carl. That makes the whole difference."

He nodded, feeling the truth that hid behind her words. Closing his eyes, he leaned in and placed his cheek on

Allie's. Her hair tickled his face, and the warmth of her breaths caressed his neck. On the other side of Allie's head, Miri did the same. While tangling their hands together over the collar that kept her captured, Carl breathed in Allie's special scent and let his thoughts wander.

Images came to him, vibrant in their colors, from the beautiful day in Lincoln Spring Park, before they understood that they loved each other. The love had flowed between them nonetheless. Thinking back, it must have been born that weekend as a result of them rearranging their relationships so they suited each other, included each other, instead of pushing someone away. It dawned on him that when Miri and Allie spent the night talking, they found an important connection that led them past him, which led them to like and respect each other for their own sake and not because of him. He stopped being their common denominator that night. Miri opened up to Allie's warmth and generosity, and Allie became deeply affected by Miri's strength and will to survive. Together they complemented each other, and becoming friends and lovers was as natural as the sun rising in the sky.

Other memories came to him; memories of him and Allie and how they had gone from a strict work relationship to becoming friends, and from there, they somehow slipped through a crack in the door to a bed somewhere, and to their surprise, found themselves loving each other.

A distinctive snap disturbed his memories, and the collar under his and Miri's hands fell on the grass and disappeared. Allie moved under their hands and blinked in confusion. With a gasp, he embraced her hard. Miri's tired face radiated of happiness and love, and she hugged Allie tenderly and kissed her cheek. Holding both of the women close in his arms, he relaxed in his whole body.

Behind him, Caesar mumbled in a trembling voice, "Sweetheart, this is not you. You're not like this."

"No, stay where you are," Olwen said in a detached voice. "You are not allowed to approach the Queen, or you will be beheaded."

Something stirred in Carl's mind when he heard those words, and he shuddered violently even though he couldn't figure out why.

"Where... where am I?" Allie mumbled disoriented as if she had woken up from a dream.

"Don't worry, Allie," Miri mumbled. "We're in Night Porter's dimension, but we're here for you now. We'll take you home."

With tears in his voice, Caesar said, "You're not a queen, Sal. You're— You're my wife. Please, stop this now. Come home with me."

Suddenly, something soft brushed against Carl's legs. When he looked down, a streaked calico cat stretched its paws up on his legs, purring. It was a perfectly normal cat, except that it had nine extremely long tails. In wonder, he crouched and petted it. *This is my cat, my Tardis. Somehow, she's come alive from my thoughts. She's a part of me.* He should think it frightening, but he didn't. Instead, he lifted the cat up into his arms. All her tails reached down to the ground, and she affectionately marked his face, before turning around, licking both Miri's and Allie's faces. Miri smiled and petted Tardis' head. Allie seemed to become more clear-minded, and she looked around as if trying to get a grasp of the situation.

Olwen spoke again in a voice void of all emotions. "You are allowed to call me Queen of Clubs, subject. We have captured Queen of Diamonds and are pleased that you've brought us Queen of Hearts."

Miriam jerked nervously and glanced at Olwen over her shoulder. Tardis put a gentle paw on Miri's cheek, and she exhaled, her whole body relaxing. Looking determined, Miri deliberately turned away from Olwen. When Carl suspiciously glanced at the cat, she watched him with unreadable amber-colored eyes. He shrugged with a crooked smile and let her be. When he looked over his shoulder,

Henry stood slumped with a gray tinge to his face, crying inconsolably. Olwen observed the older man with a blank and detached expression on the mask that didn't seem to be a mask anymore, but a part of her.

"Queen of Clubs, Queen of Diamonds, and Queen of Hearts? Where's Queen of Spades?" he asked with a hard-won casual voice, trying to intervene. Somehow, it didn't surprise him when someone sensually embraced him from behind, and a deep, purring voice whispered in his ear, "Right behind you, love."

Tardis hissed and jumped down, budging Miri and Allie away from him. In his mind's eye, he saw Miri lying on the ground – *floor* – lifeless with glassy eyes and pale skin, blood slowly spreading out under her, beside Allie, who was rocking back and forth on the ground – *floor* – with empty eye sockets and bloody tears.

"Move away, both of you," he said urgently, nauseous with terror.

As Miri dragged Allie away from them, Athena laughed, a deep, full laugh that sent trickles of disgust down Carl's body.

"Aren't you so sweet, Carl?" The embrace was hard and constraining around his waist, and he had to force himself to keep his composure, to breathe evenly, and to not shiver. "Always so caring. Do you think it will help? It's in the script that she'll die here."

"What script, Athena?" He tried to sound calm, but she saw right through him.

Laughing at him, she moved around, slithering like a snake, and let her long, protracted tongue glide over his neck and throat, licking away the dried blood. A sinking feeling of disgust overwhelmed him, but he refused to show it. She was not going to win over him. When she reached the front, she looked him wickedly in the eyes, and he had to restrain himself from not trembling, from not giving in to becoming a victim again.

"She knows," Athena whispered and leaned in toward his lips.

Desperately, he turned his head, and the kiss landed on his cheek instead. When tears welled up in his eyes, she smiled triumphantly. *No, I'm not giving in.*

"Who? Who knows, Athena?"

Athena turned and looked at the woman she resembled so much. "She opened the book."

Miri gasped where she stood some yards away, holding her arms protectively around Allie, and it was clear that she knew what Athena talked about.

"What book?"

"At the library." Miri's voice was a hoarse whisper. "The books there, I couldn't read them."

Athena's eyes gleamed in anticipation. "You can now, Mother." Miri jerked at the word, suddenly pale in her face, and Athena smirked. "Night Porter wrote it, but he likes watching spiders. I don't, so I'll tell you a little secret. You can change the book." Her smile was as full and satisfied as that of a cat in a bin of whipped cream.

"Why are you telling us this?" Carl suspiciously asked, and got a secretive smile back.

"You're all so much more fun alive, love, in your world from where I can borrow you from time to time, maybe even visit. Here, I'd only tire of you. Here, Night Porter will turn you all into spiders. So boring." Cold shivers ran down Carl's spine as he somehow recognized the truth in her words. Athena gave Henry, Olwen, and Allie a hungry look. "Now, go away, read the book, change it, and come back, while I'm going to have some fun with your friends."

"Allie's coming with us," Carl said sternly and got that secretive smile back.

"Of course, you want her to. However, I need her here. She's so talented in my special area. So gifted. But you already know that."

"Please," Miri pleaded, "we need her too."

Athena's eyes sparkled, and she showed her teeth in a predatory grin. "What do you want to trade for her? Your unborn child? Herakles would indeed enjoy a sister."

Miriam gasped and took an involuntary step back, hands protectively over her stomach.

Stunned, Carl watched her. "Are you— Are you pregnant?" His voice sounded hoarse.

Miri looked at him with big, shocked eyes and shook her head. "I— I don't— I don't think so…"

In the corner of his eye, it seemed as if Allie tried to get herself together. "I'm not for trade," she said coldly, and Carl breathed again, relieved to see her trying to get back to her old self, relieved to not have to make an impossible deal.

"Don't hurt them." His voice sounded calm, even though his whole being <u>screamed</u> at the thought of getting visits by Athena at home and getting dragged back here, again and again, all his life until she was tired of him.

Athena looked back at him, anticipatory. "Because?"

"Because otherwise, I'll follow the script."

It was an empty threat, and she knew it. Her eyes glittered. "I don't think they'll get hurt, sweetheart. That's not my game. On the contrary. They might discover things about themselves that will surprise them. Now go. It's that way."

She turned her back at them and approached the other three, but Carl lingered, didn't want to leave them with her. He knew how much damage she could do.

"Don't be stupid. Do as she says, Carl." Caesar stared angrily at him. "Why do you think you need to babysit us? Go."

When Allie glared at him too and gestured at them to go, he took Miriam's arm, and reluctantly, turned around. A lit path had opened up in the <u>mist</u>. Miri let Tardis down, and together with the cat, they hurried toward it.

Chapter 37

When they left Henry, Allie, and Olwen behind, the helpless anger gushed through Carl's body, making him warm and cold alternately. He hated this game! He hated becoming victimized and forced to make choices that always hurt someone in the end. He hated this living nightmare that would continue on and on throughout his life if Athena got what she wished for. He wanted to go home, to forget that this place existed, to forget that dreams could take physical forms and hurt the ones you loved.

With a glance toward Miriam's stomach, he wondered if there were any truth to Athena's words, or if she was just playing with them, as usual. He truly hoped it was a game this time. How would a fetus react to being trapped in this realm? Would it react at all or would something affect its brain negatively?

With a deep, sobbing breath, he caught Miriam's hand and squeezed it hard, but couldn't find any words to express his worry, and she neither spoke or looked at him. Instead, they walked in awkward silence. The mist swirled around their feet, but it was only mist, nothing that was alive.

At length, Miri asked the question he had been afraid she would, "You know her?"

To his surprise, all the shame and self-disgust he thought he had driven out of his system, came back and smothered him. He drew a trembling breath to answer her, but his throat clasped. Treacherous tears wanted to escape his eyes, and he blinked ferociously to hinder them. He hated the damn crying too! Here, he couldn't control it. All his strength went to protect his sanity instead.

Miriam finally glanced at him. Without stopping, she placed her arm around his waist underneath the backpack.

"What did she do to you?" Her voice was gentle and worried.

"I… I thought she was a dream…"

"A dream?"

He tried to compose himself, distance himself from the memory.

"It happened at the inn, after we... you know..." His voice was no louder than a hoarse whisper. "I— I had nightmares. You remember. You woke up. And she— she was one of them. She— she took physical form..."

Miri shivered violently, but her hand stroked him calmly over his back. "Do you want to tell me about it?"

He didn't dare to look at her. *No. No, I don't, but you're going to take offense if I keep it to myself.*

"You don't have to, you know. I just thought..." Her voice trailed away, and in the corner of his eye, he saw her looking away with a confused and hurt expression.

Inhaling deeply, he tried to prepare himself for her rejection but failed. Scared to death that she would pull her hand from him and stare at him in disgust, he struggled to explain. "It's— It's something that's—" He paused, searching for the right words without finding any. "It's— It's hard for me... to talk about it, but— Now when it's here, literally staring us in the face, I... I don't seem to be able to hide from it anymore..." He hesitated, and in the silence that followed, he made another attempt to collect his thoughts, to distance himself even more from the destructive feelings that wanted to break free. "I woke up from another nightmare, and it was so real. You were lying beside me and— At first, I thought you were sleeping, but you were dead. The wound in your head... It— It cracked open and— and she— she stepped out, said her name was Athena, and— and then, she— she—" He couldn't hinder the tears anymore. *Please, no more crying. It's enough! I can't... can't...* He hated feeling this vulnerable, hated not being able to stop himself. Miri put a hand on his chest, halted his step, before embracing him hard, allowing him to let all the tears of shame and self-disgust and pain fall until he felt empty. Tardis insisted on coming up in his arms. Miri lifted her up, and the cat curled together in his embrace, licking his face.

"What did she do?" Miri's voice was so gentle, and her hands on his back caressed him so calmly, so steadily.

"She... raped me." His voice was a mere whisper, cracked and filled with shame, and the words fell heavily to the ground.

Miri didn't stop caressing him. Instead, she hugged him closer, and the cat purred between them.

"The first time, at home, I had a feeling something had happened to you. You were so tense and nervous, more than I thought would be normal. I remember you were nervous here too, but not like that." Her voice was low and soft. "She's not allowed to break you, Carl. You're worth so much more than that."

He drew another deep, trembling breath. "She's not. I won't let her."

"Good." The confidence she obviously had in him, and the lack of judgment and accusation in her voice was something he hadn't expected. He let his head rest on her shoulder and sighed as the burden got lighter to bear.

Eventually, Miri cupped his face and looked him seriously in the eyes. "It won't change anything for me, Carl. Don't think it will. We're in this together, and we're going to beat it, no matter what they think they can use us for, no matter what they throw in our way. They won't win, Carl, because we're not going to let them."

The overwhelming love for her and her strength washed through him, made him feel clean and strong again. *I'll do anything for you, Miri. Anything.* Determinedly, she took his hand. The cat licked Carl's face one last time before jumping down, all nine tails high in the air, and they began to walk again.

It didn't take long before the mist faded away, and they found themselves in a large plaza. Carl shivered when he turned around and saw houses and meandering streets behind him, instead of an earthy path flanked by tall grass.

"I hate this place," he muttered, and Miri squeezed his hand comfortingly.

"That's the library over there." She pointed toward a big, dark building on their left.

He made a new attempt to compose himself, but it started to get difficult. *It really gets to me. It's like a physical weight on my mind. Let's hope it really is this easy, read the book, change it, go back to Allie and get everyone home, but… Something's hidden here. There's another trap somewhere. And where the hell is Night Porter? I swear he knows about this, laughing his ass off somewhere.* With another deep breath, he tried to shake off the ominous feelings. *I don't have a choice, do I? It doesn't matter how much I loathe her, what Athena said, it rings true. Somehow, I know she's right. Miri's going to die in here if we don't fight it.* A low voice in his head whispered, *She already has.* With dread in his heart, he squeezed Miri's hand so hard, so she gasped and gave him a surprised look.

"Sorry," he muttered. "Just having a bad feeling about everything."

"Mm, yes. That's what this place is built up around, bad feelings, nightmares, and people's worst fears, and a wicked love of creating bad things out of good thoughts." A cloud floated over her eyes, and she got a distant look on her face.

He sighed. *Here we go again.* "Miri?" She didn't answer. He let his hand tangle her hair and leaned in and kissed her lips. It was easier without Caesar around, but it didn't feel right when she wasn't really present.

When she finally kissed him back, he felt relieved. *Still hanging in there.* He let go of her and watched her concerned, but she put her hand on his cheek and gave him a straight look back.

"I'm still here."

"Good," he muttered. "Let's get going so we can get out of here once and for all."

She nodded and led him up some very steep stairs and headed toward the huge wooden doors.

"Last time they were open," she mumbled and tried them. Without a sound, they swung open, and she gave up a shaky laugh. "I was a bit afraid there for a second."

When they entered the library, a strange feeling crept upon him. It was like… *coming home.* No. He shook his head. Not coming home, there was no place here that could be called home, but there was something familiar about it, as if it tried to copy and remind him of places he visited before, places where he felt intimately connected with his soul, as if it tried to reach out to him and calm him down. Suspiciously, he looked around. *Is this the trap? Trying to influence me to relax and forget everything about what we're supposed to do?*

Suddenly, the cat hissed fiercely and disappeared into the shadows.

"Aren't you so clever, my dear friend?"

As Carl turned around and saw Night Porter standing at the once again closed doors, the calmness attempted to snare him, and he had to viciously fight the feeling.

Night Porter tilted his head and watched him with his clear pit-coal eyes. "Why do you fight?" The voice sounded genuinely curious. "You know I'll win in the end. I always win, but you don't care. You just keep on fighting."

"I'm not playing your game."

Night Porter laughed. "You're here. You're part of the game." Carl looked for Miriam, but she stood at a bookcase, searching for the right book. "She can't see me or hear me right now. It's just you and me." A hissing sound was heard from the shadows. Night Porter turned his head toward it. "And your cat. Quite a curious creation, I have to say. I think I'll let it live." Night Porter gave him a friendly look that immediately made Carl even more suspicious than he already was. "Most people who come here are no fun, but you two… you create things, discover things, manipulate things, and try to make this your own game, almost as if you understand my realm. It's very refreshing." He looked at Carl again with a little smile playing on his lips. "Let's do like this; since you have created new entertaining subjects for me, I feel like I'm in a generous mood. If you can find the right book and make the right changes, I'll let you leave, both of you, together with your friends, even my sweet, feisty Queen of Clubs. No more games. No more deaths. But if you return to my realm one more time, you and my precious Queen of Hearts will be all mine."

Night Porter made a tiny gesture with his hand, and all books got caught in something that resembled a dusty golden tornado. They whirled around in the library like crazy birds before they landed in heaps all over. When Carl looked at Night Porter again, he was gone.

He exhaled and ran a hand through his hair several times before he caught himself and forced himself to stop.

Miriam looked around with her mouth open in astonishment, and her hands stretched out as if she had been holding on to a book that just flew away.

"Did you see that, Carl?" She smiled openly like a child who had seen fairies fluttering around.

"Yeah…"

"Wasn't it beautiful?"

"I guess it was."

Then her demeanor slowly changed, and she looked tired again as she viewed the thousands upon thousands of books lying around.

"We'll never find the right book."

"Miri, don't think like that. We can't give up. We haven't even started yet."

She sighed. "You're right." For a moment, she fell silent and watched the mess around them, but soon, a determined look replaced the dejected. "Okay, let's make it organized. I look through the books, you place them on the shelves."

"Sounds like a plan."

"Okay, here goes." She sat down on the floor and randomly took a book, opened it, and looked at the first page. "*Aristotle's Main Works*. Really?"

She gave it to him, and out of curiosity, Carl opened it, but the alphabet was one he had never seen before. As he glanced at her, a cold, uneasy shiver ran down his spine, and he hurriedly placed the book on a shelf. Tardis came back from the shadows, jumped onto Miri's lap, and fell asleep, purring.

Carl had no idea how long time they spent going through book after book after damn book, without finding what they were looking for. Together they had filled nine full bookcases when Miri stretched for a book almost out of her reach, and the cat woke up and hissed at her. Her hand stopped in the air, and she got an uncertain look on her face as she met the cat's gaze.

"Um, you don't want me to take that book?"

Tardis stood up on her hind legs and placed her paws on Miri's hand. When she let Tardis put her hand down in her lap, the cat licked her cheek, yawned, and curled together in her lap again. Miri's face had an odd expression when she looked up at him.

"I don't think you should touch that one," Carl said in a faint voice.

She cleared her throat. "You might be right." Instead, she turned her back toward it and continued going through the next heap.

For Carl, it felt as if time ceased to exist. It was only the three of them in a bubble of light and silence, and the one thing showing them that time probably passed somewhere, was the bookcases that slowly filled up, and the empty space on the floor that grew yet larger. Somewhere around fifty filled bookcases, he lost count, and everything turned into a blur. Neither of them complained, however. If this was the only way to keep Miri from dying and to have even the slightest chance to go home without any more trouble or losses, it was definitely worth the tedious work. For some reason which he couldn't explain to himself, Carl didn't tell Miri about the meeting with Night Porter, and right now, he didn't even want to scrutinize his own ulterior motives for this decision.

Twice more did the cat hinder Miri from touching certain books, and they lay in tiny beacons of uncertainty on the floor, loosely shaped as a triangle. Carl was very careful to step around them, so he didn't accidentally touch them or got trapped inside their invisible borders. At this point, he completely trusted the cat's instincts.

It was when they reached the inner parts of the library, that Tardis stretched, yawned and jumped down from Miri's lap. She went over to a pile of only three books and meowed quietly. Then she buffed her head on the two top ones, so they fell to the floor, and put her front paws on the lowest-lying book. Carl and Miri shared a look before she approached the cat.

"Is that one for me?" she asked in a trembling voice, and the cat marked first her face, then the book's corner.

Miri's hands quivered when they reached for the book, and Carl held his breath. With a couple of short steps, he went over to her and sat down beside her. Shoulder to shoulder, with the cat stretching out over their laps, purring, they viewed the book in Miri's hands.

"Aren't you going to open it?" Carl whispered at length. She nodded and took a deep breath. He had expected it, but it was still a disappointment when he didn't understand the letters. "What does it say?" he asked, and when she gave him a surprised look, he explained, "I don't recognize the alphabet."

"Huh… I thought it was English, but I guess not. The title is *The Woman Who Travels the Dreams.*" She fell silent.

"Well, I guess that could be you. Does it feel like you?"

She nodded. "There's a tingling sensation in my stomach. There's just one problem."

"What's that?"

"It's in verse. I mean, yes, I liked English in school, but reading about yourself in verse, it's— I don't know… I can't relate to it. Listen here, *Wake up, your Dream is calling; the red, crimson in color, blending with cerulean blue. Leave your waking world behind, step into mysteries of old; let them guide you in your search of you.*"

      "It's kind of beautiful. It creates images in my mind."

      "Does it?" He nodded, and she sighed relieved. "Good, then I'll read aloud to you, and we'll see where we get."

      "Alright."

      She cleared her voice and began reading. Carl let his mind float with the sound of her voice and saw the images in front of him, so alive. He followed her as she relived her time here on her own, and tears trickled down his cheeks when she read about the loneliness and the fear she experienced, and the madness she lived through. She read about when she got company, the *cracked tower that still stands tall*, the *thorned rose bleeding of doubt*, and the *quiet whisper of faraway imaginings*, and how the *Dream Traveler enters the cracked tower and heals it*, how the *mind-bursting warrior of eternal pleasures* was born, how the *Land and Realm of Dreams grieves when the Dream Traveler abandons its lonesome shores* and how it rejoices when she returns again with the tower and the stronghold, and how its inhabitants now are determined to keep her. She read about how her daughter, the *warrior* destroys the hope of keeping her at the shores again and again, but—

      Tardis suddenly stood up and buffed her head on Miri's chin, so she lost the sentence. Carl immediately came out of his half-trance and held up his hand to stop her. He put a finger on his mouth to silence her when she glanced at him. Then, he cleared his throat. He had never been good at writing poetry, but he could try.

"In the Land and Realm of Dreams
where old inhabitants scream
Lost
Forgotten

Their souls downtrodden

Time will find and heal
their anguish and ordeal

The Dream Traveler explores
the realm's many lonesome shores
Grieving
Leaving
In her own world believing

Happy and of obligations free
Closing the realm's boundary

With her, the Stronghold and the Tower
will go together in the hour
Spurning
Yearning
To their own land returning

Wake up the Queens
End the go-betweens

With minds cleared and hearts healed
the visitors will never yield
Victorious
Glorious
In their own selves, meritorious..."

Tardis buffed at his hand, and he smiled at her anticipatory gleam.

"The cat with nine tails
her own boundaries prevail

Light will return in the end
Lost souls will transcend
Caressing
Evanescing
With all love's blessing."

At this point, Tardis stood up on her hind legs and placed her paws on his mouth. He couldn't help but smile at her again. Miriam glanced at the book, and for a split second, Carl thought he saw it glow. A peaceful expression spread over her face as she read the last sentences. She slowly closed the book and looked at him with a serene and solemn gleam in her whole being.

"I like that ending. Shall we try to fulfill it?"

He nodded and took her hand. "Yeah, it's time."

About the Author

A.E. Hellstorm was born in Sweden but spent several years of her youth in Portugal and Greece, before returning to Stockholm, her city of birth.

As a young adult, she took a diploma in Creative Writing, as well as a Master of Arts in Scientific Archaeology.

In 2005, she and her husband moved to Canada together with their cats and have lived there ever since.

In Canada, she took a diploma in Arts and Cultural Management, and in Photography. She opened her photography business *Flying Elk Photography* in 2012.

In the Hands of the Unknown, Lost, and *Of Darkness Born* are her first published novels, but she has had a play, *Marsvindar,* staged at Rosenlundsteatern in Stockholm, Sweden, in 1992, and she has also participated in two anthologies: *Karbunkel* in 1994, and the *2014 Wyrdcon Companion Book.*

Other than that, she is a vivid roleplaying enthusiast, and she was deeply engaged in the Swedish larping community during the 1990s and early 2000s. In the year of 2000, she organized the Greek mythology-based larp *The Song of Mycenae.*

When she doesn't write, she enjoys curling up in a recliner with a book, her cats, and a large cup of tea.

www.ingramcontent.com/pod-product-compliance
Lightning Source LLC
Chambersburg PA
CBHW060209030726
47499CB00004B/968